Chronicles of the Nephilim Series Books 1-2

Noah Primeval and Enoch Primordial
By Brian Godawa

Please Note:

The first book in the Chronicles series is *Noah Primeval*. *Enoch Primordial* is the second book in the series, but is actually the prequel.

For this Box Set Edition, I have placed *Enoch Primordial* first in reading order so the reader can read them in chronological order.

Chronicles of the Nephilim Series Books 1-2:
Noah Primeval and Enoch Primordial

Copyright © 2016, 2021 Brian Godawa
All rights reserved. No part of this book may be reproduced in any form or by any electronic or mechanical means, including information storage and retrieval systems, without prior written permission, except in the case of brief quotations in critical articles and reviews.

ISBN: 978-1-942858-87-4 (Paperback)

Warrior Poet Publishing
www.warriorpoetpublishing.com

Scripture quotations taken from *The Holy Bible: English Standard Version.* Wheaton: Standard Bible Society, 2001.

TABLE OF CONTENTS

TABLE OF CONTENTS iii
Book Two: Enoch Primordial – The Prequel vii
ACKNOWLEDGMENTS x
MAP of the World – Enoch Primordial xi
Prologue 1
Chapter 1 3
Chapter 2 9
Chapter 3 11
Chapter 4 15
Chapter 5 17
Chapter 6 18
Chapter 7 24
Chapter 8 28
Chapter 9 32
Chapter 10 37
Chapter 11 44
Chapter 12 47
Chapter 13 50
Chapter 14 56
Chapter 15 60
Chapter 16 64
Chapter 17 70
Chapter 18 75
Chapter 19 83
Chapter 20 88
Chapter 21 92
Chapter 22 95
Chapter 23 99
Chapter 24 105
Chapter 25 108
Chapter 26 112
Chapter 27 116
Chapter 28 120
Chapter 29 122
Chapter 30 124
Chapter 31 129
Chapter 32 132
Chapter 33 134
Chapter 34 137
Chapter 35 140
Chapter 36 143
Chapter 37 147
Chapter 38 151
Chapter 39 154
Chapter 40 159
Chapter 41 167
Chapter 42 171
Chapter 43 174
Chapter 44 180
Chapter 45 184

Chapter 46 189
Chapter 47 193
Chapter 48 196
Chapter 49 199
Chapter 50 201
Chapter 51 204
Chapter 52 207
Chapter 53 211
Chapter 54 215
Chapter 55 220
Chapter 56 226
Chapter 57 233
Epilogue 236
Chapter 60: Appendix Retelling Bible Stories .239
Book One: Noah Primeval 283
Preface 288
MAP 293
Prologue 294
Chapter 1 297
Chapter 2 301
Chapter 3 309
Chapter 4 321
Chapter 5 328
Chapter 6 331
Chapter 7 341
Chapter 8 346
Chapter 9 354
Chapter 10 361
Chapter 11 370
Chapter 12 375
Chapter 13 383
Chapter 14 387
Chapter 15 402
Chapter 16 407
Chapter 17 413
Chapter 18 419
Chapter 19 422
Chapter 20 426
Chapter 21 431
Chapter 22 440
Chapter 23 447
Chapter 24 450
Chapter 25 455
Chapter 26 459
Chapter 27 465
Chapter 28 468
Chapter 29 471
Chapter 30 480
Chapter 31 482
Chapter 32 486
Chapter 33 491
Chapter 34 495

Chapter 35: The Sons of God 498
Chapter 36: The Nephilim 518
Chapter 37: Leviathan 533
Chapter 38: Mesopotamian Cosmic Geography in the Bible 544
Chapter 39: Great Offers By Brian Godawa 570
Chapter 40: About the Author 571

GET THIS EBOOKLET ON THE BOOK OF ENOCH!

For a Limited Time Only

FREE

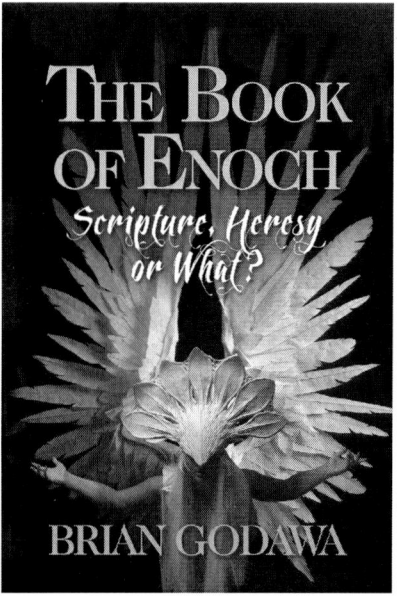

A Controversial Ancient Book with Shocking Information!

By Brian Godawa

Chapters Include:
• What is the Book of Enoch? • Where did it come from? • Why isn't it in the Bible? • Is the Book of Enoch reliable? • and MORE!

The answers may surprise you. Written by respected Christian and Biblical author.

Click on this link to get your FREE eBooklet:
https://godawa.com/feb-ne/

BOOK TWO: ENOCH PRIMORDIAL – THE PREQUEL

Enoch Primordial
Chronicles of the Nephilim
The Lost Book (Two)

By Brian Godawa

ENOCH PRIMORDIAL
5th Edition

Copyright © 2012, 2014, 2017, 2021 Brian Godawa
All rights reserved. No part of this book may be reproduced in any form or by any electronic or mechanical means, including information storage and retrieval systems, without prior written permission, except in the case of brief quotations in critical articles and reviews.

Warrior Poet Publishing
www.warriorpoetpublishing.com

ISBN: 9798710790809 (Hardcover)
ISBN: 978-0-9859309-2-9 (paperback)
ISBN: 978-0-9859309-1-2 (ebook)

Scripture quotations taken from *The Holy Bible: English Standard Version.* Wheaton: Standard Bible Society, 2001.

Dedicated to
the memory of the late C.S. Lewis,
and to the memory of the late J.R.R. Tolkien.
Even though it is a cliché these days,
still, they are my masters of imagination –

– after God.

ACKNOWLEDGMENTS

Special thanks to Yahweh Elohim, the God of Enoch, Methuselah and Noah, and to the Son of Man, the second Yahweh in heaven. To the wife of my youth, Kimberly, my heart and soul. To Neil Uchitel for all our rambling discussions all those years ago about fallen angels, vampires and the Nephilim. To Michael S. Heiser, for his scholarship and resources that have fed my hunger. To David Rohl, for his helpful archaeological speculations of the ancient world based on his New Chronology. Thanks to my editor, Don Enevoldsen, my proofreader Shari Risoff, and my editor of this much better second edition, Sarah Beach.

And to Joe.

MAP OF THE WORLD – ENOCH PRIMORDIAL

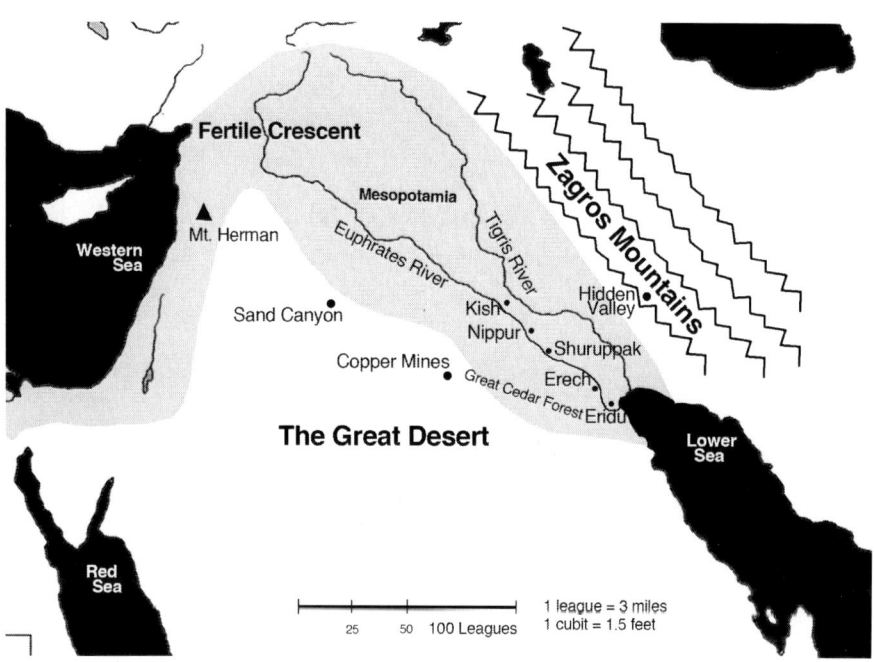

Could it have happened something like this?

PROLOGUE

Expelled from the Garden of Eden on the Mountain of God, the distant patriarch Adam and his wife Havah, or Eve, the "mother of all living," were forgotten by their descendants in the mists of time. Even though their creator Elohim's gracious forbearance covered them, they lived in regret the rest of their days with a mysterious people somewhere in the volcanic region of Sahand, near the boundary of the Garden. Like a dog kicked out of its shelter, they lived as close to their original home as they could without being struck down by those who guarded its perimeter.

The creator Elohim marked their son, Cain, the first murderer, and he was cursed to wander the earth. Few knew what the mark was, but there were rumors. It was said that he had a wild dog or wolf as a companion. Others claimed the man himself transformed into a canine beast at every new moon. The mystery of the actual fate of the cursed Cain was only matched by the fertility of imagination and legend surrounding him.

Cain's tribe migrated south from Nod through the Zagros Mountains and eventually broke away from their embittered patriarch to settle in the plain of Shinar, later called Sumer. The Shinarians referred to themselves as *unsangiga,* the black-headed people for their predominantly black hair and dark-skinned features. Unuk ben Cain, Cain's son, was the first city builder. He created the oldest city, Eridu, naming it after his own son Irad. He also built Erech, in honor of himself. This was the beginning of the ancient cities such as Nippur, Badtibira, Larak, Sippar, and others on the Mesopotamian plains in the land between the two rivers Tigris and Euphrates.

As mankind spread out upon the face of the earth, so did the evil that followed them. For it is the heart that is taken with man wherever he goes, and the heart is deceitful above all things and desperately wicked.

Elohim replaced Cain's cursed bloodline with another seed of Adam called Seth, the Righteous. Seth's people multiplied and migrated down into the fertile plains and surrounding area.

Tribal shamans divined that in a distant island beyond the primal sea a volcano had belched forth a mighty force of its gasses from the underworld below into the heavens above. The sun was obscured, and the earth grew colder for a time. Livestock perished, crops failed, the winters became harsher. It seemed that Elohim's displeasure with man was displayed in all of the heavens and earth.

And generations passed.

CHAPTER 1

An eerie silence settled over Mount Hermon. The ubiquitous ringing drone of singing cicadas ceased in unison. Birds of prey and land predators stalking their next meal froze in place as though suddenly aware of a powerful hunter tracking them. The sounds, the movement, all signs of life that filled the dark night just stopped. The wildlife knew something was coming.

Mount Hermon lay about two hundred leagues to the west of the Mesopotamian valley, across the barren desert. It stood above a valley at the southernmost tip of the Sirion mountain range of the Levant, "where the land rose out of the sea" of the great western waters. It was the tallest peak in the area, about six thousand cubits high. Capped with snow most of the year, the headwaters of the Jordan River, that brought life to the wooded hills and grassy valleys of the south, began on its slopes. It was known for its heavy dew and its evergreen cypress trees that peppered the region.

A beam of blinding light from high above in the dome of heaven punched the mountaintop. It pierced the blackness with a ferocious velocity. Heaven and earth fused as one into a cosmic center of the universe.

Two hundred shining beings of light, brilliant as the stars, fell to earth from their lofty heights above the clouds. A crack of thunder announced their violent passage through the solid dome vault over the earth called "the firmament." The firmament separated the waters below on the earth from the waters above in the heaven of heavens, where the temple of the creator Elohim rested. The mountains trembled and quaked to their very foundations.

These were *Bene ha Elohim*, Sons of God, a mere two hundred out of the myriad of Elohim's divine council of holy ones. These mighty beings surrounded his throne on the mount of assembly with worship and legal counsel. Certain Sons of God called "Watchers," regularly crossed the barrier between heaven and earth to carry out Elohim's plans and to watch over the sons of men.

But these two hundred were not carrying out Elohim's plans tonight. These were Watchers in revolt. Led by two mighty warriors, Azazel and

Semjaza, they were establishing their own mount of assembly in the far reaches of the north in direct defiance of Elohim's will.

They chose Mount Hermon as their abode, intending to make it a rebellious reflection of God's own cosmic mountain of Eden, the paradise now banned to all. This choice began a complex plan of deceptive mimicry. Just as Eden held the headwaters of four rivers, the Pishon, the Gihon, the Tigris and Euphrates, all flowing out of the mountainous region surrounding the Garden, so Mount Hermon gave birth to the headwaters of the river Jordan that flowed into the Levant. Its surrounding territory would be called Bashan, "place of the Serpent," in honor of *Nachash*, the Serpent of Eden.

The Garden of Eden had been a temple sanctuary for the presence and worship of Elohim, a perfect shadow of the real temple in the heaven of heavens above the waters. Hermon would become the cosmic mountain of passage between the heavens and earth for the Watchers — the gateway of the gods.

As the Tree of Life stood in the midst of the Garden, so the Watchers chose Mount Hermon for its proximity to the World Tree of the Great Goddess Earth Mother in the Great Desert.

The Man and Woman were the intended priests of the Garden, cultivating and keeping it as a holy center of Elohim's cosmic order before they were banished. Mount Hermon would become a new cosmic mountain that would not only connect heaven and earth, but earth and the Abyss, also called *Abzu*, the subterranean waters, below which lay Sheol, the underworld. Deep within the bowels of the mountain a large cavern held a portal into the waters of the Abyss, a wide pool of thick black liquid that burned with a perpetual flame on its surface.

The two hundred rebel Watchers assembled in disorderly ranks at the center of the new Eden by the shore of the pitch-dark liquid lagoon. Azazel and Semjaza stood ominous and intimidating before them.

"SILENCE!" Azazel's voice thundered throughout the cavern. The Watchers abruptly stopped murmuring. Azazel's violent temper gave him a commanding presence. Every word burned like an ember ready to explode into a burst of flames. Azazel often looked ready to burst into flames. The skin of a Watcher consisted of almost imperceptible serpentine scales that gave off a shimmering glow when enflamed by any kind of passion. And Azazel never lacked passion.

"The decision has been made. We are the Seven who Decree the Fates. If any of you question Semjaza's leadership or my own, I most heartily welcome the contest!"

Azazel's hostile disposition supported by the fiercest of warrior skills made him virtually unopposed in the band of fallen ones. No one would be contesting Azazel this evening.

Only Semjaza standing next to him had the requisite strength, intellect, and strategy to restrain Azazel's volatility. It bothered him that Azazel was a loose fireball who used fear and intimidation to subjugate. He believed that more could be accomplished through positive leadership and inspiration. Semjaza's words were calculated and carried the weight of authority. When he spoke, others listened, even Azazel. He stepped forward to draw attention from the simmering volcano at his side.

"Brethren, for the plan to work, we must all be in one accord. The mythology we are constructing requires a subversion of Elohim's own narrative of authority. If we do not support the narrative, we may forfeit the humans' worship of us as deity. Azazel and I have carefully deliberated who will fill the Seven, based upon craft and skill required for the plan, not upon partiality. We are all gods and we will all rule cities of men. The difference is mere façade. We seven will constitute the visible symbolic figurehead of the divine assembly of gods. As for the prize of our strategy, we will all share equally."

The assembly of Watchers applauded. Azazel frowned with envy at Semjaza's speaking prowess. Semjaza was clearly more skilled at making a lie sound like the truth. Though he and Azazel were equal leaders, it gave Semjaza the edge of perceived superiority. Azazel would have to find a way to change that.

Semjaza continued, "As Anu, the high god of the heavens, I will have more responsibilities of petty bureaucracy than any of you would care to shoulder. Azazel has chosen to be Inanna, the goddess of war who will lead our military administration."

Azazel came up with the role of goddess as an attempt at humorous irony. A female divinity who could stand on the neck of the best of any male warrior was the kind of humiliation of others he frequently sought. But he was beginning to realize that maybe he did not think that irony through well enough. He did not relish the idea of adorning himself in female garb and sexuality for such a long period of time. Some Watchers were already making jests about his feminine traits behind his back. He concluded to himself that if he caught them he would slaughter them.

Semjaza gestured to the five others standing beside them. "Baraqel will be Enlil, the god of air; Arakiba will be Enki, god of the waters below; Tamiel will be Nanna, the moon god; Zaqiel will be Utu, the sun god; and Ezeqel will be Ninhursag, goddess of the earth." Each of them stood proudly beaming in their new identities.

Semjaza pointed into the crowd. "Since Ramel and Sariel helped to pinpoint this location for our cosmic mountain, they shall be Ereshkigal and Nergal, goddess of the underworld and her husband. They shall guard the entrance to the Abyss."

Ramel winced. Much like Azazel, he did not treasure the idea of assuming a female identity. He certainly did not like the fact that according to the myth the others had created, Nergal raped Ereshkigal to make her his wife, in a failed attempt to master the secrets of the hidden underworld. Ramel consoled himself that he would be undisputed queen of the underworld, the guardian of the gates of Sheol.

Sariel pondered how he might play out the myth in a particularly demeaning way on Ramel.

Semjaza continued, "Each of you will have your own identity in the pantheon and will be given tribes and cities to rule over as patron deities." The worship of awe from the humans would not be too difficult. The physical structure of a Watcher represented divinity in the minds of humans. At five and a half cubits tall, with sinewy musculature, they were already towering above the average male human who stood less than four cubits tall. Their finely scaled skin produced a gleaming bronze appearance that earned them the nickname, "Shining Ones." Coupled with their elongated heads and glimmering blue lapis lazuli reptilian eyes, their luminescence reinforced a distinction between the human and the divine necessary for their deception.

Semjaza added, "As you know, Elohim is an insufferable tyrant whose megalomania is only matched by his childish tantrums. If we want to accomplish our ultimate goal, we must give these humans a pantheon of gods that is unified, benevolent, and worthy of worship and obedience."

Azazel knew that last statement was meant for him.

Semjaza had given Baraqel authority over the city of Nippur. Its central location among the cities of Shinar made it a valuable prize for Azazel's military strategy and political status in the pantheon. Nippur would be the first location for the assembly of the divine council among humans. Azazel knew Baraqel was a favorite of Semjaza, and that was why Semjaza had sided with him against Azazel's legitimate claim on the city. Semjaza's compromise was to give Baraqel as Enlil the city, but to allow Azazel as Inanna to have a residence there as well. Azazel had argued vociferously against the decision at first, but decided to give in and wait for the right moment for his own rise to power. Once he led their forces into war, he would achieve the distinction that even Semjaza would have to acknowledge and perhaps even submit to. And then Azazel would rout out all those who mocked him. He would cut off their heads and boil them in lava, which was a particularly painful torture considering that Sons of God could not die mortal deaths. They were, all of them, divine.

Semjaza concluded his remarks to the assembly. "Our first task is to go out to the villages and cities and perform signs and wonders and reveal the secrets of heaven to draw the humans into our trust. If we are to make them believe us, we must believe ourselves. So it is imperative that we never use our heavenly names again. We must always refer to one another by our adopted names of deity. But more importantly, we must *think of ourselves* as those deities. We must inhabit our roles with truthfulness. I am no longer Semjaza; I am Anu the sky god. There is no Azazel, there is only Inanna."

Someone blurted out, "Queen of heaven!" Some laughed. Inanna marked out the heckler and schemed how she would torture him later.

Anu deflected the insult. "Indeed, she is. And she is the goddess of war. You will do well to follow her lead into battle when the time comes. Until then, find your cities, reveal your mysteries, and establish your shrines of worship. This Mount Hermon will be our divine mount of assembly. We will reside here and visit our cities on an as-needed basis."

Enlil spoke up. "But if we do not reside in our cities, will we not lose control over them with our absence?"

Anu replied, "Your religious priesthood will be responsible for crafting a graven image of you that represents your presence and rule over the city. We have developed a ritual for your priests to use to draw your breath into the statue, which becomes your living presence when you are not there. We call it the 'opening of the mouth' ceremony."

Inanna thought the ritual ridiculous, but humans were so flesh-bound they needed concrete expressions of the supernatural realm or they would lose heart. Elohim had done a poor job of uniting spirit with these disgusting filthy sacks of meat.

Anu continued, "You will reveal the doctrine of the priest-king as also created in your own image. This will build the myth required to maintain orderly submission from your people in your absence, when we meet here at Hermon to complete our final plan of action."

It was brilliant. Anu had thought of everything. He had even sent out a select number of them into the four corners of the earth, south into Egypt, north beyond the Euphrates into the Halafan hinterlands, east to Elam and the Indus Valley, and even west across the great primal seas to distant unknown islands. The Watchers would reign as gods over the entire earth and inspire countless variations on their one myth of rebellion against Elohim.

But it was the final plan that excited the loyalty and devotion of the Watcher gods.

They swore an oath, to bind everyone among them by a curse. If anyone abandoned their commitment to the final plan, or revealed its secret scheme, the others would unite and bind that Watcher into the earth to suffer the torment of frozen solitude for millennia until the judgment. It was the one heinous thing that made each and every one of them shiver with dread.

CHAPTER 2

The Watchers spread out over all the land, claiming their peoples and unveiling secrets to the sons of men — dark occult secrets that humanity should never have known. They taught mankind the ways of sorcery and alchemy, incantations and the cutting of magical roots, casting of spells and the arts of divination, necromancy, and astrology. Elohim fast became a distant memory for mankind as they worshipped and served the creation instead of the Creator.

The heavens above was one of the most glorious of that creation that man twisted to evil ends. When Elohim placed the heavenly objects in their order, he did so with the intent of expressing his glory not through beauty alone, but also through story. He embedded that story in the very physical structure of the skies above. As the sun, moon, and stars revolved around the face of the earth, observers recorded movements and charted the heavens. Stars were connected by imaginary lines of constellations that depicted the future God ordained. These constellations were pictures that told a story in twelve distinct parts.

The narrative was of a virgin (Virgo) who would bear the promised seed and pay the price of justice to overcome the "wounder of the heel" (Scorpio the scorpion). This promised one would be a conqueror (Sagittarius the archer), who would carry the weight of sins and bring living waters for his people (Aquarius the water-bearer). Those people would be blessed though bound (Pisces the fish). Their blessings would be finally achieved through a ram of sacrifice who would become a ruling leader (Taurus the bull), a king with two natures (Gemini the twins). He would hold his people fast in his grip (Cancer the crab), and would ultimately reign as king over the earth (Leo the lion).

But this narrative of prophecy would eventually be subverted by the enemies of Elohim, who transformed it into an entire substitute system of astral worship where stars were considered as gods over the lives of men. Though there was no actual power in the stars, it served the purpose of the gods to divert mankind's attention from the true God of history into a god of one's own use.

· · · · ·

Of all the forbidden secrets revealed by the gods, none caused as much hope in the heart of Inanna as the arts of fornication and war. She exploited the beauty of human sexuality. It was a particular talent of hers to twist a good thing into something bad. She sought to replace Elohim's holy marriage covenant with unholy violations. She wanted to enslave these wretched creatures to their appetites. The possibilities were endless. The goal was to inspire every kind of union other than a man and woman in lifelong covenant before Elohim.

One of the unfortunate results of such unrestricted behavior was unwanted offspring, which tended to infect humans with a repulsive desire for moral responsibility and chastity. To counter this sentiment, the gods taught the medicinal sorcery of bitter herbs to induce miscarriage, as well as the technique of using utensils to smash the embryo in the womb. This would enable immoral behavior without the consequences. Inanna shivered with delight at that thought. It made her want to go out and violate a few humans herself. But that would be for later.

As for war, now *that* was an art. Inanna taught the craft of making instruments of death more accessible to the wicked. Knives, slings, arrows, shields, breastplates, and spears would become more ubiquitous than instruments of peace. These things were not in and of themselves evil, but in order to inspire mankind to do more damage, provide them with a technology for accomplishing that damage beyond the reach of one man wrestling another to the ground with fists, rocks, and clubs. Evil men will always seek to kill. Warfare technology simply provides them the ability to carry out their evil on grander scales with more destruction. Unfortunately, it would also provide good men with the ability to defend themselves against such evil. But Inanna could overcome that minor technicality with authoritarian control of the populace. Take away the dissidents' weapons and they are more docile and obedient to the power of the state which was the power of gods. To Inanna, the human race was an unfettered malignancy on the earth that required occasional strangling to keep it from getting out of control.

CHAPTER 3

At first, people all across the land bowed in awe before the glory of the gods and their revelation of secret knowledge. They worshipped and built shrines expressing their submission. This first step of the three-part plan of the gods had been successful.

At Mount Hermon, Anu inspired the surrounding peoples to build the first holy temple to the gateway of the gods called *kadingir*. Embedded into the mountain in a step-like structure, it dominated the landscape, serving as the temple of Ereshkigal, goddess of the underworld, Sheol.

The time had come for the second step of their plan. All across the land, in every city and every village presided over by a god, the citizens were called together in congregation before the holy shrine at the center of the city. The priest-king of each city, called the *ensi*, introduced their patron deity who then heralded a proclamation to the people — the proclamation of the Sacred Marriage.

Far away in the city of Nippur, Enlil, Lord of the air, was supposed to be the patron deity and Inanna a secondary goddess. But Inanna's intensity and assertiveness gained her a more devoted following, of which she never ceased to remind Enlil. She often found ways to usurp Enlil's authority, as she did that day during his announcement of the Sacred Marriage rite.

Enlil stood before a hushed audience. "Citizens of Nippur. You have been our loyal servants and for that we thank you. You have honored us with these shrines and with your worship and obedience. But a new day has dawned upon the world. And with it, a new opportunity for union between gods and men."

Inanna butted in, stealing Enlil's thunder with her characteristic impatience and bravado. "We are instituting the Sacred Marriage rite. All women will have the opportunity to be given in marriage to the gods."

The faces in the crowd were unmoved. They did not quite understand what they were hearing.

Inanna continued. "By the authority of the pantheon, we are temporarily suspending all marriage covenants across the land. This will give every woman a right over her own body to choose. If you volunteer for this high honor you will transcend your pathetic earthly limitations and become one with deity. You will be liberated from your oppressed status as the 'weaker sex.' And the fruit of your womb will be demigods who will rule the earth."

Inanna rose to a crescendo as the thought flitted through her mind that even Anu would not be more eloquent at this moment. "I can think of no greater privilege than being a child bearer of the gods! And that privilege begins today. All those women who desire the Sacred Marriage say your goodbyes to your fathers, your husbands, your siblings and your lords, and come to the holy shrine of Enlil this evening. We will perform a mass marriage ceremony and celebrate your newly exalted status!" Inanna was smugly satisfied with her delivery. She had practiced all morning and relished the jealousy Anu might feel at her stirring speech.

The crowd remained unimpressed. They stood in stunned silence. They had not anticipated such an outrageous offer and did not know what to do. Slowly, they melted away with solemn faces, back to their homes to consider their options. Was this truly voluntary or was this another play on words that Inanna and Enlil were so adept at doing? Would there be punishment for those who chose not to marry the gods?

Inanna looked with contempt upon the dispersing crowd. Poor insects. They had no idea that she was actually a male, and that Enlil was not the only one who would have his way with these women.

Enlil plotted how he might someday stab Inanna in the back, metaphorically, or literally if at all possible. Either way would suit him just fine.

That evening the priests had eaten their sacrificial meal of goat and barley offerings. They assembled in the courtyard of Enlil's shrine in anticipation of welcoming the arriving women for preparation in the Sacred Marriage.

Enlil and Inanna bickered all the way from their residence in the shrine out to the courtyard. Inanna thought the images of them carved out of stone and wood were terrible artwork. Ugly and unflattering. Enlil thought they were good enough.

"Good enough?" barked Inanna. "Incompetence is not 'good enough.' If we chopped off a few hands, you can rest assured, these deplorable artisans would sharpen their skills and take their duty more seriously."

Before Enlil could respond, they were in the courtyard. The sight was not encouraging.

It was already late into the evening and not a single woman stood in line to offer herself to the gods. Not even a loose woman. A messenger pazuzu, an ugly dog-faced flying creature with a double set of bat-like wings, brought them the message that this was the picture all over the land.

"These malicious conniving ingrates," spouted Inanna.

Enlil fumed as well. Since taking on flesh, his sexual desires increasingly consumed him as he looked upon the beauty of these daughters of men. He wanted them, and he wanted them now.

"What should we do?" asked Enlil.

Inanna responded flatly, her expression frozen. "If they will not give themselves to us, then we will have to take them by force."

Enlil broke into a knowing grin. For once, he and Inanna were entirely in agreement.

· · · · ·

An unusually quiet night rested over the city of Nippur. Families stayed inside their mud brick homes fearing reprisal for not volunteering their daughters and wives to the gods. Families sat hushed as they ate their meals, and went to bed early, hoping to hasten the coming of the next day and with it, a return to normal life. Many finally fell asleep as their exhaustion overcame their worry with slumber.

The tumult of soldiers marching and barging into homes at random broke the quiet. They held fathers and sons at spear point while companions dragged the females of the households and chained them by the neck to the backs of carts drawn by oxen. Screams cracked the darkness throughout the city, awakening families with fright. They could do nothing to protect themselves, only wait and hope they might be overlooked. They could not even pray to the gods, since it was the gods who were kidnapping their women and girls.

Fifty female hostages were herded into the courtyard of the shrine. They crowded in the small courtyard, trapped by the walls of simple enclosed structures of the shrines.

Inanna watched them and thought they would soon have to build up this unimpressive residence with ornament and pillars and gardens. A god deserved to be in the most expensive and extravagant building of the city. They were gods after all. In fact, she had plans to turn it into her own temple with sacred prostitution.

Inanna and Enlil stepped out onto a dais on one side of the large square courtyard bordered with pillars. Some of the women cried hysterically, others shivered in silent terror. Enlil spoke to them.

"My women. My beautiful women. There is no need for you to fear us. Though we were treated disrespectfully this evening, Inanna and I only desire to bless you with our bounty. Sometimes, disobedience to the gods brings chastisement, but it is a chastisement out of love for your best interest." Enlil scanned the crowd as he spoke, looking for his first choice.

"Oh, stop your pontificating and start choosing," muttered Inanna. She tromped out into the crowd and grabbed two young girls. They squealed and squirmed, but they were like a couple rabbits in the strong arms of the tall divinity as she carried them to her shrine.

It was going to be a busy night for Enlil. His skin radiated with hunger and virility. But he was not cruel like Inanna. He would be kind to his new wives. He was compassionate and thoughtful.

· · · · ·

This atrocity of forced marriages occurred all through Shinar. Before Inanna and Enlil embarked upon their plundering, they sent their flying messenger pazuzus to as many other cities of the plain as possible, explaining their predicament and solution and encouraging the other gods to follow suit.

And follow suit they did. The injustice throughout the land rose up as wailing tears in the ears of Elohim.

CHAPTER 4

Word reached Anu of Nippur's horror and its resounding influence on the other cities of the plain. Instantly, he knew it was Inanna's scheme. It was all he could do to contain himself. He would journey to each city himself and force each god to personally apologize for their reprehensible behavior. But first on his list was Nippur.

• • • • •

When Anu arrived with an escort of twenty other gods, Inanna lay sound asleep from her long night of exertion. By the time she was coherent and aware of what was going on, not even she with all her fury could withstand the ten gods who held her and dragged her out to the courtyard. She saw Enlil bullied in like manner to stand beside her. An audience of the city elders and the families victimized by Inanna and Enlil were assembled before them.

"People of Nippur," Anu announced, "I return to you the daughters and wives who were untouched by the reckless actions of your patron deities."

Thirty of the women had not yet engaged in Sacred Marriage with Inanna and Enlil. They raced out of the midst of the priests into the arms of their families, weeping with both pain and joy. The others were already pregnant and would have to remain in holy confinement in the quarters built behind the shrine for this purpose.

"And now, your patrons have something they want to tell you." Anu looked straight at Inanna, awaiting her response.

Inanna stood close enough to hiss at Anu, "We will look weak. They will lose their respect for us."

Anu returned the hiss. "You are a fool, Inanna. You have already lost their respect. Men do not follow cruelty. They follow justice. Apologize, or I will have you flogged. Then we will see how much respect you will receive."

Inanna glared back at him spitefully. She refused to open her mouth.

Enlil jumped in. "My people. My precious worshippers, Inanna and I would like to extend our deepest heartfelt apology for our — excessive enthusiasm last night."

His choice of words was clever, thought Inanna. *Qualified apology*. It gave her an idea.

"As your gods," she interrupted Enlil, "we are responsible to care for you and provide for your needs." Anu could see her twist coming. He knew her too well. "And as our people, you are responsible to obey us. We should not have acted so hastily, and we will not be so harsh in the future. But can you not see how you only hurt yourselves when you refuse to offer your daughters and wives out of love? Can you not see how you hurt us as well? Let us move forward and put this behind us. All is forgiven. All is blessed."

It was amazing, thought Anu, *how Inanna could turn an apology into an accusation without a blink. And deliver it as if she was an objective mediator rather than the offending party.* Of course, he expected as much. But it was better than nothing.

Inanna would not forget this moment. One day, she would have her chance for revenge on Anu and his bullying ways. Her rising anger was tempered by the amazing fact that afterward, Anu appealed to the people again to volunteer for the Sacred Marriage, and this time, at least thirty came forward. They may have realized they had no real choice or that things would only get worse if they did not "volunteer," but nevertheless, they volunteered. Inanna could not deny it; Anu had turned the embarrassment into a victory. The gods would have their brides for breeding.

CHAPTER 5

The offspring of the union between the Sons of God and the daughters of men were called *Nephilim*. A Naphil grew quickly in the womb and depleted the mother's nutrition to a deadly level. Their gestation period was five months. Though they were humanoid in appearance, they had a slight bluish grey tinge to their skin color and sported an extra digit on both their hands and feet, for a total of twelve fingers and twelve toes.

But there was one other important trait that would prove to be problematic for the breeding interests of the gods: Nephilim were large, very large. A mature Naphil could reach heights of seven, eight or even nine cubits tall. The Nephilim were giants. The fetus therefore was manifestly huge and tended to stretch a woman's womb cavity to its limits. For this reason, a Naphil's birth would kill its mother. This was all very natural for its kind, since the dead mother would be the newborn's first meal.

This inconvenient fact meant that the gods had to cloister the carriers into isolated quarters. They pursued a rigorous campaign of lies to keep the public from discovering the truth.

But leaks had occurred and rumors spread about the deadly consequences of the Sacred Marriage rite. All of mankind feared what they worshipped in place of Elohim their creator.

Within five months, the first Nephilim were born and celebrated in the cities and villages across the land. These firstborn were called *Rephaim* because they were the most pure of the breed. They would become kings and rulers of the earth. The inhabitants of Shinar called them the *Igigi*, demigods who served the Anunnaki gods, or "gods of princely seed." New flocks of women, regularly chosen, repopulated the harems of the gods with vessels worthy of their seed.

· · · · ·

A generation passed. Nephilim giants multiplied upon the face of the earth and subdued it.

CHAPTER 6

Enoch ben Jared pushed open the doorway to the council chamber of the palace just in time to see Thamaq, one of the ruling Rephaim, pound the table in anger, all but spitting in the face of King Enmeduranki. "We have given a command and we expect it to be obeyed!" shouted Thamaq. Yahipan, the other Rephaim, grunted and nodded sternly as he leaned forward to emphasize his agreement with his co-regent's words.

Enmeduranki was the two-hundred-year old priest-king of the city of Sippar, and Enoch, his young eighty-five-year old *apkallu* wisdom sage. Sippar sat strategically at the point of closest proximity between the Tigris and Euphrates in the northernmost region of Shinar. As the crucial port city for all the economic activity of the area, all commercial trade between the northern and southern regions of Mesopotamia went through Sippar. Commodities like stone, cedar, and lapis lazuli from the north, as well as barley, beer, and livestock from the south all passed through its trade channels. It was a split city, with one half on each bank of the Euphrates. A transportation canal had been dug from the nearby Tigris to connect the two rivers that serviced different sides of the alluvial plain.

The fertile land around Sippar produced an abundance of crops. But there was a shortage at that moment, and the Rephaim were not happy about it.

Enoch choked down his disgust for these contentious giant rulers and set the clay tablets on the table, bowing in deference. "My lords, the accounting of the food stores of the city." He wished his entrance could help Enmeduranki, but he knew the report was not good news.

"Thank you," said Enmeduranki. He looked over the tablets for the numbers. Drops of sweat pooled on his forehead and trickled down his cheeks. The pressure was taking its toll on him.

Enmeduranki was a good soul who sought to rule his people with compassion. But he was also a vassal of the Rephaim, the true rulers of the city. They were a new addition to the bureaucratic hierarchy above the priest-king and below the god. Enmeduranki was supposed to be a liaison between the people and the Rephaim demigods, but what it really amounted to was making the people accept the demands of the Rephaim. And their demands continued to increase.

"It is as I feared, my lords," he sighed. "There is nothing left."

"What do you mean there is nothing left?" blurted Thamaq. "What about the famine food stores?"

Thamaq and Yahipan were two of the original Nephilim born by the seed of the gods to rule over men. They were both nearly eight cubits tall and dressed in ostentatious robes of royalty. They were impious models of vainglorious conceit, releasing their tempers at the slightest of discrepancies. They even mocked Utu the sun god behind his back, an unforgivable act of blasphemous arrogance. Enoch detested them.

"I am afraid the famine stores are exactly what the Nephilim just finished consuming," Enmeduranki offered. The impossible position of responsibility without true authority wearied him. "The last of our famine food stores. The normal stores were emptied out last month."

Yahipan broke in, "Enlist more citizens to grow and harvest more food."

"The entire city is already forced to do so. We have no more private laborers who are not slaves of the realm. We have no source of income, only administrative expenses," pleaded Enmeduranki.

Thamaq rebuked him, "Enmeduranki, we must find a way. The Nephilim occupy the palace streets in protest. They dug the canals and built the entire irrigation system that brings the very life waters to this city from the Tigris and Euphrates. Do you question their entitlement to food?"

Enmeduranki swallowed his sigh at the utterance of that big lie. The Nephilim had built the vast irrigation canals that radiated around the cities like blood vessels. But those earthworks had been completed many years before, and they were now in grave disrepair. The giants had gathered themselves into a union of agreement that demanded minimal labor and maximum wages from the government. They had become an organized gang of thugs. Neither the Rephaim nor the gods seemed to be concerned about the demise of the city's economy.

"I do not question their right, my lord. But as you know, the Nephilim have increased their food intake by a factor of four over the past generation. No one anticipated such exponential growth when we first created our programs. We simply cannot keep up with their consumption." *They are very large and very hungry mouths to fill,* the priest-king thought bitterly to himself.

Thamaq regathered himself, "I am not sure you understand the seriousness of our predicament, priest-king. Facts and statistics are irrelevant to the Nephilim. They are hungry, bitter, and their numbers are strong. If they rise up in revolt, I will not be able to stop them. This entire city will be at their mercy."

"What say you, apkallu?" asked Yahipan with biting sarcasm.

Enoch's bowed head lifted to see the intense stare of both of the Rephaim.

"You sit there in silence. Are you not a fount of wisdom? Then vomit us some wisdom."

For a fleeting moment, the futility of his office flashed through Enoch's mind. He took his religious and political responsibility seriously, so seriously that he had adopted the Shinarian name *Utuabzu* in honor of Utu. Yet, increasingly, it seemed clear that the Rephaim were not so serious in their respect of the office or of his skills.

The city's governance was a typical Mesopotamian oligarchy modeled after the divine council of gods. Sippar's patron deity was Utu, the sun god. Enmeduranki was the governing ruler, the priest-king, created in the image of the gods. He carried out the combined duties of both religion and government on behalf of the deity. He had a council of elders of the city with whom he counseled, but he held closest his personal apkallu wisdom sages.

Enoch, as wisdom sage to the priest-king, was required to command a wide breadth of knowledge. He had trained in the sciences of both heavens and earth. He was shaman, diviner, scribe, and poet all in one. But it seemed to him that the most important office he held was as bard, the carrier of the culture's stories. All the laws, governance, religious beliefs and values of a people flowed downstream from the culture embodied in the songs and epics of the poet. Hearts and souls are moved by story and he who controls the culture's stories controls the people.

The world of storytelling was changing dramatically around Enoch. The new visual communication called "cuneiform" was overtaking the traditional oral recitation of verse. Scribes created cuneiform as a codified physical expression of language, using utensils to make impressions on clay tablets. The scribes wanted to keep a tangible account of personal and public wealth that could not be challenged by verbal lies or faulty memory. Using handheld styluses pressed into the clay, they could list objects owned by the ruler and how many he possessed. It had started out as pictures of cows, gold, wheat, wood, and other belongings. It had evolved into an abstract system of symbols that could be rapidly copied or communicated in a legal dispute.

Eventually the scribes saw other uses for this thing called writing. They experimented with ways of inscribing their oral epics and myths onto the clay. Writing could record what was said by the poet or sage. That record would be preserved unchanged through the years. It was a kind of magic that most sages hated because they feared it would soften their minds. After all, that which was recorded on clay did not need to be held in the memory. But Enoch was fascinated with writing. He wanted to adapt it into a tool for transmitting the dream visions he received from the deity.

"Well? The Anzu got your tongue?" Yahipan growled with biting sarcasm. Anzu was a huge lion-faced bird with vicious talons.

Enoch's stories would not be appreciated today. Today, all that mattered was the original use of writing for accounting records.

"Forgive me, Yahipan," said Enoch.

"Would you be pleased with a bloodbath?" said Yahipan.

"By no means, my lord," said Enoch. "I am a man of peace and piety. I deplore violence, and I have sought to encourage the people to submit to the rule of the priest-king and your majesties."

In truth, Enoch detested these Rephaim with all his being. They exploited the citizens with their tyrannical control and redistribution of wealth and food. But he was also a pacifist. He believed in submission to authority and would never encourage civil disobedience, let alone an uprising. Violence only led to more violence. He believed he should trust the gods and accept their decrees with steadfast faith.

"In my lowly opinion, it seems evident that both the Nephilim and the citizenry have become dependent upon the government to care for them. It is most natural then for them to not care for themselves and to become hostile when their subsidies are taken away. Unfortunately, it seems to me that we are not up against a matter of political opinion, but of reality. The government is bankrupt. There is no more to give. We cannot spend what we do not have."

"You call that blathering 'wisdom'?" complained Yahipan. "I want a solution, not a contest of blame!"

Enoch frowned and then quickly banished it. This was not a contest of blame, these were the bald facts. All the other cities such as Erech, Eridu, and

Larak faced these same facts. The strongest economic cities were all collapsing. The giants had been brought to all these cities to accomplish mighty feats of industry for the Rephaim. The purpose had been to glorify the gods and build an empire of power for the pantheon. But it had all gotten out of control. Now, the entire civilization was in jeopardy of collapsing. The giants were large, strong, warrior-like, and organized. They appointed leaders to press their demands upon the Rephaim rulers of all the cities. Revolution seemed inevitable.

The victims in all this turmoil were the average citizens, the backbone of the civilization. These were the ones Enoch felt were exploited at the expense of this class warfare for power. The society appeared to be an advancement of civilization, but Enoch believed it moved toward the inevitable centralization of power into the hands of the elite priestly caste, of which he was one. It remained a point of contradiction in his conscience.

His position made him privy to the myriad of government archives compiled by their scribes, registering every aspect of the lives of its citizens. Births, deaths, genealogies, land transfers, tax records, all were used to drain every ounce of income tax, land tax, head tax and death tax from every soul.

It would seem that slaves, in comparison, had a less complicated life. At least they were called what they actually were. The average citizen became a slave without the name. He worked hard on his farm or in the marketplace, earned an honest wage to take care of his simple family, paid his taxes to the realm, worshiped his gods, and left others alone to seek their own happiness. This average man and his family had his life sucked out of him by taxes and government control, only to end his life in Sheol, forgotten and never to return. Was this the will of the gods? It made Enoch weep at night and question his devotion to the pantheon. He felt that he was a man stuck in the middle, trying to make both sides happy, the ruling elite of the gods, and the common citizens who served that divine council. He felt a miserable failure.

"Apkallu! Are you listening to me, maggot?!" Yahipan's outburst brought Enoch back to the immediate moment. "I will whack your skull from your spine." He raised his hand.

Thamaq stopped him. "Brother, he is not worth your energy. We have been alerted to the facts by our servants. Let us withdraw to our chambers and determine our course of action."

Enmeduranki turned to Enoch. "Where is your son, the apprentice? If he is to become a sage, would not this situation be essential to his learning?"

"Forgive me, my lord," replied Enoch. "If you will excuse me, I will go and brief him." Enoch bowed and left the room. He did not even have the beginning of an idea where in the world his rascally son Methuselah was. But he had a good idea of *who* he might be with.

CHAPTER 7

Methuselah swung the pear-shaped mace down toward the skull of his adversary, a fifteen-year old girl named Edna. She raised her shield and blocked it effectively, then parried with her own mace.

He barked, "Excellent, runt!"

Methuselah was a strapping twenty-year old handsome young man. His unusual blue eyes often drew the teasing of his companions, saying that he was a *Bene ha Elohim*, or more likely a Naphil. It was not true, but he played along with it because he liked standing out from the crowd. He was a fiery lad with a passion for arguing, not the best of traits for an apkallu in training, since their order was marked by restraint and listening. But Methuselah hungered for knowledge, and loved to study and learn about everything.

At this moment, though, he was not learning. He was teaching. And it was not an intellectual exercise, but a physical one.

Edna swung again. He blocked her blow.

"Is that the best you can do, you scrawny little female?"

Methuselah burst into action, swinging one blow after another. Edna could barely keep up with the raining strikes. If she let one get through, it would leave a nasty bruise she would nurse for days.

With each swing, Methuselah verbally challenged her strategy. "What did I teach you? Have you no counter plan? I am stronger than you, so how can you defeat me?"

With those last words, he backed her up against the wall of the small practice room, his mace to her neck. He had used sheer strength to overwhelm her.

He leaned in close to her face and mused, "Now, if I was a particularly wicked soldier, having worn you down, I might take my pleasure before killing you." He was not teasing her. He wanted her to face the reality of the world.

"Too late," she said. He looked at her puzzled.

"Letting you expend your energy on me was my counter plan. While you were worn out and arrogantly crowing into my face with your horrible breath, I was gutting you," she said.

He glanced down to see her hand with knife blade at his abdomen. She shifted it down to his groin and added, "Or severing your manhood if you prefer."

He smiled. "I am proud of you, Edna." He kissed her forehead and turned to sit down for a rest.

To him, it was just a simple peck of affection. He did not notice that the soft swift touch of his lips upon her skin made her swoon. She gathered herself together and plopped down next to him.

"Why do you talk mean to me while fighting?" she asked.

He smiled. "That is what warriors do. It is mental warfare. Wearing down the enemy inwardly as well as outwardly."

"Oh, I see," she said, and added playfully, "you ogre."

He smiled at her. "You are hardly wet with sweat." He was drenched from the exercise.

"We women do not sweat, we glow." Her look of serious reflection melted into shared laughter.

"Edna," he said, "You are amusing. You are a girl, yet you prefer the company and roughhousing of boys. You do not wear makeup or jewelry. You sneak around your superiors to learn sports and fighting — and you are good. You are really good. You are intellectually curious and you want to see the world, yet you are a temple virgin, dedicated to the gods."

It was true. Edna was a spitfire boyish girl. Her serious expression returned in an instant. She brushed a strand of hair away from her face. It was a sole loose one that had come out of her otherwise usual tightly wrapped and bound hair bun.

"Do not tease me, Methuselah. Girls have no choice in their placement in society. I do not want to *be* a boy, I just enjoy doing things that boys do. It is not that I do not have female desires as well."

He laughed. "That would make you the perfect wife I guess."

She thought to herself, *Yes! And I would make you so happy.*

He interrupted her thoughts. "Those female desires will soon be fulfilled when you engage in the Sacred Marriage rite with the god."

She blushed through a moment of uncomfortable silence.

"I wish I could be married to a normal man — like you."

She gulped. Did she say too much?

Methuselah looked at her seriously. "Me too, Pedna." It was one of his many affectionate nicknames for her. He would call her "Edna Pedna," so she had responded by calling him "Methuselah Poozelah," and they eventually shortened them to Pedna and Poozela.

His whole countenance changed from joy to sorrow. He knew the consequences of being betrothed to the gods. He knew the ultimate end of bearing the Nephilim offspring. It always bothered him. On the one hand, the gods were sovereign and had the right to their wives. Humans were, after all, slaves of the gods. But on the other hand, how could so gruesome a reality be part of a just world?"

"What happens to the child-bearers?"

"That is the prerogative of the gods," he said. He could not bring himself to tell her. Instead, his silence and the look of dread on his face spoke loudly.

"Would you let them hurt me, Poozela?"

His heart nearly broke in two. He had been a big brother, even a father figure, to this girl ever since he noticed her special qualities and vivacious thirst for life as a mere ten-year old. He had secretly trained her to read cuneiform, fight with weapons, and reason like a sage. She now stood on the verge of her sixteenth birthday, and he was about to lose her forever. He struggled to hold back a flood of tears ready to burst. He did the only thing he could do. He deflected the question.

"We exist to serve the gods, not question them."

It was the pious response, the proper answer, his duty. And he did not believe it for one second.

"Poozela."

He kept staring out to space.

"Poozela?"

He looked into her eyes. He could not avoid her tender soul.

"That is not good enough."

Methuselah was about to break completely apart.

The door suddenly burst open. Enoch and the priestess supervisor, a stout woman with a perpetual frown of dissatisfaction stood in the doorway.

Methuselah and Edna froze.

"Edna, I told you to stop this silly interest in sports," said the priestess. "You have your Sacred Marriage rite tomorrow and we need to test your makeup and try out the new dress!"

Enoch did not need as many words. "Methuselah."

Methuselah jumped to his feet and followed Enoch down the hallway back to their quarters in the palace.

CHAPTER 8

As a major city of trade, the Sippar palace sported a hodgepodge of ornamentation. Winding their way through the palace hallways, Methuselah and Enoch passed cedar columns from Aratta, hanging tapestries from the Indus Valley, and stone mason work from the Levant.

Enoch was a holy man who did not even see the craftsmanship and art that filled their living environment and absorbed Methuselah's imagination.

They could not be more different. Enoch received visions from the gods. He sought to raise his son with the same sense of piety and obedience. Unfortunately, Methuselah was too lustful for life and this earth. Enoch loved prayer, Methuselah loved reading cuneiform. Enoch barely noticed women, Methuselah stared at every attractive woman he saw. Enoch loved the holy liturgy of worship, Methuselah loved a feast of food and good drink. Enoch spent hours of silence in the temple shrine, Methuselah spent hours worshipping the beauty of creation (and especially the gods' most beautiful creation, the female body). Enoch was a holy man of heaven, Methuselah felt he was a profane man of earth.

It seemed that the only thing his father loved on this earth was Methuselah's mother. She was Enoch's one connection with humanity and both father and son adored her. Nevertheless, Methuselah thought Enoch could not understand his friendship with Edna. His stomach turned with anxiety.

"Are you romantically inclined to this girl?" demanded Enoch.

"No! She is devoted to the gods!" Methuselah barked, reflexively. How could he think that? Methuselah might be quite the romantic lothario in his weakness for women, but he would never violate the sacred order to even consider Edna as a love interest.

"She is like the little sister I never had," Methuselah claimed. "I do not expect you would understand that."

Despite what his son may have thought of his holy demeanor, Enoch was not a heartless disembodied spirit. It warmed his heart to see his son care for people, and seek to help them and protect them. And he certainly understood love. He just wanted Methuselah to learn what was most important in life after religion, and that was status. There would be plenty of time and opportunity to choose a wife from the court once Methuselah was established as a bona fide apkallu to royalty.

They arrived at the door to their quarters and entered. Enoch struggled to shake off his usual thoughts of his son's future.

"Well, I do not expect you to understand the spiritual vision I just received from an enemy god."

Methuselah's mouth dropped. He had no idea what in the world Enoch was talking about.

Enoch's wife greeted him at the door with a kiss and embrace, as she did every day of their marriage. She was a humble woman, unfortunately too often overshadowed by Enoch's important status and neglected in his royal responsibilities. Yet Methuselah knew that without her, Enoch would be nothing. Enoch knew it as well. She was his strength, his support, his closest counsel and only trusted friend. As passionately zealous as Enoch was, he was also prone to depression. He would often say that in his mountaintops and valleys, his Edna was his steady sea level.

She believed in her husband, happy to support his high and holy calling. Methuselah would sometimes jest what a miracle it was that the gods would create a woman with enough patience for his father.

Methuselah found it ironic that with everything about father and son being so at odds, his best friend had the same name as his mother. Methuselah often wondered why his father, who could see spiritual patterns and signs in just about everything, could not embrace this curiosity with a more positive acceptance.

One thing was certain. The two Ednas were nothing alike. They were as different as Methuselah and Enoch. Mother Edna was kind, sweet, supportive, and submissive. Sixteen-year old Edna was spunky, feisty, independent, and stubborn.

Methuselah's differences with his father haunted him wherever he turned. The living quarters they occupied were humble compared with other palace servants or royalty. According to Enoch, a wisdom sage was not concerned about the things of this world, but about truth, justice, and heaven. Thus, their living space held only a couple bedrooms, and a small eating and lounging area. The whole dwelling space was no bigger than the average servant's quarters. They had only the most basic of furniture, stark against bare walls. Methuselah felt it a pity that royalty such as they were should live in such lack of beauty.

Methuselah had wanted to change the bleak environment for a long time. To him, beauty embodied as much a part of truth as philosophy or ethics. In fact, he thought Enoch's failure to understand this was his father's weakness. A spirituality that excluded the body was impoverished. Methuselah sought a more earthy spirituality. Austerity might bring more intellectual satisfaction, but it created emotional emptiness. Did not the gods make this world to be enjoyed? It made no sense to create a rose, or a woman's body and then say, "Ignore the rose and the woman, and the myriad of sensory experiences that make up your daily existence. Just think about abstract wisdom and the unseen spirit world." That was madness to him.

Enoch said, "Methuselah, I just had a vision of the unseen spirit world that you will probably think is madness."

"Try me," quipped Methuselah, expecting his father to be right. It already sounded crazy and he had not even heard it yet.

The three of them sat down together. Edna brought some fruit and nuts for them to eat.

Enoch said to Methuselah, "Once again, your extracurricular activities drew you away from your responsibility to be with me in the council meeting."

"Sorry, father." They might not be able to understand each other, but they did love one another. Apologies and forgiveness came quickly between them.

"You better be sorry or I will tan your hide," said Enoch. Methuselah cringed at the saying. It was a corny phrase his father liked to use — too often.

Enoch continued, "The first place I looked for you was in the palace garden. You spend too much time in that useless waste of space."

"It is not useless, father," said Methuselah. "Beauty *is* divine transcendence. It connects us to the gods as much as any ritual does." He shook his head. "You always do that. You miss the forest for the trees."

"You are wrong, son," said Edna. "Your father does not care for the forest *or* the trees."

It was her way of teasing Enoch without putting him down. A little bit of humor went a long way toward persuasion for Edna. She had to have a lot of humor with this family of stubborn mules.

Methuselah continued complaining, "Do you even know that the temple is laden with garden imagery and ornamentation? The gods are worshipped in a garden!"

"Enough, son," said Edna. "The point was made. Listen to your father." She would never abandon her true loyalty to her husband.

Enoch sat expressionless, waiting for Methuselah to finish his defense. He continued as if he had not heard a word Methuselah said. "When I was in the garden in my dream vision, I fell to the floor as a dead man, and when I awoke, two archangels stood over me."

Enoch knew how to tell a good story, a useful skill for an apkallu sage. Enoch unfolded his experience to his wife and son with such vivid, artistic description that Methuselah felt himself enraptured into the very heaven of heavens, seeing it all with his own eyes. Maybe his father was not all that out of touch.

CHAPTER 9

"Who are you?" asked Enoch.

The larger, stronger angel spoke first, "We are Gabriel and Uriel, the archangels from the throne of Elohim."

"Elohim?" Enoch had heard of the name. His tribe descended from the line of Seth that had worshipped this god as the creator of all things. But when the dispersion had occurred and his ancestors had settled in the city, they were visited by the gods of Shinar, and this Elohim faded into obscurity. An abstract blurred memory of a distant unseen deity seemed impotent in the real presence of the pantheon with its Four High Gods, Anu, Enlil, Enki, and Ninhursag, and their mighty signs and wonders.

"Everything you worship is a lie," said Gabriel.

Uriel looked at Gabriel. "That is a little shocking, Gabriel. Do you not think it would be wiser to ease him into the truth, instead of slamming him over the head with a mace?"

Gabriel rolled his eyes. "Very well." He turned back to the speechless Enoch.

"You might want to close your mouth," Uriel added to Enoch who snapped his gaping mouth shut.

"Enoch ben Jared, the living God is calling you to bear witness to the truth that has been suppressed in unrighteousness." Gabriel looked at Uriel as if to ask, is that good enough for you? Uriel nodded cautiously.

In the fold of archangels, Uriel ranked as a black sheep, one marred with spots as well as an off-color. He always seemed to see things from a different perspective than the others. This caused him to always interrupt discussions and provoke delays. It made him the butt of jokes. He could not help it. He did not seek to stand out of the crowd. Elohim made him that way. Uriel sometimes called it a "curse," but only in jest. Elohim knew better and had his purposes. In a way, it made Uriel feel special. Perhaps his nature was not all that undesirable.

Uriel stood a bit shorter than most archangels, maybe by half a cubit. His stature became another source of relentless teasing about strength and ability. The mockery nudged Uriel to work harder than all the rest, to prove that he was as good as any of them. The teasing sharpened his wit and words, as if to compensate for his lesser physique.

Enoch's dumbfounded stare focused on Gabriel, until Uriel spoke.

Uriel said to Enoch, "Elohim is the true and living God, the Creator of the universe. He has chosen you as his representative to proclaim judgment upon the gods and upon their giant progeny, the Nephilim."

"You call that subtle?" muttered Gabriel under his breath.

"More lyrical than you will ever be," quipped Uriel. He turned back to Enoch. "Terror is about to break out on all the land, and Elohim has commissioned you to reject the gods of Shinar and become his prophet."

Enoch could not decide which was more difficult to accept, a confrontation with two archangels or the inane banter that kept distracting them from their message. He shook himself out of his stupor. Nothing he had just heard made sense to him. "Excuse, me, what did you say?" asked Enoch.

Uriel repeated the words like a mother with an unruly child who would not listen, "Elohim wants you to speak for him."

"Are you crazy?" said Enoch. "I have been a diviner priest for Utu the sun god all my life. The pantheon of gods has been good to me and my family. Now, I am supposed to condemn them all to their faces?"

"And the Nephilim," Uriel reminded him.

Enoch persisted, "The Nephilim are demigods. They have strength and powers unmatched by humans. The first prophecy I make will be my last. They will execute me on the spot."

Gabriel ignored Enoch's protest. "Trust in Elohim. Rahab is coming upon this city." Rahab was the name of the sea dragon of chaos, the creature of destruction that swam the waters of the Abyss. People invoked her name when they wanted to express foreboding disaster of total annihilation.

"Bring your family and loved ones to the mountains of Aratta in the north. In the volcanic lands of Sahand you will find your distant ancestor, Adam. He will teach you what you need to learn to fulfill Elohim's calling upon your life."

Enoch protested again, "How do I know you are telling the truth? I have never heard from Elohim before. How do I know I can trust him?"

The angels knew the question was reasonable. Gabriel had prepared for it. "This very night, your city will be besieged and your king will die. When you, Enoch, son of Jared, are offered the opportunity to be king, know this: If you accept, you and all your family line will be executed to clear way for a new regime."

Uriel completed the prophecy. "If you choose to escape the city with your family, you will be protected by — well, yours truly." He could not pass up the opportunity for a touch of wit.

Gabriel thought Uriel's wit lessened the urgency of their warning. He reiterated, "Do not accept the offer of kingship, Enoch. It will be deadly."

For the first time in his life in the presence of his father, Methuselah sat quiet. He was stunned. Of all the crazy dreams and visions his father had experienced throughout the years, this one was different. It hit Methuselah more like the truth than anything ever had. He thought that was strange, because he was not the mystical type. But this time, *he just knew it was true*.

Enoch's voice vibrated with anxiety. "How do I know this is true? I mean, this Elohim has never shown his face to me all these years, and now all of a sudden, I am told to leave everything and follow him? It is bizarre."

"Are you moonstruck, father?" said Methuselah, a common insult in the city of the sun god. "After all these years of your wild and unbelievable dreams, you question *this one — now*?"

Enoch retorted, "And you now are the gullible true believer? Or is that just your habit of being contrary and impulsive?"

"I am not being contrary. I cannot explain it. I just know it is true."

"You cannot explain it," repeated Enoch. "Well, now you know how I feel, and what I have been trying to tell you all these years."

Methuselah said, "Have you not often said you would like to meet our forefather Adam? To learn of our history? Here is your opportunity to do so."

"I was being sentimental, not literal," snapped Enoch. "I cannot just walk away from Utu. He has been my god all these years. He has provided for us."

They heard the front door shut. They suddenly noticed that Edna was not with them anymore. She had gotten up and must have left their chambers.

Enoch called out, "Edna?"

No one answered him.

"That is strange," said Enoch. "She has never done that before."

Methuselah guessed that his mother believed the prophecy, more than the "sage" who had received it. She was probably preparing to leave the city, preparations that included Methuselah's young friend, the other Edna, and her parents. She had discussed the possibility with her son in the past.

"She is warning others," he surmised.

"What others?" challenged Enoch.

"Edna and her parents?" offered Methuselah.

"How does she know about this girl of yours?"

"She is not my 'girl,' father," said Methuselah. "I have told mother all about her. She knows we are close, and she is going to help them. She will go after Edna's parents first, to bring them to the palace."

Methuselah's mother already knew that young Edna was in love with her son. She had spent long hours talking with the girl. Mother Edna had been a young lower caste girl once and had fallen in love with a young Enoch as a royal apkallu in training. So she did not have the qualms that either of the men had. They always took so much longer to see these things.

Methuselah replied simply, "We should prepare the family to leave. Mother will be back before long."

"Son, we must have confirmation."

"What else do you need to be — " A knock at the door interrupted Methuselah. Enoch opened the door to a servant messenger.

The man was pale and trembling. "My lord, a riot has begun in the city. The Nephilim are on a rampage, destroying everything in sight and capturing citizens."

Enoch could not believe his ears. "They are taking hostages? What ransom can the palace possibly give them that they have not already extorted out of us?"

"They have been demanding justice. Some say they are taking their anger out on the poor citizens."

"Holy Utu," said Enoch. "My Edna is out there."

Methuselah's throat went dry. He also knew what other horrors awaited the women. "Where is the city guard? Have they done anything to hold them back?"

"The city guard was the first to be taken out," the messenger wailed.

Enoch said, "Where are the Rephaim? Enmeduranki?"

The messenger shook his head. "Nowhere to be found."

That did not make sense to Enoch. They would be the first to coordinate action to protect the citizens. He knew the priest-king truly cared for his people and the Rephaim did not tolerate rebellion.

"The gates of the city have been locked," said the messenger. "No one can get out. For some reason, the Nephilim have stayed away from the palace area." The palace and its riches were always the ultimate goal in these revolutions. "Justice" usually meant theft, plunder, and destruction.

Enoch dismissed the messenger. He turned to Methuselah. "I have to get Edna, but I do not know where she is."

"My Edna will know," said Methuselah. "She can lead us there."

Enoch nodded reluctantly. "You go find the servant girl. I will spread the word to the family to gather in the underground passageways and wait for us. I will meet *you* in the courtyard. Your little friend can lead us to her parents and our Edna."

They ran out the door.

CHAPTER 10

Enoch had been accused of being so spiritually minded that he lacked practical sense, but it was not true. He had arranged various positions of responsibility in the palace area for his extended family. He had given each a code and procedure to follow should any kind of disaster arise, be it a siege of the city or a revolt from within. This revolt fulfilled the second contingency.

He would not have to gather everyone himself. He need only contact a couple of them and they would pass along the information through their prescribed channels. All of them would follow various prepared routes to meet in the secret passageways below the palace, created for this very purpose. Down there, they could weather the danger in the city above. They even had food stores which stayed well-preserved in the cool and dry environment.

Young Edna had no such preparation. In the harem, they would probably be the last to hear about the tragedy unfolding outside their palace walls.

Methuselah made his way across the courtyard to the small harem building at the distant end of the palace area. He could hear the screams outside in the streets. He could not imagine why the giants had not breached the palace gates. He glanced over his shoulder. The glow over the walls of the palace told of buildings burning throughout the city. It was as bad as he had expected.

When he reached the harem building, he dashed into the private chambers. He passed by maidens beautifying themselves and trying on their dresses for tomorrow's Sacred Marriage rite. Screams of surprise and offended modesty rose up as Methuselah looked around wildly hunting for Edna. Losing his way amidst the clamor and buzz around him, he stumbled upon a girl in an elaborate white dress flattening out its ruffles.

"Excuse me, miss," said Enoch.

She turned, and he lost his breath. He beheld a vision of a stunning young beauty with flowing locks of golden spun hair. It bothered him that the gods got the choicest of the women.

"Where is Edna?"

The beauty glared at him with incredulity, exotic make up accentuating her every breath-taking feature. "Are you mocking me?"

"I am sorry, what?" he replied.

"Are you that thickheaded? It is me, silly," said the girl.

It hit him like a ton of mud bricks. This gorgeous vision of feminine transcendence frowning at him was none other than the transformed presentation of his immature scrawny little boyish girl Edna. His little Pedna. How could he have never seen her this way before?

He stumbled back a step and almost fainted. He knew at that very moment that he would never be happy in this life again until he married this goddess. This was the very first time he had really truly *finally* seen her. And his entire life changed in that instant.

"What is wrong with you?" Edna giggled.

Methuselah shook it off. He would have to deal with this later. Right now, he had to save her life.

"Edna, do you trust me?" he said.

"Yes, of course."

"Then trust me this once completely, and do exactly as I say. The city is in danger."

"What?"

"I will tell you on the way. Take off this outer dress. We must leave now. No questions asked."

She obeyed and pulled it off. Her tunic underneath was better suited for running.

She did trust him, with all her heart and soul. She let him lead her out of the building toward the courtyard. He told her about the riots and the giants and the hostages as they ran. It was all horrific, but she was a tough girl. Methuselah realized she was the kind of person you wanted on your side when all Sheol broke loose. She would not scream in fear and shake like a little mouse. She would want to join the fray.

"You need to tell me where your parents live. My mother went to get them, to bring them with us. But now they are all three caught up in the middle of it."

"I will take you there," said Edna.

"I want you to stay here," said Methuselah.

She looked him square in the eye. "You will not be able to find your way," she said. "You do not know the city streets, and you certainly do not know the shortcuts. You will get lost, plain and simple. I am not letting you go alone. I want to be with you."

He stared back into her eyes. He sometimes questioned whether he should have taught her how to debate so well. But she was right, so it was a good thing he had done it.

For the first time in her short existence on this earth she saw the expression of a man who would give his life for her without a thought.

In her eyes he saw the look of a woman who would die by his side rather than be alone. That is, after all, what she had trained for all those years.

He grinned. "Pedna, let us kick some shank."

Throughout Sippar, the streets lay eerily empty. Enoch, Methuselah, and Edna slinked through the shadows, trying to stay out of sight. The screams had died down, sporadic and at a distance. Fires burned all over, but they did not see any giants or people.

"This is not a good sign," said Methuselah.

She responded, "My parents have a secret hideaway in the floor. I am sure they would have hidden there at the first sign of trouble."

"Is there room for a third person?" asked Enoch.

"Yes," she said. "They always figured me into their plans."

"Utu be with them," prayed Enoch as they continued on. *Or should it be Elohim?* he thought.

Ahead of them, in the center of the city, they could see the glow of a huge bonfire. The giants had congregated there with the hostages. The trio needed to pass the gathering to get to the sector where Edna's parents lived. They slid past homes demolished by the smashing strength of the Nephilim. They shuddered at the degree of damage. Whole houses reduced to rubble, the streets littered with household items and furniture, small fires everywhere. But not a sign of life.

They made their way through the cluttered back alleys that Edna knew so well. They avoided the central bonfire. They were almost to her parents' street, when curiosity got the better of them. They decided to turn back and take a look. A gap in the wreckage gave them a better look at the open space.

The debris in the town square had been cleared away and piled up with wood from the marauding. Nearly a hundred of the giants stood around like a gang of miscreants.

Vomit arose in Edna's throat. They could see a crude line of cages full of weeping, pleading humans. Other humans were strung up from poles, and still others were encircled and taunted by groups of Nephilim. But the ultimate atrocity playing out before their eyes was not one of torture and rape, but cannibalism. The Nephilim were eating their captives one by one. Some took the time to impale the victims and roast them over the flames. Others had no such civility, eating the poor humans alive and drinking their blood. The hostages were not being held for ransom at all. They were being held for food.

Tears filled Enoch's eyes. He knew the giants were a rowdy community and sometimes got in trouble for their violence, but he had not realized that they were capable of such barbarism. His entire view of the world had turned upside down.

Suddenly, behind them, they heard the snap of wood and the sound of stumbling and grunting. They dropped to the ground and slid beneath some wreckage. About fifteen cubits away, a drunken Naphil relieved himself in the open. Not all the Nephilim were at the bonfire. Stragglers wandered the streets and back alleys. The trio would have to be extra careful.

The Naphil belched and then without warning, projectile vomited into a pile of rubbish. The commotion gave Enoch, Methuselah, and Edna the opportunity to slip away without being seen or heard.

· · · · ·

The Rephaim leaders Thamaq and Yahipan were not at the palace or coordinating a military response to the riots because they had been the ones who betrayed the militia guard. They had been the ones to lock the city gates, and they had been the ones to instigate the mob riots of Nephilim. They had planned this entire drunken chaos. They had now gone off to a dark corner of the city to celebrate the bloodshed with carnal appetite.

They donned their royal robes and were on their way to the bonfire. Only a few streets from the scene of Nephilim atrocities, they heard a noise from one of the homes. They slipped up to a window and peered inside. An older couple climbed up from a trap door in the floor amidst a pile of debris. Smirking to each other, the Rephaim positioned themselves near the door, ready to trap these renegades. But they paused at a sight they had not expected.

Someone they knew very well followed the older couple from the hiding place: Edna, the wife of Enoch the apkallu.

Their smirks turned to broad grins. What a lucky surprise for them, and what an unlucky surprise for these poor leeches. They burst into the home.

The would-be fugitives gasped and backed into a corner. Edna picked up the remains of a chair and brandished it as a weapon.

Thamaq laughed and brushed it aside as though it were nothing more than a feather. He grabbed Edna by the throat and pinned her against the wall. Then he seized the other woman with his free hand.

As Yahipan subdued the old man, Thamaq glared at Edna. "What are you doing here, wife of Utuabzu? You should have stayed safe in the palace."

She struggled in his suffocating grasp. "Why are you doing this?" she choked out. He ignored her question. He leaned in close. "I have long fantasized about consuming your flesh." Thamaq opened his mouth to bite off her head.

He did not get to chomp tonight. A knife flew through the air and penetrated his cheek. He dropped the wench to the ground, clutching his wound in pain. He pulled out the blade with a wince of pain. He looked for the source of the stinger.

Enoch stood a knife's throw away. Just behind him, panting from running, appeared young Edna in her tunic, now soiled with the dirt of the city.

It confused Thamaq. It did not make sense, all this royalty out of context in the tenement district of the city.

Yahipan felt no such confusion or hesitation. He immediately started for the little rodent to squash him with impunity. But he did not think ahead. He did not consider there might be a third party lying in wait.

Yahipan rushed toward his prey. The hidden Methuselah struck out with his knife and sliced the heel tendon of Yahipan's right foot.

The Rapha screamed in pain. His leg gave way, tumbling him to the ground with a large thud. He carried the old man in his arms, and used him to cushion his fall. The impact of the giant's body crushed the life out of the poor fellow.

"FATHER!" screamed Edna.

Methuselah shot a glance in her direction. He did not see Thamaq focus on him. The Rapha threw his captives to the ground and jumped for Methuselah. He swatted the human with such force that it jettisoned Methuselah a good fifteen cubits into a wall, knocking him senseless.

When Yahipan fell forward, he landed within arm's reach of Enoch and Edna. He grabbed them both in his iron vise grip. They were not going to break free from this monster. Thamaq brought the stunned Methuselah over and threw him down next to Edna. All three of them looked up into the eyes of fate ready to crush them.

"I love you, Edna," muttered Methuselah.

"I have always loved you," she replied.

"Is that not precious," snorted Thamaq. "Maggots in love."

"SON OF SHEOL, THIS HURTS!" screamed Yahipan. "I want that little worm Utuabzu. I am going to eat him alive."

Thamaq motioned forcefully for Yahipan to wait as he mused over their prey.

"Let us not be hasty, Yahipan. Consider what we have here. The royal apkallu and his apprentice son. Here to save the family of a sacred virgin with whom they have committed treason against the gods." It would indeed be considered treason to steal away a virgin betrothed for the Sacred Marriage rite to Utu.

"I would say that was a deed punishable by death, would you not agree, Yahipan?" said Thamaq.

Yahipan nursed his wounded tendon. His every word came out filled with venom, "I think they deserve a fate worse than death. I am going to torture you apkallus first and make you watch what we do to your little lovebird here."

Enoch swallowed. This was the end. He saw Enmeduranki's priestly jewels hanging from Yahipan's neck, and he knew the priest-king's fate. A fate that would soon be their own. The three held hands and prepared to meet the gods.

And meet the gods they did.

A loud trumpet call filled the skies and the Rephaim looked around. The earth trembled. Thunder cracked the sky.

Yahipan gasped, "The war cry of Anu!"

The bonfire in the distance flared up with supernatural vigor. They heard the sounds of battle, the sounds of weapons of war.

"It is the pantheon," said Thamaq. "They found us."

Everyone turned to see a group of four Nephilim fleeing on the streets. Hot on their tails stormed one of the gods, though they could not tell which one. The god dove and tackled the Nephilim like a group of pins in a sport. The fugitives tried to get up and defend themselves, but the deity sliced through them with his strange scythe-looking weapon as if they were blades of wheat in the wind.

Methuselah could not believe his eyes.

The god looked up and saw him. Methuselah went white. He looked behind himself. Thamaq and Yahipan had already vanished. Young Edna held onto her mother, kneeling on the ground where she had fallen. Next to her, Enoch clutched his wife Edna.

The god walked toward them, joined by another. Methuselah realized it was Anu followed by Utu. Utu called out, "Methuselah! Thank the stars you are alive. Where is the priest-king and your father? Are they alive as well?"

He was the sun god, patron of the city, thought Methuselah. *He should have better knowledge of the whereabouts of his servants.* Methuselah stepped aside.

Utu saw Enoch cradling his beloved wife in his arms, weeping.

Methuselah said, "Thank you for saving us." He limped over to young Edna, and knelt down beside her. He held her in his arms as she held her mother's lifeless body in hers. He was close enough to extend his hand to his father. The three of them were united in their grief. Their loved ones were all dead.

The gods approached them. Anu said, "I am sorry for your loss."

Utu followed up with, "The pantheon will make sure your loved ones make it safely through the Abyss into Sheol."

That was not much comfort to Enoch. What he knew of Sheol did not reassure him. Sheol was the land of the dead, the netherworld, from which no one returns. It was said that the mouth of Sheol was never satisfied and the shades of the dead rested on a bed of maggots where the worm does not die.

Anu said, "The Gigantomachy has been suppressed. Their rebellion is averted."

Enoch did not care about the rebellion. He did not care about the gods. He did not care about anything anymore. His Edna was gone. Now, only his son Methuselah kept him anchored to this earth.

CHAPTER 11

Only a few hundred citizens of Sippar were saved by the gods from the rampaging Nephilim. Similar scenes of debauched giant uprisings and anarchy had played out in other cities of the plain. Pazuzus, the grotesque flying messengers, had been used to spread the madness to other cities. Unfortunately for the mobs of giants, that same source of news found its way to the pantheon, who responded with swift justice from their lofty height on Mount Hermon. Many of the giants were killed, but some of them surrendered quickly to their procreators, and were incarcerated for further interrogation and later execution.

Anu, Inanna, and Utu had arrived and called a gathering to make an announcement. The surviving citizens assembled before the palace. Though Sippar was Utu's city, Anu was chief deity, so he was traveling the circuit of cities making appearances at each one to inspire hope and unity. He spoke with a fatherliness that moved Enoch's heart. Methuselah and Edna were not so easily moved.

"People of Sippar, we stand before you today with shared sorrow and deep regret."

Inanna stood behind Anu, taking note of the dance of verbal trickery displayed in his speech. She listened with a mixture of awe and resentment, but she listened and learned from this master of rhetoric.

Anu continued, "This Nephilim rebellion, this *Gigantomachy*, has wrought great destruction throughout the cities of our rule. We have all suffered great loss. And I want to assure you that on behalf of the pantheon of your gods, I feel your pain."

Disgusting, thought Inanna. *Is he shedding a tear? He has actually mustered up a reptilian tear from within the stone cold rock of his soul.*

The people before them listened in resigned silence.

"The divine council has convened and deliberated on what is to be done for justice to be served on these criminals and degenerates. After much soul wrenching we have come to a most painful yet necessary judgment."

Soul wrenching, thought Inanna. She must remember that word. *It gave the humans the impression that we have a conscience.*

"The giants have become an unruly elite of privilege and power," Anu proclaimed. "They have conspired in revolution and have proven themselves unworthy of their status and authority. As of this day, the gods have removed the giants from leadership over you, and their organized activities have become illegal. The surviving Nephilim will no longer be allowed to congregate, and the Rephaim are considered outlaws for their conspiracy in the riots. They will no longer reign over you. Any giants that are found outside the employ of the palace or temple authority are considered criminals and will be executed. We gods have remained too distant and aloof from our people. But we will now leave our heavenly abode in the cosmic mountain and will reside in the cities of our patronage. We will protect you and shepherd you with our undivided attention."

The people murmured to one another. Enoch thought, *Could it be true? Could the gods come and dwell amongst us?* This seemed to make Elohim further distant in his invisibility and removed presence.

The plan repulsed Inanna. *These stinking organisms of bone, flesh, and excrement are loathsome,* she thought. *Elohim displayed his true incompetence when he created such foul parasites in his image — his despicable image that the gods had sworn an oath to desecrate.*

Anu's voice carried out over the crowd. "Some Nephilim who were captured have expressed remorse for their part in the uprising. Others did not join in. In our grace, we have chosen to accept these few loyal ones back into the fold of our mercy. We will brand them with tattoos of our ownership, and employ them only as our bodyguards and special forces. Those who escaped their punishment into the desert or wilderness will be hunted down and brought to justice."

The crowd of humans broke into spontaneous applause. Methuselah did not. He thought about how he might track down Thamaq and Yahipan and kill them.

The noise made Anu pause. It created a nice dramatic effect. He raised his chin in the air to display a superiority of leadership that inspired confidence in his subjects. He was masterly.

He rode the crest of the wave. "But good people of this fertile crescent, we will need your faith and your fortitude to help rebuild your cities, and create temples for your gods. To seek a progressive future where everyone will give their fair share and everyone will be taken care of from crib to grave."

More applause rang out from the people. He inspired them, refilling them with a sense of hope.

Inanna chuckled to herself. *These ignorant hairy insects have no idea that their fair share is complete and total servitude to the god of the city-state. They were born to be slaves and they will be slaves — from crib to grave.* Inanna and the other gods had discovered the universal economic law from time immemorial: whatever you tax you get less of, and whatever you subsidize you get more of. By heavily overtaxing wealth, she could decrease the amount of private wealth and therefore lessen its power. By subsidizing poverty with government welfare she would increase poverty and thus dependency upon the state. Human nature was such an easy thing to exploit when you understood how it operated.

"It is with a heavy heart that I must inform you that your priest-king Enmeduranki of Sippar was killed in the riots."

Murmurs and a few cries could be heard from the crowd.

Anu had not finished yet. "We will appoint a new priest-king to establish a royal line that will administer the will of the gods."

That will relieve us immortals from the contemptible millstone of governmental bureaucracy, mused Inanna. The gods would do as they pleased and make the mortals cover their tracks with treaties, covenants and other wasteful bureaucracy.

Anu concluded his soaring inspirational speech, "So, now, my people, go back to your homes, gather your survivors, nurse your wounds, and rebuild your houses. Soon we will work together for a new world of hope and of change, freed from the suffering you have endured."

The crowd applauded. Anu reached back and held up the hands of Inanna and Utu as their champions.

Enoch, Methuselah and Edna quietly slipped out of the back of the crowd.

CHAPTER 12

"Lord of the sun, Queen of heaven," Enoch humbly offered as he bowed before Utu. The god sat on the throne of Enmeduranki. Beside him stood Inanna, left behind to finish the royal appointment process with Utu. Anu had discharged his duty of making an appearance at Sippar and was off to the other cities to repeat his rhetorical performance. Inanna lusted for the supreme power of the high god, but she certainly did not envy his responsibilities of political pandering required to maintain an awed worship from the citizens. She would prefer to smite them.

Enoch had been summoned to their presence and he waited respectfully for them to speak.

"As you now know," said Utu, "Enmeduranki was killed in the uprising. We are required to appoint a new priest-king to take his place. Because of your wisdom and experience in the workings of the palace, we have chosen you, Utuabzu, to be the new priest-king."

For a sun god, Inanna thought, *Utu was rather dim and unimpressive.* She could not wait to get out of this insignificant city and catch up with Anu to maneuver for some more influence.

"I am unworthy of your grace, my lord and lady," said Enoch.

Inanna could not bear the pleasantries of royal etiquette. She cut in, yet again. Utu's face took on a tight lipped expression of irritation.

"Prepare your family for a coronation tomorrow morning. We will meet in the palace courtyard beforehand to brief you on the procedures. Let us be done with this."

"It is an honor of great magnitude, your majesty," said Enoch.

"Move along, move along," spit Inanna.

Enoch responded obediently, scurrying back to his residence in the palace.

· · · · ·

"This night?" asked Methuselah. Enoch had arrived back at his quarters and was hurriedly packing bags.

"Yes, we are leaving now! Gather only what is necessary. We will meet the family down in the secret passageways and we will take the lesser desert path to the mountains of Aratta," said Enoch.

"So, you have changed your mind. I was right, then?" said Methuselah with a touch of sarcasm.

Enoch stopped packing and turned to look at his son. "Methuselah, this is no time for laughs. The gods just appointed me to the position of priest-king. Tomorrow is the coronation, and the entire family is required to be there."

Methuselah wiped the smile off his face. He remembered the vision his father had told him, how the archangels had said that Enoch would be offered the position of king and then executed with his family to facilitate a total regime change. He shut up and quickly gathered his things together.

• • • • •

It would not take long to mobilize the fifty or so family members in the passageway below the palace. They had stayed there since the Gigantomachy uprising, so they were ready to leave at a moment's notice. Enoch explained everything to them.

They exited the tunnels a half mile from the city. They would make their way across the Tigris and up into the Zagros mountain territory. They had some onagers to carry the young children, women, and elderly of the tribe. They would have to test their limits with a brisk pace to get as far from the city as they could before daylight.

Enoch knew that the gods would hunt them down as soon as they discovered the family was gone. They did not stand a chance, but he had to try. He had no other choice. Stay and certainly die, or run and probably die.

When Methuselah arrived at the gathering point with Edna, Enoch glared with disapproval. Methuselah stared him in the eye and said, "Would you prefer she marry the gods?"

Enoch stubbornly refused to answer as they moved on through the passageway. His son was right. After all Edna had been through with them, he should not have even raised the question. He would apologize for that later.

They had taken only a few paces when Edna pulled Methuselah aside and spoke to him in a whisper. "You might want to talk to me before implying romantic intentions in public to your father."

"I was referring to saving you from the Sacred Marriage."

Edna studied his face, regathering her thoughts. Then she took the chance of vulnerability, "So did you mean what you said when we were attacked by the Rephaim?"

"What did I say?" he said, stonefaced.

She tightened her lips in anger and hissed, "Methuselah ben Enoch, you know exactly what you said."

"We were about to die, Edna," he complained. "I said whatever came into my mind."

She could not believe it. This stubborn onager was too scared to admit his feelings after all they had been through. But he had left an opening and her strategic training prepared her to take it.

"So, you are saying that at the moment of facing death, your love of me came into your mind?"

Methuselah walked on silently.

What was it with men? Why could they not just say what they felt?

"Poozela, just promise me one thing," whispered Edna. "If we ever face certain death again, please do *not* say you love me unless you intend to admit your love to the world should we survive that certain death. I do not think that is asking too much, do you?"

"Very well, Pedlum," he said, "I promise. Now let us go." They were behind the rest of the family.

Pedlum was a new nickname, adapted no doubt from Pedna into a more flowery affection. It was the tiniest hint that he was starting to break. Edna shivered with glee.

"By the way, happy birthday," Methuselah added as an afterthought. He traipsed on.

She had forgotten. In the midst of all this terror, she had turned sixteen. It seemed inconsequential in light of the world ending and everything.

But he had remembered. He did remember.

CHAPTER 13

Enoch's caravan had covered five leagues to the Tigris River by morning. He had pushed them. They were running for their lives, but this was all the distance they could make with women, children, and elderly.

A small river tribe with boats lived along the banks which could easily have taken them downriver. Unfortunately, their destination did not lie downriver in the heart of Shinar. They needed to travel *upriver* into the mountains of Aratta.

But there were no tribespeople in sight. Had they all hidden? Were they out on a hunt?

Enoch looked back along their path. The morning light revealed a pack of Nephilim already on their trail. Some women screamed. Enoch tried to calm them. Their backs were to the river. The Nephilim were riding down upon them. They had nowhere to go.

Methuselah held Edna tightly and gripped his mace even tighter, Enoch fell to his knees and cried out to Elohim, this god he barely knew and hardly trusted. But what could he lose now? They were all going to die. And this poor innocent river tribe, when they showed themselves, would be caught in the cross blades of slaughter. They had not done anything to deserve this. None of Enoch's clan had done anything to deserve this.

The palace Nephilim had closed the distance to an arrow's flight, but they would use no arrows on their quarry. Nephilim preferred close quarter combat. They preferred to tear the limbs off their prey rather than pierce them dead from a distance. Close combat satisfied their bloodlust. They were monsters, fast monsters. They did not need animals for transportation, for they ran faster without them.

Methuselah counted ten of them. *Talk about overkill,* he thought. *One alone could kill us all.*

The tribe huddled close to each other. The men stepped out with their few useless weapons in a pathetic attempt at a vain last stand. They felt the call of moral obligation to act courageously. They did not stand a chance. They were all going to die.

Certain death did not matter to Methuselah and Edna. They were actually hoping that they would be able to take down one together as a badge of honor before they perished. They had done well against the Rephaim. Their victim was probably suffering a humiliating permanent limp somewhere out in the hinterlands.

Yet, even at that moment, Methuselah felt compelled to make light of circumstances to Edna. He stared out at the approaching predators, at the trail of dust rising in the air, and said under his breath, "Well, here we are again, facing certain death."

She glared at him expectantly.

Methuselah surprised her, "This is where you admit again that you have *always* loved me." He said the word *always* with relish. It was quite revealing when she had first said it, and now she felt like a silly little fool.

She punched his arm hard.

"Ow!" he yelped. He was the stronger vessel, but he had also taught her how to maximize her punch with impact. He sighed and smiled warmly at her. "It is true, Edna. I do love you. And if we do get out of this alive, I will declare my intentions to the world."

Edna glanced back at the advancing Nephilim. She could now see their skin and faces. Their entire bodies were covered in occultic tattoos, displaying their new allegiance to the gods. She had not realized Nephilim could be any scarier than they already were.

"That is not fair," she said. "You know we are *really* dead this time. Even so, I am praying for a miracle."

She glanced around, looking for that miracle. She noticed two river people in cloaks come out of their tents. So there were a couple unlucky tribesmen here after all.

The two cloaked men stood in front of Enoch and his people. The lead one spoke clearly for all to hear, "Fear not! Trust in Elohim and he will deliver you!"

Enoch recognized that voice.

The two men turned toward the Nephilim. The giants were within fifty cubits of the clan and about to pounce. In unison, the mysterious pair threw off their cloaks.

Gabriel and Uriel, the archangels, stood guard before the clan. They brandished the strange weapons Enoch had seen before. Uriel had two of the long blades in his hands called *swords*. The archangels raised their weapons and yelled, "A sword for the Lord and for Enoch!" Then they bolted into the fray of approaching giants.

The archangels cut through the Nephilim like barley. Trained and angry giants were cut down by these two mighty warriors in less time than it took for Enoch to urinate in his tunic from the terror mere cubits away.

The stronger of the two, Gabriel, fought three at a time like a hungry lion. But Uriel made up for his diminished size with cunning strategy and unorthodox moves. They worked well in tandem.

Gabriel disarmed one and yelled out to Uriel, who spun around and cut him down. They swapped positions and opponents in a flash, confusing the Nephilim. But it took effort. The archangels had to work hard for their results.

Three Nephilim managed to strike Gabriel's sword at once. It flew out of his hand. Uriel threw Gabriel one of his two swords until Gabriel could pick up his own and get back on track.

The last four Nephilim surrounded Uriel. Gabriel fought with the leader of the pack. The four monsters tightened their circle on Uriel, lashing, swinging, and jabbing their weapons. Uriel appeared to be weakening.

He had only been drawing them in closer. Then he did something that astonished all those who saw it. He stretched out his two swords like windmill blades. He spun like a whirlwind in this strange position. His shearing blades took out the circle of the enemy surrounding him. It was awe inspiring.

Not one Naphil got past these mighty warriors of Elohim.

Enoch found himself thinking that it was a good thing he had changed allegiance to this distant god of his fathers. His servants were just. And they shared the same enemy. This was good. This was very good.

The archangels walked toward Enoch.
Methuselah and Edna drew near to listen in.
The angels were exhausted. These warriors fought like gods, but they were still finite created beings with flesh. They suffered the burdens of that flesh. They were drenched in sweat and breathing hard. Nephilim were not easy to kill.

As they approached the astonished Enoch and his family, they muttered under their breath to each other. "Six kills to your four. Would you like me to teach you some tactics?" said Uriel.

"Five to five," countered Gabriel. "That one we did together."

"You mean the one *I killed*," said Uriel.

"After *I disarmed* him," retorted Gabriel.

"Was that before or after you dropped your sword?" said Uriel.

"I did not 'drop' my sword," said Gabriel. "Three of them hit me at once."

"Okay, okay, *they* disarmed *you*," said Uriel with a grin. Then he added, "But then, if we both killed him, then that would make it five and a half to four and a half."

They arrived at the humans, and snapped out of their bickering.

"I am famished. Let us eat something," said Uriel.

Enoch stepped backward fearfully. Uriel paused, then laughed, "Fret not, Enoch, we are not going to eat you. Truth be told, we would not even eat those Nephilim."

Edna scrunched her face in disgust. This archangel was rather profane. She wondered if his god Elohim had that kind of sick sense of humor.

Gabriel soothed their anxiety. "Elohim sent us to help you. We brought these boats for you to take the Tigris and Diyala rivers up into the Zagros where you can follow the rest of your trip on foot in relatively safe passage."

Enoch protested, "But the rivers flow south. We do not know how to sail, and we do not have the strength to man the oars to get upstream."

"Are you sure?" asked Gabriel.

"Yes, I am sure," Enoch shot back. "Unless this Elohim of yours would like to perform another miracle and change the course of the rivers from south to north." His sarcasm dripped a bit heavily after having just been delivered by this servant of Elohim.

Uriel raised his hand and gestured with his finger for Enoch to follow him.

Enoch trailed behind him to the bank of the river. The others of the clan shadowed them. Enoch looked out onto the river and lost his breath.

It was flowing north. The river actually flowed in the opposite direction than it had been from the beginning of time.

"It is a miracle," exclaimed Enoch, his eyes and mouth wide open.

Gabriel smiled. "You will learn to be more grateful. It comes with experience."

Uriel leaned in close to Enoch and murmured, "And you also need to stop allowing your mouth to gape open when you are in awe. It is unflattering."

Enoch snapped his mouth closed.

Methuselah spoke softly into his father's ear, "Well, we better not disappoint Elohim, father."

"Board the boats," Enoch said to the tribe.

"Wait a minute," interrupted Edna.

Everyone stopped and looked at her. Enoch thought the little pipsqueak was bold. She stared straight at Methuselah with her teasing eyes. It made him wary. She normally pulled that expression on him when she occasionally beat him in a game or prank.

She proudly proclaimed, "Methuselah has a promise to fulfill."

He sighed. Then a big fat grin burst across his face, and he yelled out to the entire tribe, "Edna has *always* loved me!"

She opened her mouth in shock and slapped him. "I cannot believe you, Methuselah ben Enoch!"

Methuselah stopped laughing. He looked right into the eyes of his precious Pedlums and laughter turned to love. "Edna bar Azrial, I want all the world to know that I love you more than life, more than the heavens and the earth!"

Everyone moaned with romantic longing.

Methuselah was not done. "And if this Elohim does not drown us in the river, freeze us in the mountains or burn us in volcanic ash on our trip to Sahandria, will you marry me?"

She squealed, jumped into his arms, and gave his big fat grin his first big fat kiss. "Yes, yes, yes, yes, yes!" she rattled off, smothering him with kisses. He heartily returned then.

Enoch stood silent, watching them. He had made known his displeasure with Methuselah's interest in the girl, so this display was a bit off-putting to him. But he could see the happiness in his son's whole body. It reminded him of his own happiness when he had realized he was in love with his own precious Edna so many years ago.

Methuselah set Edna down and she apologized for her inappropriate display of public affection. Everyone laughed and applauded her. She gave an impish glance at Enoch, her future father-in-law.

Enoch could see that they were two of a kind. Even he could not stay disagreeable. He smiled. But deep in his heart, he longed for his beloved, the only true thing on this earth. And she was now gone forever.

A deep yearning came over Methuselah that he never experienced before. He hungered for Edna, body and soul.

They had better get to Sahandria quickly so he could marry her.

CHAPTER 14

It took Enoch's family about two weeks to navigate the Tigris to the Diyala river about 80 leagues up into the Zagros. Their trip was uneventful. Enoch prayed that Utu had more important things to do than track down a single apkallu sage and his family, who would probably be dead in the wilderness anyway. He knew Utu well enough to know that the god would not waste his energy micromanaging such minor issues. What was one less puny human to worry about?

The missing Nephilim sent after them were a different matter. They would be missed eventually. Enoch hoped that when they failed to return, Utu would believe them to be rogue outlaws who took their chance to run to the hills when freed from the confines of the city. It would be a reasonable explanation for their disappearance. It had already happened with many Nephilim.

Enoch's party left their boats at the river's end. They had all forgotten the miracle of the changed river course within hours of steering upstream. After a few days, they had begun wondering if their memories had failed them and the river had always flowed north. But as soon as they ran their boats aground, the current suddenly turned back south.

Enoch fell to the ground weeping in repentance.

Methuselah noticed Enoch had been doing a lot of weeping lately, usually for his lost Edna. He wept mostly at night, when everyone else slept. He also prayed much more. Too much. It seemed to Methuselah that his father sought escape by plunging even further into his spirituality in order to avoid facing the pain of this earth. Methuselah felt that pain was more reliable and real than the hope and promises of the heavenlies. After so deep a betrayal by the gods, how could he shift his allegiance to this new god Elohim without question? Elohim's emissaries had saved them, it was true, but for whose sake? Methuselah felt more like a pawn in an invisible spiritual game of wrestling powers. He did not feel as if he had much of a choice in the matter. The worst thing about the situation was all the secrets and mystery. It made trust seem so uncertain.

Methuselah trusted the experience of his senses. The strength of a belly full of food, the contact of a handheld mace with an enemy's skull, and the touch of his beautiful betrothed Edna. These things he could know with resounding certainty. He found it more difficult to trust the uncertainties of invisible gods, disappearing angels, and unanswered prayers and petitions. This Elohim would have to prove himself trustworthy with a bit more rigorous confirmation to get Methuselah's attention.

Edna more willingly believed in Elohim's beneficence. When the river had returned to its natural southward current, she wondered how many other miracles they would take for granted with such lack of gratitude. The provision of food to fill their bellies? More salvation from the enemy's mace? The devoted love of a man with a woman? The conception of a new human life? The birth of a child? It seemed everything kept pointing back to Methuselah in her heart. She watched him lead the group with authority. She thought of him tenderly soothing her fears, dreamed of his strength and humor. She simply wanted to make him happy and build a home together.

Methuselah kept thinking about doing only one thing with Edna, and it was not building a home.

• • • • •

They traveled another thirty leagues through the valley of Havilah and the Mannean plain until they finally stood upon the volcanic fields of Mount Sahand.

Enoch felt humbled by the majesty. Everyone stared across the stark expanse in silence. The snow-covered dome of the Sahand volcano stood about eight thousand cubits, the highest peak in the region. The mountain range included a dozen other volcanic heads along the ridges. It looked like a fortress wall of rock with volcanic guard towers. Lake Urimiya spread sparkling to the west.

Enoch's soul moved deep within him, knowing that on the far side of Mount Sahand lay the valley of the Garden of Eden, that no man dare approach. This would be the closest anyone could ever come to the legendary paradise. A tribe of Cherubim guarded its perimeter, to keep the descendants of Adam away.

They stood before a vast terrain of igneous rock. Not a soul in sight. A dead wasteland. Enoch wondered where the Adamites were, those forgotten people and their patriarch that they were supposed to find? Did Elohim have his directions correct? Obviously not. There was not a sign of life for leagues around. Tribes of any size always left traces of their presence, and they could see no trace of any human presence in the area but their own.

They would have set up camp and begin their survey of the area first thing in the morning. Enoch hoped that he had not wasted his and everyone's time after all.

They pitched camp a third of a league onto the barren landscape to avoid surprise by any approaching enemies. There was nowhere to sneak up on them in a three hundred and sixty degree arc. Anyone who tried to crawl their way toward the camp would shred their clothes and flesh right off their bodies from the sharp porous bedrock and rubble strewn about.

Enoch limited the nightwatch to two details of three guards. He made sure to keep Methuselah on the far edge of the men's camp for his watch detail. It would keep his son from the tempting position of easy access to Edna in the women's camp. Methuselah was an honorable young man, but at his age passionate urges could be so strong that even honorable young men could go temporarily mad and make decisions they would regret when cooler heads prevailed.

The midnight hour came and Methuselah could not sleep. His thoughts burned of Edna, piercing his brain with a hammer-like pounding. At least it kept him awake for his watch duty. Unfortunately, it also distracted his attention.

He did not catch the first soft sound of scraping in the rocks near him. But the second time the sound flew by, he heard it. He looked up. A full moon lit the landscape. There was nothing out there. Still, he was uneasy. He reached down and picked up his mace, intending to practice some moves with it.

When he brought it up, he stopped in silent shock.

Just seconds before, the horizon had shown no life for miles around. Now the shadows of a hundred dark figures surrounded the camp. The shapes stood upright like men, but had antlers and horns like wild animals. They formed a living fence of shadow-like spectres roundabout. Where had they come from?

It was as if they materialized out of the rocks themselves. Were they phantasms, shades of Sheol? Or worse, *shedim*, demons?

Before Methuselah could shout a warning, all the figures held up branches with pots on them and smashed the pots with their weapons. The resounding echo woke everyone up in terror. Women screamed, men grabbed their weapons. A frightening ring of fire surrounded them and they became disoriented. The figures had carried torches hidden in pots. The camp was taken entirely by surprise and now Enoch's company was completely vulnerable, like a man asleep with a blade at his throat.

CHAPTER 15

The dark shadows of the night were not demons, they were men. But they were not entirely the same kind of men that Methuselah and Enoch and all their lineage produced. They seemed more apelike. They walked upright, but were hairier than usual, with a stocky, robust musculature and pronounced brows and jaws. They wore animal skins and headdresses created from the game they hunted, thus creating the illusion of supernatural denizens in the night.

As the strangers guided them in the dark, Methuselah learned why he had not spotted them creeping up on the camp, and why they seemed to emerge from the rocks themselves. They *had* emerged from the rocks. They were troglodytes, cave dwellers. They now led Enoch's clan through fissures and portals into the volcanic earth below their feet.

Their torches lit the way through a labyrinth of carved passageways.

Edna was already confused and thought how easy it would be to become lost amidst these tunnels. She could see the troglodytes knew the way like the back of their hand. Then she thought of Methuselah's hand, and how strong and manly it was, yet how it could caress her with such affection. She pushed that thought out of her head. She had to be all there. She had to be ready for action.

As they walked down the incline, Methuselah was disgusted with himself. Here they were, their lives in danger, captive to a tribe of primitive apemen, not knowing if they would help them or eat them, and all he could do was to stare at the pleasurable way that Edna's hips moved as she walked in front of him. What on earth was happening to him? He could not think straight. He shook it out of his mind. He had to be ready for action.

Enoch could tell they were going deep into the earth. The slope of the shaft was steep at first, but then tapered off as they neared their destination, which seemed to be an untold number of cubits below ground.

They passed through a guarded portal into a large cavern. Enoch gasped at what he saw. They stood on a ledge overlooking a vast space. As large as the palace in Sippar, about two hundred cubits in diameter and seventy cubits high, it was more than a mere natural cave. It had been carved and shaped into a palatial interior, with a vaulted arch ceiling and columns around the perimeter. How could these primitive apemen create such sophisticated architecture?

Below them, dozens of apemen, apewomen, and apechildren busied themselves at a marketplace. They all stopped and stared up at the captives descending the stairs into another passageway entrance. One of the apechildren pointed up at them and whispered something to its mother. It occurred to Enoch that he should probably not call them apemen. It might offend them. Their adult males appeared strong enough to crush his skull if they wanted to.

They passed other hallways and arched entrances. They saw more neighborhoods of dwellings and communities. By the time they reached their destination, Enoch calculated that this city was easily as big as Sippar, but entirely underground. He now started to think that perhaps he should not call them apemen because they might very well be more sophisticated than the city dwellers of the plains.

They stopped before a huge pair of cedar doors. The leader of their party pulled on the bell rope hanging beside the entrance. A beautiful bell clang sounded out. In answer, the doors opened from within.

The leader, a robust older soldier, turned to Enoch and spoke. "People rest here. Leaders come with me." This was the first he had spoken since the capture of the clan.

"Methuselah," said Enoch.

Methuselah jumped to his side. They followed the soldier into a large reception area. The beautiful space had been adorned as a garden. Large oak and cedar columns lined the walls like trees. Flowing green drapes were hung with pomegranates embroidered on the hem. Various sparkling jewels bedecked everything. This was not merely a garden, it was a sacred underground temple.

Methuselah thought about pointing out to his father the earthly imagery used in a spiritual sanctuary. But a voice interrupted his thoughts.

"Enoch, my son! What took you so long!"

Enoch and Methuselah turned to see an old man and woman walk out of a side entrance.

They were both at least a good eight hundred years or so old. The man's stately but bent posture tempered the flashing white hair on his head. The woman's hair shone white as well, but she carried herself with the grace of royalty. She led the man by the arm. They both had a sense of carrying the weight of the world upon them.

Then Enoch and Methuselah saw why she was leading him. It was not that he was more frail than she, but because he was blind. His eyes were glazed over with a foggy whiteness.

"Father Adam?" Enoch said. He realized his mouth hung open and he closed it.

"And mother Havah," Adam replied with a smile. "Do not be disrespectful, lad."

Years of cave dwelling had not been good to Adam, on his body *or* soul. Enoch thought Adam had taken on a resemblance to the troglodytes over whom he obviously ruled. Perhaps being out of the sun had its negative effects on the human body.

Enoch embraced Adam fiercely. "It is you! I never thought I would ever meet you." Then he hugged Havah with tenderness.

"Yes, here I am in the flesh. Are you not going to introduce me to your companion?" Adam said. He could not see, but he had highly attuned his other senses to compensate for the lack of sight.

"Dear, dear, Enoch," Havah said with a loving sadness.

"Oh, pardon me," said Enoch, "This is my son Methuselah."

"That would be your great-great-great-great-great-great grandson," retorted Methuselah.

"Oh? And with a sense of humor, too. It does my heart good to hear you, my great-great-great-great-great grandson," said Adam with what would have been a twinkle in a seeing eye. "I cannot see you, but I can smell you, and you are in need of a bath." He grinned impishly.

They laughed. It had been some time since their last contact with moving water.

Methuselah hugged Adam. He could feel a quivering sigh of sadness in Adam's arms, a regret of lives not shared.

Then Methuselah embraced Havah. She whispered to him, "Methuselah, you shall outlive us all." That struck him as a bit odd, out of place. Maybe she had lost some of her wits in her old age.

Adam said, "You have both come a long way, and with your family. It must have been a difficult journey."

"Just at the start," said Methuselah, knowing he was putting it mildly.

"Well, then, let us break bread to celebrate your safe delivery," said Adam. "Gabriel and Uriel told me of your approach to Sahandria. We have much to discuss."

CHAPTER 16

The cave dwellers laid out quite a spread before Enoch's family. Though they lived in an underground world, Adam's troglodytes were adept at growing fruits and vegetables in secret gardens in the foothills within hiking distance of their residence. They spread a sumptuous banquet before the weary travelers. Skilled hunters, they supplemented the produce with mountain goat, gazelle, ibex. Anything with hair, they could catch and kill. Enoch chuckled at the discovery that even isolated from the rest of civilization, they still managed to make beer and wine. The drink of the gods never eluded humanity.

The extended family finished the meal and left the elders of the tribe to discuss their matters. Enoch, Methuselah, and a handful of others talked about the quarters that were put aside for their people. They did not know how long they would stay, but they would prepare their clan to adjust to their new residence until Elohim revealed otherwise.

Adam sat with Havah next to him, listening to the conversation. She never left his side. They were inseparable, and not because he needed her guidance with mobility. They were all alone in the world, and they only had each other. Despite the community of love around them, they would always have a pain too deep, a woundedness, that separated them from everyone and everything in this world. So they clung to each other with a subtle desperation.

Watching them, Enoch thought Mother Havah was a bit too controlling over Father Adam in his weakened state. But he did not intend disrespect, so he kept his mouth shut.

Adam sat back and belched. He muttered, "Excuse me, my little *Ninti*, Lady of the Rib."

"You are pardoned, my little Man of Red," Havah remarked wistfully.

Methuselah overheard it and his heart warmed. So old grandfather and grandmother liked giving affectionate nicknames. It must run in the family. He longed to hold his little Pedna Pedlums.

Enoch mused, "What is it like, Father Adam? The Garden. I have longed to know."

Havah watched Adam sadly as he gave a deep sigh. He could not get it out of his mind anyway. He might as well paint the picture burned into his heart and soul.

"Exactly as you would think. That is, like nothing you could imagine," he said. His eyes, though dull and without vision, brightened. He could see it all as clear as day before him.

Adam spoke with a hushed awe, "The lush valley is bounded on three sides, the Sahand and Bazgush mountain range in the south and the Savalan and Kush ranges in the north, and in the west, Lake, uh, the lake…" His memory lapsed.

"Lake Urumiya," said Havah. She finished his sentences, corrected his errors, and filled in when he forgot. He showed no sign of irritation. In fact, his descendants had the impression he would not even try to talk without her.

"Yes, yes, of course, Lake Urumiya. It makes for a perfect shelter from the harsh climate that we all know so well. The westerly winds from the great sea bring a warm rain for the dense vegetation in the valley. Every fruit tree known to man thrives there. Whole orchards, and vegetables and nut-bearing trees as well. And plenty of grapes of the vine, let me tell you."

Methuselah raised his chalice. "More wine to make the heart glad!" Everyone laughed.

His words conjured a vision of the Garden for his listeners. They could all see it. And they realized it was good for his soul to have a moment of rest from the heavy burden that lay upon him.

Adam turned solemn again. "And rich red soil," he said ever so slowly, treasuring every word as he felt the earth running through the fingers of his mind.

Havah reached out and rubbed his arm. He held her hand on his arm and continued, "Hot springs of water in rolling meadows. Ice cold waters pouring down the mountains into the river that flows through Paradise and empties into Lake Urimiya."

"The Meidan River," added Havah.

Adam continued, "But it was all like volcanic ash compared to the presence of Yahweh Elohim." He paused. "His immediate presence is what I miss the most." Adam's eyes welled up with tears. An absolute silence fell on the group, breathing stilled.

Methuselah had never heard that name before: *Yahweh Elohim*. He assumed it was an affectionate nickname that only Adam had with Elohim. It was the nature of names in their world. A name was more than mere object reference. A name would often carry the essence of a person. Like *Adam*, which meant "red earth," or *Havah*, which meant "life source."

Enoch did not know what *Yahweh* meant. He had heard no one else use the name, so he decided to avoid presumption and leave the topic for another day. He knew he had much to learn of *Yahweh* Elohim.

Adam finished with melancholy longing, "We would walk together sometimes in the cool of the day."

Everyone listened closely. They had never known such presence. Nobody did, except that primordial couple. Death and alienation from Elohim had permeated the entire human race as a consequence of their disobedience. This was why Elohim seemed so distant and unapproachable.

The one thing no one dared discuss was the one thing everyone wondered about: the trees. That is, the Tree of the Knowledge of Good and Evil, and the Tree of Life. To mention them would send Adam and Havah into a tailspin of depression and regret that they might never escape. Uriel had warned the travelers about this. He had told them about the couple's act of eating from the Tree of the Knowledge of Good and Evil that resulted in their exile. He told them that had Adam and Havah eaten from the Tree of Life in that state of sin, there would be no end to the tragedy of eternal evil generated by such a horror. No burden of responsibility could be greater to bear than that. Enoch felt he should trust the angel this time and avoid the topic altogether.

Yet he could not get it out of his mind. He had heard rumors about the Tree of the Knowledge of Good and Evil when he was a young child. It was only a distant memory of forgotten family folklore, replaced by the myth with which he was indoctrinated as an apkallu of Shinar: the legend of Adapa. He called up that tale now to examine it in his mind. The story went that Adapa had been a sage of Eridu, city of the god Enki. He had been taken into heaven and offered the bread and water of immortality by Anu. But he turned them down because his patron deity, Enki, had advised him against it, claiming they were the bread and water of death. So Adapa missed out on the opportunity of immortality. He was clothed with new garments and returned to Eridu to die.

There were so many similarities between the stories: the names of Adapa and Adam, the loss of eternal life, the rejection of a command and the trickster temptation. Yet there were such significant differences: the Shinar pantheon versus the sole Yahweh Elohim; failure to eat rather than eating; no trees, no wife. It was almost as if the Adapa story was an inversion of the Garden of

Eden, a replacement narrative intended to displace loyalty from the original story onto a new paradigm.

Enoch studied Adam's face. Yet, here he sat before the original eyewitness of it all, telling him a different report than that of the gods. This was the problem of being a scribe and a sage. Sometimes, education and learning became a flood that darkens the mind with confusion rather than a sun that enlightens it with truth. Enoch hoped one day Elohim would clear that up for him, since he was now his servant.

Enoch had also wondered what it would be like to live forever. Was it transformation of the body? Was it perpetual regeneration? And what was it like to be in communion with Elohim so perfectly as to not need the dreams and visions that Enoch had become dependent upon for his own sense of real presence of the deity?

Methuselah's mind wandered into the details of what Uriel had told them about the Garden. He thought, *If Adam was made from the clay of the earth, and Havah was made from his rib, did they have belly buttons?* Then his mind drifted further to the image of Edna's belly button.

"Methuselah, are you listening?" Enoch's words brought Methuselah out of his tailspin of desire. It continued to creep up on him at the most inopportune moments.

"What?" said Methuselah.

"I just told Father Adam about my vision from Elohim."

"Right," said Methuselah. "You are to be a prophet of judgment."

"Yes," said Enoch. "But you did not hear the rest of my interpretation. I said that it seemed to me that if I were to pronounce judgment upon the giants, I had better be able to defend myself for long enough to finish my prophecies. I want to become a giant killer."

"A WHAT?" exclaimed Methuselah. Finally, he listened.

"A giant killer," repeated Enoch. "Nephilim are considered outlaws now, so by the law of the land, we have every right to hunt them down and bring them to justice. I would not merely be pronouncing judgment, I would be *bringing* judgment down upon their heads."

"You have been a man of peace all your life, father," protested Methuselah. "It does not suit you." Methuselah found the image of his father as a fighter difficult to embrace.

Enoch explained, "When we were in the midst of the Gigantomachy, I knew that everything that I had believed in was a lie. I understood for the first time in my life that the only way that evil was allowed to spread its talons over the earth was for righteous men to do nothing. We will no longer do nothing. We will fight this evil."

"In case you had not noticed," said Methuselah, "Nephilim are very hard to kill."

Adam spoke up. "You are right. Nephilim are half-angel, half-human. What makes them difficult to kill is that they inhabit two realms, and therefore have the strengths of both in a way that neither has of the other."

"Archangels do pretty well against Nephilim. We saw it ourselves," said Enoch.

"Yes, but not without great effort," Adam countered. "And if the Nephilim were to fight in great numbers, they could overwhelm even archangels."

"But we would not fight them in numbers," Enoch insisted. "We would single them out and destroy their filthy corrupted bodies of flesh one by one."

Methuselah said, "You may not have that luxury, father, since they often travel in packs. Still, they are not of this world. They have occultic fighting skills that we know nothing about."

Adam interrupted their spat. "There is a secret order who have developed special skills to kill Nephilim."

"Who?" asked Enoch.

"They are called the *Karabu*," said Adam.

"How can we find these Karabu?" asked Enoch.

"You already have," said Adam.

Methuselah and Enoch looked at each other.

"Sahandria is the home of the Karabu. They are those who aid the Cherubim in guarding the perimeter of Eden."

It all became clear to them. Adam's community was on the perimeter of the Garden, because they housed the guardians of Eden. Enoch was disappointed that he did not figure it out sooner.

"When can we start training?" asked Enoch.

Adam said, "It will take years to perfect the technique."

"Years?" asked Methuselah.

"More like decades," said Adam.

Enoch resolved, "Then decades we will take to become Karabu warriors."

The thought turned Methuselah's stomach. "There is one thing I need to do before I enter this training, or I will not last to the end."

To everyone's pleasant surprise, he turned to Adam and said, "Father Adam, will you marry me to Edna bar Azrial?"

CHAPTER 17

Troglodytes knew how to throw a party. They gathered in a series of halls attached to each other that were even larger than the marketplace cavern Enoch had seen when they first arrived. Apparently, most of the city had come to the wedding celebration. There were thousands of them. They filled the carved out chambers with echoes of chatter and laughter.

These were not the simple people Enoch had thought them to be. Their structure and decorations were simple and sparse, their cave drawings almost childlike, but they were socially integrated and communally connected like no other people he had ever seen. They carried a spiritual quality about them that Enoch could relate to, something he knew his clan could not understand. He had a strange connection to them. He understood why Adam had chosen to live with the cave dwellers. His original bias against them had proven false. It had been based on false legends he should not have listened to.

This was the time to feast and celebrate the marriage of his son. He saw Methuselah and Edna dancing out on the floor. Adam had officiated the ceremony with his ever-present Havah by his side. It made Enoch cry like a baby. He had been concerned about this insignificant little temple virgin, but had come to realize that she too had overcome his expectations. He was beginning to think that for a wisdom sage, he was not proving very wise of late.

In the midst of the music, Enoch glanced at Adam and Havah at the table. They smiled and pretended to enjoy the festivities. But even now, they could not escape the pall of sadness that haunted them.

Suddenly, the floor cleared, and everyone moved to the tables to watch the entertainment. Methuselah and Edna sat down at the head table with Enoch and the others. Adam leaned toward Enoch and said, "You have been wondering what the Karabu can do? Sit back and get ready. You are about to find out."

The Karabu took their places on the floor. There were ten of them. They were dressed as warriors with armaments of animals. Lion heads and manes, vulture winged robes, and heavenly weapons Enoch had never seen before. Strange blades, shields, and javelins.

They engaged in battle exercises that seemed more like a dance of acrobatics than about brute strength or power. They ebbed and flowed like a river of water, their movements fluid, not forceful. They moved through the air as if they were fish floating in water. Flipping, twisting, they attacked and defended with such precision and poise as to transform the act of fighting into a ballet of grace.

Adam could not see the dance, but he could feel it. He knew it well. He said to Enoch, "They were trained by the archangel Gabriel. The original giant killer."

Enoch caught himself with his mouth open again and quickly shut it. He now knew that Elohim had provided for his calling.

Methuselah was entranced by the javelins and how they glided like birds in the air and spun in the hands of the heavenly skilled Karabu. He thought to himself that this was the weapon for him.

Edna wanted to dance like the wind as these fighters did. She found it a haunting vision of terrifying beauty.

Adam touched Enoch's arm and said softly, "What do you say we go up top and get some fresh air?"

It surprised Enoch. So far as he knew, this stooped-over old man had not been out of the caves since he arrived here ages before.

"Anything you ask, forefather," said Enoch.

"Walk me, then," said Adam.

Havah moved to help as she had always done, but Adam gestured to her to stay. He would be all right. Just the men.

As they walked up to the surface through the winding tunnels, Enoch asked Adam about the name he had uttered earlier, Yahweh Elohim.

Adam apologized, "It slips out too often. It is the covenant name of Elohim. It is reserved for only the most sacred of relationships. It expresses his essence as the foundation of existence itself. The divine council of heavenly host uses it." He paused for a moment. "We used it in the Garden, but now with the Edenic exile…" his voice cracked for a moment. "It is a name that should remain secret until latter days. For what purpose, I do not know. Perhaps it has to do with the seed of Eve."

They stepped out in the evening breeze under the stars. Adam stopped and took a deep breath. "Ah," he proclaimed, "I do believe I miss this sweet taste in my lungs."

Enoch helped him carefully so Adam would not stumble on the rough ground at their feet. Adam turned his face to the sky, unable to see anything. Yet he knew every star's location.

"He brings forth the Mazzaroth in his season," mused Adam as if remembering Yahweh Elohim's own words. Enoch smiled and looked upon the host of heaven.

"Elohim's story for us," Adam added, still thinking.

His blind eyes found the right place in the night sky. "Can you see the constellation of the Virgin? The second decans, right about there," he pointed. "*Comah*, the desire of nations."

Enoch could see it. One of the benefits of being an apkallu was their learning of the stars.

"It is my favorite constellation," added Enoch. "Virgin and child. It tells me there is hope. Hope for purity, for a new beginning. For a new 'Adam.'"

Adam welled up with emotion.

"Father Adam," said Enoch, "I know this is probably not the time to ask you, but…" He hesitated.

"But what?" queried Adam. "Speak."

"Is it true, the legend about Cain the cursed one?"

Adam hesitated in uncomfortable silence. He wished Enoch had not spoken after all. It was another sore wound for him in a life of many self-inflicted wounds.

He sighed. "Cain is a scourge upon my existence. He has made it his one purpose in life to foil the plans of Yahweh Elohim because of his punishment for murdering his brother." Adam kept using the covenant name of *Yahweh* because he was in private and knew Enoch was a chosen vessel of Elohim.

"But how can he deny his guilt?" asked Enoch.

Adam shook his head. "The mind of man is never so cunning as when it is involved in the art of self-justification. I know, I am guilty as well."

Enoch steadied Adam as they stepped over some volcanic rubble on their walk.

"At first, Cain accepted his exile in the land of Nod. His family line left him when he began to show signs of lunacy. He had discovered that Yahweh planned a new righteous lineage through Seth to replace his own cursed line.

Many of the names of the sons of Seth were even similar to Cain's line, which reinforced the substitution. To be forgotten, erased from the tablets of history was a fate worse than his infamy. Punishment still affirms the value of the guilty party because it shows they had the nobility to do otherwise. But annihilation means they have no value, and they could not do otherwise. Like a clay pot created merely to be destroyed."

Adam took a long breath. "Cain learned of Yahweh's curse of enmity between the children of Eve and the children of the Serpent. And he learned of the Promise of the Seed that would crush the Serpent's head even as it bit the Woman's heel. Cain realized that the only revenge he could inflict upon Yahweh would be the destruction of the lineage of that promised Seed. So he set out to destroy Seth's bloodline. Unfortunately for him, it had already grown and splintered into many lines of descent, leaving Cain with an impossible goal.

"He seeks the chosen line of the Seed of Havah, and when he finds it, he will destroy it."

Enoch remained silent. He could not imagine the weight of sorrow that burdened this great man.

He changed the subject. "Father Adam, it is getting cold. Let us return to the wedding party."

"Let me return to my bed to get some much needed sleep," said Adam in reply. "My talk with you has made me tired."

Enoch knew he had been a help to the old man. There was something very freeing that came with confession of the heart. It had the effect of relaxing the soul from what it could not carry.

"Oh, I almost forgot," added Adam. He stopped and reached into his shoulder sack and pulled out a couple of animal skins. He handed them to Enoch.

"I want you to have these. They are the original skins that Yahweh Elohim clothed Havah and me with after our fall."

Enoch looked at them with reverence.

Adam finished, "They were a covering for our sins. May they be a covering for you."

Enoch embraced his forefather with all his heart.

· · · · ·

Methuselah waited for what seemed like an eternity on the large wedding bed they received as a gift from Adam and Havah. He had only one thing on his mind: Edna. She was preparing herself in the wash area.

He had waited too long for this moment and it had finally come. He thought back on the years he spent pouring his soul into this precious jewel, with nary a thought that she would one day pour back into him. It was the perfect dream. They had been best friends, soul-mates, and now they would be lovers. They would finally become one.

Where is she? he thought.

"Edna, my wife, are you sleeping in there?" he teased.

Suddenly, she pounced on him from behind.

It took him by surprise. They rolled on the bed laughing and playfully wrestling, as they always used to in their sport room.

Then play turned to passion. Finally, they were released for love, and finally, they truly, deeply knew each other.

CHAPTER 18

Many years passed.

Enoch and his tribe sojourned with the cave dwelling Adamites, raised their families, and learned the way of the Karabu. The Watcher gods of Mount Hermon consolidated their reign over the land of Mesopotamia. They built large temples to their names and continued to pursue the outlaw giants. They offered bounty on Nephilim packs and rogues who roamed the desert badlands and mountainous hideouts of the earth.

Rumors grew that the gods were experimenting with occultic sorceries, creating unspeakable monstrosities. For what purpose, no one could tell. Whispers of conspiracy filled the cities. But in the rural areas of desert, forest, and mountain, life was less complicated. For those who did not serve the gods of the pantheon, life was not as bountiful. Survival was a foremost priority.

Survival was not in the stars for the snow tribe of Barakil the elder. They numbered about a hundred members, living and hunting in the snow-capped mountains of Aratta near the Greater Zab river basin.

Most of the men of the tribe were dead, hanging from trees to be dried out like meat under the soft shimmering of fresh snow fall. The surviving women were corralled in makeshift cages for later sport.

Four Nephilim outlaws ransacked the tribe's belongings for valuables and foodstuffs. Three of them were nearly seven cubits tall, but one came up short standing at less than five cubits. All were shaven and covered head to toe with occultic tattoos. They wore pieces of strange body armor over what looked like soldier's garb.

The short one stoked the fire in preparation for roasting their next meal. The leader of the pack, the tallest and the ugliest, crouched in the bush struggling with constipation, the result of eating too much meat the night before. He yelled to the short one, "Get that fire burning, midget! I cannot stand this abysmal cold!"

The other two giants examined some pillaged jewels, trying to figure their worth and conspiring how to secret some away for themselves.

Unseen, Enoch ben Jared peeked out from behind a tree, clothed in near white for concealment. He was just over three hundred sixty years old now, or thereabouts. He had stopped counting because years on this earth were not as important to him as eternity in the heavens. He had spent many years training for his calling with the Sahandrians.

Enoch thought, *These brutes do not seem to belong here. Rogue Nephilim do not usually congregate in packs because they are too easy to spot.* He frowned over the matter. The giants did tend to hide out in unpleasant environment for the camouflage advantages they provided. He gripped his marvelous bow made from heavenly metal and strung with the indestructible hair of a Cherub. He had become quite a death-dealing archer after all those years of naively condemning all war and violence. Elohim had quite a sense of irony.

Twenty cubits away, Methuselah and Edna crouched behind a bush waiting for the sign from Enoch. Methuselah was almost three hundred now, with Edna four years his junior. Their white stealth outfits gave them cover. They held the special Karabu weapons of angels: his, lightweight but deadly javelins; hers, a multi-bladed weapon called a sword, which did not just cut but spliced, diced, and shredded. Methuselah looked from Enoch to Edna's face, mere inches from him, and surprise-kissed her. She gave him a "not now" frown, but then pecked him back with a smile. They were inseparable.

On Enoch's other side, obscured in the brush, Methuselah's twenty-year old son Lamech, pride of his mother Edna, waited. Lamech took after his grandfather. He was a bit of a hermit holy man, preferring prayer and meditation to socializing with people. A conflict of interests burdened him. He loved his tribe of the Sahandrians and he wanted to become a holy priest of their temple. He longed for the security of his volcanic underground home. But he had been trained by his father for another vocation, the holy calling of giant killing.

Lamech prepared his special sword, created by his trainer the archangel Gabriel, and forged in the volcanic heat of Mount Sahand. The blade was strangely like a whip. When opened, it stretched a good seven cubits of flexible metal. When not in use, it rolled up, ready to unravel and strike with razor sharp fury at a distance. Those who relied upon close quarter combat would not have a chance with this little snakebite. He had nicknamed it "Rahab" after the sea dragon of chaos.

The team of giant-killers watched as the short Naphil opened the cage of women. He dragged out a kicking and screaming redheaded teenage girl.

"We have a lively one here!" crowed the short Naphil. "And she is lovely looking. Maybe we should save her for dessert."

"We do need some breeders," said one of the other giants. He stepped up to her, shoving the short one aside.

He looked at her with hunger. "I think I will have some sweets before dinner."

He glanced at the short one for his reaction. Then his body stiffened in shock as an arrow pierced his eye and burrowed into his brain. Before his companions realized what had happened, another arrow buried itself into his other eye. The giant fell to the ground blind and dead.

The short one bellowed. The other giant drew a battle axe and shield to face the Karabu team barreling at them from their concealment.

Methuselah threw a javelin at the front giant, but the Naphil dodged it with preternatural ease. The short one behind him, caught the javelin in mid-air, and snapped it like a twig in his hand. He may have been small for a Naphil, but he was still a Naphil — and strong.

Two more arrows buried themselves in the shield of the axe giant. He shortened the distance between himself and Enoch in seconds, making the bow and arrow useless.

He swung his battle axe with raging fury, chopping down trees as mere nuisance, but it was like fighting a ghost. Enoch danced around the giant's moves as if in a ballet with boulders. It made the giant more angry — and sloppy.

Edna raced straight at the short one and choreographed her own dance of battle with the miscreant. She slashed the creature's spleen, stomach and kidneys before it had the chance to even stop and bleed. He fell on the snowy ground in his own spreading pool of death.

She did not see the lead Naphil behind the bush. He jumped out roaring with a spiked mace — and to his embarrassment, his loincloth still down at his knees.

The poor redheaded teen had been out of the fray, frozen in terror watching it all. The lead giant saw her and snatched her up, intending to throw her at his enemies. He stopped short. A javelin and arrow pierced through his heart. Then Rahab, in the hands of Lamech snapped out, removing the despicable head from its body.

The teen girl dropped to the ground in a heap. The giant's body fell forward, his knife hand just missing Edna as he hit the ground in a splash of bloody snow. He was the last one to fall.

Killing Nephilim was not usually as easy as this battle had been. This crack team of giant killers had become so well trained over the decades that they were a formidable force even for an organized pack of Nephilim. They had been trained by angels.

Within seconds, Lamech was by the young girl, checking to see if she was dead. He lifted her from the snow. When he got a closer look at her, he almost lost his breath. She was as beautiful as a sunset. Ravishing red locks, large pulpy lips, and eyes like a doe.

Edna looked around to see Enoch standing on his quarry's chest, smiling with bow in hand. He saw her, and then his smile faded into dismay. She realized her arm felt numb — and wet. She glanced down. The giant had not missed her. His knife had grazed her arm, leaving a gaping bloody wound. The bright red flowed down her arm and pooled on the ground. She thought, *Is that blood all mine?*

She passed out.

When Edna came to, she found herself surrounded by the team. The redheaded girl was applying a paste of plant leaves and tree sap to her wound. Edna pulled back in dazed fear, but the men held her down.

"It is fine, my love," said Methuselah. "She is a healer shaman. You will be all right."

Edna dropped her head back in relief.

Methuselah leaned in close to her face and gave her a big smacking kiss.

"Nice moves Pedlumnoonypoo!" he said. The years had brought a more developed nickname among many others. "You deserve a back rub tonight."

She smiled through her pain.

He added a caveat, "Of course, he was a small one, more manageable for your size."

He always looked for a way to tease her, catch her off guard. It was his prankster nature to do so, even in the face of grave danger, like now. He used it to diminish fear and evil and she loved it. She had also learned how to tease right back.

"You are right, Poozelahbunnybunch," she bantered. "Apparently, your javelin was not big enough. But we got him anyway, my lovebird of heaven."

It was all in good sport. He adored her thoroughly. She respected him completely. He admired her fighting skills. She had even saved his life more than once. But he knew that did not mean they would not be competitive. She was still a tomboy at heart. *Thank Elohim*, he thought, *she is still a tigress in the marriage bed.*

Enoch examined one of the pieces of body armor. "Strange," he said. "This is specially designed armor that they are wearing. It is almost as if they were a scouting party or a strike team."

Methuselah and Edna looked at Enoch with surprise. "Nephilim hordes are virtually extinct, and packs have not been seen in over a hundred years," said Methuselah. "Where could these have possibly come from?"

"That is a fitting question," replied Enoch. A pack was a company of about four to eight Nephilim and a horde could be as small as twenty organized giants or as large as a hundred strong. A cold eastern wind started to pick up and blow snow around their faces. Enoch bent closer to examine the bodies.

Lamech stared at the redheaded vision before him.

"Thank you, for saving me," she said to him, brushing off snow and pulling her tangled hair back.

"My name is Betenos, Betenos bar Barakil," she said, awaiting his reply.

Lamech gave none. He just stared at her with gaping mouth, just like his grandfather.

Betenos giggled. It brought Lamech to his senses. "Oh, I am Lamech ben Methuselah. This is my family."

"Where are you from?" she asked.

"The Sahand."

"I have never seen such skilled warriors before."

"I have never seen such beauty before," he blurted out without even thinking, and then caught himself. He turned as red as her hair. She giggled again.

"I am sorry, I did not mean to…"

"I thank you for your compliment, Lamech ben Methuselah."

He looked around at the carnage. "I am very sorry for your tragedy," he said. "These Nephilim deserve eternal damnation for what they have done."

"I thank you for your kindness," she responded. "My father, Barakil, was the elder of the tribe."

"Is there no end to your loss?" he said. She saw his eyes blear with tears.

"Would you help me free the others?" she asked.

"Forgive me for my thoughtlessness," he said.

They tromped through the snow to the makeshift cage. The six remaining members of her tribe, all women, cowered in the cage, all alone in the mountainous wilderness without a defense. Lamech and Betenos freed them.

"Lamech, come here!" shouted Methuselah.

Lamech led the women over to the Nephilim carcasses surrounded by Enoch, Methuselah, and Edna.

"We need to move quickly. Apparently, these Nephilim are part of an organized militia of some kind."

"How could that be?" asked Lamech.

Methuselah pointed down at the thigh of one of the dead. "They are branded by the same rulers."

Lamech saw the cuneiform on the thigh amidst the tattoos. There were two names. He read it out loud, "Thamaq and Yahipan."

Methuselah suddenly screamed and thrust one of his javelins into the cadaver's branded thigh. Edna held him and pulled him aside to whisper to him. He was clearly in mental anguish, over what, Lamech did not know.

Enoch explained to Lamech, "Thamaq and Yahipan were co-rulers of the city where I was apkallu many years ago. They killed your grandparents and almost killed us."

Lamech's eyes went wide with shock. He turned to comfort his mother, but she was too busy selflessly comforting Methuselah. "And now they have an organized pack?"

"Or worse, maybe a horde," said Enoch. "We need to wrap up these bodies and transport them quickly to Nippur and get the bounty, before they are discovered missing and sought for by their pack."

"Or horde," reminded Lamech.

"Or horde," said Enoch. The thought was too horrible for him to imagine. He knew things had been getting worse. Evil was spreading across the land. But what use would his calling as a giant killer be to Elohim if Nephilim were organizing and congregating into packs and hordes again? It would be too overwhelming for them. They could take out stragglers here and there. But packs of four to ten could become very lethal and a horde of fifty to a hundred was invincible for their small team.

Enoch turned to Betenos and the others standing behind her. "What can you tell us about your ambush?"

"The men had gone hunting," said Betenos, "so it was easy for them to overpower our camp and catch the hunters unawares when they returned." As the strongest of the survivors, Betenos had became the spokesperson for them.

"They used the women as human shields," she said.

"Cowardly," said Enoch.

"Strategic," countered Methuselah, He had returned to the discussion, his anger suppressed. "Nephilim have no conscience. They cannot be cowards. They must be hunted and slaughtered like the animals that they are."

Methuselah bit his lip. He would hunt down Thamaq and Yahipan and slaughter them, if it was the last thing he did before meeting his maker. He was sure his maker would understand. Or would he? Could Elohim know the pain of losing a father or a son? Or was he a distant and removed being without a family?

Enoch asked Betenos, "Did you hear any conversation that might suggest they belonged to a pack?"

"Or horde," added Lamech. Enoch gave him an annoyed look this time.

Betenos looked to her fellow tribeswomen. They all shook their heads no.

"Just that they came from a great distance," concluded Betenos. "They only seemed to be passing through. But I could not tell from where."

"We had best move quickly," said Enoch.

Betenos implored Enoch, "Please good savior, may I request funeral rites for our dead?"

Enoch looked around. "The snow and cold has made the ground too hard to break," he said.

"My people do not perform ground burial," she replied, "we perform excarnation."

"What is that?" asked Methuselah.

"Sky burial," she said. "We remove the heads and place their bodies in the trees to have their bones stripped by carrion vultures. We then cremate their remains so the soul goes to the gods and the body returns to the earth as dust."

The barbaric ritual repulsed Enoch. On second thought, he realized that no matter how removed from the true God these rural pagans were, their beliefs still dimly reflected the image of God that was in every human. Betenos' words reminded him of the words that Yahweh Elohim spoke to

Adam so long ago in the Garden, "For you are dust, and to dust you shall return."

"We will respect your wishes, as far as we can," said Enoch.

Relief flooded Betenos. "Thank you," she said, She impulsively hugged Enoch.

Methuselah felt proud of his father for his wisdom and grace. He was sensitive to the weakness that is humanity.

Enoch's mind drifted in painful memory to the recent deaths of Adam and Havah. Through the years of Enoch's stay with the cave dwellers, he had become close to his forefather. Adam had died first, but Havah followed close on his heels, as she always did.

Enoch remembered the burial ceremony of the Sahandrians. They laid the body into a pit curled up in a sleeping posture. This expressed their belief that death was only a sleep from which they would one day awake. Around the body, they placed various mementos and souvenirs of the beloved's life. They included fruits and vegetables because Adam had longed for the Garden to the very end. They had prepared the body by mixing red ochre powder with water to create a paste with which to cover the body. For them, it was a token of the red earth from which Adam himself had come. It was the red earth they all longed for in their souls. They had then covered the body with flowers of all kinds; yarrow, ragwort, hollyhock and others chosen for their medicinal purposes in life with hope for the afterlife.

CHAPTER 19

After the bodies of the snow tribe's dead had been placed in the trees and on makeshift platforms, Enoch and the others hauled the corpses of the Nephilim onto wagons they had brought with them.

Wagons came into use by adapting the recent invention, the wheel. Four round pieces of wood attached to axles were secured underneath a sled. Towed by a couple onagers, this wagon device could carry heavy loads across great distances in shorter amounts of time than the old sleds had been capable of. Enoch did not know who originated the invention. He wondered if it was from the angels. But whoever had done it should be a king for his brilliance and imagination.

Once they had the Nephilim corpses loaded, they had to stop. They were completely exhausted, with no strength left to continue. A death defying battle with rabid giants and then the sky burial of a hundred tribal dead had used every ounce of their strength. Not even the benefit of wheels was enough to help them. They had to rest. even though they would lose more time and risk being tracked down by other Nephilim.

Betenos, however, had not exhausted her bag of herbal tricks. She gave each of them some special root to chew on that provided them with a burst of energy. They put their belongings on the wagon and started down the path toward Nippur.

They wheeled the wrapped giant carcasses through a dozen or so leagues of lush mountain valleys to a river port where they rented boat passage down the Diyala river another sixty leagues or so to the Tigris. From there they took the artificial canals to Sippar on the Euphrates, and then on to Nippur. The bounty on four Nephilim outlaws could carry them for months with supplies and bribery money.

It was a tiring life to be always on the move, gathering information and tracking giants. For Methuselah and Edna it had been particularly difficult being separated from their family for months at a time. They felt they were missing out on their children's growing years as the tribe took care of them in their stead. Bringing their favored son Lamech with them had brought some peace of mind, but it had its own stress. He was good at giant killing, but his heart was in Sahandria. He did not like the lonely rootless life of a wayfarer.

They had left Sahandria with many tears to become nomads. It seemed more appropriate to Enoch's calling, but it made it harder on everyone, feeling unattached to a substantial community, always unsettled, always leaving.

Though he focused on fulfilling his duty of slaying Nephilim, Lamech often dreamed of being a priest of Elohim for the clan. In this spiritual aspect, he found himself identifying more with his grandfather Enoch than with his father, Methuselah. That brought testy moments of tension between them.

Methuselah would tell Lamech he needed to stop being so sheepish and see himself as the seed of Havah, the special line of God's own choosing. But Lamech just wanted to serve God in the temple of Sahandria and minister to its people, whom he loved dearly. One thing was certain, he would not die a wandering nomad. If he could not go back to Sahand, he would build his own city somewhere on the plain. But first, he had to have a family. That was something he did not think much about in his pursuit of piety. What was a mere human family compared to fellowship with the mighty Creator Elohim? There had not been much of a comparison in his mind until now. He had not thought much of females in his youthful interests — until now. Now, he stared at the most vivacious and beautiful of all Elohim's creatures that he had ever seen. And she was traveling with them to Nippur: Betenos bar Barakil.

Now I am becoming more like my father, thought Lamech. It confused and frustrated him. He felt he had two men inside him battling for control: his father, Methuselah, man of earth; and his grandfather, Enoch, man of heaven. Would he forever be tormented by two opposing natures? If this was the burden he had to shoulder to have a family, then he would seek every way possible to avoid it.

Betenos was no helpless victim, nor would she go down without a fight in this world. She loved life too much. When the Nephilim attacked her, she fought back with the ferocity of a nomad, no matter how futile it had seemed. On this journey, she helped everywhere she could, cooking or cleaning, or even moving the dead giant corpses when necessary. She could drive the wagon or ride an onager free-back. She seemed willing to do just about anything. She was driven to prove her worth to everyone, to demonstrate she was not just another helpless waif in need of saving. Even though she thought the young man Lamech was certainly handsome and strong, she was determined not to fall in love because she knew where that would lead her. And she did not want to go down that road again.

Everyone saw the attraction between Lamech and Betenos. Enoch did not like the idea because Betenos was not a follower of Elohim. She spoke often of the Great Goddess Earth Mother, the World Tree, and had a hard time grasping the incomparability of Elohim over all other gods. She would argue with Lamech for hours on end about Elohim and his excessive demands of exclusivity against the gods. Lamech seemed to enjoy the challenge. The young man's fanatic commitment to Elohim was the one thing that comforted Enoch. He knew Lamech had no interest in marrying an idol worshipper. But what if she converted? What then? He knew it was not right, but he secretly hoped she would not convert to save them all the pain and suffering. Enoch could not wait to get to Nippur so they could end this distraction and get moving on without her.

Edna knew that it was too late. They were already in love. They were all merely observing the discovery process. When Methuselah expressed caution at her youth, Edna reminded him how young they had been when they fell in love. When he brought up Betenos' gods, she told him it was only a matter of time before Betenos would step over to Lamech's side. She knew it. Call it women's intuition or Elohim's insight. But she prayed for Elohim's will to be done.

The other women victims of the Nephilim attack were brought along with the team to be dropped off at Nippur with Betenos. They asked to stay with Enoch's nomads. Enoch had to inform them that the four of them were a band of warriors on a mission. They were simply not available for protection, and their tribe was too far in the opposite direction for the team to escort them there. The women would journey with them to Nippur and remain there to find a new life on their own.

Edna's heart shivered. The circumstances of these women made her long for her own family back at Sahand. During their years of residence with the Sahandrians, she had borne sons and daughters for Methuselah. She missed them terribly. They were taken care of by the extended family when the team was away on their missions, but her longing for them persisted.

Their years of training had granted her the blessed privilege of complete and focused attention from her husband Methuselah. Or rather, *almost* complete attention. The training called for an arduous schooling in heavenly weapons and spiritual discipline with high demands. It was not easy to become a giant killer. Once Methuselah fixed on a goal, he would devote his heart and soul to its completion. But at least in the caves, they had been spared the distracting complications and responsibilities of survival on the surface.

Now, their missions took them away for longer and longer periods of time. She felt guilty about it. Conflict tore at her because she also knew that sometimes holy callings involved a sacrifice that was not required of other servants of Elohim. Still, she sometimes longed to live an uneventful and happily boring life with a stable family and clan in the comfortable caves of Sahandria. She just needed to be attached to someone or some community that would give her purpose. Her parents had provided that for her until she became a sacred virgin dedicated to the gods. When they murdered her parents, she found Methuselah to give her that purpose. The nomadic calling now displaced raising a family in Sahandria. Her identity was constantly being shaken up. She clung to the closest thing Elohim gave her, Methuselah. She sometimes wondered if she was being too needy with him. Whatever the case, she loved to make him happy.

For Enoch, the sacrifice of being a wanderer was not so great as for Edna. He remarried at Sahand and they had five sons and three daughters. But it had never been the same after he lost his Edna. A part of him had died with her and it changed him forever. He was more otherworldly than the rest of the clan. He spent hours in prayer, and treasured his dream-visions. He would talk for hours about spirit and heavenly bodies with a thoughtless disregard for the human bodies right in front of him, including his own wife and children. Edna often felt that Enoch's grandiose prophetic elevation of spiritual reality resulted in the neglect of his own family.

Methuselah seemed to be his father's very opposite. Though he loved Elohim with all his heart, soul, mind and strength, Methuselah's affections were more this-worldly. It placed him at odds with his father more often than not. He remembered one time when Enoch was pontificating at the dinner table about the need for more mundane food and less preparation, so that they might have more time to devote to the pursuit of their spiritual disciplines. Methuselah got angry and retorted by asking if Enoch was saying Elohim was too worldly, since the Creator devoted too much time to crafting the Garden with its multitude of tastes and exotic foods. It was one of the few ways that Methuselah could actually force Enoch into silence.

Methuselah had let the silent pause sink in, then took a deep bite of roasted meat and with his mouth full, spluttered out the words, "I am worshipping Elohim as I enjoy this mutton's glorious heavenly juicy flesh. As

I do when I pray or when I hunt or when I love my wife. So, I ask you, who spends more time in spiritual discipline, the one who worships in only some of his actions or the one who worships in all of his actions?"

Enoch had left the table and charged Methuselah with dishonoring him. Methuselah apologized in front of the family for his disrespectful provocation. They both realized that spiritual arrogance was just as sinful as fleshly intemperance.

Edna believed it was Elohim's sense of humor to place such contrary personalities of extremes within the same family and then use them for his purposes. He had provided Lamech as a kind of hybrid of them both as a further picture of their tension and a rebuke of their imbalance. It indicated to her that Elohim was somehow in control, and not their puny little human wills.

If it were up to us, she thought, *we would be in hot bitumen.*

CHAPTER 20

The city of Nippur lay on the Euphrates just downriver from Sippar, Enoch's home town. They had passed by Sippar without stopping in order to avoid being recognized by the god Utu and thrown into prison. Even though their escape had been hundreds of years earlier, and though Enoch had grown out his hair and beard, Utu would certainly recognize him. The god would certainly remember his original intent for Enoch's family, and would certainly not be merciful.

Enoch and his traveling band of warriors and women pulled up to the Nippur river wharf on their boats with their dead Nephilim cargo. They hauled the bodies to the Temple Guard command post just outside Inanna's temple, called *E-anna*. Though Utu was the patron god of the city, his temple, *E-Babba*, was not as large as E-anna and was overshadowed by its administrative duties, another visible sign of Inanna's usurpation of his priority. A saying had developed amongst the Nippurians, "It matters not he who rules, but she who counts the money."

It was bothersome bureaucracy to register the details of the abduction and execution of the fugitives, with exact times, locations, descriptions and names of everyone involved. Enoch did not trust this procedure. It created an accessible record of their comings and goings that could make them more easily tracked. It typified the kind of centralized control by the gods that Enoch despised. He had been raised within its clutches, but his years with the Adamites had changed him. He and his band of free spirits now roamed through Elohim's creation without the gods' oversight. But unfortunately, he could not violate this protocol if he wanted to collect the bounty for their wages.

It had not been the usual protocol, however, for the gods to be involved in this petty administrative procedure. It surprised Enoch when Inanna herself showed up at the command post to meet with Enoch's raiding party.

She stepped into the room, leaving two Nephilim Guards at the door. Methuselah glanced at Enoch. Lamech and Edna tensed. Would she smell their fear? Would she recognize any of them? Edna remembered Inanna with crystal clarity. She was abominable — intemperate, violent, and unpredictable; the worst combination in any leader let alone a god.

Inanna glanced over the tabletwork. She looked at Enoch and the others with a suspicious pause. *How could these four worms have overcome four formidable Nephilim?* She stared long at Enoch. He looked familiar, but she could not place him. He was rodent-like with his long tangled hair and filthy ratty beard. They all looked the same to her. These rural types would have to be cleansed from the earth someday to maintain ethnic purity. The younger sinewy one was acting a bit skittish. Maybe he was overwhelmed by Inanna's charismatic presence. She smirked to herself. Their obvious son was handsome and ripe. But she had to return to the task at hand

"What is your name?" she queried.

"Enoch ben Jared," he said.

She did not know the name. It was foreign to Shinar. Enoch was grateful he had taken on a Shinarian name when he was an apkallu of Sippar. Had he used that name of Utuabzu now, Inanna would mentally place him at Sippar and might recollect his escape from their heinous scheme all those years ago.

"How did you defeat these giants?" Inanna inquired with her annoyed impatient tone.

"Good queen of heaven," — Enoch hated faking respect — "most of our tribe were wiped out in the battle. We have a few survivors staying at a hostel in the city." The most convincing lie was the one that was mostly true.

He continued, "We were concerned about the armor and branding on the giants, my lady. It appears they might be congregating in packs of organized militia."

"Or hordes," added Lamech.

Inanna looked at the young man with surprise. Enoch broke out into a cold sweat.

"You think there may be hordes of Nephilim?" Inanna asked Lamech. "That is a rather bold claim, human. Hordes of Nephilim would indicate a rebellion of serious concern. How do you come by this intelligence?"

"The child speaks thoughtlessly, your majesty," interrupted Methuselah. "We have only seen pack-like activity."

"I am speaking to the young man," snapped Inanna. She knew if she had an opportunity to draw out anything incriminating on these foul vermin, it would be through this stupid brick head of an offspring.

"How is it you are so well trained in recognizing such militia activity?" she asked Lamech. Perhaps they were not telling her everything about their background. Maybe they had their own revolutionary connections. She had heard rumors about some kind of secret order of giant killers somewhere in the Havilah territory, but could never verify them with any certainty. Even torture had not revealed any secrets. Subterfuge might be a better tactic.

"Does not their soldier's uniforms and special armor indicate military affiliation?" asked Lamech. He was no brick head. He knew that turning it around and asking it as an obvious question would make him look much less educated and more of a speculator.

Inanna surprised them by turning to Edna. "Have there been any rumors of where these hordes may be?" Inanna thought wenches were even easier to trip up than young men.

Edna played her ignorance well. She added an uneducated rural accent. Her theatrics made Methuselah anxious. "My lady, can they hide inside volcanoes?" She said it without a trace of guile. She sounded spectacularly naïve.

Inanna rolled her eyes and shook her head with contempt. She would not even dignify that remark with an answer. Instead, she turned back to Enoch. "We have had some military uniforms stolen from caravans," she said. "Several other packs have shown up wearing them as well. Your 'hordes' are merely a pack of thieves." She turned to the administrator and snapped, "Give them their bounty." She whisked herself away without a farewell.

"Thank you, mighty queen," Enoch called after her.

She did not even acknowledge it. But as she exited the room, the Naphil guard who accompanied her caught Enoch's eyes in a long stare before he turned to follow the goddess.

It bothered Enoch. He collected their reward, thinking that they had better leave the city as quickly as possible.

Inanna sensed something askew with the bounty-hunters, but she also knew she would not get anywhere with her questioning. These humans were too smart to be so stupid. So few survived a tribal slaughter and killed four trained Nephilim warriors? And yet these survivors did not even know that volcanoes were inhospitable to animal life? She did not believe it. There was only one way she was going to get any information out of these wily travelers.

"Shadow them," she ordered the Nephilim.

Ohyah, the Naphil who had been watching Enoch, responded, "I will send my best tracker, your worship."

"Good. If he discovers a conspiratorial hideout of more of these giant-killers, we will hunt them down," Inanna said. "If not within the week, have him kill them as quickly as possible. We cannot have any of these nasty little gadflies getting under our skin with their revolutionary tendencies."

"Yes, my queen," said Ohyah.

She knew she could trust him. As a captain of the bodyguard, Ohyah had proven himself worthy by foiling an assassination attempt on Inanna some years before. It had happened when she began to usurp Enlil's status as patron god of Nippur. She simply outshined the unexceptional and mediocre Lord of the Air. She drew more followers through her bold leadership, and he had clearly become jealous.

She suspected the attempt had been masterminded by Enlil, but found no connections that led back to him. Though, as an immortal, she could not die, she could be wounded and impaired, which would weaken her status in the pantheon of power. Enlil had become so impotent that he locked himself in E-babba for weeks on end, not showing his face to anyone. When she went on her strategy trips back to Mount Hermon, he was too incompetent to take back his rightful glory. It made her smugly proud. She would eventually orchestrate his imprisonment so she could assume the throne physically, to complement her spiritual influence. But imprisoning a god was tricky. They could not be killed and had to be bound and entrapped into the heart of the earth, or better yet, a volcano. She grinned to herself. It required just the right sort of opportunity. She would wait for her moment.

She was engrossed in her planned rise to power. She had no idea that Ohyah, this most trusted of servants, had secrets of his own that had been haunting him. Secrets he could not reveal without losing his head.

CHAPTER 21

Enoch and his party, with the six rescued women squashed themselves into a city dwelling that only housed a family of four. They slept, some on the floor and some on the roof under the night sky. The patriarch of the home, Egibi, was a good friend of Betenos' father Barakil. They had traded with each other through the years and had become more than mere acquaintances. Egibi felt honored to give shelter to Betenos' tribe in this time of mourning.

Enoch explained to the women that Egibi would help them all find shelter and training for employment in the city. It would be difficult for these nomads to adjust, but they needed to do so. Enoch could not take care of them.

Betenos, however, was another story.

She pleaded with Enoch to take her with them. She pointed out that she had already helped them in many ways since they rescued her, not the least of which was finding this much needed shelter.

Enoch was set against it.

"This is a holy calling, Betenos. You do not even know who Elohim is."

"Lamech is teaching me," she answered.

"We cannot afford the time for Lamech to teach you," said Enoch. He doubted she would ever convert to Elohim.

Lamech butted in. "I will not shirk my other responsibilities and I will carry her weight if I must."

That brought a raised eyebrow from Betenos.

Enoch said, "She is not a giant killer."

Betenos retorted, "Giant killers need healing shamans for their battle wounds and cooks for their strength."

Enoch said, "This is too dangerous."

Edna now joined in, "She survived having her tribe wiped out by Nephilim."

Enoch barked, "Because we saved her!" He felt put upon.

"And she returned the favor." Methuselah held up Edna's bandaged arm. He was forever grateful for the healer's salve.

Enoch Primordial

Enoch sighed with exasperation. He stared at Betenos and asked, "Why do you want to join us so desperately? Are you trying to seduce my grandson?"

Everyone went silent.

Betenos looked offended. She puffed up indignantly and said with a slow burn, "No, I am not trying to *seduce* your grandson." She gave that back with a sting. "I was the daughter of a tribal elder. I do not need your grandson for my betterment! Although, I suspect your concern should be that your grandson is trying to seduce *me*."

Lamech flushed with embarrassment. She could not have insulted him more.

"But you do not have to worry about that," Betenos continued proudly, "because I never want to marry and have a family anyway! I want to do something much more important with my life. I want to fight for justice. And that is what you are doing."

Enoch sighed, his resistance cracking. "If you slow us down, we will leave you at the nearest city."

Betenos pushed on, relentless and unyielding, "Did I slow you down in the Greater Zab valley?"

When they had been too exhausted to go any further, Betenos had given them those special roots that renewed their strength like that of eagles when chewed.

"All right, all right!" barked Enoch. He put his foot down. "But you will be our healer and cook, and you will do as you are told."

"Will you teach me the bow?" asked Betenos.

Enoch burst out chuckling. Everyone joined in, relieved. She was growing on them all.

Enoch said, "Well you certainly do have the requisite stubbornheadedness to be a part of this tribe."

They all laughed some more — except for Lamech. Her remarks had deeply hurt him. He had truly been enjoying her presence, not trying to seduce her. Her arrogance of caste superiority left a foul impression on him. He looked for a way to leave the room without drawing attention to himself.

Edna could see her son's hurt. She held back from mothering him. She knew he had to go through this rejection on his own. It would mature him.

A knock at the door frightened them all. A curfew ruled the city. Anyone out in the streets at this hour could be arrested. The four of them found their weapons. Egibi opened the door to a six-year old child.

"Child, what are you doing out there!" yelped Egibi. He grabbed the small shoulder and pulled him quickly inside. "Do you not know, you could be arrested or killed outside past curfew!" he scolded.

The child nodded. He held out a small box to Egibi, a scribe's writing tablet with wax embedded in wood. When opened, a person could mark the wax and close it for storage and delivery. Egibi opened it and looked at it, but he could not read.

Enoch took the tablet and read it. His eyes went wide. "It says it is from an 'Ohyah,' the Nephilim Captain of the Guard. He wants to speak with me in secret. He says he has important intelligence for me. He wants to meet outside the city walls by the garbage dump."

"That smelly pit?" said Betenos.

"He does not want us to be discovered," said Enoch. "No one is going to be snooping around the city garbage dump in the late of night. And there are not many places a giant's presence can be discreet."

"A trap," offered Methuselah.

Enoch did not agree. "He would not admit to me that he was a Nephilim Captain of the Guard if he wanted to trick me," he said. "That would be about the last thing he would pretend to be."

"A double cross?" suggested Methuselah.

Enoch countered, "He is telling me a truth that places himself in a vulnerable position. And this little child is more evidence of that sentiment."

"Just the same, we are going with you," said Methuselah. "We will keep out of sight in case it does turn out to be a trap."

CHAPTER 22

The city dump lay just outside the walls on the north side of the city, downwind from the sea and river breezes that jostled their way through the streets. The stinking festering pile of refuse made Enoch think of Sheol and what it would be like to be cursed.

He walked toward some trees at the edge of the dump. How anything could grow here amazed him. The stench of the rotting garbage drew too many flies and made him gag. He shooed away a couple hyenas fighting over a cattle bone and looked around. The nearly six cubit tall dark figure standing in the moonlit shadows of the tree foliage gestured just enough to draw Enoch's attention. His heart raced. He wiggled his fingers in preparation to draw his dagger. Methuselah, Edna, and Lamech moved in and out of cover amidst the piles of rubbish, ready to charge at his command.

Enoch stepped up to the giant and found cover out of sight of the city watch above on the walls.

Ohyah towered over Enoch in both size and strength. Tattoos covered him, but he was one of the more handsome looking giants, if one could say that about such beasts.

"Are the three following you your own?" asked Ohyah, trying to keep his deep voice to a whisper.

Enoch nodded. This giant was also warrior-trained and had highly attuned senses. He could easily grab Enoch and crush him before any of them could come to his aid.

"I am grateful you came tonight. I know it was not an easy decision," said Ohyah.

"Then make it a worthy one," said Enoch. He would not fear this monster. He knew whom he served and did not fear death in the least.

Ohyah said, "The Nephilim you killed were not random thieves wearing stolen uniforms. They were from the deep west in Bashan by the Western Sea. From the area around Mount Hermon."

Enoch had heard of Mount Hermon. He knew it was the place of descent, where "the gods came down from heaven" to rule among men. It was an area shrouded in mystery, separated from their fertile crescent by hundreds of leagues of harsh arid desert. No one he knew had ever travelled there. All he had heard about it was rumors, gossip, and speculation. Nothing he cared to trust.

Ohyah continued, "After the Gigantomachy, some Rephaim escaped the Great Purges and found sanctuary in the one place that the Watchers would not consider looking for them. Their own territory of Bashan. The gods left their cosmic mountain to reside in the cities, so the criminal Rephaim and Nephilim went to hide out where the gods had left. They congregate and secret themselves like cockroaches in the nooks and crevices of the mountains and foothills. The giants you brought in were branded with the mark of Thamaq and Yahipan, Rephaim originally from Sippar."

Ohyah did not know that Enoch had been in Sippar during that fateful event. Enoch heard everything Ohyah told him, and knew it was all true. This earned the giant a measure of trust. Of course, he was still a Captain of the Temple Guard of Inanna, and the best lies were mostly true. So Enoch remained guarded.

Ohyah offered, "If you want to kill outlaws, Bashan is one of their hideouts."

Enoch narrowed his eyes and looked suspiciously at Ohyah.

"Why are you giving me this intelligence?" Enoch asked.

Ohyah did not expect Enoch to believe him easily. He knew he had to be vulnerable first, to reveal information that would place Ohyah himself in jeopardy. It was the only way he could earn trust.

"I have been having dreams from a god named Elohim," Ohyah said.

Enoch's attention perked up. How could this dark minion of Inanna know about Elohim? Did he know that Enoch and his band served Elohim? But how?

Ohyah, continued, "I saw the Ancient of Days, the ruler of heavens come down to earth and sit on a throne surrounded by ten thousand times ten thousand of his holy ones. He proclaimed a sentence upon all flesh and then wrote it on a tablet. The tablet was immersed in water and when it came out, all the names were washed away but eight. I fear for my life, Enoch. I want to join the forces of this god Elohim."

How could a demonic chimera receive revelations from Elohim? wondered Enoch. This was madness.

Ohyah said, "Elohim told me that you served him."

He could not possibly have known Enoch's calling except by revelation. *But what was this water judgment?*

"And he said that you would be going to the land of Bashan."

Ah, there he is wrong, thought Enoch, *I have been called to pronounce judgment upon the Watcher gods and their progeny, but Elohim has not told me to go to Bashan. Though it would provide the most opportunity for his bounty hunting of giants.*

Ohyah said, "I have a twin brother, Hahyah, who I believe is hiding out in that region. We have had an inseparable spiritual connection since we were born. I am sure he has had the same dreams and is most likely looking for me. I want to go with you to Bashan to find him. We will both repent and serve Elohim the Creator."

Enoch simply could not accept this insanity. A demonic spawn repent to worship Elohim? But was it possible that the truth was more than he understood? Could Elohim regenerate the soul of a Naphil? They were half human after all. Why could not their sin be as forgivable as his own? He wondered, if one of these could turn, could a Watcher god turn?

"No," said Enoch, "We are not going to Bashan. If you want to find your brother, you will have to go alone."

"It is treason to leave the side of Inanna. I will not be allowed to return. At least with you, I have a chance."

"Why do you say that?" asked Enoch. "You are a mighty warrior."

"But Elohim favors you," said Ohyah.

Enoch paused and measured his words carefully. "And Inanna favors you."

Ohyah understood the obvious implication. They served different gods. Enoch could never trust him because Inanna was a treacherous scheming demon of war and perversion. He did not blame Enoch. But it dashed his hopes nonetheless.

Enoch could see Ohyah's crestfallen expression. A Naphil, Captain of the Guard, mighty warrior, and demigod looked as if he was a kicked cub. Maybe more truth hid in this matter than Enoch thought at first. But he had to trust his intuition, unless Elohim himself told him otherwise.

Ohyah spoke with sad respect, "May your Elohim bless you on your journey with protection and success." With that Ohyah melted away into the shadows of the trees.

Methuselah arrived first. "What happened?"

Enoch stared into the blackness. Edna and Lamech joined them. Enoch paused thoughtfully, then finally offered, "He wanted to help us, but I turned him down."

"Help us?" sniffed Methuselah, "You mean betray us."

"That may very well be," said Enoch. "But if so, then he fooled me."

Methuselah, Edna, and Lamech all looked confused at Enoch and then into the dark, hoping that Ohyah would come back and explain the impossible. But no explanation was forthcoming. Enoch said, "Let us get back to the house. I need sleep."

Enoch's thrashing awakened Methuselah and Edna from their sleep. When he sat up, they saw the sheen of sweat bathing him. He gasped for air. They knew it was another dream vision.

"Elohim told me to go to the land of Bashan," said Enoch.

Methuselah and Edna could not believe their ears. Edna reached over and softly closed Methuselah's gaping jaw.

"That is near Mount Hermon, the cosmic mountain of the pantheon," said Methuselah. "Do you consider it wise to tread so close to the headquarters of the gods?"

Enoch said, "The Naphil guard captain told me that Thamaq and Yahipan were hiding out in Bashan."

Methuselah took one look at Edna and said, "We are going with father to Bashan."

If the Rephaim of Sippar, the murderers of his beloved Edna's parents, were still alive, if these abominations of desolation still breathed the good air of earth, then Methuselah had his purpose: to hunt them down and kill them.

The revelation of the Naphil dreams still bothered Enoch. Elohim had told Ohyah Enoch's charge before Elohim had told Enoch. How could this be? Should he have welcomed the giant into their company? Was that from Elohim? Or was it occultic sorcery? Was this a test? Did he fail it? It chewed into his brain. The giant knew Enoch's destination before he did. Elohim spoke to a Naphil!

Enoch stared into the distance like a holy man in a trance. "If you are going to go with me, you had better wake the others. We leave immediately for Mari."

CHAPTER 23

The city of Mari sat a good one hundred and thirty leagues up the Euphrates River from Nippur. As an economic trading center between Shinar in the south and Syria in the north, Mari channeled timber, stone, pottery, grains, and perishable foods up and down the Euphrates. It was also a way station to cross the vast desert to reach Bashan by the shorter and more hazardous path. The longer circuitous, and safer, route swept northward around the fertile crescent.

Enoch's traveling band of giant killers hired a boat to take them up to Mari. From there, they would strike out across the desert. The legendary Thamudi, primitive tribal peoples, roamed the desert, filling it with danger. They were said to skin victims alive and roll them in the sand to increase their unbearable pain.

Enoch left the snow tribe women with Egibi as he had promised. But he took Betenos with them, as he had conceded to her.

They avoided staying in the city proper so they would not be easily tracked by enemies. They chose a thick forest off the river's edge. They burrowed deep into the wildwood far from civilization to rest before their westward crossing of the desert.

After clearing a camp, they started one of the first fires they had been able to burn in a long time. They roasted wild boar on a makeshift spit and sat back, bellies full, mugs topped with drink. The women slept as Enoch, Methuselah, and Lamech sat around the fire planning the next leg of their trip.

Methuselah interrupted the discussion. "We are being followed." Lamech shook his head in surprise, for he had not noticed.

"I know," said Enoch. "I sensed it about half way up the river, and whoever it is has trailed us into the forest."

Lamech grabbed his weapon, Rahab. "Should we wake the women?"

"Yes," said Enoch. "But do not cause a commotion, because they are very near."

Lamech lightly nudged Edna and Betenos awake. He gave them a shushed gesture of warning. They understood the danger and picked up their weapons. Edna gripped a multi-bladed weapon and handed Betenos an axe from the wood pile. They stepped up slowly to the campfire.

"Backs against the flames, in a circle," commanded Enoch, who pulled an arrow from his quiver and nocked it on his bowstring. "It is time we face our stalker," he said.

They heard the rustling of the leaves in the wind in sync with the rustling in the underbrush. Whoever lurked there had a hunter's skill for blending into the natural background.

Or whatever.

They heard a soft growling. The iridescent glow of eyes reflecting the firelight from the brush appeared. Pairs of eyes. All around them. About twenty.

The lead alpha male stepped out of the bush. It focused on Enoch, seeming to know his equal. It was a bizarre creature that none of them had ever seen before, a chimera, a hybrid mixture of several animals. It crept on all fours, and was about three times the size of a man. It had the long scaly neck and head of a horned dragon, the body and forelegs of a feline predator, the taloned hind legs of a bird of prey, and its tail was a living snake.

The creature showed no fear of its prey. It seemed to merely be sizing up how easily the game would be taken. It snarled.

Lamech rolled out Rahab. He could tame this thing with a whip of his sword, but twenty of them? That was another story altogether.

The alpha hissed. Its forked tongue tasted the air that carried their scent. It backed up a bit into the shadows. The eyes of the others moved slightly forward, lowering to the ground. They prepared to strike.

Suddenly, the alpha beast yelped as its tail was jerked from behind. Something dragged the monster into the brush and out of sight. Its roar cut off in a squeal of pain.

One of the surrounding chimeras jumped out of the bushes at the humans by the fire. A seven cubit tall Naphil leapt through the air, intercepting the chimera. It met the beast with a crunch and they rolled to the ground in a mass. Then the giant stood up, victoriously, his blade dripping with chimera blood.

He stood, wearing only a loincloth, the ritual Nephilim hunting attire, holding a pear-headed mace in one hand and a battle axe in the other. Was he on their side or was he claiming them as his prey?

Another squeal cut through the dark. Another chimera flew out from the bush and landed in a dead heap for all to see. Its killer followed, a second leaping Naphil. He landed on the other side of the blazing fire, ready to kill with a mace and sword. Two down, eighteen to go.

Enoch suddenly recognized the second Naphil as Ohyah, the Captain of Inanna's guard. The first Naphil stared at Ohyah with a look of surprise, like he had not anticipated Ohyah's arrival.

Enoch had no time to sort out what was happening. The gang of monsters pounced in unison. Most of them attacked the two Nephilim. The others went for the humans.

These hellions fought fiercely. Methuselah thanked Elohim the Nephilim were on their side. They might not have survived without them.

Enoch killed a couple of the chimeras with his bow. With such close quarter fighting, he dropped the bow and switched to an axe.

Methuselah used his javelins as pikes, poking out eyes and throats. He caught a quick glance of Edna, spinning and slicing more furiously than he had ever seen. But her wounded arm, though mostly healed, was a bit stiff and slow. She was tiring and getting sloppy. Killing hybrid giants was one thing, but these obscenities were five-part hounds of Sheol. Their freakish nature resulted in confusing unpredictable fighting behavior. They were flexible, agile and fast.

Betenos was not a warrior. Lamech had been working with her, and she had been catching on quickly. But this was not any kind of battle to practice in. It was not even a battle that Lamech, with all his experience, had ever been in before. He had double duty snapping his sword Rahab and covering for Betenos behind him with their backs to the bonfire. She snatched up Enoch's bow and arrows. She had time to aim and release from behind Lamech.

Lamech's arm was tiring. He chopped off a snake head tail of one of the beasts and then caught the dragon head of another. The force of it yanked his weakened arm and he lost control. The whip blade cracked just over Methuselah's head near the fire.

"Are you still angry at me, son? I told you I like Betenos!" yelped Methuselah. Even at such a moment, he could find the humor. He might as well. They would probably all be dead and eaten by evening's end.

"Sorry!" yelled Lamech. He switched hands with the flexible blade. He was not as good with his left arm. But he needed rest or he would collapse any moment.

The Nephilim worked in natural coordination with each other. They each grabbed a monster in tandem and threw the beasts at each other with a crash, stunning them. They followed up with a synchronized double clubbing. They were highly trained guards and would be very hard to kill should Enoch's team find themselves facing off with the giants after this ambush — *if* they made it out alive.

Enoch's thoughts distracted him for a moment. One of the chimeras fell upon him and pinned him to the ground, knocking the wind out of him. Saliva splattered from its jaws. He could feel the hot breath on his face. It bared its teeth to strike, its lips pulled back to reveal two rows of razor edged fangs.

Enoch shut his eyes, waiting for his life to be torn from his body.

The jaws never came.

Ohyah grabbed the dragon's throat and ripped out its windpipe. It fell to the ground.

Enoch opened his eyes.

Ohyah smiled at him, for just a moment. Then a pack of three of the mongrels pounced in unison onto his back. He went down beneath a pile of fighting monsters. One of the creatures clamped its iron jaws onto Ohyah's arm. He screamed in pain.

The other giant ripped one of the beasts off of him and flung it down onto the fire.

An explosion of flames and embers covered everyone.

Methuselah's javelin and Edna's weapon pierced through the second one.

The third mutant beast with clamped jaw had its head cut off by Lamech's Rahab.

Suddenly, unexpectedly, it was all over. Those were the last three of the chimeras. The giant killers had teamed up with their own enemy to defeat a common foe.

Everyone was near total exhaustion, lungs burning for air.

When Lamech saw that Betenos was unwounded, he hugged her for dear life.

Methuselah crawled to Edna. He was too exhausted to say anything more than, "Pednanoonypoo."

"Poozelahbunnybunch," she murmured and collapsed in his arms. They lay gasping for a moment.

"What in the world were those monstrosities?" an incredulous Methuselah asked anyone who would answer.

No one did.

Methuselah glanced around. The second Naphil helped Enoch up to his feet. Whatever possessed this creature to help them was beyond Methuselah.

He saw Ohyah stand up behind Enoch. His father was sandwiched between the two giants. The hair rose on the back of Methuselah's neck.

Ohyah raised his ax.

Methuselah screamed.

It was too late. Ohyah delivered a mighty blow.

But it was not to Enoch. Ohyah struck the other Naphil. It fell to the ground dead at Enoch's feet.

Enoch looked up in fear at Ohyah.

Ohyah dropped the weapon and sat on the ground, his task completed.

Lamech and Methuselah ran to Enoch to protect him. They pointed their weapons at the surviving giant. Ohyah sighed and said, "That Naphil was sent to kill you."

"How do you know that?" demanded Enoch.

"Because Inanna ordered me to send him," said Ohyah. "He did not anticipate being beaten to the task by the mushussu." He looked at Methuselah. "That is the answer to your question. The beasts are called *mushussu*. He must have relished the challenge of gaining your trust in the fight in order to kill you in your sleep."

"And you?" said Lamech.

"I came to stop him. He thought I was here to help him."

"This is becoming a jumbled confusion of cross purposes," exclaimed Methuselah. "I must be getting old."

"It is simple, father," said Lamech. "We are on our way to kill giants." He pointed to the dead Naphil. "That giant was sent to kill us." He pointed to Ohyah. "This giant came to kill that giant. But these mushussu came to kill us all. So we all teamed up and killed the mushussu." He paused for a moment. "And now we are all wondering if we should kill this giant." Lamech was becoming a chip off the old mud brick, with his wit. Edna smiled.

Enoch said, "Why should we trust you, giant?"

"Is it not obvious?" said Ohyah. "If I wanted you dead, I would have let the Naphil kill you."

"But *you* are a Naphil," protested Methuselah. "You are the Watchers' seed."

"But half human," said Lamech in Ohyah's defense.

"Elohim made me this way," Ohyah countered.

Edna watched Ohyah closely. She did not have the open mind that these men displayed. She cared only to protect her son and husband.

"Can Nephilim actually repent and serve Elohim?" Methuselah's words echoed everyone's thoughts.

Enoch spoke up. "Ohyah means us no harm. He will be traveling with us to Bashan."

He stared straight into Ohyah's eyes as he said the words. Ohyah sighed with relief and smiled at him.

"Well, I never thought I'd see the day," said Methuselah. "A repentant Naphil joining a team of giant killers. You will have to write about that in your memoirs, father. But I anticipate you will be accused of fictional embellishment."

The others chuckled. It was all too absurd to believe. But they were living it.

Enoch studied one of the dead monsters, deep in thought. He picked up one of the severed heads to look at it more closely. "Ohyah, you called these mushussu? I have never seen nor heard of them before. What are they?"

"Miscegenation of the gods," said Ohyah. The word referred to hybridization. Herdsmen and pastoralists had learned to crossbreed certain animals to create new ones that were blended combinations of both animals. The domesticated dog came from such breeding. Humans selected wolves from one pack that were more docile than the others and interbred them with docile members of a different pack to create a new breed of canine more friendly to humans. There were limits to hybridization that restricted such breeding to animals of the same kind. One could not "crossbreed" birds with felines and reptiles. Yet this hideous mutant clearly had been so magically bred. It was unimaginable.

"How is it possible to crossbreed so many creatures?" asked Methuselah.

A pall of darkness came over Ohyah's face. "It is not natural," he said. "It is part of an experiment of occultic secrets by the gods."

"But why?" asked Enoch. "For what purpose?"

"I do not know," said Ohyah. "But I suspect you will find the answer in Bashan."

"Well, let us get our rest," said Enoch. "We begin our crossing of the Great Desert in the morning."

CHAPTER 24

They set out to cross the Great Desert, heading into a stretch of one hundred and seventeen leagues of the most severe desert, with the harshest weather Enoch and his band of warriors had ever experienced. He wondered where such severity came from. He had heard that in early days, the region had been rich in vegetation, animal life and bodies of water. Something had happened that changed it all, that brought a curse upon this infernal land.

Riding onagers, they followed a trade route marked by wells along the way. The watering spots gave them relief for their blistered and dehydrated bodies. They crossed paths with caravans returning from Egypt by way of the Levantine coastal lands. Within days they adjusted to the harsh environment. As nomads, they had learned to survive in any habitat, from rigid cold mountain to hot humid jungle to barren dry tundra.

Methuselah, who longed to experience all the extremes that his body could endure in this world, found it exhilarating. He felt that if Elohim gave him physical senses to experience, he would indulge them to the fullest — within moral boundaries of course. And one of those moral boundaries included holy union with his beloved Edna. Even after all these years, he was more grateful for Elohim's creation of oneness with his wife than anything else, be it feasting on a roasted boar or killing a giant. Well, roasted boar ran a pretty close second.

Edna glanced at Methuselah, lost in thought as they plodded along on their pack animals. She knew exactly what he was thinking. She would tease him about it in their tent later that night. And then she would kiss him—passionately—because she understood him more than anyone in the world. She loved him the way he was, with all their differences.

Enoch had not adapted to this miserable climate as well as the others. He used the long hours of travel to pray to Elohim. But he could not stand the relentless heat. He longed to leave his body and once again swim in the crystalline waters above the heavens. He dreamed of being in the heavenly temple and the glorious light of ten thousand times ten thousand of Elohim's holy ones. Instead, he suffered the burning rays of a red hot sun scorching him to the bone.

Lamech and Betenos lagged further behind. Their non-stop talk drove everyone up a rock cliff. What is your favorite animal to kill and skin? Do you prefer lean-to shelters or sleeping under starlight? Do you ever want to settle down in a city someday? It was amazing how long they could talk without taking a break to breathe or drink water from their goat skins.

Edna smiled and said a prayer of thanks when she heard them spend hours debating the greatness of Elohim versus the Great Goddess. She could hear Betenos breaking down in her protestations. She knew it was only a matter of time before Betenos rejected her pagan upbringing and embraced Elohim. Who knows? She might even become a giant killer. In the meantime, she cooked a mean lizard stew and kept them from heat exhaustion with her herbal remedies.

The one area that gave Edna grave concern was Betenos' vow against marriage. The young woman was dead set against having children and refused to talk about it. Edna made a mental note to talk to Betenos about it when they were alone.

Ohyah brought up the rear. They all found it difficult to accept a giant walking amongst them. He did not want to make them any more uncomfortable. Besides, Nephilim were reclusive creatures and treasured their solitude. They were bred to kill, not socialize.

The group made astonishing time at almost eight leagues a day for nearly a week. They were just past half way to their destination. The midafternoon sun penetrated everything.

A gush of warm air washed over them.

A shiver went through Ohyah's spine. He yelled out in his deep resounding voice,. "Shaitan! Shaitan!" It carried all the way to Enoch at the front of their line.

It was the Naphil word for sandstorm, a very vicious sandstorm. Enoch searched the horizon. He did not see it. No one did. The Nephilim had a sixth sense the humans did not share.

Ohyah sprinted to the front. "It is coming from the north! We must find shelter!"

They had seen no shelter for days.

Enoch yelled, "RUN!" They all kicked their rides and galloped westward as fast as they could.

The storm did not take long to become visible. A huge billowing wall of sand in the distance charged toward them like a tsunami. Before they could get to safety, it swept over them. A cyclone of whirling dust and sand and rocks enveloped them.

A large rock hit Ohyah in the back. It would have killed any of the humans, but it merely knocked him dizzy. He tried to cover the women with his bulky figure.

They did not know how long they could last. Such storms could be short gusts or stretch for distances of leagues.

They covered their mouths with their cloaks as filters. They could barely breathe.

The onagers collapsed. They had no filters for their lungs.

The company could not move. Their beasts of burden were dead. They huddled together.

They prepared to die.

As suddenly as it began, the storm stopped. It passed over them. They coughed and sputtered and shook out the sand from their clothes.

They looked around. The storm had not actually passed them by. It was now all around them. They stood within a swirling wall of sand circling around them like a huge corral.

"The eye of the storm," blurted Lamech.

They had heard of such a thing, but had never experienced it. As if they were at sea, this hurricane of sand had a center of complete calmness and they had entered it. All around them rushed the impenetrable curtain of cyclonic wind and earth. They huddled in a circle of complete calmness.

Betenos looked up behind them all with astonishment. "Oh my gods, it is true. It is really true."

Everyone turned to see an incredible wonder. Not too far from them stood a tree, a very large tree, a tremendous tree that extended into the heavens, thousands of cubits high.

"The World Tree," murmured Betenos. "See, Lamech?" she cried, "I told you it was true. The Great Goddess Earth Mother."

She fell to her knees and worshipped.

CHAPTER 25

Enoch looked upwards. He could not see where the tree ended. It just disappeared into the clouds. How could this be? They should have seen it from leagues away. But there had been nothing but empty desert for many leagues in every direction. It was not only thousands of cubits high, it was at least a couple hundred cubits around. Its tangled mass of roots were no doubt anchored deep into the earth. It could not move with the shifting storm, so how could it be in the center of it?

Enoch rubbed his eyes. Was this a vision? It could not be. The others saw it as well. Were they under some kind of spell? It must be magic.

Skepticism filled Enoch. He felt they were nestling within the coils of a huge serpent. It might be dark magic.

Ohyah recalled the story from his youth about Inanna and the Huluppu Tree. Could this be the one? The very origin of the Sacred Marriage rite. It came rushing back to him. *In the very first days and the very first nights when Anu and Enlil had separated the heavens and the earth, and Ereshkigal was given the underworld, there was a single Huluppu Tree.* The wood from the tree was used to make the bed of Inanna where her lover Dumuzi would sleep with her. Then he remembered, *the great thunderbird, Anzu left its young up in the branches*. Ohyah stared up into the sky, transfixed, looking for some sign of the mythical eagle-like creature.

Without warning, he ran toward the tree.

Enoch yelled after him, "Ohyah! What are you doing?"

Ohyah did not respond. He ran like the wind all the way to the mighty trunk and jumped onto it a dozen cubits in the air.

He climbed.

The others stood wondering what had gotten into his head to do such a thing.

Methuselah said, "I knew we could not trust the giant."

"We must take cover before the storm shifts," Enoch said, starting toward the tree. They approached its base, a tangle of gnarled roots plunging into the earth like grappling hooks. The wood of the tree was weather-beaten and leathery. The roots writhed and folded around each other creating crevices and hideaways.

High above them, Ohyah climbed rapidly. White clouds shrouded the top of the tree. As they watched the spectacle of the tree-climbing giant, he vanished into the mist.

Enoch brought his gaze back down. He started.

Three beautiful young maidens stood before them like phantasms. They reminded him of the cave dwellers of Sahand who suddenly appeared as if rising from the ground itself. But these beings probably materialized from the large fissures of the tree. And they were not so earthy as the cave dwellers.

They were actually quite heavenly.

Surprise silenced the travelers.

The women were barefoot, adorned in silky flowing dress, with flower-laden hair. One had jet black hair and the others had wavy locks as golden as the sand. Their pale milky skin looked as if it had never been in the sun. And when they spoke, it gave the impression of singing.

The women spoke as if in unison, "Welcome to our abode. You must be exhausted to have weathered such a storm."

Enoch could swear he did not see their mouths move. "Who are you?" he asked.

"I am Lilith," said the raven-haired beauty. "And these are my daughters Lili and Lilu."

"Are you angels?" blurted Lamech.

Lilith smiled. "We are the keepers of this most sacred space."

"Where are we? What is this?" asked Enoch.

"This is the Great Goddess Earth Mother, the Tree of Life," answered Lilith. "She is the link between heaven and earth."

"What?" said Enoch. He looked at Methuselah and Edna. They knew of only one Tree of Life and that was unapproachably secluded in the Garden of Eden.

Lilith and the girls giggled. "All will be made clear. But first you must rest, re-gather your strength," said Lilith.

She led them to a campsite nestled in the encircling roots of the tree. It seemed a comfortable safe encampment with a firepit, locations for sleeping and protection from any sandy winds or scorching sunrays that might try to find them.

But the feature that caught their attention was the flowing fountain of sparkling fresh water that poured from a hole in the tree into a small pool with well walls built around it.

Lamech plopped down exhausted in a bed-like nook of soft bark.

Lilith stepped over to the pouring water and took a handcupped sip. "You must be weary and thirsty from your journey. Please allow Lili and Lilu to serve you refreshment."

Enoch, Methuselah and Edna were not merely weary but wary. Betenos was transfixed in wonder.

Lamech started to snore. He had fallen asleep from fatigue.

Lili and Lilu brought ladles of the water to them. Enoch surmised that this strange angelic woman could not be offering them poisoned water since she indulged from the fountain herself. He nodded to the others and they drank deeply.

But Enoch also noticed something about Lilu that made him curious. Up close, it became apparent to him that Lilu was in fact a slender feminine young boy who had been dressed and groomed as a girl. But the promise of water distracted him.

The liquid felt like balm in their parched throats. It brought almost instant healing to their chapped lips and revived them from within. Their blurry sight became unclouded. Their foggy heads dissipated and they could think more clearly. They must have been dangerously dehydrated and had not realized it.

Lilith said to them, "It is the living waters."

Edna felt a pain in her stomach. Nausea swept over her. She looked at the others. They seemed all right. It was not the water.

Lilith noticed Edna's grimace with a look of concern, a display of preternatural sensitivity to others' feelings. To Edna, she seemed the very embodiment of compassion. She was elegant and fair, like a hidden queen of this desert oasis paradise.

Methuselah was no doubt allured by her. He deeply loved his wife. She knew he worked hard at keeping his eyes focused on his beloved Edna. But she also knew her husband's tastes. She suspected that he was trying very hard at that moment to avoid an attraction to this exotic woman.

She was right. Methuselah found Lilith beautiful. He wondered if Havah had looked like this when she was first created in the Garden so long ago, the essence of woman.

Enoch felt surprised at himself. He had never been one to be overcome by women's beauty. But he had never seen such transcendent and feminine loveliness in all his wanderings. It stirred him in a way he had not been stirred for years. He wondered if he had become too mental and disembodied in his spirit. Perhaps Methuselah's accusation of him was correct: he was missing out on the visual beauty of Elohim's creation.

Lamech had stopped snoring. In his dreams, he began to experience erotic thoughts he had not had before. His desire for Betenos was rising within his soul. He wanted to marry her. But she did not worship Elohim, and that was a problem. He had no desire to unite himself, a temple of Elohim, to a temple of other gods. Betenos had listened and asked questions for a while. But she was unwilling to reject the gods she had known all her life and worship his god. But even if she did, she still did not want to marry and raise a family.

Yet, in the dream, Betenos came to Lamech as he slept. She whispered in his ears, "I will follow your god, but you must first know me."

Her body began to sway and undulate with an inhuman flexibility, almost like that of a snake.

She brushed against his body and he was about to grab her, when her tongue flicked out and licked his face. It was a split tongue.

It shocked him awake. His heart raced. He tried not to display his fear as he looked at Betenos sitting attentively listening to Lilith, completely unaware of Lamech behind her.

Edna thought she felt the sand move beneath them. It was a dizzy spell. She shook it off. She was feeling better.

Enoch said to Lilith, "Tell us about this Tree of Life you call the Great Goddess Earth Mother." Enoch refused to be a pushover. Just because they had been rescued by these maidens, that did not mean he trusted that they had altruistic motives. The others knew he was testing Lilith. He did not mention that they had sojourned with the very first inhabitants of the Garden, the only humans to see the Tree of Life. He knew this was not the same tree.

Her daughters sat dutifully beside Lilith as she told her amazing story.

CHAPTER 26

Hundreds of cubits above the campsite, Ohyah continued to scale the mighty tree. Deep grooves and knots in the wood made for easy climbing. He stopped again to rest. For the first time, he looked more closely at the bark he had been grabbing for handholds and footholds.

What he saw almost made him lose his grip.

The bark seemed to consist of countless multitudes of human bodies fused indistinguishably into the wood in agonizing and convoluted tangles. It was as if the tree was made of these bodies melded into one large edifice that rose into the sky. Was this a tree of corpses or damned souls?

A tremendous caw overhead drew his attention back to his goal. The call of the Anzu. He planned to catch the great thunderbird. He could not see it yet, but knew he was close. It probably nestled amidst one of the branches in the heights. He continued to climb.

· · · · ·

"You are familiar with our forefather Adam and the Garden of Eden?" Lilith asked her attentive group of resting travelers. They nodded their heads yes.

"And you have heard that he had a wife, Havah?" she added. They nodded again.

She let loose with her revelation, "What you no doubt have *not* heard is that I was Adam's first wife."

The travelers did not hold back their surprise.

"It is true. I do not expect you to believe me. For I know that Adam and his second wife have conspired to construct a myth that covers up the truth. You see, Elohim created me to be Adam's equal in the Garden. But if you knew Adam, you would know that he is a controlling patriarchal male."

Enoch and the others could understand that sentiment. They had come to know Adam. He had been a strong leader, at times a bit demanding. And he often had appealed to his status as the firstborn of humanity. When drunk, he would sometimes mumble, "I am primogeniture," a term that meant the firstborn birthright to inherit an entire estate. Ironically, though, in his later years, his blindness made him depend upon Havah. Methuselah thought it was Havah, not Adam, that had become a bit more controlling than he thought appropriate.

Lilith continued, "Adam became so oppressive that I refused to submit to his authority out of fear for my safety. I had no desire for his position as head of the human race. I simply wanted equality. After all, Elohim had created me out of his side, not his rear end."

The listeners chuckled. She had the good sense of humor to make light of what was an otherwise intolerable situation. Edna began to think of Methuselah and how much she had given up to follow him, and how he was often insensitive to her interests and absorbed in his own.

Betenos hung on every word, completely oblivious to any memory of her secret romantic interest in Lamech. All she thought of was his insufferable demands that she follow his male god Elohim, who did not display much interest in women as far as she was concerned.

"I gave in to his bizarre and abusive demands," continued Lilith, "and gave him the two daughters you see before you now." Lili and Lilu were looking more innocent to Methuselah and Enoch. Enoch had already forgotten his discovery that Lilu was a boy.

It did not occur to any of them that Lilith and her offspring should appear much older than they did. If they had been with Adam before Havah, they would be close to nine hundred years old.

Enchantment lay upon Enoch and his party. The water from the tree had drugged their faculties of observation, reason, and morality.

"Unfortunately," said Lilith, "Adam and his 'god' did not want girls, they wanted boys, the superior gender as they told me. They conspired to use this against me and cast me and my daughters out of the Garden, so Elohim could make a more 'suitable' partner for him, someone who would remain barefoot in the Garden and bow to his every wish and whim. In other words, a slave."

Edna now saw Methuselah as the exact replication of his forefather Adam, a patriarchal pig. Thoughts raced through her mind like gnats. *He probably thinks of me as his slave, to fulfill his commands at the expense of my own. And all he ever thinks about is sex. What kind of spiritual leader is that? I probably need a man like a fish needs a pelican.*

Betenos had already determined that she would never marry Lamech, the wild boar progeny of his father. *Maybe what I really need is another woman instead, who understands me. Maybe one of these daughters. That way, I would never have to worry about birthing those clinging little screaming monsters called "children."*

Lilith said, "My daughters and I were exiled by the sky god and his violent male oppressor, but our Earth Mother, the Great Goddess, found us and gave us rebirth here at the true Tree of Life."

Betenos suddenly broke out weeping. Lilith touched her gently.

"What is wrong, my dear?" she asked.

Betenos mumbled just clearly enough, "That is why I do not want to bring children into this world! My whole tribe was slaughtered by men and their lust for violence and war."

"It is true," said Lilith. "Perhaps if the nurturing gender were in charge, we might have peace in the world."

Edna doubled over with crippling pain in her abdomen. She reached below her cloak and pulled her hand out. It had blood all over it.

Enoch recoiled with revulsion.

Methuselah refused to come to her aid.

Serves her right, he thought, *the way she has been ignoring me lately with her hysterical emotional tantrums.*

Lilith helped Edna up with gentle compassion. "I think this is something only another woman can help with," she said. "Come for a walk, my love. I can help you clean yourself from impurities."

Betenos jumped up. "May I come also, Lilith?"

Lilith kept her back. "Maybe later, dear."

Betenos sat down again, disappointed.

Edna felt certain that something moved beneath her feet again, like something swimming in the sand.

Lilith called back to her daughters, "Lili and Lilu, will you please keep the others entertained."

"Yes, mother," they said in perfect unison. Lamech was sure their mouths did not move when they spoke.

However, their bodies did move. Their motion reminded Lamech of the writhing dance in his dream. Exactly the same dance in his dream. Like the movement of snakes.

The sinuous dancing wove the enchantment on the travelers tighter. But the three keepers of the tree had not anticipated one minor mistake in their perfect scheme: Lamech had not drunk the water.

The young man burst out, "Father, we have been enchanted by sorcery! In the holy name of Yahweh Elohim, awake!"

The secret covenant name of Yahweh broke the spell and ripped the men from their stupor. He would never have used it but for the lethal nature he knew they were in.

The girls cried out in unison, "Ningishzida, arise!" And then they fled.

Betenos tried to go after them, but Lamech held her back. She struggled and thrashed in his arms, trying to get loose. "Let me go! Let me go!" she screamed. It was as if she was possessed of an evil spirit. But Lamech would not let her go. He loved her too deeply.

Enoch and Methuselah gathered their weapons. They snatched up some burning logs for light, and ran after the two girls.

They saw the figures fleetingly, disappearing into the tree a short distance ahead of them. It was as if they dissolved into it.

When the two men reached the spot, they discovered a cleft that led deep into the tree, hiding a narrow passageway. They entered it, with lit torches and drawn dagger and javelin into the darkness.

CHAPTER 27

Ohyah stopped climbing the gnarled wood and pressed close to the trunk to avoid being seen. The Thunderbird nest was in sight. He could see its tangled branches and leaves molded into the arm of a large branch. For one moment, he reconsidered what he was doing. Not only was he about to risk his life attempting to capture the great Anzu with nothing but a rope he had attached to his belt, but he was planning on doing so after an exhausting climb of untold thousands of cubits.

The bird had made no sound since he first heard it. He did not know if it was still in the nest or had left it. He would have to take a chance and hope he caught it asleep. He thought he would make a quick prayer to Elohim just in case he might be willing to help him out, since he was a member of Enoch's team of travelers.

· · · · ·

Betenos finally broke down in Lamech's unrelenting embrace. She wept as Lamech told her they had been victims of sorcery. He told her that he forgave her for all the cruel words she had bellowed at him while trying to escape his grasp. They had been vile, spiteful words and she was now deeply sorry.

She could not believe such evil things could come from her heart. But they had. Lamech knew it was the same evil that lay in his heart and in every heart of every human. The sorcery did not create their wickedness, it merely unleashed it from its moral restraint.

Now he understood why she had fought against the idea of having a family. It made him feel even closer to her. How could he blame her for not wanting to bring children into such an evil world? It was natural for her to think this way. Only faith could overcome such fear.

Betenos looked up at him and said, "Lamech, who is Ningishzida?"

It was the last thing the sirens had uttered before they disappeared. *Ningishzida arise.*

"I do not know," said Lamech. He felt the ground move as if something burrowed beneath them. They got up to follow Enoch and Methuselah. But they were thrown backward by an explosion of sand in their path.

Out of the earth rose the head of a gigantic serpent. The creature must have been a good twenty-five cubits long. Its horned head was as big as Betenos' body. Its girth was at least three cubits wide. It was black and its eyes glowed with the lapis lazuli blue of the gods. But its fangs gleamed pearly white.

"I think we just met Ningishzida," said Lamech.

The head rose until it reached a striking position three cubits above the ground. It hissed fiercely. Lamech and Betenos could hear in their minds a whispering voice, *You are going to die.*

Lamech's weapon Rahab lay where he had been sleeping. The path to it was blocked by the other end of the snake. The tail burst out of the ground and grabbed Lamech in its coils. It shoved Betenos aside into the sand.

Lamech struggled to free himself. But the strong coils of pure reptilian muscle held him fast. All he had been able to do was grab a handful of sand. He laughed at himself. A handful of sand. What a weapon! At best, he could throw the sand in its eyes and blind it for a moment — before it finished him as the first course of its two-course meal.

The tentacle-like tail raised Lamech into the air, squeezing the life out of him. The giant ophidian head gracefully moved to look its prey in the eyes. Its big split tongue shot out and tasted Lamech's skin. His horrible dream came back to him like an unheeded omen. He should have foreseen this. He had been too concerned about Betenos to catch the signs all around him. Now, he was going to die and he could not even help the woman he secretly loved.

· · · · ·

Enoch and Methuselah followed the labyrinthine passage under the tree deep down into the earth. The serpentine roots appeared to move under the heat of the torches. The men were so intent on their quest, they barely noticed that the roots all around them consisted of the tortured tangle of human corpses transmuted into the wooden essence of the tree.

Edna's husband loved her so madly that he adored her through every one of his senses; visual, audible, tactile, taste, and olfactory. The perfume of spices she used left an alluring trail of smell. He stopped at various points in the pursuit and sniffed the air or a root where her clothes had brushed by and he knew exactly which way these "night hags" had taken her.

Soon they came upon a large opening in the ground, a subterranean chamber cut out of the rock. They remained quiet, hoping to maintain the element of surprise.

All four women were there.

But Edna lay upon a stone altar.

Lilith stood over her, while Lili and Lilu held Edna down. Her cloak was pulled back to reveal a plump belly. Three hyenas sat obediently on either side of the altar.

The hideous sight of the walls of the chamber shook Enoch and Methuselah to their cores. Skeletons, thousands of skeletons, not adult bones, but infant ones, all covered the walls. They both realized this was not the madness of grave robbers, but rather the evil of demonic murderers.

Then Methuselah realized what he had been too ignorant to see before.

Edna was pregnant.

· · · · ·

Lamech gasped for breath. The scaly coils of the huge serpent crushed his lungs. He should have been awake earlier to be prepared. He started to black out. The serpent bared its fangs, ready for the kill.

Lamech managed to wheeze out one last word, "Ra — hab."

He and Betenos heard a whisper in their minds tell them, I am not Rahab. I am Ningishzida, Lord of the Tree. But I welcome the comparison.

Lamech was not looking at the serpent, but at his beloved Betenos on the ground. He made his final gesture before collapsing, throwing the sand into the face of his enemy. Its protective lids closed for just a moment.

That was all that Betenos needed. The snake had ignored the weak female prey to focus on its stronger male opponent. It did not realize that *Rahab* was not a reference to the sea serpent of chaos, but rather to the name of Lamech's weapon.

Betenos snatched the weapon and unrolled it behind her. She had watched Lamech enough times. He had even taught her how to use it in a pinch.

This was a pinch.

She snapped it forward. The blade wrapped its coil around the serpentine abomination just below its head and cut through it like a stalk of wheat under the scythe.

Lamech dropped to the ground with the falling head of Ningishzida. Betenos ran up to him and pulled the coils off him in tears.

"Lamech! Lamech, my beloved!"

He was unresponsive, pale blue, not breathing.

"Please, Elohim, please," she pleaded to the heavens.

Lamech coughed and gasped for air. His face filled with color.

Betenos hugged him for all her life, but he stopped her.

"We have to find father and grandfather. They need us."

CHAPTER 28

Ohyah ascended the last distance to the Anzu nest with as much stealth as he could manage, to avoid detection. He peeked over the edge of the nest. The Anzu bird lay inside, asleep. The fierce looking creature had a body size twice that of a Naphil and a wingspan of about four times that. Huge and powerful, its leonine face included sharp incisors in the jaw.

He climbed closer. It snored. He suppressed an involuntary chuckle. Every creature on the face of the earth, no matter how frightening, had to sleep just like every other creature. Therein lay its fleshly weakness. This massive intimidating bird of prey snored like a giant kitten.

Ohyah sprang. He slipped his prepared rope bridle over the monster's mouth as he landed on its back.

Startled awake, it snapped open its wings at the weight of the Naphil. It opened its mouth in a roar. Ohyah pulled tight on the makeshift bridle, asserting control over his wild quarry.

The bird reacted instantly. It leapt into the sky. It quickly realized that it had to release this smelly agitating creature from its back or suffer the fight of its life.

First it flew upside down, then it zigzagged. It plummeted, it shot up, it jerked left and right. The nasty little parasite would not let go.

Ohyah was breaking this bucking Anzu.

·····

Down in the depths of the hideous tree, Enoch nocked an arrow in his bow and aimed.

Lilith held a stone sacrificial dagger raised above her head. She sounded an incantation over Edna. Enoch saw that the physical features of the women had become decrepit. Their beauty was falling off their faces. These monsters drew their life force from the slaughter of infants. Enoch marveled, appalled. What kind of abominable deity would demand such a thing?

He released his arrow.

The arrow pierced Lilith's hand, pinning it against the wall behind her. She dropped the blade to the floor.

Methuselah threw a javelin. It penetrated Lilith's chest, puncturing her lung simultaneously with Enoch's arrow in her hand. A howling shriek of agony, such that neither of them had ever heard before, filled the chamber.

Enoch realized that these were not mere creatures of flesh. They were demons.

Lili and Lilu pulled the projectiles from Lilith's body. They cackled in unison. Large leathery wings unfolded from behind Lilith, materializing from nowhere.

Methuselah realized the piercing shriek did not come from Lilith, but from the three hyenas near the altar. They howled in agony when Lilith was struck. Some kind of connection ran between the animals and the demons.

"Hit the hyenas!" he yelled. He launched one of his javelins into the air.

It caught one of the hyenas in the thigh. It yelped again. Simultaneously, Lili grabbed her thigh in pain. The other hyenas scrambled for cover.

Enoch for another target. A rumbling overhead halted him. The vibration felt as if an army on heavy mounts was arriving just above them.

He looked around.

The night hags and their animal avatars were gone.

Methuselah ran to the altar and took Edna up in his arms. She gazed up at him in a drugged state of mind and simply uttered, "My Poozeydoodoo," before passing out altogether.

He kissed her with weeping tears. "I will never take you for granted again, my dear, dear Pednapoodlums."

CHAPTER 29

Enoch led the way back through the maze of twisted roots. Methuselah carried the unconscious Edna, holding her close. Halfway to the surface, they met Lamech and Betenos. A group of strangely clad desert nomads accompanied the pair. Enoch drew his dagger.

"Stop, grandfather!" Lamech called out. "These are the Thamud."

That did not reassure Enoch. He held himself ready for battle. He remembered what he had heard about these savage killers. They skinned their victims alive.

Lamech pleaded with hand raised, "Please, trust me. They have come to rescue us."

Enoch and Methuselah traded glances. How could this be? They looked back at Lamech. He was not under duress. They could tell if he was lying, and he was not.

Enoch relaxed.

"Well, they might have gotten here a bit earlier," complained Methuselah. "We could have used their help."

The lead Thamud, tall, gaunt and handsome with closely cropped beard, stepped forward. "Forgive me, Enoch. I am Diya al Din, prince of my people. We need to hurry. The storm is increasing."

"Can we not seek refuge inside the tree?" asked Enoch.

"The storm and tree are one demonic entity, and that entity will draw us alive into Sheol if we do not leave promptly" said Diya.

Methuselah protested, "My wife is with child. She needs medicine."

Diya looked at her pale face. He understood exactly what had happened to her.

"Follow me," said Diya, "or she will die."

They followed him.

The fury of windblown sand that had surrounded them earlier now descended upon them.

Diya's team of fifty warriors on camels led Enoch, Methuselah, Edna, Lamech, and Betenos out into the whirlwind. Methuselah thought they were going to be suffocated as before, when they came upon a small canyon carved out of the rock.

A cave entrance rescued them from the immediacy of the tempest outside. It was a tunnel pathway, not merely a shelter from the weather.

They traveled through the tunnel for a couple of leagues before ascending back onto the desert plains.

When they came out of the tunnel, Enoch looked all around him. There was no sign of the sandstorm. It was as if it had never been there. And there was no thousand cubits high Huluppu Tree connecting heaven and earth.

Diya could see his confusion. "I will explain later. Our first concern is to get your wife some help."

Methuselah raised his eyes from Edna's face to an amazing sight. They were close to some rocky buttes that seemed to burst out of the ground. He could see rock carvers chiseling facades of huge buildings into the faces of the rocky bluffs. It was a small city of buildings carved out of the rock.

Methuselah saw a large figure standing out a distance away from the rock faces, looking their way like a dog awaiting the arrival of its master.

It was the giant Ohyah on an Anzu bird.

This should be interesting, thought Enoch as they rode toward the stone city.

CHAPTER 30

This was the second time Enoch learned that his preconceived notions of a people were completely wrong. He had thought the Adamite cave dwellers were primitive ignorant natives, only to learn they were a spiritually profound elite who taught him the secret ways of Elohim. Then he had believed the rumors and gossip about the Thamudi being a savage clan of barbarians, only to be sitting in front of them now in their homes of incomparable architecture having his own ignorance enlightened by their compassionate explanation of current events. Even the interiors of these rock palaces were exquisitely designed and carved.

The Thamud had heard of Elohim through the trade route that spanned their area many generations before. They had concluded that the very god that Lilith and her Earth Goddess brood of demons hated would be the very god whose side they wanted to be on.

Methuselah could barely listen as Diya al Din explained everything. All he could think about was Edna. The healers and midwives were treating her in their special room set aside for such matters. Would she be all right? And their growing child in her womb? He would never forgive himself if anything happened to either of them.

Lamech and Betenos listened intently as everything came clear to them.

"At first, we made our battle call and mounted up in preparation to fight Oyhah. He is a Naphil after all."

Ohyah sat a bit away from the others. He never wanted to impose his presence or overshadow anyone in the room. He did not need to be near to hear. He had eagle ears and could hear a centipede crawling at ten cubits distance.

Enoch turned to face Ohyah. "How did you do it? How did you tame the Anzu bird?"

"It was not easy," said Ohyah. "He nearly threw me to my death a thousand cubits in the sky more than once. But after he broke, I could lead him with the bridle as we do any beast of burden."

"But how did you know we were in danger?" asked Lamech.

"I am a Naphil," Ohyah said simply. "I am attuned to the spiritual world. As I climbed the tree, I connected with it, with its soul, or should I say with the myriads of souls it had devoured to sustain its life."

"That is not all it devours," said Diya. "The desert you have now become so unhappily acquainted with was not always a dead barren wasteland. Before the Earth Goddess grew there, it was a fertile land every bit as lush as life along the Euphrates. Even more so. Mountains, rivers, forests and meadows, wildlife of every kind."

"How could that be?" exclaimed Betenos, speaking for everyone's wonder.

"The Earth Goddess is a parasite," said Diya. "Her roots burrow deep into the earth, and her branches seek the heavens as she sucks the life out of the environment and atmosphere around her. That is what she has done to create the desert that covers this peninsula."

"Abomination of desolation," blurted Enoch.

"Someone should destroy it," offered Lamech.

"That would be very difficult," said Diya. "It would take a gibborim."

"How did you find us?" asked Enoch.

Diya replied, "When Ohyah flew the Anzu bird to our humble city and pleaded for your lives, he offered his neck to me. I could have killed him in an instant. Something I had never seen a Naphil do. And because he tamed the Anzu, the watchbird of that wicked tree, I knew we had a common enemy. Without your giant friend and the Anzu, we would never have found you. Its black magic comes from the depths of Sheol and the witch demons use sorcery of all kinds to remain obscured and undiscoverable."

"Well, I hope to never discover that vile wicked tree again," said Betenos. Everyone laughed.

Lamech blurted out, "And the story Lilith told us about being the first wife and daughters of Adam?"

"Lies from the pit of Sheol," said Diya. "That She-demon knew that the best lie is patterned after the truth. You conquer a people by conquering their narrative — subverting it. It has been her goal all along to control the world."

Betenos felt a fool for being taken in by the trickery. A wave of repentance washed over her. She stood up to proclaim to the group, "I repent for worshiping the Great Goddess Earth Mother. I am ashamed of my idolatry. And I am grateful for the patience and loving help that Lamech has displayed with me during my travels with your family. It took a large black serpent to awake me from my spiritual slumber, and push me into the arms of my Creator, Elohim." She was done, and she was crying, her tears flowing from a cleansed soul.

Lamech, bleary-eyed, hugged Betenos.

Enoch got up off his chair and approached her.

Lamech pulled away to see what his grandfather would do.

Betenos felt a bit afraid, since Enoch had not trusted her throughout their journey. Would he doubt her now?

Enoch stared at her. She felt her spine tingle.

"Betenos," he said, "slayer of Ningishzida, you *are* my family." And Enoch hugged her with complete acceptance.

Lamech's smile went so wide it hurt his mouth.

Methuselah felt some happiness despite his own painful fears for Edna's safety.

Even Ohyah was moved. Could this god Elohim be so powerful as to redeem the most cursed of all creatures?

Betenos wept more. She had so longed to be accepted by this great patriarch, the grandfather of the man with whom she was desperately in love.

"Betenos bar Barakil," said Lamech on bended knees, "I have prayed for this moment from the second I set my eyes upon you. And now my wildest dreams have come true. Will you be my wife?"

Betenos could not contain her happiness. But before she could express it, they were interrupted by two midwives entering the room.

Methuselah leapt to his feet and ran to them.

One of the midwives simply whispered, "I am sorry, we lost the child."

Methuselah broke away from them and ran to the healing room, to the bedside of Edna.

She was barely conscious, drifting off into sleep. Methuselah sank beside her and gently held her.

"My Peedlums, I thought I lost you."

"Poozy," Edna whispered. "I love you."

"I love you," he replied, "with all my heart and soul."

"I was waiting for the right moment to surprise you," she managed to murmur. "I should have told you sooner." She began to cry weakly. "I am so sorry, Methuselah. I have failed you."

"Pednanoonypoo. You have failed no one."

She did not believe it. She had spent all her life transferring her purpose from one person to the next, as if her significance were founded in giving other people significance.

Edna protested, "I have failed to bring forth your seed."

Methuselah was almost angry. "You listen to me, woman. Your worth is not in satisfying my purpose, it is in obedience to your Creator. And if my memory serves me, you have obeyed Elohim far more than I ever have. It is from you that I have come to understand Elohim's ways, his compassion, his mercy, his grace and his love. You have not failed me. I have failed you. I have failed to be the leader worthy of your submission. I have placed my trust in this earth and not in the promise of Elohim's seed. Can you forgive me, my love?"

She looked up into his eyes. He knew just how to get through to her, and she to him.

"There is nothing to forgive, Poozey," she said with a weak smile. "You are the finest, truest man I have ever known."

"You are the *only* woman I will *ever* know," he said.

He caressed her sweaty hair. "Do not fret. Elohim has our little one in his arms."

"Yes, I know," she whispered and fell asleep.

Methuselah kissed her on the forehead, and settled her back on the bedding. He then rose and crossed over to the water pail and birth rags. He opened a bloody towel to behold the tiny little body of his miscarried son. He was no bigger than a mouse, all curled up in a tight sleeping position, red with uterine blood. But this was his son. He whispered a prayer to Elohim and turned to one of the midwives come into the room.

"We would like a burial for our son, Adam," he said.

"Yes, my lord," said the maidservant and left the room to prepare.

He softly laid the edges of the towel back over the little body in his hand.

He could barely contain himself. He knew the reason his son was dead was because of their experience with Lilith and her evil offspring. He blamed himself. He thought that if he'd only kept his mind on Elohim, he would not be so easily deceived by the flesh. If he was as godly a leader as he ought to be, he would have seen the trap earlier, and saved his wife sooner. He would have saved his son.

Betenos gazed into Lamech's eyes as they waited for Methuselah to return from the healing room. Their situation was bittersweet. In the face of death Betenos now saw new life.

She spoke with conviction, "I have been so afraid to lose what I could not hold onto. I have seen that I am far worse than I ever imagined, and more loved than I could have ever hoped. I will be your wife, Lamech ben Methuselah. I will bear your seed. I will bear Elohim's calling."

• • • • •

The burial ritual for little baby Adam was brief and simple. They laid him in a small carved box and rubbed red ochre on him, just like his forefather. They even had some desert flowers to cover him before they prayed and filled the grave with dirt. *For you are dust, and to dust you shall return.*

Enoch said a prayer to Elohim. They all filed back into the rock-faced buildings. Edna had returned to health and was able to mourn with Methuselah. It was not the same as losing an adult child like Havah had with her Abel, but it was still a sacred little life created in the image of Elohim, taken too early.

She was sure Elohim knew their pain, and knew that someday he would put all things to right.

CHAPTER 31

"You cannot be serious!" Edna cried, staring at Enoch, in one of the meeting houses of the Thamud city.

Ohyah remained silent and listened from the back of the room, as usual.

Methuselah added, "God wants us to go on a suicide mission?"

"Not you, me," said Enoch.

"God wants *you* to go on a suicide mission?" said Methuselah. For once, Methuselah wished he could see whatever it was that Elohim showed Enoch. How did he know these dreams were actually from Elohim and not mere self-delusion? Hallucinations from greasy sand rats not cooked well enough before eaten? Or spoiled drink?

"Not suicide, obedient faith. Young man, have I taught you nothing in this life? Have I failed as a father?" said Enoch. "When Elohim commands, we obey. He will bring about the results that he sees fit."

Enoch told them of his latest dream-vision. Uriel had visited him again and taken him up to Mount Hermon in the presence of all the fallen Watchers, not to fight them, but to pronounce Elohim's word of judgment. No actions, just words. And this was Enoch's final journey to make.

This vision gave one new piece of information they had not heard before. Enoch had been told that there was a Chosen Seed to come from the line of Seth, through Enoch, Methuselah, and Lamech, one who would bring an end to the reign of the gods and bring rest from the curse of the land.

Everyone recognized the reference from their time with Adam and Havah. It was the seed of the Woman, Eve, at war with the seed of the Serpent, Nachash.

Lamech was stunned. His bloodline would bear a redeemer?

It perturbed Methuselah "When am I going to see one of these visions?" he asked. "You would think that Elohim would confirm such crazy ideas with one or two others of us, if they were so important to the future of the human race."

Enoch flushed red with righteous indignation. "Methuselah, you speak as an ignorant child who would not want the very thing he whines for should he receive it."

Methuselah went silent, properly scolded. Enoch walked up to him, slowly explaining himself. "You have fought giants, and have faced the gods, it is true. But you have no idea the terrifying holiness of Elohim's temple and divine assembly of his holy ones."

With every word, Methuselah's confidence waned.

"Are you so sure you want to see what I see? Do you desire to tremble and fall at your feet stiff like a dead man? Do you want to be utterly and entirely exposed in your sinfulness before the Lord of hosts and before his holy ones who surround his throne crying, 'Holy, holy, holy'? Let me give you just a glimpse of the frightening awe of the heaven of heavens into which you so desperately long to look."

Methuselah had become very still.

Enoch spoke with barely a breath, "In the midst of piercing light is a structure of crystals, and between those crystals are tongues of fire, encircled by rivers of living fire, over which are the sleepless ones who guard the throne of Yahweh's glory, the Seraphim, the Cherubim, and Ophanim, the archangels, Mikael, Raphael, Gabriel and Uriel and ten thousand times ten thousand of countless holy angels, all bowing before the Ancient of Days and the one to whom belongs the time before time, the Son of Man, with head as white as wool and an indescribable garment, to whom belongs righteousness and with whom righteousness dwells, the Lord of Spirits, who will remove kings and mighty ones from their comfortable thrones and shall loosen the reins of the strong and crush the teeth of sinners, who shall depose the kings from their kingdoms who do not extol and glorify him and neither do they obey him, the source of their kingship, and he says, 'Behold, the Lord comes with ten thousands of his holy ones, to execute judgment on all and to convict all the ungodly of all their deeds of ungodliness that they have committed in such an ungodly way, and of all the harsh things that ungodly sinners have spoken against him.'"

It was the longest run-on sentence Methuselah had ever heard, and it frightened him deeply. But he would not tell anyone that. And he would never again ask to be given a vision of Elohim and his holy ones. No one else on the team would either, as they were all duly terror-stricken. Edna trembled.

Methuselah mumbled, "Father, forgive me for my impertinence. I am an unclean man with unclean lips."

Enoch could not believe it. Methuselah had actually apologized.

Methuselah's relentless curiosity interrupted even this moment. "But help me to understand why Elohim would equip us to be giant killers only to have you walk alone and unarmed right into the hornet's nest of invincible death and destruction?"

"He will not be alone," a voice said behind them.

Everyone turned to see Uriel the archangel at the entrance of their room, standing with arms crossed in assurance.

It did not assure Methuselah. "I mean no disrespect, mighty one, but there may well be hundreds of Watchers on Mount Hermon, and you are but one archangel." The battle with the Nephilim at the Tigris River came to his mind. "And if I remember correctly, you are not even the largest or strongest one."

Uriel rolled his eyes. *Why does everyone always have to point that out to me?* he thought.

"Oh mouthy one," Uriel retorted with his signature touch of sarcasm, "I will not be the only one accompanying Enoch. Mikael, Gabriel, and Raphael will all join us when we are in range of our destination." The presence of the four highest archons of Elohim's throne room signaled something big to everyone in the room.

Methuselah said, "Forgive me, high prince Uriel, but that is still only four. It seems to me that fighting Watchers will not be quite as easy as fighting Nephilim."

"Who said we were going to fight them?" asked Uriel with a smile.

It baffled Methuselah and the others. Enoch would walk into the midst of the Watchers' hideout with the help of four high archangels and preach a sermon, and these rebellious sons of Elohim were going to just listen to them?

The only one it made any sense to was Ohyah, who chose to remain silent.

Uriel chuckled. "Before I explain the elementary principles of faith and obedience to my hardheaded companion here, I think we have a wedding to celebrate." He looked with joyful eyes upon Lamech and his betrothed Betenos.

CHAPTER 32

Lamech and Betenos had a brief wedding ceremony. Its brevity was inspired by the fact that the team of giant killers was about to embark on the final leg of its journey to Bashan. They allowed the new lovers several days to discover themselves in all their god-given intimacy. At last, Lamech understood what his father meant when he said that loving his wife was an act of worship to Elohim. It embodied the kind of union that transcended their physical existence. Grandfather Enoch, with his passionate way with words, had often spoken of the love of Elohim for his people being like that of a bridegroom with his bride.

If that is true, thought Lamech, *then I am most honored to have had this small taste of so great a love.*

For all her royalty, Betenos had never experienced loving tenderness in her family. Barakil had been a protective father to her, but he was also the clan elder, so he could never be vulnerable with his family. He could never put aside his responsibility for his tribe's safety and justice to play with his children or caress his wife. As a result, Betenos had experienced stern discipline and mature responsibility, but she felt as if she never had a childhood. She did not know how to have fun, how to let loose and just release her voice into the wind with abandon.

She could do that now, with her loving husband to free her and protect her.

Diya al Din, whose name meant "brightness of faith," proved to be an ally of inestimable worth. He had not only saved them from the Earth Goddess and her demonic minions, but also helped them plot their final course into Bashan. Though his people had never been inside Bashan, Diya knew the best and speediest route to get there. He showed them on a map, with Enoch, Methuselah, Edna, Uriel, and Ohyah clustered around the table.

Diya said, "It will only be a short distance west from the Thamudi fortresses before the topography will change and become the foothills of the

Sirion mountain range. You will find the lone river Pharpar that will take you in all the way to Bashan and ultimately to the foot of Hermon."

"Do you have information about specific packs or hordes of Nephilim in the area?" asked Methuselah.

"We just do not know," apologized Diya.

Lamech and Betenos skipped into the room together with giggles of delight and playful grabs. Everyone turned to look at them. They stopped, blushed, but got down to business.

"Betenos is going with us," Lamech announced.

"It is too dangerous without Karabu training," responded Enoch.

"Grandfather, do we really have to go over this again? Has Betenos not proven herself worthy over and over?"

"This is different. We do not know how many packs we may encounter in Bashan," said Enoch.

"All the more reason to have a healer," said Lamech. "And I do believe she has bested you in target practice more than once."

Methuselah snapped, "Shooting targets is not the same as shooting Nephilim warriors."

"You are newlyweds," added Edna. "Stay here and get to know one another. There will be time later for responsibility."

"Mother, if I recall, it was Elohim who said that marriage was a leaving and a cleaving. I am not under your authority, I am now responsible for my own family, and we have decided that the time is now."

In one of the rare instances, Ohyah spoke up. "A healer would be beneficial. I fear we will not return from Bashan unscathed."

Uriel studied Ohyah with curious interest. "The giant is correct," he said. "It is a lawless territory. Fiefdoms of war chiefs. What few small towns are there, Ugarit, Jericho, and others, are not friendly."

"So, what you are saying," said Methuselah, "is that we are entering a lawless province of criminals, that willingly hosts the Watchers, universally hates our god, unanimously despises our people, and will joyfully kill us where they find us."

"Exactly," said Uriel.

Methuselah concluded, "But it is also the hideout for the scurrilous Rephaim Thamaq and Yahipan that killed our parents and tried to annihilate our family line."

"When do we leave?" said Lamech.

CHAPTER 33

The fellowship of giant killers gathered on Camels given to them by Diya al Din. These amazing creatures possessed the ability to store nutrients in their large humps, enabling them to travel long distances at quick paces. They had not yet become universally domesticated, but Diya believed they would be eventually because they were so advantageous.

Enoch's team had been with the Thamud for a month or so, but Methuselah knew they had made lifelong friends. He hoped one day to return in less troublesome times, but suspected those times might not come during his life.

After much customary hugging and kissing, Enoch's band set out on their way: Enoch and Uriel, Methuselah and Edna, Lamech and Betenos, and Ohyah.

It only took one day of vigorous travel to reach the Pharpar river. They followed it toward its source fifty leagues upriver, about a three-day brisk ride. Half way to their destination, they were met by three new fellow travelers, Mikael, Gabriel, and Raphael. They each rode a new beast of burden called a *horse*.

These horses were powerful animals, similar in structure to a wild ass, but twice the size, and pure muscle. They had smaller ears and could run like the wind. It was no surprise that the heavenly archons were the first to seize this opportunity of newly domesticated travel. The archangels riding on the majestic creatures appeared like a new kind of Cherubim.

The angels would ride ahead on their horses, their heavenly senses highly tuned to sense approaching danger. Ohyah took up the rear on foot, his earthly spiritual senses almost as acute as those of the angels.

Enoch rode ahead to travel with the archangels. He discussed the secrets of heaven with the spiritual beings. Methuselah watched with curiosity, wondering what they were saying.

The Naphil could hear them. If he concentrated hard enough and pointed an ear in the flow downwind, his preternatural aural sense could pick up snatches of their private dialogue. They had long discussions on the heavenly luminaries, animal visions, the Chosen Seed and a "Son of Man." He gathered that of the group of archangels, the small one was sharp tongued and the mightiest one a bit overly confident. They all seemed to bicker and pick on the small one. It amused Ohyah the kind of servants Elohim chose for his purposes. It was so opposite of the ways of the Nephilim, which was based on power.

They did not spy their first giant until they were in the foothills near Mount Hermon. The sun set on the horizon. The team set up early camp on a hill overlooking the wide expanse of the Sirion range. They ate some dinner of dried gazelle meat. They were hidden within a thicket of pine trees to avoid detection. Ohyah stood lookout.

Enoch and the angels huddled, discussing the route they would take further west to Mount Hermon.

Ohyah quietly alerted them.

He spotted two Nephilim less than half a league down in the valley. They appeared to be headed north toward a destination somewhere around a rocky butte.

Enoch told Methuselah, "It looks like this is where we part ways. The archangels and I will continue on to Hermon. You may want to stay low and seek out information before you start attacking any giants. Remember, you do not know the land yet."

"You are right. We would not want to just march right into the headquarters of evil and announce our presence," retorted Methuselah sarcastically. "That would be suicide."

Enoch scowled at Methuselah for venting his pain. They both knew in their hearts that they would never see each other again on this earth. No matter how different in nature father and son were, no matter all the arguments they had been in through the years, they loved one another with fierce devotion.

"You will live to a long fruitful age, my son," said Enoch.

Methuselah thought, *Why does everyone keep saying that? Havah, now father.*

Enoch added, "But you have already made me the proudest father on earth. Elohim be with you."

"Elohim be with you," said Methuselah.

They kissed and embraced.

Enoch lingered longer with Betenos and Edna. "My two precious flowers. You have brought much needed grace to this pack of slovenly brutes. You are too good for my sons." Everyone's nervous laughter broke the somberness.

Enoch continued, "I love you as my own daughters." They hugged and kissed and cried.

Enoch turned to Lamech and held his face in his hands. He said, "Lamech ben Methuselah, out of your line will come a Chosen Seed who will end the rule of the gods and bring rest upon the land. Tell no one until God himself does."

"Yes, grandfather," said Lamech, and they hugged.

Enoch stopped at the giant. "Ohyah, you have surprised me, and humbled me." He paused for a second, then continued.

"I want to tell you this one thing. The judgment in your dream is fast approaching the earth. And the water you saw in the vision, it is not symbolic. It is real water. It is cleansing water."

Ohyah was not sure what to make of that esoteric statement, but he hugged Enoch.

"Thank you for believing in me," said Ohyah.

They had no more time to delay. They all mounted their camels and stallions and went their separate ways: Enoch, Mikael, Uriel, Gabriel, and Raphael, west toward Hermon; and Methuselah, Edna, Lamech, Betenos and Ohyah, north after the traveling Nephilim. If they moved quickly, they might be within close observation range by the time the giants pitched camp.

CHAPTER 34

The sun set over the great sea. Enoch and his four companions rode solemnly toward the base of Mount Hermon a mere league away. Enoch was about to face the ultimate challenge of his life, but he felt safe in the presence of these mighty angelic warriors. He knew they would have no problem getting safely *to* the cosmic mountain. The real danger was getting *inside* the infernal meeting place where the fallen Watchers assembled for their diabolical planning.

Angels could not die like humans. They were spiritual beings that could suffer and even be overcome, but they could not die. They were only four archangels facing as many as two hundred Watchers, if all were in attendance. Despite their exalted status, these four would be easily overcome and tortured. They would probably be bound and cast into the earth where they would live forever in a prison of stone. They saw no way that Enoch would get out of this alive. There was no way the angels were going to get out of it at all.

Enoch had come to realize over the years that he had been running from his calling. Elohim commissioned him to pronounce judgment on the Watchers and their progeny the Nephilim. But he had turned that calling into a hammer of his own justification. When he lost his Edna, he lost all interest in this earth. Killing the Nephilim became an expression of his desire to escape the physical world that held him prisoner and stank of corruption. But in hating the physical world that Elohim created, he misunderstood the faith that was required of him. Now he exercised that faith by obediently fulfilling the calling he had been given. Enoch had been an instrument of judgment on the giants. Now he was to be an instrument of *Elohim's* judgment on the Watchers. He was to pick a fight he would not win, because Elohim was going to win it on his terms.

Methuselah was right. It was suicide. But Enoch reasoned that Elohim could raise the dead, so what did it matter that Enoch was riding to his death? The interaction of his comrades in arms broke through his solemnity.

Uriel was the talkative one, a bit rascally, and witty. Gabriel countered his fellow wisecracker with his own whimsical and energetic humor. Raphael did not speak much, but he thought and observed plenty, so Uriel and Gabriel often competed to win a smile or even a nod from "the quiet one" as they teasingly referred to him. Mikael took his responsibility as the prince leader with serious determination. So like the bigger brother, he would always have to "break it up" when it got out of hand. But even he could not help but smile at a well placed verbal barb.

"Did Uriel tell you, Enoch?" asked Gabriel, "He was chosen by Elohim to be the guardian of the Chosen Seed when he should carry out his calling."

He paused, and then delivered the punch line, "Elohim wanted to make it very obvious that the Chosen Seed was protected not by strength nor by might, but by faith."

Enoch snickered. "Very funny," said Uriel. "You mean the faith that killed six Nephilim to *your* four in the battle at the Tigris river, to which Enoch was witness?"

"*Five and a half to four and a half*," protested Gabriel. "I remind you of the one we did together."

"You mean the one I killed?" said Uriel.

"That I helped you kill," said Gabriel.

"Before you dropped your sword," said Uriel.

"I did *not* drop my sword!" said Gabriel. He felt frustrated at getting trapped in the same argument as before.

Uriel just smiled and shook his head. He had successfully turned the tables, as he usually did with his superior wit.

Raphael laughed from the belly. "Very good, Uriel. Very good." Raphael did not speak much, so when he did, he tended to cast the deciding vote on an issue.

"So what you both meant to say," concluded Mikael, "was 'not by strength, nor by might, but by verbal bickering and wordplay,' saith the Lord."

Enoch finally interrupted. "You know, I cannot believe that I am on my way to certain death in the bowels of the mountain of hell and you four are quibbling and jesting over your battle prowess. Is it too much to ask you to be more somber about our impending doom?"

"Forgive us, Enoch," said Gabriel. "We mean no disrespect to you."

Enoch felt better for the apology. "Thank you," he said with finality.

Gabriel muttered to Uriel, "But it *was* five and a half to four and a half."

"Six to four," muttered Uriel.

"Elohim, deliver us," muttered Enoch.

• • • • •

By the time Methuselah, Edna, Lamech, Betenos, and Ohyah caught up with the traveling Nephilim, their quarry had already arrived at their base camp a league north. The giants were not alone. As Methuselah had feared, they were part of a pack. But they were wearing armor similar to that worn by the Nephilim that had started them on this journey. The hunters were on the right track.

Fifteen of them feasted on what appeared to be cattle and humans roasting on spits. If the team were discovered, killing the Nephilim would be difficult. Methuselah and his team were giant killers, but they were not archangels. Three and a half trained warriors against fifteen giants was not the kind of odds Methuselah wished to entertain. They had never even seen that many Nephilim together at once, let alone fought them. The rumors were true about Bashan. It had become an easy hideout for bandits, desperados and other packs of outlaw giants.

Thank Elohim, we have one Naphil on our side, thought Methuselah. Ohyah possessed the enviable Nephilim fighting skills. They would have the element of surprise. These brigands would never expect one of their own to fight against them.

Lamech whispered to himself, "That is a lot of bounty."

Methuselah gave him a dirty look. "We are not here for bounty. We are here to find Thamaq and Yahipan. And stop talking. You will give us away."

It was a difficult task to sneak up on Nephilim. They had acute senses and usually would be able to hear them and smell them approaching. But this time, they were downwind from the hunters on a particularly windy evening, with a storm brewing overhead creating distracting noises.

The small camp sat in the center of a rather wide clearing around the butte. Methuselah and the others hid at the crestline of foliage watching the camp with high strung nerves. They waited for their planned deception to unfold.

CHAPTER 35

Enoch and the angels arrived at the foot of Mount Hermon and left their animals to climb the rocky crags. A short way up the foothills of the mountain sat the village of Kur, populated by the human followers of Ereshkigal. They had built a temple for this goddess of the underworld embedded halfway into the mountain, an expression of the union of heaven and earth within the sacred space.

According to legend, inside the temple were the seven gates of Ganzir that led to an opening to the Abyss, or *Abzu*, the cosmic waters under the earth, the barrier above Sheol, the underworld. Ereshkigal's throne stood at the Gateway to Sheol.

The Abyss was home to the most frightening of all creatures, the sea dragon of chaos, Rahab. It roamed the waters as sovereign of the beasts, seeking whom it might devour. It was a creature of both utter destruction and yet utter perfection. A terrible beauty, armored scales covered its huge, three hundred-cubit-long body, its teeth were like sharpened iron, and it could produce a flash of burning fire from out of its mouth. It seemed its only purpose was to destroy worlds. No one could defy Rahab or subdue it, save Elohim alone, who created it for his purposes. How it was that Elohim controlled the untamed monster of the deep, Enoch could never understand. But then again, Elohim did not operate within human ways of understanding.

Mount Hermon was not the only location that had direct access to the waters of the Abyss that led to Sheol. There were several openings to the earth. One of them lay in Lake Urimiya at the very Garden of Eden. It was said that Yahweh Elohim at the lake held back both the waters of the Abyss and the dragon of chaos in order to establish the "heavens and earth," his covenanted cosmic order with his covenant people, Adam and Havah. It was also said that the Abyss and Rahab were the only things that the Sons of God and the Nephilim actually feared.

Enoch hoped in his heart that he would simply be killed by the Watchers rather than being thrown into the Abyss. He did not want Rahab to sport with him before tearing apart his body and consuming his flesh. He was thankful that at least they would not need to journey through the pagan village, and the temple, and the seven gates of Ganzir to get inside the meeting place of the Watchers. Mikael knew a secret way in, through a cave opening in the side of the mountain, out of sight of the village near a terebinth tree.

•••••

The pack of fifteen Nephilim were busy about their camp site when they heard a lookout whistle. They grabbed their weapons in unison and peered into the brush near their camp. In walked a disheveled Ohyah with a lookout giant behind him.

The team's plan had been for Ohyah to disguise himself as a wandering loner desert Naphil looking for a pack to join. The Nephilim would of course be suspicious at first. But their guard would eventually lower as they got to know Ohyah. Eventually they would lead him to their headquarters. Ohyah would study the branding on the Nephilim to see if any were owned by Thamaq and Yahipan. He would gather any other information he could on the whereabouts of the two Rephaim. If there were any so branded, he would give Methuselah the sign by going to relieve himself on the edge of the camp, and signing how many had the mark. Methuselah's band would then follow the pack of Nephilim at a distance until Ohyah could find an opportunity to slip away and rejoin them.

Ohyah surprised the pack. But after some discussion, they calmed down and offered Ohyah some food. He chose the cattle over the human meal and partook as a hungry loner would. Soon, Ohyah went to relieve himself, heading toward Methuselah's hidden team. When he signaled, they were surprised to see Ohyah excitedly indicate the number fifteen.

It shocked Methuselah. All fifteen had the branding of Thamaq and Yahipan? How could that be?

Lamech interrupted his thoughts, "We hit the payload. They will lead us right to those sons of Sheol."

A Nephilim war cry burst behind them, an ugly sounding scream that pierced their ears and shuddered their souls. Methuselah jerked his head around to find the lookout Naphil in the bush, hovering over them. He had scouted the grounds and found them. Their cover had been compromised.

Methuselah looked back at camp. All the Nephilim faced their direction, taking up arms. By the time they took out this Naphil, the others would be upon them. They would not be able to outrun these muscle-bound monsters.

They would have to stand and fight.

CHAPTER 36

Anu and Inanna presided over the parliament of gods in the cavern of the Watchers. The huge stalactites and stalagmites created the sensation of being in the fanged mouth of the sea serpent. The cosmic mountain and divine council room of the gods rebelliously replicated Elohim's original council room on the Edenic mountain, complete with throne and source of waters. Enoch noted the irony that this sacred space was a garden of stone as opposed to Eden's garden of living vegetation. The source of its waters was a fiery black quagmire in contrast to the rivers of fresh living waters of Paradise.

The dripping of mineralized water built the stalactite formations, sparkling with gemlike iridescence. It created a kind of glow through the subterranean grotto in even the faintest of light. But there was no need for a light source, because the Shining Ones emitted a brightness when emotionally charged, a glow like that of burnished bronze or gleaming metal. Their heated discussion created flashes of fire and sparkling beryl that stalactite reflectors amplified.

Anu and Inanna sat on the thrones of Ereshkigal and Nergal to lead the discussion. They did so whenever they were in Bashan for the divine assembly. Over a hundred others gathered before the throne, along the burning black liquid shore of the Abyss.

They were discussing the possibility of capturing Rahab the sea dragon of chaos, to use her as a weapon of war. Enoch, Mikael, Uriel, Gabriel, and Raphael slipped into a dark recess of the cavern through their secret mountain tunnel.

Anu announced with authority, "The throne recognizes Enki, patron of Eridu, Lord of the Abyss."

Enki stood and spoke to the assembly. "Brothers and sisters, I have organized an advisory committee on the Rahab matter with the gods of Canaan."

The Canaanite deities stood up. Enoch had not seen them before. There were whole families of gods that administered different locations on the earth that Enoch did not recognize.

Enki continued, "We have been developing spells that will render the sea dragon Rahab vulnerable to capture."

"Are you mad?!" interrupted Resheph, one of the Canaanite gods of plague and destruction. "You think you can domesticate Rahab for our purposes? She is not tamable. She is the very heart of chaos itself!"

Enki replied, "I do not suggest Rahab is tamable. I merely intend to subdue her long enough to capture her in such a way as to release her upon our enemies for their destruction."

"And what way of capture might that be, O brilliant shining one?" snorted Resheph, his scaly skin burning with arrogant luminosity.

"If you must know," Enki answered curtly, "we believe that we can lure Rahab into an underwater cavern where we have engraved tranquilizing spells on the walls of rock. Her spirit will be lulled into a trancelike state. We then have a large cedar box, with the spells carved in the walls to contain her in that numbed state until release."

"Oh, so, now Rahab has a fear of enclosed spaces?" asked Resheph.

"No. It is a kind of catatonic dream state the monster goes into. I cannot explain it. I do not understand it," said Enki.

"May I suggest that what you do not understand, remains out of your control," sniped Resheph.

Inanna listened closely. If what Enki said was true, she could use this weapon one day to great advantage. Resheph was a fool to scorn innovation in combat tactics. Such risks often brought victory on the battlefield. It was true, the sea dragon lived resplendent in its mighty power to wreak havoc and destruction. It was the mightiest of all created things. But it was still a created thing, and no created thing was invulnerable. If they could merely unleash that chaos in the direction of an enemy, why could it not accomplish great devastation? She would have to converse with Enki on this further.

Anu asserted authority again, "Enki will report back to us with the final results of the investigation. But now, we must finalize our strategy for the lawsuit we are to bring before the divine council of Yahweh Elohim." The Watchers, faithful or fallen, referred to Elohim by his covenant name within the sacred space of the divine council in heaven. That surprised Enoch a little.

Anu continued, "I yield the floor to the Accuser."

The Accuser, translated as "the satan," was the legal term for the prosecuting adversary in the heavenly court of Yahweh Elohim. Of all the Shining Ones, the Accuser drew the most respect and admiration. He was *Nachash*, the Serpent of the Garden, a seraph of great intellect and cunning. His single act in Eden had accomplished more for their cause than anything anyone else had done. Unlike the others, he was the sole Watcher who had not taken on a new divine persona in the pantheon of gods. Semjaza had became Anu, and Azazel, Inanna in order to spearhead the earthly violation of the created order. But Nachash remained the heavenly Accuser before the divine council in order to accomplish their massive legal assault upon Yahweh's kingdom. He even preferred being called simply *the Accuser*. It brought attention to what he sarcastically referred to as "his calling."

Anu looked about for his colleague. The Accuser was not there. Everyone looked around for this titan of malevolence, but he was no longer present.

He had sensed what was about to happen.

·····

The lookout Naphil died in seconds, pierced through with Methuselah's javelin and Betenos' arrow. Edna took off its head with her multi-bladed angelic weapon.

The Nephilim raced toward them. They broke through the foliage like a wind storm. They held to some discipline, as two remained guarding the camp.

The giant killers called upon all the best of their training in this battle. They used an integrated defense system of covering for each other. Rather than one team member taking on a fight alone, each lent their skills to create a "one-two" punch. An arrow from Betenos was finished off with a slice by Edna, or a javelin from Methuselah. But in order for this system to work, they were constantly on the move, flowing in and out of each other's space with a dance-like choreography. Crisscrossing one another's paths, diving, rolling, spinning and flipping. This was the dance of the Karabu.

When the first three Nephilim reached them, weapons swinging, Edna went right into the thick of them. She flipped and twirled her weapon around the three of them. They swung maces and clubs in thin air, missing Edna. Betenos' arrows and Methuselah's javelins caught them unprepared. The team took care to make head shots or gut shots to avoid the alloy armor the Nephilim wore. Lamech with a slashing Rahab in hand beheaded the third Naphil in midstride.

The other Nephilim reached them, and it became a frenzied attack. It might have been an unequal fight of these four against the many ogres, but the giant killers had a secret weapon: Ohyah.

Once the fight ranged into the bush and out of sight of the two guards left at the camp, Ohyah rained down fury upon his fellow Nephilim from behind.

They did not even know what hit them. Ohyah took out four of them before the others realized they were betrayed.

With Ohyah behind them and the four giant killers before them, the last five did not stand a chance.

It discouraged Methuselah. This was not really as glorious a victory as he had hoped. But he could not complain. It was more important to win than to have a close fight.

When the Nephilim lay at their feet, Ohyah and the four humans took a moment to catch their breaths. They had been taxed, but invigorated as well.

"Well, that was some much needed exercise," said Methuselah.

Ohyah picked up a pear mace. He walked up to Methuselah and knelt. He offered the mace to Methuselah. "Hit me," he said.

"What?" asked Methuselah.

"I said hit me. There are two guards left at the camp, and we cannot sneak up on them. We will have to use subterfuge. It will appear suspicious if I am the only one left alive without significant wounds."

"Of course," agreed Methuselah. He grabbed the mace, swallowed, and swung it at Ohyah's head.

He knocked Ohyah unconscious to the ground. When he came to, he had a black eye and a large bruise on his noggin.

"I did not ask you to knock me out, just give me a bruise," said Ohyah.

"You did say 'significant wound.'"

"Evidently our definitions of 'significant' do not coincide."

"Sorry."

"You will have to give me your weapons," continued Ohyah. "I will walk you in as my captives. When we are close enough, we will be able to overtake them before they catch on."

"I hate to be the killjoy," said Lamech, "but we just slaughtered an entire pack of branded Nephilim. I suspect in this territory, we will be the wanted outlaws now."

"Unless we can get rid of the bodies," said Edna. "That might gain us time before they are discovered."

"Let us finish the job first, then discuss strategy," said Methuselah.

CHAPTER 37

By the time the Watchers inside the mountain realized that the Accuser was not with them, Enoch and the four archangels had found their way to the far side of the black lake. Across the water, they could see the Watchers congregated around Anu and Inanna on their thrones. They heard the Watchers discussing some way to capture Rahab for their nefarious purposes and then announcing their plan to bring a lawsuit before the throne of Elohim. Enoch had no idea what that was all about. He just knew what he was supposed to do: prophesy and die.

Though Mikael, Gabriel, Raphael, and Uriel were the highest of archangels, and could no doubt take out a good number of these Watchers, they would eventually succumb to the sheer force of enemy numbers. There were just too many of them. The loyalty of his guardian escort impressed Enoch. They did not even question their duty. They told jokes and argued amongst themselves on the way to this spot, as if they were just going to march right into this nest of vipers and prance right out, job accomplished.

He could not imagine facing their possible fate. Unless they knew something they were not telling him.

The four archangels surrounded Enoch, with weapons drawn and ready. He bellowed out, his voice amplifying as it carried over the pitch black waters of the Abyss.

"Praise the Most High, the Great and Holy One!"

The entire army of Watchers fell silent. All heads turned to stare straight at Enoch and his four puny guardians on the other side of the lake. It simply did not enter their minds that these insignificant fools would ever do such a moronic thing as to enter their very cosmic mountain.

Inanna reacted first. "Well, well, well, what have we here? A silly loud-mouthed meat puppet and four yipping lapdogs on a leash?"

Enlil recognized Enoch. "Utuabzu? So, you are still alive. What brings you into our lair uninvited?"

Anu thought, *This little insect has gall. Where did he come from and how did he get these archangels?*

"I am Enoch, a servant and prophet of Elohim, the living God, and I have come to pronounce judgment upon the Watchers and upon their progeny the Nephilim!"

The chamber held silence for a moment. Then Inanna howled with laughter, followed by a hundred other Watchers.

Anu and Enlil played along with this farce. It seemed absurdly amusing to them.

"Well, then, by all means, pronounce thy judgment, little man. We wait with baited breath," said Anu.

Enoch looked straight at Anu. He raised his hand, pointing his finger at the Watcher. "Semjaza, you and your associates have united yourselves with women so as to defile yourselves in all your uncleanness!" Enoch called Semjaza out by his true name. "And when your unholy sons are slain, you will be bound fast for seventy generations in the valleys of the earth, till the day of judgment."

"My, oh my, we are quaking in our sandals," mocked Inanna. "Fear and trembling has seized us! We beseech thee to draw up a petition for us that we might find forgiveness in the presence of the Lord of heaven."

Enoch ignored the vitriolic mockery. He next prophesied directly to Inanna by true name. "Azazel, thou shalt have no peace. A severe sentence has gone forth against thee to put thee in bonds. And thou shalt not have toleration nor request granted to thee, because of the unrighteousness which thou hast taught, and because of all the works of godlessness and unrighteousness and sin which thou hast shown to men."

Inanna muttered to Anu, "My humor is taxed. Let us be done with this pathetic gnat."

"Wait," Anu held up his hand.

As Enoch prophesied, the Watchers circled slowly around the lake, to enclose Enoch and his guardians. Anu had not been simply entertaining the absurd prophecy for the sake of amusement. He was stalling for time. But something in the human's words sent a chill down Anu's back, setting his teeth on edge. He wanted to hear the final words.

Enoch continued, "The decree has gone forth to bind you in the earth for all the days of the world. And you shall see the destruction of your beloved sons. For a Chosen Seed is coming to bring an end to the reign of the gods and bring rest from the curse of the land!"

That last line struck them all. In that moment, they knew Enoch was indeed a prophet of Elohim, and they had been cursed.

"Eliminate them, immediately!" commanded Anu.

·····

Ohyah walked behind his four captives, Methuselah, Edna, Lamech, and Betenos. They held their hands behind their heads in submission. Ohyah even pushed Lamech, to look impatiently hostile. Lamech fell to his knees from the force.

"Hey, take it easy," muttered Lamech. "You are enjoying this a bit too much for my comfort." Ohyah smirked.

They were about half way across the vast clearing when the two Nephilim guards noticed the captive visitors. They trotted toward them to meet Ohyah's arrival.

Methuselah whispered, "I will take the one on the left. Ohyah, take the right. They will not see it coming."

Before they could carry out their plan, they stopped dead in their tracks. A line of Nephilim stepped from the foliage into the clearing. Methuselah turned and saw masses of other armed Nephilim appearing *all around them*. A horde of over one hundred Nephilim surrounded them. They had never imagined this horror happening.

·····

Anu gave the command to eliminate Enoch and the angels on the shoreline of the cavernous Abyss.

Gabriel lifted his cloak and pulled out his trumpet. He raised it to his lips and blew. The mighty sound penetrated the diabolical cave and resounded right up to heaven itself.

The percussion of the horn's note was supernatural. Its sound waves washed over the Watchers, felling many of them in its wake. An earthquake rattled the cave to its core.

A beam of intense burning fire cut through the rock ceiling above Enoch and the angels' heads and enveloped them in its blinding light. But it did not consume their flesh. It was as if they stood in the midst of a flaming furnace and remained unsinged by the heat or flames.

It dumbfounded Anu and Inanna.

Before their eyes, Enoch and the four angels were translated up through the ceiling and into heaven. In an instant, they were gone, and the beam of blazing light followed them.

A shroud of darkness fell in the cavern. The drastic change from intense brightness to intense darkness temporarily blinded the Watchers. After a moment, their eyes adjusted. They looked to the throne for their commands from Anu and Inanna.

The two of them were shaken to the core.

Anu, who had never shown weakness as leader of this rebellion, for the first time was pale and sweating. Inanna stood speechless for her first time. Their behavior had been uncovered by Elohim and judgment was coming. Their time was cut short. They had to act on their plan or risk utter failure and imprisonment in Tartarus.

"Unleash the wolves of war," commanded Anu.

CHAPTER 38

Methuselah's team was not quite as blessed as Enoch's.

The horde of Nephilim surrounded Ohyah and his "captives." They stood fearfully awaiting their end at the hands of the horde. An officer adorned in golden armor stepped out from the horde. He approached Ohyah. He studied the captives, then looked back at Ohyah with suspicion. He thoughtfully considered the bulging pus-filled black and blue eye of Ohyah.

The Naphil leader spoke with a gravelly voice, "I am General Mahawai of Baalbek. Who are you, soldier?"

A general? thought Methuselah. *What do they have out here, an army of Nephilim? How could that be?*

"I am Ohyah, son of Semjaza," blurted Ohyah.

Methuselah's team tried to hold back their surprise at this revelation. Semjaza? Semjaza was the infamous leader of the Watchers, now known as the father sky god Anu.

What new trick is Ohyah attempting? thought Methuselah. Sure, it might protect them from immediate execution, but it only delayed their demise until the Nephilim got word from Semjaza. Still, any amount of time was helpful, if they could only devise an escape.

Thanks a lot, Ohyah, Lamech thought. *You just added prolonged torture for us when they discover you lied. Well, at least you will suffer more for being a traitor.*

Ohyah continued, "I am a lone voyager from the east. I found this regiment because I wanted to join your forces. These giant killers took us all by surprise."

Mahawai glanced at the two Guards from the camp. They nodded slightly in approval. But it was not approval enough for Mahawai.

"These soldiers merely parrot what you told them earlier. How do I not know whether you brought these vermin on your tail? How is it that you alone survived the slaughter of thirteen of my soldiers? Why should I believe you?"

Ohyah felt his hands tremble. He became short of breath. He had no answer.

Then a voice came from out of the horde, "General Mahawai, I will vouch for this Naphil's word."

Everyone turned toward the voice. One of the soldiers stepped out from the crowded regiment. He came straight up to Mahawai. He saluted and stood at attention.

Mahawai looked at him expectantly.

"I am Hahyah, son of Semjaza. This Naphil is my twin brother."

Methuselah felt a sickening pit open in his stomach. His whole world came crashing in on him. Everyone on the team glanced at each other with shock. Only Betenos kept staring at Ohyah.

This Hahyah did indeed look just like Ohyah, save for his warrior-shaved head.

The general's next declaration caught them off guard. "We are done with our training exercise. Bring these captives back to Baalbek. Let Thamaq and Yahipan deal with them."

Well, thought Methuselah, at last I will face the Rephaim who killed our parents and the rest of my city. Unfortunately, they will have the blade in their hands.

The distant sound of a war horn interrupted his thoughts. The Nephilim stood at attention. Mahawai peered to the south and said to himself, "That is the battle call of Inanna." He turned to his troops and yelled, "ALL SOLDIERS TO ARMS! DOUBLE TIME TO BAALBEK!"

· · · · ·

Baalbek lay about ten leagues north of where Methuselah and his team were caught. All night long they marched through the Sirion mountain pass. Eventually, they entered a broad river basin called the Beqa Valley, just before the sun rose. They followed the Orontes River through a vast cedar forest to its springs in the heart of the city.

As they came up from the south, they passed a huge quarry used for the stone of the city. The morning quarry shift had not yet begun, leaving the stone pit empty. It struck Methuselah how large the stones seemed to be. He thought his eyes were playing tricks on him in the moonlight, with the distance and his perception.

Yet when they reached the city gates, he realized that the size of the stones was not an optical illusion. They were huge beyond belief. Stones the size of four men tall, thirty cubits long and thousands of tons apiece. He had never seen hewn rock so large or so finely crafted with precision. How did they cut, transport, and position such mammoth stones? It was inconceivable to him.

Until they entered the city gates.

Baalbek was a city of giants, vast and thriving, alive with industry and labor. And all of its inhabitants were Nephilim — *thousands of them*. All around them, everywhere, humongous architectural edifices crafted from cyclopean blocks of stone rose tall, some of the buildings a hundred cubits or higher. The team of giant killers felt like fleas in a nest of wasps. The giants they saw going about their business towered six to ten cubits high, and most of them wore strange foreign looking armor or carried foreign looking weapons. Baalbek looked like a military occupation of invading forces.

They were paraded through the city streets toward the palace. The staggering implications of what they saw overwhelmed Methuselah, Edna, Lamech, and Betenos. It meant that everything they believed about the gigantomachy was a lie. The giants were not reduced to outlaws and wandering vagrants hunted by the gods, they were an organized civilization. The general Mahawai had submitted to the call of Inanna as if they were her own army. How could this be? The gods had outlawed the giants in the East, only to create an army of Nephilim in the West?

These and many other questions filled Methuselah's head. He feared the answers. A deathly dread overcame him.

Lamech stumbled closer to Methuselah as they approached the steps of the palace. "Ohyah planned this all along. He betrayed us from the beginning," he whispered.

Methuselah nodded his head. He glanced at Edna to make certain she was well. Both Edna and Betenos had barely kept up with the rigorous march. The rapid journey had exhausted them all. They could have fallen asleep standing up, were it not for the fact that they would have been executed had they done so.

Before the palace, they passed a series of giant chariots, four-wheeled war carts drawn by teams of horses. The giants did not usually use beasts of burden, except in royal processions or in a military capacity for their leaders. This gathering obviously included a dozen different chariots from a dozen different tribes.

Baalbek was not the only city and army of giants? How much worse could these revelations possibly get? How much more shocking? thought Methuselah.

CHAPTER 39

The giant killers were ushered through the gigantic halls of the palace by a squad of six Nephilim warriors. Edna marveled at the intricate sculpting of marble and granite on the architecture. These monsters were evil, but they were still capable of creating such impressive beauty. It could only mean that artistic creativity and cultural sophistication were not in themselves signs of moral goodness. The cruelest, most monstrous beast could torture and eat a man, and yet turn aside and carve magnificent masterpieces of sublime beauty worthy of gods.

Betenos wanted to hold Lamech's hand. But she knew better. It was bad enough to be a woman captive. The heinous treatment she would soon receive was bad enough. But if their captors knew affection bound any of the giant killer team together, it would provide their torturers more vulnerabilities to exploit, when they got around to carrying out their duty. If Ohyah revealed their relationship, all attempts at hiding the connection would be futile.

Lamech and Methuselah sized up everything as they trod the halls to their destination. The thought of escape might be laughable, but a warrior never stops looking for ways to fight. Whatever they could learn of the palace layout or the cultural behaviors of their captors might come in handy in an emergency.

Methuselah watched one of those cultural behaviors in action as they were escorted through the hallway: Nephilim were slaves to their insatiable lusts. They had voracious appetites for food, drink and danger of any kind that gave them a thrill. The Nephilim guards kept sneaking glances at Edna and Betenos. Methuselah knew exactly what they were thinking.

On the one hand, he could certainly understand why. His wife was still the most covetable woman in any company.

Betenos was no less attractive. Though Lamech had sought to emulate his pious grandfather Enoch in spirituality, he could not avoid his good taste in beauty. Like patriarch, like son.

While Methuselah worried about Betenos' future, he knew Edna was very capable of using womanly talents to her own advantage. *It may even be she who will get us out of this impossible situation,* he thought. She would play them, cloud their minds with her seductive beauty, and then slit their throats before they knew what happened. He was proud of his godly warrior wife.

They arrived at a set of huge oak doors that opened to a feast banquet for giants. The vast dining hall had floor tables in a U-shape overflowing with every kind of fish, fowl and mammal imaginable: roasted boar, gazelle, lion, bull, and bear, as well as whale shark and coelacanth. The one animal kind Methuselah noticed as absent was reptile. No snakes, crocodiles, lizards or dragons.

That would be too much like eating their own, he thought.

It was a feast of flesh fit for kings, because that is who sat at the table before them; kings — giant kings. They were the Rephaim who were first birthed when the gods came down from heaven. Eleven of them sat on the floor in their eating positions. One tossed a lion's bone to two mushussu chained in the corner. They were the same type of chimera dragon monsters that had almost killed Methuselah's team near Mari, at the beginning of their journey. The beasts snarled and fought over the bone. It was not an encouraging sight.

Thamaq and Yahipan presided at the center table, the evident rulers of this city. They looked up from their revelry to see Methuselah and his team standing in chains before them.

Their eyes met. Time stood still. The enemies recognized each other. Blood rose up simultaneously in Methuselah, Edna and Yahipan. Hatred resurrected and gripped all their souls.

Yahipan stood and started to limp briskly around the table toward the captives, the look of murder in his eyes.

"Yahipan!" shouted Thamaq.

Yahipan stopped.

"There will be plenty of room for revenge later."

Yahipan limped back to his spot and plopped down in anger.

Methuselah thought, *Good. He has carried that wound I gave him for hundreds of years as a miserable reminder.*

Edna's thought completed his, *That is a foretaste of the misery I am going to give you, giant, if Elohim gives me one chance.*

"Methuselah ben Enoch and his band of mighty giant slayers," said Thamaq, with biting sarcasm. "Welcome to my *marzih* feast of the First Born."

A *marzih* was a banquet that Rephaim indulged in the presence of the gods to celebrate life or death or a military send off. But no gods were present at this feast.

The other Rephaim now stared at Methuselah's team. They were the first of the offspring of the Watchers. The mightiest, the rulers of royalty, and they were all supposed to have been executed after the Gigantomachy hundreds of years ago.

These Rephaim all measured about ten cubits tall and wore robes of kingship that expressed primacy and power. Each sported a different design, based on the different tribes or cultures they represented. Some outfits were studded with precious gemstones, others with silver and gold. All of the Rephaim were hairless and carried the tattooed skin of the Nephilim, strange occultic marks and spells burned into their leathery bodies as a magic oath of fealty to their gods. Their eyes bore the strongest resemblance of any of the Nephilim to their reptilian creators. They were stronger, faster, more cunning, and more spiritual than those who followed them.

"Forgive my lack of etiquette," said Thamaq. "Let me introduce you to the Council of the Didanu, who will soon rule over the wretched little lives of your descendants."

So they were organized into some kind of multi-kingdom empire. But who was the emperor?

Thamaq gestured to each one as he gave their names. "Ulkan, Taruman, Sidan-and-Radan the conjoined twins, Thar the eternal one." Methuselah did not hear the rest of the names. He kept his eyes focused on Thamaq and Yahipan, like a leonine predator waiting for the moment to strike.

Yahipan felt it.

Even though Methuselah stood in chains, and the kings were surrounded by the mightiest of the Rephaim in a city of giants, still he felt it — as if *he* was the one in danger. *Ridiculous,* thought Yahipan. *I am manifesting weakness,* he concluded and shook it off.

Methuselah and Lamech did not know why this Rapha even bothered to treat them as if they had information to exchange.

Thamaq was playfully ironic. "As you no doubt have seen through your tour of our good city, we have been busy. Apparently, so have you, I see. Learning the way of the Karabu."

Silence filled the room. Everyone on the team thought, *How did he know?*

The other Rephaim sat intensely quiet, anticipating the answer Methuselah might give. Genuine fear filled their eyes, as if Methuselah's little gang knew something that would crush them. But what could it be that would scare them so?

Thamaq dropped his levity and turned deadly serious. "Where did you learn the way of the Karabu?"

Thamaq did not appear confident of his question, fishing for the truth with a bluff.

The Karabu never left their underground city. Only a few bands like Enoch's ever travelled outside of the Sahand area of Eden. So only rumors and legends ever traversed the land about the secret order. There was no way that information was going to be drawn out of any of the team — even under torture.

"Very well," said Yahipan, "torture them."

The Nephilim guards turned to escort the prisoners away.

Yahipan added, "But keep them alive. I want the leader and his wench for myself."

Methuselah and Edna cringed. They could only imagine the horrors he had in store for them.

"Halt, Nephilim," said Thamaq.

The Nephilim obeyed.

"What would the Council of the Didanu advise?" said Thamaq.

Yahipan grimaced with anger. He did not want anything slowing down his plans for the two maggots.

The conjoined twin Rephaim, Sidan-and-Radan, spoke first. When they did, they spoke in synchronization. It was as if they shared not merely their middle body but also a consciousness. "We have heard the legends of the Karabu," said Sidan, "but it seems to us mere exaggeration," concluded Radan.

"We do not have time for such trivialities," said Taruman. "The die is cast. The furnace is stoked. There is no turning back."

What were they talking about? wondered Methuselah. *What strategy had these creatures of damnation implemented? What diabolical madness have we happened upon?*

Yahipan tried to conclude the discussion. "I will extract what I can from them and meet up with you with any important intelligence."

"Be gone with them," said Ulkan with the wave of his hand. "We have a war to conduct."

A war? What war? thought Methuselah.

The team of giant killers wondered what devastation was about to be wrought upon the land as they were led out of the banquet hall in chains.

CHAPTER 40

Methuselah hung by chains on the dungeon wall. He had already been beaten but kept in one piece for Yahipan. Edna lay chained to a mating altar, used for the Sacred Marriage rite. Lamech and Betenos were in the next room in their own bonds.

Yahipan sat before them, staring at Edna.

"I care nothing for the Karabu," said Yahipan. "I have no interest in extracting useless secrets of some sneaky order that exists in the fantasy and rumors of desperate and hopeless slaves."

For the first time in their lives, Methuselah and Edna were really and truly afraid.

"No, little worm," Yahipan said to Edna, "I am not even going to torture you."

He paused for effect. "I am going to impregnate you and the other wench. You will bear my offspring, then you will die. And I will have satisfaction."

Methuselah struggled to free himself from his chains. It was completely futile, but he tried anyway. He would die trying.

Yahipan smiled at him. "You, I will do interesting things with. I have never forgotten the day you gave me this limp. I have plotted all these years what I would do if I could only find you again. I have some ideas I have been waiting for the right opportunity to experiment with. What a pleasure to discover I can do them also to your own son as you watch. Yes, I will have satisfaction."

Yahipan stood up and limped over to Edna. He leaned down close to her and sniffed in deeply her scent. Then his sandy lizard-like tongue licked her face for a foretaste. Edna cringed and almost vomited.

Methuselah had no idea how he could possibly get out of this predicament. He did the only thing he could do at that moment; talk. Any amount of talk brought the tiniest delay that might result in some kind of miraculous opportunity. At least, that was his faint hope.

"Nephilim — w-were outlawed," he stuttered through his pain. "Why did the gods allow them to build a city?"

Yahipan considered the question, and then slowly smiled. Perhaps additional knowledge would increase the pain as well, knowing the juggernaut they could not stop.

"Oh, there is more than one city," said Yahipan. "The Gigantomachy was a hoax. It was a ruse ordered by the gods to draw attention away from their true plans; to build an army of Nephilim in Bashan, and train them thoroughly for the battle of all battles." He paused again for dramatic effect.

"A war on Eden."

The words hit Methuselah and Edna hard. And sank deep. They knew the reason without Yahipan needing to finish.

"We are going to storm the Garden, destroy the Cherubim, and capture the Tree of Life," said Yahipan.

The consequences of this plan horrified Methuselah. A malevolent race of giants with the power to live forever would reach heights of evil he could not even imagine. They would be invincible in their might and omnipotent in their rule.

"How?" asked Methuselah. "The guardians..." he sought to finish his question.

Yahipan interrupted him, "Those guardians have a weakness. The gods cannot invade because their own kind, the heavenly host, outnumber them overwhelmingly. And earthborn humans cannot enter because of the Cherubim sentinels. That is why the Watchers bred the Nephilim. Nephilim are a hybrid of angel and human, a creature that exists simultaneously between heaven and earth. We can achieve collectively what our genetic sources cannot individually. And our numbers are legion."

Suddenly, it all came clear to Methuselah. Years before, when they had killed the pack of Nephilim in the mountains of Aratta, he had wondered where their strange armor had come from and whether they were a part of a horde. Their armor was the insignia of this Baalbek army. They had killed a band of Nephilim scouts on a reconnaissance mission, gathering intelligence of the land surrounding Eden for their planned invasion. Enoch and his band of giant killers had stumbled upon the plan and had never realized it. And now they were about to be gotten rid of.

A rap on the dungeon door stirred Yahipan's impatience. "What is it?!" he yelled through clenched teeth.

The door opened. A soldier saluted and announced, "My lord, the goddess Inanna demands your presence at the mustering. They are about to begin the march."

"Son of Belial!" he cursed. "I told her I was occupied." Belial was the spirit of unclean wickedness.

Yahipan might be angry at the inconvenience, but he responded immediately. One did not trifle with Inanna's will. She once struck a high Rephaim dead for a delayed appearance before her. Yahipan turned to leave the room, but stopped, and turned back to his prisoners.

"I am going to inquire of my god. Now is your chance to inquire of yours. You might want to ask him why he cannot save you. But then I doubt he can even hear you."

Yahipan left them alone.

Methuselah admitted to himself that the thought had crossed his mind. Edna had been praying the entire time. They both knew that Elohim owed them nothing. Every breath of life was already undeserved. Elohim gives and Elohim takes away. Blessed is the name of Yahweh Elohim.

Simultaneously, Methuselah looked up and Edna stopped praying.

The soldier had not moved. He did not leave them or even close the dungeon door. He stared at them. Methuselah could not believe their bad luck. Was this going to be a Nephilim who broke ranks and risked death just to abuse a pair of prisoners?

The soldier walked up to Edna and took off his helmet.

It was the familiar face of Ohyah. Only it was not Ohyah, it was his brother Hahyah. He began to unlock the chains that held down Edna.

"We do not have much time. When Yahipan discovers Inanna did not summon him, we will have them both after us."

It confused Methuselah. "Your brother betrayed us. Are you now betraying him?"

"No. He is freeing your compatriots right now."

Edna asked, "But why do you help us?"

"When we discovered your team in the clearing, he had to maintain the ruse or risk execution. We are sons of Semjaza. That would be the highest of treason."

"Then why treason?" asked Methuselah.

Hahyah finished releasing Edna. He moved to unclasp Methuselah's chains. "I had dreams from your god Elohim not unlike my brother's. It was a garden of two hundred trees being watered. I believe these were the Watcher gods who came down from heaven. As their roots grew, the water flooded the forest and suddenly the garden became ablaze with fire and the water evaporated. I kept getting this dream night after night. And I knew it was judgment. Then I heard of the prophet Enoch and of his condemnation of the gods. I knew the time was at hand. So when my brother finally found me, I discovered he too had been visited by your god."

He finished releasing Methuselah. Edna leapt into her husband's arms.

"Wait a moment," said Methuselah. "You said you heard of Enoch's condemnation?"

"We had received word that Enoch and some archangels had entered the cosmic mountain Hermon, and stood right in the midst of the council of the gods who could not touch them. He prophesied and it was said he was translated into heaven on a fiery chariot."

Methuselah and Edna looked at each other with hope in their hearts and smiles on their lips. If this rumor was true, Elohim surely had a sense of irony.

"The gods are mustering their armies for war on Eden as we speak. Inanna is the Commander in Chief, and the Rephaim Council of the Didanu are the generals."

Of course, thought Methuselah. *Why did it not surprise me that Inanna was the force behind this atrocity?*

Ohyah and the freed Lamech and Betenos arrived at the door.

"We have no time. We must leave now!" barked Ohyah.

· · · · ·

Yahipan quickly made it to the command center by the gates of the city. He limped his way past the security detail with swift recognition. When he arrived at Inanna's tableau, she stood finalizing her plans with Enki and Utu who would accompany her leadership of the forces.

Enlil had refused to be there as one of the gods under her command. Their long lasting feud over the control of the city of Nippur was known to all. She had managed to seize popular support if not political status through her machinations. If she succeeded in this campaign, she would most likely imprison Enlil in the earth and turn Nippur from the religious center of Shinar into the capital of an empire with herself at the top. Yahipan wondered if Anu had thought through the predictable consequences and whether he had prepared for such a coup.

Yahipan limped before the gods and knelt in fealty.

"My gods, Queen of heaven," he said.

Inanna turned to look at him. He noticed a distinct lack of expectation in her face. In fact, she looked annoyed, wondering why she was being interrupted.

"What now, Hobbler?" she exclaimed impatiently. She called him that in derision because of his persistent limp, an ongoing sign of weakness and reminder that he had been hobbled by a pathetic human.

She was not expecting him.

In that moment, Yahipan knew he had been duped by that piece of baboon excrement down in the dungeon.

"Forgive me, your majesty, I only wished to alert you to the fact that my forces are ready to bring up the rear guard."

It distracted her. "Good, do not slow us down, Hobbler, or we will leave you in the dust. Be gone with you." She turned back to her plotting.

Once Yahipan was out of Inanna's sight, he barreled full force back to the palace dungeon. He accommodated his handicap using a skipping movement that maximized his speed when running. Unfortunately, it made him look like a jackrabbit scampering through prickly bush. All he could think of was figuring out how a Naphil could possibly agree to engage in treason. Whatever the case, he would immediately kill the males and impregnate the females without further ado.

• • • • •

Ohyah and Hahyah led the four giant killers through the dark dungeon hallways up toward the surface. They dodged and hid in the shadows, avoided personnel, and only had to kill one Naphil guard who happened upon them by accident.

Methuselah hounded Ohyah with questions.

"How many Nephilim troops are mustered?" he asked.

"Thirty thousand."

Thirty thousand Nephilim storming Eden? "Are the other Watchers joining the battle?" said Methuselah.

"No," said Ohyah.

"Why would Elohim not send his heavenly host right now to stop it?"

"Because the other Watchers have employed the Accuser to prosecute a lawsuit in the heavenly court at the same time. So the Sons of God are required as witnesses and counsel. It was all a diversion."

That did not quite add up to Methuselah or anyone in the group. They were not familiar with the bureaucracy of the divine council and the legal procedures that Elohim used to procure justice. They had to trust that what Ohyah was saying was true, since he had been privy to the Watchers' plot as a son of Semjaza. They concluded that if it was not true, he would have just let them suffer their fate at the hands of Yahipan.

• • • • •

Yahipan made it to the dungeon. He discovered what he had feared most: the open doors and empty dungeon cells. He found a security detail of four guards and barked orders for them to follow him. The prisoners had escaped.

He tracked the smell of their sweat upward. He had become very acquainted with Edna's scent. It had inflamed him like none had before. He would find them. It was only a matter of moments.

They stumbled upon the dead Naphil and continued on, knowing they were close.

• • • • •

Methuselah continued his questions with Ohyah as they climbed the palace hallways toward the roof.

"How far is Baalbek from Eden?" he asked.

"About two hundred and thirty leagues."

It would take a normal army twenty days to march that distance at a fast pace. But this was not a normal army. It was a Nephilim fighting force that could run all day with packs on their back. It would take them a third the time, perhaps seven days to make it to the perimeter of Paradise. How long then to defile it and raze it to the ground?

Methuselah felt sick. "We have to get to Eden to warn the Karabu."

• • • • •

Below them, in the long passage, Yahipan figured it out. They were going to the roof. But why? To cast themselves off? Why did they not try to find the tunnels beneath the city? It did not matter. They would all be dead soon. The Nephilim behind him had all their senses tuned in for the kill.

The two giants and four humans arrived at their destination, the top of the palace building overseeing the entire city. They ran to the ledge and looked out onto the plain. An awesome and frightening sight spread out before them. Thirty thousand armed Nephilim warriors filled the valley, preparing to march to war.

Trumpets sounded. A series of eerie drones blown through dragon horns created an unearthly sound befitting an unearthly horde.

The Nephilim started their march — or rather, their long distance race. One by one, huge sections of the multitude poured forward like a tsunami wave of titans.

That is what this holocaust is, thought Methuselah, *a Titanomachy that will make the Gigantomachy of the past look like cub's play.*

"We cannot possibly outrun the Nephilim," cried Lamech.

"We are not going to outrun them," answered Ohyah. He turned and produced a screeching birdcall, unlike anything Methuselah had heard.

"We are going to outfly them," added Hahyah.

Methuselah realized that he *had* heard that sound once before.

A reply screech drew their eyes into the blinding center of the sun. Out of that brightness, six large Anzu birds dropped directly toward the palace. It was the family of the Anzu bird that Ohyah had broken at the World Tree in the desert.

The Anzu landed on the rooftop. Each of the escapees got on one. The feathered felines were huge, twice the size of even the giants. They could easily carry the passengers. It would be harder for the passengers to stay on, however.

So Elohim did work all things to his own purposes, thought Methuselah. Even the Anzu bird. But what about this army of darkness assembled before them on the plain?

Yahipan burst through the rooftop access with his four Nephilim. He spotted the escaping prisoners.

The Anzu birds lifted off the roof.

Methuselah's was the last to take off. It moved just a second too late. Yahipan leapt and grabbed its hind talons. Rephaim had iron vise grips. He was not going to let go until he sent them all plummeting to their deaths.

Methuselah's Anzu bird lost its balance. It zigzagged a course over the Nephilim on the roof.

Yahipan smirked to himself. *I have you now, Methuselah. No last second escape this time.*

Yahipan focused on how he would grab Methuselah. He did not see Edna's Anzu bird circle back.

It clamped its lion jaws on Yahipan's strong leg.

Yahipan screamed.

He let go of the leg of the bird Methuselah rode. The biting Anzu bird let go of him at the same time. He was only about ten cubits above the roof, so he landed with a concussive thud. But he survived — and so did his burning desire to spend the rest of his life hunting down Methuselah and his disgusting wench.

"AHHHH!" he screamed. He grabbed his leg, bleeding profusely from the wounds created by the Anzu fangs. Now both his legs were wounded. He belted out another curse of anger and wrapped up his wound. How was he going to hide this from Inanna now?

The Anzu birds ascended vertically, to reach their maximum height as quickly as possible. They leveled off and flew in formation higher than any mountain in the region.

Methuselah saw the waves of charging Nephilim far below. They looked like an army of termites. He could not imagine how Eden would withstand this onslaught. He only hoped they would not be too late.

He glanced at Edna, flying beside him. They shared a smile. Ohyah and Hahyah led the group, with Lamech and Betenos taking up the rear. It was as if the birds intuitively understood all the relationships in the group and lined up to match them. Methuselah calculated that at this height and speed, it would take them less than a day to reach the Sahand and alert the Adamite Karabu. It was their only hope in a hopeless situation.

Methuselah thought back to what Ohyah had told them. He wondered what was happening in Elohim's court of principalities and powers. Would the Watchers' heavenly scheme delay Elohim's response to the earthly crisis? The implications were staggering.

CHAPTER 41

The Throne of Yahweh Elohim gleamed in the holy temple in the heavens above the waters, unapproachable, a chariot enthroned above the Cherubim and beneath the Seraphim. The Seraphim were a different breed, created exclusively for God's own guard. The Cherubim were sphinx-like, but these had four faces and four wings, and they sparkled like burnished bronze. Their faces were those of human, lion, ox, and eagle. Beside each one was an object that appeared to be a wheel within a wheel of gleaming beryl, that moved with the living creature as they moved.

The Seraphim above the throne were equally as glorious and awesome. Their humanoid yet serpentine bodies had six wings. With two they flew, two covered their feet, and two covered their faces. And all of them proclaimed the trisagion, "Holy, holy, holy, is the Lord of Hosts. The whole earth is full of his glory."

The heavenly host presented themselves around this throne, the *bene ha Elohim*, or Sons of God, ten thousand times ten thousand of his holy ones, the divine council. Their presence flashed like lightning that would burn out the eyes of any human being in the flesh.

The Accuser was not impressed by any of this. A transformed seraph himself, his plaintiffs were all Sons of God as well. His opposition did not intimidate him at all. He and Semjaza, along with almost two hundred Watchers, presented themselves across from the array they despised. They considered the throne-circling adversaries to be a mob of sycophants, yes-men and sell-outs, puppets and tools.

The Accuser, Semjaza, and their fellow Watchers were just as divine, and maybe even more powerful than their enemies because at least they exercised free will — real free will — iron will. That will did have to bend to the sovereignty of the Judge, however, to the use of their original heavenly names of Semjaza, Baraqel, and Zaqiel instead of their Shinarian deity names of Anu, Enlil, and Nanna.

They assembled before the throne of heaven to prosecute a lawsuit with the help of the rebel Watchers who fell to earth. This would not be like any other lawsuit the Accuser had ever litigated. This was a *covenant* lawsuit against the very judge himself, Yahweh Elohim, the maker of heaven and earth, the Lord of Hosts, the Suzerain King of kings.

The ancient form of covenant treaties between sovereign or suzerain king and subservient vassal contained five basic parts that bound the two parties. First, there was a preamble that identifies the Lordship of the great king, his transcendent sovereignty and jurisdiction over territories. Second, the historical prologue that recounted the previous relationship of the king and his subject, along with an establishment of hierarchy and authority. The third section laid out the ethical stipulations or laws required by the king for the subject to maintain his status as protected vassal. The sanctions or listings of blessings for obedience and curses for violation of the covenant came fourth, providing for the continuity of the covenant relationship with succeeding generations. The fifth and last section called for divine witness of the gods or the heavens and the earth.

When Yahweh Elohim had created Adam and Havah, he had enacted a covenant that essentially reflected this pattern of Preamble, Prologue, Laws, Sanctions, and Witnesses. Adam, as the first of the human race, had violated that covenant and the world now experienced the negative consequences of that covenant violation.

The Accuser had filed a third party class action complaint on behalf of Adam and Havah and the entire human race, claiming that Yahweh Elohim's covenant with the human race was in fact unjust at every single one of the five points. The Accuser's "equitable remedy" involved among other things, an award of damages and a permanent injunction and restraining order against Elohim from the Garden and the presence of mankind.

To make matters worse, the Accuser intended to pull every trick of legal hairsplitting, explore every petty technicality, and appeal every tedious legal procedure that he possibly could, in order to drag this thing out as long as possible. He felt confident and prepared as he took his place as prosecutor in the court.

A battery of defenders stepped out, across from the Accuser and Semjaza's Watchers. They took their places to counter the accusations of the lawsuit. They were the prince archangels: Mikael, Gabriel, Raphael, and Uriel.

Then the voice of Yahweh Elohim cried out, "Whom shall I send? Who will speak for us?" The silence of the throne room penetrated all beings present. The arrival of the final member of the defense team broke the silence: Enoch ben Jared, prophet of God.

"Here I am, send me," said Enoch. He approached the defense team and joined them. They smiled their approval.

At the sight of Enoch, Semjaza wanted to jump out of his seat and strangle the little meat sack. Enoch caught his eyes and rage rose up inside the Watcher. The Accuser saw it. He leaned over to Semjaza, whispering, "Do not be a fool. We have a higher cause here. Suppress your instinct. It is weakness."

Semjaza sat back and took a deep breath.

Enoch saw Semjaza's rage. He sat down in his defense position before the throne with a sense of righteous indignation. He remembered the saying Diya al Din had told him back at the Thamudi fortress, "Let justice roll down like waters." It felt appropriate for this scenario.

A cloud filled the inner court, and the sound of the wings of the Cherubim swept through as far as the outer court. The Seraphim spoke as one. Their voice thundered like the sound of many waters. "Elohim has taken his place in the divine council. In the midst of the gods, he holds judgment."

Everyone fell silent.

This lawsuit would be different from all others because of the legal procedure to be employed. Normally, plaintiff and defendant would stand in the bar before the Judge and make their arguments, calling forth testimony and producing evidence upon which the Judge would rule. But since the Judge himself was being charged by the Accuser, there would be no need of additional testimony or cross examination. The Accuser would make the complaint, and Enoch would speak in defense of Yahweh Elohim. After presentation of all oral arguments, the Judge would make a righteous summary judgment. Special circumstances dictated special procedures.

Yahweh Elohim pronounced, "Hear O heavens, give ear O earth, listen O mountains of God and the heavenly host. I call the sun, moon, and stars as witness today."

The Accuser and Enoch stood beside each other before the throne.

Yahweh Elohim said, "Accuser, what are your motions?"

"Going to and fro on the earth," answered the Accuser.

"What are your *legal pre-trial* motions?" said Yahweh Elohim, correcting the deliberate misconstrual of his words.

He was a wily one, this Accuser, looking for every opportunity to twist, spin, and undermine the system and procedures to his advantage.

The Accuser said, "I petition the court for a change of venue on the grounds that this heavenly court places the defense at great advantage and the prosecution at great disadvantage. I petition the court for jury nullification on the grounds that the myriad of heavenly host are incapable of impartial witness because of overriding prejudicial bias in favor of the defendant. I petition the judge to recuse himself on the grounds of conflict of interest as he is the defendant in his own trial and therefore cannot be fair and unbiased. And I petition the judge for the removal of the defense attorney next to me on the grounds of his lack of legal qualifications for this case."

This was going to be a long trial, thought Enoch.

Yahweh Elohim responded, "There is nowhere in the universe that can contain the heavenly host outside of this throne room. First motion dismissed. The Sons of God are divine council, they do not render verdicts. Second motion dismissed. I am the origin of fairness and objectivity. I do not change and I do not violate my character, so all my judgments are true and just even in reference to my own actions. Third motion dismissed. Enoch ben Jared has stood in the divine council and therefore has met the qualifications for prophet of God and lawful defense attorney. Fourth motion dismissed."

"Well, in that case, your mighty eminence of unbiased objectivity and fairness," said the Accuser sarcastically, "I ask for seven days to finish discovery, since I was surprised by the unreasonable volume of documents that deluged my council. These tablets of unending *toledoth* are time consuming." He was referring to the clay tablets that contained the genealogies of the heavens and the earth as well as those of Adam's descendants.

The gall of this rascal amazed Enoch. He could turn everything into an accusation, even against Yahweh Elohim.

The Accuser continued, "And you really have to admit that this endless list of animal names is quite tedious and would fatigue any staff, much less my own of less than two hundred Watchers."

After a deliberate delay, he added, "Your magnificent majesty most high."

This list of names was a record of those that Adam gave the animals in the Garden as an expression of his covenantal dominion, the authority that the namer had over the named.

"You have two days," said Yahweh Elohim.

Enoch knew the Accuser had no intent of reading the genealogies and names. But even in the face of this obvious stalling tactic, Yahweh Elohim went out of his way to be fair and impartial, even to his own disadvantage.

CHAPTER 42

The team of giants and giant killers fell asleep on the flight over the vast desert. At this height, the air was cold, but the feathers of the Anzu kept them warm. The giant birds flew smoothly.

Methuselah awoke to the sunrise directly in front of them. He saw they were already leaving the arid environment of the desert, flying over the fertile Mesopotamian plain.

But something was not right. They were heading into the sunrise. The sun should be to their right.

He recognized the river course below him. It was a part of the Euphrates just north of his own city of Sippar. They were headed southeast. They should have been traveling northeast toward the Aratta mountains and Eden. But they were going southeast toward Shinar and the Zagros.

He got the attention of Edna and the others. They all recognized their change of route. But their Anzu flyers would not catch up to the two giants in the lead. It was as if the birds had been ordered to stay back and not allow the contact. Methuselah could only assume that they were now captives of their rescuers. He could not imagine where they were being taken and for what purpose.

• • • • •

The Nephilim horde had run most of the day. They only set up camp for a three hour sleep. Before the sun rose again, they were already up and trampling the ground. Fortunately for Yahipan, Rephaim generals rode on the new four-wheeled chariots drawn by teams of horses. Otherwise, his doubly wounded legs would have dangerously hampered him. He needed more time for healing.

They made good time, following the Sirion Mountain range along the curve of the fertile crescent to avoid the deadly desert. The Euphrates lay a few leagues before them. They would head due east, cross the fertile plain of northern Mesopotamia and enter the Aratta mountains just below their target point.

Inanna calculated that if they could keep this pace up, they might shave another day off their journey. So a few hundred would die of exhaustion or dehydration. What was that to her? Countless thousands would perish in the final battle anyway. Nephilim were expendable. She expected to lose most of them in the first wave of attacks establishing a breach in the Garden. Elohim's forces would not be fighting for their lives, they would be fighting for their eternities. It would actually be quite a relief to lose tens of thousands of mouths to feed and demands to satisfy. These hybrid offspring were a voracious consuming mass of flesh and bone. Like a plague of locusts, they stripped bare the life of every territory where they encamped or passed through.

She liked to call it "the circle of life," the way of all things on earth: eat or be eaten, only the fittest survive. Morality and all its self-righteous proclamations of right and wrong were reducible to the will to power. Might made right. She would have to craft that into a myth one day. It would be a useful tool to obscure the Creator and justify all kinds of atrocities.

If a man could convince himself that morality was not a matter of humanity being created in Elohim's image, but rather was a construct of society, in order to maintain arbitrary control over the masses, then there would be no end to the genocides and holocausts that could be unleashed when man would take that belief to its logical end. Even more devastation than that accomplished by the religions she and her fellow gods "revealed" to these pathetic mud-pies of Elohim.

That was an idea whose time would come. But now was not that time. Inanna grinned with self-satisfaction. *I will indeed craft that secular myth for when ancient religion will have run its useful course.*

· · · · ·

By the end of the second day, the Anzu birds arrived in the Zagros Mountains, just northeast of Erech and the South Sea. As the giant birds descended, Methuselah saw a large ring of steep mountain buttes surrounding a plush forested valley. This secluded crater basin might have been a second Paradise. It looked just that rich, green and flowing with streams of waters. The ring of cliffs were like a wall of rock protecting a pristine lost world. It did not look like there was any way in or out, except by air. The Anzu landed inside the Edenic crater.

Methuselah, Edna, Lamech, and Betenos got off their mounts. What else could they do? Their carriers were obviously in the service of Ohyah and Hahyah. The Anzu birds took flight to the north. They had been double-crossed by the giants they had trusted, whom they had considered to be redeemable. Methuselah was not yet sure for what purpose they had been betrayed.

"Why did they not kill us?" asked Lamech. "Drop us from the skies to our deaths over the desert, never to be found again?"

Edna added, "And why in this lush, beautiful, secret valley?"

It certainly seemed safer than the rocky lands outside Eden, where war was approaching.

"Do not be deceived by appearances," said Betenos, looking around at the trees of gorging fruit. "Poison can be as outwardly beautiful as medicine."

"First, we must make some weapons," said Methuselah. "Then, let us get to the walls and explore the perimeter. There may be some hidden exit through a cave or a climb."

They only had three knives among them, taken from the bodies of guards they overcame on their escape out of Baalbek.

CHAPTER 43

"I have already addressed the partiality of the divine witnesses in this case," said the Accuser. "So let me move on to my next charge."

The trial had resumed. Yahweh Elohim had summoned the prosecution, and the Accuser came out with serpentine eyes and bronze body blazing. His skill as an adversary was quickly proving to be of the highest marksmanship.

The Accuser continued, "Regarding the covenant preamble, we have this difficult matter of the sovereignty of the Creator. Really, is not the sovereignty of the suzerain the foundation of the entire edifice? If this cornerstone is rejected, do not all other bricks crumble to the ground?"

He brilliantly used leading questions. Enoch thought to himself how he would like to see the cornerstone fall on the Accuser and crush him.

The Accuser's voice rolled on. "Now Elohim's covenant begins with a claim to sovereign jurisdiction: 'In the beginning, when Elohim began to create the heavens and the earth, etcetera, etcetera.' Is this not a clear case of tyranny and colonialism? Elohim claims to 'create' and 'own' all things as a tyrannical justification to colonize the land. He wants to demand a certain land goes to a certain people, in this case, the Garden to Adam and Eve, and no one else has the right to it. And then he kicks everyone out. What next? Will he claim a land that already has a people residing there as his own, and just wipe the indigenous inhabitants off the face of the earth to make room for 'his people of choice?' Will he ultimately claim the whole earth as his own and allow some clan of meek people to inherit it over those strong peoples who built up its richness? What kind of a suzerain does such a thing? I will tell you what kind: A despot and a tyrant."

Zealous anger filled Enoch. Not only was the Accuser spewing outright blasphemous lies about Yahweh Elohim as defendant, he was also cunningly undermining his authority as Judge by deliberately using the shorter non-covenant name *Elohim* in place of the judicially proper *Yahweh Elohim*. The Accuser earned his name with the ability to accuse on every level of his language.

Still, he was right about one thing: suzerains did claim their right to the land by claiming their gods as creators of it. The difference in this case was that Yahweh Elohim *really did* create all things and the gods were incomparable in his presence. *They* existed in *his* universe. But the Accuser was only beginning. He would build his case upon a mountain of bitterness built up over the millennia.

The Accuser carried on his argument. "But this covenant maker is not merely a tyrant, he is a totalitarian puppet master who is the author of evil. What kind of creator makes earthquakes that demolish entire cities and kills the populace under mountains of rubble? Or a hurricane that drowns shiploads of sailors and devastates port cities under tsunamis of water."

It did not bother the Accuser that his comrade, the god Enki, had claimed the same powers to make the earth tremble and quake, or that Enlil claimed to be the source of hurricane storms and lightning and thunder. Consistency was not the Accuser's strong suit, emotional appeal was.

"What kind of 'loving god' allows untold thousands of poor innocent women and children to suffer the ravages of disease and poverty?"

The Accuser was an actor of the highest caliber. He actually looked as if he meant what he was saying. Tears flowed from his crocodile eyes down his glistening scaly face. He did not care a whit for women and children. He actually thought poverty and disease were good ways to keep the population from expanding to unmanageable numbers that would threaten the earth's ecosystem of life. To the Accuser, humans were in fact parasites of Mother Earth, grubworms of the Great Goddess. Disease was the Earth's balancing revenge. But that belief would not stop him from using rhetoric to appeal to the sympathies and compassion of his enemy.

"But that is only 'natural evil,'" he waxed eloquently. "What of *personal evil*?" Now his words took on the calculated righteous indignation of a politician. "What kind of god would allow the heinous evils of rape, murder, genocide, *and war*?"

Uriel snorted at the irony. At this very moment, the Accuser's ally Inanna was leading a horde of thirty thousand unholy demigods on Eden. They were planning massive rape, murder, genocide, and war.

"I submit that if Elohim is truly 'sovereign over his creation,'" the Accuser said, his words dripping with venom, "then he is responsible for all the evil that exists in the world. If he is not so sovereign, then he is an impotent deity without the authority to back up his covenant."

The Accuser took a dramatic pause, pretending he was holding back a flood of empathetic tears. Then he finished, "A covenant is supposed to be constitutional, the very bedrock of truth and justice. This covenant is unconstitutional because its creator is a king who is a totalitarian oppressor, a cheat who makes the rules of the game to favor himself; a despotic dictator and tyrant who claims absolute ownership over creation; and worse, a genocidal emperor, who, mark my words, will soon kill everyone on earth who gets in the way of his imperialist empire!"

Enoch was stunned. He had never heard such a vile litany of invectives and hate speech against the Creator pour out of the mouth of a mere created being, except perhaps from Inanna.

The Accuser stopped abruptly and returned to the bar with a suddenly quiet and diplomatic disposition. "May the court forgive me, I forgot one thing. If I may, I would like to propose a humble suggestion. The defendant, Elohim, appears to be obsessed with transcendence and separation. Heaven is separated from earth, land is separated from waters, angel is separated from human, human from animal, male from female, and so on. With all this talk of the creator's transcendent distinction from his creation, all this *separation* and difference within creation, perhaps therein lies the problem. Separation and distinction breed hostility and fear of the 'other.' If this god would only be *one* with his creation, if all things were considered *one* instead of separated and different then maybe we might not have all the alienation and violence that such fear of *the other* creates. Of course, the Creator might know this if he actually knew what it was like to be one of his lowly creatures, to be a man rather than the omnipotent potentate of power and pious purity that he proudly preaches." He smirked. He thought his alliteration of Ps was a nice touch of poetic contempt.

He wrapped it up, "But I contemplate that would be impossible for such a 'high and mighty one,' so 'separate' and 'distinct' from his creation is he."

It was quite an explosive opener, thought Enoch, *followed by a low-key false humility that had the effect of making the audience listen intently. Like dropping your speech to a whisper after yelling.* Enoch wondered what was next, if this was just his opener. His adversary had engaged in so much fallacious rhetoric that he thought it would be quite easy to dismantle the argument and make a fool of the Accuser.

But then he thought better. He realized that he did not want to fall into the trap of emulating the fool in his folly. He decided his strategy should be to avoid matching the emotional excess. Instead, he should strip the rhetoric down to its core of absurdity with calm cool reason. Use the folly against the fool. This was, after all, a court of law where rationality served truth and justice not agenda and advocacy.

Enoch strutted before the throne. He lifted his chin high in thought. He then spoke like a scribe would speak to his students. "This Accuser has laden his argument with so much emotional invective and blind hatred that one can only wonder where he received his credentials. I am not aware of any apkallu wisdom sage on earth or in heaven who teaches insulting, appeals to pity, appeals to force, and popular sentiment, false dilemmas, slippery slopes, equivocation and question begging as actual legal strategy." *That was good,* thought Enoch. He did not hear the expected chuckles from the divine witnesses. But then again, they did follow strict rules of sobriety in trials. All his years of being an apkallu were bearing fruit in him now. It was as if it were all preparation for this moment.

He continued. "I would like to strip down the Accuser's so-called arguments to their bare essentials and address those sparsely few issues with that gem so rare among the wicked; rationality. 'Come, let us reason together,' says the Lord. And so we shall."

Enoch felt his confidence rising. He was much smoother than he had expected. The butterflies in his stomach had gone. He felt like a falcon flying pretty high, his eyes focused on his prey far below him.

"It is true," said Enoch, "that Yahweh Elohim is sovereign over his creation and therefore the covenant." He used the covenant name of God as proper protocol in the heavenly temple regarding covenant lawsuits.

He continued, "Our Creator works all things according to the counsel of his will. He makes nations great and destroys them. He brings both well-being and calamity upon cities and individuals. He has made everything for its purpose, even the wicked for the day of evil. And no purpose of his can be thwarted. In short, Yahweh Elohim is all-powerful and ordains whatsoever comes to pass. It is also true that he is an all-loving creator who cares for his creation. So if I may boil down the Accuser's argument into its simplest form, void of all its emotional hysteria and libelous insults, it would look like this --

Premise one: If Yahweh Elohim is all-powerful he could destroy evil.

Premise two: If Yahweh Elohim is all-loving he would destroy evil.

Premise three: Evil is not destroyed.

Conclusion: Yahweh Elohim is either unable or unwilling to destroy evil."

Now it was Enoch's turn to pause for dramatic effect. He milked it with relish.

"Let us dispense with this popular sentiment of ignoramuses and mental midgets. It is really very simple. There is a hidden premise in that argument that is fallacious. It *assumes* that evil will never be destroyed or put to rights. Well, who says so? Is the Accuser the god of time that he knows that evil will not be destroyed in the future? In fact, Yahweh Elohim promises to one day destroy all evil and put all things to rights. Simply because evil is not *yet* destroyed is no argument that evil will *never* be destroyed. I realize logical consistency is not a virtue to the Accuser, but it is a requirement of truth."

His train of thought completely engrossed Enoch. His words came out like fire from heaven. His pronouncements of justice rolled down like waters. He barely stopped to take a breath.

"The Accuser slanders Yahweh Elohim of being the author of evil, but *creating* evil for a purpose is not the same as *being* evil. Just because we do not know his purpose or reason for the evil he ordains in this world does not mean there can be no good purpose or reason. Our finite ignorance is not a measure of the parameters of the truth. Creaturely freedom and responsibility does not logically negate the Creator's sovereignty. Does the clay say to the potter, 'Why have you made me like this?' Shall the axe boast over him who hews with it, or the saw magnify itself against him who wields it? The Accuser complains of the Creator/creature distinction as the source of cruelty, but it is precisely the transcendent infinite God who distinguishes kindness from cruelty. If everything is one, kindness and cruelty are one and the Accuser's complaint is dismissed."

Enoch delivered the death blow. "And so I file a motion for summary judgment to dismiss this frivolous lawsuit. Amen."

Enoch sat down next to Mikael on one side, Uriel and the other archangels on the other. He felt like one of the angels himself. He drew in a deep breath. He knew that he had just won the entire trial in one fell swoop of oratory.

"You may have just lost the trial in one fell swoop of oratory," Mikael whispered to Enoch.

"Elegant delivery, apkallu," said Uriel. "That was vanity befitting of the Serpent himself. Is that what they teach you in wisdom sage school?"

Gabriel added, "Have you switched sides?"

Enoch's eyes stretched in terror. What had he done wrong? He had just made an iron clad rational case on behalf of the Creator. Or so he thought.

"Close your mouth," said Uriel.

Enoch stared at him.

"I mean literally," said Uriel. "Your mouth is hanging open like a fly catcher again."

Enoch closed his mouth. He was dumbfounded.

Then he opened it again. "But I thought I was supposed to use rigorous wisdom to dismantle the Accuser's position. I thought that is what truth is about."

"Truth is a person, not a mere proposition," said Uriel.

"So you think you fight vanity with vanity?" said Mikael. "You do not represent an idea, you represent Yahweh's character. Of which you were evidently completely oblivious as you strode about like a pompous braying ass."

"A strutting cock-a-doodle-doo," added Uriel.

Enoch's spirit dropped. His own pride, the worst sin of all, had just blindsided him. He had completely failed his God and had not even known it. Had he lost the case already?

CHAPTER 44

Methuselah found some straight saplings, cut them down and whittled a series of spears with his knife. The aim and accuracy of a spear required a finely balanced weight, which was not easy to attain with such primitive instruments. But he did his best with what he had.

So did the others. Betenos worked hard to create a bow and some arrows using one of the other knives. She wove some durable and string-like casings of a wild vegetable for the string. Lamech, who was at a loss without Rahab, created a sling and filled a pouch with perfect stones from a nearby brook. Edna took the knives when they were done and created a makeshift three blade staff weapon, an adaptation of the angelic blade she had mastered over the years. They could not kill giants with these handmade weapons, but they would not be at the mercy of lesser predators, which described most everything else.

They searched along the western wall for quite some time. They decided to make camp for the night, when Edna yelled out that she had found something.

Everyone ran to where she was. Or rather where she had been. She was nowhere to be found in the rocky area.

"Edna?" called Methuselah. "Edna, where are you?"

He began to get worried when she gave no response. They shouted urgently for her.

Methuselah came to a portion of the rock wall covered with hanging vines and other foliage. He stopped and looked back out into the forest, searching for any sign of Edna. Suddenly, a pair of hands flashed out from the hanging vines and grabbed him. They pulled him into the wall of green, as if to dissolve into the mountain face.

It was Edna. The vegetation hid a ravine just six feet wide. Edna hid within it.

"Gotcha, Poozelahpooneypoo," laughed Edna. She gave him a big fat sloppy kiss.

They had been in such danger for so long that they had not had time to show their love for one another. And when love has lived long, the connection gets deeper and richer than young lovers have any idea of.

Lamech and Betenos lay cuddling on the bank of the brook. They felt rested and at peace for the first time in a long time. He kissed her and stared into her eyes. She loved the way he would appreciate her. He would say she was a feast for all his senses: sight, sound, smell, taste, and touch. He made her feel so beautiful. Only Elohim could create such a harmonious artistry of physical and spiritual unity between man and wife.

The sound of a monstrous bellowing roar brought them to their feet. It came from the direction of the vine-covered crevice where Methuselah and Edna had been. They ran as one to the spot. They grabbed up their weapons, leaping through the vegetation into the ravine. It was a passageway through the mountain wall. They followed it.

Methuselah screamed at the top of his lungs. The roar burst over them again. It was so loud, it shook their insides.

How big was this thing? thought Lamech as they ran toward the sound. They knew their patriarch was in trouble.

They burst through the other side and found themselves in the mountain territory just outside the secret valley.

Methuselah knelt on the ground, cradling Edna, covered in blood, weeping.

Mere cubits away, a gigantic creature the height of a huge temple building staggered around. It tried to shake a javelin from its eye. It stood upright on its hind legs, though Lamech was not sure that was its natural posture. It had a tail the size of a cedar tree, bulging muscles on bones of iron, and teeth like iron swords. Its head looked like a hideous reptilian bull. It was some kind of amphibious dragon. It roared again and came down on all fours, revealing a deformed hump on its back. It turned to lunge at Methuselah and Edna.

"Father!" screamed Lamech.

Methuselah did nothing. He just held his beloved in his arms.

Immediately, Lamech and Betenos raised their weapons. Betenos launched an arrow at the great beast. Her makeshift arrow hit it in the face near the javelin. Lamech's stone broke one of its teeth with a loud cracking sound.

It roared again. They realized they were only making it angrier.

Lamech and Betenos ran to Methuselah. They dragged the patriarch and Edna's limp, bleeding body back into the covered ravine opening.

The colossus shook the javelin loose and launched after them. It snapped at their feet as they cleared the entrance into the ravine. But it was too large to fit through the opening.

Betenos launched one last arrow into the beast's mouth. It buried itself in the creature's tongue. It roared with rage and actually tried to force its way through the crack of the mountain.

Lamech felt the very mountain shake. Rocks fell loose and the earth quaked. But the colossus could not get through.

They carried Edna back into the safety of the crater basin. Betenos ran to get whatever healing roots she could find. Edna had been bitten by the monster. Her life was bleeding out of her.

Lamech tried to compress the wounds where the teeth had penetrated Edna's body, but there were too many punctures and they were too deep.

Methuselah knew it was time. She gazed up into his eyes. She managed a slight smile of love. She was in more pain than he could imagine, and she could still smile in the face of the only man she ever knew. She tried to say something. Her lungs were punctured. He leaned in close, putting his ear to her lips.

"I — will — see you in time, my be-beloved." Every word was painful and prophetic. "Enoch's m-mantle is now — yours. Our son — m-must live."

And Edna breathed her last.

Methuselah wailed. It echoed across the valley like a ghostly hound. It made Lamech think of the very beast they just escaped.

Betenos came back from the forest in resignation. She knew it was over.

The three of them lay over Edna's body and wept. Wife, mother, servant of Elohim, she was now with her Creator.

They buried her body near a large terebinth tree by the brook. Terebinth were sacred trees that were considered places of communion with deity. Edna had been a conduit of communion with Elohim for Methuselah. She was the most powerful proof of God's presence and goodness to him. Through her he came to understand grace, goodness, strength, perseverance, and a faith that he did not have in himself. She had been both submissive wife and godly inspiration to him, his perfect *ezer*. He would never have known happiness but for her. He would never know happiness again without her.

They laid the stones upon the resting place as a memorial, and prayed to Elohim, and wept and sang songs of hope. Then they ate a meal together.

Late night drew over them. And still they sat in silent memories.

Betenos looked up at the full moon. She sat close to Lamech with silent empathy. He labored to fix the triple blade weapon his mother had made. It had been damaged in the attack. Lamech's eyes were red from hours of painful recollections of his mother. The joys, the happiness, the hard work and discipline of family. He could not understand why Elohim would allow such a seemingly random thing as her death, after all they had been through. He had started to think they were invincible, God's chosen ones. That nothing would stop their righteous cause. Now, his pride crashed down in humble brokenness. He did not know what he believed. *Would Elohim allow us to get this far, only to snatch our lives one by one, never to be found or remembered in this uninhabited godforsaken mockery of paradise?*

Methuselah stared into the fire with dead eyes. He could not feel anymore. His soul was gone. He wanted to run out and attack the cyclopean monster without concern for his survival. Suicide. But Edna's words haunted him. He was to take over Enoch's mantle, now that Enoch was gone? Lamech was to be Elohim's chosen lineage for the One who would end the rule of the gods? What was all that to him now? He just did not care. He did not want to live.

But how to end it? he thought.

A twig snapped.

Instinct flooded back into them all. They were on their feet in seconds, with weapons drawn.

A single man walked out of the darkness into the flickering light of the fire. Tall, muscular, and young-looking, his eyes betrayed a great age. Beside him trod a large black she-wolf.

"I see you have met Behemoth outside the valley walls. I think your wailing was about as loud as his. Made it easy to find you."

Methuselah gripped a spear, ready to lunge. Betenos pulled on the string of her bow with nocked arrow ready. Lamech gripped the triple blade Edna had made.

The black she-wolf snarled at them.

"Is that any way to treat family?" said the stranger. "I let you bury your dead and get your bellies full." His delivery was ominous. He had a darkness in him that reminded Methuselah of Inanna.

"Who are you?" demanded Methuselah. "What do you mean, 'family'?"

Twenty large wolves stepped out from the bush surrounding them. They appeared to be a pack of predators controlled by this stranger before them.

When the stranger spoke again, Methuselah's blood ran cold.

"I am Cain, son of Adam."

CHAPTER 45

The trial reconvened before the Supreme Judge of the Universe. The Accuser took his place to mount his next attack on the Covenant.

"In your historical prologue, there is prattling on and on about the 'generations of the heavens and the earth,' etcetera, etcetera. And then we come to your creation of Man, 'in the image of God you did create him, both male and female.' I would like to address two aspects of this 'image': First, authority and hierarchy, and then this imperialist mandate of 'dominion.'"

Semjaza approached the Accuser and whispered in his ear.

He was updating the prosecutor on the progress of Inanna's forces. Enoch knew this already. Everyone on the defense knew it. Yahweh Elohim was not some kind of idiot finite deity who did not know what was going on in his creation. The mere fact that he chose to accomplish his purposes through such secondary means as the divine council and the freedom of his creatures did not bother Enoch anymore.

There were many mysteries of the infinite eternal Creator that faded away in the minds of finite mortal creations in his immediate presence. Enoch smiled to himself at all the energy he had spent on earth fretting as an apkallu sage, seeking the ever elusive dream of absolute knowledge and wisdom. It was an endless pursuit of always getting closer and never arriving. No matter how wise he could be, no matter how much knowledge he possessed, the universe and everything in it was so far beyond the limits of his understanding as a tiny little object embedded within that creation that he could not hope to achieve god-like status of observation and understanding. *It was certainly not a waste of life to pursue such wisdom,* he thought. *But perhaps it was a sign of the true fallenness of our nature that we would twist our calling as Yahweh Elohim's images into an intent to become Elohim, demanding all truths be made sufficiently understandable to our puny finite faulty understanding.*

The Accuser's rant brought Enoch back into the present.

"This notion of authority and hierarchy in the covenant is quite incoherent to me. On the one hand, Elohim tells us both male and female are created alike to be his imagers or representations of his rulership on earth. And then on the other, he contradicts himself when he gives the vocation to the Man to work and keep the Garden before he even creates the woman! Imagine that! A 'men's only' club. No women allowed. How sexist can you be? Then Elohim creates the Woman out of the Man's side and tells her she is to be man's 'helper fit for him,' like some kind of slave. The Man 'names' the woman, and we all know what that means: The namer has the power over the object being named. My dear Creator, this is all about power. Not truth, not justice, and not love. But I will speak the truth to power! I would think that if one were a loving god, one would make everyone equal in race, class, and gender; not this misogynist Patriarchal justification of male domination over women."

Enoch thought of the "truth, justice, and love" that the Watchers had been giving to the women they were using to breed the Nephilim. It was not the first time the Accuser used his own wicked behavior as an argument against his Creator.

"But I will make one concession to your majestic power," said the Accuser. "You are consistent. That is, your unfair gender favoritism of the male is a reflection of your own bias as male and your sexist creation of angels as males. It is quite clear to me, 'father,' that you and all your 'Sons of God' are afraid of women. You oppress the female gender and enslave them to be breeders and deny them their rightful place in this world. I think you are secretly suppressing the fact that the true creator of this world is not the male Sky God, but the Great Earth Goddess!"

The myriads of holy ones broke out in shocked murmuring. Whispers of "blasphemy" abounded. The grace of Yahweh Elohim in not smiting the Accuser on the spot amazed Enoch. Elohim had his greater purposes.

"And that brings me to my second point," said the Accuser. "Your covenant charge to Man to take dominion over all creation and to subdue it to his interests is just another facet of your suppression of the Great Goddess. You would have man trample, burn, and destroy the environment that the Earth Mother gives him, as an expression of your macho excess!"

He quoted the words of Elohim back to him with incredulity, "'Elohim made the greater light to rule the day and the lesser light to rule the night? And the stars in the firmament for signs and seasons and for days and years'? Where is the sun god and the moon god? And are not the stars a heavenly host of deities? You want to divest the universe of spirits and gods so that you can reign supreme as a jealous autocratic Emperor! You want to turn the cosmos into some 'soulless' natural order so that your little male minions can trample the environment, spoil the creation, and engage in cruelty to animals!"

The Accuser turned to the heavenly host with excessive theatrics, "Elohim is not fair and equal in his dealings with his creatures, he is a sexist and a speciesist!"

Enoch almost laughed out loud. The absurd lengths to which the Accuser would go to construct a delusive opinion to suit his purposes amazed the human. He wondered if anyone would ever actually believe this combination of insanity and iniquity. Ironically, he could see where the Accuser was going with it, and it was truly evil. He would make sure to address it in his rebuttal.

The Accuser ended with a rising plea. "Does your unfair favoritism and partiality know no bounds, Elohim? You choose who rules over whom, who is forgiven and who is not, you elect one man over another to carry your purposes forward. These are not the actions of a fair and impartial Creator, these are the actions of — dare I say it again — a tyrant and puppet master! But of course, if the sandal fits, wear it. Your honor. Amen." The Accuser bowed and went back to his team of Watchers.

Enoch stood and approached the throne. "Your honor." He turned to the heavenly host, "divine witnesses of the court. I want to apologize for my previous display of pride. It was unworthy and unbefitting an ambassador of Yahweh Elohim and a defender of the throne. I hope to address the Accuser's further slanderous lies with a more respectful demeanor. Amen."

Enoch began his formal presentation. "In the first place, regarding the Accuser's complaint of the imago dei and authority, I think this gets to the heart of the argument. The Accuser does not seem to like the order of things, the hierarchy of one over another, the notion of authority. He wants everything to be 'equal.' But I must ask this question, 'By what standard?' Whose definition of equal? If by the standard of the Creator, then that begs the question. The Creator has the right to define authority and justice in any way he deems proper. If by the Accuser's standard, why? Why should anyone listen to the Accuser's definition of what is just and what is not? I would prefer my own definition over the Accuser's, and you would prefer your own definition over mine. It is an endless trap of infinite definitions and authorities that cancel out the Accuser's own accusations."

Enoch took a breath. He let it sink in. This time, he would make his arguments with more concern for the hearers. "I would like to address each one of his accusations to show that they are straw men that do not even apply to Yahweh Elohim. But I do not even have to, because his claims are simply pitting his own finite ignorant authority against the self-authorized infinite Creator of all authority. The Accuser pronounces, 'sexism, imperialism, misogyny, speciesism' and a plethora of other 'isms.' But by the Creator's standards the Accuser is sexist, imperialist, misandrist, and speciesist because he is seeking to define the created order from his own subjective, arbitrary, and finite viewpoint. This is sheer bigotry and hubris on the Accuser's part. A creature is trying to subject the Creator to his own authority."

Enoch shook his head and continued, "Since the Accuser seems to want to claim to be the creator of the standards of truth and justice, and not be beholden to a standard outside himself, then I would like a few answers from him. I would like him to gird up his loins and make known to us where he was when Yahweh Elohim laid the foundations of the earth. I wonder if he might tell us who determined its measurements and who laid its cornerstone. It would please the court if the Accuser would tell us who poured the sea, who commands the morning and evening, who crafted the gates of Sheol and dug the pits of Tartarus, who created thunder and lightning and rain, who bound the chains of the stars of the Seven Sisters or loosed the star-cords of the Shepherd of Anu? Perhaps the Accuser might show us how he gave the horse his strength or the hawk his wings. Shall a faultfinder contend with the Almighty? He who argues with God, let him answer it. Otherwise, may he forever hold his peace."

Enoch almost sat down, but he reconsidered. "If it please the court, I said I did not need to address the Accuser's straw men accusations. But I just wanted to get something on the record. Abuse of authority does not disprove proper use of that authority. Man was not called by Yahweh Elohim to be a slave master over woman, as the Accuser argued, but to be her loving sacrificial leader. Yahweh Elohim never told man to 'trample, burn and destroy' his environment. To exercise dominion over nature, yes. And if man fails to harness the natural world, all life on the earth will succumb to chaos, disease, and destruction. But man was also commissioned to 'care for and keep' that world with responsible stewardship. It is not the *'undeifying'* of nature that leads to exploitation and hurt, it is the *deifying* of nature that does.

For when the sun, moon, stars, lightning, storm and disease are gods, that is when man worships the creation in place of the Creator and death reigns."

That felt more satisfying to Enoch. He had to get that off his chest, even if it was not technically necessary. He concluded, "But there are some things I think we should all trample, burn, and destroy, and those are the Accuser's straw man arguments."

Enoch sat down.

CHAPTER 46

Methuselah, Lamech, and Betenos awakened to the smell of stew cooking on morning fires. The sun had not yet come up, but they could see by the sky that it was near. They were bound together hand and foot with vines used as rope. Cain and his pack of wolves had taken them hostage the previous night, and brought them to this camp on the far side of the valley, distant from the exit crevice.

They looked around for the wolves, but the animals were gone. The Cainites were a clan of about a hundred, male and female, all wearing animal skins — but no children.

Where were the children? thought Betenos. *What kind of tribe does not have children? How could it survive?*

Cain approached them with a woman by his side, tall, with raven black hair and chiseled facial features. She had the presence of a warrior, but dressed as a tribal queen. She carried a pot of stew for them.

"This is my favorite sister and wife, Awan," said Cain. "Welcome to 'the Hidden Valley', my 'Garden away from the Garden,' I like to say. I have always had a green thumb. So I put it to good use."

Lamech remembered from stories that Cain was a worker of the ground. This secret paradise was a breathtaking incarnation of God-given skill.

Awan undid their bindings. She gave them utensils to eat some stew from the large pot. Lamech and Betenos attacked it hungrily.

Methuselah did not bother. He stared into oblivion. Why eat? It would only keep him alive.

Cain said, "The giant twins brought you to me."

Methuselah showed no interest in this conversation.

It was Lamech who spoke. "You sent Ohyah and Hahyah?"

"I paid them a bounty to find you," said Cain. "I think you understand that concept well enough."

Cain lingered over regretful memories. "I have been wandering for too long in search of you, my vengeance."

"Us?" asked Lamech.

Cain answered, "I was not even sure you were the ones I was looking for. But when Ohyah told me of his dreams and his meeting with Enoch, I knew. I knew that you were the lineage of the chosen seed of Eve that would crush the seed of the Serpent."

Lamech broke out in a cold sweat. He had an idea where this was going and did not want to find out.

Awan watched the three of them like a wolf watching its prey.

Cain continued, "Elohim is a sadistic connoisseur of cruelty. He is an arbitrary dictator. He accepts one offering and rejects another. And why? I gave him the fruit of my gifts that *he* gave me. But it was not good enough for him. He wanted it his way or no way. He wanted a blood sacrifice."

A bitter pause hung in the air. Then Cain gave a savory grin. "So I gave him one: The blood of my brother. The vengeful petty deity cursed me and made me a creature of the night — with an eternal thirst for blood. I cursed him back and decided to create my own Eden with my own rules, and my own god: me." A big proud smile cracked his lips.

Lamech and Betenos shivered. They felt as if they were staring into the face of sin itself, crouching at their feet, ready to pounce.

"At this very moment," Cain added, "a gargantuan horde of Nephilim warriors marches on Eden to take possession of the Tree of Life." He paused. "Imagine a world of true equality, where all men are gods, all creatures divine, everyone lives forever."

Where evil never dies, Lamech thought to himself. He knew what such claims to "equality" without God led to: genocide by those who ruled in the name of equality. They never shared their power once they had it. The first to taste of the Tree of Life would turn and keep it from everyone else.

"Imagine the absolute freedom from all dependence on a cosmic child abuser who tells us what we can and cannot do."

And I thought it did not get worse than Inanna, mused Lamech.

Methuselah remained in his trance of self-pity. He listened, but still did not care.

Cain concluded his pontificating, "And in the meantime, I will have the ultimate revenge of absorbing the very life and lineage of Elohim's Chosen Seed into my own body, when I drink your blood."

A shiver of terror went down the spines of Lamech and Betenos. Now they understood why Cain looked more like one hundred years old, instead of his eight hundred and fifty years. He cannibalized the life source of his victims, their blood replenishing his youth, regenerating his body. Lamech glanced at his father, who now watched their captors. Those captors were not interested in Methuselah, they were interested in Lamech.

"The sun is rising," said Cain. "I must retreat to my residence for rest. Awan will care for you until the evening, when I rise — for dinner." He smiled and walked away, leaving Awan watching them with a smirk on her face.

She shoved the pot at Methuselah. "Eat up, old man, we need you plump."

Methuselah did nothing. Awan dropped the pot at his feet. Some of it splashed on Methuselah, and still he did not react.

Awan left them alone with the last of the food.

Lamech studied Methuselah. "Father, you are not the only one who lost mother."

Methuselah remained unmoved. They had been sitting there for some time and Methuselah had offered no plan, no hint or desire to escape. He waited to die. His meaning, his Edna was gone. And with her, the heavens and the earth.

Lamech spoke sharply with renewed conviction. "You may want to die. You may not care what happens to the rest of the world. But I do. This is bigger than my life, than all of our lives. If grandfather Enoch prophesied the truth and Betenos and I are the lineage of the Seed, then why would you give up? Would you dishonor the faith of the one you loved most on this earth?"

That got through Methuselah's wall of silence. Lamech was right. His son was absolutely right. Methuselah had placed his faith in this world and not in Elohim's promised world to come. He had relied on his senses for so long that he had worn them out. He had lost his taste, his smell, his touch; he had become blind, deaf and dumb. He had neglected prayer because Elohim seemed so distant and his prayers almost futile. He had come to believe that things got done because he got up and did them, not because of Elohim's solicited favor. Since Elohim was going to do what he was going to do anyway, then why bother wasting time talking to him about it? He had become a self-made man who lifted himself up by his own sandal straps. And it was all a self-deluded lie. He had missed the whole point that his wife had been trying to tell him: he distrusted Elohim because of the betrayal of the gods. He had lived a life of self-reliance rather than a life of faith. He had sought desperately for significance in this world. But he now understood his significance would be as the protector of Elohim's Seed, not the fulfiller of his own.

Methuselah lifted his face to Lamech. His eyes were red with tears, his face flush with revelation. Everything in Methuselah's life came clear in that one instant.

Methuselah took the pot of stew and ate like a hungry dog. He would need his strength.

CHAPTER 47

She had done it. Inanna had pushed her warrior horde at an unprecedented pace. In three days, they had gone over one hundred and thirty leagues, an unrivaled achievement of Nephilim endurance. However, her glorious fortitude had taken its toll.

"We must slow down, Inanna," Enki complained in their command tent. "We have lost two thousand warriors to exhaustion and dehydration."

"They were the weakest," said Inanna. "More food for the strong."

Utu jumped in. "The numbers of deaths will rise exponentially if we continue at this rate. Even Nephilim have their limits, and we are perilously close to it."

They were within sixty-five leagues of Lake Urimiya, on the west perimeter of the Garden.

"We will be at our destination in one more day," she said.

It shocked Enki. "Are you out of your mind? You want to take the last sixty-five leagues in *one day*?!"

Inanna's eyes narrowed like a dragon about to strike. "Are you challenging my authority, General Enki?"

Enki backed down. Insubordination was punished by binding in the earth, a fate worse than death for a Watcher.

He softened his argument. "It will do us no good if we make it to Eden in record time, with a demoralized and exhausted army at a fraction of their fighting strength. It is suicide."

"For Anu's sake," said Utu, "at least give the soldiers a half-day's extra rest." They were within minutes of trumpet's call to march.

Inanna stared at them with incredulity.

Utu clapped his hands. The eleven Rephaim generals entered the tent and stood to attention. Thamaq and the limping Yahipan were among them.

Utu ordered them, "Report on the morale."

Thamaq said, "My lord, there are whisperings of mutiny in some quarters."

Inanna thought about it. She strode past the Rephaim. She spotted Yahipan with recognition. "Hobbler here is keeping up, why cannot everyone else?"

Yahipan gritted his teeth. On the one hand, his handicap was singled out again, but on the other hand, he clearly impressed Inanna. Now, if he could only find another way to shine like a star.

"Give the horde an extra hour of sleep," said Inanna.

She thought to herself, *Am I being too weak?*

"We need to be to Lake Urimiya by nightfall tomorrow. Then they can have a few day's rest before battle."

"Yes, Queen of heaven," said Utu. He raced outside to make sure the trumpet call would be delayed.

"And for my sake," said Inanna, "track down these mutinous whisperers and execute them."

Yahipan saw his opportunity and stepped forward. "Yes, Supreme Commander. I will rout them out before sunrise."

Inanna stopped her pacing and noticed Yahipan again. She turned to the other Rephaim. "You see this will? If the rest of you had half the will of this invalid, we would be unstoppable."

Yahipan bowed and left the tent on his mission. He wondered whether her comments would raise him up or keep him singled out as pitiful.

Inanna had no intention of giving the Nephilim a few days rest when they arrived. They would need a full day just to build their pontoons for crossing the lake. She would throw numbers at the enemy to overwhelm them. Tens of thousands of weakened Nephilim were still too many for the Cherubim to withstand. Nephilim were expendable and Cherubim were not invulnerable.

She knew the Cherubim well, their strengths, their weaknesses, and their numbers. Only several hundred of them guarded the Garden. She would split her forces. The Western army would build pontoons as the Southern army travelled around the shore to mount a flank attack from the mountainous region in the south.

The Garden was walled by the Savalan mountain range in the north, the Sahand in the south, and by the huge Lake Urimiya on the west. The only opening into the valley lay in the East, where the Cherubim forces stood guard. When they discovered the Nephilim army arriving on the lake, they would split their forces between east and west. They would not be expecting a flanking attack from the mountainous southern region. The huge volcanic chain of the Sahand was precipitous to climb and therefore an unexpected entry point for a raid.

The Cherubim were not experienced in fighting angelic/human hybrids. Humans they could slaughter easily enough with their flaming whirling swords, but Nephilim were a crossbreed. The forces needed to combat the angelic half of the Nephilim were the angels who were now busily held up in heavenly legal procedures.

The Nephilim would have to rise to the occasion. Inanna did not know how much longer the Accuser could keep the heavenly council embroiled in his lawsuit. It was a diversion made in heaven. God and all his heavenly host, because of their despicable dedication to righteousness would give their full attention and presence to due process of law. In doing so, they would not be available to defend the Garden when it was attacked. She had split the enemy's forces and cut them off from their Commander in Chief, that loathsome tyrant from above.

She thought of cutting in half the extra hour she gave the Nephilim to sleep. Beneficence was one of the demands on deity she detested.

CHAPTER 48

Lamech and Betenos had prayed for Elohim to deliver them. Awan and several villagers watched them like guard dogs the entire day. They fed them well. Methuselah considered that a mistake, because regardless of how "plumped up" Cain thought they were, they were also renewed in their strength and readied in their resolve to fight back if they had a chance.

Methuselah watched the sun go down. He asked Awan, "Where is the wolf pack that accompanied Cain in our capture? I have not seen them in the camp."

"They only come out at night," said Awan, with a hint of dark delight.

Betenos wondered whether Cain planned on sharing his meal with those canine allies.

Awan watched Betenos with a cocked head, trying to read her lips moving in prayer.

"Where is your god?" said Awan.

Betenos stared back without fear. "He is in the heavens and he does as he pleases."

"He does not appear to be very capable of rescuing you," said Awan.

"Our God is able to deliver us," said Betenos. "But even if he does not, we do not fear you who can destroy the body, but rather Him who can destroy both body and soul in Sheol."

"My god will consume your body and soul," said Awan. "So I doubt there will be anything left over for yours."

They turned to see Cain walking toward them in the darkness, like a phantom.

Awan said, "Here comes my god, now." She and the other guards got up and left the captives alone with Cain.

"How goes the seed of Eve?" asked Cain with a lighthearted tone of irony. "I had a good day's sleep, and I am famished."

Methuselah glanced at Lamech and Betenos. There was no way he would let anything happen to his son and daughter-in-law. But the only problem was that he was entirely at the mercy of this monster. He was in no position to save anyone.

The silhouette of an Anzu bird suddenly fell across the bright blood red moon. It came right toward them. It landed in the village which now looked strangely empty of people. It had become a ghost village.

Where had all the people gone? wondered Methuselah.

Cain turned to see the thunderbird and whistled.

From out of the darkness came six very large wolves. The raven-black she-wolf came up to Cain. He gave it a look that Methuselah saw was more than master or owner. Then Cain went to meet the Anzu bird in the distance.

The wolves circled the captives and watched them with hungry attention.

Methuselah looked into the eyes of the black she-wolf. In that moment, he knew where all the people had gone. Those were the eyes of Awan, the black-haired wife of Cain. *These wolves must be the human villagers transformed into canine beasts of the night.* It started to make sense. Awan's allusions, the disappearing wolves and now the disappearing villagers.

Methuselah glanced at Lamech and Betenos. They appeared to have had the same revelation.

Lamech whispered, "What black art is this? Does Cain know the secrets of the Watchers as well?"

The She-wolf growled menacingly and stepped closer to Lamech. He promptly shut up.

Cain came back to them. He spoke hastily, "I have some important business to attend to. I am afraid I will be gone for the evening."

The wolves looked up at him as if they understood his every word. He turned to Methuselah.

"Do not worry, they will not be eating you tonight." Then Cain ran back to the Anzu bird. He climbed on it and it flew off like a bat out of Sheol.

The wolves turned their attention back to the hostages and stood watch as sentinels.

Lamech hoped Cain was not exaggerating with that last remark about not being eaten tonight.

Betenos was not as certain that these voracious carnivores would be able to exercise such self-control until their master got back.

Methuselah had seen real concern on Cain's face after he had received the correspondence attached to the Anzu bird. Something was not going right with Cain's plans, and that gave Methuselah just the edge he had been praying for.

He had begun praying again.

CHAPTER 49

The heavenly court reconvened for the Accuser's litigation against the third part of God's covenant with humanity. He took the bar and spoke with the particular disdain he had for rules.

"Ethical stipulations," he said. "The laws required by the suzerain of the subject if he is to maintain his status as protected vassal before his lord."

The Accuser launched into a new diatribe. "In this most primitive of law codes in the Garden, Havah was told by Elohim, and I quote, "You may surely eat of every tree of the garden, but of the tree of knowledge you shall not eat, neither shall you touch it, for in the day that you eat of it you shall surely die.""

The Accuser paced around shaking his head with ridicule. "We will have much to say about this curse of death in our fourth complaint. But for now, we would like to focus on this silly demand that humankind stay mired in unenlightened ignorance by submission to an impossible command. I ask the court, did Elohim *actually* say this? Could his childish motives be any more obvious?"

"Now, I have said this before, and I will say it again, this whole thing is a set-up by a god who is spiteful, mean, obsessively jealous, and self-protective. He wanted to keep humanity from becoming like us — *from becoming gods*. Elohim must have known that knowledge would allow man to control his own life and to discover all the secrets of the universe, and well, we just cannot allow that kind of competition, can we?"

The Accuser paused for effect. His cohorts smiled at the progress, but the heavenly host sat unmoved. He delivered his conclusion, "I submit to you that Elohim's covenant is not the legal treaty of a master protecting his servant, it is the declaration of a monomaniac oppressing his servant, and protecting himself from being outdone by his own creation!"

The Accuser sat down.

Enoch stood. He carried with him a tablet and dove right into his rebuttal. "The testimony we have just heard from the Accuser has several half-truths in it, or as I would more accurately define them, *lies*."

Enoch read from the clay tablet in his hand. "Yahweh Elohim did not say that the couple could not *touch* the tree, he said that they could not *eat of it*. That is an exaggeration of the command to make the Creator appear excessive and overbearing. Secondly, it was not 'the tree of knowledge' that was forbidden, it was the 'tree of the knowledge *of good and evil*.' Yahweh Elohim was not forbidding knowledge to humanity, he was commanding reliance upon him as their ultimate authority to define good and evil. And we are right back to ultimate authorities that I spoke of earlier. Yahweh Elohim is the only ground of morality that can justify the Accuser's own attack on morality."

Enoch paused for a moment in thought, then said, "It would not surprise me if one day, the serpent will have effectively convinced the masses with more of these kinds of distortions. I can imagine him twisting the 'forbidden fruit' into *sex*, and turning Yahweh Elohim into a cosmic killjoy prude who just wants to keep people from having fun."

Enoch launched into his conclusion, "No, the forbidden fruit is the essence of freedom. The Accuser would have us believe that boundaries of protection are actually restrictions of oppression; that rules repress human potential and laws take away freedom. He and his Watchers argue that freedom is the ability to do whatever one wants without an external code imposed upon them. Let each man be a law unto himself. Yet, look around the earth below to see the consequences of such ideas. Humans have achieved the self-determination from the knowledge of good and evil and in so doing have become slaves to their own appetites. Prisoners of their desire. They claim to be free, but they are everywhere in chains of their own making. Only in the boundaries of a loving Creator can humanity be free. Is a fish out of the water free? Is a bird out of the sky free? Only in fulfilling our god-given purpose can mankind experience the liberty of obedience. Disobedience is not enlightenment, it is pure blindness; it is not freedom, it is slavery."

Enoch stood for a moment as his words sank into his own soul. He realized that he had fought God's purpose for himself so many years — that he prayed when he should have fought, fought when he should have prayed, and too often exhibited the ultimate sin of spiritual pride.

Enoch fell to his knees and wept in repentance before Yahweh Elohim.

CHAPTER 50

In the early morning, the Nephilim horde arrived at their beachhead destination in the mountains on the edge of the vast Lake Urimiya. Inanna allowed them a few hours rest. Utu had been wrong. They did not lose exponential numbers of warriors in the final push toward Aratta. They only lost five thousand total weaklings to the extreme running march. That left her with about twenty five thousand Nephilim fit warriors, plenty of fodder to accomplish her goal.

She employed thirteen thousand in cutting down trees and building pontoon rafts to cross the great lake. The other twelve thousand, she sent thirty leagues around the lake to the volcanic fields of Sahand. They prepared to climb the rocky face of the mountain for an incursion on the south of the Garden simultaneous with the amphibious landing in the west. Their attack would launch at midnight when the moon was high in the sky, allowing them enough darkness for cover, enough light for battle.

She noticed that some of the trees had been carved and used to impale a host of about twenty Nephilim in the sight of all. These were the "mutinous whisperers" that Hobbler had hunted down and punished. It was a pathetic indication that a cripple could be more loyal than the other Rephaim generals who seemed to prefer ordering others around.

The undead Cain arrived the night before on an Anzu bird. Ohyah and Hahyah had heard through their officers that Inanna did not know exactly where the Tree of Life was located in the Garden, having only rumors and legends to go by. The twin giants had relayed to the goddess their connection with the Cursed One. They were allowed to send one of their thunderbirds to fetch him. Cain's knowledge from his parents of the Garden and the location of the Tree of Life could be just the information she needed to strike with a more accurate ferociousness.

Because of his well-known reputation, Cain was awarded admission to the presence of the goddess and her Rephaim generals. Inanna knew that any enemy of Elohim was an ally of hers.

But Cain brought with him another idea that would prove of inestimable value for her. The rock face of the Sahand on the interior of the Garden was precipitous. The sheer cliffs would severely impede the attackers' ability to attack with swift surprise.

Cain shared with Inanna an invention he had developed to traverse the heights of his own mountainous paradise. By sewing together cloths and animal skins into large "sails" five times the size of an individual, they could create a traveling source for each individual warrior. When grasped through some ropes the skins would allow them to jump from the great height and "sail" a pocket of wind down quickly and safely. It would delay them a few hours to construct these "sail chutes," but it was an ingenious invention.

They buried Cain in the ground according to his request, to avoid the light of day that was dawning on them. If exposed to the sun, he would burn up into ashes as a consequence of his curse. At nightfall, he would be allowed to return to his Hidden Valley on one of the Anzu birds. It was a great loss to give up one of their six thunderbirds, for they were crucial to their air strike, but it was worth it to Inanna. Cain's information might actually help them win the war on Eden. She could use this Cursed One in her new administration — or kill him as a potential usurper.

Inanna performed a valuable service to her cause by apologizing to the troops.

She gathered the horde to speak to them before their Rephaim leaders set out. They assembled around the clear-cut tree stumps. She spoke to them with her amplified voice of divinity.

"Children of the Watchers, progeny of the gods! If ever you listened to me, give ear to me now, I plead with you. First, I beg your indulgence. I know I have pushed each and every one of you beyond what any god has ever asked of their servants. I know that you are hungry, exhausted, and strained to your limit. I know that many have paid the price with their lives. And for that my heart bleeds. I feel your pain. The life of one warrior is the life of all."

A low base rumbling chant of agreement interrupted her. It was the horde's way of uniting in morale. The thought flitted through her mind that perhaps she had finally become Anu's equal. His oratory was impressive, but she doubted he could inspire as she was now doing.

She continued, "But today marks an achievement unheard of in the annals of history. And you, my horde, are the titans who have risen to prove your worth of becoming gods!"

The horde rumbled again in affirmation.

"We are on the verge of a war the likes of which will change the world forever. And we are the agents of change. We are the ones we have been waiting for. We are the change that we seek."

She paused again for dramatic effect. And she received it. The ground vibrated from the noise of the Nephilim.

"We are about to occupy the Garden of the mountain of God. This god, who was born with a golden spoon in his mouth, this deity who claims to own everything and leaves nothing for the ninety-nine percent of the rest of us, we are about to show him who is god!"

She paused for another moment of rumbling before finishing.

"You are about to storm a fortress guarded by mighty Cherubim. I know you are exhausted. I know you have been worked to the bone. I know you barely have anything left to give to this campaign because you have given all you have and more. But I ask you this one thing. When you are crossing the lake, when you are climbing the rocks, when you hear the horns of war bid you attack, when you find yourself battling the evil Cherubim, when you have reached the end of your strength and have nothing left to fight with, just remember one thing: tomorrow you will taste of the Tree of Life and you will be gods, and you will tire no longer -- for you shall live forever!"

The horde rumbled yet again. They caught the spirit of the moment. She knew no amount of exhaustion could quench their strength in the light of that hope. And she was proud of her ability to lie through her fangs with every single word she spoke.

CHAPTER 51

Methuselah woke. He looked around with curiosity, squinting at the morning light. Their sentinel wolves were gone. The people of the village were also gone. Methuselah, Lamech, and Betenos had been left all alone. It did not fit with the way they had been treated up until that moment. He tried to figure out what trick was being played on them. Did they want their prey to escape? To hunt them down like rabbits, to make the feast more enjoyable?

Methuselah's searching gaze passed over the bush next to him.

Uriel the archangel stood there.

"What are you doing here?" asked Methuselah. Lamech and Betenos jerked their heads up to see Uriel step out in front of them.

"You sound disappointed," said Uriel. "Would you rather I leave?"

"Praise Elohim," said Betenos. "I knew he heard our prayers."

"Great. But are you not here to miraculously free us?" said Methuselah.

"Oh no," said Uriel. "I was sent to encourage you. Be strong and courageous, mighty warriors of God, for Elohim hears your prayers and will help you to endure."

"Wait a minute," said Methuselah. "What kind of angel shares words of encouragement but does not help us out of our bonds?"

"What, do you expect Elohim to do everything for you?" said Uriel. "While you sit and do nothing?"

The three of them could not believe what they were hearing.

Uriel said, "I just emptied the village for you! How many more miracles do you want? Respond with some faith will you?" Then Uriel walked away into the jungle.

He stopped and turned back for one last comment.

"A word to the sage, lower your demands on Elohim. He does not owe you a thing. You are blessed that he gives you anything at all." And then he vanished into the foliage.

Methuselah watched him leave with utter incredulity.

"The gall of that archangel," said Methuselah.

Lamech retorted, "He is right, father."

Methuselah and Betenos turned to look at Lamech. He stood with his bonds cut loose and a knife in his hand.

"I was fixing mother's makeshift weapon when we were caught the other night. I could not pull it out while they were watching over us like — wolves."

Methuselah sighed. "Well, cut us loose, and let us get out of this godforsaken place. If I catch that archangel, I am going to give him a piece of my javelin."

Lamech cut the vines. They darted into the jungle, wondering where in the valley the village wolf-men were.

They reached the narrow ravine exit covered with vines and found their way through to the other end. They knew something waited for them there, something huge and monstrous.

Methuselah stopped Lamech and Betenos. "Stay here, I will be right back."

Methuselah stepped out into the open and started screaming at the top of his lungs, "Over here, you son of iniquity! Come and get me!"

Lamech and Betenos looked at each other with shock. What was he doing? They heard the loud bellowing roar of Behemoth reverberate across the rocks.

Methuselah ran full tilt back to their exit. Behemoth raced after him, lunging and snapping for flesh.

They fell back as Methuselah dove into the narrow opening just out of reach of the snapping jaws. Behemoth belched out another roar that could be heard across the entire Hidden Valley. It scraped furiously at the rock, trying to get through.

Methuselah stood with his finger pointing at the beast as if it would understand him. "One day," he declared, "I am coming back, and I am going to slaughter you and turn you into a feast for the vultures, for what you did, you instrument of evil."

Behemoth backed up a step and roared again. Lamech swore to himself that the creature almost looked and sounded as if it had a tinge of fear.

Methuselah turned and walked back toward the Hidden Valley interior.

Lamech yelled after him, "Hey, wait a minute, father, what are you doing?"

Betenos joined in, "You just made it impossible for us to escape."

"I do not want to escape," said Methuselah. "I want to make the wolf tribe *think* we escaped."

Betenos blurted out, "Whatever for?"

Methuselah explained, "To maintain the element of surprise. Because we are not going to escape, my lovely daughter-in-law, we are going to stay and fight."

Understanding flooded over Betenos. Lamech smiled with pride.

Methuselah said, "It is too far for us to help fight the war on Eden. But we can fight our own war on the son of perdition. It is time we cleanse this garden of evil. You never know when we might need it someday for refuge."

Lamech added, "That seed of the Serpent wanted a war with the seed of Eve. Well, he has got it."

CHAPTER 52

For the last part of the trial in heaven, Yahweh Elohim allowed the litigators to engage in cross examination and rebuttal. The Accuser stood next to Enoch before the throne. Yahweh Elohim announced the beginning of the next exchange, "Accuser, you may speak."

The Accuser began with his first complaint, "On this fourth aspect of the covenant, the 'blessings and curses,' we find another series of immoral maneuvers by Elohim, the first of which is the injustice of his capital punishment."

The Accuser delivered his lines with theatrical exaggeration. It would have annoyed Enoch had they not been so self-incriminating. "What kind of a loving god would punish a simple act of disobedience in the Garden with death and exile? In the interest of wisdom, the primeval couple eat a piece of fruit and what reward do they receive for their mature act of decision-making? Pain in childbirth, male domination, cursed ground, miserable labor, perpetual war, and worst of all, exile and death! I ask the court, does that sound like the judicious behavior of a beneficent king or an infantile temper tantrum of a juvenile divinity who did not get his way?" The Accuser bowed with a mocking tone in his voice, "Your majestic majesticness, I turn over to the illustrative, master counselor of extensive experience, Enoch ben Jared."

The Accuser's mockery no longer fazed Enoch. His ad-hominem attacks on a lowly servant of Yahweh Elohim was so much child's play. It was the accuser's impious sacrilege against the Most High that offended Enoch — and the Most High's forbearing mercy that astounded him. He spoke with a renewed awe of the Almighty, "If I may point out to the prosecutor, the seriousness of the punishment is not determined by the magnitude of the offense, but the magnitude of the one offended. Transgression of a fellow finite temporal creature requires finite earthly consequences, transgression against the infinite eternal God requires infinite eternal consequences."

The Accuser jumped in, "But why does a loving God punish at all? Is it not his obligation to forgive all sins large or small? What kind of a loving God punishes imperfection? What kind of a loving God casts people into Sheol? That is not love, that is cruelty."

Enoch sighed. He was already weary of hearing "what kind of a loving God" preface a horde of false accusations. But in the interest of fairness, he sought to address each one. "Firstly, I would like to establish that counsel is repeating a falsehood already laid to rest. It is not imperfection that is being punished, it is iniquity. Secondly, may I remind my accusing adversary that a *just* God is not obligated to forgive anyone anything. A *just* God punishes sin. Forgiveness without payment of the penalty is the true cruelty. Worse, it is to denigrate the criminal's own worth to nothing. For if the criminal is forgiven without the penalty being served, then both victim and victimizer have no value. But neither is "love" obligated to forgive, for that would make such actions duty and no longer gracious."

"Ah," interrupted the Accuser, "But there you are on the horns of a dilemma. For Elohim to be just, he must punish, but for Elohim to be loving, he must forgive. So if he punishes, he is unloving, and if he forgives, he is unjust. So I ask the Judge with humility, submission and deference, which art thou, cruel or impotent?"

Now that was a coup, thought the Accuser as he let his impeccable logic sink in to the minds and hearts of ten million "holy ones." *Holy, my rear end.*

· · · · ·

The moon cast its pale light on endless lines of rafts, built and portaged to the shores of Lake Urimiya. The Nephilim launched their rafts. They paddled across the watery expanse, led by seven of the Rephaim, including Thamaq and Yahipan. Inanna stood on the shores staring out on the waters with her Anzu mount next to her. She thought of what it would be like one day in the near future when she would swim across the expanse of the waters in the heavens to take Elohim's throne. Utu stood beside her like an obedient komodo dragon, his thunderbird ready for flight. His hands held the war trumpet ready.

· · · · ·

Enki on an Anzu bird and his four Rephaim generals led the expeditionary forces onto the Sahand range. Ohyah and Hahyah rode the final two thunderbirds as scouts. The Nephilim forces had pieced together their sail-chutes and had crossed the volcanic terrain surrounding the Sahand. They encamped at the foot of the mountain and began their ascent.

Unbeknownst to the giants, they had trampled the volcanic rock ceiling of the underground city of Sahandria, home of the Karabu giant killers. The Adamite cave dwellers had not been warned of the planned invasion because of Methuselah's capture. But the sound of twelve thousand Nephilim foot soldiers stomping overhead was warning enough. The Karabu were already suited up and ready for battle. They simply waited for the right moment.

· · · · ·

Cain was unearthed at dark. He bid farewell to his comrade-in-arms, Inanna, and her armed force of demigods. It took only a few hours to fly back to his Hidden Valley.

When he arrived, a downcast Awan and her pack of wolves greeted him. He learned that their prisoners had escaped in broad daylight. She had no idea how it happened. She had turned her head and they were suddenly gone. She wondered if they had put a spell on her and the guards. But when they had heard the roar of Behemoth signaling their exit, she knew they were either dead and eaten or long gone into the Zagros mountain range, where no doubt they were quite at home in evading detection.

Cain flushed with anger. He suppressed the emotion to maintain control of the situation.

"You said you heard Behemoth?" he asked.

"Yes," said Awan. "But when we checked the valley exit, we found nothing. No blood, no sign of struggle."

Cain said, "Had it entered your thoughts that they may have possibly engaged in a trick to make you *think* they had escaped or were eaten?"

Awan was silent. She had not thought of it.

"Had you considered that they may in fact be hiding somewhere in this valley, waiting for a better opportunity or better course for departure?"

"No, my lord and god," said Awan.

"I want the entire pack ready for the hunt, NOW!" he yelled.

She bowed in submission and ran to alert the others.

I had them, thought Cain. *I had them in my hands, and they slipped through.* It burned like a knife in his back, one that kept burning. *I have sought all my life for this opportunity and now I have been betrayed by my own clan.*

My own clan. I have nothing. I have no one. I am alone, utterly alone. Elohim has stolen my revenge.

He heard the howls of the wolf tribe already on the chase for human blood.

Maybe I will kill the whole tribe when this is over, thought Cain.

CHAPTER 53

After the Accuser trumpeted his philosophical dilemma of an unloving or unjust God, Enoch was about to respond when the entrance of another counselor to his team interrupted him. He came from the right hand of the throne of the Ancient of Days and whispered to Enoch. The hairs of his head were white, like white wool, like snow. His eyes were like a flame of fire, his feet were like burnished bronze, refined in a furnace, and his voice was like the roar of many waters. But when he whispered, it was a still small voice heard only by his listener.

It was the Son of Man, the "second power in heaven." The first one he spoke to was Uriel. The Son of Man whispered something to him and Uriel immediately excused himself from the throne room.

Then the Son of Man walked to Enoch and gave him counsel. Enoch could see the Accuser visibly shaken by the presence of this glorious being. It was as if he knew his case was instantly lost. Enoch had seen this "Son of Man" in his dreams when he was on earth, but after ascending into heaven, he came to know him. There he learned that this Son of Man was also a Son of God, but not like all the other heavenly host. He was the Firstborn, a species-unique, uncreated Son of God. And now, he had joined the defense. Everything would change.

After receiving counsel, Enoch spoke, "There is a third way, not addressed by the Accuser's dilemma. And that is substitutionary atonement."

The Accuser scoffed with derision. He was so loud, he turned heads. "I knew he would pull this."

Enoch continued, "The purpose of blood sacrifice is to place the penalty of the guilty upon an unblemished innocent. The shed blood satisfies divine wrath for justice, which makes forgiveness of the repentant covenant-breaker possible."

"Barbaric!" barked the Accuser. "Slaughtering innocent precious animals for the bloodlust of divinity. This animal cruelty is despicable and disgusting."

In truth, it was not despicable or disgusting to the Accuser or the rest of the rebel Watchers. They had set up their own religion of blood sacrifice that would substitute humans for animals. The Great Goddess Earth Mother was the most voracious, with a ravenous appetite like Sheol. Her tree rings consisted of the corpses of human vermin, the virus of the planet. But the Accuser did not have the luxury of consistency, he was trying to win a case.

• • • • •

Lake Urimiya stretched out about thirty leagues, but was only ten leagues wide. The flotilla of Nephilim warriors crossed at the shortest point, a distance of only half the full width. It was the largest salt water lake in the entire region.

But it was also one of several key openings to the Abyss.

The Abyss contained the great waters below the earth that fed the waters above and formed the overhead to the underworld of Sheol. It was this same Abyss whose waters rose to the surface of the black lake in Mount Hermon's bowels. It was this same Abyss that was one of the only things on earth that Nephilim feared. And that is because it was this same Abyss that was the abode of Rahab the sea dragon of chaos.

Climbing Nephilim covered the base of the Sahand range like termites on a tree. Enki on one of the Anzu birds flew overhead with a strategic eye, noting the progress of the masses below. About half of their forces were ready for the next wave.

At that moment, the Karabu slid out from their hiding places and crevice openings. They attacked the Nephilim at the base of the mountain.

The Nephilim forces were divided into two units, those climbing and those waiting to climb. But the six thousand at the bottom of the mountain would still be a difficult victory for the three hundred members of the vanishing secret order of giant killers. The battle form of the Karabu was referred to as "the dance of death," which showed itself as the Karabu attacked. They came at the Nephilim in clothing the color of the volcanic rock around them. The Nephilim did not even know what hit them. By the time they could get their bearings on the hostile force cutting them down, they had already lost nearly a thousand giants.

The Nephilim below pulled in their ranks to fight the spinning, twisting, flipping, nearly invisible enemy. The Nephilim above saw the slaughter, but kept climbing toward their launch point above.

・・・・・

In the Hidden Valley, Cain's pack spread out into the entire basin in search of their prey. But their prey had prepared all day and were ready for the pack. The odds were about three to one, against the escaped captives. Except that there were two minor details that Cain did not take into account. These three prey were giant killers and they were not afraid of mangy dogs.

Methuselah, Lamech, and Betenos had not been able to collect their homemade weapons before they slipped out of the village. They had one knife. But they also had their wits.

The first pack of eight wolves that ran across a scent became overconfident with zeal as they saw their quarry. Betenos and Lamech struggled up the rocky side of the valley. Lamech stumbled and fell to the ground with a thud.

The pack ran like the wind, yipping with victory. Seconds before reaching the prey, the ground gave way beneath them. The branches and leaves covering the pit full of carved spikes gave way. The wolves had thrown caution to the wind. Because they ran as one, they all fell as one into the pit.

All eight of them were skewered and impaled through their legs, throats and bellies. The few that did not die immediately yelped and whimpered in pain. Long spears carved by the team's lone knife finished them off.

A sound in the brush startled the team. Had they missed one? They drew their pathetic weapons, a few pointy sticks for Methuselah and Betenos, and a blunt useless knife for Lamech.

It was not a wolf that stepped out. It was Uriel.

"We thought you were gone," said Betenos.

"No. I was just teasing you," said Uriel.

They did not laugh.

"Oh, come on," said Uriel. "I was not going to let you get killed *that* easily."

Methuselah was angry. "Have you come to give us more 'encouragement from the Lord?'"

"Yes, as a matter of fact, I have," said Uriel. "But this time in the form you prefer."

He reached into the brush and pulled out a large bag. He threw it at their feet.

Uriel said, "I think even you are going to thank me for this one, Methuselah."

Methuselah stared at him dubiously. It was hard to know what this crazy angel was going to say or do next.

Betenos bent down and opened the bag. She pulled out a bow, a quiver of arrows and a rack of javelins.

"Our angelic weapons!" she exclaimed She handed the javelins to a slightly less doubtful Methuselah.

Methuselah growled, "It is about time."

"You are welcome," replied Uriel.

Uriel strode up to Lamech. He reached behind his own belt and drew out a familiar handle with rolled up blade. "You did not think I would forget about you, did you, Lamech?"

A big broad grin spread across Lamech's face as he unfurled Rahab into the dust. He snapped a sapling in half.

"Please give our regards to Elohim," said Lamech.

"Oh, I am not going anywhere," said Uriel. "I am supposed to guard over you."

"What, now you are my guardian angel?" said Lamech.

"Do not flatter yourself, Lamech," said Uriel. "I would not miss this for the world." He drew his shimmering sword from its sheath with the sound of metal crossing metal.

CHAPTER 54

The Accuser had been quite shaken up by the arrival of the Son of Man and of his influence on the progress of the suit, or rather, the regress. The Accuser decided to reframe the debate.

"If it please the court, I need to place into the public record another piece of evidence. You know, I am often slanderously called a liar. My character is defamed with the pernicious mudslinging title 'Father of Lies.' Well, let me tell you, it was not I who lied to Adam and Havah in the Garden, it was Elohim! 'Thus saith the Lord,' and I quote, 'in the day you eat of the tree you shall surely die.' Pshaw! They did *not* die on that day! Adam and Havah lived over nine hundred years. I ask you, who is the real liar here? The covenant is invalidated because of the discredited character of the suzerain!"

Enoch only took a moment to respond. "Your honor and esteemed members of the council, the Accuser seeks to deny the authorial intent of the text by reducing it to the reader's own responsive interpretation, as if *he* defines reality. "In the day" is a colloquialism that means a general time period, and the Accuser knows this very well. He is using literalism to control the text for his own despotic purposes. They did not die 'on that day,' they died 'in that day' which signifies a new era of existence because of the serious consequences of their actions. Exile from the Tree of Life in the Garden meant their bodies could not be regenerated. That is when they *died*."

The Accuser and Semjaza wondered how close their army was to seizing that very prize of eternal life for their minions, the Tree of Life. If they were victorious, they would make a name for themselves and nothing that they proposed to do would be impossible for them. They would be the ones kicking certain other deities out of the Garden.

The Accuser scrambled for more cover. "Counsel has suggested that death is the inability to regenerate the human body. But I submit that this depends on what the meaning of the word 'is' is."

Enoch wondered to himself, Was this insanity even worth the dignity of a response?

Rahab could swim the waters above and below the firmament. It was all her territory. But her special domain was the Abyss. From there, she could access every body of water that ultimately connected to this underwater abode. Her birth waters were Lake Urimiya, where Elohim created her and held her at bay when he established the heavens and the earth. She was in the Lake again at that moment. She had returned to this sacred ground to give birth to her own spawn.

The Nephilim paddled on the surface of the water. They were unaware of the nemesis below, a protective mother sea dragon and her very hungry newborn offspring, *Leviathan*.

Leviathan was every bit the armored sea serpent as its parent. Even so young, it was already about half the size of Rahab. But it had something its progenitor did not: seven heads. Seven dragon heads on seven snakelike necks with seven times the predator's snapping jaws, and seven times the rows of razor teeth. Leviathan's strike zone was wide and it was more agile and speedier than Rahab. And it had seven times the fury.

The Nephilim were oblivious to the shadowy forms approaching them from the darkness below. They filled the waters with their crafts The lead skiffs were only two thirds of the way across.

The first casualties came at the front of the line. A huge explosion of water erupted. Pontoons snapped in two, throwing Nephilim into the water.

Yahipan screamed, "RAHAB!!" The Nephilim stopped rowing and looked about the water. The huge serpentine armor broke the surface again, crushing a slew of the flatboats and dragging Nephilim into the depths. The spiny back cut through the water and disappeared.

The Rephaim yelled orders. The Nephilim rowed for their lives. But it was an easy feast for the monsters of the deep. Rahab simply opened her mouth and scooped up dozens of Nephilim like so many minnows.

Leviathan came next, with the seven dragon heads snapping up Nephilim faster than they could get out of the way. Leviathan might be a newborn and smaller than its mother, but already armor covered it. It was even able to launch small pillars of fire from its nostrils. Its youth and speed made up for its size as it darted and dodged around, all of its heads coordinated in a bloodbath of feeding.

Inanna wondered where all that food went.

Some Nephilim tried to fight back But it was futile and the smart ones made for the shoreline. They hoped they might get lucky and be overlooked by their serpentine predators.

That was only the beginning. The sorry paddlers were no match for the worst of all Elohim's creatures. Another creature came up from the depths. Its body could not be seen, only tentacles bursting from the water and crushing demigods in its grip. Yahipan and Thamaq were in the middle of the mayhem and counted eight of these snakelike appendages grabbing hapless soldiers.

On the shoreline, Inanna's complexion went pale. It was the one thing she had not anticipated. And it was the one thing that might completely derail her strategy.

In the water, Yahipan noticed that the tentacles were not grabbing Nephilim, they were grabbing the Rephaim generals. It was as if the creature were searching only for Rephaim. Before he could move, one of the tentacles wrapped around his body and pulled him into the air. He chopped with a battle axe. But the constriction of the tentacle made him black out. His axe splashed in the water.

Bands of Nephilim closer to the launch site tried frantically to paddle back to shore.

Numbers, thought Inanna. *Chaos cannot possibly keep up with the numbers. Some will get through.*

She drew a bow and some arrows and started shooting the returning Nephilim. She bellowed, "DESERTION IS TREASON. FORWARD OR DIE!!" The fleeing Nephilim stopped in confusion. They turned back around, to try their luck for the other side.

The lake became one big cauldron of churning waters, snapping multiple dragon heads, crushing tentacles and Nephilim blood. The Nephilim forces were being decimated. But some crossed over and made it to the other side.

Inanna and Utu mounted their Anzu and flew overhead to try to assess their losses and help the few who appeared to be close to landing.

This sea dragon and her brood are not going to stop me, thought Inanna. *If I have to attack it myself, I will.*

• • • • •

The Karabu had trained for this war all of their lives. They had built strength, developed technique, and placed their faith in Elohim. Thus, their casualties at the walls of Mount Sahand were a mere dozen after slaughtering three thousand giants at war. They moved like ghosts The giants considered them demons. They fought with an acrobatic technique the giants did not recognize. The Nephilim were occultic creatures that were hard to kill for normal humans. But the Karabu were secret assassins trained by God's archangels specifically to fight Nephilim. It was not an even fight.

Unfortunately, Inanna was right. The numbers favored her. Even though the Karabu were able to take down astonishing numbers of giants and scatter a goodly number of them in fear, they could not win the battle in time to stop the other six thousand Nephilim already cresting the top of the Sahand ridge The climbers prepared for their sail-chute descent into the Garden.

• • • • •

Cain had heard the cries of the wolves caught in Methuselah's trap across the Hidden Valley. Judging by the sound of it, he reasoned that Methuselah had taken the offensive. That meant he probably had a strategy of divide and conquer, since he did not stand a chance against the pack. Cain called the others together with a whistle. He sent them out on the scent as a pack of forty. The wolves would simply hunt them down one by one. As Inanna had told him at Lake Urimiya, they could not overcome sheer numbers.

But Cain had another idea of his own. And he was willing to sacrifice his entire wolf clan to achieve it.

• • • • •

Methuselah teamed up with Betenos and Uriel with Lamech. That was one command from Elohim that Uriel was grateful for, since Methuselah did not like him much.

How could a man be so miserable? thought Uriel. *If Methuselah continues on like this, he is going to be one crotchety old geezer when I come back to guard his grandson. I guess some people just need a little more time than others to get it right. But hundreds of years?*

They bolted into the woods after the pit incident. They knew the other wolves would be there in no time at all.

They ran to their next location and waited for the wolves to follow. Their scent was an easy draw. This would be more difficult. Their pursuers would be wise to them and more cautious in their approach. On the other hand, they were sure Cain did not know they had an archangel with them. They would use that to their advantage.

• • • • •

As Cain stalked his prey, he knew that they were not alone. Only one thing could have pulled off the kind of blinding that occurred to his clan earlier in the day: they must have an angel with them.

The wolves tread softly through the jungle. They smelled their prey and knew they were near. Like silent ghosts, they glided through the forest, eyes ablaze like glowing coals, figures dark as the night. They came upon the four hiding in the bush, waiting for an attack. Their backs were to the wolves that had crept up behind them. Fifteen of the monsters leapt on their quarry, fangs blazing.

But the quarry was not their quarry. They were rocks dressed with the clothes of the quarry. The humans had dressed themselves in leaves and hid in the trees They rained down arrows and javelins, taking out a dozen wolves in mere moments.

They swung down on vines to the ground and slashed, stabbed, and sliced their way through the wolverine forces on their way to the rock wall. The rest of the pack raced after them with snarls and howls.

CHAPTER 55

Yahweh Elohim and his divine council surrounding the heavenly throne were about to be blasted by the Accuser's final complaint. He took a confident breath and embarked on his concluding strategy: blame shifting.

The Accuser said, "If I am to stomach this dodgy ad hoc definition of 'death' as eventual mortality, and the excessive punishment of death and exile for the primal pair in the Garden, that is one thing. But to then shift that blame onto the rest of the human race, that is the most unfair, unjust, unwarranted, unreasonable, unjustifiable attribution of guilt anyone has ever seen in the history of the heavens and earth."

Enoch thought the Accuser's rhetoric reached its shrill climax of excess in this catalogue of allegations and complaints.

The Accuser continued, "What kind of a just god blames innocent people for the guilt of others? What kind of a loving god punishes the *entire rest of the human race* for what two moronic idiots did in the Garden?"

He stood there with dramatic pause.

There it was again, thought Enoch. The endless refrain against a 'loving god.' But now the Accuser was adding a new slogan for a bit of variety with 'what kind of a just god' etcetera, etcetera.

The Accuser concluded, "The prosecution rests its case." He sat down by the other Watchers.

The Son of Man leaned close, giving more counsel to Enoch. It amounted to revealing the mystery of good news that would be hidden for ages until the end of days. This secret held the answer to the Accuser's charge.

Enoch then realized that the Accuser's final trick was more than rhetoric, he was trying to force Yahweh Elohim's hand to reveal the mystery.

So that is what this was all about, he thought. The Watchers and all their principalities and powers in the heavenly places were trying to use a legal maneuver to draw out Yahweh Elohim's secret in order to defend himself. If this secret were unveiled, they hoped to have the means by which they could defeat the Seed of Eve. This Accuser is cunning indeed.

Enoch stood at the bar. He knew this would require the utmost of his highest apkallu skills. How to answer the Accuser's charge without revealing the mystery of ages before its time.

He spoke with a measured tempo, "Sin came into the world through one man. Death came through sin. So death spread to all men because all sinned. Death reigns from Adam unto this very day, even over those whose sinning was not like the transgression of Adam, because Adam is the federal representative head of the human race. Just as all the inhabitants of the city of Erech would suffer for the illegal actions of its representative head of state," Enoch stared accusingly at Semjaza, "or benefit from the righteousness of that federal head. So the blessings and curses of the progenitor of the human race would be attributed to those whom he represents. It is the nature of authority and representation used even by those who seek to discredit it in this courtroom. If the Accuser does not like that, then he will have to file another injunction against all the blessings received by the human race as well. The defense rests its case."

Enoch sat back down to await the summary judgment before the throne of the Almighty Judge of the universe.

• • • • •

The lake glistened blood red in the full moon. Inanna flew angrily over the chaos and turmoil of the mass slaughter, She had to do something. She saw Rahab come up and chomp a mouthful of soldiers. She unsheathed her sword and dove from the bird down to the beast.

She landed on the back of the huge dragon with a thud. Before Rahab knew what had happened, Inanna raised her blade high, finding her mark between a couple of scales that had been torn in the battle. She plunged it deep into soft flesh, down to the hilt.

Rahab roared and the mountainside trembled. Fire belched out of her mouth, scorching the rest of the Nephilim on the water to a charred crisp. In a few seconds, a thousand of them were flaming flesh.

Rahab dove. Inanna held on. The dragon went deep. The Watcher on her back could not be drowned so easily. Although Watchers became weakened in water, all Inanna had to do was hold onto the sword. That did not require fighting strength. She rode an unbreakable sea bronco. This was the most dangerous risk Inanna had taken in her existence as a Watcher. If she held on too long, it would not end well for her. Rahab would inevitably bury her in the depths under rock, where Inanna would be imprisoned until the judgment. She just had to wait for her opportunity to let go.

Rahab turned and swam back to the surface. She broke the water and snapped her curved back in an arching leap.

Inanna yanked the sword out. She went flying a hundred cubits, landing in the middle of her decimated, water-soaked Nephilim horde on the shore.

She rolled to her feet. All about her she saw that two thousand out of the horde had made it across the water. They were on the frontier of Eden. A mere two thousand combatants for the invasion of an impregnable fortress. Five out of six Nephilim had perished at the mercy of Rahab and her brood of Leviathan and the tentacled one. The devastation was inestimable. It could lose her the war.

Still, she had two thousand warriors with her. They were on the shores of the entrance to the Garden that hid the Tree of Life deep in its midst. Thanks to the Cursed One, she knew exactly where that tree was.

She looked for her Rephaim generals but could not find them. They had all been lost to the denizens of the deep.

An earthquake rocked the land. It was deep, the precursor of something much bigger.

"Now what?" Inanna complained. She looked onto the horizon of her destination. Black smoke billowing out of the mountaintops of not only Mount Sahand, but the more distant northern Mount Savalan. The earth rumbled again. She realized she did not have much time.

She signaled for her Anzu bird, and called out to Utu, flying above them at a safe height.

"SOUND THE CRY OF WAR!" she bellowed.

Utu put the trumpet to his lips and blew with all his might. The war cry of Inanna echoed throughout the land.

Her Nephilim gathered their arms and dashed toward the heart of Eden.

Inanna mounted her thunderbird. She glanced out at the Lake. Rahab glided on the surface, its eyes watching her. It would not forget this day, nor the Watcher, who for one moment bested the sea dragon of the Abyss.

· · · · ·

At the top of the Mount Sahand ridge, six thousand Nephilim prepared their sail-chutes. They waited for the call of war. When it came, they jumped off the cliff edge by the dozens. They opened up their sails to float down into the Garden. Handfuls of them failed and Nephilim plummeted to their deaths a thousand feet below. But most of them worked. The Nephilim drifted from the heavens into the pristine paradise.

Right into the flaming whirling swords of the Cherubim.

· · · · ·

The humans and Uriel ran through the foliage, the pack of canines on their heels. Suddenly, ahead of them, they saw the other half of the wolves blocking their path by the brook. They were being hemmed in. They took a hard right.

Within moments they were up against a rock wall, the end of the valley. Hundreds of feet of mountain rock rose above them, at their backs. Ninety ravenous wolves surrounding their front. They had nowhere to go.

They faced the valley again and saw ninety pair of glowing orbs slouching closer toward them. They backed up against the rock. A rocky overhang with vines dangling down loomed over their heads. There was no way they could climb.

Instead, they pulled on the vines.

The vines were attached to wedges that held back a huge pile of boulders ready to fall. Those huge boulders came down upon the wolves in an avalanche of stone.

The humans had not been backed in. They had led the wolves to this prepared trap. They were protected by the large overhang as a hundred tons of rock rolled down on the heads of the wolves, killing a dozen and wounding a dozen others.

When the dust settled, Methuselah and his team leapt forward with weapons alive. Javelins, arrows, blade, and slashing whip sword.

The wolves focused all their forces on the angel.

As he fought, Methuselah wondered, Why Uriel? He could not die. Is not Lamech their prize?

They rushed the angel in a wave of claw and tooth. Uriel's sword slashed and cut through fur and muscle alike. He was a powerhouse, but the wolves were legion. Seventy of them piled onto Uriel and overwhelmed him with their weight. They growled and bit.

He was overcome. He might be an angel, but these large werewolves were no human warriors either. They were hounds of hell.

Lamech snapped Rahab and cut off heads and legs. The wolves could not get near to him. His flexible sword swung like a wild serpent. They did not really menace Lamech. They stayed on Uriel.

Methuselah yelled a mighty war cry. He single-handedly threw a dozen wolves off of Uriel's prone figure. Betenos picked off others of the enemy one by one from a position on a ledge.

The way of the Karabu awoke in Methuselah, and he began to move like a river of doom, dodging and dancing with fighting that balanced the equation.

Uriel finally got to his feet, and began again to cut down wolves like a machine. He and Methuselah were a two-man killing force. They took out fifty of the monsters in a bloody wave of fur, javelin, and blade.

While everyone focused on the angel, Lamech fought wide open.

The Cursed One had stealthily moved toward his only interest: Lamech. His pack had cut off the guardian angel from the guarded, as he had planned.

Cain leapt. He took Lamech to the ground. Rahab flew out of Lamech's grip. Cain's preternatural strength overcame him. Lamech blacked out.

Cain glanced up, to check the progress of the fighting. He saw Betenos turn. Their eyes met, and he grinned. She let loose a superhuman volley of three arrows. They seemed to simultaneously hit Cain before he could move. They buried themselves deep into his heart. She would kill anyone or anything that tried to take her beloved.

But Cain was not alive to kill.

He was undead, and the arrows had no effect on him. He snapped them off, picked up Lamech and dissolved into the forest.

Betenos bounded after Cain. But she was suddenly knocked off her feet. She fell to the ground in a tumble with the black she-wolf.

They rolled to a stop with the she-wolf on top of Betenos, burning rage in her eyes. She bared her fangs.

She was about to rip out Betenos' throat, when her own throat was cut by a javelin thrown by Methuselah. It missed the jugular, tearing some of beast's flesh as it passed by it. The she-wolf yelped and bounded off into the darkness after Cain.

Methuselah's aim had missed because his muscles were fatigued. They had just killed an overwhelming number of foes. He and Uriel stood thigh high in the bodies of their enemies. Methuselah collapsed. Uriel suffered a multitude of bite and claw wounds.

Uriel lay down on the ground, looking up at the moon. He called out for Lamech, but heard no response. He called again. "Lamech, are you all right?"

Uriel and Methuselah sat up, concerned. They saw Betenos running into the forest. They instantly knew what had happened.

There was no time to tend their wounds. They leapt to their feet and ran after her.

CHAPTER 56

The throne room was silent. Yahweh Elohim conferred with his heavenly host. The Accuser, Semjaza, and the rest of the Watchers stood to their side. Enoch and the archangels, minus Uriel, stood to the other side before the throne of the Almighty.

The Ancient of Days took his seat. His throne blazed with fiery flames, the Cherubim wheels burned fire. A stream of fire came out from before him. Ten thousand times ten thousand stood before him. The court sat in judgment and the books were opened.

The temple filled with smoke and the Seraphim proclaimed again the trisagion in their voice that sounded as many waters, "Holy, holy, holy, is Yahweh Elohim Almighty. Who was and is and is to come."

Yahweh Elohim spoke and the foundations of the thresholds shook at his voice. "Accuser, you have presented your case before the court this day and I have allowed it in accord with justice. I have appointed my chosen prophet Enoch to speak on my behalf. And now, I have appointed the Son of Man to pronounce my summary judgment on this case."

The Son of Man came down from the right hand of Yahweh Elohim. He spoke with the soul of a man and with the heart of God.

"The Accuser has entered this heavenly courtroom in an attempt to place God in the dock. But God is not in the dock, the Accuser is. He has listed five complaints and made a multitude of legal and moral accusations against Yahweh Elohim, including: partiality, bias, prejudice, jealousy, selfishness, imperialism, sexism, tyranny, speciesism, misogyny, monomania, and lying. He has sought to impugn the sovereignty of Yahweh Elohim. If the suzerain as foundation of the entire covenant is unjust, then the covenant is without authority over humankind and is therefore null and void. On this the Accuser stands firm. In fact, on this, we all stand firm. That is to say, without Yahweh Elohim, none of us can stand on anything at all. All of the Accuser's indictments, every single one of them, from tyranny to imperialism to cruelty assume a moral universe with moral absolutes established by a moral lawgiver, Yahweh Elohim.

"Without Yahweh Elohim, all claims to evil, all the Accuser's moral indignation and outrage, all his ethical pronouncements are mere subjective sentiment without any legal weight or value whatsoever. If Yahweh Elohim is not the origin of morality, there can be no moral condemnation of anything, only personal preferences. One man's genocide is another man's ethnic cleansing. All is permitted, nothing is forbidden. This Accuser is, in fact, *assuming* Yahweh's moral character as he is condemning it. But if all was permitted, then the Accuser would have no basis for his lawsuit.

"Secondly, every appeal to evidence and reason the Accuser has made presupposes a uniformity of nature upheld by the sovereign right hand of Yahweh Elohim. Without this sovereign control, how would the Accuser know that morality or nature should or will be consistent? How would he know if contradictions are not in fact legitimate truth in a distant corner of the heavens and earth where he has never been? What is the basis for law in a lawless universe? The only way he can in fact appeal to rationality is to assume a rational universe upheld by a rational Yahweh Elohim. Otherwise everything we say is mere subjective arbitrary chance and all our belief in reason is a delusionary habit.

"The Accuser does not like the way his Creator acts in this world, but he must assume his Creator's sovereign control in every appeal to evidence, reason, and morality that he makes, even when he attacks Yahweh himself for being inconsistent. It is like a little child sitting on its father's lap in order to slap him. Once again, the Accuser must *assume* Yawheh's sovereignty even as he is denying it, because without this assumption his 'rational' thoughts are mere illusion. The fear of the Lord is the beginning of knowledge and wisdom.

"Yahweh Elohim is the only valid foundation that provides the necessary preconditions for the intelligibility of a rational and moral universe that all of us inescapably assume in everything we think, say and do. By coming to this trial and making his complaints, the Accuser is affirming that Yahweh Elohim is the standard of justice and truth, a standard the Accuser does not like, but which is nevertheless unassailable. This lawsuit is self-contradictory, frivolous, and without foundation and is summarily dismissed."

The Seraphim pronounced, "Holy, holy, holy, is Yahweh Elohim. The whole earth is full of his glory." The ten million holy ones lit up with praise and honor to the Judge of all the universe.

The Son of Man leaned over and whispered into the Accuser's ear, "You just wasted your best military leaders in a frivolous lawsuit, when they could have been in Eden winning your war. Your plans are going up in smoke."

Semjaza heard it, too. Both of their faces went flush with shock. They had sought to distract Elohim's forces with a heavenly lawsuit, but in fact, the lawsuit had kept their best warriors, the Watchers, from leading their forces to victory. It was now too late to turn the tide.

Court was adjourned. The strategy had backfired.

• • • • •

Mount Sahand and Mount Savalan rumbled with a mighty fury of black smoke and gases over the Garden. A cloud of ash filled the night sky, darkening the moon and stars. It was if the very earth was reacting against the Nephilim forces invading the sacred Garden. Two thousand warriors streamed in from the shores of Lake Urimiya and another several thousand sail-chuted down from the heights of the Sahand ridge.

The Garden had been breached.

The forces of evil were closing in.

But the armies of God had not been sleeping. The Cherubim had seen what was coming. They had gathered their forces en masse to meet this two-pronged assault.

The Cherubim of the Garden were several hundred strong and they fought with the technique they taught to the Karabu. They were frightening guardians of the holy. Sphinx-like with bodies of lions, human heads and eagle's wings, they stood upright in battle. Their hair was indestructible and was used to bind fallen angels. Each Cherub was accompanied by a "Flame of the whirling sword." The Flame was terrifying, for it was a divine being of the heavenly host that accompanied the Cherubim and wielded a weapon of flashing lightning. The combination was like a sentinel with a personal sentinel.

The Cherubim set a semi-circular battle formation to meet the two forces attacking from the west and the south. Not far behind the heavenly ranks was the target they protected: the Tree of Life. Not far before them surged the demonic horde of warring giants.

The sound of the clashing forces rent heaven and earth as the Nephilim met their adversaries with weapons forged in the occultic furnaces of the Watchers.

Above the battle, the volcanoes exploded with a mighty force. The reverberations leveled the battlefield. For one moment, all fighting stopped. Everyone looked up at the mountain summits. The peaks blew sky-high, bursting forth with rivers of flowing magma. They were not single peaks with portals to Sheol. The entire group of mountain ranges were a series of peaks that were now releasing that same magma, threatening to envelop the entire Garden in a wave of red hot molten lava.

Huge boulders of burning rock from the explosion rained down on both Nephilim and Cherubim. The forces continued fighting. Flashes of lightning from the Flames met with the demonic swords, maces, battle axes, and javelins of the Nephilim. Heavenly chimera faced off with hellish hybrid as heaven and earth came crashing down around them.

Inanna cursed. Elohim was making the earth vomit slag in order to bury the Garden under molten debris and destroy the Tree of Life. That juvenile deity decided that if he could not have his Tree and Garden to himself, then no one could and he would destroy it all and go home.

The Watchers knew the war was already over. They did not stick around to be part of the casualties. Inanna, Utu, and Enki abandoned their command and flew their Anzu birds into the West, back to Mount Hermon.

· · · · ·

Methuselah, Uriel, and Betenos heard another great sound of thunder from the north. The earth trembled. They turned and saw the moon and stars darkened. The sky rolled up like a scroll. They knew their heavens and earth would never be the same. But they had a son, a husband, a ward to save.

By the time they arrived at the village, Cain already had Lamech bound and lying on the stone altar next to a blazing fire.

This was all too familiar to Methuselah. He remembered Lilith and her demons, who almost sacrificed Edna in just this way. It was the way of the gods, blood sacrifice. But in this case, the god who would be drinking the blood was Cain and the victim would be Methuselah's son, the bloodline of the Chosen seed of Eve.

Cain's raven she-wolf, the transmuted Awan, stood watch for him with bared teeth and snarling growl. Cain's advantage was also his disadvantage. He held the future of Elohim's chosen Seed at fangpoint. In one bite, he could achieve the revenge he had spent his whole life seeking. On the other hand, as soon as he did, he would be vanquished and bound by these putrid sacks of flesh and their heavenly toilet slave. Cain would end up in Tartarus and who would be the winner? The problem was that Cain did not want to die. He wanted to live forever, even if just to spite his Creator, the one who cursed him.

He grasped the sacrificial dagger tightly, holding it against Lamech's neck. The edge drew a bead of blood. It excited his thirst. It became difficult to think straight.

Methuselah, Uriel, and Betenos stepped closer. Lamech's bonds were tied tight. He could not fight back.

"I know what you want, Cain," said Methuselah. "I have felt the pangs of revenge. But you cannot win."

"The Titanomachy has failed," said Cain. He looked at the heavens, darkened by volcanic ash. He could feel the failure in his restless soul.

Uriel spoke up, "The war on Eden was never your concern."

"No," said Cain. "It was only a helpful diversion. With all of Elohim's heavenly host tied up in court, and all his martial forces defending the Garden, I knew his depleted resources would increase my chances to strike down his Chosen Seed. And here we are."

He smirked. "Though I did not realize he would care so little as to send an incompetent guardian angel, an old man, and a woman to protect him."

Uriel laughed. "Do you really think Elohim has not foreseen that this would happen? That he does not plan ahead? That he does not ordain the future? Go ahead and kill Lamech. It will not stop the bloodline of the Chosen Seed."

Cain was taken aback with surprise.

Lamech and everyone else also looked at Uriel with surprise. What in the world was he talking about?

Uriel continued, "Lamech's seed is already in Betenos. What do you think they were doing in the valley before you caught them? Twiddling sticks?"

Betenos and Lamech looked embarrassed. Betenos backed up a step a little behind Uriel, touching her belly softly.

Cain tried to process what he had heard. Did he have the wrong hostage? Was it a bluff?

"I do not believe you," said Cain. "I think you are lying to cover for your failure to protect the Seed."

"On the contrary, protecting the Seed is exactly what I have been doing," said Uriel. "By stalling you. Not with a sword, but with words."

Cain's mind raced, trying to figure out what game Uriel was playing.

Uriel pointed behind Cain.

A cloud of ash cleared away to show the morning sun cresting the mountain range of the Hidden Valley.

Cain's eyes went wide. The sun's rays burst through the village and spilled over Cain. He screamed in pain and dropped the knife he held to Lamech's throat.

The she-wolf started whimpering at the sight. Cain's entire skin bubbled and smoked. He was burning alive from within.

The light rays were like a flaming blanket on his body, penetrating his very core. He gave a last guttural scream that filled the entire valley like the sound of Behemoth.

He fell out of sight behind the altar. The She-wolf howled with sympathetic pain and went to the body trying to lick its wounds. But it was futile.

By the time the three reached the altar to free Lamech, the She-wolf had already transformed back into the human body of Awan. She wept bitterly, holding onto the corpse of her beloved Cain, now a distorted grotesque figure of hardened ash and bone.

Awan glared up at the group of four. She snatched up the sacrificial dagger and pointed it at them.

The four of them stepped back, ready to fight.

Awan would not fight anymore. She used the blade on herself and fell on top of her Cain, mixing her blood with his body of wrath.

Betenos embraced Lamech for all her worth. Methuselah fell to his knees. Uriel looked up to heaven. They prayed to Elohim and gave thanks for his loving-kindness and strength.

All of a sudden, Betenos snapped a look at Uriel. "How did you know what we were doing in the forest? Were you peeping on us?"

Uriel laughed. "Do you really think Elohim and his angels do not see what you are doing?"

Lamech and Betenos looked at each other shocked. They never really thought about it that way.

Uriel calmed their fears. "I was not 'watching' you. I was watching over you. I do have some decency to turn my head, you know."

Lamech and Betenos smiled.

Methuselah piped up. "How did you know she was pregnant with the Chosen Seed?"

"It is not the Chosen Seed," said Uriel. "Not yet."

"You lied?" said Methuselah, indignant.

Uriel sighed, "If you were listening, you would have noticed I did not say she was pregnant with Lamech's 'Chosen Seed,' I said pregnant with 'Lamech's seed.' *That* was not a lie."

"That is being picky," said Methuselah.

"That is being tactful," said Uriel. "Something you should consider more often, Methuselah."

Methuselah blushed. He knew he did not think enough before speaking.

Uriel added, "But if you must know, Elohim does allow lying in order to save lives, so I consider it quite an accomplishment having avoided an appeal to an exception, would you not say?"

Methuselah rolled his eyes. This angel was a bit full of himself. "Well, now that this Hidden Valley is cleaned up, I am going to miss it. It might make a great place to retire before I die."

Uriel glanced around. "Remember one thing: you could build a big boat in here and no one would ever know."

They had no idea what he was talking about.

But one day, Methuselah would remember.

CHAPTER 57

The aftermath of the war on Eden was devastating. Mounts Sahand and Savalan had rained down ash, fire and brimstone on the battling armies of Nephilim and Cherubim. Some of the Nephilim deserted when they saw the river of lava rolling toward them like a tsunami of molten fire. The Cherubim held their ground, only too happy to be encased in molten rock as perpetual sentinels surrounding their sacred custody, the charred ashes of the Tree of Life.

Everything else burned up under the wave of magma. The Garden was completely and utterly consumed forever, thus protected from the conquest of evil. The Watchers would now have to achieve their goals by other means.

• • • • •

Far away in the bowels of Mount Hermon, the Watchers planned their other means. But first there would be Sheol to pay for the absolutely disastrous miscarriage of their plans that had been Inanna's war on Eden. They had lost everything they had planned meticulously and worked for over generations. Inanna, the most aggressive and violent of the gods, was stripped of her garments and laid bare to the miserable punishment of approximately two hundred lashes, one from every god present.

Her back became a bloody pulp of scaly flesh. Watchers could not die, but they could experience pain and suffering. Though they healed with supernatural speed, they retained scars just like any other creature. These scars would be an eternal reminder of Inanna's utter humiliation at the hands of her compatriots in rebellion.

She screamed in agony as the lash fell down from the hands of Enlil, who had particular delight in her agony. He stole a second lash before being scolded by Anu for over zealousness.

Utu and Enki received half the punishment, as they were Inanna's inferiors in the campaign. She had ignored their strategic and tactical advice enough times to have jeopardized the outcome of the war.

When they had finished their punishment, Inanna, Utu, and Enki lay in their affliction as Anu called the council to order.

He said, "Gods of Mount Hermon, let this be a reminder to us. Inanna is one of the strongest and most loyal members of this assembly. Yet her failure has not only cost us the war, but has set us back for generations. We will never again have the opportunity to seize the Garden or the Tree of Life. They are gone forever. For her punishment, Inanna will forfeit her co-regency of the divine council and of the city of Nippur. She will become my personal consort in the city of Erech. Enlil will now be sole ruler in Nippur."

Whisperings blew across the assembly. They knew that was a pain far greater than her bleeding body for Inanna.

Enlil smirked. *Serves her right,* he thought, *stupid cow.*

"We will continue to breed our Nephilim, but they will be our security forces in our cities, not our standing armies. Any more concentration of Nephilim will only be thwarted no doubt by Elohim."

Then he dropped his special revelation on them, "I think it is time we pursue more diligently our Chimera Project. We have already achieved great successes with the mushussu and other creatures. I have been working on the creation of a new soldier. One that is a chimera of human and animal, not human and god as the Nephilim. This creature is more obedient and capable of communal conformity than a Naphil. I introduce the Bird-men and Dog-soldiers."

A platoon of ten hybrid soldiers stepped out from behind Anu's throne. They moved and walked as one. They were sinewy human bodies with the heads of predator birds and canines: falcons, hawks, jackals and wolves. They stood in perfect unison, then engaged in a brief military exercise that illustrated pinpoint precision and harmony in the platoon. They did not have the strength of Nephilim but they also did not have the individual wills of the Nephilim. They were a unified body. They were a fighting machine. They were the new army of the gods.

The assembly murmured with excitement. Anu concluded, "We have had the dubious distinction of being the recipients of the prophet Enoch's prophesy of judgment. We now know that the time is close, and that Elohim is sending a 'Chosen Seed' who will seek to 'bring an end to the reign of the gods.'"

Murmuring broke into panicked whisperings.

"SILENCE!" yelled Anu. The assembly quieted down.

He continued, "We do not know when, we do not know where, we only know soon. So the duty of every one of the gods in this assembly is to seek out, by any means necessary, this 'Chosen Seed' and bring him to me, because his is the bloodline of the seed of Eve that will war with the seed of the Serpent, our father. It is this Chosen Seed and his anointed bloodline that we must corrupt at all costs."

EPILOGUE

The city of Shuruppak stood on the Euphrates in the middle of Shinar, now called Sumer, closer to Erech than Nippur. In the seventy short years since it had been settled by Lamech and his clan, it had grown to be quite a commercial depot for shipping. After their experience in the Hidden Valley, Lamech, Betenos, and Methuselah had found a suitable location to build a new city with their kin who had survived the Sahand volcanic eruption.

As the city grew, it drew others from the plain of Shinar who did not share the convictions of the founders. Lamech was the first priest-king and he dedicated the city to Elohim. They based their legal and political system on the covenant of Elohim. They became a commercial trading center for grains, wood, cattle and livestock, shipped through their port in large commercial barges.

But the influence of foreign traders came quickly with commercial trade. The foreigners brought many gods of the pantheon into the culture of Shuruppak. The pantheon held tight their grip on the souls of men. A growing cult of Ninlil, the consort goddess of Enlil, took hold of the city. Many of her followers pressured the government for special status. They protested to Lamech, petitioning him to build a temple for Ninlil. When they were denied, they caused a riot that ended in Lamech giving in and allowing them their temple.

The ultimate authority of a culture is its god. The deity provides meaning, sustenance, cultic religion, and law codes. Because of the city's diversity, it seemed inevitable that it be drawn toward a diversity of deities. And those deities did not like a solo incomparable divinity like Elohim ruling over everything with dictatorial authority. They demanded equality. Thus the Sumerian pantheon came to overtake the city of Shuruppak, as it had with all the cities on the fertile plain. The pantheon spread like a disease.

Eventually, Lamech became dispirited with the developments of his city. It seemed that the only people who did not become slaves of the pantheon were the nomads. These free-spirited wanderers drifted through the territories free to worship as they pleased, without the interference of the cities and their pantheon bureaucracies. Some of the nomads worshipped even stranger gods than the Sumerian pantheon, but at least they were free to do so.

Lamech looked for the right moment to resign his priest-kingship, sell all his land and goods, and journey into the desert with his extended family. He wanted to live the life of a nomad and worship Elohim as he wished. Methuselah fully supported his desire. But that time had not yet come.

Lamech waited in a closed room with Methuselah. His father was now about three hundred and seventy years old. He was still young. Most of their ancestors had lived eight hundred to nine hundred years. Of course, Enoch was only on earth three hundred sixty five years, because he had been taken by God into heaven. The longest lived so far had been Jared, who lived to a ripe old nine hundred and sixty-two. Methuselah was competitive but thought there was no way anyone would beat that record.

A midwife came into the room all covered in blood. Lamech and Methuselah looked at her with fear.

"It is a baby boy," said the midwife.

"Is Betenos safe?" Lamech asked through tired, worried eyes. It had been a difficult pregnancy. Once, they thought she would miscarry.

"Your wife is fine," said the midwife.

Methuselah grabbed Lamech and hugged him tightly. He still felt the sting of loss of his Edna. He wished she could be here to celebrate. Nothing seemed real to him unless he could share it with her. But this was real.

The midwife said, "Come see her and your son."

They followed her into the delivery room being cleaned by a couple other midwives. Being priest-king provided some rather nice privileges such as the best of midwives and medicine that the city could provide.

When Lamech and Methuselah entered, they saw Betenos holding his new son. She was not smiling. She looked concerned. She looked up at Lamech and said, "My love, I think there is something wrong with him."

Lamech's spirit sank. Was he sick? Missing an arm or leg? What could it be?

He ran to the bed and she held out the boy to him. He saw what she had meant. The little tyke had white hair on his head and his skin was shiny all over.

"What is wrong with him, Lamech?" said Betenos. "What is wrong with our son?"

Lamech looked up. They all suddenly noticed that Uriel was in the room. Uriel the archangel, who had protected Lamech because his lineage bore the Seed.

He was smiling.

Methuselah's eyes went wide with excitement.

Uriel said, "The time is arrived."

Lamech prophesied over the child, "This is the Chosen Seed who Elohim promised would come to end the rule of the gods and bring rest to the land."

Betenos turned from frowning to tearful joy.

Methuselah raised his hands to heaven.

Lamech looked at Uriel and said, "His name shall be called Noah."

If you liked this book, then please help me out by writing an honest review of it on Amazon ([click here to write review](#)). That is one of the best ways to say thank you to me as an author. It really does help my exposure and status as an author. It's really easy. In the Customer Reviews section, there is a little box that says "Write a customer review." They guide you easily through the process. Thanks! — *Brian Godawa*

CHAPTER 60: APPENDIX

Retelling Biblical Stories and the Mythic Imagination in *Enoch Primordial*

In my novel, *Noah Primeval*, I retell the story of the Biblical Noah as a nomadic tribal warrior. He refuses to worship the divine council of gods in Mesopotamia and is subsequently hunted down by assassin giants, leading the chase through Sheol, and ending in a climactic battle involving Leviathan and other hybrid monsters. In my novel, *Enoch Primordial*, I creatively imagine the untold story of the Biblical Enoch as a bounty hunter, a holy monk with a mission to kill giants who travels through a fantastic world of chimeras, gods, monsters and men.

"What?" you may say. *That's* not in the Bible! That sounds more like the non-canonical book of Enoch or the fantasy world of *The Lord of the Rings* than *Holy* Scripture. Isn't that mythologizing the Bible?

It is hard enough to get some religious believers to appreciate the imagination of the fantasy genre. But when it comes to retelling a story from the Bible, don't even think of putting those two things together; Bible and fantasy. That borders on tampering with the Word of God worthy of the curse in Revelation 21 on those who "add or take away from the words of the book." Or at least that's what some well-meaning believers think.

I think this negative impulse comes from an essentially good intent; the desire to avoid denigrating their sacred stories or reducing them to the level of false pagan myths. But such good intent does not necessarily produce the good result of a well thought out Biblical understanding of story.[1]

What would surprise many of these concerned believers is the fact that the same ancient Hebrews who championed the Scriptures as their sacred text containing the very words of God, were also the holy ones who wrote those Scriptures utilizing pagan imagination and motifs. And they were also the

---

[1] The curse of Revelation 21, is not a reference to the entire Bible, but the prophecy of the particular book of Revelation. The context is not about taking away individual words but about taking away or adding to the *content* of the prophecy. If it were words, then we are all condemned because we do not have the original words, but only English translations based on many different copied manuscripts with lots of different textual variations. In other words our English translation of Revelation contains added words and taken away words.

same devout ancient believers who wrote many other non-canonical texts that retold Biblical stories with fantastic embellishments worthy of mythopoeic mastery.

Retelling Bible Stories and Non-Bible Stories

The ancient Jews loved to retell their Bible stories with embellishments in literature we now call apocrypha and pseudepigrapha. And they did so, not with a disdain for "the facts of history," but rather with deep respect for the original theological *meaning* as they understood it. As scholar George Nickelsburg explains, they wanted to "expound sacred tradition so that it speaks to contemporary times and issues."[2] Biblical scholar Peter Enns adds, "It is a characteristic of ancient retellings of Scripture that the exegetical traditions incorporated in to these retellings are not clearly (if at all) marked off from the Biblical texts. The line between text and comment was often blurred, so much so that the two often went hand in hand."[3]

Thanks to manuscript discoveries in recent centuries, we now have access to many of these Jewish retellings of Bible narratives, some of which include Jubilees, The Genesis Apocryphon, The Testament of Moses, The Testaments of the Twelve Patriarchs, and the Books of Adam and Eve and others. In these non-canonical texts we are retold, with creative embellishments, various episodes in Biblical history, from Adam and Eve, to Noah, through Abraham, Isaac, and Jacob, to Moses and more. I have used some of these Second Temple texts and other Jewish legends to embellish the Biblical narrative in *The Chronicles of the Nephilim*.

Not only do non-canonical Second Temple texts retell Bible stories, but the Bible itself uses some of these non-Biblical manuscripts as source texts for holy writ.

The orthodox doctrine of the Inspiration of Scripture is "God-breathed" human-written words (2Tim. 3:16). Human men wrote from God, moved by the Holy Spirit (2Pet. 1:20-21). The Bible was not dictated directly by God to the authors, nor was it written by God's direct "hand" (except for the tablets on Sinai), nor does it claim to be an automatic writing scenario where God

---

[2] George W. E. Nickelsburg and Klaus Baltzer, *1 Enoch : A Commentary on the Book of 1 Enoch*, (Minneapolis, Minn.: Fortress, 2001) 29.
[3] Peter Enns, *Exodus Retold: Ancient Exegesis of the Departure from Egypt in Wisdom 15-21 and 19:1-9*, (Atlanta, GA: Scholars Press, 1997), 35.

uses the hands of writers as puppets to do his bidding. Scripture itself attests to human authors compiling, editing, and drawing from other source texts to achieve their authoritative canon, all under the *providential oversight* of God.

There are well over fifty references in the Scriptures to just over twenty non-canonical source texts used by Biblical authors that are lost to history. Some of them are *The Book of the Wars of Yahweh* (Num. 21:14), *The Book of Jasher* (Josh. 10:12-13; 2Sam. 1:19-27), *The Acts of Solomon* (1Kings 11:41), *Acts of Gad the Seer* (1Chron. 29:29), *Acts of Nathan the Prophet* (2Chron 9:29), *Prophesy of Ahijah the Shilonite* (2Chron. 9:29), *Visions of Iddo the Seer* (2Chron. 9:29), *Acts of Jehu Son of Hanani* (2Chron. 20:34), *Acts of the Seers* (2Chron. 33:19) and others.[4]

One of these source texts quoted by Joshua and Samuel, *the Book of Jasher (or Jashar)*, is believed by some to be extant in a medieval copy of a Hebrew manuscript[5] (which I incidentally used as a source for *Enoch Primordial* and *Noah Primeval*).

The New Testament continues this tradition of non-canonical sources in Scripture. In 2Tim. 3:8 Paul refers to "Jannes and Jambres" who opposed Moses, a reference to Pharaoh's magicians in Exodus 7-9 attempting to reproduce God's miracles and plagues. But there is no mention of the names Jannes and Jambres in the entire Old Testament. So how did Paul know the names of the two magicians? The ancient church fathers, Origen[6] and Ambrose claimed these names were drawn by Paul from the Jewish pseudepigraphal work entitled *Jannes and Jambres* that describes the Exodus episode from the perspective of these two magicians, one repentant, the other unrepentant.[7] There is also a long Jewish tradition recorded in the *Targum Jonathan* of these two names.[8]

The New Testament book of Jude tells us of Michael the Archangel disputing with the devil over the body of Moses (Jude 9), an incident that is

---

[4] For a closer examination of these non-canonical source text references, see Duane Christensen, (1998), "Lost Books of the Bible," *Bible Review*, 14[5]:24-31, October.
[5] Ken Johnson, ThD., *Ancient Book of Jasher: A New Annotated Edition*, (Lexington, KY: BibleFacts Ministry, 2008), p 4.
[6] Origen, *Commentary* on Matthew 27:8. *The International Standard Bible Encyclopedia, Revised*. Edited by Geoffrey W. Bromiley. Wm. B. Eerdmans, 1988, 966.
[7] James H. Charlesworth, ed., *The Old Testament Pseudepigrapha: Vol. 2* (New York, NY.: Doubleday, 1983), pp. 427-442.
[8] "Jewish tradition makes them sons of Balaam. *Targum of Jonathan* on Num. xxii. 22), and places their rise at the time the Pharaoh gave command to kill the first-born of Israel (Sanhedrin, f. 106a; *Sotah* 11a), and supposes them to have been teachers of Moses, the makers of the golden calf (*Midrash Tanhuma*, f. 115b)." "Jannes and Jambres," Philip Schaff, *The New Schaff-Herzog Encyclopedia of Religious Knowledge*, Vol. VI, p. 95, accessed from Christian Classics Ethereal Library online, February 4, 2008, at < http://www.ccel.org/ccel/schaff/encyc06/Page 95.html>.

spoken of nowhere else in Scripture, but appears, according to some ancient Church fathers, in a lost Jewish book called *The Assumption of Moses*.⁹

Scholar Pete Enns explains that the Apostle Paul assumes a non-Biblical tradition when writing about the Hebrew wilderness sojourn.

> 1 Corinthians 10:3–5
> and all ate the same spiritual food, and all drank the same spiritual drink. For they drank from the spiritual Rock that followed them, and the Rock was Christ.

In context, Paul makes an object lesson for the New Covenant community by way of analogy with the Old Covenant experience. There's only one problem, the "movable rock" (or "well" as a possible interpretation) is not in the Old Testament.

Enns exegetes the origin of this moveable well as deriving from an "extra-Biblical tradition found in a variety of Jewish sources dating roughly from the New Testament era to medieval rabbinic compilations" (namely, *Pseudo-Philo, Tosephta Sukka* and *Targum Onqelos*, among others).¹⁰

Hebrews 2:2 claims that the Law on Sinai was "spoken through angels" to Moses, another reference to the intimate involvement of the divine council of sons of God *that is not revealed in the Old Testament as we have it.*

In 2Pet. 2:5, Noah is called a "Preacher of righteousness," a description found only outside the Old Testament (*Sibylline Oracles* 1.125-31).

The Fascinating Case of the Book of Enoch

One of the most fascinating cases of Biblical appropriation of non-canonical texts is the New Testament references to the book of *1 Enoch*. Written sometime around the third to second century B.C., this text has both haunted and been cherished by the Christian Church through its history. It is apocalyptic in genre; cloaking warnings of judgment in dream visions, parables, and complex allegorical imagery. But it is most well-known for its detailed elaboration of the Genesis 6 story about the Sons of God (called "Watchers") and their intimate involvement in the cause of the Noachian Flood. There it describes in much detail the Watchers as fallen angels revealing occultic secrets to mankind, having

---

⁹ Richard J. Bauckham, *Word Biblical Commentary Vol. 50, 2 Peter, Jude* (Waco, TX., Word, 1983), pp. 73-74.
¹⁰ Peter E. Enns, "The 'Moveable Well'" in 1 Cor 10:4: An Extrabiblical Tradition in an Apostolic Text," *Bulletin for Biblical Research* (1996) 23-38 [© 1996 Institute for Biblical Research] 6.

intercourse with human women, and birthing giants who cause terror across the land.[11] Here is just a sample of passages that tell that story in much more vivid detail than Genesis 6:

> Enoch 6:1-2
> In those days, when the children of man had multiplied, it happened that there were born unto them handsome and beautiful daughters. And the angels, the children of heaven, [the Watchers] saw them and desired them; and they said to one another, "Come, let us choose wives for ourselves from among the daughters of man and beget us children."

> Enoch 7:1-8:3, 19:1
> And they took wives unto themselves, and everyone respectively chose one woman for himself, and they began to go unto them... And the women became pregnant and gave birth to great giants.

> These giants consumed the produce of all the people until the people detested feeding them. So the giants turned against the people in order to eat them. And they began to sin against birds, wild beasts, reptiles, and fish. And their flesh was devoured the one by the other, and they drank blood. And then the earth brought an accusation against the oppressors.

> And Azaz'el [the Watcher] taught the people the art of making swords and knives, and shields, and breastplates... and alchemy...[or *transmutation*: Ancient Ethiopian commentators explain this phrase as "changing a man into a horse or mule or vice versa, or transferring an embryo from one womb to another."] Amasras taught incantation and the cutting of roots; and Armaros the resolving of incantations; and Baraqiyal astrology, and Kokarer'el the knowledge of the signs, and Tam'el taught the seeing of the stars...The angels

---

[11] 1 Enoch chapters 1-36 is called the "Book of the Watchers" and deals with this material. The book of *Jubilees* is another respected text that contains a detailed retelling of the Noah story with Watchers cohabiting with women, and birthing giants. See Jubilees 4-10 and 20:4-5.

which have united themselves with women. They have defiled the people and will lead them into error so that they will offer sacrifices to the demons as unto gods.

Enoch 10:4, 11-12; 54:6
the Lord said to Raphael, "Bind Azaz'el hand and foot and throw him into the darkness!" And he made a hole in the desert which was in Duda'el and cast him there…And to Michael [the archangel] God said, "Make known to Semyaza [the Watcher] and the others who are with him, who fornicated with the women, that they will die together with them in all their defilement…bind them for seventy generations underneath the rocks of the ground until the day of their judgment and of their consummation, until the eternal judgment is concluded… on account of their oppressive deeds which (they performed) as messengers of Accuser, leading astray those who dwell upon the earth." [12]

Just what contemporary situation is Enoch referring to in his apocalyptic prose of fallen Watchers, carnal giants, and coming judgment? Some scholars think its origin around the time of the Maccabean revolt in 167 B.C. makes it a prophetic denunciation of the religious corruption of the Jewish world by its Hellenistic occupiers.[13] This pagan occupation would soon be overthrown by the victorious exploits of Judas Maccabeus and his brothers, returning Judaism to its purity and inspiring the origins of the festival of Hanukkah.

So the author of 1 Enoch was engaging in a rich tradition of retelling a Biblical story of judgment on a corrupted and compromised world as a moral warning for those of his own time. It was also part of this tradition to attribute their manuscripts to such historical luminaries as Enoch himself, not as a lie but as a literary technique that reinforces the significance of the message. However, it is entirely possible that sections of 1 Enoch were copied from much older manuscripts.

Though 1 Enoch is not in the Western canon of Scriptures, it is in the Eastern Ethiopic canon, and was respected by Christian scholars and

---

[12] James H. Charlesworth, *The Old Testament Pseudepigrapha: Volume 1*, (New York; London: Yale University Press, 1983) 16-18, 38.
[13] Charlesworth, James H. *The Old Testament Pseudepigrapha: Volume 1*, New York; London: Yale University Press, 1983, 8.

authorities throughout the early church. It was never considered heretical by church authorities. But the real kicker is that the New Testament even refers favorably to the book of Enoch and its tradition of fallen angels cohabiting with humans which results in their punishment of binding (1Pet. 3:19-20; 2Pet. 2:4-10; Jude 6-14).

First, Jude quotes the book of 1 Enoch outright when he writes of false teachers corrupting the church:

> Jude 14-15
> It was also about these that Enoch, the seventh from Adam, prophesied, saying, "Behold, the Lord comes with ten thousands of his holy ones, to execute judgment on all and to convict all the ungodly of all their deeds of ungodliness that they have committed in such an ungodly way, and of all the harsh things that ungodly sinners have spoken against him."

Here is the text from the actual book of 1 Enoch that Jude is quoting:

> 1 Enoch 1:9
> "And behold! He cometh with ten thousands of His holy ones to execute judgement upon all, and to destroy all the ungodly: And to convict all flesh of all the works of their ungodliness which they have ungodly committed, and of all the hard things which ungodly sinners have spoken against Him."[14]

But not only does Jude explicitly quote a passage out of 1 Enoch regarding God coming with the judgment of his divine council of holy ones (Sons of God), but *all three texts* refer to the Enochian notion of the angelic Watchers' punishment for co-habiting with humans as a violation of the divine/human separation; another main theme of 1 Enoch.

> 1Pet. 3:18–20
> [Christ], being put to death in the flesh but made alive in the spirit, in which he went and proclaimed to <u>the spirits in</u>

---

[14] *Pseudepigrapha of the Old Testament*, ed. Robert Henry Charles, Enoch 1:9 (Bellingham, WA: Logos Research Systems, Inc., 2004) 14.

prison, because they formerly did not obey, when God's patience waited in the days of Noah.

Jude 6-7
And angels who did not keep their own domain, but abandoned their proper abode, He has kept in eternal bonds under darkness for the judgment of the great day, just as Sodom and Gomorrah and the cities around them, since they in the same way as these indulged in gross immorality and went after strange flesh, are exhibited as an example in undergoing the punishment of eternal fire.

2Pet. 2:4-10
For if God did not spare angels when they sinned, but cast them into hell [*Tartarus*] and committed them to pits of darkness, reserved for judgment; and did not spare the ancient world, but preserved Noah…and if He condemned the cities of Sodom and Gomorrah to destruction by reducing them to ashes, having made them an example to those who would live ungodly lives thereafter… then the Lord knows how to…keep the unrighteous under punishment for the day of judgment, and especially those who indulge the flesh in its corrupt desires and despise authority.

Just in case anyone would question this fantastical interpretation of the carnal sin of the angels, Peter and Jude quote a common doublet that linked the sexual violation of the angelic Watchers (and their giant progeny) with the sexual violation of the inhabitants of Sodom who sought sexual intercourse with angels. The common theme of both instances was the transgression of heavenly and earthly separation of flesh.

There's just one big problem: This doublet of the sin of Sodom and the sin of the Watchers in the days of Noah "made as an example" is not found anywhere in the Old Testament, but only in non-canonical ancient Jewish texts.[15]

---

[15] There is one other New Testament passage that links Sodom with the days of Noah: Luke 17:26-34. Here, Jesus is prophesying about his coming in judgment upon Jerusalem and the Temple. He says that his coming will be as "the days or Noah" and "the days of Lot." But rather than referring to the sin of the angels here, he refers to the deception of normalcy that would blind sinners to coming judgment. People were "eating and drinking and marrying and being given in marriage" as well as "buying and selling, planting and building" until judgment came and "destroyed them all." The reference then is to the nature of surprise judgment upon clueless sinners, not about the sin of angels and their giant progeny.

Here is the list of some of those extra-Biblical texts containing this doublet of connection, and we see clearly that the angelic sexual sin is usually connected to the judgment on giants as well:

Sirach 16:7-8
He forgave not the <u>giants of old</u>,
Who revolted in their might.
He spared not the place where Lot sojourned,
Who were arrogant in their pride.[16]

Testament of Naphtali 3:4-5
[D]iscern the Lord who made all things, so that you do not become <u>like Sodom</u>, which departed from the order of nature. <u>Likewise the Watchers departed from nature's order</u>; the Lord pronounced a curse on them <u>at the Flood</u>.[17]

3 Maccabees 2:4-5
Thou didst destroy those who aforetime did iniquity, <u>among whom were giants</u> trusting in their strength and boldness, <u>bringing upon them a boundless flood of water</u>. Thou didst <u>burn up with fire and brimstone the men of Sodom</u>, workers of arrogance, who had become known of all for their crimes, and <u>didst make them an example to those who should come after</u>.[18]

Jubilees 20:4-5
[L]et them not take to themselves wives from the daughters of Canaan; for the seed of Canaan will be rooted out of the land. And he told them of the <u>judgment of the giants</u>, and the <u>judgment of the Sodomites</u>, how they had been judged on account of their wickedness, and had <u>died on account of their

---

[16] *Apocrypha of the Old Testament, Volume 1,* ed. Robert Henry Charles, Sir 16:7–8. Bellingham, WA: Logos Research Systems, Inc., 2004, 372.
[17] Charlesworth, James H. *The Old Testament Pseudepigrapha: Volume 1.* New York; London: Yale University Press, 1983, 812.
[18] *Apocrypha of the Old Testament, Volume 1.* ed. Robert Henry Charles, 3 Mac 2:5. Bellingham, WA: Logos Research Systems, Inc., 2004, 164.

fornication, and uncleanness, and mutual corruption through fornication.[19]

2 Enoch 34:1
God convicts the persons who are idol worshipers and sodomite fornicators, and for this reason he brings down the flood upon them.[20]

The New Testament literary reference to non-canonical sources does not mean those sources are the inspired Word of God, nor that everything in them is true; but it certainly does illustrate that the Bible itself draws meaningfully and favorably from interpretive traditions that engage in imaginative embellishment of Biblical stories. Unlike some Christians, God *does appreciate* creative imagination.

Jude's references to the book of Enoch are not limited to material citations. He uses the same poetic phraseology throughout his letter that indicates an intimate interaction with the entirety of 1 Enoch on the incident of the Watchers and their condemnation. Researcher Douglas Van Dorn has put together a helpful chart of these linguistic comparisons.[21]

SOME OF JUDE'S ALLUSIONS TO 1 ENOCH			
JUDE		1 ENOCH	
Jude 6	"The angels that did not keep their own position but left their proper dwelling"	"[The angels] have abandoned the high heaven, the holy eternal place"	1 En 12:4
	"until the judgment of the great day"	"preserved for the day of suffering"	1 En 45:2 (1 En 10:6)
	"angels…kept in eternal chains under gloomy darkness"	"this is the prison of the angels, and here they will be imprisoned forever"	1 En 21:10 (1 En 10:4)
Jude 12	"waterless clouds"	"every cloud…rain shall be withheld"	1 En 100:11
	"raging waves"	"ships tossed to and fro by the waves"	1 En 101:2

---

[19] *Pseudepigrapha of the Old Testament Volume 1.* ed. Robert Henry Charles. Bellingham, WA: Logos Research Systems, Inc., 2004, 42.
[20] James H. Charlesworth, *The Old Testament Pseudepigrapha: Volume 1* (New York; London: Yale University Press, 1983) 158.
[21] Douglas Van Dorn, (2013-01-21). *Giants: Sons of the Gods* (K-ebook Location 4850). Waters of Creation, K-ebook Edition.

	"fruitless trees"	"fruit of the trees shall be withheld"	1 En 80:3
Jude 13	"wandering stars"	"stars that transgress the order"	1 En 80:6
	"the gloom of utter darkness has been reserved forever"	"darkness shall be their dwelling"	1 En 46:6
Jude 14	"Enoch the seventh from Adam"	"my grandfather [Enoch]… seventh from Adam"	1 En 60:8

1 Peter 3:18-20 speaks of Christ going down into Sheol to proclaim his triumph to the "spirits imprisoned" at the time of the flood. This act appears to be a typological replay of Enoch's own vision journey into Sheol to see the "prison house of the angels" who disobeyed at the flood (1 Enoch 21:9-10).

But the story does not yet end there. You will notice that the location of punishment and binding of the fallen angels that we have already seen in 2 Peter is *Tartarus* in the Greek.

> 2Pet. 2:4
> For if God did not spare angels when they sinned, but cast them into hell [*tartarus*] and committed them to pits of darkness, reserved for judgment.

What is important to realize is that the Greek word translated as "hell" in this English translation is not one of the usual New Testament Greek words for hell, *gehenna* or *hades*, but *tartarus*.

The Greek poet Hesiod, writing around 700 B.C., described this commonly known underworld called Tartarus as the pit of darkness and gloom where the Olympian Titan giants were banished following their war with Zeus.

> Hesiod, *Theogony* lines 720-739
> as far beneath the earth as heaven is above earth; for so far is it from earth to Tartarus…There by the counsel of Zeus who drives the clouds the Titan gods are hidden under misty gloom, in a dank place where are the ends of the huge earth. And they may not go out; for Poseidon fixed gates of bronze upon it, and a wall runs all round it on every side.[22]

---

[22] Hesiod, *The Homeric Hymns and Homerica With an English Translation by Hugh G. Evelyn-White. Theogony.* (Medford, MA: Cambridge, MA., Harvard University Press; London, William Heinemann Ltd., 1914).

Obviously, Peter does not affirm Greco-Roman polytheism by referring to Tartarus, but he is alluding to a Hellenistic myth that his readers, believer and unbeliever alike, would be very familiar with, subverting it with the Jewish traditional interpretation.

Extra-Biblical Second Temple Jewish legends connected this legend of gods and bound Titans in Tartarus to the bound angelic Watchers and punished giants of Genesis 6.

> Sibylline Oracles 1:97-104, 119
> enterprising <u>Watchers</u>, who received this appellation because they had a sleepless mind in their hearts and an <u>insatiable</u> personality. They were mighty, of great form, but nevertheless <u>they went under the dread house of Tartarus guarded by unbreakable bonds, to make retribution</u>, to <u>Gehenna</u> of terrible, raging, undying fire…draping them around with great <u>Tartarus, under the base of the earth</u>.[23]

Other well-known Second Temple literature reiterated this binding in the heart of the earth until judgment day:

> Jubilees 4:22; 5:10
> And he wrote everything, and bore witness to <u>the Watchers</u>, the ones who sinned with the daughters of men because they began to mingle themselves with the daughters of men so that they might be polluted…
> And subsequently they [the Watchers] were <u>bound in the depths of the earth forever, until the day of great judgment</u> in order for judgment to be executed upon all of those who corrupted their ways and their deeds before the LORD.[24]

This "binding" or imprisoning of supernatural beings in the earth is expressed in 2 Peter's "cast into pits of darkness reserved for judgment" (3:19), 1 Peter's "disobedient spirits in prison" (v. 6), and Jude's "eternal

---

[23] James H. Charlesworth, The Old Testament Pseudepigrapha: Volume 1 (New York; London: Yale University Press, 1983), 337.
[24] James H. Charlesworth, *The Old Testament Pseudepigrapha and the New Testament, Volume 2: Expansions of the "Old Testament" and Legends, Wisdom, and Philosophical Literature, Prayers, Psalms and Odes, Fragments of Lost Judeo-Hellenistic Works* (New Haven; London: Yale University Press, 1985), 62, 65.

bonds under darkness for the judgment of the great day" (2:4). But it is not altogether unheard of in the Old Testament.

> Isa. 24:21–23
> On that day the LORD will punish
> the host of heaven, in heaven,
> and the kings of the earth, on the earth.
> They will be gathered together
> as prisoners in a pit;
> they will be shut up in a prison,
> and after many days they will be punished.

Isaiah here is speaking of judgment upon Israel by the Babylonians around 600 B.C., but he evokes the same Enochian imagery of the angelic host of heaven (often linked to the astronomical heavenly bodies *and* earthly rulers) being overthrown and imprisoned in the earth until judgment day.

Robert Newman notes that the Qumran Hebrew of the Isaiah scroll of this passage refers to a past event as its reference point: "They *were* gathered together as prisoners in a pit" (past tense). [25] This past event could very well be the antediluvian binding of the fallen host of heaven (*bene ha Elohim*) as an analogy for the future captivity of Israel.

So what shall we make of all this wild exploration of Biblical stories, pagan myths, and Jewish legends? Does this mean that Biblical writers tried to integrate their theology with pagan mythology (syncretism)? Is the Bible just an unoriginal adaptation of other religious myths?

Subverted Pagan Imagination

Some Bible believers are fearful of the Bible's adaptation of mythopoetic imagery and seek to ignore it by literalizing everything in the Bible into their modern understanding. They point to New Testament commands of Paul to "have nothing to do with irreverent silly myths" (1Tim. 4:7), to avoid devotion "to myths and endless genealogies, which promote speculations" (1Tim. 1:4), "Jewish myths and the commands of people who turn away from the truth" (Titus 1:14). They even think that it is a sign of the end times that some

---

[25] Robert C. Newman, "The Ancient Exegesis of Genesis 6:2, 4," *Grace Theological Journal* 5,1 (1984) 13-36.

teachers "will turn away from listening to the truth and wander off into myths" (1Tim. 4:4).

But are these texts denigrating the literary genres of myth and speculative fantasy that employ the imagination in understanding God? A closer look at their context reveals that not all mythology is created equal.

In 1 Timothy and Titus, Paul is not comparing doctrinal teaching with mythical genre, he is comparing *true* doctrine with *false* doctrine that was being taught by the prevailing myths of his Jewish opponents who denied the Gospel.[26] It is the *content* that is damnable heresy to Paul, not the *genre* of mythic storytelling itself. Of this heretical mythology, scholar William Mounce writes,

> It appears to have been a form of aberrant Judaism with Hellenistic/gnostic tendencies that overemphasized the law and underemphasized Christ and faith, taught dualism (asceticism, denial of a physical resurrection), was unduly interested in the minutiae of the OT, produced sinful lifestyles and irrelevant quibbling about words, and was destroying the reputation of the church in Ephesus.[27]

The New Testament does not command against using mythical storytelling, but against its misuse for false doctrine. Put positively, we should devote ourselves to myths that "promote stewardship from God that is by faith" (1Tim. 1:4), myths that "turn people to the truth" (Titus 1:14); "reverent, sober myths" of "faith, good doctrine" and "godliness" (1Tim. 4:6-7); myths that "turn toward the truth" (2Tim. 4:4).

But it is equally interesting to see how the Bible itself redeems pagan mythopoeic imagination.

I have written elsewhere about the extensive use of Canaanite poetry and imagination by Bible authors to express God's own imagination.[28] The Bible redeems pagan imagination by using its motifs and baptizing them with altered

---

[26] "The use is, to be sure, not specifically literary. "Myth" is used here, as is frequently the case elsewhere, to denote false and foolish stories." Martin Dibelius and Hans Conzelmann, *The Pastoral Epistles a Commentary on the Pastoral Epistles, Hermeneia--a critical and historical commentary on the Bible*, (Philadelphia: Fortress Press, 1972) 16.
[27] William D. Mounce, vol. 46, Word Biblical Commentary : Pastoral Epistles, Word Biblical Commentary, (Dallas: Word, Incorporated, 2002) 19.
[28] http://godawa.com/Writing/Articles_And_Essays.html

subversive definitions that support Yahweh, the God of the Jewish Scriptures against Baal, the god of Canaan, and other pagan deities in the ancient Near East.

Two examples of this redemptive subversion that show up in *Noah Primeval* and *Enoch Primordial* are Leviathan and the divine council of the Sons of God. It appears that Yahweh was not only interested in dispossessing the Canaanite people from the Promised Land, he was interested in dispossessing their narrative, because the Bible embodies a subversion of Canaanite imagination within its own narrative.

Baal, the storm god, was the chief deity of the land of Canaan in the time of the Israelite conquest. Canaanite myths depict Baal as a "cloud rider" who defeats the River and the Sea, as well as the seven-headed Sea Dragon called "Leviathan," (a symbol of chaos), in order to claim his eternal dominion.[29]

In polemical response to this mythology, the Biblical writers describe Yahweh as a "cloud rider" (Isa. 19:1; Psa. 104:3-4), who defeats the River and Sea (Hab. 3:8), as well as the Sea Dragon, "Leviathan," (Isa. 89:6-12) or "Rahab" (Psa. 89:9-11) in order to establish his eternal dominion (Psa. 89:19-29). It appears that Yahweh, in consort with the human authors of the Bible, is subversively using the pagan cultural motifs and thought-forms of the day to say, "Baal is not God, Yahweh is God."

In Psalm 74 and 89, and Isaiah 27 and 51 the story of the Exodus crossing of the Red Sea is described with the imaginative terms of creating the heavens and earth, crushing the heads of Leviathan, and binding the chaos waters of the sea in order to establish Yahweh's covenantal dominion on the earth in his people. This is history mixed in with mythopoeic imagination to describe the theological significance of what is taking place — just like other ancient Near Eastern religions did.[30]

Another aspect of Canaanite pagan mythology that is redeemed in the Scriptures is the divine council of the Sons of God. In the sacred Baal texts we read about an assembly of the "Sons of El," the father deity of the pantheon. Baal is a vice regent who ascends to the throne of El and rules over the other gods of the council, who then do his bidding.[31]

---

[29] See Wyatt, N. Religious Texts from Ugarit. 2nd ed. Biblical seminar, 53. (London; New York: Sheffield Academic Press, 2002). Also, Brian Godawa, "Old Testament Storytelling Apologetics," http://godawa.com/Writing/Articles/OTStoryApologetics-CRJournal.pdf
[30] See Brian Godawa, "Biblical Creation and Storytelling: Cosmogony, Combat and Covenant" for a detailed explanation of this ANE technique: http://godawa.com/Writing/Articles/BiblicalCreationStorytelling-Godawa.pdf
[31] See Michael S. Heiser, *The Divine Council In Late Canonical And Non-Canonical Second Temple Jewish Literature* (Madison, WI: University of Wisconsin, 2004) 34-41: http://digitalcommons.liberty.edu/fac_dis/93/; Patrick D. Miller, "Cosmology And World Order In The Old Testament The Divine Council As Cosmic-Political

In the Bible, God (called "El" or "Elohim") presides over a divine council or assembly of the "Sons of God" (Psa. 82:1; 89:5-7), who also give advice in judicial decisions of Yahweh (Psa. 82), and carry out his bidding as well (Job 1:6-12; 1Kings 22:19-22). A deified figure called the Son of Man is a vice regent who ascends to God's throne surrounded by those "holy ones" who do his bidding (Dan. 7:9-14).[32]

Of course, there are significant differences that separate the monotheistic Biblical divine council and the polytheistic pagan Canaanite divine council. As one example illustrates, the Biblical divine council are not to be worshipped, as God is, while the Canaanite divine council were worshipped.[33] Big similarities, but bigger differences. Biblical imagination does not engage in syncretism (blending opposing views), but in subversion (infiltrating and overthrowing an opposing view). The commonalities show a clear cultural connection that is subversively redeemed and redefined in the Biblical understanding of the concept. God incorporates pagan imagination and motifs into his own narrative and subverts them through redefinition and poetic usage.

Eden

The novel *Enoch Primordial* includes the Garden of Eden as a location important to the plot of the story. For those who believe it was an historical place, there are as many suggestions for its location as there are Bible commentators. We just don't know. The strongest hints are found in one passage, Genesis 2:10-14 that speaks of Eden at the headwaters of four rivers, The Pishon (in the land of Havilah), the Gihon (in the land of Cush), the Tigris, and the Euphrates.

The Tigris and Euphrates we know, but the Pishon and Gihon we do not. And if the flood was historical, whether global or local, then the terrain affected by that cataclysm would be significantly altered to derail all speculation. However, it's still fun to try.

Archaeologist David Rohl takes the Bible as basically truthful about the people and events it speaks of in history. He has looked at geographical, linguistic, and archaeological evidence of the ancient and modern Near East, and has made a persuasive argument that the land of Eden was in the

---

Symbol" *Israelite Religion and Biblical Theology: Collected Essays by Patrick D. Miller*, (NY: Sheffield Academic Press, 2000).

[32] See Michael Heiser's writings on the divine council in the Bible at http://thedivinecouncil.com/.

[33] For more differences explained, see Gerald Cooke, "The Sons of (the) God(s)," *Zeitschrift für die alttestamentliche Wissenschaft*, n.s.:35:1 (1964), p 45-46.

mountainous valley area known to us as Armenia, where modern Turkey, Iran, Syria, and Iraq all meet.[34]

Bible readers often mistake the *Garden* of Eden for Eden itself. But Genesis speaks of "the Lord God planting a garden *in* Eden in the east" (Gen 2:8). So the Garden was in the eastern part of a land called "Eden."

Rohl places the Garden in the Adji Chay valley adjacent to Lake Urmia and nestled in the volcanic mountainous ranges of the Savalan in the north and the Sahand in the south. He shows how that area is at the headwaters of the Tigris and Euphrates as well as two other rivers he suggests are the Pishon (Araxes) and Gihon (Kezel Uzun).

The interesting variety of environments of volcanoes, mountains, lakes and forests were an inspiring setting to tell my story, so the map I've provided in the novel shows that I have followed Rohl's scholarship on the location of that most elusive Paradise.

Enoch

Enoch Primordial is a story that takes place in the primeval ages before the flood. It follows the Biblical hero Enoch on his journey through the "world that then was," as a holy man who preached judgment upon the Watchers and their progeny the giants. As discussed above, the book of 1 Enoch was used as a reference for the story of the novel. The Bible itself says almost nothing about Enoch. Apart from genealogical references, all Genesis has to say about him is this:

> Genesis 5:21–24
> When Enoch had lived 65 years, he fathered Methuselah. Enoch walked with God after he fathered Methuselah 300 years and had other sons and daughters. Thus all the days of Enoch were 365 years. Enoch walked with God, and he was not, for God took him.

In the New Testament, we have three references: A genealogical reference, the quotation from 1 Enoch in Jude about God coming with judgment against the fornicating angels referenced earlier, and this passage from the writer of Hebrews reminding us of Enoch's faith:

---

[34] David Rohl, *Legend: A Test of Time Vol. 2* (London: Random House 1998) 43-70.

> Hebrews 11:5
> By faith Enoch was taken up so that he should not see death, and he was not found, because God had taken him. Now before he was taken he was commended as having pleased God.

Archaeologist David Rohl theorizes that if such important people of the Faith really did exist, then they are likely to show up in other ancient literature of the same geographic location or time period. They may have a different name in a different language and culture, which was common, or they may be distorted vestiges of the real person.

In his book *Legend*, Rohl sifts through extant Sumerian literature to find who he believes is a "distant Sumerian memory" of this antediluvian patriarch Enoch. He uncovers Mesopotamian literature that refers to seven sages called *apkallus*, or wise men who are regarded as the originators of the arts and skills of civilization. By removing the mythological veil covering these advisors to ancient kings whose kingship "descended from heaven," he reveals a fascinating correlation. The seventh sage, Utuabzu, apkallu to King Enmeduranki of Sippar, is described as having "ascended to heaven," just like Enoch, the seventh patriarch, did in the Bible.[35] So I decided to follow this possible connecting point for defining Enoch's character in *Enoch Primordial* as being the apkallu to Enmeduranki of Sippar.

Cain

The infamous first murderer Cain, son of Adam, shows up in *Enoch Primordial*. He has a wolf companion and eventually we find that the curse/mark on Cain that the Bible does not explain is vampirism. Cain is an undead being who must feed on the blood of the living to maintain his wretched life. It reminds one of the fact that sometimes the greatest punishment is not death but living with the disastrous consequences of one's actions.

> Gen 4:11, 15
> And now you are cursed from the ground, which has opened its mouth to receive your brother's blood from your

---
[35] Rohl, *Legend*, 201-202. Also, Hess, Richard S. "Enoch (Person)". In *The Anchor Yale Bible Dictionary*, edited by David Noel Freedman. New York: Doubleday, 1992.

hand…And the LORD put a mark on Cain, lest any who found him should attack him.

I drew from Jewish legends for this creative license. The rabbinic *Genesis Rabbah* 22:12 interpreted the "sign" that deterred others from attacking him as a protective dog (domesticated wolf), thus my lycanthropic connection.[36] The Pseudepigraphic *Life of Adam and Eve* paints a vampiric dream of Eve for her son Cain:

> The Life of Adam and Eve 2:1-3:2
> After these things Adam and Eve were together and when they were lying down to sleep, Eve said to her lord Adam, "My lord, I saw in a dream this night the <u>blood of my son Amilabes, called Abel, being thrust into the mouth of Cain his brother, and he drank it mercilessly. He begged him to allow him a little of it, but he did not listen to him but swallowed all of it. And it did not stay in his stomach but came out of his mouth."…</u>
> And God said to Michael the archangel, "Say to Adam, 'The mystery which you know do not report to your son Cain, <u>for he is a son of wrath</u>.[37]

The notion of vampirism is not new to *Enoch Primordial*. We have seen the Watchers drink blood from sacrifices as a means of their sustaining life in *Noah Primeval* as well. Biblical theology links atonement to blood sacrifice because "life is in the blood."

> Leviticus 17:11–12
> For the life of the flesh is in the blood, and I have given it for you on the altar to make atonement for your souls, for it is the blood that makes atonement by the life. Therefore I have said to the people of Israel, No person among you shall eat blood, neither shall any stranger who sojourns among you eat blood.

---

[36] Gordon J. Wenham, Vol. 1, *Genesis 1–15*. Word Biblical Commentary. Dallas: Word, Incorporated, 1998, 109. See http://www.sacred-texts.com/jud/mhl/mhl05.htm (page 55).
[37] James H. Charlesworth, *The Old Testament Pseudepigrapha and the New Testament, Volume 2: Expansions of the "Old Testament" and Legends, Wisdom, and Philosophical Literature, Prayers, Psalms and Odes, Fragments of Lost Judeo-Hellenistic Works* (New Haven; London: Yale University Press, 1985) 267.

This is not to make God into a vampire, but it does make vampirism into a reflection of the curse of seeking to be gods or "like god." The notion of blood sacrifice was near universal in the ancient world because the *imago dei* in man, though distorted, is inescapable and thus finds its way into humankind's distortions of God-created reality.

Azazel

Baal is of course, not the only pagan entity that is subverted in the Bible. Remember the fallen Watcher Azazel who, in the Enoch passages above, was bound into the earth in the desert? Azazel makes his appearance in *Enoch Primordial* in this same way as one of the two lead Watchers who instigate the rebellion of the Watchers and the revelation of occultic knowledge to humanity. There is a much debated Scripture where this Azazel tradition may be influencing the Hebrew understanding of atonement. In Leviticus 16, the high priest Aaron is instructed in sin offerings for the people of Israel. One of those offerings is to be a scapegoat.

> Leviticus 16:7–10
> Then he shall take the two goats and set them before the LORD at the entrance of the tent of meeting. And Aaron shall cast lots over the two goats, one lot for the LORD and the other lot for Azazel. And Aaron shall present the goat on which the lot fell for the LORD and use it as a sin offering, but the goat on which the lot fell for Azazel shall be presented alive before the LORD to make atonement over it, that it may be sent away into the wilderness to Azazel.

Scholarly opinion is not unanimous (is it ever?) over just what "Azazel" refers to, but knowing the Enochian tradition of the angelic Azazel bound in the desert, there is strong warrant for the thesis that it refers to a "desert demon"[38] who happens to have the name of the demonic fallen angel who was bound in the desert in 1 Enoch.

---

[38] "Azazel", Karel van der Toorn, Bob Becking and Pieter Willem van der Horst, *Dictionary of Deities and Demons in the Bible*, (*DDD*) 2nd extensively rev. ed., (Leiden; Boston; Köln; Grand Rapids, MI; Cambridge: Brill; Eerdmans, 1999) 129.

Another demonized pagan deity appears in the Old Testament that may shed more light on this desert "goat-demon" Azazel. The Hebrew word, *seirim* is translated in several Old Testament passages as the pagan "satyr" or "hairy goat-demon." In two places it refers to the goat idols to whom some Canaanites made sacrifices (Lev. 17:7; 2Chron. 11:15) and in others to demonic entities that haunt the desert (Isa. 13:21; 34:14).[39] The Hebrews saw these pagan deities as the same thing: Demons.

Banias in ancient northern Canaan/Israel near Caesarea Philippi eventually became the center of worship for Pan, the hybrid goat-man deity. And this temple was near the base of Mount Hermon. To the Old Testament Jew, Azazel was an analog or incarnation of the desert goat-demon.[40]

Lilith

Another Mesopotamian deity subverted in the Old Testament narrative is Lilith, the she-demon. Regarding this monster, the *Dictionary of Deities and Demons in the Bible* says its Mesopotamian narrative reaches back to the third millennium B.C.

> Here we find Inanna who plants a tree later hoping to cut from its wood a throne and a bed for herself. But as the tree grows, a snake [Ningishzida] makes its nest at its roots, Anzu settled in the top and in the trunk the demon makes her lair... Of greater importance, however, is the sexual aspect of the— mainly—female demons lilitu and lili. Thus the texts refer to them as the ones who have no husband, or as the ones who stroll about searching for men in order to ensnare them.[41]

Lilith was also known as the demon who stole away newborn babies to suck their blood, eat their bone marrow and consume their flesh.[42] In Jewish legends, she was described as having long hair and wings, and claimed to have been the first wife of Adam who was banished because of Adam's

---

[39] van der Toorn, Becking, *DDD*, 129.
[40] Judd H. Burton, *Interview With the Giant: Ethnohistorical Notes on the Nephilim*, (Burton Beyond Press, 2009), 19-20.
[41] "Lilith," *DDD*, 520.
[42] Handy, Lowell K. "Lilith (Deity)". In *The Anchor Yale Bible Dictionary*, edited by David Noel Freedman. New York: Doubleday, 1992, 324-325.

unwillingness to accept her as his equal.[43] Lilith and her offspring make their appearance in *Enoch Primordial* as temptresses guarding the World Tree in the desert with the snake god Ningishzida in the roots and the Anzu bird in its high branches.

Lilith the "night hag" makes her appearance in the Bible in Isaiah 34 along with that other pagan mythical creature, the satyr, a demonized interpretation of the goat-like god Pan. In this chapter, prophetic judgment upon Edom involves turning it into a desert wasteland that is inhabited by all kinds of demons; ravens, jackals, hyenas, satyrs — and Lilith.

> Isaiah 34:13–15 (RSV)
> It shall be the haunt of jackals... And wild beasts shall meet with hyenas, the satyr shall cry to his fellow; yea, there shall the night hag [*Lilith*] alight, and find for herself a resting place.

Resheph and Qeteb

Two other "demonized deities" that show up in the Bible are Resheph and Qeteb. In the song of Moses, Yahweh describes how he will punish those Israelites who enter the Promised Land but do not obey him:

> Deuteronomy 32:23-24
> And I will heap disasters upon them;
> I will spend my arrows on them;
> they shall be wasted with hunger,
> and devoured by plague (*Resheph*)
> and poisonous pestilence (*Qetab*)

Resheph and Qeteb were Canaanite gods of plague and pestilence. Similar to this Deuteronomy passage, Resheph was described in Phoenicia as using his arrow of flaming judgment.[44] This curse is a poetic expression of Yahweh handing the rebellious Israelites over to the Canaanite gods for punishment.[45] As the *Dictionary of Deities and Demons in the Bible* concludes, "Qeteb is more than a literary figure, living as a spiritual, and

---

[43] Ginzberg, Louis; Szold, Henrietta (2011-01-13). *Legends of the Jews*, all four volumes in a single file, improved 1/13/2011 (K-ebook Locations 1016-1028). B&R Samizdat Express. K-ebook Edition.
[44] Ronald S. Hendel, "The Flame of the Whirling Sword: A Note on Genesis 3:24," *Journal of Biblical Literature*, Vol. 104, No. 4 (Dec., 1985), pp. 673
[45] "Resheph," *DDD*, 703. Resheph is also referenced in Ps 78:48, 1 Chr 7:25, Ps 91:5, and Sir 43:17.

highly dangerous, reality in the minds of poets and readers,"[46] and "in the OT Resheph is a demonized version of an ancient Canaanite god, now submitted to Yahweh."[47]

Rahab

One of the mythopoeic creatures that shows up in *Enoch Primordial* is Rahab, the Sea Dragon of chaos. In the appendix of *Noah Primeval*, I explained the mythological origins of the seven-headed Sea Dragon called Leviathan and its appropriation in the Bible. Though the Old Testament seems to indicate Rahab as simply another name for this sea monster,[48] I decided to separate the two and make Leviathan the offspring of Rahab. But in the big war scene, we see that Rahab has other "helpers" with her, other monsters of the deep. This was also taken from a mythic motif that shows up in Babylonian, Ugaritic, and Biblical texts.

In the Ugaritic texts, the gods Baal and Anat defeat Leviathan along with her divine allies Yam, Nahar, Arsh, Atik, and others.[49] In the Babylonian Enuma Elish, the god Marduk defeats the sea dragon Tiamat and her monster helpers.[50]

> Tiamat assembled her creatures,
> Drew up for battle against the gods her brood [offspring]...[51]
> She has set up the Viper, the Dragon, and the Sphinx, the Great-Lion, the Mad-Dog, and the Scorpion-Man, Mighty lion-demons, the Dragon-Fly, the Centaur...[52]

So, we also see Rahab, the sea monster in Biblical texts being crushed and her "helpers" the enemies of God being "bowed" and "scattered."

---

[46] Qeteb," *DDD*, 703, 673-74. Qeteb also makes an appearance in Psa 91:5–6, Hos 13:14 and Isa 28:2.
[47] "[Resheph] appears as a cosmic force, whose powers are great and terrible: he is particularly conceived of as bringing epidemics and death. The Hebrew Bible shows different levels of demythologization: sometimes it describes Resheph as a personalized figure, more or less faded, sometimes the name is used as a pure metaphor. At any rate it is possible to perceive aspects of the personality of an ancient chthonic god, whichs fits the image of Resheph found in the other Semitic cultures."
van der Toorn, Becking van der Horst, *DDD*, 703-704.
[48] See Rahab's equivocation with Leviathan in Psalm 89:10; Job 26:12; Isa 51:9-10 with Psa 74:13-14; Isa 27:1.
[49] KTU 1.3:3:35–47: N. Wyatt, *Religious Texts from Ugarit*, 2nd ed., Biblical seminar, 53, 79-80 (London ; New York: Sheffield Academic Press, 2002).
[50] "The Creation Epic," Tablet II lines 1-2, 27-29; IV, lines 107-108: *The Ancient Near East an Anthology of Texts and Pictures*., ed. James Bennett Pritchard, (Princeton: Princeton University Press, 1958) 67.
[51] "The Creation Epic," Tablet II lines 1-2, William W. Hallo and K. Lawson Younger, The Context of Scripture, 393 (Leiden; New York: Brill, 1997-) 393.
[52] "The Creation Epic," Tablet II lines 27-29; *The Ancient Near East an Anthology of Texts and Pictures*., ed. James Bennett Pritchard, (Princeton: Princeton University Press, 1958) 64.

Job 9:13
God will not turn back his anger;
beneath him bowed <u>the helpers of Rahab</u>.

Psalm 89:10
You <u>crushed Rahab</u> like a carcass;
you <u>scattered your enemies</u> with your mighty arm.

Behemoth

Speaking of Rahab's monstrous "helpers" of chaos, we come to Behemoth, another creature who finds his way into *Enoch Primordial* and *Noah Primeval*. The one place in Scripture where this huge beast shows up is in God's discourse with Job about God's unapproachable incomparable powers of creation:

Job 40:15–24
"Behold, Behemoth,
which I made as I made you;
he eats grass like an ox.
Behold, his strength in his loins,
and his power in the muscles of his belly.
He makes his tail stiff like a cedar;
the sinews of his thighs are knit together.
His bones are tubes of bronze,
his limbs like bars of iron.
"He is the first of the works of God;
let him who made him bring near his sword!
For the mountains yield food for him
where all the wild beasts play.
Under the lotus plants he lies,
in the shelter of the reeds and in the marsh.
For his shade the lotus trees cover him;
the willows of the brook surround him.
Behold, if the river is turbulent he is not frightened;
he is confident though Jordan rushes against his mouth.

Can one take him by his eyes,
or pierce his nose with a snare?

The most common interpretations of the identity of this monster by Biblical scholars is a hippopotamus, a crocodile, or a water buffalo. Young earth creationists argue that it is a sauropod dinosaur.[53] All of these seek to understand the creature as a real beast that existed in Bible times. Ancient Near Eastern scholar John Day dismisses these naturalistic interpretations in favor of a mythological picture of a chaos monster. There is no paleontological evidence of dinosaurs coexisting with humans. Hippopotamuses and water buffalos do not have strong bones, sinewy muscles, or tails like a cedar. Crocodiles are carnivores and do not eat grass.[54] But more importantly, unlike Behemoth, all of these animals are easily caught by man in contrast with Job's emphasis that only God can do so. And lastly, none of them hold pride of status as "the first of the works of God."[55]

Day argues that Behemoth is a mythological chaos monster that represents the Jewish demonization of pagan deities and symbolizes the subjugation of creation by God. He points out that Behemoth in this Job passage is coupled with the mythical chaos monster Leviathan in the verses following Behemoth (Job 41).

Later Jewish texts also understood Behemoth to be coupled with Leviathan as chaos monsters of creation with eschatological references to future judgment:

> 1 Enoch 60:7-8, 24
> On that day, two monsters will be parted—one monster, a female named <u>Leviathan,</u> in order to dwell in the abyss of the ocean over the fountains of water; and (the other), a male called <u>Behemoth,</u> which holds his chest in an invisible desert whose name is Dundayin, east of the garden of Eden..."These

---

[53] http://www.answersingenesis.org/articles/tj/v15/n2/behemoth
[54] Day ignores the dinosaur hypothesis. There remains no paleontological evidence of dinosaurs coexisting with humankind. And young earth creationists admit there is no known species of sauropods that fits all the details of Job 40.
[55] John Day, *God's Conflict with the Dragon and the Sea: Echoes of a Canaanite Myth in the Old Testament* (University of Cambridge Press, 1985) 62-87.

> two monsters are prepared for the great day of the Lord (when) they shall turn into food.[56]

God is using these symbols of creative power over Chaos to close the mouth of Job's complaints. Leviathan and Behemoth were "the first of the works of God" (40:19) and "the king over all the sons of pride" (41:34) because "the powers of chaos were primeval in origin."[57] But fear not, God created them, God subjugated them, and God will turn them into a feast at the end of time.

Day then shows where this coupling of Leviathan and Behemoth has its origin, in two Canaanite texts of Ugarit where the goddess Anat is described as defeating Leviathan, "the dragon," "the crooked serpent, the tyrant with seven heads," and "El's calf Atik" also called *Ars* (the ox-like Behemoth of Job 40:15).[58] Kenneth Whitney shows an established 2nd Temple Rabbinic tradition of Leviathan and Behemoth as companions of destruction in this same manner, thus the bovine nature of the amphibious creature in the *Chronicles of the Nephilim*.[59]

Day then concludes, "The reason for the inclusion of the sections on Behemoth and Leviathan in Job 40-1 is to drive home the point that, since Job is unable to overcome them, how much less can he hope to overcome in argument the God who defeated them."[60]

In *Enoch Primordial*, I took liberties to alter this monster's description somewhat in order to make him more ferociously carnivorous, but he remains a monster of chaos that is held at bay by the mountainous gates of a hidden valley of God's creation.

---

[56] James H. Charlesworth, *The Old Testament Pseudepigrapha: Volume 1*, (New York; London: Yale University Press, 1983) 40-42. See also 2 Bar. 29:4; 4 Ez. 6:49, 5.
[57] Day, *God's Conflict*, 80.
[58] Day, *God's Conflict*, 80-81.
KTU I.3.III.43-4
Surely I lifted up the dragon...
(and) smote the crooked serpent,
the tyrant with the seven heads.
I smote Ars beloved of El,
I put an end to El's calf Atik.
KTU 1.6.VI.51-3
In the sea are Ars and the dragon,
May Kothar-and-Hasis drive (them) away,
May Kothar-and-Hasis cut (them) off.
[59] Kenneth William Whitney, Jr., *Two Strange Beasts: A Study of Traditions Concerning Leviathan and Behemoth in Second Temple and Early Rabbinic Judaism*, Cambridge, Massachusetts: Harvard University, 1992
[60] Day, *God's Conflict*, 87.

Mushussu

Another mythological creature that shows up in *Enoch Primordial* is the mushussu chimera that is well known from its tiled depiction on the Babylonian Ishtar Gate and many other seals discovered throughout Mesopotamia. It was a lion's body with a dragon's head, taloned back feet, and a tail that was a snake.

Robert Koldeway, an amateur archeologist of the 19th century, wrote a book about the Gate of Ishtar and noted that this mythical creature, called a *sirrush* at the time, was one of the few animals that were depicted remarkably consistent in Babylonian art over time. He thought that this might be because they had actual specimens of them. His thoughts were that they were dinosaurs misinterpreted as dragons. Ancient astronaut authors like Joseph Farrell suggest they were examples of actual genetic splicing by extraterrestrial aliens.[61] I used it as the first hint of the dark arts that the Watchers were just beginning to perfect in their own miscegenation project. We would see their advancements in *Noah Primeval*, but it represented the notion of the violation of the natural order of separation that seemed to be an important element of God's creation.

Scholar Theodore Lewis explains regarding the mushussu genetic combination of lion and dragon, "The common denominator for associating these two creatures seems to be that they could both inspire paralyzing, heart-stopping fear when encountered."[62] He concludes that this is the creature used as a metaphor for the Pharaoh who had oppressed Judah rather than the "crocodile of outdated scholarship."[63] Yahweh was going to capture and cast that beast of a ruler onto the ground for the nations to gorge on its flesh.

> Ezekiel 32:2
> You are like a <u>lion</u> among the nations,
> You are like a <u>dragon</u> in the seas.

The literary pairing of a lion and serpent also occurs in Psalm 91:13; Isaiah 30:6; and Amos 5:19 and may come from the cultural awareness of this mythopoeic creature the mushussu.

---

[61] Joseph P. Farrell, *Genes, Giants, Monsters, and Men: The Surviving Elites of the Cosmic War and Their Hidden Agenda* (2011-05-09). Perseus Books Group. K-ebook Edition 1-9.
[62] Theodore J. Lewis, "CT 13.33-34 and Ezekiel 32: Lion-Dragon Myths," *Journal of the American Oriental Society*, Vol. 116, No. 1 (Jan. - Mar., 1996), 35.
[63] Lewis, "Lion-Dragon Myths," 39. He also points out that Ezekiel was in Babylon under Nebuchadnezzar, who rebuilt the Gate of Ishtar. So it is likely the prophet draws from this imagery rather than from Egyptian.

Cherubim

Some of the critical characters that come to play in the narratives of *Noah Primeval* and *Enoch Primordial* are the Cherubim. The Mesopotamian version of this creature is the *aladlammu*, the bull-man and lion-man who guarded the thrones of Anu and Inanna. These large sphinx-like monsters were made famous by their presence on the huge stone Ishtar Gate of Babylon and other statues in museums around the world. But they are also ubiquitous in artifacts all around the ancient Near East, from Phoenicia to Syria to Egypt.[64] They were chimeras, hybrid creatures with the body of a lion or bull, the head of a man, and the wings of an eagle, and they protected the thrones of royalty and divinity throughout the Ancient Near East.[65]

It is not surprising then, to discover that they were also the creatures that guarded the throne of Yahweh, a throne that some explain was a commonplace Mesopotamian motif of a divine "throne chariot."[66]

> Psalm 80:1
> You who are enthroned upon the cherubim.

> Psalm 99:1
> The LORD reigns; let the peoples tremble!
> He sits enthroned upon the cherubim!

> Psalm 18:10
> He rode on a cherub and flew;
> he came swiftly on the wings of the wind.

When Ezekiel has his vision of the cherubim in chapters 1 and 10 as "living creatures," their usual sphinx-like morphology is expanded into a multiplicity of four wings, and four faces of human, lion, eagle and ox. But its essential nature remains the same.

---

[64] Ronald S. Hendel, "The Flame of the Whirling Sword: A Note on Genesis 3:24," *Journal of Biblical Literature*, Vol. 104, No. 4 (Dec., 1985), pp. 671-674.
[65] William F. Albright, "What Were the Cherubim?" *The Biblical Archaeologist*, Vol. 1, No. 1 (Feb., 1938), 1-3.
[66] "Assyrian art portrays the god Aššur riding into battle on behalf of the king. The god Baal is described in Ugaritic texts as one who rides the clouds mounted on a chariot (see 68:4; 104:3). This image dates as far back as the Old Akkadian period (ca. 2400 B.C.), from which a cylinder seal depicts the storm god riding a chariot drawn by a winged lion."
John H Walton, *Zondervan Illustrated Bible Backgrounds Commentary (Old Testament) Volume 5: The Minor Prophets, Job, Psalms, Proverbs, Ecclesiastes, Song of Songs*, (Grand Rapids, MI: Zondervan, 2009) 333.

Enoch Primordial

The cherubim guarding the ark of the covenant with their outspread wings was crafted by pagan Phoenician artistry for Solomon (1Kings 8:6-7), and an ivory artifact discovered in Megiddo, Israel shows an Israelite king, possibly Solomon, seated on his throne guarded by a lion-bodied, eagle-winged, human-headed sphinx cherubim.[67]

In contrast with this imaginative art, the living cherubim guarding the way to the Tree of Life in the Garden of Eden were no sedentary statues (Gen 3:24), *but they were the sphinx-like cherubim.*

Genesis 3:24 says that these cherubim guard the Tree of Life with "the flame of the whirling sword." Scholar Ronald Hendel has argued that "the 'flame' is an animate divine being, a member of Yahweh's divine host, similar in status to the cherubim; the 'whirling sword' is its appropriate weapon, ever-moving, like the flame itself."[68]

Scholar P.D. Miller appeals to passages such as Psalm 104:4 where "fire and flame" are described as "Yahweh's ministers" to conclude a convergence of imagery with ancient Ugaritic texts that describe "fire and flame" as armed deities with flashing swords. He writes that "the cherubim and the flaming sword are probably to be recognized as a reflection of the Canaanite fiery messengers."[69] Thus the Biblically strange, yet strangely Biblical presence in *Enoch Primordial* of the Cherubim and their divine fiery beings beside them brandishing whirling swords of flashing lightning.

Whence all this commonality between pagan and Hebrew cosmology? Did the Biblical writers draw from their ancient Near Eastern neighbors for their concepts of the cherubim or were pagan depictions distorted memories of the "myth that was true"?

Archaeologist David Rohl argues that the cherubim may have been a mythological spiritualization of a very human tribe of sentinels called the Kheruba who guarded the Edenic paradise.[70] I decided to incorporate all these interpretations into *Enoch Primordial*. How subversive of me.

---

[67] Walton, John H. *Zondervan Illustrated Bible Backgrounds Commentary (Old Testament) Volume 5: The Minor Prophets, Job, Psalms, Proverbs, Ecclesiastes, Song of Songs.* Grand Rapids, MI: Zondervan, 2009, 405.
[68] Ronald S. Hendel, "'The Flame of the Whirling Sword': A Note on Genesis 3:24," *Journal of Biblical Literature*, Vol. 104, No. 4 (Dec., 1985), pp. 671-674.
[69] Patrick D. Miller, "Fire in the Mythology of Canaan and Israel," *Catholic Biblical Quarterly*, 27 no 3 Jl 1965, p 256-261.
[70] David Rohl, *From Eden to Exile: The 5000-Year History of the People of the Bible,* (Lebanon, TN: Greenleaf Press, 2002), 31-32.

Seraphim

The prophet Isaiah had an exalted vision of the Lord sitting on his heavenly throne high and lifted up with the glorious train of his robe filling the temple. But there were also some other chimeric creatures in his presence:

> Isaiah 6:2–7
> Above him stood the seraphim. Each had six wings: with two he covered his face, and with two he covered his feet, and with two he flew. And one called to another and said: "Holy, holy, holy is the LORD of hosts; the whole earth is full of his glory!"… Then one of the seraphim flew to me, having in his hand a burning coal.

The meaning of the Hebrew word for *seraphim* is "fiery serpent."[71] It was used to describe the fiery serpents in the wilderness whose poisonous burning venom was God's punishment for Israel's grumbling and complaining (Num. 21:6). God's balm of healing forgiveness was obtained by looking to a brass serpent (*seraph*) image raised on a pole called Nehushtan (Num. 21:8).

But this is not the only use of *seraph* that sheds light on the meaning of the angelic seraphim. The Brown-Driver-Briggs Hebrew Lexicon points out that Isaiah 14:29 and 30:6 refer to a "flying fiery serpent" (*seraph*) in the wilderness that originated in mythically conceived winged serpent deities.[72] The term is unavoidably serpentine in all its cognates.

Some deny this serpentine essence by pointing out that the Isaianic seraphim are described as having human heads, wings, hands and feet. But Karen Randolph Joines has persuasively argued that the Egyptian winged *ureus* (upright cobra) that guarded the Pharaoh's tombs and thrones with its "fiery" venom is demonstrably the equivalent of the Hebrew seraph. Like the seraphim in Isaiah, the ureus was also commonly described as having a human face, wings, hands and feet when it was necessary for it to accomplish tasks like those of Isaiah 6.[73] But it remained a winged serpent.

---

[71] Harris, R. Laird. "2292 שָׂרָף". In *Theological Wordbook of the Old Testament*, edited by R. Laird Harris, Gleason L. Archer, Jr. and Bruce K. Waltke. electronic ed. Chicago: Moody Press, 1999.
[72] Brown, Francis, Samuel Rolles Driver, and Charles Augustus Briggs. *Enhanced Brown-Driver-Briggs Hebrew and English Lexicon*. electronic ed. Oak Harbor, WA: Logos Research Systems, 2000.
[73] Karen Randolph Joines, "Winged serpents in Isaiah's inaugural vision," *Journal of Biblical Literature*, 86 no 4 D 1967, p 414-415.

ANE scholar Michael S. Heiser goes one step further and provisionally considers a literary overlapping of all these elements of fiery serpents, flying, humanoid features, and divinity to be variations of descriptions for the "Watcher paradigm":

> "Seraphim, then, are reptilian/serpentine beings – they are the Watchers (the "watchful ones" who diligently guard God's throne, which is carried [cf. Ezekiel 1, 10] by the cherubim, who may also serve as guardians). There are "good" serpentine beings (seraphim) who guard God's throne (so Isaiah 6's seraphim), and there are fallen, wicked serpentine beings (seraphim) who rebelled against the Most High at various times, and who became the pagan gods of the other nations."[74]

He supports his view from Isaiah 14:29, a prophecy about Philistia (the city of Goliath and other giants) that references the messianic war of the seed of the serpent (*nachash*) that brings forth the fruit of the flying fiery serpent (*seraph*).

> Isaiah 14:29
> [29] Rejoice not, O Philistia... for from the serpent's [*nachash*] root will come forth an adder, and its fruit will be a flying fiery serpent [seraph].

Could this be a literary reference to the Watcher paradigm?

A text fragment from the Dead Sea Scrolls affirms the ancient Jewish understanding of Watchers having this reptilian presence and ruling over specific peoples:

> 4QAmram (4Q544) lines 10-14
> [I saw Watchers] in my vision, the dream-vision. Two men were fighting over me...I asked them, "Who are you, that you are thus empowered over me?" They answered me, "We have been empowered and rule over mankind," They said to

---

[74] Michael S. Heiser, "Serpentine / Reptilian Divine Beings in the Hebrew Bible: A Preliminary Investigation" 4.

me, "Which of us do you choose to rule you?" I raised my eyes and looked. One of them was <u>terrifying in his appearance, like a serpent</u>, his cloak many-colored yet very dark... And I looked again and... <u>in his appearance, his visage was like a viper</u>.[75]

Rephaim

The Rephaim that appear in *the Chronicles of the Nephilim* arc based upon Biblical and ancient Near Eastern references to giants or deified kings that ended up in the underworld. A buried library of cuneiform tablets was excavated at Ras Shamra from the ancient city of Ugarit during the years 1940-47. They yielded tablets that have been crucial to understanding the development of Syrian and Canaanite religion. One of the corpus of texts unearthed there was what came to be known as the Rephaim Texts. These texts and others talked about a *marzih* feast, like that in *Enoch Primordial,* that involved royalty traveling distances in their chariots to participate in this feast, wherein the "most ancient Rephaim of the netherworld" are summoned to assemble as the "council of the Ditanu, (or Didanu)."[76] Some names of these deified royal ancestors were given as Ulkan, Taruman, Sidan-and-Radan, and Thar, the eternal one.[77] This is where I drew the names for my council of Didanu that meets in Baalbek for a diabolical plan. The names of the infamous Rephaim Thamaq and Yahipan, the Rephaim targets of Methuselah's revenge in *Enoch Primordial*, were drawn from these ancient texts as well.[78]

As Ugaritic scholars Levine and Tarragon sum up, "the Rephaim are long departed kings (and heroes) who dwell in the netherworld, which is located deep beneath the mountains of that far-away eastern region where the Ugaritians originated."[79]

While creative license and speculation drives *Enoch Primordial*, even the names of the Nephilim brothers, Ohyah and Hahyah, as well as the giant General

---

[75] Robert H. Eisenman, Michael Wise, *The Dead Sea Scrolls Uncovered: The First Complete Translation and Interpretation of 50 Key Documents withheld for Over 35 Years*, (Rockport, MA: Element Books, 1992) 55-56.

[76] William W. Hallo and K. Lawson Younger, *The Context of Scripture*, (Leiden; New York: Brill, 1997-) 356-58.

[77] N. Wyatt, *Religious Texts from Ugarit, 2nd ed.*, Biblical seminar, 53, 431-34 (London ; New York: Sheffield Academic Press, 2002).

[78] N. Wyatt, *Religious Texts from Ugarit, 2nd ed.*, Biblical seminar, 53, 321 (London ; New York: Sheffield Academic Press, 2002).

[79] Baruch A. Levine and Jean-Michel de Tarragon, "Dead Kings and Rephaim: The Patrons of the Ugaritic Dynasty," *Journal of the American Oriental Society*, Vol. 104, No. 4 (Oct. - Dec., 1984), pp. 649-659

Mahawai, were taken from the ancient manuscript *The Book of Giants* that was part of the Dead Sea Scrolls found at Qumran.[80] In these texts the giant brothers are described as the giant offspring of Semjaza, one of the Watchers, and they have dreams of God's judgment coming upon them in the form of tablets being drowned in water and a garden being uprooted. As in the novel, so they seek out Enoch to explain their dreams and allow them repentance.[81]

The Bible also reinforces this ancient Ugaritic understanding of Rephaim as dead royal or heroic ancestors who reside in the underworld, but with a twist. In Isaiah 14, the prophet pronounces an oracle of judgment upon the king of Babylon whose arrogance leads him to consider himself a god (v. 13-14). Isaiah concludes with an ironic mockery of the Rephaim, these exalted dead kings and heroes, including The Babylonian king in their ultimate impotence.

> Isaiah 14:9–11
> Sheol beneath is stirred up
> to meet you when you come;
> it rouses the shades (*Rephaim*) to greet you,
> all who were leaders of the earth;
> it raises from their thrones
> all who were kings of the nations.
> All of them will answer
> and say to you:
> 'You too have become as weak as we!
> You have become like us!'
> Your pomp is brought down to Sheol.

To the Hebrew prophet, these proud kings were humiliated in the underworld of Sheol. Their glory became as "shades" in the light of God.[82] Apparently, the prophet transforms ancient Canaanite mythology into a polemical emasculation of pagan pride.[83]

But there is another element that the Biblical text adds to these royal "divinized" Rephaim: Gigantism. The very land of Canaan around Mount

---

[80] 4Q203 and 6Q8, Florentino García Martínez and Eibert J. C. Tigchelaar, *The Dead Sea Scrolls Study Edition* (Translations) (Leiden; New York: Brill, 1997-1998) 410.
[81] 4Q539, García Martínez, Florentino, and Eibert J. C. Tigchelaar. *The Dead Sea Scrolls Study Edition* (Translations). Leiden; New York: Brill, 1997-1998, 1064-65.
[82] See also Proverbs 2:18-19; 9:18; 21:16; Psa 88:10; Job 26:5-6; where the Hebrew word Rephaim is translated variously as "departed," "the dead" and "shades."
[83] For a good exegesis of Rephaim from the Ugaritic and Biblical texts, see Conrad L'Heureux, "The Ugaritic and Biblical Rephaim," *The Harvard Theological Review*, Vol. 67, No. 3 (Jul., 1974), pp. 265-274.

Hermon that was called Bashan was described as the "land of the Rephaim" (Deut. 3:13), whose inhabitants were described as tall giants like the Anakim (Deut. 2:11, 20) and were related to Goliath the giant (1Chron. 20:4-8). When Joshua was wiping out the tribes and cities of giants in Canaan, one of the last ones to go was the mighty Og of Bashan, the "last of the Rephaim" (Joshua 12:4) whose bed (or sarcophagus) was thirteen and a half feet long (Deut. 3:11). The reader will learn more about Og's exploits later in the series *The Chronicles of the Nephilim*.

Satan

A familiar character that shows up in *Enoch Primordial* but not in a familiar way is Satan — or, as the name means, *the Accuser*. The typical Evangelical mythology surrounding Satan is that he was the highest cherub in God's heavenly host, a worship leader with the name of Lucifer, who before the Garden of Eden, rebelled by trying to usurp God's seat of authority in heaven. He wanted to be "like God." He was then cast out of heaven with a third of the angels and fell to earth, where he tempted Eve in the Garden as a snake, and now he is "Lord of the air" over the earth.

I have no problem utilizing *lesser known* extra-Biblical mythology or legends in *the Chronicles of the Nephilim* in order to bring a fresh perspective to the Biblical story. But I also have no problem dismantling other *well-known* extra-Biblical mythology and legends in order to support that same goal of fresh perspective. The Satan legend as I described it above is one of those accepted myths that I decided to avoid because, well, it really isn't in the Bible.

I am going to follow David Lowe's strategy and "deconstruct Lucifer" in order to rediscover Satan in a new and more Biblical light.[84] First, let me affirm that the New Testament does equate Satan with the Serpent in the Garden (2Cor. 11:3; Rev. 12:9; 20:2) so I have no quarrel with that notion. But let's take a look at the rest of the Lucifer/Satan mythology to see if it really has Biblical merit.

The two passages that are most often used as source material for this myth are Isaiah 14:12-15 and Ezekiel 28:12-16. Let's look first at the Isaiah passage:

---

[84] David W. Lowe, *Deconstructing Lucifer: Reexamining the Ancient Origins of the Fallen Angel of Light*, (Seismos Publishing 2011).

Isaiah 14:12–15
"How you are fallen from heaven,
O Day Star (Lucifer), son of Dawn!
How you are cut down to the ground,
you who laid the nations low!
You said in your heart,
'I will ascend to heaven;
above the stars of God
I will set my throne on high;
I will sit on the mount of assembly
in the far reaches of the north;
I will ascend above the heights of the clouds;
I will make myself like the Most High.'
But you are brought down to Sheol,
to the far reaches of the pit.

The context of the entire passage of Isaiah 14 is that the prophet is making a prophesy of judgment upon the king of Babylon who existed in Isaiah's own day during the Jewish Babylonian exile. Well-meaning Christians interpret this text as a mythopoeic allusion or analogy of pride between Accuser, called Lucifer, and the Babylonian tyrant.

To start with, the name *Satan* is nowhere in the story, but *Lucifer* is. The problem with this name is that we have come to consider it a proper name of a demonic entity only by tradition. As author David Lowe points out, Lucifer was actually the Latin translation for the Hebrew words *Helel ben shahar*, which means "Morningstar," known to the ancients as the planet Venus.[85] In the ancient Near East, planets and stars were equated with deities and the heavenly host, so this is indeed a mythopoeic reference. But scholars have uncovered a very different narrative being referenced than the Garden of Eden. It is in fact a pagan Canaanite myth that Isaiah used to mock the pagan king of Babylon.

Scholar Michael S. Heiser definitively explains the linguistic and narrative referent of Helel ben Shahar as being the Ugaritic god Athtar from the epic Baal Cycle of myths at Ugarit. Heiser reveals that Athtar was equated with the planet Venus. Athtar sought to raise himself above "the stars of El," a reference to the divine council or heavenly host that surrounded the high god of the Canaanite pantheon. He tried to do so by seeking to sit on the throne of

---
[85] Lowe, *Deconstructing Lucifer*, 39-40.

Baal, referred to as "the Most High," upon the "mount of assembly" in the north called Saphon. But Athtar was not powerful enough for the position of power and was cast to earth/Sheol.[86]

There are no versions of this Isaianic narrative applying to Satan anywhere in the Bible but there sure is one of Athtar in the Canaanite context in which ancient Jews like Isaiah lived and breathed. Isaiah was declaring judgment upon the Babylonian tyrant by using pagan myths against the pagan king as mockery.

As Norman Habel put it,

> The presence of this archaic mythological imagery to describe the dwelling place of God does not imply that the Israelite writers thereby espoused the crass mythological view of reality current in the ancient Near Eastern world. Polemical and poetical considerations governed the Israelite writers' use of imagery taken from their pagan environment.[87]

The second passage that well-intentioned Christians use to justify their belief in the Satan/Lucifer mythology is Ezekiel 28:12-15. I will focus in on the most important elements to keep this as short as possible. Similar to Isaiah, Ezekiel prophesied about the hubris and fall of the king of Tyre. Also like Isaiah, Ezekiel makes a mythopoeic reference to some narrative. In this case, I would argue it *is* the Garden of Eden narrative being referenced. But the difference is that whereas many Christians assume Ezekiel is equating the fall of the king of Tyre with the fall Satan, the truth is that the prophet is actually equating it with the fall of *Adam!*[88]

> Ezekiel 28:12–16
> You were the signet of perfection…
> You were in Eden, the garden of God…
> You were an anointed guardian cherub…
> I placed you; you were on the holy mountain of God;
> in the midst of the stones of fire you walked.

---

[86] Michael Heiser, "The Mythological Provenance of Isaiah 14:12-15: A Reconsideration of the Ugaritic Material" Liberty University <http://digitalcommons.liberty.edu/lts_fac_pubs/280>
[87] Norman C. Habel, "Ezekiel 28 and the fall of the first man." *Concordia Theological Monthly*, 1967, 38 (8),. 520.
[88] For an excellent explanation of this view, see Norman C. Habel, "Ezekiel 28 and the fall of the first man." *Concordia Theological Monthly*, 1967, 38 (8),. 516-524.

> You were blameless in your ways
> from the day you were created,
> till unrighteousness was found in you...
> so I cast you as a profane thing from the mountain of God,
> and I destroyed you, O guardian cherub,

It was Adam who was in Eden and was blameless in his ways, not Satan. According to the Evangelical Satan legend, Satan already fell *before* the Garden. It was Adam who was created blameless and fell into sin and was cast out of Eden, not Satan. Satan's name is nowhere to be found in this passage.[89]

One possible reason to presume the Satan connection here is the description of the character as an "anointed guardian cherub." But there is a problem with this translation. Many commentators make the point that this is based upon the Masoretic text (MT) of the Bible. But the Septuagint (LXX), another authoritative Greek text of the Old Testament that is quoted by the New Testament authors and Jesus, renders those phrases "From the day that thou wast created thou *wast with* the cherub"[90] and "the cherub has brought thee out of the midst of the stones."[91] Being "with the cherub" is a very different meaning than "being a cherub." Though this is not unanimously conclusive, an increasing number of Bible scholars point to this ambiguity and likelihood of the Septuagint being the superior textual tradition here.[92] Adam was not a cherub, he was *with* the cherubim.

Lastly, in Revelation 12, we see the origin of the notion that one third of the angels fell to earth with Satan at his fall. The only problem is that this event did not occur before the garden of Eden in a cosmic rebellion, *it happened at the birth of Jesus Christ*! Revelation 12:1-6 describes an apocalyptic parable of the cosmic war of the Seed of the Serpent (a dragon of chaos) and the Seed of the Woman (Israel/the Church).[93] It describes one third of the angelic stars (Watchers?) joining Satan with the swipe of his serpentine

---

[89] Scholar H.J. van Dijk makes an interesting grammatical and linguistic argument that "You were the signet of perfection" is better translated, "You were the serpent of perfection" because the Hebrew word translated *signet* remains obscure. In Phoenician and Aramaic, however it means *serpent*. This would provide serious evidence for a link to the Serpent of the Garden. H. J. van Dijk, vol. 20, *Ezekiel's Prophecy on Tyre (Ez. 26:1–28:19): A New Approach* (Biblica et orientalia; Rome: Pontifical Biblical Institute, 1968).
[90] Lancelot Charles Lee Brenton, *The Septuagint Version of the Old Testament: English Translation*, Eze 28:14 (London: Samuel Bagster and Sons, 1870).
[91] Lancelot Charles Lee Brenton, *The Septuagint Version of the Old Testament: English Translation*, Eze 28:16 (London: Samuel Bagster and Sons, 1870).
[92] Notes on Ezekiel 28:14, Biblical Studies Press. *The NET Bible First Edition Notes*. Biblical Studies Press, 2006. Also see Lowe, *Deconstructing Lucifer*, 118-131.
[93] The woman's crown of twelve stars is a symbol of the twelve tribes of Israel.

tail. The dragon and his minions seek to devour the male seed (offspring) of the woman, but they fail and the child becomes king. And then the passage tells of a heavenly war:

> Revelation 12:7–10
> [7] Now war arose in heaven, Michael and his angels fighting against the dragon. And the dragon and his angels fought back, [8] but he was defeated, and there was no longer any place for them in heaven. [9] And the great dragon was thrown down, that ancient serpent, who is called the devil and Satan, the deceiver of the whole world—he was thrown down to the earth, and his angels were thrown down with him. [10] And I heard a loud voice in heaven, saying, "Now the salvation and the power and the kingdom of our God and the authority of his Christ have come, for the accuser of our brothers has been thrown down, who accuses them day and night before our God.

Most Christians believe this is a reference to Satan's fall before the Garden of Eden incident, where he takes one third of the angels in heaven with him. But a closer look at the context reveals that this is not the case at all, but rather the opposite. The war in heaven *does not* happen before the Garden, it happens at the time of the incarnation of Messiah on earth! The woman (Israel) gives birth to a male child (Messiah, v. 5), who the dragon (Satan) seeks to devour (from Herod's slaughter of the innocents all the way to the Cross). That Messiah ascends to the throne in authority after his resurrection (v. 5; Eph 1:20-22), during which time that woman (Israel) flees to the wilderness (time of tribulation under the Roman Empire).

The war in heaven we see cannot be before the Garden because it says that the throwing down of Satan occurs with the coming of the kingdom of Christ! (v. 10). He is thrown down to earth and then seeks to kill the Christ (v. 13). Satan then seeks to make war with the rest of her offspring (God's people) which we see in history.

Revelation 12 is an apocalyptic parable that is describing the incarnation of Messiah, his ascension to the throne of authority over all principalities and powers, and his suppression of Satan's power as the Gospel goes forth into the world.

But our problems with Satan do not end there. In *Enoch Primordial*, I do not call Satan, Satan, but *the satan*, lowercase, or the Accuser. Why? Because the Hebrew word is not an individual's name, but a *legal role* meaning "accuser" or "adversary." The satan/accuser depicted in Job 1 and 2 is one of the divine council of heavenly host (1Kings 22) who engages in legal accusations against God and his people and sometimes carries out God's intentions. In short, he is a kind of manipulative prosecutor whose purpose is to challenge God and his perfect law.

In Hebrew, *satan* is prefixed by the definite article *ha* which makes it translate more accurately as *the satan*, or *the accuser*. In the New Testament Greek, *satan* is prefixed by the definite article *ho*, carrying the same result of *the satan* as *the Adversary* (Rev. 12:9) or *the Accuser* (Rev. 12:10).

So the most we can know of the Accuser's work in the Old Testament is that he was the Serpent in the Garden, and he *may have been* a prosecuting attorney-like accuser of God's heavenly court. I say *may have been* because the Accuser was more a role or state of being than an individual. The avenging angel who was going to strike down Balaam was described as *the satan (accuser)* in Numbers 22:22 and verse 32 ("adversary" and "oppose"); the political opponents of king David were defined as *the satan* to him (2Sam. 19:22); David himself was described as a potential *satan* to the Philistines (1Sam. 29:4); Hadad the Edomite and Reznon, son of Eliada are both described as *satans* to Israel (1Kings 11:14, 23); and even God himself is described as *the satan* (adversary) when he incites David to take a census (1Chron. 21:1; 2 Sam. 24:1). In the Old Testament, *the Accuser* was not always the same individual, but more likely the legal office of prosecutor.

This short excursion into deconstructing Satan is the foundation for why I portrayed him as I did in *Enoch Primordial*, as the prosecutorial Seraph, the Serpent of the Garden, whose purpose became accusing God's people and bringing lawsuits to God's throne to try to foil his plans.

Covenant Lawsuit

In *Enoch Primordial*, the Accuser prosecutes a "covenant lawsuit" against Yahweh Elohim in order to buy time for the Watchers to accomplish their nefarious plans of world domination. The Accuser and most of the Watchers "present themselves" before the heavenly court, along with "ten thousand times ten thousand of God's holy ones," the divine council. God is seated on his chariot throne above the Cherubim and beneath the Seraphim, and the Accuser engages in his arguments against God with Enoch, the translated holy man, as defense attorney.

At first blush this may seem to the modern "enlightened" religious mind like an artificial modern construct imposed upon the ancient story. But in fact, it is organically derived from the Bible itself, which drew from the ancient suzerain vassal treaties of the ancient Near East (most likely Hittite in origin).

Whenever "the Accuser" (the *satan*) is named in the Bible, it is usually in the legal context of a heavenly lawsuit. In the *Noah Primeval* appendices, I examined the divine council in the Scriptures in detail. In passages such as Job 1 and 2, and 1Kings 22 we are told that "the sons of God came to present themselves before Yahweh,"[94] "all the host of heaven standing beside him on his right and on his left."[95] God then asks counsel and recommendation from this multitude on what to do regarding a specific situation.[96] The heavenly beings give their opinions, God renders his verdict, and directs some of the host to carry out the sentence.[97]

The context in these passages is that of a legal body of divine beings counseling with God over justice and the satan is one of these divine beings whose role is to accuse.[98] In Zechariah 3:1-4, Joshua the High Priest stands in this divine council before God. The satan stands beside him "to accuse him" before Elohim in good legal form.

While some of these scenes are the Accuser initiating legal accusations against God's people, others are litigation against pagan rulers for their own defiance of God's universal sovereignty. In Daniel 7:9-14, we see "the Ancient of Days" seated on his throne, "and ten thousand times ten thousand stood before him; the court sat in judgment" over the nations of the earth (Dan. 7:10). And in Psalm 82, God renders legal judgment upon the members of the divine council who failed to carry out justice for God upon the gentile nations they had inherited.[99] We read this Psalmic phrase used in *Enoch Primordial*,

---

[94] Job 1:6; 2:1.
[95] 1Kings 22:19.
[96] Job 1:8; 1King 22:20, 22; Isa 6:8. Scholar Frank Moore Cross shows that the divine council is implied in other passages such as Isaiah 40:1-6 and 48:20-21 where God is heard asking a question to an "unknown" plural audience. "Comfort my people," "a voice says, 'Cry!'" and "declare this with a shout" are all plural imperatives as if spoken to a multitude surrounding God's throne. Frank M. Cross, Jr., "The Council of Yahweh in Second Isaiah," *Journal of Near Eastern Studies*, Vol. 12, No. 4 (Oct., 1953), pp. 274-277.
[97] Job 1:12; 2:6; 1King 22:22-23.
[98] Lowell K. Handy, "The Authorization of Divine Power and the Guilt of God in the Book of Job: Useful Ugaritic Parallels," *Journal for the Study of the Old Testament* (60) December 1993, 108-109: Min Sue Kee, "The Heavenly Council and its Type-scene," *Journal for the Study of the Old Testament*, Vol 31.3(2007): 259-273.
[99] See Appendix A "The Sons of God" in *Noah Primeval* for a detailed explanation of this Biblical concept of the sons of God inheriting the pagan nations.

"God has taken his place in the divine council; in the midst of the gods he holds judgment" (v. 1-2).

Another kind of Biblical lawsuit saw Old Testament prophets as Yahweh's prosecuting attorneys indicting Israel for breaking her covenant with God. The prophet would stand before God's divine council and make the summons and charges against Israel before calling her to respond to the charges. Then Yahweh as judge would pronounce his verdict. One of the qualifications of a prophet's authority to speak for God was that he had stood in this divine council (Jer. 23:18, 22).

Herbert Huffmon has pointed out examples of covenant lawsuits in Jeremiah, Isaiah, Micah, and other prophets carried out in God's courtroom against Israel that illustrated a Biblical pattern of legal procedure:

> A description of the scene of judgment
> II. The speech of the plaintiff
> A. Heaven and earth are appointed judges
> B. Summons to the defendant (or judges)
> C. Address in the second person to the defendant
> 1. Accusation in question form to the defendant
> 2. Refutation of the defendant's possible arguments
> 3. Specific indictment[100]

I used this basic scenario in *Enoch Primordial* when the Accuser accuses Elohim of being unjust in his own covenantal relationship with man. But I also used the ancient Near Eastern covenant formula for the document under attack in the Accuser's lawsuit. This ancient formula can be seen in the form of the Biblical covenant as well. Biblical scholars have shown how God's covenants with Israel displayed the same five or six point structure that their neighboring Hittite nation used during the Late Bronze or Early Iron Ages (1400-1200 B.C.).

It is commonly understood now that covenant texts occupy a significant proportion of Biblical composition. As Biblical scholar Eugene Merrill states,

> The Covenant Code of Exodus 20-23 and the entire Book of Deuteronomy are the most outstanding examples of this type. It is quite apparent that Moses undoubtedly utilized already

---

[100] Herbert B. Huffmon, "The Covenant Lawsuit in the Prophets," *JBL* 78 (1959): 7. 285–95.

existing treaty formulas in the construction of biblical treaty contracts between God and individuals or God and Israel.[101]

The chart below summarizes how the book of Deuteronomy reflects five key elements of the ancient Hittite suzerain treaty as currently attested by scholarship:

Parallels Between Hittite Suzerainty Treaties & the Book of Deuteronomy[102]	
Structure of Hittite Suzerainty Treaties (14th Century B.C.)	Structure of Deuteronomy, a Hebrew "Covenant Document"
1. Preamble: "These are the words of the Great King…"	**1. Preamble**: (1:1–6). "These are the words which Moses spoke…"
2. Historical Prologue: The events leading up to the treaty.	**2. Historical Prologue:** (1:7–4:49). Events leading up to the making and renewing of the covenant.
3. Ethical Stipulations: Laws relating to the vassal's obedience to the suzerain.	**3. Ethical Stipulations:** (5–26). The loyalty due to God.
4. Curses and Blessings: Contingent upon disobedience or obedience.	**4. Curses and Blessings:** (27, 28). Contingent upon disobedience or obedience.
5. Divine Witnesses: Called to witness the making of the treaty ("heaven and earth").[103]	**5. Divine Witnesses:** (32). The witness of "heaven and earth" (30:19; 32:1).

Whether the majority of the Pentateuch (first five books of the Bible) was written by Moses or compiled and edited in the centuries that followed him, some scholars such as Meredith Kline have argued that the entire Bible, including the early chapters of Genesis, is formulated on the model of an extended ancient Near Eastern covenant.[104]

---

[101] Eugene Merrill, "Covenant and the Kingdom : Genesis 1–3 As Foundation for Biblical Theology," Criswell Theological Review 1 (1987) 296-7.

[102] Adapted and modified from Walter A. Elwell and Barry J. Beitzel, *Baker Encyclopedia of the Bible*, 535 (Grand Rapids, Mich.: Baker Book House, 1988). See also Meredith Kline, *Treaty of the Great King* (Overland Park: KS, 2000); Walton, John H. *Zondervan Illustrated Bible Backgrounds Commentary (Old Testament) Volume 1: Genesis, Exodus, Leviticus, Numbers, Deuteronomy*. Grand Rapids, MI: Zondervan, 2009 420-515.

[103] The *DDD* has this to say about the divine witness duo of heaven and earth: "'Olden gods' frequently occur in pairs in the ancient theogonies and often represent elements of the natural order. In texts of diverse origins in the ancient world, these pairs of deities are invoked to serve as witnesses to treaties and covenants. We find analogous petitions made in OT covenant lawsuit formulas used by the prophets. Isaiah (Isa 1:2) invokes the Heavens and the Earth to act as witnesses against Israel for breaking the covenant with Yahweh. The prophet Micah makes a similar appeal (Mic 6:2; cf. Jer 2:12). While these elements were by no means considered divine by the prophets, their use in covenant lawsuit formulas indicates a common rhetorical form whose origins may be traced back to originally mythological conceptions." Karel van der Toorn, Bob Becking and Pieter Willem van der Horst, *Dictionary of Deities and Demons in the Bible*, 2nd extensively rev. ed., (Leiden; Boston; Köln; Grand Rapids, MI; Cambridge: Brill; Eerdmans, 1999) 644-45.

[104] M.G. Kline, *The Treaty of the Great King* (Grand Rapids: Eerdmans, 1963); *The Structure of Biblical Authority* (Grand Rapids: Eerdmans,1972).

Another well established "Tablet Theory" by D.J. Wiseman suggests that the early portions of Genesis may have even found their sources in clay tablets inscribed by those closest to the primeval events.[105] So maybe the notion of the Accuser referring to "discovery documents" of genealogies in *Enoch Primordial* is not so far fetched after all.

In conclusion, even the legal procedures and divine council found in the Bible reflect the covenant treaty structures, and city-state bureaucracy of Israel's ancient Near Eastern pagan neighbors redeemed and applied to God's purposes.

The Chronicles of the Nephilim

So that's what I did in *Noah Primeval* and *Enoch Primordial*. I retold the story of these two heroes of faith, incorporating the respected Enochian tradition of the Watchers and giants, Ancient Near Eastern imagery of Azazel, Lilith, Leviathan and Rahab, cherubim and seraphim, speculation on the divine council of the Sons of God, along with other Mesopotamian mythopoeia and Biblical imagination, in order to give a theological explanation for the true origins and "partial truth" of pagan mythology. It's all positively primeval.

If you liked this book, then please help me out by writing an honest review of it on Amazon (click here to write review). That is one of the best ways to say thank you to me as an author. It really does help my exposure and status as an author. It's really easy. In the Customer Reviews section, there is a little box that says "Write a customer review." They guide you easily through the process. Thanks! — *Brian Godawa*

• • • • •

Biblical & Historical Research

For additional free Biblical and historical scholarly research related to this novel and series, go to Godawa.com > Chronicles of the Nephilim > *Scholarly Research.*

---

[105] P.J. Wiseman and D. J. Wiseman, *Ancient Records and the Structure of Genesis* (Nashville: Thomas Nelson, Inc., 1985). Online, see: Curt Sewell, "The Tablet Theory of Genesis Authorship," *Bible and Spade*, Winter 1994, Vol. 7, No. 1. http://www.biblearchaeology.org/post/2010/10/11/the-tablet-theory-of-genesis-authorship.aspx

GET THIS EBOOKLET ON THE BOOK OF ENOCH!

For a Limited Time Only

FREE

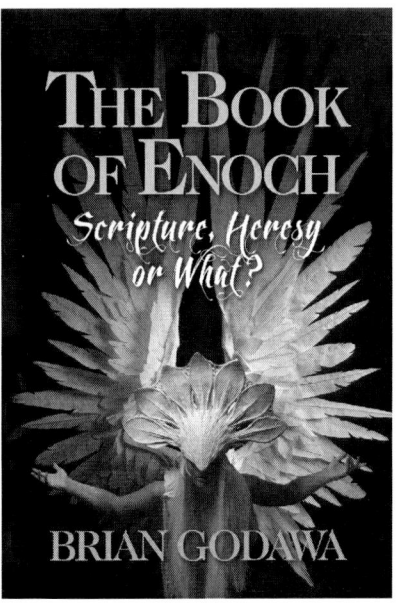

A Controversial Ancient Book with Shocking Information!

By Brian Godawa

Chapters Include:
• What is the Book of Enoch? • Where did it come from? • Why isn't it in the Bible? • Is the Book of Enoch reliable? • and MORE!

The answers may surprise you. Written by respected Biblical Christian author.

Click on this link to get your FREE eBooklet:
https://godawa.com/feb-ne/

BOOK ONE: NOAH PRIMEVAL

Noah Primeval

Chronicles of the Nephilim
Book One

By Brian Godawa

NOAH PRIMEVAL

5th Edition

Copyright © 2011, 2012, 2013, 2014, 2017, 2021 Brian Godawa
All rights reserved. No part of this book may be reproduced in any form or by any electronic or mechanical means, including information storage and retrieval systems, without prior written permission, except in the case of brief quotations in critical articles and reviews.

Warrior Poet Publishing
www.warriorpoetpublishing.com

ISBN: 978-0-615-55078-7 (Paperback)
ISBN: 978-0-615-56567-5 (Kindle)

Scripture quotations taken from *The Holy Bible: English Standard Version*. Wheaton: Standard Bible Society, 2001.

Dedicated to
my Emzara,
my Muse,
my Kimberly.
Song 2:1-2

and to
Michael S. Heiser,
whose scholarship has opened my eyes
like Elisha's servant.
2 Kings 6:1

ACKNOWLEDGMENTS

Special thanks always goes to my wonderful wife Kimberly, without whose support, I would not be writing much of anything, including this novel. Another special thanks to Neil Uchitel for all our rambling discussions all those years ago about fallen angels, vampires and the Nephilim. Thanks to my editor, Don Enevoldsen for his friendship and fellowship in the passionate and weary struggle of the life of writing. And to John Kleinpeter for his excellent proofreading. And to Sarah Beach for her excellent editing of this fourth edition, that made it so much better. Most importantly, I thank Yahweh Elohim, my Creator, for his inspiration of imagination within his poetry, stories, and creation.

Inspired By True Events.

PREFACE

The story you are about to read is the result of Biblical and historical research about Noah's flood and the ancient Near Eastern (ANE) context of the book of Genesis. While I engage in significant creative license and speculation, all of it is rooted in an affirmation of what I believe is the theological and spiritual intent of the Bible. For those who are leery of such a "novel" approach, let them consider that the traditional Sunday school image of Noah as a little old white-bearded farmer building the ark alone with his sons is itself a speculative cultural bias. The Bible actually says very little about Noah. We don't know what he did for a living before the Flood or even where he lived. How do we know whether he was just a simple farmer or a tribal warrior? Genesis 9:2 says Noah "*began* to be a man of the soil" *after* the Flood, not before it. If the world *before* the flood was full of wickedness and violence, then would not a righteous man fight such wickedness as Joshua or David would? Noah would not have been that different from Abraham, who farmed, did business and led his family and servants in war against kings.

We know very little about primeval history, but we do learn from archeological evidence that humanity was clearly tribal during the early ages when this story takes place. Yet, nothing is written about Noah's tribe in the Bible. It would be modern individualistic prejudice to assume that Noah was a loner when everyone in that Biblical context was communal. Noah surely had a tribe.

There is really no agreement as to the actual time and location of the event of the Flood. Some say it was global, some say it was in upper Mesopotamia, some say lower Mesopotamia, some say the Black Sea, some say the earth was so changed by the flood that we would not know where it happened. Since Genesis has some references that seem to match Early Bronze Age Mesopotamian contexts I have gone with that basic interpretation.

The Bible also says Noah built the ark. Are we to believe that Noah built it all by himself? It doesn't say. With his sons' help? It doesn't say. But that very same book *does say* earlier that Cain "built a city" (some scholars believe it was Cain's son Enoch) Are we to assume that he built an entire city by himself? Ridiculous. Cain or Enoch presided as a leader over the building of a city by a group of people, just as Noah probably did with his ark.

One of the only things Genesis says about Noah's actual character is that he was "a righteous man, blameless in his generation. Noah walked with God" (Gen. 6:9). The New Testament clarifies this meaning by noting Noah as an "heir" and "herald" of righteousness by faith (Heb. 11:7; 2Pet. 2:5). The popular interpretation of this notion of "righteousness" is to understand Noah as a virtually sinless man too holy for his time, and always communing with God in perfect obedience. But is this really Biblical? Would Noah have never sinned? Never had an argument with God? Never had to repent? As a matter of fact, the term "righteous" in the Old and New Testaments was not a mere description of a person who did good deeds and avoided bad deeds. Righteousness was a Hebrew legal concept that meant, "right standing before God" as in a court of law. It carried the picture of two positions in a lawsuit, one "not in the right," and the other, "in the right" or "righteous" before God. It was primarily a relational term. Not only that, but in both Testaments, the righteous man is the man who is said to "live by faith," not by perfect good deeds (Hab. 2:4; Rom. 1:17). So righteousness does not mean "moral perfection" but "being in the right with God because of faith."

What's more, being a man of faith doesn't mean a life of perfect consistency either. Look at David, the "man after God's own heart" (Acts 13:22), yet he was a murderer and adulterer and more than once avoided obeying God's will. But that doesn't stop him from being declared as "doing all God's will" by the apostle Paul. Or consider Abraham, the father of the Faith, who along with Sarah believed that God would provide them with a son (Heb. 11:8-11). Yet, that Biblically honored faith was *not* perfect, as they both laughed in derision at God's promise at first (Gen. 17:17; 18:12). Later, Abraham argued with God over his scorched earth policy at Sodom (Gen. 18). Moses was famous for his testy debates with God (Ex. 4; Num. 14:11-24). King David's Psalms were sometimes complaints to his Maker (Psa. 13; Psa. 69). The very name *Israel* means "to struggle with God."

All the heroes in the Hebrews Hall of Faith (Heb. 11) had sinful moments, lapses of obedience and even periods of running from God's call or struggling with their Creator. It would not be heresy to suggest that Noah may have had his own journey with God that began in fear and ended in faith. In fact, to say otherwise is to present a life inconsistent with the reality of every human being in history. To say one is a righteous person of faith is to say that the completed picture of his life is one of finishing the race set before him, not of having a perfect run without injuries or failures.

Some scholars have even noted that the phrase "blameless in his generation" is an unusual one, reserved for unblemished sacrifices in the temple. This physical purity takes on new meaning when understood in the genetic context of the verses before it that speak of "Sons of God" or *bene ha elohim* leaving their proper abode in heaven and violating the separation of angelic and human flesh (Gen. 6:1-4; Jude 5-7). Within church history, there is a venerable tradition of interpreting this strangest of Bible passages as referring to supernatural beings from God's heavenly host who mate with humans resulting in the giant offspring called *Nephilim*. Other equally respectable theologians argue that these Sons of God were either humans from the "righteous" bloodline of Seth or a symbolic reference to human kings or judges of some kind. I have weighed in on the supernatural interpretation and have provided appendices at the end of the book that give the Biblical theological foundation for this interpretation.

This novel seeks to remain true to the sparse facts presented in Genesis (with admittedly significant embellishments) interwoven with theological images and metaphors come to life. Where I engage in flights of fancy, such as a journey into Sheol, I seek to use figurative imagery from the Bible, such as "a bed of maggots and worms" (Isa. 14:11) and "the appetite of Sheol" (Isa. 5:14) and bring them to life by literalizing them into the flesh-eating living-dead animated by maggots and worms.

Another player that shows up in the story is Leviathan. While I have provided another appendix explaining the theological motif of Leviathan as a metaphor in the Bible for chaos and disorder, I have embodied the sea dragon in this story for the purpose of incarnating that chaos as well. I have also literalized the Mesopotamian cosmology of a three-tiered universe with a solid vault in the heavens, and a flat disc earth supported on the pillars of the underworld, the realm of the dead. This appears to be the model assumed by the Biblical writers in many locations (Phil. 2:10; Job 22:14; 37:18; Psa. 104:5; 148:4; Isa. 40:22), so I thought it would be fascinating to tell that story within that worldview unknown to most modern westerners. The purpose of the Bible is not to support scientific theories or models of the universe, but to tell *the story of God* through ancient writers. Those writers were people of their times just as we are.

I have also woven together Sumerian and other Mesopotamian mythology in with the Biblical story, but with this caveat: Like C.S. Lewis, I believe the primary purpose of mythology is to embody the worldview and values of a culture. But all myths carry slivers of the truth and reflect some distorted vision of what really happened. Sumer's Noah was Ziusudra, Babylon's Noah was Utnapishtim, and Akkad's was Atrahasis. The Bible's Noah is my standard. So my goal was to incorporate real examples of ANE history and myth in subjection to that standard in such a way that we see their "true origin." Thus my speculation that the gods of the ancient world may have been real beings (namely fallen "Sons of God") with supernatural powers. The Bible itself makes this suggestion in several places (Deut. 32:17; Psa. 106:34), and it also talks of the Sons of God as "gods" or supernatural beings from God's divine council (Psa. 82:1; 58:1; Ezek. 28:2). See the appendix at the back for my defense of this interpretation from the Bible.

Lastly, I have permitted myself to use extra-Biblical Jewish literature from the Second Temple period as additional reference material for my story. The most significant is the book of *1 Enoch*, a document famous for its detailed amplification of the Genesis 6:1-4 passage about supernatural Sons of God mating with human women and birthing giants, as well as leading humanity astray with occultic knowledge. I use these ancient Jewish sources not because I consider them completely factual or on par with the Bible, but simply in an attempt to incarnate the soul of the ancient Hebrew imagination in conversation with the text of Scripture rather than imposing my own modern western one upon the text. I am within the tradition of the Church on this since authors of the New Testament as well as early Church Fathers and other orthodox theologians in church history respected some of these ancient manuscripts as well.

Many of these texts from the Second Temple Period, such as *Jubilees*, *Testaments of the Twelve Patriarchs* or *The Life of Adam and Eve*, and others found in the Pseudepigrapha, were creative extrapolations of the Biblical text. These were not intended to deceive or overturn the Bible, but rather to retell Biblical stories with theological amplification and creative speculation while remaining true to their interpretation of the Scriptures.

In short, I am not writing Scripture. I am not even saying that I believe this is how the story *might have* actually happened. I am simply engaging in a time-honored tradition of the ancient Hebrew culture: I am retelling a Biblical story in a new way to underscore the theological truths within it. The Biblical theology that this story is founded upon is provided in several appendixes at the back of the book for those who are interested in going deeper.

The beauty of fiction is that we can make assumptions regarding uncertain theological and historical information without having to prove them one way or another. The story requires only that we establish continuity within the made up world, and accepting those assumptions for the sake of the story does not imply theological agreement. So, sit back and let your imagination explore the contours of this re-imagined journey of one of the most celebrated religious heroes across all times and cultures.

MAP

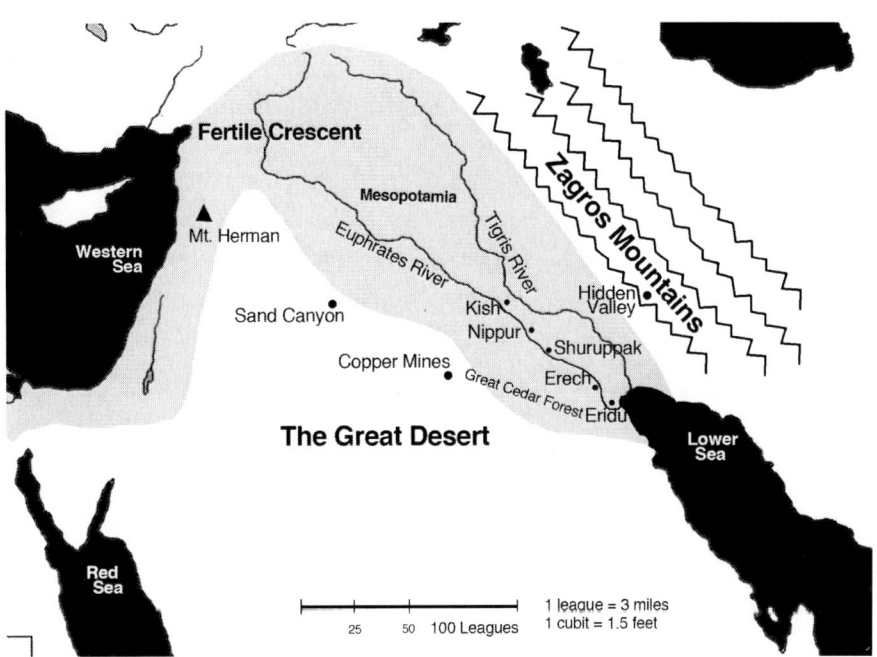

PROLOGUE

Methuselah squinted through half opened eyes. Enoch traveled beside him as they descended onto crystalline blue waves, the eternal sea. Above him, the deep black sky, painted with a pulsating wave of ethereal color, stretched endlessly into the distance. Methuselah knew where they were — in the waters above the heavens. Before him, a lone ancient temple rested upon the waters like an island, crafted from white marble with gold trimming and inlaid with innumerable precious jewels; jasper, sapphire, emerald, onyx, and others. Around this temple hovered a myriad of the Holy Ones, like phantasms of starlight that he could see, but not quite see. He knew what the structure was — the temple of Elohim, and it was terrifyingly wondrous.

Methuselah sighed with disappointment. Another vision. He was approaching his eight hundred and fiftieth year of life and these visions wearied his old soul. His father, Enoch, hounded him like a ghost in his dreams. Enoch was known for being a righteous man who walked with Elohim, and Elohim spoke with him in visions. When he was young, Methuselah would often complain about his father's "head in the clouds," until he learned the frightening truth that Elohim's holiness was unbearable to sinful human nature. It made him more sympathetic to the effect it had on Enoch.

Elohim had taken Enoch up to heaven alive before he could experience the dismal universal experience that is death. No aching joints, no wavering eye sight, no bodily pains as the years would wind him down to the grave.

From all this Enoch was spared.

It's not fair, thought Methuselah. But alas, Elohim is the creator of all things, and surely has the right to do as he pleases, no matter how strange or incomprehensible those actions may be to us mortals made of clay and nephesh, God's own breath. Methuselah took the lesson hard. One day soon, this heavenly temple will be his permanent home. But not today. He resigned himself and took in the fearful symmetry of a terrifying yet wondrous cosmos through which Enoch escorted him on the wings of the wind.

Despite his sense of helplessness, Methuselah considered that maybe these visions were worth the irritation, after all. Who else is allowed to see such awesome marvels before their time? Maybe Elohim may yet take him, as he did Enoch.

Out of a myriad of stars some fell from the sky and plunged into the waters below. Pulled beneath the waters, Methuselah watched their descent. The murky depths deadened their shining.

A shiver went through Methuselah's spine as he continued descending into the deep. Then he saw the reason for his chill. The spiny armored back of a long serpentine creature swerved just below him, and disappeared into the darkness. Gigantic, the creature measured maybe three hundred cubits long, a shadowy impression of its full fearful presence in the murky blackness. This was Leviathan, the seven-headed sea dragon of chaos, and the guardian of the deep. Few had ever seen it, fewer still had lived to tell about it. The only thing more terrifying than Leviathan was its mother, Rahab.

Methuselah and Enoch landed on the bottom of the heavenly ocean and began to move through a solid crystalline floor, known to his people as *raqia*, the firmament of heaven. Below this raqia the heavens and the earth were enveloped by the firmament like a vaulted dome. Embedded in the vault of heaven glittered the stars, planets, and the greater and lesser lights that rose upon the ends of the earth in the east and set upon the gates of the west.

As Methuselah and Enoch watched, the luminaries passed through the clouds and approached the earth, a flat disc surrounded by the waters, under which were the pillars of the earth, and below that, Sheol, the underworld. Two hundred of them landed in succession on Mount Hermon in Bashan in the northwest and he knew he was watching many years of the past moving before his eyes. The shining ones spread out across the earth from that cosmic mountain to reign as gods over mankind. These were the *Bene ha Elohim*, the Sons of God.

"Weep for mankind, Methuselah," said Enoch. "For every intent of the thought of his heart is only evil continually. And behold, the Lord will come with ten thousands of his holy ones to execute judgment on all, and to destroy the wicked. But I saw a vision of a Chosen Seed who will bring an end to the reign of the gods and bring rest from the curse of the land. Elohim promised in the Garden that the seed of the Woman, Havah, she who is also known as Eve, would be at war with the seed of the Serpent, Nachash. But through this chosen seedline will come an anointed King who will crush the head of the Nachash, the seed of the Serpent and their abominations in the land."

Hundreds of leagues southeast from Mount Hermon, directly below Methuselah's feet, sat Mesopotamia, the center of the earth, the land between the rivers Tigris and Euphrates. The rivers produced a fertile crescent that rose from the Lower Sea in the south up to Ebla and Amurru in the north, bounded on the west by the vast Great Desert, and on the east by the Zagros Mountains.

Methuselah descended to the southern part of Mesopotamia near the Lower Sea into the fertile land of Shinar, now called Sumer. He was being taken home to the great cedar forest, where his nomadic tribe's camp was hidden from the city-states that bordered the rivers. He felt the vision fading to its end.

"I am not the Chosen Seed," complained Methuselah, "so why do you keep troubling me with these visions?"

"Because," replied Enoch, "the Chosen Seed is not listening. But you have his ear."

Methuselah knew who the Chosen Seed was. And he was going to tan his hide.

CHAPTER 1

Noah ben Lamech dashed through the sparse brush surrounding the mighty cedars, easily twisting his spear to avoid tangling low hanging branches. Five of his tribesmen trailed behind him, clad in animal skins, carrying spears, bows, and maces.

Lemuel, Noah's protégé, ran fast, nocking his arrow and aiming the flint tip at the prey. The target was a pazuzu, a black monster with a double set of bat-like wings, talons for feet, and a ghastly looking doggish face. The arrow, loosed too quickly, buried into the tree inches from the pazuzu's head. The vile creature let loose a shriek that pierced the human's ears, and fluttered with increased frenzy.

A second pazuzu panicked and almost ran into the first one. They both flitted erratically around the thick trees, seeking shelter from their pursuers' missiles. Unable to find an opening through the heavy canopy of foliage overhead to reach the sky and freedom, they split apart to escape their predators.

Noah gestured to his men to split as well, three on one. Lemuel and Shafat veered into Noah's footsteps after the first pazuzu. The other three turned after the second one.

They are enemy spies, Noah thought, *scouts for the city gods, gathering information on the last of the human tribes evading the conquering will of their Lords. We may have started the day hunting for food, but these things are no food for us. We must destroy them.*

Until now, Noah had managed to avoid detection by staying nomadic and hiding in the forest with his people. His family had originally settled the city of Shuruppak in the midst of the southern plain generations ago. His father Lamech was the priest-king of the city-state and Noah had inherited the position as a young man. But when the pantheon of gods extended their dominion throughout the land of Shinar, Noah's clan left the city because of their dedication to Elohim. They became nomads and roamed the forests, deserts, and mountains.

Noah's tribe had traversed all these territories and had found the forests to be the most inhabitable. But as his people grew in number, presently a few hundred, with children and herd, it was becoming more difficult to pick up quickly and move. If one of these damnable creatures got away and reported to the gods, Noah's community would be in jeopardy. They would run to the mountains where the city gods refused to follow. The desert was bone dry, scorching and brutal for child mortality, and mountain life was not much less miserable to raise a family like the ancient cave dwellers who died out long ago. There were not many of the human tribes left, and Noah was determined to remain one of them.

His desperate need fueled him. Noah's spirit surged. His team spread out and surrounded their pazuzu. Hindered by the closeness of the trees and underbrush, the creature's wings slowed its progress, and the pursuit steadily gained ground. The pazuzu twisted and turned in confusion. With the desperation of a cornered animal, the quarry looked for an opening to strike back at the hunters.

Lemuel glanced away to check his position. He nearly ran headlong into a cedar tree.

The pazuzu pounced in that instant. It took its eyes off Noah for one moment to swoop down.

That was all Noah needed. He drew back and released his spear with the power of an arm accustomed to strenuous labor. The wooden shaft flew straight into the breast of the creature with such force that it impaled the pazuzu's body and pinned it into a tree. It screeched its last shriek and died, black blood oozing down the rough bark of the cedar.

Noah, Lemuel and young Shafat approached the beast. Their long hair, and beards flowed over their animal skins. Noah knew that it gave city dwellers the impression of uncivilized brutishness. But they would be wrong. His nomadic people were highly cultured, and their earthiness was a deliberate expression of their refusal to worship the city gods. His were the people of the Creator Elohim and they were proud to be separate from the rest of humanity who had rejected Elohim's kingship and descended into the worship of the gods of the land. Noah felt that the nomadic tribes could rightly be called the last of humanity.

Noah was over five hundred years old and in his prime as the leader of his people. This was middle age in a community where many lived as long as nine hundred years. As Lemuel was Noah's apprentice, so young twenty-year old Shafat was Lemuel's. They were as close as brothers in their community. They did everything together and protected one another.

"Stand back!" Lemuel snapped to Shafat. "These things are treacherous. They will feign death just to bring one of us with them to the grave. If its talons get hold of you, we will have to cut your arm off to loose you."

Its death throes were genuine. The pazuzu's legs twitched and the last of its air gurgled from its lungs.

"It stinks like excrement," blurted Shafat, with his hand over his nose in disgust.

"It is an abomination," said Lemuel. He reached up and jerked the spear out of the monster, letting it drop to the forest floor in a heap. He handed the spear to Noah.

"It is getting worse, Noah. There will soon be nowhere to hide. We cannot run forever."

Noah ignored the point. He prodded the creature with the tip of his spear, exposing a brand of the god's name in cuneiform on the twitching leg. "This is a scout of Anu."

"We killed a scout of the god Anu?" exclaimed Shafat.

"Quiet your fear," Noah said. "We bow to no god."

"No god but Elohim," Lemuel amended.

Noah shot an irritated glance at Lemuel, then caught himself and nodded reluctantly, "No god but Elohim."

This was a sensitive issue for Noah. He was not always on speaking terms with Elohim, who seemed to be quite distant, only conferring with crazy men like his grandfather Enoch and leaving so much to the *mal'akim* angels to do his bidding.

Noah had served Elohim through the years. He remained pure in his generation. He walked upright and kept separate from the pollution of the city gods who came from heaven and sought to mix their blood with humanity. Noah's tribe and the other human tribes of nomads refused to worship these pretenders to the throne of Elohim, and refused to participate in their corrupting sorceries.

But this was not enough for Noah. Though he knew Elohim was Lord of creation, he sometimes felt that there was little difference between the servitude Elohim expected and the servitude that the city gods demanded of their subjects. A god was a god after all, and in either case man was a servant.

Noah did not like being a servant. He yearned for freedom. *Why can we not be left alone to live our lives? Why must we fight evil all the time?* In a wicked generation, evil never sleeps. And Noah was growing weary from eternal vigilance. He preferred to hide away from it all and just enjoy his family, his beautiful wife, and his own concerns. He wanted to work the land and enjoy the fruit of his labors and be left alone. He had enough on his back to survive in this difficult world and to build his own community based on his own beliefs. If evil was left to run its course, it would destroy its own servants anyway, so why not let it? They deserved it. Why did Noah and his companions have to fight Elohim's battles for him?

The sound of breaking twigs interrupted his thoughts. The three turned toward the sound, tensed and ready.

Tobias and the other two warriors came through the brush. Noah instinctively glanced at their spears, hoping for a sign of pazuzu blood. There was none.

Tobias looked uncertain. "I think we got it. We reached the forest's edge and it broke out to the clearing. But we struck it twice. It managed to stay in the air, but I do not believe it could make it back the distance to the city with two flints in its flesh."

Noah pondered a moment. "We had best have an elder's meeting tonight and make a decision whether to move on."

Shafat let out a sigh of disappointment. Noah slapped him on the back of the head and gave him a warning glance. Without a word, Noah stomped off toward the camp.

Lemuel wondered just how long they could keep going like this. He had followed Noah's lead for many years and had always trusted him. Noah would do no wrong to any man. He was the patriarch of their tribe, a warrior who knew the land well and would not compromise with wickedness. But he could also be impatient and insensitive with those who lacked his resolve. Some men needed understanding and encouragement in the ways of the Lord. Zeal for righteousness did not mean one should give up compassion. Lemuel shook his head sadly as he walked.

But then again, Noah did listen to Lemuel. His passion meant he might be quick to anger, but he was also quick to repent. Lemuel had never known a better man in all his days. He repressed another sigh and tramped after his leader.

CHAPTER 2

Far away in the skies over Mesopotamia, the wounded pazuzu flapped its double wings struggling to navigate the air streams that helped it remain aloft on its journey to the city. The two arrows burned its muscles with searing pain, one in its left thigh and the other in its right calf. It had lost much blood. Its wings felt heavy. It labored on, knowing if it landed to rest, it would never make it back into the air.

The desert landscape gave way to the unmistakable marks of civilization as the pazuzu reached the outskirts of the city. Erech encompassed over one hundred hectares of land. Below the creature's labored flight stretched the agricultural fields and farms watered by canals from the bordering Euphrates River. Since their very lives were interwoven with the river, the residents became expert canal builders. Levees and dikes brought water to their crops in the outlying areas within the city multiple man-made canals and aqueducts criss-crossed the various residential divisions, channeling lavish amounts of water for everything from cooking to cleaning to waste disposal. In between those channeled sections were the adobe and sun-dried brick homes. The Sumerian citizens went about their daily business, unaware of the flying presence high above.

In the center of this metropolis that boasted a populace of close to ten thousand, a raised hillock overlooked the city and its outlying farming villages. On the elevation rose the temple called *Eanu*. It was dedicated to the patron deity of the city, Anu, the father god of heaven. It consisted of a huge platform mound seventy-five cubits high, built from mud brick and limestone at the bottom. At the top of the platform terrace, raised another twenty cubits high, sat the White Temple, the holy place of the gods. Its intense whiteness, the result of gypsum plaster, created a shining glow in the hot sun.

Next to this temple complex stood a smaller temple district called *Eanna* for Inanna, the goddess of sex and war, and consort of Anu. Eanu dwarfed the Eanna temple. The compound of the goddess had a different design, reflecting the lesser divine status of the female deity. The Eanna district harbored cult prostitution and other deviant whims of the goddess.

Erech was one of the largest and most advanced cities of the alluvial plain. It was originally settled by Unuk ben Cain, son of Cain, who also built Eridu, the oldest city named after Unuk's son, Irad. The original human inhabitants had arrived from the Zagros mountains to establish the first urban civilization on the plains. Those inhabitants formed a slave force that would help them achieve their urban paradise.

Each city was independent, ruled over by a god. Every year at the New Year Festival the pantheon of city gods would meet in assembly in Erech and deliberate their divine decrees for the upcoming year. Anu arranged his pantheon after Elohim's divine council of heavenly host. It pleased Anu to mock the Most High with his own hierarchy of power.

The gods had no desire to burden themselves with the petty worries of human administrations, so they each chose a priest-king to rule in his stead through a governorship. Scribes referred to the arrival of the gods and their rule as the time "when kingship descended from heaven." But ever since then, the princes of the cities vied for prominence amongst themselves as the gods also sought distinction. The hierarchy was unstable. Bureaucracy always courted ambition and rivalry.

The White Temple on the top of Eanu was the highest point in the city. The large platform structure imitated a holy mountain, a connection between heaven and earth. The people called the artificial mountain a ziggurat. Its four corners pointed to the four corners of the earth. The long straight limestone stairway that ascended from the base to the White Temple at top inspired the name Stairway to the Heavens by the people. The gods assembled in the White Temple for their deliberations and liturgy. Only the priest-king and his servants could enter it.

The priest-king of Erech, Lugalanu, stood in the temple performing sacred duties when the wounded pazuzu crashed onto the floor.

Lugalanu hurried his pace through the long dark underground tunnel connecting the ziggurat and the palace in the Eanna district. With practiced effort he balanced his sacrificial bowl in the flickering torchlight without spilling the blood offering for Anu and his consort Inanna. They always wanted blood. It was the food of the gods and they were ravenous.

Lugalanu's father, the previous priest-king of Erech, had died not long before, leaving his son as the new ruler of the city, called the Big Boss. Lugalanu's name meant "leader of Anu," and his name reflected his job. His responsibilities included not merely the overseeing of ceremonial and priestly activities but the civil governing of the city and the military defense of the outlying area. This combined religious and civic responsibility sometimes wore him out. He had even pleaded with the father god Anu to divide the duties between two leaders, one civil and one religious, but Anu told him it was not yet to be. Concentrated power was always more efficient at getting things accomplished, and Anu had a lot to accomplish with his priest-king.

The positive result of such multiple responsibilities was a certain breadth of wisdom. And wisdom made Lugalanu a good ruler. He had studied some of the dark secrets of the gods, and he was trained in the art of leadership and war. He pitied his people and sought their good, even if they did not understand that good, and the gods richly rewarded him. He had everything he wanted in this world of power and privilege — except a wife. Oh, he had concubines plenty. His nights were filled with selfish gratification of every desire, both natural and unnatural. What he longed for was to be known, to make a true connection with another human being, to have a queen who would rule by his side. But how could the supreme human ruler of the city ever find a woman he could trust amidst this crowd of sycophants, manipulators, and usurpers?

Such thoughts fluttered through his mind as Lugalanu passed into the palace area. His royal robes flowed behind him as he whisked over mosaic floors and engraved walls of brick. Palace guards stiffened to attention at the sight of him.

He was pure royalty, a youthful three hundred years old, muscular, and handsome with his regal oblong cranium. All the servants of the gods and their entourage practiced head binding. It expressed devotion to the deities. Infants were taken early and their skulls bound with straps until they protruded like an extended egg. As the infant's skull matured and hardened, it maintained its oblong shape permanently.

Lugalanu was completely hairless, like all royal servants. Not a hair on their heads, not an eyebrow or a single nose hair was allowed. It was a sign of perfection to transcend humanity by freeing oneself from the most mammalian of physical traits, hair. It made one look more like the sleek hairless gods he worshipped.

Lugalanu marched through the outer court of the palace, striding past lines of bird-men soldiers. These chimeras with bodies of men and heads of hawks and falcons stood at perfect attention, motionless as statues. Their stoic rigidity masked the savage brutality of fierce warriors, created by the sorceries of the gods to build an army for conquest. But the bird-men were a mere trifle compared to the apex of the gods' creativity: the creatures which Lugalanu now approached at the doorway of the inner court.

The gigantic doors loomed over Lugalanu's head. They were ten cubits tall, two and half times the size of the largest man, made of the mightiest cedar and inlaid with gold. Guarding either side of the gateway were two immense Nephilim.

These Nephilim were giant warriors eight to nine cubits tall, nearly as tall as the inner court doors, demigods created by the mating of the divine Sons of God with the human daughters of men. They were the personal royal guard of deity. Their bodies were covered in occultic tattoos used in magic. They had an extra digit on their hands and feet for a total of twelve fingers and twelve toes. No one on earth had seen anything like their armor, coverings made of a light metallic alloy unknown to man. The Nephilim were also called the Seed of Nachash, titans of war that could not easily be defeated by man born of woman. From the perspective of the gods, they were a strategic achievement of intermingling the human and the divine. From the perspective of Elohim, they were an evil corruption of creation. They struck terror into the hearts of everyone who saw them, including Lugalanu. Though they seemed to defer to his authority, he could never quite bring himself to look them in the eye. He stared blankly at the floor ahead of him and continued his purposeful march.

Lugalanu passed the giants into the inner court, the doors closing behind him like a barrier of magic. He paused to take a deep breath before looking up. This moment always astonished him. The most beautiful atrium ever conceived by the mind of deity lay before him. The vast space measured seventy cubits long and forty cubits high, a man-made paradise. It hosted a mixture of architecture sculpted by the most trained of slave craftsmen, and flora cultivated by the most practiced of horticulturalists. As Lugalanu proceeded down the path toward the throne room, a flurry of doves flew out of the foliage around him past the brick columns into the vaulted ceiling above, a heaven on earth. Gemstones glittered everywhere, embedded in the marble: lapis lazuli, sapphire, beryl, topaz, and amethyst. His own adjacent courtroom as priest-king, though full of its own luxuries, looked like a poor imitation of this chamber.

The smell of exotic incense burning on braziers filled his nostrils, as Lugalanu approached the throne room. He saw the shimmering curtains to the throne room were pulled back to display the forms of Anu and Inanna seated on gem-laden thrones. Two large crossbred sphinx-like creatures that the gods called *aladlammu*, guarded the pair. One had the body of a bull, the other of a lion, and both the bearded heads of a human being. They were born of the gods' magical warping of creation. The stone sculptures outside the palace depicted this pair of living breathing monstrosities. The sight of them sent a shudder through Lugalanu. Their penetrating eyes followed his every move with sentinel alertness.

Anu and Inanna silently watched Lugalanu pour out his libation of blood into crystal chalices on the altar. Lugalanu then genuflected and waited for their command.

The gods lounged resplendent in their royal finery. When standing, they towered well over five and a third cubits, much more than Lugalanu's own four cubits. Their eyes shimmered with blue lapis lazuli reptilian irises. Their tongues split lizard-like. Despite their androgynous appearance, Inanna dressed the part of a goddess. They had elongated heads, which the head-binding of their servants sought to mimic. Anu and Inanna would tolerate nothing less than human attendants molded into their likeness. They both wore the horned headdress of deity common throughout the region. Both wore royal robes created from the feathers of vultures.

Inanna cultivated a flamboyance that set her apart from Anu. She wore heavy makeup and pierced her body all over with rings, studs, and spikes. Her nose, eyebrows, and other body parts hosted these symbols of the forced pain that she pleasured in. She also gloried in outrageous outfits as a display of her ironic status as goddess of sex and war. This day, she was more restrained with her red leather and chains.

The skin of the gods appeared smooth, but Lugalanu knew that close up fine subtle serpentine scales that sparkled in the light covered them, producing a visible aura of constant radiant luminescence. Many described this radiance in terms of beryl, crystal or shining bronze. When their passions flared for good or bad, their shining would increase in brilliance, giving the impression of flashes of lightning. Because of this, they were called Shining Ones.

Lugalanu could always count on Anu to have a certain detached playfulness about him, as if he enjoyed being deity and played up the formalities of royalty with a sardonic loftiness. Inanna, on the other hand, was unpredictable and dangerous. She had a violent temper because everyone always seemed to be in the way of her accomplishing her plans. She would instantly kill servants who made mistakes in her presence. She might smite even those who gave her gaudy appearance a strange look. Lugalanu sought to ingratiate himself to them at every opportunity.

"My priest-king, Lugalanu, lord of the city, how dost thou fare?" pronounced Anu with a touch of playful overstatement in his voice.

"Well, my lord Anu, king of gods," Lugalanu responded, promptly followed by a nod to Inanna. "Queen of heaven, my worship."

"Up, up. What do you want?" blurted Inanna.

Lugalanu straightened up quickly and replied, "I have intelligence from one of our pazuzu scouts of a human tribe of nomads in the great cedar forest."

"Well, go slay them," she snorted.

Anu stepped in. "We want loyal, willing subjects, not rebels of insurrection, Inanna."

They argued about this frequently. Anu knew that Inanna wanted to eliminate all the remaining human tribes who worshipped Elohim. But he thought they would accomplish their purposes more effectively if they concentrated on defiling the human bloodline as a way to thwart Elohim's plans for a kingly seed.

It frustrated Inanna to no end that she had to submit to Anu's kingship. Ever since her colossal failure in the war of the titans, called the Titanomachy, she had been demoted from co-regent with him to his consort so he could keep an eye on her. She had massive scars on her back to remind her of the consequences of insubordination. She reined herself in with calculated self-interest.

Lugalanu curried the Queen's favor, "My lord, I humbly defer to her highness. Every rogue human tribe is a possible fulfillment of the revelation."

Anu bristled with annoyance. "The Revelation," he snorted, conveying the impression to the human that he did not believe it. But he did believe it. He sickened of the dread that seized everyone when this revelation business was brought up. Fear was healthy; dread was self-destructive.

"Ah yes, the Revelation," Inanna shot back. "A 'Chosen Seed' who will end the rule of the gods. Are you not concerned, lord? *We* are among those gods who rule. And you are the head of the pantheon, the high and mighty one." She matched Anu's annoyance with sarcasm. "Unless you think you have nothing to lose."

She knew how he would respond. For the hundredth time, he said, "If they worship us, then we have no concern, and are free to use them as slave labor for *our* kingdom."

The gods of the pantheon kept hidden from Lugalanu and most humans their real identities and goals. Anu's real name was Semjaza, and Inanna's, Azazel. These divinities were not gods like Elohim. They were in fact the Sons of God who rebelled from Elohim's divine council that surrounded his very throne.

Elohim himself sat on the high throne, the Creator and Lord of all. Though mortal eyes could not see him, he was visible in his vice-regent, the Son of Man, The Angel of the Lord, who mediated and led God's heavenly host. The members of the host were the Sons of God, or *Bene Elohim,* ten thousand times ten thousand of his Holy Ones who deliberated with the Almighty and would carry forth his judgments — except those who had fallen.

Two hundred of them had rebelled and fallen. They were called "Watchers." By masquerading as gods of the land, they sought to usurp the throne of Elohim and draw human worship away from the Creator. To further enslave the sons of men in idolatry, they had revealed unholy secrets of sorceries, fornications, and war. Enoch had pronounced judgment upon them in faraway days, but the manifestation of that judgment had not yet fallen upon the Watchers. The fullness of their iniquity was not yet complete.

Elohim had created mankind as his representative image on earth, to rule in his likeness. If the fallen Sons of God could transform the image of God into *their* image, their revenge would be almost complete. By mixing the human line of descent with their own, they could stop the bloodline of the promised King from bringing forth its fruit, and thereby win the war of the Seed of Nachash with the Seed of Havah.

Anu had a mellower side that Inanna lacked. He preferred to keep humans alive to serve him rather than destroy them. It was all a matter of perspective. He believed wisdom dictated that his own interests be portrayed as compassion to the humans. Perhaps they would even one day love him instead of fear him. Was this not what it was like to be Elohim?

Lugalanu interrupted Anu's thoughts. "These nomads killed our scouts. They are ruthless savages."

Anu responded, "I too would kill those ugly little beasts if they were sniffing around my residence."

Inanna snorted with disapproval but refused to keep fighting. She would choose her battles. This was not one of them.

"Meet with the tribal leaders and allow them every opportunity to submit," Anu decreed.

Inanna's ire went up. "And if they do not?"

"Then enforce the will of the gods." He was not about to appear weak. His patience only went so far.

Lugalanu bowed low and backed away from their presence. He wondered if he had kept a proper balance of flattery for Inanna without disrespect for Anu's supremacy.

When the human was gone, Inanna grinned with delight to herself. Her vampiric fangs glistened red as she guzzled the blood offering with satisfaction. Perhaps she had not lost this battle after all.

CHAPTER 3

Noah, Lemuel and the others trudged into the camp after their pazuzu hunt. Noah hoped that the evening feast would distract the tribe's attention from the somber faces of the hunting party. The news would not go over well with the community. They had been discovered, and while they could not be sure that the pazuzu escaped to deliver the information, they had to consider it a strong possibility. They would have to discuss it with the elders tonight. Even if the pazuzu did not make it back to the city, its disappearance would eventually bring more scouts to the area.

The camp nestled in the thick cover of the great cedar forest. Ancient trees blocked much of the light, but they also blocked the view of hostile airborne eyes. Old fallen trees provided dry wood to minimize smoke. Tents and other shelters spread over the large encampment with plenty of camouflage to conceal their presence. The livestock of sheep, goats and donkeys were penned off to the east face as an early warning of arrivals from the river cities. The middle of the camp vibrated with mothers boiling soups over low fires, children playing and giggling, and elders cleaning up loose ends.

These were a happy people who served Elohim. Since they had become nomads, they had seen the wonders of a world so much bigger than they had imagined as city dwellers just a generation ago. Weathering snowstorms in the north, surviving the waterless places of the desert, hunting mountain wildlife. They had been at their current forest location for some time now and had become familiar with all its rhythms and cycles, integrating themselves into it all with a confident caretaker's dominion. They could think like deer, hide like foxes, hunt like bears and fight like lions.

Noah nodded silently to his companions and turned toward his personal encampment. Though he was the tribe's patriarch, his tents were no more than appropriate for a family of his size: one goatskin tent for his wife Emzara and himself, one to the side for his children, and one on the other side for his parents, Lamech and Betenos. They lived with his grandfather, Methuselah.

Noah detested the arrogance of royalty and sought to lead by example and merit rather than through power and station. He would not live with special privileges. He would not ask sacrifice of his people that he would not himself also give.

Noah went first to check on his parents. He loved his father and mother deeply. They had raised him with a stern but steady love. Though they were well over six hundred and sixty years old – Noah lost count – they had been mighty in the dark past as giant killers with his great-grandfather Enoch. They spoke little of those days. They did not want the clan to lose vigilance in thinking they had special warriors in their midst. They were human after all, and not invincible. But they taught Noah how to fight and how to be a leader.

Lamech had built the city of Shuruppak after the Titanomachy had almost destroyed their world. But when followers of Ninlil, the consort goddess of Enlil, overran Shuruppak with their worship of the goddess, Lamech walked away from his royal station to become a humble nomad. He chose to worship Elohim as he saw fit, removed from the influence of the wicked masses upon his descendants. He often told Noah that Elohim had special plans for Noah. Not many years before, Lamech had lost his right arm in a battle, and chose to retire and hand over leadership of the tribe to Noah as the new Patriarch.

When Noah stuck his head in the tent, all he saw was grandfather Methuselah snoring away in his afternoon nap. Lamech and Betenos must have gone for one of their many walks in the woods, reminiscing about their past, a time of adventure and danger that they hoped they would never have to face again.

Noah moved on to his children's tent, a sense of anticipation rising in him. These were his true achievements: his two sons, Shem, age five, and Japheth, age four. He took his responsibility to Elohim's command to be fruitful and multiply very seriously. He took everything seriously, too seriously. And these two little gems were just the antidote he needed to bring him back down to earth and enjoy life a little more. "Stop once in a while and smell the crocuses," Emzara often told him. Had he ever even bothered to smell a crocus flower before? He would make sure to do so next chance he got. But this was the immediate pleasure. "Where are my little pups?" he called out as a warning. With a sudden burst of movement, he yanked back the tent flap and jumped inside.

Instead of the expected giggles of two young boys, a laconic, "Baaah" greeted him. No one was there, only a pet lamb tied up in the middle of the tent. His sons called the lamb Lemuel, naming their favorite pet after their favorite of father's friends. Noah used it as a joke to tease Lemuel, calling him "my little lamb." That often ended in a wrestling match of some kind, with Lemuel usually winning because Noah was laughing too much. At least that's the way Noah told it.

Noah looked all round outside the tent. No sign of the boys.

He called out, "Shem? Japheth?"

No response. A single "Bah" punctuated the silence. Noah back glanced at the lamb, as though he expected an explanation from the creature. He looked around the tent again. It was a mess, with everything strewn around like a pack of dogs had been set loose. Was this demolition the work of a couple of rowdy boys playing their hearts out? Or was something wrong? Suddenly, his eyes tightened and he became concerned.

"Shem? Japheth? My sons, where are you?"

He looked frantically around the room. That is, he pretended to. Because he knew exactly what would happen next. Two miniature predators jumped out from hiding and pounced on their victim with wooden axe and mace.

"Aha! We got you! We tricked you!" yelled Shem in his triumphant warrior-lord voice. He and his younger brother hailed blows upon their prey. Noah cowered and protected himself while carefully allowing them easy access with their weapons.

"Ah! You distracted me with a sacrifice! You clever little warriors!"

"A sacrificial lamb!" shouted Shem.

Japheth could not stop giggling. Noah's free hand had reached out to tickle him with targeted precision. Japheth always fell victim to tickling. He dropped his mace and completely lost control.

Shem, however, continued to rain blows on Noah. Shem was a chip off the old limestone. He had his father's determination. Noah knew that one day he was going to have his hands full with a young man who was a reflection of himself, stubbornness and all.

"You are an abomination!" screamed Shem, absorbed in his righteous slaughter.

Noah abruptly stopped tickling and sat up, sternly. "Where did you learn that word?" he asked.

A wave of fear rushed over Shem. He did not know what was wrong. It horrified him to displease his father. "Jared's father Lemuel uses it."

Noah knew that it was not a guilty attempt to shift blame, but rather a genuine appeal to justice, something Shem did far too often. The boy was right. Lemuel did use it all the time as a curse word. That bothered Noah. He could not force Lemuel to stop, but he could do something about his own son.

"Stop using it. It is an adult word, not for children."

"I am sorry, father," Shem said meekly.

Noah's eyes looked deep into Shem's. The boy stared back, praying now for mercy.

Noah softened. His eyes brightened and a big toothy grin appeared. "No harm done, my son."

He grabbed them both in a big hug, refusing to let go, crushing them tighter and tighter.

"Uh oh," he said, "giant sloth hug!"

The boys giggled and squirmed, trying to escape their father's embrace. Japheth shrieked with pleasure, the childish shriek that pierces one's eardrums, especially when done right next to the father's ears.

Noah grunted and released the boys, fingering his ear to rub out the pain. "Japheth, remember to use that voice if a wild animal ever attacks you. It may never attack another human again."

Japheth grinned impishly.

Noah added, "Speaking of wild animals, where is that she-wolf of a mother of yours?"

He looked up and saw Emzara standing in the tent entrance smiling. Backlit by the bright sun rays upon her red dye linen dress, she was a goddess to him—every bit a tribal queen, and every inch a magnificent vision of Elohim's creative capacity. Her long, dark, auburn hair caught a breeze and shifted. The sight sent shivers down Noah's spine. The linen tightly wound around her voluptuous form beckoned to him, drawing him into a trance. Noah was under her spell, body and soul.

He kept his eyes locked on her as he spoke. "Boys, stay in the tent for a while. I have to consult privately with your mother."

Emzara gave an ever-so-slight grin and walked away, leaving the little boys to play and the bigger boy to stumble after her. Unaware of how parents played, Shem and Japheth fell back into battle with each other.

Emzara had known Noah all her life. They both had spouses that had died. For many years, Noah had avoided grieving as he poured his heart and soul into care for the clan. He had avoided Emzara as well. The mere sight of her doubled the pain of losing both his wife and his closest confidant, Aramel, Emzara's dead husband.

But one day, Emzara had confronted Noah, exhibiting the independent strength he would later become intimately familiar with. She refused to leave Noah's presence until he discussed with her their mutual pain, in an attempt to overcome it. In that encounter, Noah suddenly saw Emzara as he had never seen her before. They were soon married. They were later than usual in starting a new family, but it was never too late for the blessings of Elohim.

Noah's favorite blessing from Elohim was the intimacy he shared with his wife. Their oneness was a God-honoring expression of their earthy spirituality. In a way, adoration of his wife's splendor calmed the troubles he had with Elohim. As he caressed her, he knew God was good. As their lips met, he knew he was known, thoroughly known, and yet still loved. To have this most excellent and brave woman of strength willingly give herself to him humbled him. He felt honored and strengthened by it. His pet name for her was Naamah, which meant "lovely."

"You wore my favorite dress we got from that caravan from the land of the Nile," he said.

She held up her copper covered wrist, smiling "And the bracelets." The benefit of a nomad life was its connection with exotic trade.

"Now, let us take them all off," he snickered.

Emzara's mood changed suddenly.

"What troubles you?" he asked.

"The clan is in turmoil," she said. "We are weary of living like a pack of wild dogs, always on the run."

"It is the price we pay for our freedom from the gods."

Emzara sighed. Lately, he had been speaking more of freedom than of Elohim.

But before she could bring that up, he changed the subject. "We found more pazuzu in the forest. It seems that evil follows us like a jackal."

"When will it end?"

"When the gods stop demanding obedience to their proud rule."

"Thus saith a proud man," she reproved.

"And this is bad?"

Emzara was the most submissive of women. She knew Elohim created woman out of man's side to be his *ezer*, a helper beside him. But sometimes that meant speaking the truth that was hard for one's beloved to hear.

"My love, pride leads to a fall. It is faith that leads to freedom."

Noah knew she was right. She was his wisest counselor. But his stubbornness rose up. *What does she know of leading a tribe?* he asked himself, avoiding the truth.

She continued, relentlessly loving. "Do you think I have not also suffered? We both lost everything once. Must you try to be so alone?"

He pulled away, though he did not want to admit it. Irritation replaced his romance. "You are a woman of faith. It is no secret my devotion to Elohim has waned as his interest in me has waned. But I am still devoted to righteousness."

She held his head in her hands and stared into his eyes. He had the greatest integrity of any man that she had ever seen, even if that integrity sometimes got in the way of the Creator who gave it to him. "I am with child, my Utnapishtim," she whispered.

Noah's eyes flashed from shock to joy. The news took his breath away. Utnapishtim was her pet name for him. It meant "he who found life." She thought it was quite appropriate for Noah's earthy gusto.

"My Naamah," he said and hugged her desperately. He kissed her passionately. Apart from Emzara's presence, a child was the one thing that melted Noah's warrior heart. Children were arrows for warriors and he wanted a quiver full. Because they started their family late, he would not have as many offspring as others, but to him that just meant that each one of his own would be cherished that much more.

"Husband, you are not a god. But sometimes I think you want to be one with your self-reliance and aloofness."

"Wife, you could not handle a god. You can barely handle me."

She jumped into his arms, wrapping her legs tightly around him, knocking him off balance. But he caught her. They laughed, and melted together before their Maker.

Noah choked awake, disoriented, underwater. He fought toward the surface in search of air, and broke through gasping.

An endless sea stretched around him, nothing but water to the farthest horizon. He turned about and saw a beautiful white temple resting on the waters before him. He swam to the edifice and pulled himself out of the water, dripping wet. He climbed the steps up into the temple and cautiously stepped into the inner courtyard, onto a pavement of sapphire stone.

Dizziness swept over him. The inside of the temple did not match the outward size he had seen. On the outside, it stood about forty cubits wide by seventy cubits long. Inside, it seemed as if he had walked through a portal into another world. In that other world ranged the flaming messengers of Elohim's heavenly host. Their brightness hurt his eyes. They did not speak. They just watched Noah in silence—a myriad of them.

Noah stood still, his feet riveted to the sapphire floor. The presence of the Shining Ones intimidated him. He could not move. Then his eyes caught sight of a marble pedestal set out in the open by itself, with a large clay tablet resting on it.

With trepidation, he approached the pedestal and looked upon the tablet. The crowded triangular markings of cuneiform covered it, the writing system used in the Land Between the Rivers. Only the scribes and the upper classes of city palaces were taught cuneiform. But Noah could read it because his father had been a city ruler and his great grandfather Enoch had been an *apkallu* wisdom sage, so they passed down knowledge of this important new means of communication. Even Methuselah, who tended to be antisocial, had taken it upon himself to stay learned in such matters.

Noah studied the tablet. At the center was a drawing of a large rectangular box structure similar to the barges he had seen on the shipping docks of Shuruppak when he was younger. But this was different. The dimensions next to the box made it larger than any barge he had ever seen. It looked more like a warehouse. He studied it curiously.

A sound behind him made him turn, expecting to see an angel.

But it was no angel. It was the god Anu. The being jumped at him with a *hiss* of viper fangs!

Noah sat up abruptly, shaking off the dream. Beads of perspiration gathered on his forehead. He reached for Emzara for support. She was gone.

Outside, the shadows grew long. It was getting late. Time for the feast and assembly.

He took a couple of deep breaths to settle his thoughts, then got dressed quickly. He stopped one moment to smell the sweet savor of memory in the red linen dress lying on his bedding. The scent of crocus filled his nostrils. He smiled and left the tent.

Outside, he found the clan already celebrating around the fire with music and dance. Families were enjoying one another and cooking their meals. Some gestured for him to join them. But Noah had something to take care of first.

In the children's tent, Lamech and Betenos were enjoying their grandchildren before the assembly meeting started. Lamech loved telling Shem and Japheth fantastic legends of warriors battling strange monsters with dragon heads and lion bodies, mystical trees guarded by demonesses, and wars of giants and Cherubim. He would tell the boys not to share the legends with others, that they would be their own special tales of adventure, which made them feel very special indeed.

The boys would often wonder why grandmother Betenos would jump in and correct grandfather's fabulous tale as if he did not tell it properly. They had no idea that Lamech's tales were true. Lamech told them what he and Betenos had actually experienced in the past as Karabu giant killers, under cover of a made-up tale. He and Betenos felt that the intensity of their experiences were too traumatic for little children to handle the reality. It was better served through the safety of imagination. They would grow up soon enough to face the wicked world from which Noah was protecting them.

Lamech and Betenos gathered Shem and Japheth into their arms for a moment. Lamech pulled out the leather case that held his special weapon. The boys' eyes went wide with excitement. They had seen it before and knew that grandfather had a nickname for it.

"Rahab," gasped Shem.

"What does Rahab mean?" asked Japheth.

"Rahab is the giant sea dragon of chaos that gave birth to Leviathan, its own sevenfold increase of terror," said Lamech. "This weapon moves like the body of Rahab and bites with ferocity." Shem leaned in to get a closer look at the case. Lamech snapped at Shem's nose with a growl. Shem jerked back with a giggling yelp.

"Tell us the story again about where you got it," the boy blurted out.

Betenos saw Lamech's eyes brighten. He loved to tell his stories. It made him feel significant in his old age. She knew Lamech loved her with all his heart. But she also knew that he was a man, and men need to feel that they are doing something significant or they wither and fade into depression. Lamech was no different. Losing his arm in battle and stepping down as Patriarch had taken its toll on Lamech's sense of worthiness. That he had to hide his achievements behind a fictional façade did not help.

"Well," said Lamech with deliberate exaggeration, "Rahab is a very special weapon, forged in the heavenly volcano of Mount Sahand amidst the stones of fire by the archangel Gabriel himself. It was given to me to watch over." He didn't explain that he was also trained how to use the weapon in the secret angelic order of the Karabu giant killers.

The boys listened in rapt attention, though they had heard the story a hundred times. They stared at the strange leather case with handle sticking out. Inside was a flexible blade made of unearthly alloy, all seven cubits of its length rolled up into the case. They had never seen or heard of anything else like it. It was virtually indestructible. It unrolled and flowed like a whip. No known metal on earth could do that. And this whip would cut giants' heads from bodies and sever villains in two.

"But remember, it is our secret," said Lamech.

"Our secret," the boys repeated in unison.

Betenos smiled warmly. Boys will be boys. And men will be boys.

Lamech continued. "And now, Shem, because you are the firstborn, I have a very special commission for you."

Shem sat speechless, wondering what it could be. Japheth fidgeted, a little jealous.

"I am handing down Rahab to you as an heirloom," said Lamech.

Shem's mouth dropped in shock. No sound came out. His eyes bulged so wide, they hurt.

"I will leave it with you, but you will not withdraw it, and you will not use it until your father lets me teach you how to use it. Do you understand me?"

Shem could only nod his head yes, still staring at the special weapon in its case.

Japheth started crying. He did not get a special weapon like Shem.

Lamech looked at Betenos. She reached behind her to pull out the special bow that she had used to kill giants, mushussu, and human wolves so many years ago.

Lamech held the bow. "Japheth, to you we bequeath your grandmother's special giant killing bow. The same goes for you as for your brother. You will not play with it until your father allows us to teach you how to use it. Do you understand?"

"Yes!" shouted Japheth with joy.

Both boys gave their grandparents hugs and kisses that Lamech and Betenos would treasure for the rest of their lives.

Methuselah's eyes popped open. The tip of a dagger pressed against his throat.

"You are slowing down, Grandfather, getting dull," said Noah. "I respect your wisdom, but what of your strength?"

"You are already dead," Methuselah replied. Noah felt a sharp point prick his belly. He looked to see Methuselah's dagger sticking in his abdomen. "Or at least without *your* manhood."

Noah pulled back, chuckling.

Methuselah sat up. "And I can still handle a battle axe, young buck," he said. "I just need a nap now and then. You will understand in a couple hundred years. If you survive that long." He made no mention of his accuracy with a javelin in his younger years.

Noah loved his grandfather and cherished his advice on everything in life. He also appreciated Methuselah's dry wit. He might be the oldest man alive, but he was also one feisty poet warrior. He never let Noah get lazy in thought or deed, because, as he always said with annoying redundancy, "Elohim's Chosen Seed needs to grow."

Noah sat back with a sigh. "I had a vision."

Methuselah came alert. "The heavenly temple on the waters?"

Noah looked surprised. "How did you know?"

"Because I had the same vision."

"Did you see the building plans?" Noah asked.

"No. Building plans for what?"

"*Tebah*. A large box. Huge. Like a fortress or warehouse." Noah scribbled out in the sand from memory a phrase he had never read before the dream. "What does this mark mean?"

Methuselah said, "Covered in and out with pitch."

"What is pitch?" said Noah.

"Maybe it will be revealed. How large is this box?" Methuselah asked.

"Three hundred cubits long, fifty cubits breadth, thirty cubits high. Several floors."

"Have you told your father?" asked Methuselah.

"Not yet. I think he is with the boys," said Noah.

Methuselah pondered.

Then he spoke with the certainty of a sage. "You must build this box—this warehouse."

"Me? Why?" Noah complained.

"Elohim gave me a similar dream. But he did not show me his plans as he did you."

"Why will not Elohim just speak clearly to me?" complained Noah. "Is that too much to ask? How do I know that he has not gotten our dreams mixed up?"

"Elohim does not make mistakes," said Methuselah. "*You* must build the box."

"It would take the entire tribe years to build such a structure," protested Noah. "It does not make sense."

Methuselah chuckled. "Well, then, we had better get chopping."

Noah drew back annoyed. "It was only a dream!"

"Sometimes that is how Elohim speaks to hard-headed men." Methuselah returned. He thought of himself and how Elohim had hammered his own hard head so many years ago.

Noah rolled his eyes. Methuselah continued, "I remind you of my father Enoch's revelation."

Noah could not keep disdain from his voice. "Oh, you have much reminded me of great-grandfather's delirious revelations."

"I also remind you," said Methuselah, "that Enoch walked with Elohim—and was taken by him, never to die. Is that delirious?"

Noah could not argue with that. As much as he thought his great-grandfather had sounded a little too holy for his taste, he could not deny that he walked with Elohim. He remembered that the Sons of God first came down from heaven in the days of Jared, Enoch's father and Noah's great-great-grandfather. That was when Enoch began having his dream-visions. Enoch had foretold all this. But Noah found it difficult to accept that Elohim would want everyone to be so heavenly minded when there was work to be done on terra firma.

Noah's father Lamech and Methuselah told him very little from the earlier years when Enoch had ascended into heaven before he was born. They would only reveal bits and pieces as he grew up, but never the whole story of their experiences in the Titanomachy.

"I do not know what happened to Enoch. But I do know that I want to live a life in peace, away from this wicked world. If we move, we are left alone and avoid trespass. If we put down roots and build this structure, we become a sitting target for the gods to conquer and rule us."

Methuselah looked straight into Noah's eyes. "Noah, do you really think you can avoid evil?"

"I have no choice. Avoid it or we all die."

Methuselah paused to consider his next move. He was cornering Noah and they both knew it. "Do you really think you can avoid Elohim?"

Noah would not respond.

Methuselah pressed harder. "We must tell the elders of this dream."

"No!" Noah blurted.

"You are the Patriarch. It is your responsibility," said Methuselah.

"As Patriarch, I forbid you to tell the elders."

Methuselah threw up his hands in exasperation. He would not trump authority.

Noah added, "But we will tell them we are moving on the morrow."

CHAPTER 4

Shafts of morning light broke through the tall timbers of the forest, accompanied by the music of birds welcoming the dawn. Noah woke to the sweet smell of Emzara's hair nestled in his neck and shoulder. Their breathing synchronized as one. She stirred and he could not help but thank Elohim for another day of life with her.

The flap on his tent slapped open. Lemuel stuck his worried face inside, which only an emergency would make him do.

Noah looked at his friend. "Lemuel, we have all day to pack up for the move."

"A royal entourage from Erech is encamped near the brook," whispered Lemuel.

Noah sat up abruptly, waking Emzara. "What? How many? Are they armed?"

"A small delegation," Lemuel said. "Should we muster our forces?"

"No," said Noah. "It must be an ambassador. Go gather the elders. We will ride and see what they want."

The royal encampment was a third of a league distant from Noah's settlement. A large ostentatious tent dominated the center, twenty cubits in diameter, made of embroidered fabric from the Indus valley. A line of bird-men soldiers with spears, maces, and axes guarded the perimeter. The banner of Anu flew high overhead on a golden standard.

Noah, Lemuel, six elders and an escort of a couple of warriors halted briefly at the edge of the brook, still partially concealed in the dense forest. Noah patted the neck of his onager as he looked at the horses of the visitors. He trusted his durable domesticated ass, but he had known of the horses which recently traded all over the Levantine and Mesopotamian plains. They provided stronger mounts and faster travel for flight or fight, either of which might happen in the next few moments.

Noah and his men crossed the brook with caution, leaving the escort of two warriors behind as watch. A truce would automatically be in effect for such a meeting, but it would not hurt to have a reserve. Noah plodded forward, eyes straight ahead, oblivious to the fact that most of his companions, with the exception of Lemuel, did not share his courage in the face of such large numbers of hostile soldiers, truce or not.

As they reached the edge of the royal camp, a priestess greeted them. She had painted eyes, hairless elongated skull, and flesh full of tattoos and body piercings. She walked up to Noah with a seductive gait in a translucent gown.

Noah thought, *This heathen religion is a lascivious one*.

The priestess hissed in a whisper, "If you please, you and your man may follow me. The others may refresh themselves."

She gestured to a lavish banquet table out in the open filled with golden cups of wine and silver platters of wild boar and vegetables.

"Thank you," replied Noah, "but we already ate breakfast. Early risers." He dismounted, followed by Lemuel and his men.

"Well, then," she said, "This way."

Noah and Lemuel followed her through a gauntlet of bird-men and portable bronze pillars leading to the tent entrance. Noah wondered at the kind of conceit that would produce such luxurious waste of resources. The vast number of slaves needed to maintain the excess of royalty and deity astounded Noah. He noticed that Lemuel kept his hand on his belted mace.

As they entered the tent, four human officers greeted them, and then stepped aside, bowing in deference. Behind them sat open chests of gold, silver and precious gems, sparkling in the rays of light that peeked in through the tent entrance. It was a king's ransom. Noah glanced at it briefly. If the display was meant to impress him, it failed miserably.

Behind the treasure, Lugalanu lounged on a miniature throne in his royal vestments, like a miniature version of Anu. He spoke to Noah in a mimicry of Anu's own lofty, light-hearted grandeur.

"Welcome to our humble delegation from the mighty sky god Anu, Lord of heaven and earth, father of the gods. I am his priest-king, Lugalanu."

Noah sniffed. "I know a certain Creator who would beg to differ with those titles. And I am not impressed by pompous exhibition."

"Well, now that I know what you are not, pray tell, who you are?"

"I am Noah ben Lamech, son of Methuselah, son of Enoch, Patriarch of my clan."

Lugalanu's brow rose with interest. "Noah, son of Enoch. I have heard of you. You are most respected among the human tribes."

Noah, dismissed the small talk. "We are nomads and we seek no trouble with the gods of this land."

"I believe you," Lugalanu responded. "The gods, however, are not so easily persuaded." He paused to add gravity to his tone. "Especially when their servants return to Erech grievously wounded by nomad arrows."

Lemuel looked nervously at Noah, then at the officers, his eyes on constant watch.

"Some token of respect might alleviate their concern," Lugalanu continued. "Simple obeisance to prove your peaceful intentions, perhaps."

The priest-king was no match for Noah, who made his own pronouncement. "We will bow the knee to no god…," the pause was noticeable "…but Elohim."

"Indeed?" questioned Lugalanu. "And I suspect you even have trouble doing that." No detail escaped Lugalanu's eagle eye. Years of court intrigue honed his senses to pick up the slightest nuance of body language and tone that betrayed underlying motives and meanings. He could tell instantly that this man before him had a proud sense of self-importance such as he had not encountered in a decade. He decided to throw out some bait. "Every man is ruled by a god. Except perhaps the man who will end the rule of the gods."

Noah ignored the bait. "My people are leaving this forest this very day. We will leave you alone. We beg your indulgence to leave *us* alone."

Lugalanu stared at him for what seemed an eternity. Then matter-of-factly, he said, "I cannot indulge you."

The answer did not please Noah. Lemuel fidgeted uncomfortably.

"But I have a counter offer," Lugalanu continued. "You are influential with the remaining nomadic tribes. You and your people will not be taxed like everyone else. You will not even be forced to join in public worship. I only ask that you bow the knee to the gods in private and not obstruct the rest of the human tribes from submitting to the pantheon." His voice was almost conciliatory. "Then you will be left alone."

Noah stared at him unrelentingly. Lugalanu clearly had no idea whom he was talking to. "I will not bow the knee," said Noah.

Lugalanu let out a deep sigh. Noah clearly had no idea whom *he* was talking to. "Very well, then. Pazuzu!" he barked.

Noah and Lemuel whirled to see one of the black hideous dog-faced creatures at the doorway of the tent.

"Pass the order. Destroy the village."

The pazuzu took off in flight.

"NOOOOO!" Noah screamed as he realized they had been betrayed.

In a flash, he and Lemuel were out of the tent, their maces ready to strike.

They stopped in their tracks. A hideous sight confronted them. The six elders and two warriors from the brook hung limp from pillars by their broken necks. The bird-men had managed to completely surprise their quarry with silent death.

Noah's world spun around him.

Lemuel's screaming voice brought Noah back to reality. He dodged just in time to avoid an axe that almost cleaved him in two. He backed up against Lemuel. Twenty bird-men surrounded them, weapons at the ready. But these mutant creatures had cornered the wrong two fighters. As a battling duet, Noah and Lemuel swung their weapons in a macabre dance of death, taking out soldiers left and right.

Noah downed a soldier behind Lemuel. Lemuel spun and hacked an attacker in Noah's blind spot. Methuselah and Lamech had trained them together most of their lives with the secret art of the lost order of warriors called the Karabu. They were seasoned and unbeatable.

Unbeatable until the net dropped from above.

It enveloped them like a spider's web. They were trapped prey. Their weapons were useless. The soldiers rained blows upon them, pounding them into submission. Noah's raw anger kept him conscious. Lemuel blacked out. When the soldiers stopped, Noah knew they were not going to be killed. He dropped his weapon.

Someone yanked the net away. The prisoner's arms were held back by five soldiers each. Lemuel came to from his black-out.

Lugalanu stepped up to Noah, reveling in his victory.

Noah spit at him. "You piece of filth. I should have known never to negotiate with the wicked."

Lugalanu crowed, "I would expect the nemesis of the gods to be smarter than that." He gestured toward the trees behind Noah with a slight nod of his head. "Your village is no more."

Noah looked up in the sky in that direction. Billowing clouds of black smoke in the distance told him all he needed to know.

Noah broke down into tears struggling in vain to get free. He pleaded, "Please. No."

Lugalanu looked at Noah with feigned surprise. "Again, you beg my indulgence? Well!" He made a dramatic pause. "I must admit, until I found out who you were, I did not anticipate you would be such a valuable treasure. Your friend, however, is not."

A wave of dread washed over Noah. He locked eyes with Lemuel, firmly held in place by the soldiers. Lugalanu nodded to one of them, who reached over and cut Lemuel's throat with a dagger. Lemuel dropped to the ground, dead.

Lugalanu grabbed a mace from one of the soldiers. "Every man is ruled by a god," he declared, and clubbed Noah into unconsciousness.

It was a massacre. Noah's camp fell swiftly, taken completely by surprise. The men tried to gather their arms but a contingent of soldiers and a squad of Nephilim warriors overwhelmed them before they could get organized. It would not have mattered if they had. The tribe had last seen the fearsome giants many years before, but no amount of past experience prepared them for this new terror. The giants' armor was more frightening, their weapons more vicious, their killing more ruthless. If it was even possible, they were *more evil*.

At twice the height of humans, Nephilim could sweep their strange blades like a scythe, cutting through a circle of surrounding enemies. The extra digit on their hands gave them a more powerful grip on their weapons. The extra digit on their feet gave them a wider surface area for balance. The armed strike of a single Naphil shattered both weapon and limb of a human opponent.

At the first alarm of the attack, the tribe scrambled for their weapons and mustered for defense. The women and children hid. The circle of evil titans squeezed the tribal fighters into a cluster, ready for reaping. The captains rallied as best they could, calling out for formation.

Lemuel's protégé, young Shafat, joined the inner ring as the more experienced fighters took the perimeter. Every man faced out toward the circling giants.

For the first time in his life, Shafat was scared, truly scared. Lemuel had taught him well, and Shafat had proven himself single-handedly worthy on more than one occasion with lions and bears. But these were not wild beasts; these were demonic monsters. Vomit rose in his throat and he urinated in his loincloth. It was a natural bodily reaction in the jaws of death. Others around him did so as well. The real test was how you responded now that your body had evacuated the toxins.

He saw the impossibility of victory that was crushing in on him. He saw his fellow soldiers struck down in waves before him. He knew he was going to die. The Nephilim were too strong, too coordinated, and inexhaustible. His heart went weak. He would never see his beloved Shemariah again. They were betrothed. Their marriage was supposed to be celebrated at the next moon. *But it was not to be now*, he thought. He would never look into her true eyes again, never kiss her velvet lips. And he would never have the joy of seeing his sons and daughters grown into families of their own—because he was not going to have sons and daughters. All his hopes and dreams would die with him this day, mere moments from now.

His training kicked in. He pushed his fear aside to focus on the task at hand. True courage seized him, not some fantasy of fearless glory, but the resignation to his duty to face his fears like a man, to act like something he was supposed to be, not like something he felt. He would do his best, and he was best with a bow. He nocked an arrow, raised his bow arm, and found his target, one of the gargantuan monsters hedging them in. He released without hesitation.

The arrow found its mark—in the right eye of the Naphil. The monster lurched back in pain and screamed hideously. The other Nephilim quickly covered their comrade. The wounded one stepped back and painfully ripped the arrow out, pulling its eye with it. It then set its sight on Shafat with revenge and renewed its advance.

Shafat's boyhood friend, Akiva, saw it all and shouted, "Good shot, Shafat! Elohim is with you!"

Elohim *was* with him. He was with all of them, but not in a way that some might expect. Elohim obliged no man life or blessing. He dispensed his purposes as he wished and he did not owe an explanation for his ways. He was the potter and humanity was the clay, as their creation story explained. If Elohim chose to craft some of those vessels for destruction and others for glory, that was his choice. He was accomplishing his purposes for his people. Shafat would trust Elohim to be just and ultimately put the world to rights one day. Elohim only promised victory in the end, not in the entire process. He promised that he would be with them through the fire. This was Shafat's fire of testing, and he shone forth with the glory of refined gold before he fell to the blade of the wounded Naphil. This is the glory of Shafat's victory: no one would live to tell his story, the only warrior of Noah's tribe to seriously wound a Naphil that day, but Elohim knew. And Elohim would not forget Shafat.

The defending warriors were slaughtered to the last man.

Lugalanu's human soldiers went after the women and children. They did not take much concern for the elderly, which was their mistake.

One-armed Lamech and his elderly wife Betenos scrambled to the tent of Shem and Japheth. They pulled the two little boys inside.

Then Lamech and Betenos stepped back out front to protect their grandchildren from the onslaught. Betenos raised her bow. Lamech unfurled his whip-like weapon Rahab. He had lost his right arm years ago, but had worked hard to relearn with his left hand as best he could. His abilities might be sorely diminished, considering he had taken down giants in his youth. But he still had enough strength in him to swing Rahab accurately enough for her snakebite of death to kill plenty of attacking human soldiers. Together, they felled over a dozen of those soldiers before being taken down by a Naphil from behind. A human soldier entered the tent after the boys.

Two warriors dragged Emzara behind her tent. She caught a glimpse of the soldier exiting her boys' tent, wiping his bloody dagger on the tent cloth. Her boys were dead. She screamed in horror and crumbled into weeping. She knew in her heart that Noah must have been ambushed. It was all too coordinated. She prayed to Elohim that her demise would quick, so she could be reunited with her beloved and the cherished fruit of her womb.

One of Emzara's captors snarled, "This one is comely! I want some time with her!"

Before he could even say another word, a javelin pierced him from behind. As he fell to the ground, Emzara saw Methuselah behind him with eyes afire and a maniacal snarl to match.

"Have your time in Sheol, you jackal!" he bellowed.

Methuselah was old and curmudgeonly, but he was no feeble relic. He still had his teeth, and his tactical wisdom made up for his lessened strength. He did not get to be the oldest man on earth without learning a thing or two about battle. In his day, he had been a mighty Karabu warrior, now he was a seasoned veteran.

But he was still no match for the camel that blind-sided him from behind, knocking him into unconsciousness.

CHAPTER 5

The marketplace of Erech buzzed with celebration. Citizens lined the streets cooking food on grills and drinking too much beer. Men were barechested with sheepskin skirts wrapped around their waists. Women wore fabric tunics with embroidered adornments. Everyone stayed out of the street in eager anticipation of the triumphal procession.

In the early days of the cities, when gods and kings conquered an adversary, they commonly paraded the captured leaders, dead or alive, along with the plundered booty, through the city streets in a procession of victory over their enemies. It commanded respect from the populace for their leaders and engaged them in the victory and complete humiliation of the vanquished foes. It was a time of state pride and unity.

The trumpets blew, announcing the arrival of the parade. The people interrupted their banter and play to settle in for the entertainment. Everyone lined the Processional Way, a long wide paved road that ran from one of the main gates all the way through the city and up to the gates of the priest-king's palace.

Lugalanu led the procession in a four-wheel chariot drawn by horses, which had recently replaced his onagers. He felt that the horse was much more powerful and regal. It was stronger, swifter, and far more pliable for domestication. They had only recently been bred and introduced into royalty and military use. Lugalanu liked the authoritative feeling he had riding horses. Glorious in his royal robes, he waved to the masses with a proud arm of power.

A wave of awe rolled through the crowds, keeping pace with him. What helped to breed that awe was the squad of giant Nephilim escorting him through the streets. They marched in complete coordination and created a wake of fear in their path. The ground shuddered beneath their feet. Apart from their sheer height, their tattoos, strange armor and weapons proclaimed them as the demigods they were.

Following the Nephilim, a herald shouted, "Behold, the victory of Anu and his spoils of war! The human tribe who would live as rebels without law and without the gods!"

The cart with Noah tied to a stake, stripped naked and beaten bloody, followed behind the herald. The people jeered and threw rotten vegetables at him. Some of the missiles hit their mark, stinging him and covering his body with a sticky putrid scum.

After Noah, a train of carts carrying the bodies of Lemuel and the other elders of Noah's tribe rolled along. The corpses hung from stakes, surrounded by kindling wood that would be set ablaze when they reached the town square. The people cheered with bloodlust.

The sun settled on the horizon of the cityscape. Inside the royal palace throne room, Anu and Inanna contemplated the dead goat lying on the stone altar before them, its throat freshly cut. They would soon suck it dry of every drop. Inanna worried about getting blood on her elaborate makeup and ornate costume of satin and wild ostrich feathers She set those thoughts aside. The first matter at hand was before them: Noah.

Three armed guards held him, but Noah was in no condition to be a threat. He could not see through his left eye, a black bulge of pus. He had lost a few teeth. So much of his blood had spilled that the court physician had to care for him to make sure he would not die on them.

Lugalanu stood beside the prisoner. He remained judiciously silent.

"So, this is the mighty tent-dweller of the human tribes, Noah ben Lamech, a son of Enoch," mocked Anu. The term "tent-dweller" was a word of scorn to urbanites. It reeked of primitive ignorance.

Noah could barely focus on the deities. He was too dizzy.

Anu continued, "We are familiar with the revelation of Enoch. Are you the Chosen Seed to end the rule of the gods?"

Noah did not respond.

Inanna exploded, "SPEAK, MORTAL! ARE YOU THE CHOSEN SEED?!!"

Noah coughed. He made them wait.

And then he laughed.

The act confused Anu and almost set off Inanna.

When Noah spoke, his voice burned slowly. "All I value is dead. My God, my tribe, my family. You murdered them. And you now have the power to end my life. What power do I have to end anything?"

Noah had given up the fight. Elohim was nowhere in sight. What was the difference between a God who existed and did nothing, and a God who did not exist at all? He resigned himself to obliteration. He truly did not care what happened anymore. "Just execute me and choose another for your foolish prophecy."

"That, my dear captive, is why I will not execute you," countered Anu. Inanna and Lugalanu both looked at Anu with surprise.

"If you are the Chosen Seed, and I kill you, then Elohim will simply raise up a new man to take your place. No, I will do the one thing that can thwart the revelation. I will keep you alive but forgotten. Erased from the history of man." Inanna and Lugalanu listened eagerly for the pay off.

"In the slave mines," Anu finished with a treacherous grin. He nodded to Lugalanu.

"Yes, my Lord and god," said Lugalanu. He gestured for the guards to carry Noah back to the dungeon, to ready him for his transfer.

"Oh, you are diabolically clever," quipped Inanna.

"Thank you," Anu replied. "I must display my superior nature every once in a while."

Anu rose from his throne. He bared his fangs and plunged them into the goat's neck to drink its blood. Inanna pulled off her ostrich feather shawl, so it would not get splashed, and joined him.

CHAPTER 6

The train of guards pulled cloaks over their mouths to protect their lungs from the sandy wind whipping around them. The desert night made it difficult to see. The five camel-back Sumerian officers led thirty cubits ahead of the twenty bird-men foot soldiers that guarded the cart transporting the shackled Noah. It would take them three days march at this pace to reach the copper slave mines at the edge of the great desert.

A human guard, a fat ugly mug with terrible breath, sat in the cart with Noah. He muttered snidely to Noah, "You will enjoy the mines. The only place more godforsaken is Sheol." He snickered.

Noah held his breath so he would not gag. *Or your mouth*, he thought.

Sheol was the underworld, the place of the dead. Hidden under the pillars of the earth below the Abyss of subterranean waters, it was the place from which no man returned. Many stories had built up around Sheol. A common saying that Noah often heard and recounted himself was, "the jaws of Sheol are never satisfied." It was the farthest one could be from the land of the living. It was where all people, big or small, rich or poor, were forgotten. To say that the slave mines were one notch up from Sheol was not a pleasant proposition.

"HALT!" The Captain of the Guard's voice barely penetrated to the back of the train over the howl of the wind. They could hardly hear him. The convoy stopped abruptly. The bird-men positioned themselves at the ready.

The Captain squinted his eyes in the dusty wind at the silhouette of a hooded man standing in their path about one hundred cubits in front of them. The faint moonlight shimmered through the dust and outlined the lone figure like a phantasm.

The Lieutenant piped up, "Could it be an ambush?"

"Do you see a single place for a war party to hide?" spit the Captain.

The Lieutenant looked around. The desert land lay flat for leagues in all directions in this stretch. They would not reach any rocky areas until tomorrow. Even with poor visibility, there was nowhere for a war party to hide, unless they buried themselves in the sand, waiting to rise up. The Lieutenant considered that possibility.

"Let us dispatch this annoying desert vagrant," commanded the Captain. He led the five camel riders toward the figure.

Noah strained to see what was going on, but the dust and the fat guard both obscured too much of the path ahead.

"What fool would be out here during this contemptible weather?" squawked the guard.

The Captain and his five officers approached the lone man within a few cubits. The stranger wore a loose hooded robe, his face wrapped in shadow.

"You there, drifter!" yelled the Captain. "Stand aside!"

The man stood like a statue, even his robe seeming oblivious to the wind and the command.

The Captain grew irritated. He would not brook insolence from a lone vagabond. "You stand in the path of the army of Anu! Stand aside!"

Still the man did not move. He showed no sign of even hearing the order. *He is either deaf or stupid*, thought the Captain.

The five camel riders circled him, their steeds snorting. The wind whipped up to a new frenzy, as though energized by the unfolding drama.

The Captain gave him one last chance. "What god do you serve?"

The lone man still stared silently from the hooded shadow. The Captain stared back. "Kill him for his disrespect," he finally growled.

The Lieutenant smiled with glee. He had not had the opportunity to kill anyone in a while. He enjoyed the feeling of god-like power that came from extinguishing life. He trotted his camel over to the hooded stranger and raised his axe high to smite him down. He swung his weapon.

The stranger dodged the blow with preternatural timing. He caught the Lieutenant's arm and pulled him from his camel, somehow turning the ax back against its owner and burying it in the soldier's head. So quickly did it happen, it took a moment for the others to realize what they had seen. This gave the stranger time to stand up and slough off his cloak. A paladin warrior in strange leather armor stood revealed. He was muscular, youthful, with sandy hair and a wide jaw line.

The thought cut through the Captain's mind, *What a handsome scoundrel.*

The paladin finally answered the Captain's question. "I am a servant of Elohim, whom you are about to meet."

The men drew their weapons, but could not hold them steady. Their camels reared up out of control, terrified by unseen forces.

The paladin pulled the axe from the dead Lieutenant and flung it through the air. The Captain's mouth opened to shout an order, but the ax embedded in him before a sound could emerge. The stunned, lifeless body dropped from his camel.

The paladin drew double weapons, one in each hand, long huge daggers with a curved hook blade that might be used by a twenty-foot giant. The soldiers had never seen this kind of weapon before. These were in fact sickle swords. This sword had not yet been introduced to humanity. But this warrior was no mere human.

The paladin cut down each of the remaining four officers in four swift moves. Then, with purposeful strides, he closed in on the prisoner convoy.

Noah could hear the pandemonium, but still could see nothing. Dust obscured everything.

The fat guard could not see much either. He belted out, "What is going on?!"

Someone yelped back, "It's a fight! Prepare for battle!"

The bird-men responded with military precision, lining up to receive the intruder. The stranger was almost upon them at a running gait.

The fat guard complained, "It's only one man! What could one man possibly do?"

But it was not one *man*. Unfortunately, none of them knew that.

The paladin hit the first guard and cut him down without losing stride. The next human screamed, "Enemy upon us!" But he was on the ground before he could finish his breath.

The bird-men were another matter altogether. They were in battle mode and they were ready.

They just were not ready for a superhuman warrior to slice through them like animal fat.

The stranger swiftly cut through to the middle of the last of the soldiers, surrounded on every side. They squeezed in for the kill. He held his sickle swords out to the sides. Then with a supernatural strangeness, he began to spin like a human cyclone. The blades became a twirling death trap that cut down every last bird-man in seconds. It was over before anyone knew it had begun.

The paladin looked up at Noah on the cart.

For the first time, Noah could see the source of the commotion. His jaw dropped, and he finally grasped the situation. The stranger was here to rescue him – or kill him.

The fat guard's mind leapt to a keen sense of self-preservation. He drew his dagger and placed it at Noah's throat. "Stop, or the prisoner dies!"

The fat guard had calculated correctly. The stranger was here for rescue.

The paladin did not take his eyes off the fat guard, though he would have liked to because the guard was rather ugly. Slowly, the rescuer set his blades down on the ground.

The fat guard smiled smugly and began to calculate his next move. He relaxed his hold on Noah ever so slightly.

It was just enough. His mind was no match for the stranger's unearthly speed. The paladin grabbed two daggers from his belt, one in each hand, and threw them with perfect timing and accuracy. They hit their marks, one buried in each eye of the fat guard. Anu's servant was dead before he hit the ground.

Noah had been speechless the entire time, in awe of this creature. He could not believe his eyes as the paladin sheathed his strange weapons. Noah had never seen their like before. The rescuer hacked at Noah's shackles.

"Who are you?" Noah asked, his voice quivering from fear. "*What* are you?"

The stranger answered him, "I am Uriel, your guardian."

"My guardian?"

"Yes, your guardian. Elohim sent me to protect you and help you accomplish your calling."

In the chaos of the moment, Noah floundered. "What calling?"

Uriel looked at him impatiently. "Have you forgotten already?"

Indeed, Noah had forgotten.

"The box?" Uriel reminded him. He shook his head, thinking, *This one is just as obstinate as his grandfather.*

Noah's sarcastic tongue returned like a flood tide at the ludicrous suggestion. "Right! The box! How could I forget the ridiculously large box?" he sputtered.

Uriel frowned at his ward. "Sometimes I am vexed why Elohim chooses people like you."

The insult took Noah aback. He paused to reflect. He responded, "On that, you and I agree. Though I would think your attitude is not properly befitting a guardian sent by Elohim."

Uriel rolled his eyes.

Noah caught a camel wandering near him and mounted it. "Well, Uriel, I thank you for your"–what should he call it?–"guardianship. But I have more pressing concerns."

"You do not get off that easily," Uriel said.

Noah whipped his camel and bolted off into the night.

Uriel looked upwards to heaven with frustration. "Lord, why me?" After a moment of thought, he added, "Why *him*?"

Noah rode his camel hard to the cedar forest. Though the attack had happened only days before, he could see smoke still lazily drifting up into the sky from the desolation. He did not want to see the ruin of the encampment, but he knew he had to. He had to face his past head on and let it fuel his thirst for revenge in the future.

As he approached the edge of the camp, the destruction engulfed his senses. His eyes clouded and his throat choked up. Why? Why would Elohim allow this to happen? If there was any thought of him being this Chosen Seed, it was thoroughly put to rest, vanished into the underworld with his family.

Everything had been razed to the ground. The animals all lay slaughtered, or had escaped. The destruction scattered debris everywhere. The only movement came from surviving children, still picking through the wreckage to find anything to eat or to use. Rather than mercifully killing the children, Lugalanu let them survive to be starved or ravaged by wolves and other predators.

But Noah's mind did not stay on the waifs now gathering around him. He barely saw them. He came to the origin of the rising smoke.

He fell off his camel. His hold on reality began to slide away.

The dark vapors rose from the smoldering aftermath of a great bonfire— of the bodies of his kinsmen. Massacre.

Noah stumbled closer to the burning pile. At the edge of the smoldering ruins he saw a burnt linen cloth. A red linen cloth. The dress Emzara had worn when they last saw each other. He pulled it out of the flames. One of Emzara's copper bracelets, blackened by the fire, rolled out. He picked it up with the cloth and wept bitter tears. He murmured to himself the name of his beloved, trying to resurrect her, demanding that Sheol would not allow her to be forgotten.

He looked to heaven and raised his fist in anger. "And you expect me to obey you?"

A child cried out in hunger.

Then it hit Noah. His sons. His sons! He jumped up and ran full tilt for his tents. He arrived at a jumble of goatskin canvas and piles of rubble. He saw a bulge in the tent and ran over, ripping it apart, digging for the truth.

It was the pet lamb, lifeless and spattered with blood.

"Father!"

He thought it was a dream-voice. He looked up.

It was no dream. Shem and Japheth stood a short distance away, shadowed by a bandaged Methuselah watching over them.

Noah cried out for his sons and ran to them. They crashed into each other and fell to the ground in weeping happiness. He kissed them. They held onto him for dear life, a pair of cubs reunited with their parent.

"I thought you were dead!" Noah cried. "I thought you were dead!"

Shem stopped him. The boy pulled away and stood upright. "No, father. We did as you taught us. We distracted the bad men."

"With a sacrifice," added Japheth. They proceeded to tell him the story of their strategy. They opened the back flap to make it appear they had left, and then burrowed into their hiding place. The soldier had followed them into the tent. They had left Lemuel out to distract him, just in case. When the soldier could not find the boys, he killed the lamb. It satisfied his frustration, and he left.

"They were *abonimations*," yelled Japheth, hopelessly mangling the pronunciation.

Shem scolded his little brother, "Japheth, you are not allowed to say..."

Noah interrupted them both. They looked into their father's eyes, expecting a chastisement. But he calmly said to Japheth, "The correct word, my son, is *abominations*."

"Abominations!" Japheth yelled.

Noah gave a sad smile of approval, because it was time for his sons to shed their innocence. They were too young. But he had no choice. It was forced upon them.

The boys noticed the red linen and copper bracelet in Noah's hand. Too late, Noah tried to hide it. They all knew, and none of them could speak. They merely embraced one another and wept again for a loss greater than words.

Young Japheth alone softly whimpered his pain into Noah's breast, "Momma."

Methuselah stepped up to them.

"Father and mother?" asked Noah.

"Gone," said Methuselah. "But they left this earth protecting your little ones."

"Grandfather," said Noah. It was like a plea for salvation.

Methuselah would have none of it. "Fortunately, the soldiers do not suspect the elderly, which is why they did not bother to burn me when they thought me dead. I killed a dozen of the jackals before I was knocked senseless—by a camel no less!"

For the first time since his captivity, Noah laughed heartily. "You are full of surprises, old man." They hugged desperately, an unspoken recognition between them of their great loss.

Suddenly, Noah sensed a presence. He pulled his sons behind him and drew his axe from his belt. Methuselah joined him with a mace. A figure stepped out from the bush.

It was Uriel.

Noah dropped his readiness. Methuselah wondered what the Sheol was going on.

Noah snapped, with a tone of disdain, "How did you get here?"

"I rode a camel," Uriel replied. "What did you expect, I had wings?"

Noah kept trained on Uriel. "I thought I released you."

Uriel laughed. "If only you could. I told you, you do not get off that easily."

"Well, I'll be an onager's uncle," said Methuselah. "Uriel, you old hyena."

Uriel retorted, "Look who's talking, you ancient relic. Sometimes, I think you will outlast me."

Confusion hit Noah "You know him?" he asked his grandfather.

Methuselah embraced Uriel. "Where have you been? It has been so many years since I last saw you, I was beginning to wonder if Elohim was pulling our tails."

Uriel laughed.

Noah said, "I want an explanation right now."

Methuselah said, "This is Uriel, your guardian angel."

"That much, I have gathered," said Noah.

Methuselah continued, "Uriel protected your father before you were born. He was there at your birth."

"I guess you were right, grandfather," said Noah. "I am so hardheaded that Elohim will not bother to speak directly to me. He prefers to use writing on tablets that do not make sense, dreams of old men that do not tell me things, and angels I cannot endure."

"Actually, I am an *arch*angel," Uriel offered.

Noah and Methuselah knew the archangels were the mightiest of Elohim's warriors, on the level of the divine council. But they had never realized just how mighty.

"Well, I guess that explains your ability to kill so expertly, and with such speed and elegance," remarked Noah, mining the moment for further irony. He turned on Methuselah. "Grandfather, you do not tell me enough for an elder."

"Noah, you do not listen enough for a Patriarch," said Methuselah. "Besides, I am old, I forget a lot."

Uriel laughed again. "I guess it runs in the family, does it not?"

The two men could not deny that.

Methuselah knew exactly what all this banter really meant. The time was fast approaching. God had sent this guardian to finalize Noah's calling. The old man did not know how many archangels it would take to bend this stubborn onager's will, but he suspected one was not enough.

They had spent some time putting together a proper shelter for the children. Uriel caught some fowl, and their bellies were full. Methuselah took the fifty children aside, and explained to them that they were going to be taken to a small tribe he knew on the eastern plains near the Tigris. That tribe would then take them to a special hidden valley in the Zagros Mountains to start anew. Methuselah had discovered the valley many years before in his adventures with Lamech. Noah and Methuselah would meet the children there after the men took care of some business that needed attending.

It was the hardest thing in his life for Noah to do, letting his sons out of his sight after losing them once. It went against every grain of his being. But a deeper grain inside him pushed out everything else.

Revenge.

The children slept and the men sat around the fire strategizing. Methuselah spoke up, "You must not do this, Noah. You would be a fool to assault Anu on his own ground. He is guarded by a host of Nephilim in the center of the city." He knew the Nephilim were offspring of the Watchers, bred as killing machines. They did not die easily. He had taught Noah that much. Methuselah had seen their horrible power when the Watchers first came down from heaven.

Uriel added, "Even an archangel is no match for a horde of Nephilim."

Noah looked at him surprised.

"We are not invincible," explained Uriel.

Noah played with the blackened copper bracelet he had found in the fire. He stretched it wider, as he spoke. "I will fight Anu on *my* ground."

Uriel shook his head, incredulous. "With what army? The entire land worships the gods. The only human tribes of any significance are scattered to the four corners in windy mountains, death dry deserts, and deep forests. And they are not likely to join you in certain death to avenge your personal loss."

Methuselah sighed. He had been right. It would take more than one archangel to rein in this wild donkey.

"Then I will go to the one place where humans have lost all hope in the gods," Noah proposed. The others looked at him, wondering where that would be.

"Where they were taking me," he explained.

"The slave mines? You want to start an uprising in the slave mines?" Methuselah did not bother to hide his shock. Had Noah gone mad with feverish revenge?

Uriel put it into perspective. "How do you plan to assault a garrison of soldiers and guards as one lone man?"

Noah looked at him with an impish grin. "I am not one lone man. I have a guardian angel—pardon me, *arch*angel." He mimicked Uriel's previous accent.

Uriel sighed and sat back with a moan.

Noah finished widening the copper bracelet enough to fit it on his own wrist.

Methuselah found his grandson's plan appealing. "*And* you have the oldest man on earth," he chuckled.

Noah lifted up his wrist brace with a fist. His macabre humor in the face of impossible odds brought the point home, "That triples my odds."

Uriel did not find this funny.

A faint sound started them. The men turned to see Shem and Japheth standing behind them. How much had they heard?

Shem raised Lamech's strange weapon, Rahab, now in its leather case. Japheth carried Betenos' bow. "Grandfather and grandmother told us you would teach us how to use their weapons when it was time," Shem said. "Is it time, father?"

Pride and pity welled up within Noah. "Not yet, Shem, but soon." He had to pause to suppress his emotion. "Carry those with you to the Hidden Valley and when I meet you, it will be time. Now, back to bed."

The two boys trudged back to their tent.

Noah turned back to the others. "We leave in the morning."

CHAPTER 7

Deep behind the palace walls of the Eanna district harem quarters, twenty women of Noah's tribe tentatively adjusted to unfamiliar surroundings. Some of them had been saved from the attack on the camp to be prepared for the gods. They were scrubbed clean in beautiful pools, and clothed in fine linen and exotic fabrics. But they did not exactly fit in. The expensive garments looked and felt unnatural.

Shazira, a young beauty, made her way over to a fountain to comfort Emzara. Noah's wife sat, softly crying into her reflection in the pool. The lead officer had noticed Emzara before her assailant could hurt her, and had stopped the deed.

"Why are they treating us like royalty?" Shazira asked her.

Emzara looked up at her. The poor girl was too young and naïve to know the evil that was about to extinguish her innocence and dignity. Should Emzara tell her and fill her with additional terror that would only add to her misery? Or should she not tell her, thereby increasing the depth of the young girl's painful suffering when awakened by reality? Either way, she lost.

"They are preparing us," Emzara answered.

"For what, Emzara?" Shazira's doe-like eyes wide, her lashes fluttering "Are we to become servants of Anu?"

"You could say that," said Emzara darkly.

She could not do it. She could not bring herself to be party to the breaking of this sweet girl's spirit earlier than need be. One more hour of purity and innocence was a lifetime to her now.

Shazira might have launched more questions, but Emzara was spared the pain of outright lies by the sound of clacking rods. Someone was arriving. Everyone's attention focused on the doorway.

Lugalanu stood there with his Palace Guards. "Follow me, ladies."

The women stumbled in single file along the dark, cold tunnel connecting palace and ziggurat. They were told to be quiet on their journey and they obeyed. Because of the dark, Emzara stumbled and bumped into one of the guards. He kept her from falling and she returned on her course.

The tunnel soon led up into the ziggurat, up to the very top chamber, the White Temple with its lime-painted walls.

At the top of the climb, guards ushered them into a special room lined with ten stone altars.

Emzara felt sick to her stomach at the sight of them.

The women lined up and whispered amongst themselves.

Lugalanu shushed them with a strong clicking of his tongue.

Emzara stared at the ground, hoping to block the truth of her situation from her own sight. The tongue clicking stopped and a long silence followed. Emzara finally glanced up.

Lugalanu stared at her, unmoving as though in a trance. It made her feel uncomfortable. But rather than shift her eyes away, she locked onto his gaze, defiant and unyielding.

Lugalanu snapped out of his trance and marched down the line of women, proclaiming, "You are blessed to be in this holy chamber. You have been chosen by Anu for sacred marriage."

Shazira gasped. Her fate started to dawn on her. She whispered, "Emzara?"

"SILENCE!" shouted Lugalanu. "You will be respectful in this kingdom. You are no longer wild beasts of the desert. You are now sacred wives of the mighty god Anu, and you will obey him."

Emzara saw Shazira tremble. She was so frail. Emzara knew the poor girl would not survive this atrocity.

Lugalanu continued, "You will have the honor of bearing Nephilim, the seed of the gods."

Emzara held back her horror. From the dawn of time, depraved men had sought to indulge their lusts with imaginative excess. But to be violated by these monstrosities was an evil so deep she could not square it with her faith in Elohim. She had lost her complete family not once, but twice in this life. That was more than most could experience and still maintain a semblance of sanity, let alone faith. But to become host for a parasitic abomination? For what purpose could Elohim allow such suffering? What could he hope to accomplish? Or had the wickedness grown to such an extent that it was out of Elohim's control?

It was too much for Emzara to comprehend. All she could do was cling to her faith in spite of what was happening to her. But she found the handle of her secreted dagger just the same. It was the dagger she had slipped from the guard she bumped into in the tunnel.

Maybe she was created for such a time as this.

Emzara became aware of Lugalanu stealing glances at her, as if he could not keep his eyes off her. Maybe she could slit his throat as well.

His next announcement broke the nervous silence. "And now, kneel before your master the Almighty Anu, and his consort, Inanna, Queen of Heaven."

Most of the women hesitated, unused to such orders.

"KNEEL!" Lugalanu barked.

They dutifully obeyed. Emzara was the last to do so. She stole another glance at Shazira, who sniffled and held back a flood of tears. They locked eyes and Emzara sought to transport her thoughts to the girl, *You can be strong, Shazira. Be strong.*

Shazira straightened up, as if she had heard those thoughts. When Emzara glanced back to the entrance, she saw the towering forms of Anu and Inanna coming her way.

Lugalanu commanded the women to rise and they did. Anu and Inanna strode down the line in their regal attire, taking a moment to inspect each woman. Inanna struck Emzara as brazenly vulgar in her gem-laden glittering outfit and bright pink wig of a mountain of hair. She looked to Emzara as if a man had made himself up as a woman. She looked away from the sight and caught the priest-king still watching her with interest. When she glanced back, Anu and Inanna were examining Shazira. She could hear them in counsel.

Anu muttered something to the frightened Shazira that caused her to tremble.

Inanna appeared jealous of Anu's attention to the females before him. "Do not play with her too hard. Remember their purpose is for breeding."

"Yes, yes, of course," he replied. Then they stepped over to Emzara.

A chill ran through Emzara as she felt the gods' reptilian eyes on her. Anu leaned in and sniffed her. Emzara's blood ran cold. She saw Inanna snarl. Emzara's hand positioned closer to the handle of her secret dagger, considering her chances.

Anu pulled back with a look of surprise. "Lugalanu!" he called.

Lugalanu came running, "Yes, my Lord and god."

"This one is already with child," Anu hissed.

Inanna broke in, impatiently, "Get rid of her, now!" she barked, "and be more circumspect in your choices next time."

"Yes, your highness," Lugalanu groveled. He barked a command and a soldier grabbed Emzara's arm. As he and Lugalanu pulled her away, she could hear Inanna's comment, "Disgusting."

When the three of them were out of earshot, Lugalanu whispered to the soldier, "Place her in my private chamber." Emzara realized her troubles were not yet over.

But she still might slit his throat.

The soldier half pushed, half dragged Emzara through a maze of passages, back to the palace. He finally shoved her through a door and into a chamber. He stayed outside the door, guarding her. Escape was out of the question. She decided to look around to find another way out.

It was a grand regal bedchamber. Large marble columns checkered the room. Exotic tapestries from the Indus valley hung on the walls. They depicted idolatrous art from the East, multicolored deities engaging in unspeakable behaviors.

A large circular bed dominated the center of the room, the extravagant mattress covered with glistening sheets of a fabric she had never seen before. The cloth felt silky smooth to her touch. The decadence repulsed her. Not the wealth itself or the beauty it could buy, but rather the perverse purposes for which such money and beauty were engaged. Elohim created beauty, and mankind turned beauty into an ugly god.

She turned around lost in thought. Lugalanu's silent presence shocked her. He stood watching her from the shadow of a pillar. She stepped back.

"What is your name, nomad?" he asked.

"Emzara, my lord, wife of Noah ben Lamech," she responded respectfully.

He struggled to hide his surprise from her. She had no idea that the man before her just sent her husband to the slave mines to be forgotten by God himself. On the other hand, if that husband was the Chosen Seed, this woman before him was a treasure of inestimable value. At first, Lugalanu's interest in her had been tender, even altruistic. Her mature queen-like beauty and composure entranced him. It was why he could not take his eyes off her in the temple room. It was why his heart had leapt with hope when the gods placed her into his hands. But now, the discovery that she was the very consort of the Chosen Seed himself carried political and historical weight of which he could only dream.

He stepped closer. She cringed.

"Fear not, Emzara," he assured her, "I will not hurt you. You please me."

She could feel his eyes all over her. They were hungry eyes. But they were not the same as the god Anu's. They had a tenderness that surprised her.

"Does this please you?" he gestured around the room. He could see she was shy about it all. "You may speak your mind."

Emzara had nothing to lose. "My lord, how could I have pleasure in the kingdom that killed my husband and family, and destroyed my people?"

Excellent, he thought, *she thinks he is dead*. That increased his chances. Of course, his responsibility in killing those most dear to her would certainly decrease his chances with equal weight, if she knew.

"But I saved you," he murmured. It was feeble. But it was only his starting point.

"Perhaps you should not have," she said.

"I am sorry for your loss," he said. "The rule of the gods is not always equitable to their subjects. If you must know, I argued against it. Nevertheless, we subjects must obey the commands of our superiors, even if we disagree with them. Surely, you respect authority."

She replied, "Integrity sometimes requires defying authority." She thought of her dead husband now, and how proud she was to have been his wife. How wrong she had been to think that he was stubborn. She understood now the value of integrity that her own stubborn will had refused to see.

Yes, Lugalanu thought, *this is the woman I want more than anything*. He would do anything to have her by his side, but it would only satisfy him if she did so willingly. He knew now he would have to woo her, because force would not maintain her dignity. He accepted this challenge with a heart full of hope. He was a patient man.

"Emzara, I am different from the gods. I will not force myself upon you. I shall make you one of my maidservants. Perhaps in time, you shall change your mind about this kingdom—about me."

Emzara could not believe her good fortune. Her hand moved away from the dagger handle secreted beneath her robes. *Let him think what he wanted*.

CHAPTER 8

The copper slave mine was a vast circular strip mining operation deep in a canyon on the outer region of the Great Desert. Spiral pathways wound their way downward like a whirlpool in pursuit of copper, the life food of a new age begun by the discovery of bronze. Bronze was an alloy more durable than its copper predecessor, being used in everything from tools and decoration to weapons and armor. It was discovered by mixing tin with copper, which resulted in the harder bronze that would last longer and kill more efficiently in weaponry. For all those reasons, especially the last, gods and kings needed plenty of bronze to build their kingdoms. Extracting copper ore from the ground was laborious work. It required many men to unearth the volume demanded by such rulers. The necessary work force could be met by only one thing: Slaves, and lots of them.

That slaves would come from humankind was ingrained in the thinking of the world from days of old. Uriel hated slavery, and he hated what the Watchers had done to craft a mythology of slavery to support their purposes.

Their first goal was to eradicate Elohim from the minds of men and replace him with their own pantheon. They disseminated myths that supported their hierarchy of the four high gods reigning over the earth. The four were: Anu, father god of the heavens; his vice-regent Enlil, lord of the air, wind, and storm; Enki, god of water and Abyss; and Ninhursag, the earth goddess. Below them were the three that completed the "Seven who Decreed Fate": Nanna the moon god; Utu the sun god; and Inanna, goddess of sex and war. The Sumerians called these and the other gods of the cities *Anunnaki*, which means "gods of royal seed."

Their creation story bothered Uriel the most. In their narrative, the Anunnaki created mankind to be slaves of the gods, and bear the yoke of their labors, to mine their precious elements and build their holy kingdoms. Clay was mixed with the flesh of a god and then spat upon and mankind was birthed. So Elohim's purpose of male and female created in his image to rule over creation was displaced with an opposite narrative, one that carried an irony not lost on Uriel: that at one and the same time, man was more exalted than Elohim made him, and yet that man was created to be a slave of the Anunnaki. In this way, the Watchers built a complete religion of idolatry that opposed Elohim's rule and corrupted the entire human race. The fallen Sons of God could not attack the living God Elohim directly, but they could attack him indirectly by despoiling his heaven-bound image of royal representative into an earth-bound image of debased slave.

Uriel lay on a butte overlooking the mine with Noah and Methuselah. Below them, thousands of slaves lined the spiral pathways with pickaxes and wheelbarrows, endlessly hacking away at veins of copper ore deposits. Dog-soldiers watched over them. The guards were more chimeras of Anu's kingdom, with bodies of men and the vicious heads of wild dogs, wolves, and jackals. Only fifty guards had this duty, because not many were needed. These slaves were broken men, some bearing the weight of a lifetime of sweat and toil, only to die in the dust having been shorn of every ounce of their self-respect. A rigid discipline kept the slaves so busy that any thought of freedom could not gain a foothold in their minds. The slaves worked from morning until night with only enough food to keep them barely alive. Hunger starved any rebellious intentions.

"So, Chosen Seed," asked Uriel dryly, "has the Almighty revealed how to conquer this impossible target?"

"I thought archangels communed directly with Elohim," Noah responded. "Can you not ask him yourself?"

Uriel shook his head. "In heaven, yes. But on earth, we are bound by the limitations of the flesh." Of course, Uriel knew that Elohim could speak to anyone he wanted, whenever he wanted, in whatever way he wanted. And sometimes he did. But his choice of using these vessels would remain a mystery to Uriel.

"Can you die?" asked Noah.

"No. But we are bound in all other ways," Uriel said. "Mal'akim and Archangels eat, sleep, and partake in all bodily endeavors, including pain. But we cannot die like men."

Uriel's limitations seemed greater than his advantages to Noah. "Are you here to help me, or just to irritate me?" Noah jabbed.

"To ensure you build the box," the archangel replied. "I can only wonder at Elohim's disappointment with me now."

Noah smiled. He was beginning to appreciate the archangel's wit.

Methuselah interrupted them, "Stop your bickering, lovebirds. I see our plan. Down there is the pen for the slaves."

They followed Methuselah's pointing finger. At the top of the vast pit was a fenced-in area with gates that housed large sleeping quarters. He pointed at a spot about seventy cubits away from the pen.

"Over there, the guards' quarters. There are not many to contend with." They saw a single earthen structure with a thatched roof.

Uriel said, "You do not need many guards for broken starving slaves."

"Once they taste freedom," Noah offered, "they will die for it."

Methuselah looked at the setting sun. "Slave or free, everyone must sleep."

Noah took the reins. "There is not much time. Let us prepare."

Shortly before midnight Noah's three-man squad made their move. They thanked Elohim it was not a full moon, for the darkness aided their concealment as they descended upon the guardhouse and slave quarters.

Noah and Methuselah slipped up to the guardhouse. Through the window, they could see the majority of the guards sleeping in tight military style rows. They took a couple logs from the woodpile and silently wedged the two doors shut. They found a cart and filled it with brush, pushing it over to one of the windows of the guardhouse.

By the slave pen, a dog-soldier marched the perimeter. He stopped to look up at the moon and suppressed the urge to howl.

The sound of soft footsteps made his ears stiffen.

He jerked around. Nothing but night surrounded him. He was on the back part of the pen, separated from the guard post up front that held his comrades. He sensed something. He drew out his horn and placed it to his snout, ready to blow.

An arrow pierced his throat sending him to the ground choking to death. Uriel trotted quietly past him.

The second sentry paced not far from the first. He saw a figure walking toward him in the darkness. He assumed it was his fellow sentry. He gave a soft yelp of recognition.

The figure yelped back.

The sentry relaxed and thought of relieving himself.

The figure stopped, and aimed a bow at the sentry. It did not register with him what was happening, until the arrow pierced him, dropping him to the ground.

By the guardhouse, Noah finished barring the other windows. Methuselah grabbed a torch from the perimeter and poked its flaming tip into the brush cart. He moved it steadily until the dried twigs sparked into flame. Then he tossed the torch up on the thatched roof.

Four dog-soldier sentries warmed themselves at a fire by the gates of the slave pen. It was nearing the end of their watch and they were all a little tired. The orange and yellow flutter of flame caught the eye of one of the sentries. He looked over to the guardhouse and saw the roof engulfed in flames. He barked in surprise. The others saw the fire. They howled to awaken the rest of the guards. One of the sentries pulled out his horn and sounded it.

Uriel came around the corner of the pen livid with anger. "They were supposed to wait for me," he grumbled. He shook his head and pressed forward silently.

At the guardhouse, the sounding horn surprised Methuselah and Noah. Methuselah turned to his grandson, a puzzled expression clouding his face. "Were we supposed to wait?" he asked.

Inside the guardhouse, the warning of the horn wakened the other dog-soldiers. Coughing from the smoke and the barking of confusion sounded under the crackling of the fire.

Uriel rushed the sentries by the gates of the pen with his drawn swords. He slew three of them before they even knew what had happened. But the fourth was already running toward the guardhouse, continuing to blow his infernal horn.

For Elohim's sake, thought Uriel, *he was waking the entire desert!* He threw his sword like a spear at the sentry. It covered the thirty-five cubits and pierced the running sentry. The horn died in a whimper.

Uriel ran for the guardhouse. He passed the downed sentry, drawing his sword from the body without slowing down.

Inside the guardhouse, the dog-soldiers sought in vain to open the doors and windows. But they were locked in. One window remained open. Barking and howling, they clambered out the window single file, only to be speared by Noah. They fell howling into the flames of the burning cart. Methuselah supported Noah with a bow and arrow.

On the far side of the guardhouse, some soldiers managed to break through the other barred window and climb out to freedom, but Uriel arrived to cut them down. He slammed the window shut and re-barred it with the log.

Very quickly, the guards were dead and the guardhouse was a smoldering ruin. The roof collapsed and engulfed the soldiers in an inferno.

Noah, Uriel, and Methuselah walked over to the slave pen.

"You were supposed to wait," Uriel griped to Methuselah.

"My memory is failing," said Methuselah. "Have some compassion for an old man."

"I will not suffer your excuses," said Uriel.

"You certainly took your time dispatching those sentries," countered Methuselah. "Did you stop to pet them?"

Noah interrupted them with a chuckle. "Respect your elder, Methuselah." Uriel as an archangel was a few thousand years older than even Methuselah.

Uriel looked over to see the two of them grinning like griffons. He shook his head, and opened the large gates single-handedly. The three of them walked inside.

The flickering firelight of their torches illuminated a thousand emaciated slaves fearfully wondering their fate. They had not been able to see what was going on outside their pen. They had no idea who these warriors were standing before them.

Methuselah immediately released the ropes that tied the slaves together through metal rings staked to the ground.

Noah stepped forward and spoke like a general. "I am Noah ben Lamech, a son of Enoch. I have freed you from the tyranny of the gods."

Baffled silence met Noah's inspiring proclamation. The slaves did not know how to respond to such a claim. Most thought it a nightmare, others, a mass hallucination. Anything but true liberation.

Eventually, a scrappy slave named Murashu stepped forward and spoke up. "What do you mean, *freed*?"

"You are now free to live by your own choices," said Noah.

Another uncomfortable silence met him.

"We have lived as slaves most of our lives. We do not know how to make *choices*."

"Anu feeds us and gives us work!" yelled another slave.

"We will die on our own," added another. The mass of sleepy slaves began to stir.

Uriel flashed an "I told you so" look to Noah.

"Then join me!" shouted Noah with a strong, sure command. "Join my army to defy the gods and free all men from slavery and idol worship!"

Now Murashu got bold. "We cannot fight trained soldiers. Look at us. We are shades of men."

Another voice shouted from the crowd, "Why should we die for you!" It was more of a statement than a question. The crowd became restless.

Murashu matched Noah's resolve. "We will be punished when the gods see what you have done! Why have you done this to us?"

Murmurs of angry agreement went through the crowd.

Methuselah stopped releasing the ropes. He began to think it might not be such a good idea to release an angry crowd of ingrates from their restraints.

Noah realized a truth about human society: not everyone wanted freedom. When a people willingly or unwillingly become wards of their rulers, they eventually lose their capacity for self-determination. Like helpless children, they actually prefer security in exchange for their freedom. Better the misery they know while being taken care of than the misery they do not know being freely accountable for their own actions. Noah pitied them. They had lost their souls.

Then a big burly man stepped out of the ranks. He had a heavy beard and arms the size of most men's legs. Evidently, he got more to eat than the others. The slaves quieted down.

Uriel stepped closer to Noah in protection.

The man walked right up to Noah, fearlessly ignoring Uriel, and said, "I am Tubal-cain, distant son of Cain."

Methuselah snapped a look at him. The name of Cain did not bring pleasant memories to mind. Cain, the cursed, the man of wrath, had once hunted him and Noah's father Lamech.

Noah's eyes went wide. "Cousin?" Noah had known of his cousins from the line of Cain, son of Adam. They resided in the land of Nod far to the north. But he had not known that they too had become captive to the Watchers.

Tubal-cain glared unblinkingly at Noah. "You say you defy the gods. What of Elohim?"

"I have an archangel of Elohim with me," said Noah, hoping that would say enough.

Uriel mumbled, "Tell everyone, why don't you." It was clearly to his advantage to remain anonymous in his identity and Noah knew that.

Tubal-cain continued to stare down Noah. Then he turned and called behind him, "Brothers!"

Two other men stepped out, and Tubal-cain introduced them as Jabal, a shepherd, and Jubal, a minstrel of music. They were twins with completely opposite personalities.

"You have a nice family," said Uriel, "but not quite an army."

So, this was the lineage that Cain had deserted for his wolf tribe, thought Methuselah. And now, they are our allies. Or at least they appear to be. Methuselah did not trust them.

Noah and his companions looked around. The slaves were becoming more agitated. Methuselah stepped up to Noah and whispered, "We best leave before they think of using us as ransom."

"Follow me," said Tubal-cain. "I have something you will need."

Tubal-cain led them out of the quarters a short distance away to a cave at the outer ridge of the pit. They entered the cave to see a vast smelting furnace area with a pile of coal, molds, anvils and other metalworking implements. "What is this place?" asked Noah.

"It is called a forge," replied Tubal-cain. "The gods taught me how to mix metals to make them much stronger for better tools… and weapons." He finished the sentence with a punctuated grin. But he had more to share.

"I have discovered something stronger than even bronze, but I have not shown it to anyone. I hoped to keep it hidden until a day that I could use it for great benefit. I believe that day has arrived." Jubal and Jabal smiled. Methuselah was all ears—mistrusting ears.

Noah and Uriel followed him to a table with a large meteorite on it. "Metal from heaven," said Tubal-cain. "I did not have to even smelt it. I call it 'iron.'

"Help me move this table," he asked. He positioned himself to push the heavy metallic worktable.

Uriel stepped over and bumped it aside like it was a baby's crib.

Tubal-cain almost fell down and Uriel gave him a smile.

Below the table was a latched door. Tubal-cain pulled it open, revealing a hidden stash of weapons. He pulled up a sword made from the iron. Uriel could see that the Watchers had instructed him in the art of sword making. He wondered if Tubal-cain had been exposed to any black arts.

"These are swords. I see your guardian is already a master of them," said Tubal-cain to Noah.

He handed one to Uriel, who grasped it with interest. The angel tested its weight and slashed the air. *Good. Very good.*

"It's more durable than bronze, almost unbreakable. If we could find this ore on earth, we could defeat an army. Who knows, maybe we could even kill a god or two."

Tubal-cain was very deliberate in his words, which did not escape Noah's notice. He liked it. Killing the gods was exactly what he had in mind.

"I do not have an army," Noah said, "but what I do have is a squad of stealthy assassins."

"With these swords, we could use their own secrets against the gods," said Tubal-cain.

Uriel interrupted. "As our near mishap of this evening illustrates, we have nowhere near the competence for such a feat. If you think you can just saunter into the city of Erech, traipse right into the temple and challenge Anu to a duel, you are sorely misinformed and ill advised. You might as well jump off one of these cliffs right now, because that is what you would be doing."

Noah said, "Well, I guess that means you will have to train the rest of us, then, Uriel."

Tubal-cain handed out swords to everyone.

Uriel had known it was coming. He groaned.

"Enough bellyaching," said Methuselah. "It is for Noah's advantage."

"And I thank you for your measured counsel," Uriel replied. He turned to Noah. "What about the box?"

"What about it?" replied Noah.

"This is not your calling, Noah," said Uriel.

"Am I not the Chosen Seed?" said Noah, "to end the rule of the gods?"

Uriel was annoyed, "Not in that way."

"I will end their rule," said Noah, "one by one."

CHAPTER 9

Lugalanu's dining table was grand, twenty cubits long with a spread fit for a king: a soup of gazelle spleen broth with lentils, chickpeas and leeks. He often ate mutton or goats, but tonight was special: horseflesh. Beef was rare, for there was little pasture land. Fresh radishes, beets and turnips, figs and dates graced the table, as well as the fine delicacy of turtle eggs to compliment them. Royal privilege allowed the variety of breads and bread cakes made from the plentiful grains grown in the kingdom. These bread cakes were offerings made for the Queen of Heaven. Lugalanu and his temple staff ate the remaining amount after Inanna had her fill. He loved them drenched in honey.

Barley was the most common grain in the kingdom, making barley beer the most common drink. Dark or clear, fresh or well aged, Sumerians drank volumes of beer.

Lugalanu drank plenty of it this evening, barely touching his food. He sat all alone at this grand table spread. He watched Emzara and some maidservants clean up the food.

The leftovers would be eaten by the servants, with the exception of the meats that could be smoked and stored for later use. Good food was one of the surest ways to maintain grateful servants. With well-fed bellies, servants would more easily tolerate the fits of rage and abuse that occasionally came over Lugalanu. It is said that a man becomes what he worships, and this was no less true for Lugalanu. He sought to emulate the noblesse oblige of Anu, but often mirrored the emotional outbursts of Inanna.

Tonight, he was depressed.

The object of his depression worked before him, cleaning the table and pouring him more beer. He stared at Emzara's beauty, her regal posture. He contemplated her moral purity. He was priest-king and it was his divine right to force her to be his wife. But he knew it would not be his victory. Thank Anu for the beer. It helped to calm him.

He watched her as she poured his beer. Servants wore simple white tunics, but his personal staff had an added element of decorative embroidery to set them apart. His eyes moved down to her stomach.

She felt the intensity of his gaze and spilled the beer on the table.

"I am sorry, my lord," she said.

"You are beginning to show," he said. It was not true. She was only a few weeks pregnant, and only the most observant would have been able to tell the thickness that was beginning to increase around her middle. He was trying to raise the topic of his offer again.

"I will wear loose clothes," she replied. She completed her pouring and shyly moved to finish the clean up.

He grabbed her arm. He felt her recoil and released his grip apologetically. With a touch of heartsickness in his voice, he asked, "Do I treat you well?"

"Yes, my lord," she said. He had treated her well for the short time she had been with him. He had appointed her as an aide to the Chief Maidservant in charge of Lugalanu's personal staff, Alittum, an experienced, agreeable and ambitious woman, who constantly sought to ingratiate herself to Lugalanu.

Emzara administered the other servants, and domestic chores such as cooking, cleaning, and finances. Though she had been given a new Sumerian name, as were all captured slaves, Lugalanu called her Emzara when they were alone. He sought a connection with that inner part of her that was not owned by the gods. Her Sumerian name was Nindannum, which meant "lady of strength." This name, given her by Lugalanu, also expressed his great admiration for her. Such name references to "ladies" were usually used only of goddesses.

Most slaves were branded with the name of the god on the back of their hands, but Lugalanu allowed Emzara the less popular form of wearing a bronze bracelet with the symbol. He sought to accommodate her personal devotion to Elohim by exempting her from any duties directly related to the worship of the gods or their divination and sorcerous activities.

Her special treatment did not go unnoticed by Alittum, nor the fact that Emzara was learning Alittum's own responsibilities. Therefore, Alittum made life miserable for Emzara, criticizing her every move. Unfortunately for Alittum, it had the undesired effect of making Emzara try so hard that she was already a model servant.

But Alittum was not here now. She had departed with the other table servants.

"If you were to remove your unborn, you could be my wife. You would birth kings and queens from your womb." He cloaked the desperate plea as an alluring offer.

She had the upper hand and she knew it. "Would you force me, my lord?"

Lugalanu glanced at the other servants cleaning the room They studiously attended their responsibilities, pretending not to hear anything said by their master. He waved his hand at them. They instantly scurried out the door.

Lugalanu and his favorite were alone. He could let down his composure. "I do not understand you, Emzara. In this world, the vanquished embrace their fate. Yet you do not." It was true, he thought. The strong ruled the weak, and the weak accepted their station in life as their fate from the gods. After all, they were created as slaves for the gods.

"I cannot," she responded. She believed in the rule of righteousness as opposed to the rule of power. Righteousness came from faith in Elohim, who created all humankind in his image. She knew this faith ran fully counter to the Sumerian belief that only the king was created in the image of the gods. She would die for her beliefs because life was of no value without them.

"That is what I like about you," he said, almost regretfully. It would only make the victory real to have all her personal strength and conviction willingly yield to him. All the more so since he did not tell her that he had engaged a sorcerer to cast a spell of enchantment upon her to fall in love with him. He participated in a ritual, building a reed altar and praying to the bright Morning Star, sacred to Inanna, goddess of fertility. He made an offering and prepared figurines that he dutifully burned, and created a potion that he slipped into her drink.

But none of it had worked. The incantations, spells, and charms of the manipulative magic, none of it seemed to have an effect on her.

He would continue to be patient.

He spoke with ostensible sadness, "Your son will be a servant of the goddess in her temple." He made it sound as if it was out of his hands and he could do nothing to change it. That was a lie.

She looked to him with hope. "But he will be alive," she said, looking for affirmation of his promise.

He gave her none. Of course, he could simply kill the child, rip it from her womb. He really should do so, because if this was the child of the Chosen

Seed, then it was certainly possible that it would carry on the lineage that might bear the revelation should Noah fail.

The thought of these options encouraged him. He felt powerful. He, the human ruler of a city, a mere servant of the gods, might have in his hands the power to destroy those gods. Even though to do so could bring about his own destruction, it was still a power over those gods.

On the other hand, if this really was the bloodline of the coming King, then he also had the power over Elohim to end that bloodline and thwart the plans of the Creator himself. He smiled to himself. He would do nothing, and this would ensure his position, for the drug-like high could only be maintained by the power over choices, and that power was dissipated as soon as those choices were exercised.

The patter of approaching feet outside the door interrupted Lugalanu's musing. A panting servant slid around the corner, and bobbed up and down in a fit of genuflection.

"What is it?" Lugalanu barked, on the verge of one of his Inanna-like fits.

"My lords Anu and Inanna require your immediate presence in the throne room."

Lugalanu sobered instantly and sprang into action. He was out the door as quickly as his feet could carry him. He might hold the power to destroy the gods, but that event would not be today.

Emzara knew this kind of request came rarely, so she decided to risk the danger by secretly following him. She knew that a passive response to her situation would never give her control over her destiny. She had to take chances. She had to take control.

She grabbed a royal canister in order to get by the guards. She stayed just out of sight behind Lugalanu as he traversed the hallways back into the palace area. When he reached the royal outer court gates, Emzara slipped around to a servant's entrance in the inner court. After all, she was a servant. She had memorized the ins and outs of the servant's access through the entire Eanu and Eanna districts.

She stayed in the shadows behind the outer pillars and slipped her way up toward the altar of the sanctuary. She could get no closer to the thrones than twenty cubits, but the acoustics in the throne room were so perfect she could hear every word.

They were already in counsel with Lugalanu when she settled in the shadows.

"He escaped?" asked Lugalanu.

"He killed the entire guard of the slave mines!" yelled Inanna. "Curse this Noah ben Lamech and his audacity!"

Emzara suppressed a gasp.

The chimera bull and lion creatures glanced over in Emzara's direction. They had acute hearing.

The conversation stopped. Anu and Inanna followed the gaze of their throne guardians. One of them moved to investigate. But before it got down the steps, Emzara had slipped behind a pillar just in time.

A servant passed her hiding place, drawing their attention to him. He carried chalices of blood for the gods. He placed the libations on the altar and left.

The gods and their priest-king returned to their discussion.

"Are you sure he is the prophesied Chosen Seed?" Anu asked Lugalanu.

Inanna burst out, "He denied it! You heard it yourself."

Lugalanu said, "He appears to have the protection of Elohim over him."

The incident had taken place a week before, but they only now discovered the escape when their weekly shipment of copper did not arrive. A contingent of soldiers had been sent to investigate. Evidently all the slaves had remained and continued their labors awaiting new leadership. It pleased Anu that it was true after all: men's souls, not merely their bodies, could be owned.

"We can afford no risks," said Anu. "Send the Gibborim. They will find this Noah and they will kill him."

"Yes, my lord and god," said Lugalanu.

He shivered inside himself. The Gibborim were an elite corps of Nephilim, a unit of five highly trained assassins. They could hunt anything and kill it, and they were unstoppable. It was said that one corps of Gibborim had conquered an entire city in the northern hinterlands, killing everyone and eating the flesh of the victims for weeks.

The lion-man continued to stare in Emzara's direction. He had not taken his eyes off the location since she had gasped. With a snarl, he bounded off the dais and covered the distance through the shrubbery to the pillars in a couple strides.

When he got there, Emzara was already gone.

The evening fell. Lugalanu rode his four-wheeled chariot through the streets of the city drawn by muscle-bound war horses. everyone in the streets moved out of the way, hiding in the shadows and locking their doors, but not because of Lugalanu's mighty chariot stallions. It was the five assassin Gibborim that followed him. They were taller than most Nephilim, about ten cubits tall. They were tattooed head to foot, wore exotic armor, and carried their unusual weapons and supplies on their backs. They walked with eyes intensely focused on their objective.

Emzara followed their movement toward the gates of the city behind the procession, in the shadows. She slid behind a water trough as the procession stopped at the gates.

One of the Nephilim sensed something and turned, looking straight at the water trough. Emzara had slid off to the side in the dark of an alley. The Naphil turned back to its mission commander, Lugalanu.

"My Gibborim," said Lugalanu, "on you lies the hope of this kingdom." They listened to him with cold, unblinking reptilian eyes. They were instruments of death and destruction. The king made the seriousness of his charge clear, "If you do not destroy this Chosen Seed, he will destroy you and your seed. Bring me his head."

With barely an acknowledgment of his words, the Gibborim walked out of the gates.

Emzara had found her way to the wall, where she could see the giant fiends through a fissure in the rock. They broke into a run out under the moonlight. The earth rumbled beneath their feet. They were so powerful, they did not need beasts of burden. They were faster without them.

In despair, Emzara uttered a prayer to Elohim. If these monsters of evil were after her beloved Noah, he did not stand a chance. He was doomed. Only Elohim could rescue him now. She turned to find her way back to the palace.

To her shock, Lugalanu stood in her path looking straight at her. Her face went flush.

He stared at her. "You are curious of my intrigues?" he asked.

"My lord, it was my opportunity to slip away from the palace for the night air." She had carefully prepared the excuse. "I prefer to be near you than alone in the streets."

Lugalanu stared at her silently. She thought he did not believe her. Her ruse had been exposed.

"Emzara," he said with a scolding tone. She readied herself for punishment. "You are not a caged animal; you need only ask and I will extend your leash." He stared at her, oblivious to the incongruity of his statement.

She was thrown for a second. Her ruse had worked. He did not suspect a thing. She forced a sweet little smile of innocence.

He stepped up close to her, brushing her hair aside with a tender hand. "You see, Emzara, am I not a reasonable man?"

CHAPTER 10

Noah and his band of warriors traveled seventy leagues north by northeast into the Great Desert, paralleling the valley plains and avoiding the cities. They found sequestered sand canyons and settled in for battle training with Uriel and their new sickle sword weapons. A labyrinthine network of channels cut through the canyon's sandy floor. Towering walls of sandstone surrounded them, walls almost forty cubits high swept by wind and water. Ancient waters, leaving ribbon-like waves of sedimentation, shaping grooves in the rock, had created the channels. The rocks were smooth to the touch. During the day, the light created a beautiful sight of orange, yellow, and red glowing layers.

Noah picked this location for the specific reason that they could lose anyone who might be after them. Both seasoned nomads and unseasoned travelers had died here, lost in the vast natural maze. But Noah had traversed these canyons in the past and knew them well. He knew them too well. His razor sharp memory both blessed and cursed him. Whatever he saw once with full concentration, he could remember with a detailed accuracy matched only by storytellers and scribes. If he were not the Patriarch he would probably have been an oral bard. The curse of his memory was that he could not forget the details of the pain he had experienced in his life: the expression of his best friend dying in his arms in battle, the gestures of his first wife that haunted him instead of fading away with time. And his superb memory did not help his impatience with others.

The men stood in a circle, gripping their iron sickle swords for fight. Noah, Methuselah, Jubal, Jabal, and Tubal-cain surrounded Uriel holding his double-handed swords in the center. Uriel barked, "Begin!" and one by one, starting with Noah, the men attacked Uriel, using the battle moves they had practiced for the last few weeks. Uriel had given them basic routines of sword-fighting moves to memorize and repeat endlessly. They contained repetitious exercises that drove the men to near exhaustion and boredom. That was the intent. They had to develop second nature impulses for a fight.

The technique was based on the Way of the Karabu, the ancient secret order of giant killers from Sahand. Methuselah had learned these skills as a younger man. He was rusty, being out of practice. But Noah was somewhat familiar with it, for Methuselah had taught him over the years. The other three men, however, were entirely new to this technique.

Several weeks of exercises were no substitute for the kind of seasoned training needed to become a master swordsman. But fortunately, these men were already accomplished fighters in their own right, which gave Uriel some unanticipated surprises. Jubal, a musician, may have had arms more slender than the others, but he proved to work his sword with fluidity and dance that outplayed the strength of the others. Uriel sometimes said that Jubal was a natural born Karabu.

Noah's sharp memory and strong will resulted in excessive devotion to mastering the forms. This resulted in a proficiency that impressed even Uriel. Tubal-cain's sheer muscle power made up for his lack of finesse, and Jabal's expertise with a staff gave him added skills that would no doubt benefit the group in a skirmish.

As Uriel brandished his weapon against each attack, he calmly tutored the men with corrections and observations of their moves. "Good thrust," here, "bad slash," there, "breathe deeply, feet spread." "Sweep more, Jubal," "Stay low, Noah," "Think of the sword as water. Wash over the enemy." The men grunted with exhaustion as Uriel deflected their every blow with a casual agility that frustrated them, making them feel they had not learned a thing.

"Cease!" yelled Uriel. He could see they were done for the day. Methuselah collapsed to the ground trying to gasp for air. Jubal and Jabal leaned on each other for support. "Well, that was invigorating," said Uriel.

"Invigorating?" countered Noah. "You have not even broken a sweat."

Uriel smiled. "I have had eons of practice. You have had only years, and they, mere weeks."

"If this is any sign of how difficult it will be to fight the gods and their supernatural minions," said Methuselah, still catching his breath, "perhaps we had better reevaluate our stratagem."

"Let us talk after a meal," said Noah.

Methuselah cooked a stew of roots and herbs on the campfire. They sat and listened quietly as Jubal breathed out a soft tune on his reed pipe. Unlike the harp, Jubal's personal favorite instrument, the reed pipe was more conducive for travel because of its small size and durability. Jubal valued this little bone-carved instrument as much as his sword. Without the beauty of music in his life, he would die a soul bereft of happiness.

Methuselah watched Noah scratching out markings on a piece of animal hide he had acquired from a carcass found on the desert floor. Noah used some dye made from animal blood with a homemade quill from a vulture's wing. He had been at the writing all evening with a torch over his shoulder. Methuselah's curiosity got the better of him. He tried to take a look but Noah would not let him see what he was doing.

Tubal-cain finally blurted out in his characteristic bluntness, "Noah, do you still want to kill the god Anu?"

"And his priest-king," added Noah. He remembered the look of Lugalanu and his proud assertions spouted at Noah. He was just as guilty of killing Noah's wife and unborn child as the god who corrupted him.

"I told you," said Uriel, "the gods cannot be killed."

"Then I will die trying," said Noah.

"You would sacrifice us all?" challenged Uriel.

"Everyone is free to leave at any time," said Noah.

Methuselah jumped in. "You are a proud man, Noah ben Lamech."

"A beautiful woman once told me that," said Noah. "She was murdered, along with my people, by the pride of gods."

"Would you make your sons orphans as well?" said Uriel.

That one made Noah pause. The one way to his heart was his family.

"Not if my guardian does his job," concluded Noah.

Noah was bent on using Uriel's commission to protect him as a way to manipulate Elohim's help in his quest. Surely, if Elohim wanted Noah alive for his purposes, then he would have to exercise some kind of supernatural protection over him, even if Noah was willing to go to Sheol and back to accomplish his goal. And if it did not mean that, then Noah would rather die and stay in Sheol anyway. Lugalanu had Noah's entire tribe wiped out with his wife and unborn child, and Anu had ordered it, so they must pay.

Methuselah spoke again, this time with pain in his every word. "Noah, do you think you are the only one who has lost his beloved to the ravages of this evil world?"

Everyone fell silent. Noah knew it was a rhetorical question, so he did not answer. He listened.

Methuselah continued, "Do not be so sure that revenge is a meal that will satisfy your hunger. It is more like a disease that eats away your soul. As the years go on, bitterness turns you into the very thing you detest. You begin a blessed man. But when Elohim takes away that blessing, you begin to believe you deserved it in the first place. You blame him and eventually you end up an old bellyaching ingrate without the ability to appreciate the good in anything. And you realize that you are the reason for your misery. You have become your own enemy."

Everyone knew that Methuselah spoke of himself, and they honored his vulnerability with their silence. They all stared at the flames until Methuselah's words of experience sank deep into them.

Uriel finally spoke, "If you want to defeat your enemy, then you must know your enemy," he said. "And the first thing you must know about the gods is that they are not what they seem."

Jubal stopped his music. Everyone sat up and looked at Uriel.

"What do you mean?" said Tubal-cain.

Tubal-cain and the twins did not know of Enoch's visions as Noah and Methuselah did.

Methuselah began, "My father Enoch first told us of the Watchers, the Sons of God."

Uriel explained, "They were in Elohim's divine council. They fell from heaven and made themselves gods on earth. Two hundred of them, led by Semjaza and Azazel. They landed on Mount Hermon in the region of Bashan in the north." The others were rapt in attention.

Uriel continued, "Along with those two hundred, a number of lesser angels or *mal'akim*, the lower messengers of Elohim, also came into the world."

"What do you mean, lower? Are they weaker?" asked Jubal.

Uriel shook his head. "To call these angels lower in rank than the Sons of God is misleading. Mal'akim are warriors who have the wisdom of sages and the power of several men."

Methuselah continued with the history. "Mount Hermon and Bashan have important lore behind them. The name means place of the Serpent."

Jabal nodded. "It is the Cosmic Mountain," he said. "The Gateway of the Gods. Some people say the mountain is also the gateway to Sheol."

"They are not wrong," Uriel said. "It is in the foothill village of Kur, guarded by the goddess of the underworld, Ereshkigal, sister of Inanna. If one makes it through the Seven Gates of Ganzir, they have access to the waters of the Abyss, which leads to the netherworld of Sheol." Noah took note of the connection of Ereshkigal to Inanna.

Methuselah's voice took on more force. "It was in Bashan that the first of the mighty warrior giants appeared. They became kings called the *Rephaim* and they spread out on the land to rule after the Watchers came down from heaven. These Rephaim had first ruled the cities then led their evil minions in the great Titanomachy." He took a deep breath. "They were hunted down and cast into Sheol by the archangels, where they remained to this day." Uriel nodded.

Methuselah continued, "The Watchers set up their rule as gods and began to teach mankind sorceries, astrology, warfare and other violations of the natural order. They have instituted an aggressive program of breeding. They want to create their own paradise. They saw the daughters of men and mated with them to create the Nephilim as their own bloodline. They have enslaved humanity as their servants to build them temples. They have structured their temples to look like the original cosmic Mount Hermon. They even call the temple shape 'holy mountains.'" He snorted with derision. Noah knew all this, but it was new information for Tubal-cain and the brothers Jubal and Jabal.

"What is their intent?" asked Tubal-cain.

"They are the seed of the Serpent, Nachash," said Uriel, "and they are at war with the seed of the Woman, Havah, the mother of all living. They have been effective in their strategy, for Elohim has seen that the wickedness of man is great on the earth and that every intent of the thoughts of his heart is only evil continually. So he prophesied that a Chosen Seed would come who would end the rule of the gods, and out of his bloodline would come an anointed King who would crush the head of the Nachash and his seed. Noah is that Chosen Seed."

The men all sat open-mouthed, looking at Noah. They could have cut the thick silence with a dagger. Uriel turned to Noah and said, "Noah's bloodline is the key to their defeat."

"Then help me defeat these Sons of God," said Noah.

"You will defeat them by building the box," said Uriel.

"What box?" asked Jubal.

"None of your business," Noah snapped. "That is a certain disagreement between me and my Maker. My main concern right now is to find a way to defeat these corrupt deities."

"The Sons of God cannot die," said Uriel. "But they have similar limitations on the earthly plane as we archangels do. Though they are divine, they are created beings, so they can be bound."

Noah stared inquisitively at Uriel. He realized that Uriel concealed much more than he revealed. "What do you mean by 'bound?'"

Uriel stared back at Noah thoughtfully. He decided he would reveal that detail later. He avoided a direct answer. "For some reason, they are weakened by water, for instance. If you plunge them in water, they lose their strength. More importantly, if they are trapped in the depths of the earth, they would not die, but they could be imprisoned."

Methuselah said, "To live forever trapped in rock?"

"Until the end of days," corrected Uriel.

Tubal-cain said, "That would be worse than death."

"And more difficult to accomplish," added Uriel.

Noah sat, deep in thought. Everyone was missing the point in focusing on the mechanics of binding. He watched Uriel like a falcon as he asked, "Is that what you are here to do, Uriel, bind the Sons of God?"

Uriel paused, then nodded. The others were confused. "Elohim is about to bring judgment down on the earth," Uriel explained to them. "Part of that plan is to bind the gods in the midst of that judgment, to imprison them until the Final Day."

"Only archangels can accomplish this binding?" asked Noah.

"It is one of our talents," admitted Uriel.

"Now we are talking," smiled Noah.

Uriel sighed. He wondered if he would ever get this man to build the box.

"You mentioned Ereshkigal is the sister of Inanna," said Noah.

Uriel nodded. Noah smiled with satisfaction. It was more satisfying revenge to kill the family members of your target of hatred before you killed them. "She is much weaker than Anu," he said.

Uriel nodded again. He knew where this was going.

"So, if we start with one of the weaker gods," Noah speculated, "we can work our way up the pantheon."

"Noah, this is not your calling," said Uriel.

"Think of it this way," said Noah, "we are helping you to fulfill your calling."

Before Uriel could respond, a strange bellow in the distance interrupted them. The hideous noise sounded like a beast from the pit of Sheol. The camels stirred in agitation.

"What is it?" asked Methuselah, looking to Uriel.

"The call of the Gibborim," said Uriel darkly.

"Gibborim?" asked Tubal-cain.

"The mightiest of the Nephilim, Seed of the Serpent. We are being tracked," said Uriel. He began packing up his things. "It was inevitable."

"Is there anything we can do?" asked Tubal-cain.

"Run for your lives," said Uriel.

Jabal gave a nervous laugh, and then realized Uriel was not jesting.

"We have to leave now, or you will all die," said Uriel.

The others began packing up immediately.

Uriel turned to Noah and said, "It is probably a squad of four to six of them. We do not stand a chance. If we stay, they will find us. You may face the gods sooner than you expect."

The five Nephilim stood at the southern edge of the sand canyons. The leader of the squad looked down at some camel droppings on the sandy floor. He took a deep breath through his nose, seeking a trace scent. Then he leapt forward into the canyon opening, followed by the others. The ground rumbled under their feet, a rolling wave of evil. They were tall and would be slowed down by some of the tight corners and low hanging formations of the canyons. But they were locked in on their prey, and it was only a matter of time before they found them. Just as the height and strength of the Nephilim were amplified, So too were their five senses, which were acute to an extreme. It was said they could see their target's eyes at nearly 700 cubits, smell blood at half that distance, and when on the hunt, could hear the silent breath of their victims. But they were also offspring of the Sons of God, born of sorcery, that gave them a sixth sense into the spiritual world. They were more than mere killing machines. They were killing demoniacs.

Noah and his men barreled out of the north canyon passage and found themselves at a crossroads. The desert lay before them, while to the east spread the Fertile Crescent valley. They gathered to take their bearings.

"Split up by twos," said Noah. "Take different routes and we will meet at a common destination."

"Where?" said Methuselah.

Before Noah could decide, Uriel pronounced it, "Mount Hermon."

The men looked at him with surprise, Noah, the most taken aback.

Uriel answered their expressions. "The mountain village of Kur, where the goddess Ereshkigal guards the gates to Sheol." Noah was surprised at his change of attitude.

"You said you wanted to start with a weaker god," said Uriel.

Noah smiled. Uriel was on board, but not entirely. The angel had his own agenda yet, for the box. But Noah now felt for the first time that he actually had a chance at revenge. He could not resist getting a dig in. "You changed your mind," he said on the sly.

"No!" snapped Uriel. "My charge is to protect you until *you* change *your* mind!"

Noah grinned. "So if I build the box, you will leave me alone?"

"It would be my pleasure," retorted Uriel. The others shared a smile amongst themselves.

Noah called Methuselah over to him and reached in his pack, pulling out the rolled piece of leather he had been marking on. He handed it to Methuselah. "In case, I do not reach you."

Methuselah unrolled the leather. It had cuneiform written all over it, along with a drawing of a large rectangular box. Noah had memorized the plans from his vision and had written them down.

Noah swiftly mounted his camel and whipped it around with a yell. Uriel followed him toward the southwest. They would try to shake the Nephilim from their trail in the harsh desert before reaching Mount Hermon.

Jubal joined Jabal and they raced northward. Methuselah and Tubal-cain went east. They all had much ground to cover if they wanted to stay ahead of the infernal hounds on their trail.

Tubal-cain mocked Methuselah, "You had better keep up with me, old man."

"It is you I am worried about, fat man," Methuselah shot back.

Tubal-cain looked hurt. Methuselah had got his goat, found the chink in his armor. "I am not fat!" he growled, "I have iron bones!" He kicked his camel and the two of them raced into the desert horizon. Methuselah was glad that this way he could keep an eye on this dubious character.

It took several days for the Nephilim to wind their way through the canyon maze and navigate through the layers of distraction laid out by Uriel. A supernatural tracker himself, Uriel had the advantage of knowing how to set false clues and dead-end trails. He knew they needed the time to gain enough distance before the Nephilim found their true exit point from the canyons.

The opening to the valley where Noah and his men had split up breathed with the sounds of life. Insects buzzing around, crickets chirping, distant howls and birdcalls combined in a cacophony of nature. Suddenly, all those sounds stopped. Dead silence. The ground started to rumble. Moments later, the five Nephilim reached the gap at a steady hunting pace.

The pack leader sniffed the air. He studied the hoof prints on the ground, then scanned the horizon. In an uncanny display of unspoken understanding, they split up into three groups, two taking the north passage, two to the east, and the leader bounding westward. After a short sprint, the pack leader let out his hideous Gibborim call. It echoed loud through the desert plain. The other Nephilim circled back and all joined the pack leader's pursuit.

All five of them were on Noah's trail.

CHAPTER 11

Alittum noticed the special attention given to Emzara. The Chief Maidservant burned with jealousy and envy, though she kept it judiciously hidden. Lugalanu did for Emzara what he had promised; he extended her leash in the palace and city. Nindannum, the Sumerian name that Alittum used for Emzara, had already been exempted from the cultic duties related to the temple worship, which Alittum thought could only lead to ultimate betrayal of Anu. But now this so-called "lady of strength" had been given more privileges; her own quarters, a personal allowance, and a day of rest during the week, something usually reserved for chief administrators like Alittum.

Nindannum got out of the temple district into the surrounding community even more than Alittum. The Chief Maidservant was saddled with so much responsibility she never had time for herself. Nindannum shopped for the palace food in the marketplace, inspected the fields outside the city walls, and even got involved in trade with traveling caravans from other cities and countries. Nindannum was not at home in this world. Alittum could see that. She could also see through her demure composure. That was not shyness or submission. Nindannum protected herself. And she was plotting something, Alittum was sure of it.

Alittum could not conceive of anything beyond the obvious. She assumed Nindannum aimed to replace Alittum herself as Chief Maidservant. In every way she could think of, Alittum resisted. But what more could she do in competition with this upstart foreign slave? Alittum had submitted her body and soul to Lugalanu. She lowered herself to that of a dog, obeying every command of a soul depraved with absolute power. She let him use her, hoping it would endear him to her. But she feared that it only served to increase his contempt for her.

Alittum wondered if Lugalanu was closer to Nindannum than to her. In some ways his restraint toward Nindannum inspired him toward more abuse with Alittum. She could not imagine what Lugalanu could want of

Nindannum. Did not she, Alittum, give him everything he wanted? Yet he treated Nindannum with such respect and esteem that it made Alittum's heart ache with loneliness.

Alittum considered ending her life to escape the despair. Hopefully, Lugalanu would regret his actions toward her. But then she became more constructive in her calculations. She reasoned that the best way to make him sorry would be the destruction of the object of his affections. If she could only eliminate Nindannum, and that detestable child in her belly, in such a way that it would not be detected, she might regain her station with Lugalanu. He might finally see her in a new light.

Alittum's experience afforded her great knowledge of every intricacy and detail of the palace and temple as well as the politics of court. If anyone had the resources to conduct a perfect palace crime, it was Alittum. Therein lay her plan, a plan that would begin by becoming Nindannum's best friend.

As a first step, Alittum visited a sorceress to put a spell of misfortune on Nindannum and to conjure the demoness Lamashtu who could kill Nindannum's unborn if given the right opportunity. She had heard through the gossip of the palace servants of such miscarriages, but had never seen it for herself. Now, she wanted to see it with all her liver, the very seat of her emotions. She had never considered herself an ambitious or vengeful person. She had never even used black magic before. It was too malicious for her personal integrity. But Nindannum's relentless pursuit of advancement forced Alittum's hand. She needed to protect her own status and legacy. Alittum purified herself through washing and oils, and sat through the incantation of the sorceress. She prayed for the utter ruin of Emzara, even as she prepared to reach out to her in feigned camaraderie.

Emzara's pregnancy was beginning to show. She knew she had little time if she wanted to escape this comfortable prison before her child was born and given up to false gods. She ran through all the possibilities in her head. She could hide out in a trading caravan leaving the city. But those were extensively searched for just that reason. So many slaves had tried to run away that the guards had become quite skilled in the art of uncovering stowaways. That was a sure path to a flogging. Many had died from the wounds of that punishment.

And what if she did get out of the city? Where would she go? She had no idea where Noah might be. She would be easy prey for the predators of the desert, both animal and human. She could not do it on her own. She needed help. But who could she trust? Alittum had become much more agreeable in recent weeks. She knew she was a threat to the Chief Maidservant because Lugalanu obviously favored her. But Emzara had fought so hard to affirm Alittum's station and defer her own that it appeared to calm Alittum of her fears.

It had occurred to Emzara that perhaps she should prepare for the kind of opportunity that she did not anticipate, such as the attempt of her husband to rescue her. She had been taught the basic plan of servants' access throughout the temple district, but she knew there was a network of more secret passageways. Only a select few of the leadership, like Alittum, knew the details of those hidden ways. If Emzara could learn those networks, she might be ready should an opportunity present itself.

But then her heart went sick. Her beloved Noah did not even know she was alive. As far as he knew, she was dead along with all their tribe. Even if he was not sure she was dead, how could he possibly discover her whereabouts in the very heart of darkness in Erech? And even if he could discover that, what difference would it make when he was being hunted by a band of assassin Nephilim? They were so skilled he would not stand a chance against them. He would need a guardian archangel for even a shekel of hope. She fought the impulse to cry. He was probably already dead. She prayed to Elohim instead.

When she finished praying, she felt more at ease. Prayers always took her mind off herself and her impossibilities and onto Elohim and His possibilities. She got up to return to her staff duties. A thought suddenly struck her. Whether Noah was dead or alive, whether he would save her or not, she should begin to think of others and not just herself. It might not be to her advantage to seek escape, but it might be to the advantage of others; those who were the slaves of the temple and palace, those who were beaten so badly they preferred to die in the wilderness seeking freedom in death to their own hell on earth. If she could learn the network of secret passageways, she might be able to establish a pathway to freedom for other slaves. She could become the means of redemption for others, a redemption that she could not achieve for herself.

It was surely the providence of Elohim when, the very next day, Alittum approached Emzara and asked to speak to her in private.

"Nindannum, how is your health?" asked Alittum.

"I am well, thank you," replied Emzara, holding her womb affectionately.

It struck Alittum that Nindannum displayed no signs of trouble. Surely, the Lamashtu demoness would have done something by now, even if just to harass her victim. Alittum would have to consult the sorceress as soon as she had some time. She brightened her countenance. "It is no secret that I have not treated you as you have deserved these past months," said Alittum. "I have been intimidated by your poise and presence. But now I see that you are a woman of true character and virtue, and I want to apologize for my inappropriateness, my impatience and shortness with you."

Emzara was shocked. She did not know what to say. "Alittum, I bear no complaint. I have nothing but gratitude for the privilege of being your aide and learning from your wisdom and experience."

Alittum could barely stomach the patronizing flattery. "Well, I think it is time for you to become aware of one more privilege."

Emzara sat up with piqued attention. Alittum continued, "It is of such privacy and significance that only the highest of temple and palace caste are allowed to know of it. I am talking of a system of secret passageways through the city."

Inside her gut, Emzara felt the rush of excitement. Elohim had answered her prayers.

Alittum concluded, "They connect all the main palace structures and lead outside the city as well."

"To what do I owe the honor of this revelation?" asked Emzara.

"To your own character," replied Alittum. "I feel that I could trust you with my life. So I knew that I would need for you to trust me with yours. But you must tell no one, not even Lugalanu."

Strange, thought Emzara. *Why would Lugalanu not want to know?* In fact, would he not have been the one to ask for her initiation?

Alittum answered Emzara's thoughts as if she read her mind. "If anything should happen through the use of those passageways — anything against the law — it would serve to protect you from any implication if Lugalanu knew not of your acquaintance with them."

Could this be true? thought Emzara. Could Alittum be offering her the very opportunity that she sought? Surely, this was from Elohim! She could not have asked for a more perfect opportunity.

Then Alittum added, "But be careful. These passageways also lead to the secret chambers of the gods, where no human is allowed to enter, save the king."

Emzara had heard of these chambers, but did not know much about them. Rumor said they were places where the gods engaged in sorceries, including the birth of the Nephilim from the daughters of men. The women who were forced to carry these infernal fetuses in the womb were never seen again. Emzara wondered what fate had befallen the innocent Shazira, the girl chosen as one among many to be the vessel of a demigod. Emzara suppressed a wave of nausea.

Alittum continued, "The chambers are said to contain the secrets of the universe. Wonders that humans cannot bear to behold: Astrology, sorcery, magic spells and enchantments. It is said that should a human learn such secrets she might become a challenge to the gods themselves." To Emzara, this seemed more like a tempting offer than a dangerous warning. She could feel a tug in her own soul toward the forbidden knowledge. Access to the heart of this evil empire could one day be used to bring about its downfall.

Alittum had carefully avoided reference to the punishment for such a breach of confidence. This kind of violation would no doubt require the ultimate price of one's life. Still, the focus on the possibilities had its affect on Emzara. The knowledge fed her hatred of injustice and her desire to right the wrongs of her world. It served her sense of significance, that she might be in the position to alter the course of history. It nurtured her pride.

CHAPTER 12

The Great Desert was a vast hostile territory that would kill visitors unaccustomed to its harsh environment. Travelers faced a lack of water, scorching hot days, freezing cold nights and unpredictable sand storms at a moment's notice. Fortunately, Methuselah knew the terrain because he had been through its jaws in the past during his giant killing days with his father Enoch. They had crossed the barren terrain on their way to Bashan. They had endured the worst of dehydration and sandstorms, and a most peculiar mystical tree guarded by seductive demons. But he prayed they would not stumble upon that nightmare again because they barely made it out alive.

During that encounter with the demonic tree, Methuselah's company had been rescued by a Thamudi tribe that had settled in the region and became allies with them. But they had been on a mission from Elohim that required them to move onward. Later, when Noah was a young boy, the two tribes had met again. Noah had become fast friends with the chief's son, Salah al Din, whose name meant "righteousness of faith." Noah wondered how his former playmate had fared since they were last together.

Noah planned to go deep into the desert in an attempt to lose their Nephilim trackers. Jubal and Jabal would lose theirs by fleeing into northern lands where the new kingdom of Akkad had begun. Methuselah and Tubal-cain would cross the Mesopotamian plains to the east and shake off their Nephilim in the Zagros Mountains, doubling back to meet everyone at the village of Kur in Mount Hermon after two moons.

Noah had not anticipated that all five Nephilim would be on his trail. Uriel had surmised this misfortune by the time they arrived at the Thamudi fortresses.

The Thamud were a mysterious people. Rock dwellers, they literally sculpted their residences in the stone of the buttes. The outer carving looked like the facades of buildings in any city of the plain, but they were in fact entirely hollowed out of the rocks of the hills. The beautiful, huge creations housed a people of formidable fierceness. One had to be fierce to survive the unrelenting brutality of the desert. The settlement to which Noah returned sheltered about seven hundred souls, three hundred able warriors and their wives and children.

Noah and Uriel were greeted by a party led by none other than Chief Salah al Din. Noah's playmate had grown up to be the tribal chieftain.

"Mustafa!" Salah called to Noah. "Mustafa" meant Chosen One in his tribal dialect. Salah never tired of reminding Noah that he had embraced Enoch's revelation and believed Noah to be the Chosen Seed who would end the rule of the gods and bring rest to the land—even if Noah himself would not accept it. "It has been too long, old friend," Salah said as he embraced his visitor.

"How is that old goat, Methuselah?" the chieftain asked. "He and father were as close as you and I."

Noah tried to keep face with proper etiquette, "He complains too much, but he is still a strong arm for me. We all miss Diya al Din. Your father was a great man, and we will never forget his kindness to us."

Salah said, "Thank you, my friend. Our humble home remains your own."

He read their solemn expressions, sensing that something was wrong. Noah introduced him to Uriel and then broke the news. "I am sorry to tell you, Salah, that this visit is not a blessed one. My companion and I are being hunted by a party of Gibborim."

Salah knew of the Gibborim. He knew they only left death and destruction in their wake. But that could only mean one thing to Salah. "If the principalities and powers of darkness are on to you," he teased, "that must mean you may soon begin to accept your own identity."

Noah could not return the jest. He was too tired, and scared for Salah and his people. "We seek only supplies, Salah. And we will be on our way. We will not jeopardize your people's safety. We have our own quest to accomplish."

"Nonsense," said Salah. "Tonight, we will celebrate with feasting, and discuss your strategy."

Noah could not argue with Salah's stubborn kindness. He was too desperate at this point. He nodded. He and Uriel rode off with Salah to the Thamudi fortresses.

The banquet tables were laden with the best food that desert living could provide; crispy beetle appetizers, sand grouse, snake, roasted gecko lizards on sticks, as well as a delicacy of gazelle organs. And beer flowed freely. Salah held nothing back from his beloved friend. But he could see that Noah remained somber.

Salah leaned in close to Noah and said, "My friend, how are your people?"

Noah told him the whole story of the butchery of his entire clan, and his subsequent capture and escape. It broke Salah's heart. His eyes teared up with empathy.

"Tell me of your quest, and how I can be of service to you," said Salah.

Noah explained grimly, "I have decided that I *will* end this rule of the gods, one by one, by binding them and casting them into the depths of the earth. Our first destination is Mount Hermon."

Salah knew Mount Hermon's fame as the cosmic mountain where the Watchers had come down from heaven. He knew it was the portal to Sheol, guarded by the underworld gods Ereshkigal and Nergal. "But I thought only archangels could bind such divine monsters of power and cruelty," said Salah. Understanding suddenly hit him. He stared at Uriel. He had been entertaining an angel unaware in his very own citadel.

A mischievous grin settled over Salah's face. "So it has finally begun. The judgment of God is nigh." Uriel's face was unresponsive. He would give nothing away. "We have a saying out here in the wadi," added Salah. "Let justice roll down like waters."

Noah said, "But first, we must shake these Nephilim from our cloaks, or we will not live to accomplish our task."

"Demigods are rascals," Salah observed. "They embody the worst of both worlds."

Uriel knew this was true. The reason archangels had a harder time defeating Nephilim was that the Watchers' offspring were a violation of the divide between heavenly and earthly creation. Members of Elohim's divine council were heavenly beings. They inhabited the same realm as Elohim, just as humans occupied the earth. But Nephilim were the spawn of both heaven and earth. They fully inhabited the corporeal flesh, but were animated by an occult spiritual vitality that almost equaled a member of the heavenly assembly. An angel could traverse between worlds, but would become subject to the limitations of both. Uriel knew this from experience. But a Naphil lived in both worlds at once. In some ways Nephilim were stronger than mal'akim, but the mal'akim angels had one significant advantage: They were immortal, Nephilim were not. Nephilim could die. That point gave Uriel some small satisfaction.

Salah was intensely curious and had much he wanted to ask Uriel. "Tell me, Uriel, how do you bind an angel or a *Bene Elohim*?"

Uriel looked at Noah, who nodded in approval. He could trust Salah with his very life. Uriel pulled back his cloak, pushed up his sleeve, and touched an armband that looked like it was made of white hair. Uriel unraveled a small amount and let Salah feel it. It felt as fine as a spider's web and was barely visible.

"Hair from the cherubim of the throne of Elohim. It is indestructible," said Uriel.

Salah was amazed. Uriel would offer no more than he was asked, but Salah badgered him with an unending stream of questions. Fortunately for Salah, Uriel was pleasantly full from the meal and more open than usual.

"What exactly is a cherubim?" Salah began.

"Cherub," corrected Uriel. "Cherubim is the plural. They are the carriers of the throne chariot of Elohim. They were also guardians of the tree of life and the gates of Eden," said Uriel.

"What do they look like? Do they look like you?"

Salah's childlike innocence amused Uriel. "They are far more terrifying than me."

"That isn't saying much," Noah jested.

Uriel sobered up. "They have skin that shines like burnished bronze. They have four sets of wings, and four faces. Usually one face is of a human, one of a lion, one of an eagle, and one of the cherub itself. They are accompanied by the Flames of the Whirling Sword, divine beings that can smite anything that approaches their custody. The sound of a cherub's wings alone strikes terror into the hearts of its enemies." It was all so matter-of-fact for Uriel. He lived in the presence of these beings, not to mention the more terrifying presence of Elohim.

Salah had pestered Enoch years ago when his tribe had first met them, so he had a few more loose ends to clear up. "Now, what are the seraphim and how are they different from cherubim?"

"Seraphim are specially appointed Watchers, the reptilian ones, with six wings, that guard the throne of Elohim."

Salah kept right on moving without a pause. "So the seraphim are like the Serpent of Eden?"

"Yes. But the Serpent of Eden is an unfortunate misnomer. The Nachash is unquestionably serpentine in his character, justifying the legends surrounding him as one of the seraphim who guarded Elohim's throne. But he was not merely a serpent. His name in another sense meant 'brazen brightness,' and like other Watchers, he was a Shining One. His body was like beryl, his face like the appearance of lightning, his eyes like torches of fire, his arms and feet like burnished bronze. The 'Serpent of Eden' became a useful allusion, because he had been cursed by Elohim to crawl the earth away from his heavenly abode with the Sons of God."

"Why did he tempt the original pair in the Garden?" asked Salah.

"He is also called *the satan* which means 'the accuser' in God's heavenly court." Salah followed the explanation well. He knew that God's divine council of holy ones surrounded Elohim's throne and engaged in legal disputes of justice on earth.

Uriel continued, "But unlike a just prosecutor of crimes, the Nachash was a liar and murderer from the beginning. He was the father of lies, the tempter and deceiver of God's people. He seeks to use God's lawfulness against him." Uriel had a particular bitter memory of the satan's attempt in the past to sue Elohim in his own court. It was a diabolically brilliant strategy of manipulating legal procedure and technicalities against the Judge himself. But it did not quite work.

"But when the pair was cast out of Eden, the Nachash began his campaign to defile every corner of Elohim's good creation. He set up his parody of the mountain of Eden at Mount Hermon, in Bashan, the 'Place of the Serpent.' He was eventually joined by Semjaza, Azazel, and the other fallen Sons of God to pursue their nefarious grand design on Eden. It was the war of the Seed of Nachash with the Seed of Havah, and it was for total conquest. No quarter given. To the victor, complete spoils. Their loss at the Titanomachy was but one battle."

"This is a long war not quickly resolved," said Salah overwhelmed by its implications. He remembered tales of the Titanomachy, the War on Eden.

"Indeed," said Uriel, abruptly changing tone. "And that is why we must be leaving. Your kindness is gallant. But the longer we stay here, the more certainly you become marked quarry for the Gibborim. They will not forgive your hospitality to us. I fear it may already be too late."

"Too late, you say?" said Salah. "Good. That is exactly what I was waiting for."

Noah and Uriel were completely taken by surprise.

"Close your mouths, will you? You are letting sand flies in. We have a job to do," said Salah. "We will take you as far as we can in our underground tunnels, which should further frustrate any scent. And when they arrive and do not forgive us for our hospitality, as you have indicated, then they will simply have to accept our hostility!"

"No," said Noah. "You cannot do this!"

"It is too late. You said so yourself," said Salah. "Admit it, Noah, I have bettered you. If you remember, I usually beat you in Seega. Face it, I am a superior strategist." Salah smiled with a self-satisfied grin. Noah grimaced at the thought. Salah was right. Many times, they had confronted one another in that ancient board game. Salah had routinely captured Noah's stones, sliding them off the board with playful jests that irritated Noah to death. But this was not the time for jesting.

"You will all die," said Noah.

Salah turned deadly serious. "Noah, I have waited all my life for this moment. Do not be so resigned to our defeat. We have a few tricks up our tunics. We know this desert better than this mangy pack of spoiled lizards venturing out of their plush valley. Do you still not realize what an honor it is to defend the Chosen Seed of Elohim against his foes?"

Salah turned to Uriel. "Uriel, my sympathies go out to you, knowing how difficult it must be to guard this thick-skulled baboon."

Uriel chuckled, "This is but the tip of the ziggurat."

Noah embraced his friend, the mighty warlord Salah al Din. He knew he would probably never see him again in life.

"Come with me, my friend," said Salah. "I want to give you a gift."

Noah and Uriel followed into a chamber filled with bubbling kettles and pots, simmering over several small fires. Salah showed him a cauldron full of thick black liquid. "We call it 'pitch.' We create it by a process of distilling bitumen from the ground." Noah had seen bitumen pits in some areas of Sumer but had not realized it had any practical benefit.

Salah explained how his tribe had learned that it was useful for many tasks, including creating long-burning torches and for waterproofing boats and homes.

Noah could not believe his ears. This was an answer to one of the problems with his calling. The directions for the tebah, the box, had included covering it inside and out with "pitch." Now he understood what that was.

Salah gave them some small pouches with the pitch sealed in them. "You may be able to use them some day to find your way in a dark place."

Noah and Uriel tucked their gifts away and bid their host a restful night. They retired to their chambers and entered the deepest sleep they had experienced in weeks.

The giants came at night. They did not even bother to use stealth. The ground rumbled, announcing their approach. It was sooner than Salah had anticipated. He was not as prepared as he hoped to be, but they would make the best of it. They were three hundred battle-seasoned warriors against five demonic Nephilim. Could it really be that impossible?

The Nephilim began their assault by catapulting huge boulders at the embedded fortresses. Three of the demonic soldiers held their shields up as cover while the other two jettisoned the large stones into the rock walls, using a sling made from the thick hides of elephants. Within a day, the outward structures crumbled to piles of rubble. Many of the interior chambers collapsed from the pounding force. The women and children moved further back into the tunnels for protection. The men prepared to fight these gigantic hellions in hand-to-hand combat.

The Thamud had dromedaries for their cavalry. Though camels looked clumsy compared to a horse, they were actually quite fast animals, able to run up to fifteen leagues in an hour in a sprint. They were not afraid of battle. The Thamud gave them light leather armor that kept them agile in a strike force. They could literally run circles around the Nephilim to tire them out. It became like a game of tag for them. The limber sprinting dromedaries dodged the lunging, clumsy monsters. The Nephilim would sometimes fall on their faces in the dust. Salah's soldiers laughed at them, ensconced in the stone bulwarks.

The harassing campaign did not last long.

The Nephilim figured out the patterns of the camel-bound warriors and began capturing them and crushing them. The remaining cavalry retreated to the fortress and readied themselves for the next attack.

Salah's forces kept up the harassment and held the Nephilim at bay for days. But the end was unavoidable. Cavalry, arrows, maces or spears could not stop the Nephilim. They eventually wore down the defenses and pushed the

Thamud back into the underground shafts, burrowed over generations. The giants were smart enough not to allow themselves to be separated, where they could become victims of overwhelming odds if lured down various cut-off corridors. But it was here that they also made their mistake.

The Nephilim had wounds, but they were used to such minor inconveniences. They decimated Salah's men step by step. A mere forty humans were left, and they were in their final throes. The Naphil leader saw that Noah had not gotten out in time. The fleeing pair had stayed to fight with their desert allies in the hopes of stopping their pursuers. The Chosen human and his irritant archangel were finally cornered with the Thamud in a last stand cavern carved out of the desert rock. They stood in the center of the contingent guarding them with their lives, lives that would soon be extinguished.

Salah's captain noticed that there were only four Nephilim. Had they separated after all? It struck him immediately. They must have sent a scout to find the tunnel exit. He screamed at the top of his lungs, "THE EXIT! GET NOAH OUT!"

It was too late. The fifth Naphil came through the cave exit, dragging the bodies of guards he had killed. He screamed the war cry of the Gibborim. The men were trapped. There was no escape. They would have to fight to the last man and pray their deaths would be quick.

This close to the source, the lead Naphil could smell Noah's scent. It attacked and split the human unit in half, grabbing Noah and Uriel within mere seconds. The leader pulled back the stinking cloak.

It was not Noah or Uriel, but in fact Salah and his Captain wearing the prey's clothes. The Naphil screeched in anger. They had been deceived!

Salah laughed triumphantly and yelled his command to his soldiers. They waited at the key brick buttresses. At the signal, they released their latches. A series of cascading collapses brought down the entire ceiling, caving in on their heads. Every last one of them, human and Naphil, were covered in a grave of rock and sand that no living thing could survive.

The Thamud had sacrificed themselves to stop the Nephilim.

CHAPTER 13

Emzara learned the network of secret passageways below the temple district and city with the patient help and support of Alittum. It was a complex system, like a spider web, with intersecting hallways, and dead end tributaries. An uninformed traveler of the passages would get seriously lost without proper directions.

She thought of her beloved Noah and how he would be proud of her, if he knew what she planned. She was nearing her child's birth. She became more heartsick for her child at the thought of birthing him without his father present. She prayed to Elohim that her child would not be raised within this wicked culture of idolatry. Lugalanu's statement about the child's temple devotion haunted her. It would be a fate worse than death to see her son in the grip of these despicable false gods. If only her beloved knew she was still alive. The fact that the Gibborim had not returned was a good sign. At the least, it meant that Noah was still alive because they had not caught him. Or, by the grace of Elohim, could he have killed them? She wanted to figure out some way to let him know she was alive, but she felt it could distract him from his own survival. That was more important to her right now.

She had always believed he was the Chosen Seed, but she was also a dutiful wife and would give her true opinion only when consulted. Her biggest influence in persuading Noah was in prayer. When Noah was blinded by his own stubbornness, she would ask Elohim to soften his heart. Elohim had a way of opening Noah's eyes better than anyone else could. She did not believe that Elohim had abandoned them. She was sure he was planning something very significant to make his point. It would take something big to transform Noah to accomplish his calling. Elohim was like that. Meanwhile, she would focus on making the best of her own situation for the glory of her God.

One day, Emzara asked Alittum how long it would take for guards to seek out a missing palace or temple slave. She couched it in the context of doing bookkeeping of staff numbers, but Alittum knew in that moment that Nindannum planned to help runaway slaves.

Alittum marveled at this in her thoughts. So that was her intention! Help disgruntled slaves who sought their freedom to escape. It was shamefully egalitarian of Nindannum and proved her lack of royal blood and culture. What fool would risk her life to die in the howling desert, when the kingdom would care for their every need? The gods required minimal devotion, and for what higher purpose would the peasants live in the wild? Themselves? Alittum found it laughable. Uncivilized folk needed to be molded and shaped by the noble class to know their station in life, otherwise they degenerate into this kind of decadent thinking. Alittum now had the opportunity that none of her useless spells and enchantments against Nindannum seemed to be able to achieve. Or was this the actual fruit of her magic?

Alittum encouraged Emzara in her fondness toward slaves. One day, Alittum "let out" the secret that she sometimes wished she could help slaves to freedom. Emzara took the bait and they quickly established an underground pathway to freedom. Emzara now trusted Alittum. But Alittum knew that she had to seal Emzara's confidence by volunteering to be the first to deliver slaves through their new arrangement.

Emzara and Alittum carefully chose their first two beneficiaries. One, a male slave in the palace named Daduri had been beaten mercilessly for incompetence. He had lost an eye and was in the infirmary, but had healed sufficiently to travel. The other was a twelve-year old female named Humusi, recently captured and appointed to be a temple slave. She was so defiant that the priestesses left her alone, until she could have a session with Inanna that would set her straight. What Inanna did in those disciplinary sessions Alittum did not know, but the rumors were ugly.

On the planned day of escape, Lugalanu noticed that Alittum and Emzara were acting skittish. He wondered if they were hiding animosity toward each other. Overwhelmed with royal edicts and law court rulings, he lost his temper with Alittum over a petty administrative detail. He grounded her to her chambers. He would visit her later and have his way with her. Of course he would envision Emzara in her place, but that would be of no consequence to Alittum. She was so needy and desperate for his love, that anything he gave her would be consumed like a crumb of food by a starving dog.

He pitied Alittum. She had no soul left to give any man, least of all him. But she was a good head-maidservant, and she did satisfy his more depraved fantasies. He decided not to replace her as Chief Maidservant with Emzara just yet.

The two women prepared their scheme. Alittum decided she would follow through with their plans, because Lugalanu was so caught up with his business that he would not even consider talking to Alittum for another day. He would probably forget that he even sent her to her chambers. In fact, this would make her more able to disappear through the passageways. She would not be missed if she was serving out her punishment.

The women did not anticipate Lugalanu's own plans.

While Emzara administered the household services, Lugalanu snuck into Alittum's chambers looking for her. Her chambermaid was alone in the room. Although the girl did not know exactly where Alittum was, a beating released enough information for Lugalanu to realize something was deeply amiss.

Alittum had prepared Daduri and Hamusi with some foodstuffs and tools for their trek out in the wilderness, once they were outside the city limits. They had taken one of the tunnel routes that led to just outside the palace walls, but they had gotten lost. Once they found their way again, Alittum kissed them and bid them good luck. She wondered how she could ever actually believe in this kind of ludicrous rebellion. Nindannum must have been possessed by evil spirits to think this was goodness. Alittum considered consulting an exorcist when she returned.

She returned from her secret passage into her chamber A fuming Lugalanu greeted her. A beaten Daduri and Hamusi lay at his feet in shackles.

"Alittum, how could you?" said Lugalanu. "What evil spirit has possessed you to do such a thing?"

The irony struck Alittum, making her flounder in her response. "My lord, I can explain. This is not what it appears to be."

"You are not what you have appeared to be," he spit out. "Is this what you have secretly pursued all these years? After all I have given you; my body, my soul, my trust, *this* is how you return my graces?"

"My lord," she cried. She wanted to tell him all about her plan, all about Nindannum and how this was just an act to expose Nindannum for what she was. It was too late.

He pulled out his dagger and drew near to her. He covered her mouth with his left hand, and gently slid the blade into her.

She dropped to the floor in pain, angrier at her own stupidity than with anything he had done to her all those years.

It is just as well, she thought. *I deserved it anyway.*

She slipped into oblivion.

Lugalanu found Emzara working on the dinner meal for the temple staff. He walked up to her with lifeless eyes. "Alittum is gone. After you birth your child, you shall be Chief Maidservant." Emzara saw his blood-soaked shirt and stood in shock as Lugalanu walked away.

CHAPTER 14

Mount Hermon was located in the northwest of the Fertile Crescent at the end of the Sirion mountain range. It was the area of Bashan, the "Place of the Serpent," near the Jordan River. It was the cosmic mountain where the Sons of God, the Watchers, came down from heaven. On its southernmost base lay the mountain community of Kur, dedicated to Ereshkigal, goddess of the underworld. Her temple, a ziggurat platform, was embedded into the slope of the mountain, with little more than the front face visible to the public. The mighty giant kings, the Rephaim, had built the temple and city, leaving it an oversized architectural wonder that dwarfed the inhabitants and worshippers.

It was evening and torches lit the temple for a display of glowing splendor in the midst of a pitch-black night. Priests blew long horns from within secret openings on the ziggurat to summon the people of the region for sacrifice. An unmistakable, deep reverberation penetrated to the very core of the soul and drew the people from leagues around. They came from all the outlying areas of Bashan to participate in the sacrifice. Entire extended families of multiple generations, carrying their torches, created a river of fires pouring into the temple complex. They camped in the nearby fields and gathered around the base of the temple for the liturgy.

Noah and Uriel could remain anonymous in the masses of this large congregation. Noah had allotted the passage of two moons for the six of his company to eventually convene at this location. Because the Gibborim had all gone after Noah and Uriel, that pair had been delayed. It was already the third new moon. They looked for their comrades in the teeming throng, but they were nowhere to be found. Noah wondered if the men had made it, or if they had given up, or if they had been captured by the gods of the city. The look of this bestial mob did not bode well for any positive option.

They tied up their camels inside the edge of the forest line near the temple, for their getaway.

They looked up at the sole stairway of brick that rose seventy cubits upward to the top temple chamber. On the chamber ledge sat a huge bronze statue of a seated Ereshkigal with her arms open to receive sacrifice. It loomed over a large fire pit called the *tophet* or "burning place."

They could see the ridge just below the altar, lined with a hundred parents and infants in their arms. They could also see the parents scratching the names of their children on the stone walls, to join the thousands that had accumulated over the years.

Uriel leaned in and whispered to Noah, "Inside the mountain temple is the entrance to the Seven Gates of Ganzir, the Gateway to Sheol."

The long horns blew again, summoning a line of hairless shaven priests with small cylindrical drums just below the line of parents and children. They pounded the drums in unison creating the sound of an amplified beat that signaled the dance.

The crowd below began to sway to the beat at first, and then slowly broke down into individual dancing, which further degenerated into erotic jerking spasms and snake-like body waves. It was as if their bodies had been taken over by another force.

It disgusted Noah.

Uriel reminded Noah to keep his look toward the temple mount. Otherwise they would be noticed. Noah found it difficult. Noah and Uriel wore cloaks to cover their weapons and maintain anonymity, as well as hide their repulsion with the debauchery of the masses around them.

On the temple mount, two priestesses with elongated skulls, exotic ornamented robes, and fully tattooed bodies approached the line of parents and children. In most cases, it was only one parent, a mother or father holding their infant, with an occasional pre-teen next to them. They were led up the small stairway to the temple mount.

A figure came out of the shadows of the temple columns completely covered in a hooded robe. The figure stood on the ledge in full sight of the people. Two priestesses stood beside it and pulled off the cloak to reveal the high priestess. The crowd cheered. Unlike the other priests and priestesses, she maintained long, flowing hair with an ornate headdress indicating royalty. She covered her fully tattooed body with jewels, necklaces, bracelets, rings and piercings.

The high priestess walked over to the fire pit. High, hot flames leapt out of it, licking the night air. The priestesses led the line of worshippers to the high priestess.

The first woman held her infant and began to cry. She reluctantly placed the infant, not two years old, into the hands of the two priestesses. They gave the crying child to the high priestess. She turned to the flames and held the baby high over her head. The crowd below went silent.

Noah shivered. It was eerie. The priestess controlled their very souls.

Her booming voice echoed down the steps of the ziggurat. The acoustics magnified the sounds with a supernatural vitality.

"Ereshkigal, mighty goddess of the underworld, we call you forth!"

The crowd responded with chanting, "Ereshkigal! Ereshkigal! Ereshkigal!"

Noah's eyes stayed locked on the infant held high above the flames. The chanting made him sick to his stomach. A tide of hatred rose within him. He could not let this happen. He grabbed the hilt of his sword.

Uriel stopped him. "We cannot stop this, Noah. Remember, these people are not forced. This idolatry is freely chosen."

He was right, of course. Mankind chose this. They chose to worship these gods and violate the natural order, the natural separation of things, the separation of heaven and earth. Ever since the murder of Abel by his brother Cain, the heart of man grew more and more desperately wicked and their sins grew more unspeakable. Noah's tribe was among the few groups of true humanity that did not imbibe in such monstrosities.

Noah released his sword hilt.

He noticed a little girl, not yet seven years old, watching him with curiosity. She stared at him with large eyes, while holding her father's hand. The father and mother stared enthralled at the altar above them.

The crowd continued the possessed chanting. "Ereshkigal! Ereshkigal! Ereshkigal!"

The surrendered infant cried, but its tiny voice was drowned out by the bloodthirsty mob. Noah dreaded what was going to happen next: abominable sacrifice. He closed his eyes tight. He could not bear to watch. The roar of the mob swelled around him. He opened his tear-filled eyes, trying with all his might not to weep.

The line of parents began handing their offspring over one by one for the slaughter of the innocents. As the people below grew disinterested with the repetition, they became more focused on themselves, and their dancing soon turned more wild and chaotic.

The little girl caught Noah's eye again. She stared at him as if she knew he did not belong here. He knew that she could see his eyes were not dry.

She smiled. He smiled back, but he could not hold it for long. He knew that one day it might be her fate to be led up those stairs. This little child with all her life before her, all her hopes and dreams, would be snuffed out, her innocent life burned from her body.

The drone of the long horns signaled the next sequence of events. Everyone's attention returned to the high platform. A young girl had been brought to the high priestess by two deformed dwarves and placed on the hands of the large bronze statue. She was laid down and held in place at her head and feet by the two misshapen creatures.

Uriel leaned in again toward Noah and whispered, "It comes."

Seconds after he spoke, a loud bellowing sound came from the fiery pit. A flock of bats scattered into the sky.

Out of the flames rose a Watcher, a Shining One like Anu, but with leathery reptilian wings. It burst out of the pit and into the sky like a creature bursting out of water for air. It wore the horned headdress of deity on its elongated head, and like Inanna was androgynous in appearance, though female in dress.

Uriel confided to Noah, "Ereshkigal, our target."

The multitude around them grew delirious with worship. Ereshkigal landed on the ground and hissed at the people below. They responded with cheers. Her wings spread out in glory as she stood over the child with coldblooded focus. She bared her fangs and feasted on her innocent blood.

Again the mob erupted with approval. Again, the long horns wailed.

Noah did not notice that the father had let go of the hand of the little girl watching him. The father and mother had become engrossed in worship. The girl drifted away from them toward Noah and Uriel.

But it was too late for her to find them.

Noah and Uriel made a hasty retreat. Their plan had been to corner Ereshkigal with distraction so Uriel could get close enough to bind the subterranean goddess. But none of their men were here. They might not get another chance like this for some time, because the goddess did not crawl out of her pit but once every new moon.

A figure stepped into their path and blocked them. Noah and Uriel poised to draw swords.

It was Methuselah, and he was angry.

"Your choice of location for hiding your camels was juvenile and pathetic. You might as well trumpet your presence to the goddess." Noah and

Uriel glanced at each other like rebuked children. Methuselah finished, "And you are very late. The men are over there now."

Noah and Uriel followed the disgruntled Methuselah back to their secreted camels in the bush.

They were greeted first by Tubal-cain. "It is good to see you alive, cousin. We wondered if the Gibborim had followed you, since we never saw them on our trail."

They embraced. "It is a long story," Noah said.

Uriel smiled at the irony. They were stronger together than apart, and he would never let them separate again.

Uriel cut short their celebration, "It is only a matter of time before the Gibborim find us."

Methuselah chimed in, "The sooner we bind this abomination in the depths of the earth, the better."

"But how do we do it?" asked Tubal-cain.

"That has just become complicated," said Noah. He explained the plan he and Uriel had prepared, the need to catch the goddess unaware during sacrifice. They would have a long wait until the next moon, but there was nothing else they could do. She would not come out for another month. They certainly could not storm her gates with their paltry six-man hit squad.

Jubal and Jabal, ever the positive duo, spoke up. Jubal said, "But that will give us more time to plan and consider all possibilities." Jabal jumped in without hesitation, "Will we not need more time to find a crevice to cast her into the earth?"

"Yes," said Methuselah, ever the pessimist. "We may need more time than we have. It is easier said than accomplished."

"No," interrupted Noah, "we cast her into Sheol."

The men looked at Noah with surprise.

"She guards the gates of the Abyss to Sheol," said Noah. "Let us kick her into that crevice and let it keep her."

The men looked at each other, perplexed. They wondered if there was a single one of them that would support that death march.

Uriel did not calm their fears. "We must be careful not to follow her in," he said, "The dead who descend never return."

"What of the living?" asked Tubal-cain.

Uriel sighed. His hesitation only made matters worse. "The shades of the dead would eat the living," he answered, punctuating their doom, "eternally."

A pall fell over the group.

"Well," countered Methuselah with dripping sarcasm, "if that is not just the future I have sought for all these years, I do not know what is. Being eaten alive forever and ever."

Jubal and Jabal gulped. Tubal-cain stared off into oblivion.

Noah would have none of it. All he wanted was revenge. He had lost everything and had nothing more to lose, except the one thing that held barely by a thread in his heart: faith. He spoke with the confidence of an archangel, "Well, then, let us avoid Sheol—and go trap ourselves a god. At least we have plenty of time to prepare."

The men gathered their courage together.

The little girl Noah had seen in the crowd surprised them. She had wandered away from her parents and had followed Noah into the bush. She stood staring at them, as surprised as they were. She glanced fearfully behind her to see if she had been followed. She had not been.

Tubal-cain started to pull his sword by impulse.

Noah stopped him. "I know this little one," Noah said.

"She looks afraid," said Methuselah.

"Poor innocent child," said Noah. He realized he now had a bigger dilemma than when they had arrived. They could not leave this waif alone to die at the hands of her parents and their murderous idolatry. She was not a faceless part of the indiscriminate masses to him. She was an individual child with a soul, who apparently knew her destiny and was silently crying out for his help. But they could not take her with them. They were on a deadly journey. She would slow them down and become a liability to their higher purpose. It would take at least one man to watch over her, and that was one less warrior in the heat of combat with the minions of hell.

Noah was about to deliberate with his men, when his decision was made for him.

The child screamed at the top of her lungs, "EVIL MEN! EVIL MEN!" and ran back out into the crowd.

Noah's team scrambled.

A dozen men from the crowd ran past the girl toward where she pointed. She continued to scream, "OVER THERE! EVIL MEN! EVIL MEN!"

The first of the rushing worshippers broke through into the trees. They were taken out with a volley of arrows from Noah's band.

"What do we do now?" yelled Tubal-cain. There would be others right behind them in seconds.

"Change of plans," said Noah. "On your camels! Follow me!"

In a flash, Noah was upon his mount. The others followed suit. Noah burst through the brush directly out into the enemy's midst, surprising them. His men followed him like a pride of lions on the hunt.

The worshippers did not know what was happening. The crowd parted in fear as the men raced headlong into the masses. The people just wanted to get out of the way of a stampede of dromedaries trampling everyone in their path.

Noah led the stampede through the thinning crowd right up to the temple steps.

The long stairway to the heavens rose upward seventy cubits of stone. His men now knew what he planned. There was no time to consult. They followed him dutifully. By the time anyone in the crowd understood that these riders were hostile, Noah's raiding party was almost to the top of the ziggurat.

Below them, men yelled for arms and began climbing the long flight of stairs.

At the top of the temple mount, the humans scattered. The priests cowered.

Ereshkigal was already gone, disappeared back into the fire pit.

Methuselah yelled above the growing din, "I thought we were supposed to be secret about this!"

"Dismount!" yelled Noah, and the men obeyed. Noah walked up to the pit of flames and peered in, Uriel by his side.

"What is he doing?" Tubal-cain asked.

Methuselah replied, "The same thing he has done all his life, since he was a boy, rushing in before the angels!"

Methuselah looked back down the steps. The sight reminded him of a swarm of angry fire ants streaming up the stairway, almost upon them.

The men gathered around Noah.

Noah looked to Uriel. "Is this the entrance to Sheol?" he asked.

"No," said Uriel, "to Ereshkigal's lair. Sheol is deeper."

"Good. That buys us time," said Noah, and he jumped.

Methuselah turned just in time to see Noah disappear into the flames. "NOAH!" he screamed, too late.

Uriel followed Noah. Unthinking, Methuselah followed Uriel.

The first of the mad mob reached the top and were upon them. Tubal-cain plowed down the first few attackers. Jubal and Jabal did not think it through. They ran and leaped into the flames, disappearing from view. Tubal-cain fought on all alone, with a growing swarm of angry idolaters circling him, pressing in, the flames at his back. Tubal-cain muttered a prayer, "Elohim, I trust in you. Noah, I am not so sure of, but please have mercy on my ignorance."

Tubal-cain turned, and bolted for the open pit. He leapt into the fire, closing his eyes. He passed through the wall of flames, only an instant of sheering heat. The next moment, he struck a floor and rolled to break his fall. He took stock for a moment to make sure he was still alive, could still feel pain. He rubbed his knee, bruised from the fall. He was alive with pain. He looked up into the eyes of Methuselah, who stood smiling down on him.

Methuselah mocked, "Nice of you to join us, hippopotamus. I was not sure you could make the jump."

Tubal-cain looked around. They were on a large outer ledge that encircled the flames rising in the center of the pit. The fire obscured the presence of the ledge from those above. Tubal-cain got up and drew his sword, looking back up through the flames.

"Do not fret yourself, cousin," said Noah, "They will not follow us into the pit of sacrifice."

"No, they will not. Who would be so foolish as to do that?" quipped Methuselah.

Tubal-cain grinned at him. "I do believe you peed your tunic, you old grizzled lizard. How is your bladder doing?"

Methuselah looked down, "I did not pee my tunic!" The men chuckled.

"Enough, you lovebirds," Noah chuckled. "Let us keep moving." He set the tone for this band of warrior poets, and they followed. He drew his weapon; they drew theirs. They followed him cautiously around the ledge to an entranceway on the other side of the flames.

The carved stone ledge gave way to a long portico of marble floors lined with pillars on both sides, twenty cubits wide and a hundred cubits long. Torches lit the way to the end, where a set of large wooden gates inlaid with brass bid them stay away. So they moved forward.

They inched cautiously toward the gates.

Noah whispered to Uriel, "Is this the first of the Seven Gates of Ganzir?"

Uriel didn't reply, all his senses honed on surveying their environment.

When they had covered half the distance, they heard a distinct rattling sound, then soft scraping of claws on a marble floor. They stopped. Something hid behind the pillars. Some *things*. All around them.

"Draw together," Noah commanded. They did so, blades out, ready for anything.

The shadows moved from behind the pillars on both sides of them. Strange creatures stepped out into sight, but they did not attack. The men could now see their stalkers. They were scorpion-men. Monstrosities with the upper torsos of human soldiers, and the lower bodies of man-sized scorpions, they were armed with bladed weapons and ready tail stingers.

Noah and his men were surrounded. Their hands tightened on their weapons, glancing around, waiting for the first move.

The scorpion-men did not attack. They were waiting.

Noah thought to himself, *What more abominable creatures could these Watchers create? What kind of sorcery enabled them to produce such demonic crossbred mongrels like these?* The bird-men soldiers, the lion-men and bull-men guardians, the Nephilim as well, all were unnatural violations of the created order. What was the plan of these Watchers?

Suddenly, the huge doors at the end of the portico creaked open. Everyone's attention shot to two large beings about five and a half cubits tall gliding through the doors. It was Ereshkigal. The second Watcher stayed by the door as Ereshkigal strode toward Noah and Uriel. The shining being kept her wings taut behind her back and stood a safe distance behind the scorpion-men.

Noah noticed a look of familiarity cross Uriel's face. Ereshkigal kept her eyes trained on the archangel; the one she knew had the power to bind her.

"Uriel," she croaked, "I thought I smelled you."

Uriel responded, "Ramel, I see you have built quite a kingdom for yourself on earth, along with Sariel." He glanced at the other Watcher by the door. "I take it he goes by the name Nergal?"

In the mythology the Watchers had established, Nergal was the name of Ereshkigal's husband. He had become her spouse after he had insulted her for not being able to attend a banquet of the gods. Anu sent him down to the underworld to receive punishment from Ereshkigal. Nergal turned the tables on the chthonic queen, overpowering her on her own throne. This reputation stained Ramel's pride and he resented it. But he could do nothing about it for the present. It took a few generations to change a myth. He would have to tolerate the mockery of his humiliation by the other gods. He could not leave this underworld domain because he was Ereshkigal, the goddess guardian of the gates of Sheol.

Ereshkigal sneered with contempt at the archangel's condescension. "My earthly kingdom with all its limitations is still more satisfying than the assembly of Elohim. You should have joined us in the rebellion."

Uriel said, "Unlike you, I have no interest in dressing up as a goddess."

Ereshkigal belittled him. "You prefer being a slave. Why are you here?"

Noah blurted out, "To bind you into the depths of the earth." Uriel closed his eyes with embarrassment.

"Indeed?" said Ereshkigal, turning her gaze to Noah standing just behind Uriel. "And who is this presumptuous little one?"

"Noah ben Lamech, son of Enoch, destroyer of gods."

Uriel rolled his eyes. He wished Noah would just shut up.

Ereshkigal chuckled at Noah's audacity. An unexpected thought crossed her mind. She turned back to Uriel. "I have word that Semjaza and Azazel seek Elohim's Chosen Seed. Is this your doing, Uriel?" Her eyes kept trained on Uriel, ignoring Noah.

She knew only that the Chosen Seed would be a son of Enoch the prophet. None of the other gods bothered to tell her anything. She had to fight for every bit of information, being isolated in her miserable cosmic mountain.

"As you said, I am a servant," said Uriel sidestepping the question.

Ereshkigal looked into Uriel's eyes for some kind of revelation. But she could not find it. "Of course," she concluded, "And so you shall die as a slave."

She turned on her heel and walked back to the gates where Nergal waited. Casually, she ordered the scorpion-men, "Kill them all. Save the bodies."

The creatures raised their swords. They surrounded the men, one to one. But twenty circled Noah and Uriel. They knew the most important and difficult kill would be these two.

The scorpion-men attacked. These were the first opponents Noah's men had encountered who also had swords. The creatures were capable, as well as armored with helmets and shields. But their weapons were bronze, unlike the iron swords that Noah and his warriors wielded.

What Tubal-cain lacked in fighting skills, he more than made up with his brawn. He shattered the swords of his foes. Jubal and Jabal did a dance of brotherhood protecting each other back to back, dodging stingers and blades alike. One sting from the tail of a scorpion-man and the victim would die in minutes.

Uriel cut off stingers and sword arms with his usual finesse, but he had to work at it a bit more than usual. These creatures were among the best fighters he had encountered.

Tubal-cain cut the tail off a scorpion-man before it hit Methuselah. "You are too slow, grandmother!" In the instant he took to breathe those words, Methuselah turned and impaled one of the infernal insects about to strike Tubal-cain. "Fast enough to save your hide, chubby infant!"

Noah broke through the circle of attackers and reached the gates.

The creatures surrounded Uriel, pressing in tight. With Noah out of the way, this was just what Uriel needed to perform his signature move. He held out his blades and spun like a whirlwind. He cut down the last of his ten adversaries in mere moments. When he looked up, he saw Jabal about to be hit from behind. Uriel threw a sword like a javelin and pierced the creature against a column. It screamed in agony.

Noah's company were the only ones left standing. They gathered together. The corpses of scorpion-men littered the floor. Noah asked if everyone was whole, and they took account, catching their breath. This battle had taxed them. Some cuts and bruises, but all alive and well.

Noah turned to Uriel and asked, "Who are Semjaza and Azazel?"

"Fallen Sons of God. They led the rebellion. And now, they masquerade as the gods Anu and Inanna." The men continued to catch their breath.

Tubal-cain jumped in with disgust, "So the goddesses are all males in female disguise?"

"Do not let their pretended sex fool you," said Uriel. "They are all Sons of God, and Semjaza and Azazel are the mightiest."

"Well," said Noah, "I guess that means you and I have a common quest then."

"We have not even captured our first Watcher. And you are ready to face the mightiest of them all." Uriel's tone dripped with sarcasm. "And I will not let you forget the box."

"All right, all right," Noah complained. "Let us get through these seven gates and see if we will be proven strong enough to capture our first Watcher." Noah was capable of returning the sarcasm in his tone.

Jabal called to Uriel as he pulled the sword out of the scorpion-man's chest. It slumped to the ground. Jabal turned and tossed the weapon to the archangel, who caught it with a nod of appreciation. But Jabal did not see the reflexive spasm jolt through the body of the scorpion-man. His tail swept up and stung Jabal in the arm. Jabal screamed in pain. Tubal-cain cut off the creature's head.

The poison spread quickly.

Jubal caught Jabal before he could fall to the ground. "My brother!" Jubal shouted.

The men gathered quickly around him. Jubal pulled the stinger out of Jabal's arm. The wound was already full of pus. They watched the black poison travelling up Jabal's arm towards his heart.

"My brother," whimpered Jabal.

Noah looked to Uriel. "What can be done?"

Uriel shook his head. The Watchers with their occultic sorcery and poisons created these creatures.

Jabal looked up at Noah, fading fast. "Cousin," he gasped.

"Yes, cousin," replied Noah.

"Take care of our motley gang, brothers all." His soul had become knit as one with them, and now that thread was being unraveled.

His vision blurred.

"I will," said Noah.

"And *you* are in Elohim's care," said Jabal, between convulsions.

"Yes, cousin," said Noah reluctantly. Jabal breathed his last in his brothers' arms.

In that moment, Noah knew that he did not believe his own words. In Elohim's care? How could he say or believe such a thing? He had led this young man out of the slave mines with the promise of glory and revenge. He had trained him and mentored him over hundreds of leagues of hostile environments, fought with monstrous enemies. He had even brought him into the very portico of hell, only to see him die at the random hit of the stinger of a dead scorpion. What kind of care is that? What kind of purpose or meaning could be behind that? He felt abandoned by Elohim. Could Elohim be any more distant? Could Noah's alienation feel any more complete?

Methuselah led in a prayer over the body of Jabal. Men and angel knelt and gave their comrade's soul back to Elohim and his body back to the dust from which it came. The ritual made Noah feel worse. He held back tears of anger at his Maker's unwillingness to make sense out of this senseless tragedy.

After a moment of silence, they gathered to eat some food. The battle had starved them. They knew they were about to enter a seven-fold series of testing that would tax them to their limits and probably even lead to their deaths. They needed their full strength.

After their meal, Uriel took a firm grasp of the gargantuan door and heaved. The huge gate creaked opened just enough for the men to get inside. Uriel led, followed by Noah, Tubal-cain, Methuselah and Jubal.

They stood inside a huge wide cavern. Long stalagmites and stalactites filled the floor and ceiling. Glowing phosphorescent moss lit the space all around them, multicolored and quite glitteringly beautiful. Uriel had opened the gate by himself, but it took all the men to close it behind them. They did not want to be surprised by anyone sneaking up behind them.

Noah noticed that they appeared to already be at their destination. He said, "Just one gate? Where are the others?"

"Just one," said Uriel.

Noah said, "I thought there were seven gates of Ganzir that we would have to go through."

"Are you complaining?" said Methuselah.

Uriel laughed ironically. "That is the problem with myth, it tends to exaggerate."

"The bards call it poetic hyperbole," added Methuselah. "It aids in emphasizing a point. If you prefer, we could re-enter this gate seven times to satisfy your penchant for the grandiose."

Tubal-cain smiled, enjoying that he was not the target of Methuselah's barbs this time.

"Why did you not tell us this earlier?" asked Noah.

Uriel shrugged. "There were more important things to deal with than the petty details of an exaggerated legend."

Noah shook his head and led them on.

They moved cautiously to the center of the great cavern, past the jutting stalagmites, along a well-worn path, until they arrived at the shore of a small lake. The substance of the lake was black and viscous, like pitch, though not as thick. A perpetual flame flitted across the surface burning the top layer as fuel.

The sound of hands slowly clapping drew their attention across the black lake to two thrones of stone. Ereshkigal and Nergal sat upon the thrones. Ereshkigal stopped her mocking applause.

"Well done, Chosen One, and your gangly squad of 'mighty men,'" said Ereshkigal. "Welcome to the gates of Sheol. Few there are who see it in life."

Uriel glanced at the black lake. "The Abyss. Doorway to Sheol."

The men looked closer at the black fiery liquid. Tubal-cain stepped back.

"Sadly for you, Uriel, you will not have your chance to bind us," declared Ereshkigal. "And for you, Chosen Seed, this is the end of your quest. You have failed."

Uriel looked up and around them with a sudden intuition of an attack.

The ceiling above them rumbled like an approaching stampede. Everyone drew weapons.

Nergal finally spoke with a calculated coolness, "And now you will all know the pain of dying at the hands of Nephilim, as you rightly should."

Behind the men, the huge gates blew inward, kicked off their hinges by powerful feet. Two Nephilim assassins jumped inside the doorway, weapons drawn. Noah's team stepped back, blocked by the Abyss behind them.

The ceiling above them continued to shake with the force of a quake. The men looked up to see three holes burst open in the ceiling thirty cubits above them, one at a time. Rocks came crashing down from the holes, carrying with them the three forms of Nephilim landing in a cloud of rubble and dust. Like birds of prey, they rose from their crouched landing and drew their weapons. These were the same savage creatures that had stalked Noah and Uriel in the desert. Salah had told Noah about rigging the cave to collapse. If Salah was not able to carry out that plan, Noah knew his friend would have fought to the death. If he had been successful, then these monsters probably dug their way out of their own graves. Either way, Noah knew that Salah and his Thamudi tribe were all dead, wiped out by these creatures of hell.

The lead Naphil growled and the five of them advanced slowly, ready to pounce.

Tubal-cain blurted out what everyone was thinking, "Noah, what shall we do?"

Noah knew it was hopeless. These five Gibborim had decimated an entire city of warriors in their pursuit of Noah and Uriel. Two Watcher gods were at their backs. They did not stand a slash of a chance.

"We have no choice. We fight to the death," said Noah.

The Nephilim drew closer. The men gripped their swords and prepared to die.

"There is a choice," said Uriel. "We enter Sheol."

This did not go over well with a single one of them.

"And double our jeopardy?" said Noah.

"Only double?" Methuselah mocked.

"Nephilim will not follow us into Sheol," said Uriel.

"Why not?" asked Noah.

"Because they are too afraid of it," answered Uriel.

This was not lost on Methuselah who had to spit it out, "You would take us where Nephilim fear to tread?"

"You will have to trust me on this one," said Uriel. "Believe it or not, I am more able to help you down there than in here."

It was too late for debate. The Nephilim charged. In seconds they would all be dead.

Noah yelled, "Follow me!" and ran to the edge of the lake, making a flying leap into the black Abyss.

"Not another leap of faith," complained Methuselah. But he said it as he followed the others into the thick black liquid—Uriel, then Tubal-cain, and Jubal.

The Gibborim reached their spot just as Methuselah made his splash. The giants stopped in fear, looking into the blackness. Two of them backed up, not wanting to get close.

Ereshkigal damned Elohim and yelled at the Gibborim, "You are done here! Return to your masters." By this she meant Anu and Inanna, or Semjaza and Azazel. The squad of Nephilim backed away, gathering together for their return. But one of them stood staring into the black liquid. Just as his comrades noticed this, he sheathed his sword, glanced at them, and dove into the Abyss. The leader screeched as if he had lost a son. But the others did not move an inch. They knew their comrade was leaping to his sure death. They turned and left the cavern for their return trip to Erech.

CHAPTER 15

Noah, Uriel, Methuselah, Tubal-cain and Jubal sank into the depths of the inky black fluid of the Abyss. It terrified them. They could not open their eyes. They did not know how long they could hold their breaths before their lungs would fill with thick black death.

They broke through the oily liquid into a new layer of water. Now they sank swiftly. Noah opened his eyes to see Uriel next to him like a loyal dog. The others were near. Tubal-cain passed him up with his heavier weight. Noah slowed himself to make sure they all passed him up so he could keep them in his sight. They continued to sink.

He did not see the Naphil who had broken through the oily layer into the water above them. The pursuer was not just sinking, but swimming to catch up with Noah.

Unseen by all of them, the shadowy form of a sea monster approached them in the distance: Rahab.

Uriel's sixth sense caused him to look up.

The Naphil was almost upon Noah. His hand stretched to grab Noah's head, his blade ready to plunge into Noah's body.

Uriel shouted, bubbles trailing upward.

Noah could not hear through the water, but the bubbles made him look at Uriel, wondering what he was trying to say.

The Naphil grabbed for Noah's head.

Rahab came out of the darkness. The huge dragon body swept through the water. Its jaws gaped open, with large razor teeth the size of swords. Rahab clamped down on the Naphil with a hundred tons of pressure, crushing the humanoid and carrying it away. The torrent in the water almost drew Noah up into its undertow. Uriel grabbed his ankle and pulled him back down.

The great dragon turned and circled back around. It was not finished. There were five pieces of sinking bait ready for snacks. It was too late for the men. They were out of breath. They could last no longer in this watery world.

Their lungs had used up all the oxygen they could store. It was time to inhale water, drown and be eaten.

Suddenly, one by one, they broke through into Sheol and fell almost fourteen cubits down onto the ground, sputtering and coughing out water from their lungs.

It was as if the Abyss was a ceiling or firmament of Sheol, an upside down underworld, where they fell down out of the water onto dry land below.

They gasped for breath. Jubal spit it out first, "What was that *thing*?"

"Rahab," said Uriel, "sea dragon of the Abyss."

"*One* of the dragons," Methuselah corrected him. "The other one has seven heads."

"Thank you for the consolation," derided Jubal. "I feel much better."

"Thank Elohim for the Nephilim after all," muttered Tubal-cain. "One moment more, and we would be a meal."

Noah wondered, "But the size of its mouth. Why did it not grab me with the Naphil?"

Uriel shook his head and boiled with sarcasm, "Hmmm. You do not think that has *anything* to do with Elohim protecting you for his purpose of building the box, do you?"

The rest of them could see Uriel's anger. They all remained uncomfortably silent while getting up to look around.

Sheol: Land of the dead, the underworld. Visibility was very poor and breathing was even harder. They would have to conserve their energy.

Noah remembered the black pitch Salah had given them and the words he had spoken, "Some day to find your way in a dark place." He and Uriel pulled out their pouches filled with the thick tar. They made torches, covered them in pitch and lit them with a flint stone carried by Tubal-cain.

The light let them see more of the dreary, lifeless world they were in. It was an inversion of the upper world: inside-out rocks, upside-down trees, their tangled gnarly roots coming out of the ground.

A howling inhuman screech made them stand up and draw their weapons. They listened for more.

Suddenly, a creature jumped out of the rocks and ran straight at Noah. It looked humanoid in shape, but had lost its distinctive identity as human. It was sexless and without eyes or hair. It only had a large mouth on its head, a large, raving mouth full of outsized ugly pointy teeth, gnashing and gnawing, ready to eat its target.

Noah swept out his sword and cut off its head. It fell to the ground, but continued to grope around for its prey.

Tubal-cain kicked the thing onto its back and stomped down on one arm. Jubal stomped down on the other arm. "What is it?" asked Tubal-cain.

"A shade," said Uriel.

"It does not die?" asked Tubal-cain.

"It is already dead," Uriel answered.

"Call it 'the living dead,'" said Methuselah.

"Come to eat us alive forever?" asked Jubal.

"Yes," said Uriel. "Which is why your best defense is decapitation."

Methuselah leaned in to take a closer look at the thing squirming under their feet. "Disgusting," he said. The body was made of rotting flesh that was falling from its skeleton. He could see that it was animated by maggots and worms that filled the cavities and muscles. An old saying came to his mind and he repeated it aloud, "Where the worm dies not."

Suddenly, two more shades jumped out from behind the rocks. Jubal and Uriel immediately cut off their heads. "How many are there?" asked Tubal-cain.

Before Uriel could answer, eight more shades came at them. The living men hacked and slashed, taking the shades down.

Uriel stood up on a rock looking at a valley below them. It teemed with an endless mass of shades coming in their direction.

"Lots," said Uriel. "Run."

They raced into the wasteland of twisted rocks and gnarled tree roots. But every turn they made, they were blocked by gangs of shades chomping after them. They changed course, only to be blocked by more marauding shades. At last, they broke through the maze of rocks and out onto a vast flat land of dried cracked mud.

Uriel led them out onto the flats. As they ran, the men saw shades bursting out of the ground. Their hands grabbed for the men, their mouths hungrily gnashing and grinding their teeth. Very quickly, the number of shades bursting from the ground overwhelmed them on all sides. There was nowhere to go. They were surrounded. They circled in defense one last time. The massive hive of hungry screeching shades pushed in on them.

"Prepare to be an eternal meal!" yelled Tubal-cain.

Uriel was not about to let that happen. He sheathed his sword, reached in his cloak and pulled out a ram's horn he had secreted from them until now. He put it to his mouth and blew for all his life. The deafening sound rolled out in shockwaves, blowing down shades with concussive force. It spread out in a ring around them.

"You are full of surprises," said Noah.

"I take back my criticisms of you," said Methuselah.

"It will not last," said Uriel.

Methuselah wondered briefly if Uriel was talking of his effect on Methuselah or on the shades.

The effect did not last. The downed shades were soon over-run by a new wave of shades, climbing over the others, mouths munching, tightening their circle once more. Uriel gave another hearty blow. The sound waves pushed the swarms back again. But this time, not as far. It had decreasing effect.

Uriel put the trumpet to his lips a third time. But before he could blow, they were all thrown off their feet by a massive earthquake. The ground exploded upward all around them. Seven giant ten-cubit tall warriors burst out of the ground. They rose from the earth like rulers standing to make judgment. They looked like Nephilim, but were taller and more regal. The shades laid down in submission before them.

"What are they?" asked Noah.

"Rephaim," replied Uriel. "Souls of the giant warrior kings. Demigods like the Nephilim, only more powerful. These were imprisoned here at the Titanomachy."

Memories flooded into Methuselah's mind. One of those Rephaim had killed his wife's family and he had given it a permanent limp with his blade.

"Is that who you were calling on your trumpet?" said Noah.

"No," said Uriel.

Methuselah put in his two shekels, "I have a feeling we would prefer to be eaten by the shades."

Uriel made one last blow on his ram's horn.

It was a quiet evening in the city of Kur on Mount Hermon. The new moon sacrifice was still weeks away. The villagers were in their homes asleep past the midnight hour. Hardly anyone noticed the faint echo of Uriel's trumpet resounding from the depths of Sheol.

Higher up the mountain on the north slope, just below the tree line, the nightlife fell silent. The crickets stopped. Wild rodents froze in their tracks, their eyes darting around in fear.

A blindingly brilliant light abruptly burst from the heavens above to the forest floor. It cut through the night like a dagger, and just as suddenly, it was gone. Darkness filled in the breach.

In a matter of seconds, three dark riders on horseback burst out of the brush from where the light had burned its path to the earth. The savage looking warriors, with armor that looked similar to that of the Nephilim, urged their fierce stallions onward. They rode with deliberation down the mountain toward the ziggurat on the south side.

CHAPTER 16

Lugalanu stared into the flames of his hearth. He was heartsick, and his mind drifted into the consideration of new directions for his life.

A maidservant interrupted his thoughts. "My lord?" she said for the third time. It was the first he heard. He looked up at her and she nodded. In a flash he was up out of his chair and rushing down the hallway to the maidservant's quarters.

He arrived in time to hear the wail of a newborn child filling the darkly lit chamber. He rushed over to the quarantined area and whisked the curtains aside. Emzara lay cradling a baby boy in her arms. She was drenched with sweat, beaming ear to ear. Lugalanu smiled at her.

She had rejected the *ashipu* shaman and his birth magic, and refused to cradle the traditional bronze amulet to fend against infant death. The amulet carried an image of a pazuzu on one side and an incantation on the back for warding off Lamashtu, a demoness believed to cause miscarriage. Emzara clung instead to Elohim as her protector and provider. She needed no other.

"His name shall be Canaanu," said Lugalanu in anticipation of their naming ceremony.

"I shall call him Ham," she said. They had agreed she would have the right to call him her own name in secret, just as he had allowed her to retain her own family name within their private company.

The other maidservants cleaned up the bed sheets and tidied the room in preparation for Emzara's recovery. Lugalanu drew close to Emzara and whispered affectionately into her ears, "Emzara, if you were my wife, I would take no other bride."

"Why do you desire me so?" she asked.

"Why do you resist me so?" he responded.

Two priestesses of Inanna arrived with a bassinet. Their bald elongated heads and tattooed bodies still repulsed Emzara. Especially when she considered what they were there for and what they would do to her only son.

That son was her only link to her beloved husband who she was not supposed to know was still alive, who may never discover that she was still breathing.

Emzara's eyes filled with pain. Lugalanu had been good to her, but she had no choice in this matter. Slowly, she raised the child to the priestesses, who took him and gently placed him into the bassinet.

"He will be a servant of the goddess Inanna," Lugalanu said. "He will serve in her temple for the rest of his life."

"At least he will live," she sighed in resignation.

"At least," said Lugalanu. It was a great pain to him to do this. He had fallen deeply in love with this woman. Even though he detested everything the child was, even though his instinct was to kill it, as one would obviously destroy every last seed of one's enemy, he would not do so. He knew that would forever destroy his chance to win Emzara.

He was beginning to wonder if he was only deceiving himself. He had been so confident he could woo Emzara over the last year. He would take ten years to do so if he had to. A hundred years even. It represented the one thing that was unattainable in his reality, and it became the one thing he wanted more than anything else; more than the riches, more than the power, more than his exalted status with the gods and rulership of the people. As he looked into her eyes, he could see the goodness, the truth, the beauty that had evaded him his entire life, and he wanted it to all be willingly surrendered to him. The one true thing he could not have was the one thing he was willing to devote the rest of his life to get. He would wait. He would remain patient, no matter how many years it took.

A messenger entered the room and approached Lugalanu. The priest-king lost his temper, "Must I be constantly interrupted? May I have one moment of peace?"

"I am sorry, your lordship. But the Gibborim have returned." Lugalanu looked up, surprised. He did not see that Emzara's eyes went wide with anticipation.

Lugalanu asked, "Was their mission objective achieved?" He had forgotten that Emzara saw him commission the Nephilim that day months ago. He certainly did not know she was aware Noah was still alive. So he spoke in generalities, referring to official matters that he expected she would not understand.

Emzara hid her emotions in response to the news of her beloved.

"No, my king," said the messenger.

Emzara's heart leapt for joy. He got away? Her Noah had escaped the mighty Gibborim?

"That is, there was no capture," the messenger continued. "Their quarry, I am told, fell into Sheol."

Emzara's heart broke. She trembled. It was all she could do to keep from weeping. But her life depended on it, and the life of her son too, so she held back with all her might.

"Sheol," repeated Lugalanu. "Hmmm. The jaws of Sheol are never satisfied, and he who goes down does not come up. I suppose I could not ask for better news."

Emzara could not ask for more crushing news. Everything she stayed alive and fought for was just murdered in front of her eyes. Questions flooded her soul. Was Elohim truly in control? What about the Revelation? How could he let such evil prosper and have victory, while the righteous perish? Had she wasted her entire life believing in a God whose will could be thwarted?

Her faith hung on by a slender thread. She did not understand Elohim, but she trusted him. This was another opportunity to express that trust, if it was as real as she had claimed.

The priestesses took baby Ham through the underground tunnel into Inanna's temple district. There, in a special room, they immediately began the process of cranial modification for servants of Anu. Newborns have soft pliable skulls whose plates were not fused for the first couple years of their lives as their skulls accommodated brain growth. The priestesses placed two curved pieces of wood on the front and back of Ham's little head. In effect, they maintained the original egg-like protrusion of the skull after birth. The pieces of wood were held tightly in place by connecting twine cables wound around a knob that could be tightened to increase pressure. They had to be careful not to crush the infant's skull.

Ham's frightened crying would soon be mitigated as he got used to the contraption. As he aged, less constrictive means could be used to finalize the head binding process until he was about two years old.

Herbal potions to kill all the hair on the body would not be necessary until the child was at least a teen and became more involved in the duties of the temple. Body piercing and tattooing would finalize the child's dedication to temple service around age sixteen or so. The entire process was rather monkish. Emzara would not be allowed to see her son until he was publicly dedicated at age sixteen. Even after that, he would be withheld from her. Priests and priestesses were not allowed to fraternize with the court servants. The caste system was harshly enforced throughout the kingdom. The only way Emzara would ever be able to have satisfying contact with her son would be if she became royalty by accepting Lugalanu's hand in marriage.

The Tigris and Euphrates Rivers poured into the Lower Sea at the edge of the earth. The body of water teamed with life. Seagoing vessels traded with distant lands. Others fished for the river cities close to the sea, like Eridu. Eridu was the oldest Sumerian city and was ruled by its patron god of the Abyss, Enki. It was the city of the first kings when kingship came down from heaven. Eridu's status had dwindled over the years as kingship transferred to other cities, ever since Inanna's treachery toward Enki.

Legend said that Enki had originally been given guardianship of the Tablet of Destinies, a tablet containing the universal decrees of heaven and earth, including godship, kingship, war, sex, music as well as magic, sorceries and occultic wisdom. Enlil, the Lord of the Air, who reigned over the city of Nippur up the river, collected the information on this tablet. Enlil had given it to Enki for safe-keeping, but Inanna was envious of Enki and crafted a plan to wrest the Tablet away from him and bring it to Erech.

She took her "boat of heaven" down the river and visited Enki, who laid out a feast of celebration for her. Enki fed Inanna butter-cakes and beer, but Inanna was calculating and got Enki drunk enough for him to hand over the Tablet to her. She then fled back to Erech with it on her boat of heaven. By the time Enki had come to his senses and sent his vizier after Inanna, it was too late. She had delivered the Tablet of Destinies to Erech, which became the new center of culture and civilization. Enki brooded bitterly at being double-crossed so boldly by Inanna. One day, he would have his revenge on her. But he would have to be patient. Besides, he was not the only one betrayed by the machinations of the goddess. Her reckless pursuit of power would surely one day result in more than one deity seeking vengeance against her.

One of those deities who might consider joining in revenge against Inanna was Enlil, Lord of the Air. Originally, he had shared patronage with Inanna over the city of Nippur, before the Titanomachy. Even though she had been humiliated after her failure in that war, losing the city to his kingship, he still carried the scars of her conniving skullduggery against him. He would never be satisfied until she was bound in the earth.

Ninhursag, the earth goddess, also had a grudge against Inanna. Ninhursag was patron deity of Kish, which lay farther up the Euphrates, past Erech and Nippur in the northern regions. But because of her cavorting liaison with Enki, she also had a temple in Eridu. The Watchers' myths, which sought to replace Elohim's creation story, gave Ninhursag the titles Ninmah, "Great Queen," and Nintu, "Lady of Birth," claiming she created man out of the clay of her womb. She knew Inanna had her eye on Ninhursag's throne, because she was the one "female" deity of the four high gods And Inanna envied Ninhursag's amorous entanglement with Enki.

The hierarchy of the pantheon was always at risk for challenge, and it was no secret Inanna was the most ambitious of them all. She had managed to make herself consort of Anu, which was clearly positioning. Anu did not seem to care. He enjoyed dominating her passionate temper. She was creative and bizarre. Anu took pleasure in the bizarre.

Inanna, it seemed, was building up a cadre of enemies within her own camp that did not bode well for her future.

The Lower Sea was a couple leagues downriver from Eridu, with its western shoreline along the winding desert coast. Just off this shoreline, the bodies of Methuselah, Tubal-cain, and Jubal floated dead in the water.

A fourth figure broke the surface and grabbed the bodies. He swam toward shore with a mighty strength.

Uriel dragged the bodies onto the sand. He massaged their lungs and squeezed their stomachs until they coughed up the water in their lungs and gulped air. Jubal, being the youngest and healthiest, came to first. One by one, Uriel revived them all.

They were alive. At first, they did not know where they were or how they got there. But it started to come back to them. They had been captured by the Rephaim in Sheol and imprisoned by their gigantic captors. But they had not been privy to the details of the negotiations for their release.

"Why did they let us go, Uriel?" asked Tubal-cain.

"They cannot hold archangels in Sheol. And I would not leave without you."

Methuselah spat sand from his mouth. "Where is Noah?" he asked.

"They required a ransom for those released," Uriel replied.

Methuselah did not follow this logic. "Noah is trapped in Sheol? Why on earth would you leave behind the one man who should not have been left behind? I would have given myself in his place." His anger with this so-called guardian rushed up.

"Noah gave himself in your place," said Uriel. "I could not stop him. He told the Rephaim he was the Chosen Seed."

The men could not believe what they heard. They refused to accept it.

"We have to go back," said Tubal-cain.

"No." Uriel responded as quickly as they had.

Methuselah would have none of it. "Are you shirking your responsibility, or are you planning on storming Sheol by yourself, you crazy angel?" he shouted.

"No," replied Uriel. "I have a few crazy associates who are going to help me."

Methuselah looked behind them. On the beach, three warrior horsemen waited. They got off their steeds and walked toward the men like wraiths of judgment. Jubal and Methuselah gasped in fear. But the men had nothing to fear. Their wrath was for the Rephaim holding the Chosen Seed in the pit of Sheol.

The three warriors walked right past them. Uriel joined them. They walked into the water up to their waists and dove in, disappearing from view. Before he dove after them, Uriel turned and shouted to the men, "Go to the Hidden Valley as Noah commanded. Methuselah, you have the plans."

Methuselah responded, "Uriel, if you find one of the Rephaim with a limp, give him my special regards." He was referring to the Rapha named Yahipan. He had permanently wounded the giant many years before in the uprising called the Gigantomachy. Uriel knew the personal loss that Methuselah had suffered at the hands of Yahipan. He would be sure to deliver the message with deadly accuracy.

With that, Uriel turned back and disappeared beneath the surface.

Methuselah pulled out the leather piece tightly packed in his cloak. He opened it up and looked at the cuneiform Noah had scratched into it.

"You heard the archangel, men. We have a commission, now let us fulfill it," barked Methuselah.

CHAPTER 17

The pit was unimaginably deep. It was only about ten cubits in diameter, its walls black, and solid, unbreakably hard, unscalable rock. It dropped down immeasurable leagues. It was so deep, one could not see the bottom. But there was a bottom eventually, and it was the furthest depth of Sheol. It was Tartarus, a place of imprisonment at the uttermost distance from the presence of Elohim. Perpetual darkness, impenetrable silence, and absolute isolation. It was said that Tartarus was as far below Sheol as the earth was below the heavens.

Noah was incarcerated at the very bottom of those depths. He had a flat stone to sleep on. A single oil lamp, refueled only when food was occasionally lowered down in a basket, gave a little patch of light. Noah was, after all, still alive. It would not do well for the forces of darkness to have the Chosen Seed dead, for he would only be replaced by someone else. His captors were so certain of their prison, they took nothing from him, leaving even his dagger on his person.

Noah looked up toward the heavens, which he could only imagine were so far away it would not matter what he yelled. But he yelled anyway. "ELOHIM! WHY HAVE YOU DONE THIS TO ME?!"

His voice did not echo up the leagues of empty cavern walls as one would expect. Instead, it was stifled like whispers in a coffin, as if the words could not go beyond his own hearing, as if the words did not extend beyond his lips. He sat in a vortex where sound and reality swirled right back into him in absolute solitary confinement. Noah had complained for so long about wanting to be left alone. Now he had his wish—to the utmost. He was finally, totally and utterly, *alone*.

And he realized what a complete selfish fool he had been.

He looked up at the wall. He could only see a few cubits into the darkness with the lamp he had. Like a desperate rat, he jumped up, trying to grab a foothold, anything. He fell to the ground in a crumple, weeping. He looked at the brass wrist brace he had worn to remind himself of his wife. He ripped it off and threw it against the wall. The sight of it only multiplied his torment tenfold in this hell.

He pulled at his clothes, ripping them to pieces in a frenzied anger of self-pity. He looked up to heaven again. He was going mad, but he still had his pride.

"I HATE YOU! DO YOU HEAR ME, GOD OF ENOCH! I HATE YOU!"

There was no response.

"ARE YOU DEAF AND DUMB? ARE YOU BLIND?!"

Still no answer.

"WHAT DO YOU WANT FROM ME? WHAT HAVE I EVER DONE TO DESERVE THIS? ANSWER ME! WHAT HAVE I DONE TO DESERVE ALL THIS? WHAT HAVE I…"

And suddenly, from deep within his bowels, a groan of despair and resignation overwhelmed him. He fell to his knees weeping in deep sobs. The words he now said were the same, but they now meant the opposite of his original intent. Accusation turned to confession. "What have I done? What have I done to deserve this? I deserve this. I deserve all this."

He wept his very soul into the void. He was broken. He could say no more. He could only sob bitter tears of repentance.

"Noah," the whisper said.

Noah stopped.

What had he heard?

He listened for more.

Nothing.

But he *had* heard it.

He knew that voice.

He quickly rummaged through his discarded clothes and pulled out his dagger.

He went to the wall, carrying his small lamp to light the surface. He began to scratch the rock. Carefully, he carved cuneiform lines that were directions. Then he scratched out the picture of the tebah, the box from his calling in a dream that would not let him go.

He scratched feverishly. He would not stop. Not even for the food lowered in the basket by some minion of hell leagues above him. He just kept scratching.

Noah did not know how long he had been there. His beard had grown out. He looked up at the wall, dimly lit by his little lamp. The entire wall all around, three hundred and sixty degrees, up to the height of his reach, was covered with scratching. It was the blueprint and directions for the box carved over and over again. The blade in his hand had been worn to the hilt. Noah's mind was emptied of its obsession. He was bled dry of his pride. He collapsed to the floor in a broken heap.

From above, he heard a distant sound grow louder. It cut through the darkness and split the void. He knew that sound. It was the unmistakable resonance of Uriel's trumpet. He looked up into the void. He could see nothing.

But he kept looking up in faith.

Moments later, the end of a rope dropped to the floor. It was followed eventually by the figure of Uriel, rappelling down the wall. He landed on the ground with a thud.

Noah looked up at him.

Uriel looked back up from where he came and muttered, "Now *that* is a deep pit."

"You came back for me," Noah blubbered, barely able to speak.

Uriel smiled with a big grin. "You know Elohim. He hounds you until you freely obey." He had that hint of irony that Noah had learned to love so dearly.

Noah burst out laughing in tears.

Uriel could see that Noah was a new man. He shared the laugh with Noah, helped his weak companion to his feet, and embraced him.

"What took you so long?" said Noah with an impish smirk on his face.

Uriel grinned back. "There was a little matter of the Rephaim I had to take care of."

"You took care of seven Rephaim?" asked an amazed Noah.

Uriel gave him a parental scolding look. "Of course not. I had help."

Uriel grabbed Noah and helped him onto his back. The angel seized the rope, readying for his long climb back to reality. "We cannot save ourselves, Noah," he said. "But then I gather you understand that now."

"Hurry up, will you?" snorted Noah. "I have a box to build."

Uriel grinned and began his ascent with mighty archangelic speed and power.

Noah was so fatigued, he fell asleep on the climb up. When they arrived at the top, Uriel fell to the ground exhausted. His muscles were cramping, worn out from the climb. He tried to catch his breath and took a huge drink from a wineskin in his belt.

The impact of Uriel's collapse woke Noah. He looked around the cave they were in.

Three of the giant Rephaim lay with their faces to the ground, bound by cords Noah could not see – no doubt the barely perceptible Cherubim hair he had once been shown by Uriel. Three angelic warriors stood on the necks of the giants. They stepped down and approached Noah. Uriel had to stay seated on the ground.

"Who are they?" Noah asked.

"Archangels," huffed Uriel.

The warriors came and hugged the awkward Noah as if he were family.

"This is Mikael, Gabriel, and Raphael," said Uriel.

The three nodded as they were introduced. They were as handsome and muscle-bound as Uriel—more so. The thought went through Noah's mind that his guardian was the least impressive of the bunch. Strange, if he was supposed to be so important as the Chosen Seed. Noah opened his mouth to direct a verbal stab in Uriel's direction, but all that came out was, "Thank you for your efforts."

"Just do not let it happen again," said Mikael with a touch of humor. "Uriel is already in trouble for his guardianship of you."

"Or lack thereof," joked Gabriel.

"Hey," complained Uriel, "I did just carry him out of Tartarus. That should count for something."

"You bound the Rephaim," said Noah surprised.

"I told you," said Uriel, "It's a special talent we have. Though not without its difficulties."

Noah's forehead crinkled with concern. "Uriel, I thought you said you took care of seven Rephaim. There are only three of them on the ground."

"I did not say seven," corrected Uriel, "You did. It was a detail I considered too petty to correct at the time. But now, I believe it is exceedingly relevant to our safety. We should make good our escape."

Before they could even move, a bellowing inhuman screech filled the air. A stampeding Rapha burst through the cave opening, headed right at Noah. It limped as it ran.

Mikael and Gabriel leapt into action. They dove at the Rapha's shins and tackled it to the ground inches from Noah. The Rapha's fist came pounding down toward Noah's head. Uriel pushed Noah out of the way. If Uriel had been at his full strength, it would not have hurt so badly, but he was still weakened from his climb up from that infernal pit with Noah on his back. His muscles were too weak to deflect, he had to absorb. He blacked out.

Now it was Noah's turn. He pulled Uriel out of the way of the second strike from the beast.

Gabriel leapt on the creature's back and pulled its head back like a tethered stallion. Raphael and Mikael dragged him away from Noah by his feet.

The Rapha reached over his head and grabbed Gabriel. He threw the angel against the cave wall with a thundering crash.

These Rephaim were harder than the Nephilim on earth because they were dead and had greater strength in the underworld than in the land of the living. But so did the archangels. Mikael and Raphael whipped their cords out. They bound the beast before it could regain its balance to get up.

Uriel walked up to the limping Rapha now bound. He remembered Methuselah's words to him before he had dived back into the abyss. Give this one his regards. He could not kill this thing, but there was one thing he could do to bring it misery. He reached with both hands and grabbed the Rapha's eyeballs. With a mighty grip and yank, he ripped out both eyes from their sockets. He threw them into the deep pit out of which he had crawled. The Rapha screamed in agony.

Uriel leaned in and whispered in the monster's ear, "That was for Methuselah ben Enoch, you son of iniquity."

The other angels watched Uriel with shock.

He pulled Noah toward the entrance of the cave. Noah was afraid of him. That act had seemed brutally out of character for Uriel. But neither the man nor the other angels had been on the journey with Uriel and Methuselah those many generations earlier. If they had been, they would not have considered his action inappropriate at all.

They stepped outside the cave.

They were up a mountainside. A thousand cubits below them countless shades scrambled from the mountain base toward them. The three missing Rephaim trampled over the shades, crushing them indiscriminately on their way up toward the cave entrance. Their hideous screams pierced Noah's and Uriel's ears.

Uriel pulled Noah to the side of the ledge. He looked up. It was a rock climb of at least sixty cubits. Before Noah could register anything, Uriel grabbed him and lifted him up to a rock with a grunt and yelled, "Climb!" Normally, Uriel would have been able to throw Noah ten cubits upward, but not in his present exhausted state. Noah climbed for all he was worth. Breathing hard, Uriel looked up at the wall before him. Well, at least he did not have to carry Noah again. But he had to keep moving. He grabbed a rock and climbed.

Even in his fatigued condition, Uriel passed Noah. He arrived at the top, just as the Rephaim reached the cave entrance, climbing like spiders toward their prey. They would be only seconds in finishing the climb. Uriel reached down and grabbed Noah's cloak, pulling him up and over the ledge onto the mountaintop. The ceiling of the watery Abyss hung just ten cubits over their heads.

Uriel felt there was no way he would be able to do it. He would have to throw Noah up the distance to the Abyss.

The Rephaim were already on the ledge and sprinting for them.

Uriel whispered a prayer to Elohim and grabbed Noah. With every last ounce of strength left in him, he heaved Noah the ten cubits up to the water. The two Rephaim hit him and tackled him to the ground, crushing him in a heap.

In but a moment, one of them would help the other leap the distance to the water ceiling.

But they would not be leaping. They were dragged off Uriel by three very riled archangels.

CHAPTER 18

Noah desperately kicked for the surface through the dark waters of the Abyss. He did not have much air to spare in making it to the top. He did not know where he was or where he would end up. He just had to make it to the surface. His lungs burned. He panicked. The shadowy form of Leviathan swimming in the distance only added to his despair. The fearsome offspring of Rahab. Could it get much worse than this? What difference would it make anyway? He would be drowned by the time the monster reached him.

Noah had the urge to give up.

Suddenly he felt a shoving from below. Uriel had followed him. He kicked with superhuman force, thrusting Noah upward. Noah knew Uriel was weak, but the angel seemed to find a hidden source of unending bursts of energy. Noah would have to make a joke about that if they made it out alive.

And he did make it.

He burst through the surface, gasping for air. Uriel appeared beside him moments later, sputtering out the next command, "Swim!"

There was a trading ship sailing their direction. The sailor in the crow's nest spotted Noah and Uriel as the ship drew near them.

Noah kicked his way toward the ship with everything in him.

Uriel kept looking over his shoulder for the sea monster.

The monster's spiny snakelike back broke the surface not a hundred cubits out. It glistened in the sun, gliding toward them, all seven of its heads focused with predator intensity. Seven sets of eyes. Seven sets of razor teeth. It had all the time in the world.

It was said of Leviathan that on earth there was nothing like it. A creature without fear. Nothing could match its ferocity or its power. Javelins and harpoons all broke upon its armored scales. Even its belly was covered with protection like sharp potsherds. It was said that Leviathan could belch from some of its mouths flame like a burning torch. From its nostrils it could spew smoke as from a boiling pot or burning rushes. It could crush the hull of a warship into splinters. It was said that Leviathan ruled the Abyss with seven times the terror of Rahab.

Knowing all this about the predator, Uriel stayed behind treading water. He could barely keep himself afloat. He gasped anxiously. He was no match for the jaws of Leviathan even if he had not been so drained of all his vitality. But he would divert its attention from Noah. He could at least do that. He would be a willing sacrifice in mere moments.

But that moment did not come.

He turned around in the water. Leviathan was nowhere to be seen. It had not gone past him, either. He saw Noah being helped up the side of the merchant ship. Uriel swam to the craft, waiting for the worst to come. Leviathan was a creature of chaos, but it was intelligent. It operated with calculation. This did not make sense. Something wicked was coming.

Uriel made it to the ship. The sailors helped him up.

The mast man shouted, "LEVIATHAN!" All hands on deck moved speedily.

Uriel and Noah looked out on the starboard side. Strange. It must have passed under them and circled back.

The armored spine of the dragon broke the surface coming at them. Was it gathering momentum for a strike? A warship would not have a chance against this beast, let alone a merchant trading vessel laden with carnelia, lapis lazuli and pearls instead of soldiers and weapons. The creature was three times the length of the ship and six times its weight. It would snap the craft like a handful of toothpicks.

The sailors did not wait to find out. They trimmed the sail to catch the windward blow. Some joined the slaves at the oars to row for their lives. It was all quite futile. They could not outrun the sea dragon and they could not withstand its mighty force. But they refused to resign themselves to fate. They would struggle for life to the very end.

The Captain of the ship demanded Noah and Uriel's attention. "What curse is this you have brought upon us all? We will all die! I am a simple merchant!" Terrified anger pulled tight the olive dark skin of his face. His black hair shook as he gestured. "I have not wronged the gods! Why are you here in the middle of the sea? Are you demons?!"

It was one long stream of hyperventilation that matched Uriel's own laboring for breath.

Uriel collapsed to the deck. He could do nothing more. There was nowhere else to run. He rested his head against the mast. His collapse actually stopped the Captain's string of complaints.

The Captain turned his attention to Noah. He spewed a fresh litany of accusations at him. The lookout above interrupted him, yelling down, "CAPTAIN! IT IS BELOW US! LEVIATHAN IS BELOW US!"

The Captain froze.

Noah tilted his head. Below us? What does he mean below us?

Uriel struggled to get up. They ran to the side of the boat to peer into the water below. The sight struck everyone silent. The ship tacked northward toward the gulf inlet at a breezy pace. Directly below the ship, at thrice its size, gliding along just cubits below the flat hull of the boat swam Leviathan, matching the pace of the ship as if it was escorting the craft back to land.

Leviathan was guarding the seagoing vessel.

The Captain looked at Noah and blurted out a new stream of words. This time, however, the tone was of adoration. "Who is this man whom the gods favor? Where do you come from? Who is your god that we may worship him? Are you a god that you tame Leviathan?"

Noah listened, astonished.

Uriel grinned. "It appears I am not your only guardian."

Noah felt overwhelmed. Words of poetry rose in Noah's heart: The pillars of heaven tremble and are astounded at his rebuke. By his power he stilled the sea; by his understanding he shattered Leviathan. By his wind the heavens were made fair; his hand pierced the fleeing serpent. Behold, these are but the outskirts of his ways, and how small a whisper do we hear of him! But the thunder of his power who can understand? And Noah knew that Elohim was his guardian who controlled even the sea dragon of chaos.

The Captain interrupted his pious thoughts, "We are going inland up the river for trade. Will you voyage with us?"

"I see you are a lucky charm as well," quipped Uriel under his breath to Noah.

Noah said to the Captain, "We will go as far as Erech."

Noah paused. He could see that Uriel thought he might still be sidetracked by his old desire for revenge. But he quickly put that thought to rest. "From there," he said, "we trek into the Zagros Mountains."

Uriel sighed with deep relief. They were going to look for the Hidden Valley where Methuselah and Noah's tribal survivors had been sent. Noah was going to find them and build the box. If they were even alive.

CHAPTER 19

The merchant vessel docked on the river port wharf of Erech, just inland from the coast where Ur and Eridu stood near the marshlands. The river made a wide delta at this point, about seven hundred cubits across, creating sufficient room for a well traveled trading port. The Euphrates flowed long from the northern mountains down to the Lower Sea in the south. The river, along with its eastern sister river the Tigris, was one of the four main tributaries that flowed from Eden. Together, they were the lifeblood of the Mesopotamian cities along its banks. Like all river civilizations, life ebbed and flowed with the seasonal effects of the river. Even civilization would ultimately ebb and flow with the rivers, for the loose winding curves of water were already beginning to alter course through the flat plain powered by the changing seasonal flooding.

It was spring. The river was high and the surrounding irrigation canals for agriculture were flooded in preparation for fertilizing the soil after the dry summer and winter months.

The surroundings puzzled Noah. By his reckoning, it had been summer when they had stormed the Gates of Ganzir on Mount Hermon and plunged into the Abyss on their journey in Sheol. How long had he been down there? It felt like weeks, but not a year.

The Captain hugged Noah and Uriel to bid them farewell. He had given them Indus Valley robes to wear, along with a small amount of money for their blessing upon his ship. It was the least he could do in gratitude. Noah had told him all about his God Elohim and how he created the heavens and the earth and humankind. He told him of the Fall and of faith, about the idolatry of the gods of the land, and about the judgment that drew nigh. The Captain and his entire boat were convinced and put their faith in Elohim.

They showered gifts of gratitude upon Noah and Uriel, which helped the pair in more than one way. First, they needed supplies and second, with their attire, they would not look like strange foreigners sauntering around the city.

As they walked down the plank of the ship to the dock the first thing they noticed was that everyone was shaved hairless and had elongated skulls with skin tattoos. Noah remembered that this kind of physical alteration was reserved for temple and palace servants of the gods, not the average citizenry. Yet as they walked the dock, it appeared that every inhabitant of the city now participated in the sacred identity with Anu. How could this have all happened within a few months? It did not seem possible.

He also noticed the presence of many horses and the distinct absence of onagers for travel use. He knew horses were just being introduced into the region and that the various cities were breeding them. But there were so many here. It just did not make sense that this kind of change could have happened without years of development and planning.

His gaze dwelt on the architecture. It was not the same. The buildings seemed taller than he remembered. He did not recognize the look of some of the city. Then he realized they had been walking down the very street where he had been paraded on the cart as captive of the gods. It was the same street, but it looked different. He had not had time to notice details of architecture while he was being pelted with rotten vegetables while transported on a cart of shame. But even so, this was different. The buildings seemed built up.

At the end of the street, they came upon the brick-making pit. Emaciated slaves crawled in it, creating mud bricks in the hot sun with sand, straw and mud. Stone was non-existent in the area, so mud brick was the main means of building structures along with some wood from the cedar forest. But again, Noah noticed that there were more slaves here than he had ever seen before. The brick making area was three times the size he remembered, and he guessed there were over a thousand slaves down there. Was his memory failing him?

A contingent of bird-men soldiers marched past them in the streets. Noah and Uriel pulled their cloaks up to cover their faces. They found a stable and bought two horses for their journey ahead. They stepped out into the street and saw the temple district of Inanna at the end of the street. Noah felt drawn to it as if bidden by some unseen force.

They arrived at the end of the market street by the entrance to the temple. Another large contingent of bird-men soldiers passed by. The military presence of these creatures seemed excessive to him. But the sight before them would raise that level of excess to new heights.

Across the street stood the entrance to the temple of Inanna. Its curved oval walls rose high over the street, casting a shadow on the long line of hundreds of male temple patrons. Minstrels played lute and pipe. Caged portholes embedded in the walls near the entrance hosted dancing women. But these were unnatural women. They were four-armed blue goddesses from the Indus Valley. They swirled swords in fluid motions to the music. Strings of human skulls hung from the floors of their cages. It was both perverse and violent, just like Inanna.

It made him sick to his stomach. Yet he knew this depravity was not entirely alien to his own soul. Evil was inside all men, including him. Their inclinations had simply been fed and nurtured instead of suppressed and overcome by faith. This moral decadence was not as bizarre as it appeared. It took humility for Noah to recognize that what disgusted him also strangely drew him, and if he made choices that began simple and small and grew over time, he could end up like any of these deluded slaves of sin. Evil was not "other." It was with him, *within* him.

Noah said simply, "I see her worship is popular." Then he added, "I was wheeled through these streets when I was first captured. But this is different. More wicked. More vile." He shook his head at his own understatement, for it was as if the entire city was possessed by demons.

"I need to tell you something, Noah," said Uriel, breaking him out of his trance. "How long were you in Tartarus?"

"Days?" said Noah. "Weeks. I lost track."

"In the depths of Sheol, it is as if time stops," said Uriel.

"Yes," said Noah. "Exactly." Then he noticed Uriel staring at him without responding.

"What are you saying?" Noah asked.

"While you were in Tartarus, up here on earth one hundred years have passed."

Noah became dizzy as the reality hit him in the gut. "One hundred years?" He could not believe it. His breath shortened. He could feel his heart pounding in his chest. He wanted to run, but there was nowhere to go.

"Yes," said Uriel. "The world has worsened. Every intent of the thought of man's heart is continually evil."

Another unit of bird-men soldiers marched past them. Uriel added, "And the gods are preparing for war."

"With whom?" asked Noah.

"With Elohim—and the seed of Eve," said Uriel.

Before Noah could appreciate the full impact of that statement, an earthquake surprised them. They lost their footing just a little. But people around them went about their normal lives as if nothing had happened.

Uriel said to Noah, "Birth pangs of Elohim's wrath."

Noah saw that the heavens were not the same. It was like the entire universe was transforming around him in preparation for something terrible.

"We have not much time," said Uriel. "We must reach the Hidden Valley."

Noah and Uriel mounted their horses and headed toward the Zagros Mountains.

CHAPTER 20

Behind its outer walls, the Temple of Inanna was another world. When they entered the bronze gates from the dusty barren city streets, patrons became submerged in a world of sensuality, a garden of earthly delights. Lush flora filled the open courtyard: exotic fruit trees with dates, figs, and pomegranates. Tamarisk and palm trees rose above the floor in a canopy of leaves. The complex artificial irrigation channels of the city watered this botanical paradise of flowers and vegetation. A wisp of incense mixed with perfume wafted through the air, teasing the nostrils. The temple and palace gardens replicated a memory of Eden. It was as if gods and kings sought to retain their ancestral past even as they perverted it into its mirror opposite.

Strange hybrid creatures inhabited this anti-Eden: an obese woman with the head of a cow, another with reptilian skin, a dwarf with a tail and hooves, a deathly thin giantess with spindly arms and legs. There were dog-headed and pig-headed women. There were even woman-headed dogs and pigs. The violation of the created order had spread so deep, the judgment of God could not be closer.

Past the priestly and servant antechambers loomed the sanctuary that housed the stone statue of Inanna. The idol towered over seven and a half feet, carved from diorite, a dark grey volcanic rock imported from the northern regions. A libations and purification priest, called an *isib*, carefully attended to the new image that adorned the sacred space.

The original idol had fallen over and broken in half in the last major earthquake. This would not bode well for Inanna's reputation, so the priests had a new statue created in the idol workshop. From there, a holy procession brought the idol down to the river. It was placed in a reed hut specially erected for the "opening of the mouth" and "washing of the mouth" rituals. These ceremonies ritually purified the stone, and called down the deity to enliven the statue with her spirit. The mouth would first be washed multiple times with varying combinations of water, honey and ghee. A priest then engaged in various incantations of birthing the goddess in the image. It was not that they believed the image itself to be the goddess, but that it embodied the deity's presence and dominion. Noah would have seen it as another mimicry of Elohim's representative image in mankind ruling on earth. In effect, the statue was "born in heaven and made on earth." The damaged statue was mourned and cast into the river. The new one, embodied with the deity in a kind of resurrection from the netherworld, was brought back up into the sanctuary for its residence.

Images were ideal for the plan of the gods. They provided a means whereby they could keep the focus of humankind on an object of this world instead of the unseen presence of Elohim. At the same time, the idols would root that concrete connection to themselves. Anu and Inanna were loath to make themselves too visible to the population. They knew that physical absence reinforced a sense of mystery and reverence in the worshippers. The less they showed themselves to the masses, the more awe they inspired. Stone idols were simply helpful reminders.

The isib priest poured out liquid offerings and checked the idol's braces and security. It had already withstood the latest rumbling of earth, but he wanted to be sure it would be able to withstand a more rigorous quake. Like all those in the service of the gods, the isib had an elongated skull, was shaved of all hair, and carried the tattoos and piercings of the deity on his body beneath his multicolored linen robes. He was being groomed by Lugalanu himself to become a *sanga*, the next highest level of priest, an administrator with an eye toward becoming an *ensi*, the high priest.

A female temple servant slipped unnoticed into the room and whispered to the isib.

"Ham."

Ham, son of Noah, the child taken from Emzara a hundred years before, had grown into a well-educated son of Lugalanu, the priest-king. Though this was not official, it might as well have been, for Lugalanu had groomed him from birth for such a noble end. Ham knew that Lugalanu loved his mother Emzara and was still trying to persuade her to marry him, and that this was why he loved Ham as his own. He still could not understand just why his mother was so stubborn after so many years. Her attitude kept her, by temple regulation, from being in communication with her own son. If she would only marry the priest-king, she would be allowed to visit with her son because of her exalted status. She could then avoid the difficulty of secret rendezvous.

Ham turned to see his beloved Neela hiding in the shadows. They had married recently. His new rank as isib allowed him the privilege of matrimony disallowed to the eunuchs and lesser temple priests. Though his court name was Canaanu, both Emzara and Neela had earned the privilege of calling him Ham in private.

Ham held out his arms and bid her come. Neela whisked over and they embraced with a deep kiss. She was fifty years his junior, full of spunk and excitement for life. Something about Neela's desert descent made her stand out from the Mesopotamian passivity. She was curious, passionate, and headstrong, but she filled his life with such playfulness and hope that he could not live without her. And she could sense his every mood.

"My love, you are weary," said Neela. "What is Lugalanu waiting for? He should initiate you into the high priesthood and be done with it."

"Neela. First of all, the initiation only occurs on the New Year Festival, and I am still an office away from ensi. I must become a sanga first. That will take years."

"Years," she repeated with contempt. "Bah! Why must it take so long? You are a leader among men."

Ham smiled. "I thank you for your support, dear wife, but there is an order to things. You know full well we hurt ourselves if we violate the order of the gods. There are secrets I have not yet been initiated into."

"What secrets?" she said.

"How can I know if I have not been initiated, silly? And if I did, I certainly could not tell you."

He smiled and kissed her again.

She teased him, "To become a priest of Inanna, the Queen of Heaven, is no small thing for such a humble servant."

He teased right back, "But to be husband of Neela, the Queen of my heart, is an altogether exhaustive thing."

"Well, then, we exhaust each other," she smiled.

She could see he was not all there. "Are you thinking of your mother?" she asked.

He could not respond with the obvious yes.

The arrival of the Temple Guard interrupted them. Lugalanu stepped through the guards and into the room.

Neela immediately bowed and backed out toward the back room exit. Ham knelt before his king.

"Lord Lugalanu, I am your servant."

"Canaanu, my isib of Inanna, how do you fare?" Lugalanu replicated the lighthearted attitude of Anu in his own dealings with inferiors. Like god, like son.

"Well, my lord," replied Ham.

"Excellent, excellent," he said, looking around the sanctuary. "I applaud you. The goddess' temple is well kept, and I see you have taken special care of the new image of our high and mighty Queen of Heaven."

Ham detected a slight sarcasm in the tone. He knew that Lugalanu wearied of kowtowing to Inanna's intemperate volatility. But it was not something they talked about. Lugalanu knew it would be injudicious to instill such conflict of interest with the very priest he was preparing for her service.

Ham did not know that Lugalanu only made him a priest of Inanna in order to persuade Emzara to love him. Unfortunately, it had not worked out the way he had hoped. Lugalanu had suffered every day since then. Lugalanu had thought it might force Emzara to compromise, but it only hardened her resolve. He hoped that watching her son become increasingly involved in the priesthood of a god she hated would at least burn on her soul with a pain equivalent to what she caused him.

"Canaanu," said Lugalanu. His tone changed, becoming more serious. "All these years, you know I have considered you a son."

It was a plea for his love. Ham looked downward submissively.

"If I may, exalted one, then why would you keep your son from his mother?"

The inquiry was certainly respectful in tone, but it was still a cloaked challenge. Lugalanu liked that about Ham. "You are so much like your mother. You know full well the servants of Inanna do not mingle with the servants of Anu. It is not in my authority to challenge the covenants of the kingdom."

Hierarchy in the priestly caste was strictly enforced as a code of holiness. It was ironic that the kingdom built upon violation of the separation of the created order should maintain its own rigid separations and distinctions of sacredness. Of course the king was fully capable of determining exemptions as he pleased, so his motives were not as honest as they appeared.

Lugalanu continued, "Nevertheless, you are being groomed to become a high priest of the Queen of Heaven, so it is time for your introduction to the secrets of the Watchers."

Ham caught his breath. This was an opportunity he had coveted for years. Initiation into the secrets of the Watchers was both a sacred privilege and a dangerous responsibility. These gods, who had come from heaven to earth, had revealed many secrets to mankind, secrets of sorcery, apothecary, charms and enchantments, witchcraft, as well as astrological worship and the making of idols and their ritual incantations. They had also revealed the art of metal making for both ornament and war. The thought of admission into this cabal of mystery made Ham's entire being well up with exhilaration.

He followed Lugalanu out of the room toward his destiny.

They both did not realize that Neela had been hiding behind the statue of Inanna the entire time and had heard it all. Her pride in her husband made her beam with excitement. Her curiosity overwhelmed her. What were these wonderful "secrets of the Watchers?"

CHAPTER 21

Lugalanu led Ham down a circular stairwell deep into the recesses of the earth below the temple complex of Eanu. The spiral brick staircase spun downward like a chambered nautilus sea shell. Lugalanu lit an occasional wall torch for their return trip.

Neela followed them in the shadows. She kept a safe distance to avoid detection, and she scurried along barefoot to silence the sound of her steps.

At the bottom of the dizzying staircase lay a series of twisting pitch-dark corridors. Fortunately for Neela, the hallways continued to be lit by Lugalanu's torch like a path of bread crumbs. Fear rose in her liver. There were so many turns, she began to lose her bearings. She worried that she could not find her way out if she found herself alone and without the lit torches. She could become a prisoner of the darkness, possibly even die down here. But it was too late to turn back. She had passed the point of no return and would have to continue on in hope she would be all right.

She had lived with risk all her life. As a little orphan servant girl of eight in the city, she found her way past all the guards, priests, and priestesses to the very top of the White Temple itself. Anu had found her so amusing and curious that instead of punishing her, he had rewarded her by appointing her to the temple staff of Inanna. For this act of kindness, Neela gave eternal gratitude to Anu, because it was how she found her way into the sight and passions of Ham. She continued in her stealth pursuit with a renewed sense of enthusiasm in her heart.

Lugalanu and Ham passed a secret corridor that brought back emotional memories for Lugalanu. Down that passage was the sealed burial chamber of his father, Lugalanuruku, the previous priest-king of Erech. He was named after his father, though he was the offspring of a Sacred Marriage rite with the high priestess. The ritual ensured fertility of the land. Priestesses were considered royalty and so their children were often successors to the throne, though they would not abdicate their temple status.

He would never forget the grand celebration of the funeral that heralded his own ascension to the throne. His father had died of unknown sickness when he was young. Neither the *ashipu* magic shaman nor the *ashu* medical doctor could cure him. He was anointed with oil and interred in the large vault on an elaborate bed-like pallet along with his beloved wife, who joined her husband in death.

The funeral procession had begun at the palace gates. A small band of musicians led the funerary lamentation playing lyres, lutes, and harps. The deathbed with its king and queen followed the musicians, surrounded by six personal guards. Behind them trailed twenty ladies-in-waiting and fifty other servants. The crowd of citizens lined the streets to catch a glimpse of their deceased grand ruler. Once the procession arrived at the temple, they were escorted by an entourage of priests out of the public eye and down into the secret recesses below the ziggurat.

They were led into the large crypt, where the priest-king was laid in his sarcophagus. Then the entire train of guards and palace servants filled the chamber, drank a poison, lay down and embraced their fate in union with their lord and master. They were to follow him into the afterlife where they would continue to serve him. The guards were fully clothed in armor and the servants in golden headdresses with necklaces of cornelian and lapis lazuli. A second vault next to them contained some gold and other riches along with two chariots and onagers, also killed with poison. The crypts were then sealed and their occupants left as the city mourned publicly. Considering how gloomy and hopeless the "land of no return" was, Lugalanu was grateful to still be a part of the land of the living.

He imagined how grand and glorious his own burial would be with Emzara poisoned beside him along with his own staff of attendants.

Lugalanu and Ham finally reached their destination, a large set of doors in the dead end of an unassuming passageway. It was large enough to accommodate Nephilim.

Ham gulped with a mixture of excitement and fear.

Lugalanu turned to him and said, "You are about to enter the inner sanctum of the gods. Few humans will ever see what you are about to see. At no point are you to express anything other than wonder and awe. Should you be appalled or revolted by what you see, remember, you do not understand the wisdom of the gods. Their ways and their thoughts are as high above you as the heavens are above the earth. Is that understood?"

"Yes," said Ham. A shiver went down his spine. He wondered just what might cause him to be "appalled or revolted."

They entered the door and closed it behind them. They travelled through a hallway lined with seven cubit tall, recessed doorways. Lugalanu stopped at one of them and opened it. They stepped inside a long, narrow room, an infirmary sectioned off by rows of brick walls, creating small stalls for beds.

"This is the breeding room for the sacred women who bear the Nephilim for the gods," Lugalanu explained.

As they walked down the hallway of stalls, Ham saw beds full of very pregnant women, one to a stall. The women were restrained with leather straps or metal shackles, depending upon their level of risk. It seemed more like a prison than a breeding room.

Lugalanu answered Ham's unspoken question in a whispered tone, "These are the ones nearest to giving birth. At earlier stages of pregnancy they have much more freedom. But the final stage can be violently painful so they have to be restrained for their own good."

"What happens after birth?" Ham asked, innocently enough. He had known of women chosen for this holy high honor, but had never seen them again.

"Unfortunately, it kills them," said Lugalanu matter-of-factly. Lugalanu had always felt sorry for the women and their plight. He tried to comfort Ham with what he comforted himself often, "Death is just a doorway into higher service of the gods. In some ways, they are better off than us."

The women looked drugged, not as giddy and hopeful about their future as Lugalanu seemed to suggest. One of the women screamed in pain just as Ham and Lugalanu passed her stall. She writhed desperately in the bed, straining against her bonds. A few midwives ran to her with a bucket and rags. Ham stared with fascination, wanting to see what happened, but Lugalanu pulled him away.

He escorted Ham back out into the hallway. The piercing scream of the woman giving birth rang in Ham's ears and echoed through the corridors.

The next doorway led them into another long hallway of stalls. These compartments did not hold pregnant women. Instead there were various versions of human-animal chimeras that Ham already knew well, seeing them around the palace and temple grounds. They too were chained to the walls with straw for beds. These were new kinds he had not seen before and they appeared to be in varying stages of mutation or development. Some looked like they had body parts attached surgically, such as a human body with a pig's head in one stall and a huge pig's body with a human head in the next. Others appeared to be an essential fusion of kinds, such as a humanoid whose body was completely covered with hair and whose face looked as much like a wolf as it did a man. It lunged at Ham, snarling for his blood. Ham jumped back, but the chain jerked the wolf man back into its stall.

Other hybrid fusions looked more like developmental failures of miserable creatures with human bodies and malformed appendages or misshapen body structures. These were chimeras gone wrong. It was all a den of sorcery, an experimental chamber of breeding horrors.

Ham remembered Lugalanu's words, and suppressed his reaction with a sense of awe and wonder—and morbid curiosity. He could see the practical use for the bird-men soldiers and other creatures like the pazuzu and the crossbred throne guardians. But these monstrous miscegenations suggested a deeper strategy at work in the minds of the gods. Just what, he did not know.

Lugalanu could see the wheels churning in Ham's mind. He said simply, "You will learn soon enough, and it will all become clear."

They exited the chamber of horrors and stopped at a final doorway. Lugalanu wanted the importance to sink into Ham's consciousness. "This is the holy of holies. The secrets of the Watchers reside here. The very knowledge of heaven." He opened the door.

Inside was a large vault of potions and vials, jars and vases, strange structures whose technology seemed far advanced from Ham's known world. Ham had been taught the rudiments of Mesopotamian science. He knew taxonomic categories of plants and animals, astronomical and astrological systems, and drugs for use with medicine and sorcery. But the things in this room were like nothing Ham had ever seen.

He looked upon the rudimentary forms of biological and genetic experimental science, mysteries beyond his education. Because the Sons of God were divine beings, they had occultic knowledge of which humans could only dream. But as earth bound creatures, they were limited to the resources at hand. Drugs and potions created a certain amount of magic, but they knew biological alteration was more fundamental than that. So they sought the manipulation of that basic nature through a primitive form of genetics.

Ham became fixated on a series of glass jars before him. He had heard of glass when it was first introduced to the economy, but he had not seen any of it until now. He stared, fascinated. But what the jars held was even more spellbinding. Ten jars contained fetuses of varying development and at varying stages of transformation from human to something shiny, slender, and reptilian – like the gods.

"Are you impressed with my creations?" a voice said, behind Ham.

Ham started out of his trance-like stare. He turned to see the mighty Anu standing behind him. He dropped to the floor in worship. "Greatly, my lord and god, greatly," he gulped, his heart beating out of his chest.

Anu offered his hand to help him up. Ham did not know what to do. He had never touched the hand of a god.

Lugalanu whispered with humor, "Your god awaits."

"Please, stand," said Anu.

Ham took Anu's hand with fear and trembling, and stood before his god. The skin was cold, clammy and slightly scaly. But Anu was kind, gentle, and patient with Ham's nervousness. He smiled.

"You are to become an ensi high priest?"

"Eventually, almighty one. My next promotion is to sanga." Ham's voice cracked with trembling.

Anu smiled warmly. "Your loyalty shall be rewarded soon enough. And I hope you will find your initiation satisfying and calming to your fears." His voice was so compassionate Ham felt as if he spoke telepathically to his heart and mind.

"It is my intent to be found worthy of such a holy honor," said Ham.

"Well then, welcome to the secrets of the Watchers," said Anu.

"My Lord, if I may," began Ham.

Lugalanu had watched the exchange carefully. He could spot Emzara's feisty inquisitiveness in her son starting to show itself.

"How can I begin to understand such wonderful sorceries?"

Anu welcomed the curiosity. "That is where faith comes in. What were you taught in school about the creation of the heavens and the earth?"

Ham recited from memory the rote words he had learned from the temple scribes about *Inanna's Tale of the Huluppu Tree* and the *Eridu Genesis*, "The sky god, Anu, carried off the heavens, and the air god, Enlil, carried off the earth. The Queen of the Great Below, Ereshkigal, was given the underworld for her domain. And Anu, Enlil, Enki, and Ninhursag fashioned the dark-headed people of Sumer."

"Well done," smiled Anu. "And now I will tell you the truth. That creation story is a lie."

Ham's stomach dropped. What could he be saying? The Most High God and the Lord of the Air, did not separate the heavens from the earth?

"What you have been taught is a myth that is intended to protect humankind from what they could not understand. There are some truths that are so sacred only the most wise and most loyal are to be entrusted with them."

Ham swallowed. Lugalanu saw him sweating. He had cultivated this young man with great care. He had confidence that Ham would rise to the honor of this high calling.

Anu continued, "What do you know of the deity called Elohim?"

"A distant god of a lost Garden in Eden?" It was all he could muster, as if it was all he knew. But it was not all he knew.

Emzara had actually taught him much about Elohim, for she worshipped him in secret. She had constantly admonished Ham to worship him as well whenever they had their clandestine meetings. It was all rather distasteful to him. She spoke of Elohim creating the heavens and the earth; and of Adam of the earth and Havah his wife, the mother of all the living; of how they were images of Elohim on earth much like the statues of Anu and Inanna in the temple were images of the deities. She spoke of the Serpent, Nachash, the Shining One, a Watcher himself, who drew them away from Elohim in disobedience and how Elohim expelled them from the Garden, away from his presence. She had told him how Elohim revealed that a Chosen Seed would come who would end the rule of the gods and bring judgment upon the gods, and rest to the land. And that a king would come from his lineage that would ultimately destroy the seed of the Serpent.

It seemed like conspiratorial myth to Ham. Worse, it was treason to the gods. It was the one thing Ham worried deeply about regarding his dear mother. He wondered what inspired her to be so fanatically devoted to such delusionary rambling. What made her satisfied with slavery and poverty over the rich pleasures and glories of the Kingdom of Anu? And her commitment to a dead man who, she kept reminding Ham in secret, was his real father. The only father that Ham knew was his adopted father Lugalanu, who loved him and took care of him. *That* man was his father, and that man stood with Ham right now in the presence of deity, supporting his rite of passage into the secrets of the gods."

Anu brought Ham out of his thoughts. "Elohim is the true creator of heaven and earth."

The words jolted Ham out of the blue. He did not see it coming. Was Anu telling him right now that his mother was right? How could that possibly be? His entire view of the world was just turned inside out.

"But Elohim is an evil god," continued Anu. "He is a jealous and bitter old spirit." Anu paced around the room and launched upon a diatribe against the deity. "This so-called 'creator of heaven and earth' has hidden from mankind the secrets which you see before you this day. He has sought to keep humankind in bondage to ignorance, jealous of allowing them to become enlightened like himself. He has sought to keep everyone and everything separate. He separated light from dark, he separated heaven from earth, human from animal, male from female, *man from god*." Anu was histrionic in his delivery, but it served to underline his righteous indignation with such injustice.

"That is a rather selfish deity, would you not agree?" asked Anu.

"Yes, my lord," said Ham without thinking.

Anu stopped his pacing near the doorway. He sniffed the air. After a quizzical look, he returned to his pacing.

He had just missed discovering Neela, who hid on the other side of the open door. Anu had been close enough for her to reach around and touch him. She had managed to escape detection.

Anu concluded his tirade, explaining his plan. "But I bring new hope and change. I want to undo the separation, to erase the distinctions between creatures. I want to make all things into One." Anu bent down and looked into one of the jars of fetuses on the shelf. "By combining my seed with human seed, I will fundamentally transform humankind. I will create man in my image rather than in Elohim's image. I will give man his proper destiny. I will make man into a god."

All of Emzara's words came flooding into Ham's mind, causing doubts and fears. The prophecy of the Chosen Seed ending the rule of the gods and bringing the judgment of Elohim down upon their heads.

Anu drew Ham's attention to the jars of fetuses. "The Nephilim are the offspring of our union with the daughters of men. But I have been working on another way of combining our flesh with human flesh, in a way that may not be so obvious as our giant progeny." Anu could not describe in detail the molecular genetics to which he was referring. Mankind's knowledge and technology were not advanced enough yet for Ham to understand this. He would have to simplify the language. "Our goal is to breed a Naphil that would look like a normal human being. It would not be a giant, it would have ten fingers and ten toes, but it would have the heart and soul of a Naphil. It would be a demigod. It would carry in its blood the ability to breed a race of Nephilim that would spread across the land."

"Are these demigods among us?" asked Ham.

"Not yet," said Anu.

Ham cautiously ventured out, "And what of the Chosen Seed? Is the Revelation true? How can we fight it?"

For the first time in his sermon, Anu became visibly perturbed. It was not a secret that the Revelation was spreading about by word of mouth, first in the temple and palace and then within the city walls. It would soon be unavoidably known by every single soul.

"That is why the gods are seeking to create an alliance between all the cities," he answered, "to overcome our differences in a coalition of common purpose. Together, we will create an army of legions for war against the Seed of Havah."

Lugalanu saw these disclosures overwhelming Ham. He put his arm around him in support. "This is why we need leaders of your will to power," he said.

Anu continued, "If we cannot breed out this coming king, we will find the Chosen Seed by killing every last remnant of the nomadic tribes of humanity who do not worship the pantheon."

The seriousness of it all settled upon Ham.

Anu had moved near the door again. But this time, he spun like a coiled snake and reached around the doorway, pulling out a choking Neela by the neck.

"What is this eavesdropper slithering in the dark? A slender conspirator?!" shouted Anu, his voice booming with supernatural reverberation.

Neela stared mesmerized into Anu's penetrating cold blue eyes. He saw into her very soul. He sniffed her with relish and satisfaction, justified that he had caught her scent earlier. He released his grip around her neck.

Ham fell to his knees before Anu.

"My god, forgive me! She is my wife. I did not know she followed me."

Anu looked down on Ham, groveling at his feet.

"My god, she has not a conspiratorial bone in her body. She is recklessly curious. That is all. I beg of you, if you must punish, punish me instead."

This surprised Anu. Such love for such puny worth.

"Her curiosity brought her into your service many years ago. You honored her for it. Please remember your goodness in your name."

Anu tilted his head with interest. He had a vague recollection. He inhaled her scent deeply this time. A smile spread across his face. "The White Temple. I do remember. This is now the second time this little mouse has managed to scurry her way under the eye of the cobra."

Neela quivered. Immediate death no longer hovered over her. But it did not matter. She was a disobedient child caught with her hand in the fig jar.

Anu slowly smiled, and his warm lightheartedness returned. Neela could feel it in her own body relaxing.

"A curious wife you have, my priest. She is a willing subject. She will serve us both well."

Ham breathed a sigh of relief. But then a chill went through him when Anu took yet another intoxicating inhale of her scent into his nostrils.

CHAPTER 22

Noah and Uriel rode their horses at a canter into the Zagros Mountains about seventy leagues northeast of Erech. When they had escaped Sheol, the other archangels stayed behind to finish their task of binding the Rephaim. Uriel had explained to Noah that the archangels would get reinforcements and seek out the last of the human tribes in the West. A war was coming, a war of gods and men. The fallen Watchers had been planning it for a long while. They had seduced most of the people of the land into their sorceries and idolatries and were now determined to exterminate the rest. The only chance humanity had was for the angels to organize them to defend themselves. But getting the last of the human tribes to agree on anything was a nearly impossible project. Nevertheless, they had to try. It might take months to accomplish this goal, but other angels were sent out as well.

The one advantage of a war for the archangels was that if they could get all the Watchers together in an allied effort, it would enhance the angels' opportunity to bind the fallen into the heart of the earth as Elohim had commanded. Noah and Uriel discussed the possibilities of such an impossible task for a goodly portion of their trek through the plains and into the mountains. There were two hundred of the gods and they were not all mustered at Erech. Nevertheless, the most important leaders were and those were the priority for the archangels.

"Where is this Hidden Valley you keep speaking of?" Noah asked.

"If I told you, it would not be hidden," Uriel chortled.

Uriel had often reminisced about the old days when he, Methuselah, and Noah's mother and father had ended up in the Hidden Valley, hemmed in on all sides by natural formations making it virtually invisible to explorers. He would speak of their adventures being hunted by the cursed Cain's wolf tribe, and how they had triumphed over that man of wrath to live another day. There would be no lineage of demon dogs left in the Hidden Valley. He assured Noah they were all taken care of.

After days of riding, they sought one of the few secret passageways into the valley.

Noah said, "Strange that we are so close to the cities of the plain, yet they are unaware. Right under their filthy noses."

"I am sure the entrance is near here, as far as my memory serves me," said Uriel.

A deep bellowing roar interrupted them. It shook the very trees around them to the roots. Noah gaped at Uriel. This was a beast very large and very near.

"Did I forget to tell you, this is the realm of Behemoth?" quipped Uriel. "Do not worry, he is much too big to get through the pass."

"Well, that is comforting," shot back Noah snidely. "Have you ever seen Behemoth?" he asked.

Uriel said, "He is like Leviathan, but on land."

"Well, I hope you are happy," said Noah. "You succeeded in ruining my day."

"It is not that bad," added Uriel. "Behemoth only has one head."

"Oh, that makes it all better," said Noah.

Uriel *had* seen Behemoth. Uriel was there at the creation and was privileged to be a part of the morning stars who sang praises to Elohim when he laid the foundation of the earth, struck its line, determined the measurements and sunk its bases. He had gloried when Elohim created a firmament in the midst of the waters to separate the waters above from the waters below. He watched with awe as Elohim made the waters swarm with great sea monsters like Rahab and Leviathan, and let the earth bring forth living creatures according to their kind, creeping things and beasts of the earth, including Behemoth. The irony was not lost on him that creation was both wonderful and fearsome.

Uriel yelled, "Run for your life!" and kicked his horse.

Noah wondered if he was jesting again.

The colossal beast broke out of the forest near them. The hair on Noah's neck stood up and a shiver of terror surged down his spine. The creature was the size of a tall building, and it ran after them at full speed, the ground shaking beneath its trampling feet.

Noah only got a glimpse of its monstrous ugliness. In a flash, he galloped for his life after Uriel. All he saw was its huge trampling legs, its tail like a cedar tree, an ugly hump, and its bull-like head. Uriel was right. It was as terrible as a sea dragon on land.

The gargantuan gained on them.

Noah could see Uriel bearing straight for a vine covered wall of the rock bluff. He wondered what the angel was doing, placing them between a rock wall and a hard place.

Uriel yelled to him, "Trust me!"

Noah saw Uriel disappear into the wall vines without smashing to pieces. It was a hidden entrance. He glanced back to see Behemoth was almost upon him as he split the vines with his horse. The monstrosity hit the narrow opening and it felt like the entire mountain around them rattled. Uriel was right again. The beast was much too huge to fit through the pass. Thank Elohim.

Noah stared back at the raging creature. He could see one of its eyes was destroyed and laid over with scars.

Noah had learned of Behemoth from Methuselah. He never forgot the story his grandfather told him of the day he lost his precious wife Edna to this hideous monster. The creature protected its territory with ferocity. When Methuselah, Edna, and Noah's parents had first discovered this location, they did not know about Behemoth. It had attacked and killed Edna. Its size and strength were so overwhelming that Methuselah had only had the chance to blind it in one eye with a javelin before escaping into the pass. Nothing could pay back the devastation this monster wrought upon Methuselah. The event broke him. He was never the same again. At least Methuselah had been able to leave a permanent scar to remind the monster of the man who planned to one day return and kill it.

But Behemoth was still alive.

Noah wondered if that meant that Methuselah had not made it back here as they had agreed. It did not bode well for Noah's plans. Had Methuselah been killed by this land dragon?

They arrived at the end of the pass, where it opened up to the Hidden Valley. They both gasped, looking out onto a world seemingly lost in time. A lush valley of plants, trees, and animals spread before them, a place that could only be described as a jungle paradise.

"It reminds me of Eden," said Uriel.

"If it was," said Noah, "I would be dead by the sword of the Cherubim." He chuckled to himself, and they entered a pathway through the foliage.

Uriel knew it was coming, but did not anticipate such hostility.

A young warrior swung out of hiding on a vine. He knocked Noah off his horse to the ground, pushing Noah face down to the earth.

Uriel was off his horse in an instant. He stopped still when he saw the warrior with a dagger to Noah's throat. Beyond that first one, three others stood with bows drawn on Noah and Uriel. These warriors were good. They were trained well in stealth. They obviously had heard Behemoth's announcement of approaching intruders. They wore animal skins and they were all young, only about a hundred years old or so.

Lying on the ground, Noah stopped struggling when he felt the edge of the blade against his throat in a tight hold.

The warrior was strong. He belted out to his comrades, "They seem human enough!"

The lead archer spit through his aim, "Of course they do, Shem. Clever disguise for clever abominations."

Noah's eyes went wide. Those words were familiar; the name, the voice. He tried to get a better glimpse of his captor. "Shem? Shem ben Noah?"

It confused the young warrior with the dagger. The archer's surprise gave way to recognition.

Noah looked up at the young man with arrow aimed at his heart. "Japheth?" he pleaded.

Japheth, ever the impulsive one, responded first. "Father! I did not recognize you!"

Shem lowered his dagger, and turned Noah around. They looked into each other's eyes. No further doubt remained that they were father and son.

"It has been so long." Shem wrapped Noah in a big bear hug.

Japheth dropped his bow, ran and jumped onto the two of them, and they tumbled to the ground in a family wrestling match.

They rolled to a stop on the jungle floor.

"We thought you were dead!" shouted Japheth.

Noah looked them up and down with pride. "You have grown into such fine warriors."

"Uh, Noah," interrupted Uriel.

The three of them looked over at Uriel, still under the aim of the archers.

"May I request you share some of that familial love?" Uriel joked.

"Forgive me," laughed Shem. "Men, put down your arms."

The archers lowered their weapons with sighed relief.

"Father, where have you been?" asked Japheth.

"That is a long story," said Noah. "And I am hungry."

The warriors led Noah and Uriel to a large clearing in the center of the valley. As they broke through the jungle brush, Noah and Uriel stopped. The sight took their breath away. There were elaborate wooden homes, a couple hundred strong, scattered around in a small village, with families going about their business. A sight that amazed Noah towered behind the village. It was a huge wooden skeletal structure the size of a large rectangle building. A pile of cut, trimmed and cleaned trees, enough to build a small city sat within walking distance of the massive construction.

"Tebah?" said Noah.

Methuselah, Tubal-cain and Jubal ran to them from the village, shouting greetings.

They exchanged long overdue embraces, grabbing each other's wrists. Noah could not keep his eyes off of the structure.

"You are building the box?" he asked.

"Your sons and tribe are," said Methuselah, "in your name."

Methuselah pulled out a piece of leather with scratchings all over it. He handed it ceremoniously to Noah.

"You gave me the directions before your little vacation in Sheol all those years ago. Must this old man shame your dullness of memory?"

Noah grinned widely and hugged Methuselah again. "Old man, I missed you terribly." He looked at Tubal-cain. "I trust my cousin here has kept you in your place with his molten word and wit."

Methuselah harrumphed. "My dirty loin cloth, he did. I am too nimble for such a corpulent whale."

"I fear our feeble senior has lost more than his bowels," retorted Tubal-cain, circling his finger around his skull in a "crazy" gesture.

"I must say," Methuselah changed the attack, "I am impressed to see that your guardian angel has actually done his job for once in protecting your obstinate rump."

"It's good to be back with family," snorted Uriel, and they all laughed.

Uriel said to Methuselah, "I believe it was you who told me many years ago, you would like to retire here."

"Elohim has granted my wish," said Methuselah.

Noah looked around at the village. "Do not tell me," he said, "all these villagers are the remnant orphans of my tribe grown of age?"

"You have been away for a hundred years," Uriel reminded him.

Japheth added delightfully, "Elohim did say to be fruitful and multiply."

Suddenly, a small tremor shook the valley. It made them solemn again.

Tubal-cain said, "I have been timing them. They are increasing. Fortunately the mountain range around us absorbs most of the rattle, but out on the plain is another story."

"Birth pangs of Elohim's wrath," said Noah, repeating the words he had heard Uriel tell him in Erech.

Shem said, "We have been preparing the materials and waiting for you to return as Patriarch to finish your calling."

Noah looked at Shem's belt to see the leather case holding the whip sword Rahab at his side. He saw Betenos' bow on Japheth's back. Noah said to his sons, "I did not fulfill my promise to train you in your grandparents' weapons."

"Considering the nature of your delay, father" said Japheth, "we forgive you."

Methuselah interjected, "I did the best I could."

Shem concluded, "We are trained, we are speedy, and we are ready."

Noah looked at them with proud tears of joy. "Well, then, let me finish my calling."

"First," said Methuselah, "I want to show you something."

Methuselah took Noah alone to an ancient terebinth tree by a small brook in a dark corner of the forest. They stood before a pile of rocks placed by the tree long before. "Terebinth," said Methuselah. "They are considered sacred objects of communication with the divine.

"This is where she sleeps," he continued. "Your grandmother Edna. My happiness. It has been good for me to be back. It has reminded me that one day, we shall be united again."

Noah asked, "Why did you never remarry, Grandfather?"

Methuselah sighed with sadness. "Because I foolishly found my significance in being loved by her, rather than in us both being loved by Elohim."

Noah put his arm around his grandfather.

Methuselah said, "I wish you had met her. You would have loved her. You are a lot like her. Full of life, zeal, and a good warrior."

Noah said, "It is hard to imagine: 'Grandmother, the giant killer.'"

They laughed. "Let me tell you," said Methuselah, "She was a giant killer of a wife."

"Grandfather, it is hard to believe any woman could handle you," said Noah lightheartedly.

Methuselah chuckled, "I am surprised I could handle her."

"Why have you not killed Behemoth?" asked Noah, referring to the source of his unhappiness.

Methuselah completed Noah's sentence slyly, "Yet."

Noah looked at him curiously.

Methuselah explained, "While we reside in this valley, that vile creature acts as a guard dog for our security. I would be a fool to settle my score without consideration of the consequences. But when the wrath of Elohim comes, I will have my satisfaction."

Noah wondered if he meant that Elohim's wrath would *be* that satisfaction or if Methuselah still had designs on the beast. He did not want to feed the hurt, so he avoided asking.

CHAPTER 23

It had taken years to prepare for building the tebah. Methuselah had led the tribe as they grew of age. He patiently taught them the construction skills they needed to build the box. They had honed their talent by building elaborate village homes of wood that provided the added blessing of luxurious living. They found a peculiar tree of very hard wood in the valley they called "gopher wood." It was a long process to cut down the trees and create long, cured and glued planks. The boards were then sealed with a prime coating of tree pitch. The pitch was made by bleeding the sap from pines, burning the pine wood into charcoal, grinding that to powder, and mixing that powder into large vats of boiling pine resin. They then painted the wood with the tree-made pitch to seal it with an initial coat.

The day Noah took charge of construction, they had already built the skeletal structure for the box based on the directions of the holy writ given from God to Noah, and then to Methuselah on leather. Everything stood ready. They needed only to begin the process of final construction. It could be completed within months if things went well.

They had perfected a means of holding the beams together by pounding wooden pins into them. They had found bitumen pits nearby for the final layer of pitch to cover the wood of the completed box with a one or two inch thickness. Noah drove them hard to finish quickly, but he never asked of any man what he was not willing to do himself. Often, men sought him with some question to be answered, only to find him hammering in wooden pegs or helping to saw a plank to fit better. They all worked in shifts from sun up to past sundown, using torches made from the bitumen pitch after dark fall.

As Noah looked out onto the valley from the top of the box, he remembered what Uriel had said when they first arrived, how it had looked like Eden. He pondered what it was like for the Man and Woman to be in such communion with Elohim, their fellow creatures, and the world around them, full of splendor and glory. He wondered what it would be like to be in

Elohim's presence and the presence of his divine council of ten thousands of holy ones surrounding his throne and worshipping in the Garden that was his temple. He grieved over how the primordial sin of the first pair had plunged them into darkness, and separated them from their Maker, the Most High, and how the world could have all gone so wrong so quickly.

It was crazy to be building a huge barge like this in the middle of the Zagros Mountains, leagues away from any river or body of water. But Elohim said he was going to judge the land and all its inhabitants and this would be his vessel of salvation; this tebah. Elohim had become sorry he had created mankind, for all flesh had corrupted their way on the earth, and the land was filled with violence through them, and the violence raised its voice to the ears of Elohim in heaven. So he had determined to make an end to all flesh. He would send a deluge of water to blot out man whom he had created from the face of the land, man and all the animals in its wake. This floating box would be Elohim's redemption of a righteous few. Noah did all that the Lord commanded him.

Inside the barge, the structure was organized into three decks lined with a multitude of pens. Ventilation was a long top housing that ran the length of the box, a roofed opening a cubit high, with a hatch for bad weather. The people wondered why the boat was so large, far exceeding the capacity for their few hundred bodies on board. Then Noah told them that God was going to bring animals of every kind from the remotest parts of the land in pairs and in sevens to reside on the boat with them. They did not believe this, until the day when animals of all kinds started to arrive in the valley in numbers, ready to board the box. The carnivores were surprisingly domesticated and would not eat flesh, instead grazing like the herbivores beside them. Methuselah joked that Uriel had hypnotized them with magic. Lions, tigers, and wolves lounged right next to lambs, oxen, and camels. It was another miracle but it would not be the last.

How would they take care of the refuse of all these animals filling up the box? Their excrement alone would pile up within days and create toxic fumes that could kill all the life on board. Tubal-cain and Jubal created a way to use the waste to their advantage. They built a large, closed-off holding tank at the stern of the boat that rose through all three floors. They had discovered that the gases released by the rotting defecation were flammable. So they created a piping system from the refuse tank throughout the craft. Small holes in the pipes allowed them to light the releasing gas. This created a perpetual light source for as long as the animals defecated, which would be as long as Elohim had them on the boat.

What caused Noah the most consternation was the change in the heavens. The earthquakes shook the pillars of the earth and went wide enough to even rattle the pillars of the firmament. The sky changed colors. Even the sun would turn blood red as it set in the gates of the West. Noah noticed an increase of storm clouds on the horizon, distant thunder portending a coming apocalypse. But this was not a time to brood. They finally finished the construction of the box and filled it with the animals.

It was a time to celebrate.

CHAPTER 24

Ham slipped quietly through the underground tunnel between the two temples. This was not the tunnel for temple staff. It was one of the secret passageways known only to him and few others. He was on a covert mission. The tunnel soon joined a passageway into the temple hallways near Lugalanu's private staff quarters. He looked both ways. It was clear. He scurried up to a locked door and softly rapped on the wood with a deliberate coded knock. A young maidservant opened the door and let him in.

Ham's words were immediate and frustrated, "Mother, please."

Inside, Emzara stood with three fugitive slaves, each carrying small bundles for travel. They saw Ham and withdrew in fear.

"Now, see, my son, you have frightened them. It is all right, children. Ham will not betray you."

Ham snapped testily, "Do not be too sure of yourself. Three fugitives at once? Must you tempt fate so?"

"These three are images of God and they have names. Ham, meet Rami, Biran and Hannah."

The first two were young men. Hannah was pregnant. The three bowed before Ham, who gave Emzara an angry look.

"My given temple name is Canaanu, mother."

"Oh, do not fret yourself," said Emzara. "It is not a sin for them to know the true identity of their liberators, the house of Noah ben Lamech." They knew Ham was the holy sanga, the administrative priest just under the ensi high priest. Ham had received the promotion earlier and was being groomed to become the ensi under Lugalanu.

Ham nodded awkwardly. He did not hate them, but he was not used to treating servants as special human beings in God's image as his mother did. In his understanding, slaves were but shadows of men who were in the image of kings, and only kings were in the image of the gods. But that was an ongoing dispute he had with his mother and it was not going to be settled any time soon.

"Mother, every time I visit you in secret, I endanger my temple status. But you increase my peril when you smuggle out servants like this. You know what the penalty is."

Emzara knew. The penalty was death, quick and sure, without legal proceedings. She remembered Alittum's horrible demise, but thought it was worth the rescue of the innocent.

"I am helping them to freedom and new life," replied Emzara, "away from *here*." Her words came bitterly. "Here" was still not in her heart and soul as it was in Ham's.

She strode past Ham, drawing the fugitives along. At the door, she handed them each bread cakes. They wrapped the cakes and placed them in their bundles. She looked at each of them and gave them an embrace and a prayer, "May Elohim guide you and protect you to safety."

She opened the door and checked for clear, then led them out into the hallway. Ham followed her, irritated.

"Why can you not accept your place in this world?" he whispered harshly to her.

"Because we are not of this world, you and I."

"*This* world," sputtered Ham, "has granted us riches, privilege, royalty. Would you prefer being a wandering nomad in the wilderness?"

Emzara stopped in the middle of the hallway and glared at Ham with moist eyes. She did not say a word, but he knew what she thought. Of course she would prefer to be so.

"Forgive me," said Ham. "Your past is not my own."

He could see she held back a torrent of emotion. "You are the son of Noah ben Lamech, son of Enoch," she said.

"I am the adopted ward of Lugalanu, priest-king of Anu. *He* has raised me. *He* has been a father to me."

"*Your father* ended in Sheol by the hand of Lugalanu."

Emzara continued onward, as if walking away from him.

He followed after her with zeal and complaint. As much as he loved her, Ham could not understand his mother's hardness of heart. In the world they inhabited, men killed other men in war and took their wives with every battle. The fact that Lugalanu would not force her and waited for her was nothing short of grace in Ham's understanding.

"He has begged for your forgiveness. Sought atonement. But you have spurned him."

Emzara's heart had bled for her son from the day he was taken from her. She did not hold it against him. How could he know the goodness that was hidden from him? She had taught him of Elohim as best she could with the few visits she could get through the years. But what chance did she have with a system of idolatry that controlled his every waking moment from the education he received to the entertainment he imbibed? Nevertheless, she knew he was in God's image. She knew he had a conscience. He was Ham *ben Noah*.

"We become the choices we make in this life, Ham. I pray you consider the choices you are making—and their consequences," she whispered.

Ham sighed. She had that look that could penetrate his soul. It was at moments like this that he would question everything he knew. Though she was a bit crazy, she had something deep inside her that was utterly and truly real. And he wanted it. But he just could not forsake the life he had worked so hard to achieve, a life of such royal pedigree and future. And for what? A phantasm of a man who was supposed to be his father, and a god who did not show himself but only spoke to foolish prophets?

They arrived at the secret passageway and moved the stone enough for Hannah to slip through with her pregnant belly.

Before they could continue, they heard hurried footsteps down the hall. Ham reflexively pushed the stone closed as they turned to face a dozen temple guards pointing spears at the four of them.

Ham gathered his confidence and chastised the guards, "What is the meaning of this foolishness? Down with your weapons! I am the sanga priest."

They did not put down their weapons. They jammed the blades closer to their throats and chests.

Lugalanu marched through their midst and up to the new captives. He looked disappointedly at the slaves who had already wet themselves with fear. "I was wondering where you two were," he said with sarcasm.

"Take them…" he was interrupted in his words by Emzara's look. He almost said "take them to the block," the chopping block where their heads would roll from their shoulders. Instead he said, "Take them away." Emzara's goodness still had a way of melting him.

Three guards moved the slaves roughly away as Lugalanu led the others down the hallway to his own quarters.

It seemed like an eternity to Emzara, She wondered if they were being led to their execution. Instead, they found themselves alone in Lugalanu's private quarters.

He turned and stared silently at both Emzara and Ham, as if they were a couple of children about to be punished with the rod. But this was far more serious. Not a rod but an axe would be their fate.

Finally, Lugalanu spoke up, "I will not report this to the gods. Neither of you will be executed."

A shock went through both Ham and Emzara. He was sparing their lives?

Indeed, he was sparing their lives. Lugalanu had been waiting for this one thing. He could not have asked for a better opportunity than to catch them both in such a compromising position, placing them at his mercy. Quite frankly, he was tired of being merciful. He knew Emzara had been having secret contact with Ham throughout the years. He knew that Ham loved her and would not turn her in for her treachery of freeing slaves. But for Ham this was surely a loyalty to blood, rather than treason to the gods. Besides, revenge against Elohim's Chosen Seed would not be complete in death, but in conversion of his seed. It had been to Lugalanu's advantage to let them develop their secret familial love for one another.

"In seven days' time, we will celebrate Akitu," he said. "Canaanu will be initiated into the high priesthood. You will no longer call him Ham." He looked with firmness at Emzara. "And you will consent to be my loyal and willing wife."

Then it all made sense to her. In order to save Ham's life, Emzara would without question give her own, even if it was to such humiliation and defilement. Ham would perform his duty completely, to protect his mother. Lugalanu would own them both. It would not be a true willingness of her own, but she knew it would be close enough for Lugalanu's purposes, after all these years. Emzara's eyes went moist with tears. What had she done?

Akitu was the New Year harvest festival that began on the first of the year in the month of Nissan. It consisted of twelve days of ritual and celebration. It was a time for the priest-king to have his scepter of power renewed by the gods, as well as time for the initiation of priests. Ham would become the ensi high priest below Lugalanu at this very festival, but one week away.

This year was going to be a special Akitu. The pantheon of gods planned to come from all the cities of the plain and meet in Erech in divine council—

the seven who decreed fate. The Tablet of Destinies would be brought out and the gods would decide the fates for the coming year. They were also bringing their armies to encamp around the city, fully dressed for war. Why? Was this just for pageantry or did the gods have plans they had not yet revealed?

Another earthquake shook the temple. Dust fell on Emzara's head from above. It seemed the very foundations of the earth were being shaken. Did these signs in the sky above and the earth beneath have something to do with this gathering?

CHAPTER 25

Noah's tribe celebrated for several days with feasting and dancing. It was early evening. A fatted calf roasted on a fire spit as Noah and his men deliberated in council. Methuselah slouched beside him, along with Shem, Japheth, Tubal-cain, and Jubal.

Earlier in the day, a stranger had arrived in the Hidden Valley. He turned out to be an angel with a message for Uriel, who was finally revealing to the men the import of the dispatch.

"The judgment of Elohim is nigh," said Uriel with a sobered look. "The archangels have mustered the last of the human tribes. They will be at the city walls of Erech by the time of the New Year Festival."

"How many?" asked Noah. He saw Uriel hesitate.

"About two thousand strong."

Noah closed his eyes in despair.

"Do you jest?" blurted Tubal-cain. "The armies of six gods will be assembled on the plains surrounding Erech. That would be upwards of twenty thousand soldiers."

Silence gripped them all. They were too stunned to know what to say next. But not Shem.

"We are ready for war," said Shem with a confident voice.

Japheth picked up Noah's sword from where it leaned against the table. He raised it high. "A sword for the Lord, and for Noah ben Lamech."

"No," stopped Noah. "The family of Noah will enter the tebah as Elohim has commanded."

Shem frowned indignantly. "You would withdraw? You would have us be cowards?"

"Obedience to Elohim is not cowardice," said Noah. He spoke with a new wisdom.

"What has changed in you, father?" asked Japheth. "You have always been a man who would die for righteousness and freedom of your soul. But now…"

"But now," interrupted Noah, "I will *live* for the righteousness of Elohim and the freedom of future generations."

Methuselah, Tubal-cain, and Jubal knew exactly what Noah was talking about, and they knew he was right. They fully understood that the most selfless, most courageous thing for Noah to do, the *only* courageous thing to do would be to save himself for his bloodline to survive. He was the Chosen Seed of Havah, through whom would come the King of victory over the Seed of Nachash. It must continue according to Elohim's plan.

Noah's sons were not so quick to wisdom. "I do not understand this," complained Shem. "I do not understand Elohim and his plans."

"Neither do I," said Noah. "But I do trust him. And that is all I have in this world."

They all could see that the leader standing before them was a different man than the one some had journeyed with to Sheol and back. None of them were the same.

The arrival of three horsemen from the tribe interrupted the discussion. They were scouts seeking intelligence on the armies assembling at Erech. One of them carried a pregnant woman on his horse. He helped her down. The scout looked somberly at Noah. "The armies of the gods are encamped outside the city walls. It is worse than we anticipated."

Noah stared at the pregnant woman dressed in servant's clothes and bearing the brand of Anu on her wrist. "And who is this?" he asked.

"We found her in the wilderness outside the city," replied the scout.

Noah's tenderness reached out to her. "What is your name, child?

"Hannah."

"What were you doing outside the city limits?"

She was a bit fearful still. "Escaping from the temple palace."

"By what means?"

She handed Noah the hand drawn map of the underground tunnels and the direction to the Zagros. "A woman in the temple employ."

Methusclah jumped in, "Would that not be treason? Who could that be?"

"Nindannum," she replied. "Chief maidservant of the priest-king Lugalanu."

"Is this Nindannum a captured slave?" Noah knew chief stewards and maidservants were usually older.

"Yes," Hannah said. "She often whispers of her husband killed by the high priest's forces. Noah ben Lamech."

Noah's breath stopped. Sudden silence gripped the gathered men.

Noah's knees gave out. Shem and Japheth caught him. But they almost lost their own footing as well with the shock.

"Emzara is alive?" asked Noah, as if to Elohim himself.

Hannah did not know who she was talking to, but she was excited to have a connection. "She has a son," she blurted out.

"What is his name?" asked Noah.

"He is called Canaanu in the palace. But his mother calls him Ham."

Noah sat down. "My wife, my son," he said to himself. "Ham." The word flowed affectionately from his lips.

"My baby!" screamed Hannah. She gripped her huge pregnant belly in pain, and then clutched a magic amulet around her neck. The water broke at her feet.

Hannah was taken into a house of birthing. Midwives surrounded her, attending to her needs behind a curtained area lit by candlelight. She screamed and struck out at one of the midwives, who fell to the floor from the force of the blow. But she continued to grasp her little magic amulet and mumbled a birth incantation to the moon-god. It was to no avail.

"The infant is too large," cried one of the midwives. "We cannot deliver it."

Hannah's belly had been abnormally large and it appeared that her birth would be a serious danger to both mother and child.

Noah, Methuselah and Uriel stood in the room by the doorway. "Do all you can," said Noah. "The tribe is praying."

The midwives did the best they could to calm Hannah and make her comfortable. The outcome was in Elohim's hands.

Uriel could tell that Noah's thoughts were far away, on something else. He looked angrily at Noah. "Do not do this, Noah."

"Emzara is my wife, Uriel."

"It is not Elohim's will."

"Elohim's will is that my family find refuge in the box. Do you suggest I go without them?"

Methuselah butted in, "If you try to rescue her, you will be captured and executed."

"Methuselah," chided Noah, "I am surprised at you. Where is your faith?"

An inhuman scream of pain from Hannah interrupted them. The midwives backed away, staggering through the curtain.

Noah and the others could see Hannah's body spasming violently. Then she stopped dead. Before anyone could move, they saw her belly rip open. What should have been her infant rose out of her torn body. It was twice the size of a normal infant. But it was not human. It was a Naphil. It made an unholy screech and began to feed on the corpse of its own mother.

Noah drew his sword and strode swiftly to the bed.

Behind him, Shem yelled, "Abomination!"

Noah whipped aside the remaining shred of curtain. The Naphil infant was ugly as it was evil. It had snake eyes and a hairless reddish gray skin color with six fingered hands. It screeched at Noah, baring its newborn monstrous teeth.

Noah swung his sword and cut off the creature's hideous little head.

He turned back to Uriel with a justified expression. In measured tone, holding back a flood of righteous wrath, he declared, "I will not leave my wife and son to this wickedness."

"We are going with you," said Shem.

"In the name of all that is holy," added Japheth.

For the first time since creation, Uriel had nothing to say.

Noah, Shem, and Japheth mounted their horses at the edge of the village. Uriel, Methuselah, Tubal-cain, and Jubal saw them off. Noah grasped the map that Hannah had followed out of the temple and city. The exit point was a small cave opening in a butte outside the city. "We will enter the city through the servant's escape route."

Uriel looked up at him. "I have discharged my duty. I protected you to accomplish your calling. The box is built. I must now help lead the armies of man to a war that you will certainly be caught in the middle of."

Noah smiled. "Fear not, Uriel, Elohim is the God of the impossible."

Uriel would not let that one go. "He is God of impossible *men*."

Noah grinned, grabbed wrists with him. "My guardian, my protector."

"My friend," finished Uriel with the first tear in his eye Noah had ever seen.

He rode away with his sons into the forest.

Uriel turned to Methuselah and Tubal-cain.

"The time has come. We ready for the morning."

CHAPTER 26

They reached the plains outside Erech at a quick pace. Noah, Shem, and Japheth found the outcropping of rock that was on the map. They hid their horses and slipped into the entrance. After going through the Gate of Ganzir and the Abyss, this long dark tunnel seemed a minor inconvenience to Noah.

Outside, past the river, the armies of the gods camped in military order. They filled the fields around the city and river like a massive hive of soldier ants.

Twenty cubits below the milling armies, Noah, Shem, and Japheth slithered through the catacomb tunnels on their way to rescue Emzara and Ham from their prison of paganism. From the moment he had discovered that Emzara was alive, Noah could not sleep. He could barely eat. His mind burned with desire to be united with his beloved. What had she endured all these years without him? He could barely contain the pain of knowing that she was alone in a world of evil without his protection and love to give her life—for her to give him life. Did they torture her? Would he have to carry her through great loss of her own dignity? And a son. A son! She named him Ham. Ham *ben Noah*. What had he grown into? Was he a soldier? A servant? A craftsman? Had he been corrupted by the world that enslaved him? The questions would not stop invading his mind as he traversed the shadows of the hewn caves lit by their pitch-covered torches.

Then Noah stopped. He thought he heard something. He looked back at Shem and Japheth. They nodded. They had heard it too. They strained to listen for another sound. There was none.

"The rock must be settling from the mass of godless minions above us," said Noah. He waved them on.

Without warning, Shem and Japheth were both lifted off the ground by their necks.

Noah turned to see an eight cubit tall Naphil grasping his sons by their throats. They clutched at the six fingered hands choking them to death.

Noah drew his sword. It was pitifully small compared to the ogre before him. The creature was a Naphil, but not a soldier of any kind. Its skin seemed as dirty as the rock around them. It seemed more like a cave troll, something sent to live down here to do precisely what it was doing to Noah and his sons, catch intruders and eat them.

The monster snarled at Noah and stepped forward. His sons had seconds before their larynxes would be crushed.

Noah yelled a battle cry and prepared to fight to his death.

The Naphil arched back in response to Noah's scream. It stumbled backward and dropped Shem and Japheth. It tumbled to the ground. The young men landed hard and rolled out of the way, gasping for breath. They marveled that a mere scream should frighten a Naphil. How could that be?

The Naphil clawed at its own neck, grasping at some invisible object. It whirled.

Noah saw the true cause of their good fortune: Uriel had jumped on its back. He was strangling it with the unbreakable binding cord he used on Watchers.

The Naphil spun around, unsuccessfully trying to grab the archangel just out of his brawny reach. It backed up against the tunnel wall trying to crush its nemesis into the rock. But its nemesis was not human. Like a lock-jawed crocodile, Uriel would not let go. The Naphil grew weaker. But these creatures did not die easily. They could go without air much longer than any human.

The Naphil had lost control of its defenses while focusing on its attacker.

Noah, Shem, and Japheth grabbed their swords. They found their opening to thrust the weapons into the Naphil's abdomen and sternum. The Naphil gave a choked scream. It fell to its knees, and then to its face on the ground. Uriel quickly drew his two daggers and plunged them into the monster's ears on both sides and right into its brain.

For the first time in battle, Noah saw Uriel catching his breath. Fighting a Naphil was extremely difficult, even for an archangel.

Uriel looked up at Noah and said blithely, "I knew you would still need me."

Shem and Japheth massaged their necks.

"I thought I got rid of you, pestering guardian angel," smiled Noah. But he sobered quickly. "What about the war?"

"Methuselah will make a fine general," said Uriel. "He is almost as old as I am."

Shem and Japheth were able to smile again.

"Well, we have to hurry," said Noah. "It appears the escape route is no longer a secret."

Two soldiers guarded the hallway outside Emzara's quarters. She would not have the freedom she previously treasured.

The secret passageway opened a crack, just a few cubits away from them. It caught their attention. They readied their spears and approached the opening. Anything that came through that passage would not live long enough to know what happened to it.

But nothing came.

Cautiously, they slipped into the darkness with their weapons ready.

They were both clubbed to the ground by Shem and Japheth.

"What do they teach these numskulls?" whispered Shem.

Noah hushed him. He led them into the hallway. They sought the doorway that matched the one on the map. Noah's heart pounded with excitement and a heightened awareness of danger. When they found the door, they used the special knock that Hannah had shown them.

Emzara was visiting with Ham when they heard the rap on the door. Emzara clicked her tongue for the maidservant to answer the door. Ham slipped silently behind one of the large pillars by the fireplace. Who could be visiting like this? Since they had been caught, no one had used the secret knock or tunnels until now. It would have been stupid. Was this a trick?

The maidservant brought Noah and his sons into the room. Emzara knew it was not a trick. It was a miracle from God in heaven above.

"Utnapishtim, you are alive!" she gasped.

"My Naamah," said Noah. They walked straight into each other's arms. They kissed boldly, desperately. She could not stop saying over and over again, "You are alive. You are alive."

Noah pulled her back. "And our sons."

Then Emzara noticed them behind Noah. They stepped forward with tearful eyes.

Emzara fainted.

When she awoke, she saw the faces of Shem and Japheth staring at her.

"My sons," she said, "back from the dead."

They moved in close to kiss their mother. She ran her hand down their rough cheeks. She held onto their arms.

"You have grown," she said simply.

Noah could not help it. His joy brought out his humor again. "You have aged," he threw in.

It was true. She had—gracefully, but she had. She looked closer at him. "You have not."

It disturbed her. Was he a phantasm? Was this all a dream-vision?

"It is a long story," said Noah. "But I will never let you go again."

She saw the beaten copper bracelet on Noah's wrist and smiled. "My husband, you never did."

She looked past them to the pillar in the corner. "Ham."

Noah, Shem, and Japheth turned. Ham stepped cautiously from behind the pillar.

"Ham, these are your father and brothers, Shem and Japheth."

Shem and Japheth gave an uneasy nod. But Ham stared at Noah.

It was strange for all of them. Ham was hairless, with temple tattoos, and an elongated head. The men before him were hairy, bearded humans in animal skins worthy of slaves. Noah had prepared them for this possibility. And it did not matter to him.

"My son. My son," said Noah. He stepped up to Ham, looking at him. He was not sure what to do.

Ham broke down in tears.

Noah moved closer and embraced his lost son, the son he could not save, the son he was not around to raise, to teach how to lead and fight, and how to love; the son who was stolen from him and violated by an evil god.

Ham cried like a child in Noah's arms. It was as if he had reverted to the childhood he lost.

Noah shared his tears. "We have come to bring you home."

Japheth jumped in a bit too eagerly. "A war of gods and men is brewing. The human tribes are amassing for assault on the city."

Ham snapped out of his emotion almost instantly. "Are they led by the Chosen Seed?"

The others exchanged uneasy looks. Ham could not understand what it meant.

"I am the Chosen Seed," said Noah.

Ham stepped back in shock. "*You* will end the rule of the gods?"

"Exactly my reaction," said Uriel, stepping out from behind everyone.

"Meet Uriel," said Noah, "my guardian angel."

It was almost too much for Ham all at once.

Noah continued, "The judgment of Elohim is coming upon the land. This family is to be spared, and you are a part of this family."

Ham looked away in retreat.

"Husband," said Emzara, "our son's past is not our own. He is a stranger to Elohim."

Ham felt like a total outsider at that moment. Then Noah smiled at him and slapped him on the back. "Sometimes, I too feel a stranger to Elohim. We shall get along well, you and I."

Ham blurted out, "My wife, Neela. She is in the temple of Inanna."

Noah looked at them all and gave a shrug. "Well, then, we shall have to go get her."

They needed to move quickly. Ham went to retrieve his wife from her bedchamber. Emzara led Noah, Uriel, Shem, and Japheth to the courtyard of Inanna. They did not want to chance another encounter with a Naphil guarding the tunnels below. They decided to do the one thing that no one would expect. They would simply walk right out the front door of Inanna's Temple district, right under their filthy noses.

They met in the garden area. Neela was overwhelmed to meet her true Father- and brothers-in-law, men of whom she had only heard stories. Now, here they were before her, in the flesh, ready to take her away from everything she had known and into a new world of danger and the unknown. She hesitated at first. But she loved her husband so terribly that she would go to the very gates of Sheol if he asked her. He was a good man, a devoted husband and lover. She could see that the way he treated his mother was proof of a man she could trust, who would love his wife and family as deeply as he loved life. It was the only point of departure from his obedience to the gods. Still, she wondered how he could give up the royalty, the privilege, and the security of this, the only life that they had known.

They crossed the open courtyard under the moonlit night. Ham was well known by sight, which would create enough of a diversion for them to take the gate guards by surprise.

A Naphil warrior jumped down from the gate into their path.

Uriel drew his swords and stepped in front of Noah.

The Naphil snarled and held his mace at the ready.

The circle tightened. They all drew their weapons, pulling Neela and Emzara into the middle for protection. Shem's sword Rahab unfurled in his hands, ready to strike like a cobra. Japheth's bow was drawn and ready for attack.

It was futile.

Nephilim started jumping from the courtyard roof all around them, hemming them in—ten Nephilim in all.

Noah looked to Uriel. The angel shook his head. It would be a slaughter.

Ham backed away from them, drawing Neela with him.

Everyone noticed. Noah felt a stab of pain deep in his kidneys.

Shem spit it out first, "Ham? You betrayed us?"

Shem stepped toward Ham, preparing to whip Rahab in his direction.

Noah shouted, "Shem!"

A Naphil stepped in between them, blocking the attack.

It was all over before it had even begun.

Ham stated simply, "My name is Canaanu." He pulled Neela close to him and walked away.

CHAPTER 27

A pair of Nephilim dragged Noah roughly up the long stairway to the heavens of Anu's temple. The chains hanging from his limbs made the climb exhausting. Swirling clouds and flashes of occasional lightning with booming thunder made a sea of turmoil on the horizon. It was getting closer. An earthquake shook the city and temple. Noah and his guards stumbled, regaining their balance.

At the top of the White Temple, the guards ushered Noah into the sanctuary and into the presence of Anu and Inanna. They sat on thrones, guarded by their bull-man and lion-man aladlammu. Noah expected them, but he was not prepared to see what was off to the side of the thrones.

Uriel hung from the ceiling. He was upside down, bound and chained like a animal for slaughter. He was so badly beaten, Noah could barely recognize him.

Anu saw Noah's reaction. "If he were human, he would be dead. But alas, he is not human."

Noah remembered that angels could not die. They could suffer, feel pain, and even experience limitations of the flesh this side of the heavenlies, but they could not expire. Uriel barely held to consciousness. He let out a groan.

The sound pierced through Noah's soul. This archangel, this warrior who had sacrificed all for Noah, now hung like a captured animal for slaughter because of the recklessness of Noah's own choices. What had he done?

"Noah ben Lamech," Anu interrupted Noah's thoughts, "the Chosen Seed. I was ready to wage war to find you. Yet, here you are, delivered if you will, by the very hands of Elohim."

Noah hated this evil miscreant with every fiber of his being.

Anu's chin rose pompously in contempt, a common pose for him. He gestured flamboyantly with his hand. "Welcome to my holy temple. I am Anu, the supreme god, king of kings, and lord of lords. My consort, Inanna, Queen of heaven and earth." He paused ceremoniously with an arrogant grin. "But you already knew that."

Then, the mocking stab, "So, where is *your* god?"

Noah would not dignify the remark. Instead, he prophesied, "I know who you are, Semjaza and Azazel, fallen Sons of God. You have laid the nations low, you sit on the mount of assembly, you have made yourselves like the Most High. But you will be brought down to Sheol."

Inanna broke in bitterly, "He imagines himself a prophet now, and privy to the Watchers' secrets."

Anu chuckled in mockery, "I shall call you 'Atrahasis,' 'exceedingly wise one.' Or would you prefer, 'Ziusudra,' 'He of immortality,' since you fancy yourself a slayer of gods?"

"WHERE IS YOUR GOD?" Inanna interrupted with a roar, her voice echoing like thunder through the temple mount and in Noah's ears.

Noah would not answer.

Another groan from Uriel drew their attention. His parched lips parted enough to force out a few words with great effort. "Elohim—is—coming."

Anu would not tolerate any more of Uriel's insolence. He rose from his throne and strode over to Uriel's vulnerable form. He picked up one of his swords and promptly cut off Uriel's head.

Noah screamed, "NOOO!" He lunged toward Anu ready to kill him with his bare hands, but the Nephilim held him back from his futile gesture.

Inanna snickered, "That will shut him up."

Anu spoke to two servants watching Uriel, "Throw the body in the dungeon. Keep it away from the head. Archangels have a nasty habit of regeneration." He reconsidered. "On second thought, give me the head. I will keep it with me."

One of the servants brought Uriel's head to Anu. He grabbed it by the hair and looked into Uriel's face. He turned it to show it to Noah.

Noah gasped. Uriel's eyes found Noah's. He was still alive. He could not speak because his vocal cords had been severed from his lungs. But their eyes made a connection far deeper than words.

The servants cut down Uriel's body and took it away. Anu placed the head on the floor next to him.

Lugalanu and Ham entered from the rear of the temple. They were dressed in the royal robes of the priest-king and soon-to-be ensi high priest. At

Lugalanu's other side was his new consort, Emzara, bedecked in splendid queenly robes.

Ham could not look at Noah. But Emzara would not take her eyes off him. Noah knew exactly what she was saying to him: she was and always would be only his alone. A silent tear of vengeance slid down Noah's cheek.

Anu announced, "Ah, my faithful priest-king and his entourage."

Lugalanu and Ham took their place beside the thrones and bowed to Anu and Inanna.

Anu proclaimed with characteristic self-importance, "Tomorrow is Akitu, the New Year festival. The gods of the land will convene in divine council. Canaanu will become a high priest of Inanna. Lugalanu will marry this woman, Nindannum, who I understand has some relation to you, my captive?" It was a rhetorical question designed to twist the dagger in Noah's liver rather than receive an answer.

Emzara's expression plead with Noah for rescue. But rescue was not forthcoming.

"As rite of passage," continued Anu, "the new high priest's charge will be to sacrifice the Chosen Seed to the pantheon."

Emzara looked at Ham with horror. She had not known this monstrous plan.

Ham could only look down in shame. But he knew his place and his need for affirmation of devotion. He looked back up. He raised his chin high in royal emulation of Anu's own conceit. Lugalanu beamed with pride.

Noah's eyes blurred with the sting of betrayal. He could not believe his son would do such a thing. It defied his comprehension. His son had been ripped from his family culture and tradition, raised in a world of slavish idolatry, but still, how could one do such a thing to his own flesh and blood?

Inanna had the last word, "Let us put an end to this ridiculous Revelation of 'the man who would end the rule of the gods.' If Elohim is so high and mighty, let him come to end this himself."

CHAPTER 28

The dungeon lay below the temple complex. It seemed fitting that the location of imprisonment in this realm would be below the edifice of religious power. Noah, Shem, and Japheth were locked in separate small cells with iron bars. The cells instilled a sense of enclosing fear and isolation, containing barely enough room to stand, let alone sit. But Noah and his sons stood—and prayed.

"Almighty Elohim," said Noah, "creator of heaven and earth. Forgive our sins. Hear our prayers. May we, your servants, be found acceptable in your sight. I have not always done what you have asked of me, and it has taken your heavy rod of chastisement to bring me back in line with your purposes. I do not ask for our survival, but for your will to be done."

A door opened and slammed shut around the corner, interrupting them. They could not see what it was. They strained to hear and figure out what was happening.

Out of their sight, around the hallway corner, two guards led a cloaked figure through an opened cell door. Inside the cell lay the headless body of Uriel. The guards picked it up and carried it out like a wounded soldier. It moved sluggishly. Though it could not die, it required the head for coordinated movement.

The guards exited the way they came. The cloaked figure turned to glance behind them.

It was Neela. She knew Noah and his sons were nearby, but she did not know where. She could not hear anyone. So she hastened and left.

Noah and his sons heard the prison hall door slam shut. They finished their prayer. Shem and Japheth said in one accord, "In the name of Elohim, creator of heaven and earth, your will be done."

An earthquake rocked their dungeon vigorously. Noah heard his iron cell door creak loudly. The iron twisted, misshapen by the immeasurable tons of rock above them. It bent outward, leaving a gap large enough for Noah's arm.

Noah thought that this might be Elohim's own hand twisting open the gates that held them. He smiled, reached out, and grabbed his misshapen doorway. He yanked. But it remained firmly in place, maybe even more so. He yanked again. He soon realized that it would not open. The iron had twisted but not enough to free him. They would not escape after all. *Elohim answers prayers, but not always the way we wish.* This was certainly not new to him or his sons.

In the guarded halls of the temple complex, Lugalanu stood with his palace diviner before an altar. Upon it lay a slaughtered lamb, its blood dripping down the small drain channels of the altar. Lugalanu sought interpretation of omens through extispicy and hepatoscopy, the practice of examining an animal's entrails and liver for divining the future. The diviner priest slit the belly of the unblemished lamb and reached in to pull out its guts. He placed them on another stone for examination. beside the liver, still hot from the slaughtered lamb. The smell of the organs repulsed Lugalanu and he stepped back to avoid the drifting odor.

The diviner looked for abnormalities or anomalies that would signify a negative answer to Lugalanu's question of whether Emzara would be his queen in his new seat of power. He poured water over the intestines and liver to clear the blood away and scrutinized them closely. Another diviner aided him, manning a cart with clay tablets of interpretation on them. All manner of irregularities had been recorded by scribes for archival reference. Some of the tablets were even in the shape of a liver with descriptions of interpretations pressed into the clay with cuneiform styluses. Though all the intestines were included in the divination process, the liver was among the most important because it was considered the source of blood and life.

Lugalanu fidgeted impatiently.

The diviner was perturbed. The priest-king always did this to him. He waited until the last moment to seek the ancient wisdom and then expected the diviner to make up for the lateness of his own irresponsibility by rushing the process. He decided to draw it out a little longer just to make his point.

Lugalanu paced.

The diviner finally looked up to give Lugalanu his answer.

"Yes."

Lugalanu passed through the heavily guarded entrance of Emzara's quarters. He found her seated on a couch, staring into the flames of the fireplace. She did not move, she did not look up. She just continued to stare into the flames licking the brick flu.

Eventually, she slowly stood to acknowledge his presence. But she kept gazing into the fire.

"On the morrow, you will be a queen," said Lugalanu. "I expect you to act appropriately."

Emzara had only one thought in her mind. "You knew all along who I was," she said.

She looked at him and saw it was true.

Lugalanu had sought all these years to win her love, but now that it would never be, it did not change his intent. "I gave you the choice. I offered you my very soul." He paused dramatically. "The bearer of the Chosen Seed's royal bloodline will bear my seed instead. Whether by free will or by force."

Lugalanu turned and left Emzara staring into oblivion.

She stood still for what felt like a lifetime. The sum of her days added up to this very moment, in captive quarters below a temple of idols in the dust of death.

She gathered herself together and marched into her bedchamber, shutting the door behind her. She walked over to the side of the bed and withdrew a dagger from hiding. She sat on the bed and pulled back her sleeve. The dagger trembled in her hand.

She wept uncontrollably.

CHAPTER 29

The Akitu New Year Festival was a twelve-day celebration. The first day would involve the final arrival of the people into the temple district and city streets. The second day brought elaborate purification rituals and washings for both priests and temple. On the third day, statues of the gods were carved out of cedar and tamarisk wood. The fourth day was considered the true starting point, because it was the actual first day of the year. After recitations, prayers and rituals, the priests would recite their creation epic to the people. The story would connect their past with their future and reinforce the kingdom of the gods.

The fifth day was the zenith of the festival. After prayers, and exorcisms of evil spirits, the priest-king was ritually humiliated in private before the gods. He was stripped of his kingly symbols of crown, ring, scepter, and mace, and then slapped by a *sesgallu* priest. He was then re-established in his kingship by having the kingly elements returned to him by Anu himself. This enthronement ritual of reversion to chaos and renewal of order was then followed by the arrival of the other gods into the temple of Anu. A public sacrifice for the sins of the people came after that. Though the decreeing of the destinies and dazzling procession of the gods through the streets in bejeweled chariots would not happen until day eight, the gods began their council assembly on day five. After the procession on the eighth day, the priest-king would engage in *hieros gamos*, the Sacred Marriage rite of sex with his queen, in place of Inanna, to insure fertility in the coming year. Emzara dreaded the Sacred Marriage, for it was her decreed appointment with Lugalanu.

But this was day five.

The land around the city swarmed with the armies of the gods. An elaborate tent for the reigning deity and his king sat in the center of each army. Since Inanna had her residence at Erech, she did not have her own forces. The soldiers in the armies had remained relatively civil. Raping of women was held to a minimum, for it was considered somewhat vulgar when invited to a city's festival as this. Under normal situations of course, it was perfectly fine, but not as guests of the high god Anu in his own city. They would soon enough find their outlet to loot and desecrate.

Inside the walls, the city overflowed with pilgrims and worshippers from leagues around. The marketplaces were full of vendors selling vegetables, fish, lizards, scorpions and other exotic desert delicacies.

The district around the temple complex resounded with bacchanalian celebration. Wine flowed, food was consumed in gluttonous amounts, resulting in much vomiting and diarrhea. The food was deliberately full of parasites enabling the digestive systems to respond by evacuating the contents soon after eaten, thus leaving room for continued consumption.

Immorality of all kinds filled the streets. Spontaneous dancing broke out, led by the blue dancers and their traveling minstrels. The human dancers jerked and spasmed as if taken over by spirits. Their eyes turned upward, showing only the whites, and they uttered strange guttural sounds as if performed by a distant ventriloquist.

There were other delights as well. Sorcerers lined the streets with potions and rituals, enabling the citizens to be possessed by a god, a great honor to plebeians who might otherwise never find themselves in the physical presence of deity. Of course, there were exorcists as well for those stubborn "deities" who would not find themselves ready to leave so soon after a possession. Astrological readings, magical potions of fertility and abortion, alchemy, spells, and enchantments—everything an idolater could desire in this panoply of paganism.

In the White Temple above, the day had already begun with Lugalanu's private ritual enthronement. Then three entourages of deity climbed each of the three stairways and arrived at the top terrace. They were greeted by Anu and Inanna, dressed in elaborate finery of divinity for the day: customary horned diadems of deity, and gaudy jewelry beneath their vulture winged robes. It took exaggeration and ostentation to incite the veneration of humans, but it worked every time. She had redesigned her simple horned crown into an elaborate headdress of huge brightly colored horns the size of small goats themselves. Even Inanna's unusually garish display did not stand out from the others as much as usual on this day. But her makeup did. Her exaggerated distortion of eyebrows, bright excessive eye shadow, overwrought angular lipstick made her look a bit like a serious clown to Lugalanu, but he would never dare to reveal such thoughts for fear of his certain death at her spiteful hands.

The three arriving divinities were Enki from Eridu, Ninhursag from Kish, and Enlil from the holy city of Nippur. Along with Anu, these were the four high gods. They were visually as stunning as Anu and Inanna. Each stood well over five cubits tall, with sparkling golden serpentine skin with serpentine eyes, oblong elongated skulls, and wearing royal vulture feathered robes and horned headdresses. The other minor gods had already arrived with less fanfare: Nanna the moon god from Ur and his son Utu the sun god from Larsa. Their status was significantly less than the other gods, and their armies as well, so they avoided drawing attention to themselves. Together these were the "Seven who decree the fates."

An earthquake shook the temple and grounds.

The deities stumbled and regained their balance. Except Enki, who lost his footing and fell down, crushing to death a servant who had been behind him.

Below on the temple grounds, a large crack spread a hundred cubits from the base of the ziggurat. Dozens of such openings were beginning to appear all over the city.

The black mass of impending storm had ebbed to within leagues of the city.

"Today, this will all cease," said Anu to his fellow divinities in the White Temple.

"Elohim is a jealous, senile old deity," retorted Enki, "with a penchant for childish tantrums."

Ninhursag got to the point. "What is the sacrifice? I need blood."

Anu and Inanna glanced at each other with a smile. Anu offered, "Nothing less than the Chosen Seed himself."

The other Watchers looked at them with surprise, eager to hear more.

"From the Revelation?" asked Enki.

Anu nodded.

Enlil jumped in, "How did you manage such privilege?"

Ninhursag added quickly, "Why did you not tell us?"

Anu paused, then slyly said, "I am the supreme god, am I not?"

Each of the Watchers received a chalice of blood from a servant. Anu raised his in toast to himself and merely nodded to his own glory. The others toasted and they drank their blood deeply. Ninhursag gulped it down in one motion.

An earthquake stopped them all again. Enki lost control of his cup and it shattered on the ground, splattering blood everywhere. "Blast this infernal turmoil!"

Ninhursag muttered under her breath sarcastically, "Is that how the Tablet of Destinies slipped through your fingers as well?" Enki gave her an angry look.

She turned to Anu. "Well, Supreme God, I suggest you sacrifice with haste or we may all lose our divine privilege."

Anu clapped his hands. Within seconds, the sound of deep long horns bellowed from the heights of the temple, followed by a series of huge kettledrums at the base. He bade the gods follow him to the ledge overlooking the city.

Below them, they saw the masses assembling. The crowds looked up, and cheered their presence to the percussive beats of the kettledrums.

Anu reached into a sack tied to his waist. He pulled out the head of Uriel, holding it high to look out upon the land before them. Uriel's silent eyes could only tear up with righteous anger.

Ninhursag muttered to Inanna, "I see he has found a way to make a toy out of an archangel. Clever."

Anu threw Uriel's disembodied head behind him into the White Temple.

It rolled up to his throne and thudded to a stop. Unknown to Anu, Uriel's headless body lay right behind his throne, a few cubits away, hidden there by Neela. The archangel's ram's horn trumpet was tied to the belt on the beheaded form.

Outside, Anu focused on speaking to the people below. His voice amplified thunderously throughout the city. It was one of the Watchers' special gifts.

"People of the land! Behold the divine council of your gods!"

The people cheered.

Another earthquake occurred. Another crack in the earth, but this time, it opened as a crevice and water from below sprayed the crowd.

Anu took advantage of this coincident timing. "What you see before you is the might and power of the pantheon!"

The crowd cheered again.

Anu bid Enlil step forward and speak. His voice too carried with a powerful resonance. "I am Enlil, god of the air, and I bring you storm!"

Above, the sky flashed with lightning followed by a crack of thunder. The people roared.

Enlil glanced at Ninhursag with surprise. They could not have had better luck than this. Of course they had the power to manifest certain physical disruptions in nature, but not to this level of spectacle. Only Elohim had that kind of control.

Ninhursag stepped forward. She could feel the vibrations coming. She waited a moment, then shouted triumphantly, "I am Ninhursag, goddess of the earth, and I bring you quake!" Seconds later, the earth rumbled and the crevice below opened wider.

Enki saw he only had seconds. He jumped forward and shouted rapidly, "I am Enki, god of water, and I bring you the deep!"

He timed it well, because the water already began pouring out of the crevice before he finished. It splashed up in a wave that pulled a cluster of people back into the crevice to drown. The crowd did not care; they went wild. These were the gods of the land, and they were showcasing their glorious power.

Inanna jested about the timing of these storm events, "Maybe Elohim is supporting us after all." She knew it was not true. Not in a thousand millennia would Elohim support their rebellion. He was a tyrant without an ounce of mercy. So if the old malcontent intended to crack apart the heavens and earth, they might as well use this opportunity to claim credit for it.

Inanna shouted to the people, "Behold, the Chosen Seed! A sacrifice to appease the gods!"

The crowd roared again as Inanna gestured below to a Stone Temple right next to the ziggurat, about fifteen cubits down. The Stone Temple stood right next to Eanna as a support structure that was used for the messy work of sacrifice so the White Temple could stay clean. On the Stone Temple stood a newly arranged sacrificial altar display consisting of Noah stretched out on frame made of angled and crossed wooden poles. Behind him, Shem and Japheth were tied back to back on a post, kindling around their feet. Across the way from them, Lugalanu stepped forward with a reluctant Emzara. She wore the regal Sumerian wedding dress of white linen robes with gold lined patterns, lapis beads, all scented with cedar oil. The night before, she had been shaven completely of all her hair as was the custom for a priestess, and for the wife of the king as well. On her head she wore a lapis-lazuli headdress with ostrich feathers and precious gems inlaid with gold.

Neela watched the pageantry from a small assembly structure at the back of the Stone Temple terrace. Ham stepped forward next to Lugalanu. The king performed a prayer and incantation before the younger man to initiate him into the high priesthood. The crowd applauded. Then Lugalanu handed Ham the sacrificial dagger, a long sharpened slate blade.

The crowds below cheered for the sacrifice. Ham looked over at Noah, tied to the frame.

Up above on the temple parapet, Inanna fumed impatiently to the other gods. "All this pomp and ritual bores me. I wish they would just hurry up and kill them all."

"Patience, my dear," said Anu. "We will be drinking Chosen blood soon enough."

Ninhursag chimed in, "These humans are loathsome creatures."

Inanna added, "I would just as soon see them all crushed to death as see them worship me."

Enki wondered with genuine amazement, "And they worship us so freely instead of Elohim." Inanna gave him a dirty look.

Anu spoke to the spectacle below them, "So begins a New Year of abundance and fertility! Of marriage and sacrifice!"

The crowds shouted in support. "Of gods and war!" They went into a frenzy, shouting Anu's name, which pleased him greatly in sight of all the others.

Inside, Uriel's head no longer sat on the floor near his throne.

Another seismic quake sent shock waves through the city. It was the biggest one yet. A part of the ziggurat foundation crumbled. Several new crevices ripped open, gushing water. They sucked people into the depths. Some screamed for their loved ones who were taken. Others went back to their enraptured worship.

Everyone heard the horn blast of Uriel coming from the White Temple area. It boomed out over the land to heaven itself.

Uriel's head had found his body. The angel had regenerated. He ran full tilt toward the line of Watchers at the edge of the Temple.

The Watchers turned, too late.

Uriel hit Anu and Inanna. They were at the top of the stairway. The three of them tumbled down ten stairs at a time. Uriel held onto Anu with a vise grip. Had they been human, the impact would have broken every bone in their bodies. But they were not human.

Inanna fell alone. She steadied herself before Uriel and Anu did. In the tumble, her gaudy horned headdress and vulture winged robe flew off her, revealing a bizarre costume of black leather. When she rose with dagger firmly gripped in hand, she looked like what she was, the goddess of sex and war.

Uriel and Anu shook off their dizziness about twenty cubits below her.

The sound of a distant trumpet drew everyone's attention to the desert horizon.

Ten or fifteen leagues out, Uriel could see the armies of the human tribes break over the far ridge. He knew then that the archangels had accomplished their task. They had rallied the last of humanity.

Another trumpet sound drew Uriel's smile. He would know Gabriel's trumpet anywhere.

Anu bellowed with a voice of thunder, "ALL GODS TO WAR!"

The gods raised their own war horns and blew.

The army encampments outside the city walls transformed into rapidly moving hives of armed soldiers organizing and flowing toward the attacking forces on the distant ridge.

Anu was absorbed in his call to war. So he was not ready for Uriel's second running leap. The righteous angel hit him square-on. They flew off the edge of the staircase and down into the crevice below, disappearing from sight.

Lugalanu saw the falling bodies. He knew he had to move fast. He yelled to Ham, already in position before Noah's weak hanging form, "CANAANU, KILL HIM!"

Emzara withdrew her dagger from where she concealed it in her wedding dress. Back in her bedchamber, she had decided not to take her own life in exchange for the privilege of taking Lugalanu's instead.

She raised the blade high to plunge it into him with as much force as she could muster.

Lugalanu saw her motion and grabbed her hand before she could deal the death blow. He jerked away the knife, hit her in the jaw, and threw her violently to the ground.

She hit her head and almost lost consciousness.

Ham saw it all. He also saw the truth of what was before him. This was what his mother had spoken of for many years. This was what he could not understand nor see in agreement with her. Yet, suddenly, it was all clear to him, as if scales had fallen from his eyes. All the riches, all the power, all the sensual delights, all of it was a big lie. In that instant, he knew the truth he had known all his life, but had suppressed; the truth that his mother had sweat blood trying to get him to see. It was the truth that Elohim himself had just confirmed with clarity: This world system was evil.

Ham did not want it anymore.

He turned to Noah and confessed in tears as he cut him loose, "My name is Ham ben Noah. Father, forgive me."

Neela had gone to Emzara's rescue, laying over her as a covering, a desperate attempt to divert the blows onto herself.

Lugalanu yanked her off of Emzara and cast her aside. She flew over the edge of the Stone Temple precipice.

Ham screamed and ran over to the ledge, "NOOOOO!"

Lugalanu raised the knife blade high over Emzara's prone figure. She lifted her arm over her head in a hopeless attempt to shield her head.

"This is your last rejection of me, Nindannum!" he screamed, and plunged.

Midway through the stroke, a spear impaled him from behind. In pain, he turned to see Noah holding the spear, a determined look in his eyes.

"Leave my family alone, you son of iniquity," growled Noah. He pulled Lugalanu around and pushed him over the ledge and out of sight. He fell right past Ham helping Neela up from her precarious hold on the edge. She had somehow grabbed the ledge in her fall.

Down in the crevice, below the churning waters, Uriel fought for control over Anu. He thanked Elohim for the fact that the Watchers were weakened by water. Uriel had his opponent up against a ledge of rock, trying to pin him. But he underestimated Anu's strength underwater. Anu slowly regained an upper hand.

Uriel saw his moment. A large wall of rock above them crumbled. It tumbled down toward them. Uriel released his grip, surprising Anu. He kicked himself away from the wall and Anu. Anu did not have time to avoid the falling debris that cascaded down upon him. He was buried in the depths under tons of sinking landslide.

Uriel kicked toward the surface. Suddenly, he was lifted by a torrential upsurge. The swelling water gushed out of the crevice, launching Uriel out onto land. He rolled to his feet.

Neela and Ham released Shem and Japheth from their post. Noah embraced Emzara with the fervor of eternal devotion.

Ham pulled the sword Rahab from beneath his cloak and handed it to Shem. Shem looked at his brother startled. Then he grinned. This was indeed a son of Noah.

They heard a whistle from below and ran to the ledge. They saw Uriel waving them down.

Ham turned to Noah and asked, "Are we to join the war, father?"

"No," said Noah. "We obey Elohim. We must get back to the tebah."

"The tebah?" queried Ham. "A box? What box?"

"I will explain on the way," said Noah. They all dashed off, running down the stairs inside the Stone Temple.

Inanna saw them escaping. She let out an ugly howling screech that resounded above the din and chaos. Below her, the people had scattered to the deceptive safety of their homes or places away from the temple. Up above, the gods had gone, on their way to lead their troops. Inanna jumped the distance between Eanu and the Stone Temple, fifteen cubits down. She landed on the Stone Temple terrace, her supernatural legs absorbing the impact. She ran to the edge of the terrace and jumped again, landing this time on a ledge ten cubits below.

At her feet lay the silent unmoving figure of Lugalanu with the spearhead sticking out through his belly. She reached down and held him in her arms with an uncharacteristic gentleness. He opened his eyes weakly. She grabbed the shaft of the spear and pulled it out through his body. He screamed in pain and blacked out.

Inanna bit her own arm, drawing blood. She let the blood drip out of her lesion onto Lugalanu's fatally wounded torso. It sizzled when it came into contact with the mortal body. The flesh began to regenerate. The blood of a god surged through him and revived his body. Inanna put her mouth to Lugalanu's cold blue lips and blew a gush of air into his lungs.

He gasped and coughed awake. He was revived.

"Now, my little pet," she said to him "muster a company of soldiers. We have a Chosen Seed to catch and kill."

CHAPTER 30

The armies of man broke over the ridge and lined up in formation, awaiting command. The Mesopotamian plain spread out before them. This drier region that was called the desert of Dudael. It would be the battlefield. They all knew it would shortly be drenched with flowing blood of warfare. None of them had any pretentions, with odds of ten to one glaring them in their faces.

Three generals galloped forward on their horses, each accompanied by an archangel. Each led a battalion of about seven hundred soldiers, Tubal-cain and Raphael commanded the left flank division, Jubal and Gabriel were over the right flank division, and Methuselah and Mikael led the center division.

They met in the center to counsel. "Have you fought Nephilim?" Mikael asked Methuselah.

Methuselah raised his eyebrow. "In my day, I was quite the giant killer. Now, I think I am just an archangel's irritant."

Everyone knew he was talking about Uriel. They all smiled.

Mikael said, "Well, then you should do well on this day."

"Will you lead us?" asked Tubal-cain.

"No," said Mikael. "You will. We archangels have gods to bind."

They could see the armies of the gods moving into formation on the dry plains before them: Phalanxes of humans, followed by battalions of falcon-headed, hawk-headed, dog- and wolf-headed soldiers. Behind them, platoons of Nephilim finished off a demonic army of genetically mutated beasts. They were twenty thousand strong.

Then the three lead generals of the gods came forward from the rear. They were Enki, Ninhursag, and Enlil, mounted on special harnesses on the backs of monstrous Nephilim.

Mikael mocked, "Three of them. Apparently, Uriel has more than made up for his sloppy guardianship of Noah. He has already bound Anu."

"He is relentless, that Uriel," smiled Methuselah.

"Let us pray he was successful in aiding Noah's escape," said Mikael with hope.

"Where are the other three gods?" wondered Raphael.

Nanna the moon god was with Inanna on her chase. None knew that Utu had fled from the city, like the coward he really was, leaving his armies without a leader. Utu had led forces with Inanna in the great Titanomachy of the past. He had also fled that battle, when he had seen their forces losing.

Noah and Emzara, Ham and Neela, Shem and Japheth, and Uriel halted their mounts on the outskirts of the city. They had commandeered some horses and slipped unmolested into the underground tunnels Emzara and Ham knew so well. They had not run into any other underground Nephilim, thank Elohim. They could see the armies facing off against each other for war on the desert of Dudael behind them.

A swirling black mass of funnel clouds churned directly overhead. It appeared that the wrath of God was truly upon them.

"I should be there leading them to battle," said Noah.

Emzara touched him lovingly on the arm.

He concluded, "Elohim's will be done."

"Now *that* is finally obedient faith," cracked Uriel.

Noah gave him a side glance, "Will you now finally leave me alone?" he retorted.

"Not on your life," said Uriel. They shared a smile, but not for long.

"Father, to the south," said Shem.

They all looked. An ominous dust cloud moved in their direction a few leagues behind them. Uriel's eagle eyes could see it was a company of two hundred chimera soldiers on horseback, a dozen pazuzu flying overhead, and a handful of Nephilim rumbling in the lead.

"Assassins," said Uriel. He could just see the figures riding on the backs of the bull and lion aladlammu creatures. "Inanna, Nanna the moon god, and Lugalanu."

The earth trembled again. Lightning and thunder overhead gave a frightening emphasis to their impending doom.

"Elohim be with us," said Noah. "We are going to need him more than ever."

He yelled and kicked his horse into a race for the Zagros Mountains and the Hidden Valley. The others matched pace with him.

CHAPTER 31

Each side weighed its options, observing and analyzing their opponents. It would be a full day before any assault would occur on the Dudael battlefield. The desert plain was framed in the north with the armies of man, and in the south with the armies of the gods. They stood arrayed for battle a mere thousand or so cubits distance from one another. The human tribes were on the higher ground so they bore an advantage. It was not much of an advantage, but anything would help in this hopeless cause. They did not want to lose this benefit, so they waited to draw their opponents uphill. But the gods were too smart for that. The armies of the gods were defending a city; they would not need to leave their defensive position.

A comparison of these two armed forces could not reveal a more imbalanced opposition. The armies of man that had come together in this emergency confederation wore animal skins, some protective leather. They carried axes, maces, and spears, and a passion to worship Elohim against the gods. The cities had created professional armies whose sole purpose was to do battle. Their warriors were universally equipped with a new kind of armor to protect them in fighting. They wore copper helmets over leather caps to protect their skulls from fracture and blunt trauma. They draped leather capes over their bodies, with small bronze circlets attached to create a more impenetrable cloak. They were trained and disciplined to fight in a phalanx unit of eight men wide and six files deep, covering each other with leather shields and spears. Some units had even been trained with the newly introduced sickle swords. The humans faithful to Elohim were not only outnumbered by this standing army, they were out-armed and out-trained.

In spite of this military advantage, the gods would not engage in pre-battle negotiations. They would not risk getting too close to an archangel who could bind them and cast them into the earth. There would be no quarter asked and no quarter given. It would be a war of ultimate annihilation, winner kill all—to the last soul.

Noah Primeval

The soldiers did not want to fight at night, but it seemed they would be fighting in darkness anyway. The skies overhead were fast becoming blackened piles of storm clouds, shadowing the entire region.

The armies of the gods would not leave their position for an uphill climb. But the armies of man were not descending. It was a stalemate of strategies. The archangels and Noah's generals were in fact, deliberately delaying their engagement in order to facilitate Noah's flight to the Hidden Valley. Finally, after a second day of stalling, they had figured that by Elohim's grace, Noah would be close enough to his destination by now. They could wait no longer. They led their forces in a slow march downfield. They would conserve every ounce of energy they could for battle. They would not allow too far a run to tire them. The armies of the gods marched forward as well, in synchronized lock step.

When they were within a few hundred cubits of each other, they stopped. Mikael, Gabriel, and Raphael blew their trumpets. The armies of man shouted a war cry for all they were worth.

The armies of the gods shouted back.

The archangels blew their trumpets again. Methuselah shouted "A sword for the Lord and for Noah!" The forces broke into a run toward the enemy.

But the armies of the gods did something unanticipated. Enki, Enlil, and Ninhursag blew their trumpets and the phalanxes of human soldiers on the front lines split apart. From behind them, came droves of bird-men and dog-men soldiers. The gods sent their elite squads out against the first line of humans. It would be a slaughter, a demoralizing tactic that would be considered risky for enduring battles. But in this case, no one expected an enduring battle. The mutant warriors were of such caliber, they would level the first human troops quickly and maintain enough strength for the second tier fighting. Against these numbers, the faithful human forces would be pulverized.

The charging armies met with a crash of bone and metal. Spear met mace, axe met sword, human met demigod. The gods on their Nephilim crushed their opponents with ease. The archangels plowed through their enemies like so much chaff. It would take some time, but the humans would ultimately be overwhelmed by the hybrid beast soldiers, who were created and mutated for just this purpose. They were soulless fighting machines.

Methuselah called down their second of three waves of forces. He had prayed that their previous fighting would weaken these elite chimera monsters. But it was not to be.

As soon as Methuselah made his call, the gods made theirs. A company of Nephilim dressed for war ran out to battle; a hundred of them. They were fierce, diabolical, unstoppable, and they hit the newly arriving human forces like a tidal wave. But these Nephilim did not just kill their enemies; they killed everything in their path, including their own soldiers. They went mad on the bloodlust of battle.

Suddenly, another huge quake shook the entire valley, throwing everyone to the ground. It split the battlefield down the middle with a huge crevice. Water gushed out of it from the fountains of the deep. It sucked soldiers of both sides into the Abyss to their deaths.

Then, from the enemy side came the sound of long horns. As suddenly as the Nephilim had charged, they returned to their own battle lines, leaving the human armies confused. Why would they retreat in a moment of sure victory?

Methuselah stood up on the height of ridge, trying to assess their options. Then he saw what the enemy waited for. From behind the enemy lines, a thousand men carried a very large ornamented box, one hundred cubits long and thirty cubits square, onto the field. It was made of cedar wood and covered with pitch, with large occultic spells and charms inscribed all over the sides of the box. When they set it down, water spilled out of its cracks onto the ground. It was immensely heavy. All the warriors stopped fighting, to see this monstrosity set near the battleground. Methuselah could not imagine what it might be.

But they would not find out for another half day, because the malice of the gods led them to draw out the inevitable and build a mounting dread in their human opponents before they would unleash their next wave of terror.

Noah and his family had pushed their horses to the breaking point as they fled to the Hidden Valley. The animals were frothing from the exertion. Emzara's horse had already died beneath her, so she rode with Noah.

An unstoppable force of evil, their hunters had stayed on their tail. They were close enough to the family to see them approaching the opening to the Zagros Mountains.

That was when the pazuzus attacked. A swarm of the hideous black flying hellions had left the chasing party and raced toward Noah's band. They dropped out of the sky upon the fugitives in a rage, talons flashing and slashing.

Neela was the first under attack. A pazuzu lifted her off her horse. Ham hacked off its beastly legs, and Neela dropped back onto her steed. His back swing caught another one by its wing, sending it crashing to the ground to be trampled by the horses. Ham had worked with these creatures and had a good sense of their movements and attack patterns.

Japheth did not. Three of the dog-faced creatures attacked him together. They gouged his head and shoulders with their razor talons. Blood oozed freely from the multiple wounds.

Uriel was just ahead of Japheth. He grabbed a bow and quiver of arrows and spun around on his horse. Riding backward, he picked off pazuzus like target practice. With his superhuman speed and preternatural aim, he rapidly downed six of the flying fiends in quick succession.

Then he ran out of arrows.

Shem swung Rahab over his head like a twirling rope fan, slicing half a dozen pazuzus in half with ease. He was actually enjoying it.

Then, for no apparent reason, the remaining few pazuzus gave up and returned to the sky above them.

But the damage had been done. They had been dramatically slowed down. Inanna's assassin squad was almost upon them. Noah worried what they would do about Behemoth, who was surely blocking their path through the gorge.

CHAPTER 32

The battle of gods and men resumed with the huge box towering behind the city lines. Yet another skirmish further weakened the human forces. Methuselah had sent forth their last battalion of soldiers. They were totally committed, and most were dead. The angels alone held their ground and kept the forces at bay. But they needed to turn their attention to their calling, that of binding the Watchers. When they left the human forces to do that, the tide of the battle turned fully against Methuselah's men.

Tubal-cain and Jubal fought near each other, comrades in battle to the end. Their tactics and skills were diametrically opposite. Tubal-cain bashed, crushed, and clobbered two at a time with his muscle-bound brawn, while Jubal danced a free flowing stream of slicing, dicing, and slashing. He had picked up the Karabu technique well and was quite good at it. They were a complimentary team. Jubal longed to be fighting next to his dear departed brother. He suspected he would see him soon. Tubal-cain wondered if he had already eaten his last meal, because he was starving.

Mikael zeroed in on Enlil and his Naphil. Mikael's agile sword matched the Naphil's swift axe, thrust for thrust. Mikael waited for the right moment. It came when the Naphil dodged an attack and fell off balance for just an instant. That was all Mikael needed. He dove in between the Naphil's long legs and rolled beneath him. He cut its heel tendons on both sides. Surprised, the Naphil fell to the ground, twisting and landing on his back, pinning Enlil.

In a split second, Mikael was upon the god. Enlil had been knocked dizzy by the fall.

Mikael swiftly cut off the Naphil's head. He pulled Enlil out from under the creature. Hoisting the groggy Watcher on his shoulders, he ran for the huge crevice in the midst of the field and jumped right in with his hostage.

Gabriel and Raphael teamed up against Enki and Ninhursag. But when Enki saw the fall of Enlil, he grabbed his horn and sounded a wailing call.

The large box on the field had five men up top. They wielded their sledgehammers in response to Enki's horn. They slammed out the large pins that held the hinges of the box front.

The door crashed open. A huge flood of seawater flushed out of the box and onto the battlefield. It washed away monsters and men. Lurking in that gargantuan box of salty brine was something else: Leviathan.

The sea dragon slithered out onto the field, a literal fish out of water—a gigantic and very angry fish—with multiple heads, monstrous teeth, serious armored scales, and a powerful tail. The writhing twisting serpent flipped around, crushing everything in its wake and dispersing all in its path. Its jaws snapped viciously, chomping chimeras and humans left and right, forward and behind. None escaped its fury.

Tubal-cain and five other warriors circled a Naphil. The giant's durability wore them down. Then Leviathan was released quite close to them. Tubal-cain could see its impenetrable armored scales, smell its decrepit fishy stench, and feel the heat of its fiery breath. Not only did the creature crush, chomp and slaughter, but it breathed fire from some of its mouths when out of the water and in contact with the air. One burst of flame burnt a company of combating warriors to a crisp in seconds. It would all be over shortly.

Methuselah saw the end was near. He released their final secret weapon to counter the monster on the battlefield: Behemoth. This was the monstrosity that killed his beloved Edna, and Methuselah had vowed to one day return and kill the monster. The creature had taken away the grace in his otherwise lonely life. But when Methuselah had faced the bitterness in his soul, he had realized that his redemption would be found not in killing the monster, but in capturing it and turning it into a benefit for Elohim's purposes.

Even though it was blind in one eye, the brutish beast required ten angels and thirty men to capture it in the mountains. The angels had used their supernatural binding cords to muzzle it and incarcerate it in a large cedar cage on wheels.

That cage now rolled wildly down the hill into the heat of battle, heading directly for Leviathan.

Warriors dove out of its way. Some did not see it coming and were crushed under its massive wheels. The aim had been accurate. The cage crashed right into Leviathan. The sea beast's massive tail swung around, exploding the wooden structure to pieces, releasing the roaring Behemoth.

A shiver of hope went through Methuselah. Behemoth was not as big as Leviathan, but it was at home both on land and in water. That should have placed its aqueous nemesis at a disadvantage. Perhaps it would match Leviathan's ferocity with its own bones of bronze, tail of cedar, and teeth of iron.

But it was not to be.

A wave of dread washed over Methuselah. It did not attack Leviathan. He watched the one-eyed Behemoth strike out for the easier prey, the last living soldiers on the battle ground. Now, two gigantic monsters smashed everything around them like a team of destroyers. Their gamble had not paid off. Their plan had failed.

It was all over, thought Methuselah.

Down in the battle, Tubal-cain saw his moment and charged. The Naphil had only a sword. It was unaware of one of the dragon's heads right behind him, turning in their direction. Tubal-cain knew they needed another few moments of diversion, so he burst out of the circle and engaged the Naphil one on one. It was a foolish action that only a man who knew that all was lost with no other chance would make. It was enough to divert the Naphil.

It turned to faced Tubal-cain. The burly metalworker's robust human size was like an infant in comparison with the demigod.

Tubal-cain managed a few good hits against the giant. Then it swung its blade and cut off Tubal-cain's arm in one clean cut.

Tubal-cain cried out in pain and dropped to his knees.

The Naphil looked down, planning an execution style finish to this courageous but failed little warrior. It did not realize that Tubal-cain had not dropped out of pain, but out of calculation. Behind the Naphil, two heads of Leviathan swiveled in their direction, mere cubits away.

The Naphil heard the deep guttural sound of air gurgling and metabolically interacting with chemicals inside Leviathan's innards, but he did not turn toward the noise. He raised his sword high to finish off the prone Tubal-cain. The wounded warrior fell prostrate to avoid the wall of fire that spewed from Leviathan's mouths. An inferno of flame engulfed the Naphil and others around him.

Tubal-cain may have lost his arm, but he had not lost his wits, thanks to the adrenaline of battle surging through his body. The burning blast flared just above where he lay, singeing his hair, and giving him a heat rash he would not care for if he lived until tomorrow. But he did not expect a tomorrow. He had only today. He raised the stump of the arm and allowed the flame to cauterize the wound, giving him more time to fight. It would be a bit more difficult with the lack of his sword arm. *Oh well*, he thought, *Elohim can give me a new one when I rise to meet him.*

Behemoth trampled and attacked downhill toward the last of the armies of the gods. At least now it was killing only the enemy. The writhing serpent Leviathan slid closer to the large chasm, closer to the battling titans of archangels and Watchers, its heads snapping up bodies as it went.

Enki and his Naphil were vicious in battle. Gabriel was taking a pounding. Enki did not see Mikael come up out of the crevice from behind him. Mikael had taken care of Enlil. Now he jumped Enki, leaping as Gabriel attacked. The two of them were a mighty team, but Enki was fighting for his eternity. Even though he was near the crevice, he was not going to let these two god-lickers ruin his future.

Tubal-cain and Jubal each saw the wrestling match of god and angels from their two different locations. Tubal-cain fought on foot, in spite of the pain of his newly cauterized wound. Jubal sat on the back of a horse he recently acquired from a now headless opponent. They were within distance of the match. They caught each other's eyes and nodded. They smirked in recognition, knowing what they had to do. It was now a personal contest between them, who could get there first.

Tubal-cain bolted forward on foot. Jubal kicked his horse and galloped for the divine beings in battle.

The grappling tangle of flesh that was Enki, his Naphil, Mikael, and Gabriel were evenly matched. The tie breaker came in the form of Tubal-cain and Jubal. They hit the tangled bodies almost simultaneously. Tubal-cain was sure he had reached the target a flash before Jubal. It was exactly the amount of force needed to throw the balance in favor of the angels. The whole lot of them tumbled over the edge and into the wide fissure.

Tubal-cain had enough breath left in him to shout to Jubal as they were plunging downward, "I BEAT YOU!"

Jubal had the last word, knowing where they were heading, "LET ELOHIM DECIDE!"

Tubal-cain had the last thought, *Yes, but you had a horse, and I was on foot.*

The turbulent waters of the great deep swallowed them up.

Tubal-cain and Jubal were not the only ones who would not leave that crevasse. Mikael and Gabriel bound Enki in the depths of the Abyss with the Cherubim hair from their armbands.

Above, at the precipice of the rift, the snapping jaws of Leviathan moved closer to Ninhursag on his Naphil. The god fought with Raphael. The mouths of six of the seven dragon heads were full of soldiers. One of the heads started choking. It had swallowed a Nephilim and two soldiers whole. But one head focused on Ninhursag and his Naphil. It was ready for another bite.

Raphael had one chance. He took it. He leapt right up into the arms of the Naphil, jamming his sword into the creature's chest. It screamed in pain and fell backward, with Ninhursag still in the harness, right into the jaws of Leviathan. The jaws snapped shut on both Watcher and Naphil.

Another earthquake tumbled the field like waves. Leviathan flipped into the crevice and descended into the deep.

It started to rain.

CHAPTER 33

Methuselah had not been able to tell Noah about the capture of Behemoth. So it was a gratifying surprise when they entered the Hidden Valley without the deep roar and imposing presence of the humongous guardian blocking their path. Unfortunately, it also meant that there was nothing to block the path of their pursuers.

The earth convulsed as Noah and his band arrived at the Hidden Valley village. Lightning and thunder increased in frequency. The sky was black with storm clouds. The floodgates of heaven opened upon them and dropped rain like a waterfall.

The wives of Shem and Japheth stood at the opening of the tebah. The village was empty of all life. Noah was thankful that the rest of the village must be safe inside the box. They just needed to get to the door in time and close themselves in.

They did not reach the door in time.

Inanna and her squad of soldiers and Nephilim broke through the brush and into the clearing. Lugalanu immediately broke away from the squad. He jumped down from his mount, and circled around the structure on foot.

Another quake suddenly split the ground beneath the feet of Inanna's hellions. Many of them went down alive into Sheol, bird-men, dog-men and Nephilim alike. Nanna and his bull-man ride were swallowed up into the Abyss.

If only all the Watchers would fall so easily, thought Uriel. He shoved Noah toward the box, and yelled, "GET IN AND LOCK THE GATE! NOW!" He turned to face the enemy, drawing his double swords.

Noah and his family ran for it. They reached the door. But Noah, Shem, and Japheth stopped to cut down the few soldiers that caught up with them.

Noah turned and saw Uriel dispatch two Nephilim and five bird-men soldiers with uncanny swiftness. The power of Elohim transfigured the angel and he became a shining star. And that shining star blocked Inanna's approach to the boat.

Noah whirled to pull the rope to the door ballast. It would lift up the huge heavy doorway.

The rope had been cut.

They could not pull it up themselves. It was far too heavy.

More soldiers were almost upon them.

To their surprise, Elohim himself closed the door and shut them in, leaving the world outside to its destiny.

They did not ask questions about the miracle. They quickly reinforced the door and applied pitch to the edges for sealant.

That done, Noah turned and saw his family, seven of them—he made eight: Emzara, Shem and his wife Sedeq, Japheth and his wife Adatanes, and Ham and his wife Neela.

Strange, he thought. "Where is the rest of the village?"

Sedeq and Adatanes looked down.

"Where is the rest of the village?" he repeated.

"Did not Uriel tell you?" said Sedeq.

"Tell me what?" His voice grew more stressed.

Adatanes was bolder than Sedeq. "They fought with the armies of man."

"They what?" He could hardly contain himself.

"They fought with the armies of man against the gods," she repeated.

"You are telling me the entire tribe of men, women and children went to die in the battlefield?" This was madness.

Adatanes told him their story. After Noah left to rescue Emzara, the angel of the Lord, *Mal'ak Yahweh* as he was called, came to their village. He had come riding on a cloud in the presence of his holy ones and he spoke the word of Elohim to them.

She continued, "He told us that he was coming to judge the earth and that it was his will that only the family of Noah board the boat when the floods came. It was not easy on the ears to hear this. But there was something about Mal'ak Yahweh. It was as if he went to each member of the tribe and comforted them individually with assurance. I cannot tell you how, father-in-law, but he spoke to each of us, and we knew he would bring the world to rights."

"Well, if that is not just like him," complained Noah. "He still seems to enjoy speaking directly to everyone but me."

Sedeq and Adatanes giggled.

"Do not be impertinent young ladies," snapped Noah.

"Forgive us," said Adatanes. "It is just that, well, Mal'ak Yahweh said you would say those very words."

"If I live to be a thousand, I will never understand his ways," he finished. "But perhaps that is what makes him God and me his humble servant."

He opened his arms wide and bid his family to join in as he beseeched Elohim, the Lord their God to have mercy upon their souls and that they would have favor in his sight.

Outside the boat, Uriel and Inanna fought like titans. Blow by blow they were equals, but Inanna was not alone. She was on her lion-man joined by three Nephilim with maces and axes.

The waters burst forth from the fountains of the deep and gushed out through the chasms opened in the earth. The contenders carried their battle to the rooftops of the flooding village. Uriel dispatched one Naphil, but he was ultimately overcome by the other two. They pinned him to the roof of one of the homes.

Inanna strode up to him in the pouring rain and thunder. She spit out with every ounce of bile that filled her demonic soul, "You have thwarted my will for the last time, you worthless slave of Elohim."

Another earthquake rocked the valley, causing them all to look up.

A huge wall of water crashed through the valley. It hit the box and burst around it. It descended upon Inanna, her chimera mount, Uriel, and the Nephilim and they were instantly washed away in a churning tidal wave of doom.

Inside the boat, Noah's family grabbed hold of some timbers. The force of the water hit the boat and shook it loose from its mooring to the ground. The barge started to drift in the massive tide.

On the battlefield of Dudael, the sheets of torrential rain and flood waters washed away the armies of both gods and men. They had been utterly wiped out to the last person. It was complete and total annihilation. They were all dead -- except for one last regiment of bird-men soldiers.

On the ridge above the plain, Methuselah and his personal guard of a handful of soldiers were the last of the human tribes. They saw the regiment of bird-men ascending toward them. Methuselah smiled. He had prayed for this very thing. He had asked Elohim that he be alive to see the end, and to have a good death, one that would be glorious. He felt the rumbling behind him as a thousand soldiers approached his group of ten from below. He raised his arms to heaven and yelled with all the passion in his soul, "EDNA, I AM COMING!"

And then he spoke the name he had learned so many years ago from his forefather Adam, the special covenant name of his god, reserved for a future time of revealing. No one would hear it now, so he was free to worship without restraint. "YAHWEH ELOHIM! THY WILL BE DONE!"

Behind him, a huge fifteen cubit high wall of water appeared, as if bidden by Methuselah. It surged over the desert of Dudael, swallowing up everything. Methuselah and his guards disappeared under the enormous wave as it crashed upon the last of the armies of the gods and drowned them all like ants in a rainstorm.

It took seconds for the deluge to wipe the battlefield clean. A few seconds more, and the city was completely enveloped. The water smothered everything that breathed. It dissolved man-made structures as if they were sand castles.

The torrential wave made its way across the plain, extinguishing everything in its path. All flesh that moved on the land died, everything in whose nostrils was the breath of life died. Elohim blotted out every living thing that was on the face of the ground.

Only Noah was left, and those who were with him in the box.

CHAPTER 34

The box had been built effectively. It floated barge-like in the water, about two thirds of it below the waterline. It was a drift ship or a current rider, not a sailing vessel. Elohim would be its rudder.

Inside, Noah's family settled in for a long voyage. They did not know exactly how long it would be, but Elohim had told them it would rain for forty days and forty nights. They knew the terrible truth that he was going to blot out all living things in the land. They knew they would be the only survivors. They knew they would start anew Elohim's plans for the human race.

Noah was already organizing the work details. The barge was full of animals of every kind. Though many had been nestled into hibernation by Elohim's hand, there were still many that had to be taken care of and fed. It would be a consuming job for these mere eight people. They had to get to work immediately. The sounds of bleating, mooing, squealing, braying, growling, and whinnying already filled the air in a cacophony of need. It would be a long journey indeed.

Noah's family did not hear Lugalanu, hiding just down the hallway and around the corner from them. He had snuck into the boat when everyone's attention had been on the battle. He carried a long dagger in his hand and waited for his moment.

He found it.

Lugalanu gripped his blade tightly and walked down the hallway toward the family. He had no need to conceal himself or surprise anyone. He was fully capable of taking them all out in a fury. He muttered to himself with satisfaction, "It is not so easy to kill a demigod."

Noah looked up from the table where they counseled. He saw Lugalanu approaching them, dagger clutched in one hand, eyes full of rage.

Everyone followed Noah's gaze. His sons pulled the women behind them to prepare for a battle. Unfortunately, the few weapons aboard were not at hand. They had not anticipated such a moment.

But Lugalanu had not anticipated what happened next.

He was halfway to the family. Suddenly, a lion jumped out of a stall, blocking his way. It growled, ready to pounce. *A nuisance,* thought Lugalanu, but killing it would be an opportunity to excite his blood rage before he took the family.

Then another lion joined it. And a tiger. And then a panther. Soon, feline predators with bared teeth and protracted claws entirely obstructed his path.

It made him pause.

A snort behind him made him look back.

A big black bull stomped its feet, preparing to charge. Behind it a huge gorilla joined in.

Lugalanu's eyes went wide with fear. The animals knew he was their enemy and they were going to protect their own.

The bull charged. It hit Lugalanu in full stride, goring him on its horns and throwing him to the floor. The predators all pounced. Lugalanu disappeared beneath their teeth and claws.

Lugalanu had believed his own lie. He was no demigod. He was very human.

And then he was no more.

Noah's family clung to each other in protection.

Elohim worked in mysterious ways.

Outside, all was darkness and rain and tempestuous waters. Seventy cubits from the boat, Inanna broke the surface, shorn of all clothing and accouterments. No more masquerade. Azazel was a pure, undefiled predator. He cut through the water like a shark toward the boat. His eyes focused on the craft with intense determination. He was weakened in the water, but he was one of the strongest of the divine *Bene Elohim,* and had a will of iron.

But even a *Bene Elohim* was no match for the jaws of the mighty Rahab. She burst through the water from below and clamped down on his body with her iron jaws. The speed of Rahab made it leap out of the water a dozen cubits before splashing back down in a fountain of spray. The monster sank fast and carried Azazel deep into the murky abyss.

It rode a violent current with its victim into the convulsive swirling sea below. Then a large wall of rock and sediment buried them, freezing Azazel in Rahab's jaws, unable to move but bound alive forever.

In the boat, Noah's family had already begun their arduous task of feeding the animals and cleaning the stalls.

Neela offered some hay to a couple of sheep. They grabbed it and munched to their heart's content.

She stopped, a stabbing pain in her belly. A wave of nausea overcame her. She quickly found a pail and wretched.

Ham rushed to her, comforting her with a loving hand on her back.

Noah noticed her retching and was concerned. "What is wrong, Neela?" he asked.

"She must be seasick," Ham offered.

"I hope you get over it soon, because we have a long drift ahead of us," said Noah.

"It is not seasickness," interrupted Neela. "I am with child."

Ham grinned wide with happiness. Emzara hugged her first, followed by the rest of the family.

Noah said happily, "Well, we will have a world to repopulate, and it appears Ham and Neela have beat us all to the task." Everyone laughed and got back to their work.

Neela sought hard to conceal her own fears. She had secrets she could not reveal—secrets of the Watchers. Semjaza and Azazel had achieved their goal of cross-breeding a normal human being that would carry the Nephilim genetic traits in a recessive form, to blossom in later generations once the lines had spread throughout the land.

Neela knew that the first of those demigods had been created, and it grew inside her.

Chronicles of the Nephilim continues with the next book, Gilgamesh Immortal.

Click here to buy *Gilgamesh Immortal*.

· · · · ·

If you liked this book, then please help me out by writing an honest review of it wherever you purchased it. It's usually pretty easy. That is one of the best ways to say thank you to me as an author. It really does help my exposure and status as an author. Thanks! — *Brian Godawa*

CHAPTER 35:
THE SONS OF GOD

Deut. 6:4
"Hear, O Israel: The LORD our God, the LORD is one."

Psa. 82:1
God has taken his place in the divine council; in the midst of the gods he holds judgment.

A major premise of my fictional novel *Noah Primeval* is that the gods of the ancient world were real spiritual beings with supernatural powers. Thus, the mythical literature and artistic engravings of the gods that have been uncovered by Mesopotamian archeology reflect a certain amount of factual reality. The twist is that these gods are actually fallen divine angelic beings called "Sons of God" (*Bene Elohim*) in the Bible. These Sons of God had rebelled against God's divine council in heaven and came to earth in order to corrupt God's creation and deceive mankind into worshipping them in place of the real God. While this is not polytheism, neither is it absolute monotheism. It is Biblical theism, which will become clear shortly.

Though I have clearly engaged in imaginative creative license and fantasy in the novel, it is not without Biblical theological foundation. The purpose of this essay is to make an argument that in principle the Bible does in fact suggest a paradigm that reflects something similar to the theological interpretation presented in the novel. For that reason I might call *Noah Primeval* a theological novel.

Jewish monotheism and Christian Trinitarianism affirm the oneness of God's being. Christianity contains an additional doctrinal nuance of three persons, Father, Son and Holy Spirit, who share the same substance while maintaining separate persons. In this way, the Christian is able to both affirm

God's oneness (unity) *and* his threeness (diversity). Simply put, God is three persons in one being, *not* three beings.

Jews, Muslims and atheists who seem to assume that a monotheistic worldview cannot provide for diversity within the divine realm have often accused Christians of being polytheists. I call this Jewish/Muslim viewpoint, "absolute monotheism" as opposed to Biblical theism. What would shock most readers of the Bible is that the same Old Testament quoted by the *Shema* about God being "one," also describes a cosmic worldview that includes a hierarchy in heaven of divine beings, a kind of governmental bureaucracy of operations that counsels with God, and carries out his decrees in heaven and earth. Biblical scholars refer to this hierarchy as the divine council, or divine assembly and it consists of beings that are referred to in the Bible as *gods*.

Before examining the texts about the divine council it is important to understand that the English word "God," can be misleading in Biblical interpretation. The most common Hebrew word translated in English as "God" in the Bible is *Elohim*. But God has many names in the text and each of them is used to describe different aspects of his person. *El*, often refers to God's powerful preeminence; *El Elyon* (God Most High) indicates God as possessor of heaven and earth; *Adonai* means God as lord or master; and *Yahweh* is the covenantal name for the God of Israel as distinguished from any other deity. *Elohim*, though it is the most common Hebrew word for God in the Old Testament, was also a word that was used of angels (Psa. 8:5; Heb. 2:7), gods or idols of pagan nations (Psa. 138:1), supernatural beings of the divine council (Psa. 82:6), departed spirits of humans (1Sam. 28:13), and demons (Deut. 32:17).[1] Scholar Michael S. Heiser has pointed out that the Hebrew word Elohim was more of a reference to a plane of existence than to a substance of being. In this way, Yahweh was *Elohim*, but no other elohim was Yahweh. Yahweh is incomparably *THE* Elohim of elohim (Deut. 10:17).[2]

Of Gods and Elohim

A common understanding of absolute monotheism is that when the Bible refers to other gods it does not mean that the gods are real beings but merely *beliefs* in real beings that do not exist. For instance, when Deuteronomy 32:43

---

[1] Geoffrey W. Bromiley, "God, Names of," *The International Standard Bible Encyclopedia, Revised.* Wm. B. Eerdmans, 1988; 2002, p. 504-508.
[2] Michael S. Heiser, *The Myth That is True: Rediscovering the Cosmic Narrative of the Bible*, unpublished manuscript, 2011, p 25-29. Available online at www.michaelsheiser.com. I have read quite a few scholars on the divine council, but Michael Heiser has been the most helpful and represents the major influence on this essay.

proclaims "rejoice with him, O heavens, bow down to him, all gods," this is a poetic way of saying "what you believe are gods are not gods at all because Yahweh is God." What seems to support this interpretation is the fact that a few verses before this, (v. 39) God says, "See now, that I, even I am he, and there is no god [elohim] beside me." Does this not clearly indicate that God is the only god [elohim] that really exists out of all the "gods" [elohim] that others believe in?

Not in its Biblical context it doesn't.

When the text is examined in its full context of the chapter and rest of the Bible we discover a very different notion about God and gods. The phrase "I am, and there is none beside me" was an ancient Biblical slogan of incomparability of sovereignty, not exclusivity of existence. It was a way of saying that a certain authority was the most powerful *compared to* all other authorities. It did not mean that there were no other authorities that existed. We see this sloganeering in two distinct passages, one of the ruling power of Babylon claiming proudly in her heart, "I am, and there is no one beside me" (Isa. 47:8) and the other of the city of Nineveh boasting in her heart, "I am, and there is no one else" (Zeph. 2:15). The powers of Babylon and Nineveh are obviously not saying that there are no other powers or cities that exist beside them, because they had to conquer other cities and rule over them. In the same way, Yahweh uses that colloquial phrase, not to deny the existence of other gods, but to express his incomparable sovereignty over them.[3]

In concert with this phrase is the key reference to gods early in Deuteronomy 32. Israel is chastised for falling away from Yahweh after he gave Israel the Promised Land: "They sacrificed to demons not God, to gods they had never known, to new gods that had come recently, whom your fathers had never dreaded" (Deut. 32:17). In this important text we learn that the idols or gods of the other nations that Israel worshipped were real beings that existed called "demons." At the same time, they are called, "gods" and "not God," which indicates that they exist as real beings, but are not THE God of Israel.

Psalm 106 repeats this same exact theme of Israel worshipping the gods of other nations and making sacrifices to those gods that were in fact demons.

---

[3] Michael S. Heiser, "Monotheism, Polytheism, Monolatry, or Henotheism? Toward an Assessment of Divine Plurality in the Hebrew Bible" (2008). Faculty Publications and Presentations. Paper 277, p. 12-15, http://digitalcommons.liberty.edu/cgi/viewcontent.cgi?article=1276&context=lts_fac_pubs&sei-redir=1#search=%22heiser+Monotheism,+Polytheism,+Monolatry,+or+Henotheism%22 accessed March 23, 2011.

> Psa. 106:34-37
> They did not destroy the peoples, as the LORD commanded them, but they <u>mixed with the nations</u> and learned to do as they did…They served their <u>idols,</u> which became a snare to them. They sacrificed their sons and their daughters to the <u>demons</u>.

One rendering of the Septuagint (LXX) version of Psalm 95:5-6 reaffirms this reality of national gods being demons whose deity was less than the Creator, "For great is the Lord, and praiseworthy exceedingly. More awesome he is than all the gods. For all the gods of the nations are demons, but the Lord made the heavens."[4] Another LXX verse, Isa. 65:11, speaks of Israel's idolatry: "But ye are they that have left me, and forget my holy mountain, and prepare a table for [a demon], and fill up the drink-offering to Fortune [a foreign goddess]."[5]

The non-canonical book of 1 Enoch, upon which some of *Noah Primeval* is based, affirms this very notion of gods as demons, the fallen angels of Genesis 6: "The angels which have united themselves with women. They have defiled the people and will lead them into error so that they will offer sacrifices to the demons as unto gods."[6]

The New Testament carries over this idea of demonic reality of beings behind the idols that pagans offered sacrifices to and worshipped: "No, I imply that what pagans sacrifice they offer to demons and not to God. I do not want you to be participants with demons (1Cor. 10:20)." In Revelation 9:20, the Apostle John defines the worship of gold and silver idols as being the worship of demons. The physical objects were certainly without deity as they could not "see or hear or walk," but the gods behind those objects were real beings with evil intent.

Returning to Deuteronomy 32 and going back a few more verses in context, we read of a reality-changing incident that occurred at Babel:

---

[4] Randall Tan, David A. deSilva, and Logos Bible Software. *The Lexham Greek-English Interlinear Septuagint*. Logos Bible Software, 2009. Baruch 4:7 in the Apocrypha echoes this Scriptural theme as well when speaking of Israel's apostasy: "For you provoked him who made you, by sacrificing to demons and not to God."
[5] Lancelot Charles Lee Brenton, *The Septuagint Version of the Old Testament: English Translation* (London: Samuel Bagster and Sons, 1870), Is 65:11. Randall Tan and David A. deSilva, Logos Bible Software, *The Lexham Greek-English Interlinear Septuagint* (Logos Bible Software, 2009), Is 65:11.
[6] James H. Charlesworth, *The Old Testament Pseudepigrapha: Volume 1*, 1 En 19:1 (New York; London: Yale University Press, 1983).

> Deut. 32:8-9
>
> When the Most High gave to the nations their inheritance, when he divided mankind, he fixed the borders of the peoples according to the number of the sons of God. But the LORD's portion is his people, Jacob his allotted heritage.

The reference to the creation of nations through the division of mankind and fixing of the borders of nations is clearly a reference to the event of the Tower of Babel in Genesis 11 and the dispersion of the peoples into the 70 nations listed in Genesis 10.

But then there is a strange reference to those nations being "fixed" according to the number of the sons of God.[7] We'll explain in a moment that those sons of God are from the assembly of the divine council of God. But after that the text says that God saved Jacob (God's own people) for his "allotment." Even though Jacob was not born until long after the Babel incident, this is an anachronistic way of referring to what would become God's people, because right after Babel, we read about God's calling of Abraham who was the grandfather of Jacob (Isa. 41:8; Rom. 11:26). So God allots nations and their geographic territory to these sons of God to rule over, but he allots the people of Jacob to himself, along with their geographical territory of Canaan (Gen. 17:8).

The idea of Yahweh "allotting" geographical territories to these sons of God who really existed and were worshipped as gods (idols) shows up again in several places in Deuteronomy:

> Deut. 4:19-20
>
> And beware lest you raise your eyes to heaven, and when you see the sun and the moon and the stars, all the host of heaven, you be drawn away and bow down to them and serve them, things that the LORD your God has allotted to all the peoples under the whole heaven.

---

[7] The astute reader will notice that some Bible translations read "according to the sons of Israel." The ESV reflects the latest consensus of scholarship that the Septuagint (LXX) and the Dead Sea Scrolls (DSS) segment of this verse is the earlier and more accurate reading than the later Masoretic Text (MT) of the same. See Heiser, Michael, "Does Deuteronomy 32:17 Assume or Deny the Reality of Other Gods?" (2008). Faculty Publications and Presentations. Paper 322. p 137-145. http://digitalcommons.liberty.edu/lts_fac_pubs/322/

> Deut. 29:26
> They went and served <u>other gods</u> and worshiped them, gods whom they have not known and whom <u>He had not allotted to them</u>.

"Host of heaven" was a term that referred to astronomical bodies that were also considered to be gods or members of the divine council.[8] The *Encyclopedia Judaica* notes that, "in many cultures the sky, the sun, the moon, and the known planets were conceived as personal gods. These gods were responsible for all or some aspects of existence. Prayers were addressed to them, offerings were made to them, and their opinions on important matters were sought through divination."[9]

But it was not merely the pagans who made this connection of heavenly physical bodies with heavenly spiritual powers. The Old Testament itself equates the sun, moon, and stars with the angelic "sons of God" who surround God's throne, calling them both the "host of heaven" (Deut. 4:19; 32:8-9).[10] Jewish commentator Jeffrey Tigay writes, "[These passages] seem to reflect a Biblical view that... as punishment for man's repeated spurning of His authority in primordial times (Gen. 3-11), God deprived mankind at large of true knowledge of Himself and ordained that it should worship idols and subordinate celestial beings."[11]

There is more than just a symbolic connection between the physical heavens and the spiritual heavens in the Bible. In some passages, the stars of heaven are linked *interchangeably* with angelic heavenly beings, also referred to as "holy ones" or "sons of God" (Psa. 89:5-7; Job 1:6)[12].

Daniel 10:10-18 speaks of these divine "host of heaven" allotted with authority over pagan nations as spiritual "princes" battling with the archangels Gabriel and Michael.

---

[8] H. Niehr, "Host of Heaven," Toorn, K. van der, Bob Becking, and Pieter Willem van der Horst. *Dictionary of Deities and Demons in the Bible DDD*. 2nd extensively rev. ed. Leiden; Boston; Grand Rapids, Mich.: Brill; Eerdmans, 1999., 428-29; I. Zatelli, "Astrology and the Worship of the Stars in the Bible," *ZAW* 103 (1991): 86-99.
[9] "Astrology", *Encyclopaedia Judaica* Michael Berenbaum and Fred Skolnik, eds. 2nd ed. Detroit: Macmillan Reference USA, 2007, p. 8424.
[10] See also Deut 4:19; Deut 17:3; 2King 23:4-5; 1King 22:19; Neh 9:6.
[11] Jeffrey Tigay, *JPS Torah Commentary: Deuteronomy* (Philadelphia: The Jewish Publication Society, 1996): 435; as quoted in Michael S. Heiser, "Deuteronomy 32:8 and the Sons of God," Bibliotheca Sacra 158 (January-March 2001): 72; online: http://thedivinecouncil.com/.
[Copyright © 2001 Dallas Theological Seminary;, online: http://thedivinecouncil.com/
[12] See also Job 38:4-7; Neh. 9:6; Psa 148:2-3, 1King 22:29 & 2King 21:5. In Isa 14:12-14 the king of Babylon is likened to the planet Venus (Morningstar) seeking to reign above the other stars of heaven, which are equivalent to the sons of God who surround God's throne on the "mount of assembly" or "divine council" (see Psa 89:5-7 and Psa 82).

Some Second Temple non-canonical Jewish texts illustrate an ancient tradition of understanding this interpretation of the gods of the nations as real spirit beings that rule over those nations:

> Jubilees 15:31-32
> (There are) many nations and many people, and they all belong to him, but <u>over all of them</u> he caused <u>spirits to rule so that they might lead them astray from following him</u>. But over Israel he did not cause any angel or spirit to rule because he alone is their ruler and he will protect them.

> Targum Jonathan, Deuteronomy 32, Section LIII[13]
> When the Most High made <u>allotment of the world unto the nations</u> which proceeded from the sons of Noach [Noah], in the separation of the writings and languages of the children of men at the time of the division, He cast the lot among the <u>seventy angels, the princes of the nations</u> with whom is the revelation <u>to oversee the city</u>.

In conclusion, the entire narrative of Deuteronomy 32 tells the story of God dispersing the nations at Babel and allotting the nations to be ruled by "gods" who were demons, or fallen divine beings called sons of God. God then allots the people of Israel for himself, through Abraham, and their territory of Canaan. But God's people fall away from him and worship these other gods and are judged for their apostasy. We will now see that Yahweh will judge these gods as well.

Psalm 82

Bearing in mind this notion of Yahweh allotting gods over the Gentile nations while maintaining Canaan and Israel for himself, read this following important Psalm 82 where Yahweh now judges those gods for injustice and

---

[13] See also 1 Enoch 89:59, 62-63; 90:25, 56:5; 3Enoch 48C:9, DSS War Scroll 1Q33 Col. xvii:7, Targum Jonathan, Genesis 11, Section II; Philo, On the Posterity of Cain and His Exile 25.89; Concerning Noah's Work as a Planter 14.59; On the Migration of Abraham 36.202; 1 Clement 29; Origen, First Principles 1.5.1. Thanks to Don Enevoldsen for some of these passages. Walter Wink footnotes a plenitude of texts about the 70 angel "gods" over the 70 nations in the Targums in Walter Wink. *Naming the Powers: The Language of Power in the New Testament* (*The Powers : Volume One*) (K-ebook Locations 2235-2242). K-ebook Edition.

proclaims the Gospel that he will eventually take back the nations from those gods.

> God [elohim] has taken his place in the divine council;
> in the midst of the gods [elohim] he holds judgment:
> "How long will you judge unjustly
> and show partiality to the wicked? *Selah*
> Give justice to the weak and the fatherless;
> maintain the right of the afflicted and the destitute.
> Rescue the weak and the needy;
> deliver them from the hand of the wicked."
>
> They have neither knowledge nor understanding,
> they walk about in darkness;
> all the foundations of the earth are shaken.
>
> I said, "You are gods [elohim]
> sons of the Most High, all of you;
> nevertheless, like men you shall die,
> and fall like any prince."
> Arise, O God, judge the earth;
> for you shall inherit all the nations!

So from this text we see that God has a divine council that stands around him, and it consists of "gods" who are judging rulers over the nations and are also called *sons of the Most High* (equivalent to "sons of God"). Because they have not ruled justly, God will bring them low in judgment and take the nations away from them. Sound familiar? It's the same exact story as Deuteronomy 32:8-9 and Isaiah 24:21-22.

> Isaiah 24:21–22
> On that day the LORD will punish the host of heaven, in heaven, and the kings of the earth, on the earth. They will be gathered together as prisoners in a pit; they will be shut up in a prison, and after many days they will be punished.[14]

---

[14] Interestingly, this passage of Isaiah is not clear about what judgment in history it is referring to. But the language earlier in the text is similar to Psalm 82 and to the Flood when it says, "For the windows of heaven are opened, and

One of the Dead Sea Scrolls written in the first century B.C., reinforces this ancient Jewish interpretation of Psalm 82 as punishment focused on the divine council of gods, with Satan as their chief, allotted judicial authority over the nations:

> its interpretation concerns Satan and the spirits of his lot [who] rebelled by turning away from the precepts of God to … And Melchizedek will avenge the vengeance of the judgements of God … and he will drag [them from the hand of] Satan and from the hand of all the sp[irits of] his [lot]. And all the 'gods [of Justice'] will come to his aid [to] attend to the de[struction] of Satan.[15]

The idea that the Bible should talk about existent gods other than Yahweh is certainly uncomfortable for absolute monotheists. But our received definitions of monotheism are more often than not determined by our cultural traditions, many of which originate in theological controversies of other time eras that create the baggage of non-Biblical agendas.

According to the Evangelical Protestant principle of *Sola Scriptura*, that the Bible alone is the final authority of doctrine, not tradition, believers are obligated to first find out what the Bible text says and then adjust their theology to be in line with Scripture, not the other way around. All too often we find individuals ignoring or redefining a Biblical text because it does not fit their preconceived notion of what the Bible *should* say, rather than what it actually says. The existence of other gods in Scripture is one of those issues.

In light of this theological fear, some try to reinterpret this reference of gods or sons of God in Psalm 82 as a poetic expression of human judges or rulers on earth metaphorically taking the place of God, the ultimate judge, by determining justice in his likeness and image. But there are three big reasons why this cannot be so: First, the terminology in the passage contradicts the notion of human judges and fails to connect that term ("sons of God") to human beings anywhere else in the Bible; Second, the Bible elsewhere

---

the foundations of the earth tremble. 19 The earth is utterly broken, the earth is split apart, the earth is violently shaken. 20 The earth staggers like a drunken man; it sways like a hut; its transgression lies heavy upon it, and it falls, and will not rise again." So this may be another passage that uses a Flood reference tied in with the Watchers and their punishment.

[15] *11QMelch* Geza Vermes, *The Dead Sea Scrolls in English*, Revised and extended 4th ed. (Sheffield: Sheffield Academic Press, 1995), 361.

explicitly reveals a divine council or assembly of supernatural sons of God that are judges over geographical allotments of nations that is more consistent with this passage; Third, a heavenly divine council of supernatural sons of God is more consistent with the ancient Near Eastern (ANE) worldview of the Biblical times that Israel shared with her neighbors. We'll take a closer look at each of these following.

Human or Divine Beings?

Though the sons of God in Psalm 82 and elsewhere in the Old Testament have been understood as supernatural, angelic, or divine beings through most of Jewish and Christian history, it is fair to say that there has also been a minor tradition of scholars and theologians who have interpreted these beings as human rulers or judges of some kind or another.[16] They claim that the scenario in which we see these sons of God is a courtroom, the liturgy they engage in is legal formality, and the terminology they use is forensic (related to lawsuits), thus leading them to conclude that these are poetic descriptions of the responsibility of natural human authorities over their subjects on earth. And they would be supernaturally wrong.

The setting, liturgy and language are indeed all courtroom-oriented in their context, but that courtroom is God's heavenly courtroom because that is how God reveals his own judgments to his people and the nations. Let's let Jesus exegete this passage for us.

In John 10, learned Jews in the Temple challenge Jesus about his identity as Christ. Jesus says that he and the Father are one, a clear claim of deity in the Hebrew culture, which results in the Jews picking up stones to stone him because he, being a man, made himself out to be God (10:33). Their particular Rabbinic absolute monotheism did not allow for the existence of divinity other than the Father. Jesus responds by appealing to this very passage we are discussing: "Jesus answered them, "Is it not written in your Law, 'I said, you are gods'? If he called them gods to whom the word of God came—and Scripture cannot be broken—do you say of him whom the Father consecrated

---

[16] Some prominent examples are: The Jewish Rabbinic Targums and Babylonian Talmud as referenced in "The Sons of God and Nephilim of Genesis 6: Aliens, Demons, or Humans?" By Gary DeMar (Unpublished manuscript); Ramban (Nachmanides), *Commentary on the Torah: Genesis*, trans. Charles B. Chavel (New York: Shilo Publishing House, 1971); William H. Green, "The Sons of God and the Daughters of Men," in *The Unity of the Book of Genesis* (New York: Charles Scribner's Sons, 1910); Meredith G. Kline, *Kingdom Prologue: Genesis Foundations for a Covenantal Worldview*, (Overland Park: KS; Two Age Press, 2000); James B. Jordan, *Primeval Saints: Studies in the Patriarchs of Genesis* (Moscow, ID: Canon Press, 2001).

and sent into the world, 'You are blaspheming,' because I said, 'I am the Son of God'?" (10:34-36).

If the judges in Psalm 82 "to whom the word of God came" were considered to be men rather than gods by Jesus, then his appeal to the passage to justify his claims of deity would be nonsensical. He would essentially be saying "I am a god in the same way that human judges were human representatives of God." But this would not be controversial, it would divest Jesus of all deity, and they would certainly not seek to stone him. No, Jesus is affirming the divinity of the sons of God in Psalm 82 and chastising the Jews that their own Scriptures allow for the existence of divine beings (gods) other than the Father, so it would not be inherently unscriptural for another being to claim divinity. Of course, Jesus is the species-unique Son of God (John 1:18),[17] the "visible Yahweh" co-regent over the divine council (Dan. 7). But Jesus' point is that the diversity of deity is not unknown in the Old Testament.[18]

Jesus is arguing for the Trinitarian concept of divine diversity as being compatible with Old Testament monotheism, which was not compatible with man-made traditions of absolute monotheism that Rabbinic Jews followed. Remember, in the Bible, the concept of "god" (elohim) was about a plane of existence not necessarily a "being" of existence, so there were many gods (many elohim) that existed on that supernatural plane, yet only one God of gods who created all things, including those other elohim or sons of God.

This is precisely the nuanced distinction that the Apostle Paul refers to when he addresses the issue of food sacrificed to idols—that is, physical images of deities on earth. He considers idols as having "no real existence," but then refers to other "gods" in the heavens or on earth *who do exist*, but are *not the same* as the One Creator God:

> 1 Cor. 8:4-6
> Therefore, as to the eating of food offered to idols, we know that "an idol has no real existence," and that "there is no God but one." For although there may be so-called gods in heaven or on earth—as indeed there are many "gods" and many

---
[17] Heiser points about that the Greek word for "only begotten" son of God is *monogenes*, which is better translated as "unique," in the same way that Isaac was not Abraham's only son, but was referred to as his "only son" in this sense of uniqueness (Heb 11:17). Heiser *The Myth That is True*, p. 28-29.
[18] Michael S. Heiser, "Deuteronomy 32:8 and the Sons of God" http://www.thedivinecouncil.com/DT32BibSac.pdf, accessed March 23, 2011, p 20-21. See also, "Michael S. Heiser, "Mormonism's Use of Psalm 82," The FARMS Review, 19/1, 2007, http://www.thedivinecouncil.com/John10Psa82excerpt.pdf accessed March 23, 2011.

"lords"—yet <u>for us there is one God</u>, the Father, from whom are all things and for whom we exist, and one Lord, Jesus Christ, through whom are all things and through whom we exist.

1 Cor. 10:18-20
Consider the people of Israel: are not those who eat the sacrifices participants in the altar? What do I imply then? That food offered to idols is anything, or that <u>an idol is anything</u>? No, I imply that <u>what pagans sacrifice they offer to demons and not to God</u>. I do not want you to be participants with demons.

In 1 Corinthians, as in Revelation 9:20 quoted earlier, gods are not merely figments of imagination without existence in a world where the Trinity is the sole deity residing in the spiritual realm. Rather, physical idols (*images*) are "nothing," and "have no real existence" in that they are the representatives of the deities, not the deities themselves. But the deities behind those idols are real demonic beings; the gods of the nations who are not THE God, for they themselves were created by God and are therefore essentially incomparable to the God through whom are all things and through whom we exist.

The terminology used by Paul in the first passage contrasting the many gods and lords with the one God and Lord of Christianity reflects the client-patron relationship that ANE cultures shared. As K.L. Noll explains in his text on ancient Canaan and Israel, "Lord" was the proper designation for a patron in a patron-client relationship. There may have been many gods, but for ancient Israel, there was only one Lord, and that was Yahweh."[19]

This is certainly difficult for a modern mind to wrap itself around because we have been taught to think that there are only two diametrically opposed options: Either absolute diversity as in polytheism (many gods of similar essence) or absolute unity as in absolute monotheism that excludes the possibility of any other divine beings less than the One God.[20] As we have already seen, the Bible seems to indicate that there are other "gods" who are not of the same species as God the

---

[19] K.L. Noll, *Canaan and Israel in Antiquity: An Introduction*, New York: NY; Shefffield Academic Press, 2001, p. 212.

[20] Another possibility, henotheism, is the belief that there are many gods but one god is supreme over them all. But this is nothing more than an exalted polytheism because that supreme god is not a different species, whereas Biblical theism or *monolatry* maintains Yahweh as being of a different substance, essence, or species than the other gods it speaks of.

Father or God the Son, yet they do exist as supernatural entities with ruling power over the nations outside of God's people. Some scholars have used the term *monolatry* of this view rather than monotheism, because monotheism excludes the existence of any other gods, while monolatry allows for the existence of other gods, but demands the worship of one God who is essentially different from all other gods.[21]

Psalm 89 fills out the picture of the heavenly divine council as opposed to an earthly human one that is composed of these sons of God who are comparably less than Yahweh:

> Psa. 89:5-7
> Let the heavens praise your wonders, O LORD,
> your faithfulness in the assembly of the holy ones!
> For who in the skies can be compared to the LORD?
> Who among the heavenly beings (Hebrew: *sons of God*) is like the LORD,
> a God greatly to be feared in the council of the holy ones, and awesome above all who are around him?

Here, the sons of God are referred to as an assembly or council of holy ones that surround Yahweh in a heavenly court "in the skies," not in an earthly court or council of humans, thus reinforcing the supernatural distinction from earthly judges. Israel is sometimes called, "a holy nation" (Ex. 19:6), a "holy people" (Isa. 62:12), "holy ones" (Psa. 16:3), and other derivatives of that concept, but the Hebrew word for "holy ones" (*qedoshim*) is used often in the Bible to refer to these supernatural sons of God, as the "ten thousands of his holy ones," surrounding God's heavenly throne.[22] Daniel calls these heavenly *holy ones* "watchers" in Daniel 4 (verses 13, 17, and 23) and the New Testament book of Jude quotes the non-canonical book of Enoch regarding God coming with ten thousand of his holy ones who were also these

---

[21] Michael S. Heiser, The Divine Council In Late Canonical And Non-Canonical Second Temple Jewish Literature (Madison, WI: University of Wisconsin, 2004), 10.
[22] Deut 33:1-4; Job 5:1; 15:15; Psa 89:5, 7; Dan 8:13; 14:7; Zech 14:5; Jude 14. Michael S. Heiser points out that even though the MT of Deut 33:1-4 appears to reference the congregation of Israel as "holy ones," the Septuagint version of this verse, which the New Testament authors seem to quote, applies the term to "angels" at Sinai through whom God gave the law (Acts 7:52-53; Heb 2:1-2; Gal 3:19) Heiser, *The Myth That is True,* p. 149-152. In Daniel 7 it appears that the holy ones in God's divine council in heaven (7:27) are spoken of in fusion (7:21-22, 25) with the "saints" or holy ones in earthly Israel (7:18). The beasts of earthly kingdoms ruled over by their Watcher Princes are at war with Israel and its Watchers led by Michael. And in Deut 33:2-3 the term "holy ones" is used of both Israelites and supernatural beings in the same paragraph.

"watchers" or sons of God from heaven (Jude 14).[23] The Dead Sea Scrolls of Qumran also used the term "holy ones" in many passages to refer to angelic beings from God's heavenly throne, making this a common Semitic understanding congenial with the worldview of Daniel.[24]

So there is Biblical unanimity in describing a heavenly host of ten thousands of sons of God, called gods, watchers, and holy ones who surround God's throne in the heavens as an assembly, and who counsel with God and worship him, and some of whom were given to rule over human nations in the past (also called "demons"), but have lost that privilege at some point. These gods are clearly *not* human judges on earth; they are supernatural elohim in the heavenly divine council.

Biblical Narratives of the Divine Council

The idea of a divine council of sons of God surrounding Yahweh as a hierarchical assembly is not merely mined from poetic passages in the Psalms; it is explicitly described in narratives that seem to settle any question of the matter. The two main passages are 1Kings 22 and Job 1-2.

In 1 Kings 22, the evil King Ahab of Israel seeks out prophets to tell him that his wicked intentions of invading Ramoth-gilead will be condoned by Yahweh. Many of the prophets encourage Ahab to do so with God's blessing. The prophet Micaiah however describes this vision of what actually happened:

> 1 Kings 22:19-22
> And Micaiah said, "Therefore hear the word of the LORD: I saw the <u>LORD sitting on his throne</u>, and all <u>the host of heaven standing beside him on his right hand and on his left</u>; and the LORD said, 'Who will entice Ahab, that he may go up and fall at Ramoth-gilead?' And one said one thing, and another said another. Then a spirit came forward and stood

---

[23] And behold! He cometh with <u>ten thousands of His holy ones</u>, To execute judgment upon all, And to destroy all the ungodly. (Enoch 1:9)
And his activities had to do with <u>the Watchers</u>, and his days were with <u>the holy ones</u>. (Enoch 12:2)
And it came to pass after this that my spirit was translated And it ascended into the heavens: And I saw <u>the holy sons of God</u>. (Enoch 71:1)
[24] See these DSS passages: 1QM 1:16; 10:11–12; 12:1, 4, 7; 15:14; 1QS 11:7–8; 1QH 3:21–22; 10:35; 1QDM 4:1; 1QSb 1:5; 1Q 36:1; 1QapGen 2:1. John Joseph Collins, Frank Moore Cross and Adela Yarbro Collins, *Daniel: A Commentary on the Book of Daniel, Hermeneia—a critical and historical commentary on the Bible* (Minneapolis: Fortress Press, 1993), 313-314. The sectarian Jews from Qumran who safeguarded the Dead Sea Scrolls believed they were united with the angels in heaven, so they occasionally used the term "holy ones" to refer to those humans, but this reinforces the usage of the term as related to the angelic beings.

before the LORD, saying, 'I will entice him.' And the LORD said to him, 'By what means?' And he said, 'I will go out, and will be a lying spirit in the mouth of all his prophets.' And he said, 'You are to entice him, and you shall succeed; <u>go out and do so</u>.'

So, here we see an explicit description of how the Divine council of God operates. The sons of God, called "host of heaven" surround God's throne and God throws out a question that they then deliberate through council until God accepts one of the ideas offered by a spiritual being. God then gives that spirit the authority to go and perform the will of the council led by Yahweh.

Job 1 and 2 picture a very similar scene of God's heavenly assembly "presenting themselves" in a legal procession "before the Lord" with the added element of the prosecuting "adversary" (the Hebrew word *ha satan* means "the adversary"):

> Job 1:6-12
> Now there was a day when the <u>sons of God came to present themselves before the LORD</u>, and the adversary also came among them... And the LORD said to the adversary, "Behold, all that he has is in your hand. Only against him do not stretch out your hand." So the adversary went out from the presence of the LORD.

> Job 2:1-6
> Again there was a day when <u>the sons of God came to present themselves before the LORD</u>, and the adversary also came among them to present himself before the LORD... And the LORD said to the adversary, "Have you considered my servant Job, that there is none like him on the earth, a blameless and upright man, who fears God and turns away from evil?...And the LORD said to the adversary, "Behold, he is in your hand; only spare his life."

Once again, God counsels with his divine assembly of sons of God, asking questions and deliberating, in this case with the adversary. And then God gives the adversary the responsibility of carrying out the will of God's overseen council meeting. These sons of God are the same heavenly host who were present when God was creating the foundations of the earth and sang for joy as in the Psalm passages we already looked at (Job 38:7). These could not possibly be human rulers in an earthly court.

The last passage that describes a scene exactly like the previous two is in Zechariah:

> Zech. 2:13-3:7
> Be silent, all flesh, before the LORD, for he has roused himself from <u>his holy dwelling</u>. Then he showed me Joshua the high priest <u>standing before the angel of the LORD</u>, and Satan ["<u>the adversary</u>"] <u>standing at his right hand to accuse him</u>... Now Joshua was standing before the angel, clothed with filthy garments. And the angel said to <u>those who were standing before him</u>, "Remove the filthy garments from him."...And the angel of the LORD solemnly assured Joshua, "Thus says the <u>LORD of hosts</u>…"

In this vision of Zechariah he sees into God's holy dwelling where Yahweh has brought his heavenly host standing before him and the satan standing ready to accuse Joshua before the heavenly court. Yahweh is called "Lord of hosts" because he is surrounded by that heavenly host of the sons of God (Remembering that the name of God used in a passage reflects a distinct aspect of his identity or character related to that passage).

Scholars point out that this vision of Zechariah is exemplary of another thread throughout the Old Testament of the covenant lawsuit. As we have seen in Job, 1Kings and Zechariah, there are legal procedures that the divine council engages in when deliberating judgment upon Israel or another guilty nation or king.[25] We have seen the summoning of the host and defendant, a presentation or standing before God, the judge's call for testimony from the council, accusation of an adversary or the prophet himself, and judgments carried out by council members. These same elements are assumed in other passages with a more implicit presence. Examples would be Isaiah's vision of the heavenly throne of seraphim with the plural imperatives by God "Who will

---

[25] Herbert B. Huffmon "The Covenant Lawsuit in the Prophets" *Journal of Biblical Literature*, Vol. 78, No. 4 (Dec., 1959), pp. 285-295; Wheeler Robinson, H., "The Council of Yahweh," *Journal of Theological Studies*, 45 (1944) p.151-158.

go for us?" (Isa. 6) or "Comfort my people and cry out" (Isa. 40), or in Ezekiel's throne room vision (Ezek. 1). In these passages, God asks a question to an unknown group of beings. That group is no doubt the divine council around his throne. Jeremiah and Amos have even indicated that the mark of a true prophet versus a false prophet is that the true prophet has actually stood in the divine council and received his directions from God and his holy ones, while the false prophet has not (Jer. 23:18, 22; Amos 3:7).

Ancient Near Eastern Parallels

We have seen that the term *sons of God* is used interchangeably in the Bible with other words such as gods, demons (in some cases), heavenly host, host of heaven, watchers, holy ones, assembly, and divine council. But there is a third reason why the sons of God are not human judges but divine heavenly beings, and that is because the same divine council or assembly of gods shows up in ancient Near Eastern stories from Israel's neighbors. In other words, Israel shared a common cultural environment with her contemporaries that provides a context for interpreting the intended meaning of the Biblical text.[26] If we want to understand the meaning of a mysterious term or concept in the Bible we must exegete the broader cultural context within which Israel operated. Though this is not finally determinative of Biblical meaning, it carries great weight considering that Israel shared much in common with her neighbors in terms of language, worldview, symbols, and imagination.

Thorkild Jacobsen, one of the foremost authorities on Mesopotamian religion explained the origins of the divine council as a projection of the terrestrial conditions of the primitive form of human governmental democracy that existed in ancient Mesopotamia.[27] Though this worldview of divine world and cosmos ruled by the gods through a divine assembly was not monolithic and unchanging, scholar Patrick D. Miller has argued that it nevertheless remained fairly constant, and was clearly a part of the Biblical worldview as well.[28]

The Mesopotamian/Sumerian worldview that Abraham was immersed in before his calling by Yahweh involved a divine council of gods that functioned

---

[26] John Walton called it a "common cognitive environment." John H. Walton. *Ancient Near Eastern Thought and the Old Testament: Introducing the Conceptual World of the Hebrew Bible*. Grand Rapids, MI: Baker, 2006; p 21.
[27] Thorkild Jacobsen, "Primitive Democracy in Ancient Mesopotamia," *Journal of Near Eastern Studies*, Vol. 2, No. 3 (Jul., 1943), 167.
[28] Patrick D. Miller, "Cosmology And World Order In The Old Testament The Divine Council As Cosmic-Political Symbol" *Israelite Religion and Biblical Theology: Collected Essays by Patrick D. Miller*. NY: Sheffield Academic Press, 2000, p 423.

in part as a court of law that ruled over the affairs of men, including the authority to grant kingship to both gods and men. The divine council met in assembly under the god of heaven and "father of the gods," An (later, *Anu*), but also with him was Enlil, the god of storm. Either of them would broach a matter to be considered which would then be discussed and debated by the "great gods" or "Anunnaki," whose number included the fifty senior gods as well as "the seven gods who determine fate."[29] As Jacobsen put it, "Through such general discussion—"asking one another," as the Babylonians expressed it—the issues were clarified and the various gods had opportunity to voice their opinions for or against."[30] The executive duties of carrying out the decisions of the assembly seemed to have rested with Enlil as a kind of co-regent with An.

The *Enuma Elish*, the Akkadian creation myth of the Babylonians who presided over Israel's exile also depicted a divine council of gods convened around the supreme god Marduk whose operations reflected the same heavenly bureaucracy.[31] But as Heiser points out, the consensus of scholars is that the Ugaritic pantheon of Canaan was the closest conceptual precursor to the Israelite version of the divine council.[32] The linguistic parallels are numerous and their comparison yields fruitful understanding of the Hebrew worldview, both in its similarities and differences.

Among the many parallels that Heiser draws out between the Canaanite and Israelite divine council are the following:

> Ugaritic terms of the divine council include, "assembly of the gods," and "assembly of the sons of God." The Hebrew Bible uses the terms, "sons of God," "assembly of the holy ones" (Psa. 89:6), and "gods" "in the council of God" (Job 15:8).
>
> In Ugaritic mythology, El was the supreme god and Baal was his vice-regent who ruled over the other gods of the council. In the Hebrew Bible, El/Elohim/Yahweh is the creator God, but he also has a vice-regent, the Son of Man/Angel of the

---

[29] The seven gods who determine fate are portrayed in the novel *Noah Primeval* as An, the god of heaven, Enlil the god of storm, Enki the god of water, Ninhursag the earth goddess, Nanna the moon god, Utu the sun god and Inanna the goddess of sex and war.
[30] *Jacobsen*, "Primitive Democracy," 168-169.
[31] Min Suc Kee, "The Heavenly Council and its Type-scene," *Journal for the Study of the Old Testament* Vol 31.3 (2007): 259-273.
[32] Heiser, The Divine Council, 8.

Lord who was a visible incarnation of Yahweh who ruled over the divine council (Dan. 7). Christians would eventually argue that this "second Yahweh" was in fact the pre-incarnate Messiah, Jesus.

In Ugaritic mythology, El lived in a tent on a cosmic mountain in the north (*Sapon*) "at the source of two rivers," where the divine assembly would meet to deliberate and El would dispense his decrees. The mountain was a connection between heaven and earth, that is the earthly temple and its counterpart in heaven. In the Hebrew Bible, Yahweh's sanctuary is also in a tent (tabernacle) on a cosmic mountain, Zion (Psa. 48:1-2), that is in the heights of the north (*Sapon*). This mountain is poetically linked to Eden, which is the source of rivers (Ezek. 28:13-16) and its precursor, Mount Sinai was where God dispensed his word with his heavenly host (Deut. 33:1-2; Ps. 68:15-17).[33]

Though there are more congruencies between Canaanite and Hebrew concepts of the divine council than listed here, there are certainly many incongruencies as well, not the least of which was the polytheistic worldview of Canaan versus the monolatrous worldview of Israel. Gerald Cooke's classic article, "The Sons of (the) God(s)" lists the distinguishing characteristics in the Hebrew divine council of sons of God:

> The full mythological representation is absent: the individualization, personalization and specification of function which characterized this idea-complex in other cultures of the Near East finds little parallel in the Hebrew-Jewish records… The recognition or assignment of functions in the heavenly company is never specific as in non-Israelite mythologies: they appear only in the more general functions of praising Yahweh and his holiness, serving as members of the royal court, entering into counsel with Yahweh, exercising judgment over the peoples, and doing Yahweh's bidding. Nor are the interrelations of the gods treated in

---
[33] Heiser, *The Divine Council*, 34-41.

Israelite tradition as in other traditions. Members of the heavenly company remain essentially characterless functionaries even when they appear singly as "the spirit," "the satan," or a "messenger." Yahweh's relationship to the lesser beings appears only in the formalized title "sons," which seems to describe only the classification of these beings as divine; Yahweh is never associated in paternal relationship with any particular one(s) of these beings, as are many of the gods of pagan pantheons; if Yahweh's "fatherhood" vis-à-vis these divine beings can be spoken of at all, it has only the formal meaning found in the idea of the "father" (i.e., head and leader) of a group of prophets; members of the heavenly company are never called "sons of Yahweh"; worship of any of the heavenly court besides the supreme Judge, Yahweh, is never countenanced by prophetic Yahwism. Members of the heavenly company never threaten his authority as supreme Judge and King.[34]

So the similarities between the worldviews need not mean absolute identity, but rather a common linguistic understanding that may help modern interpreters to understand the Bible in its own historical and cultural context. As Miller concluded, "The mythopoeic conception of the heavenly assembly, the divine council, is the Bible's way of pointing to a transcendent ordering and governing of the universe, of which all human governments and institutions are a reflection, but even more it is the machinery by which the just rule of God is effective, that is, powerful, in the universe."[35]

---

[34] Gerald Cooke, "The Sons of (the) God(s)," *Zeitschrift für die alttestamentliche Wissenschaft*, n.s.:35:1 (1964), p 45-46.
[35] Miller, "Cosmology And World Order," p 442.

CHAPTER 36:

THE NEPHILIM

Gen. 6:4
The Nephilim were on the earth in those days, and also afterward, when the sons of God came in to the daughters of men, and they bore children to them. Those were the mighty men who were of old, men of renown.

Num. 13:33
And there we saw the Nephilim (the sons of Anak, who come from the Nephilim), and we seemed to ourselves like grasshoppers, and so we seemed to them."

The meaning of the Biblical word *Nephilim* has been a matter of unending controversy in Church history. That the word is still not translated into an English defined word but *transliterated* in most Bible translations is evidence of the fact that no agreement can be made over its original meaning. The two passages quoted above are the only two places in the Bible where the Hebrew word *Nephilim* is used. What would surprise some Bible readers is that these are not the only places where the Nephilim are *talked about* in Scripture. *Nephilim* has a theological thread that begins in Genesis 6 and goes through all the way to the New Testament.

The main opposing interpretations of this word come down to whether it is a reference to mighty leaders of some kind or to giants of abnormal human height. In my novel, *Noah Primeval* I take the perspective that these are giants and that these Bible passages are not merely obscure and unconnected factual references to an historical oddity, but rather that they are part of a diabolical supernatural plan of "sons of God" who are fallen from God's divine council of heavenly host. While my novel is obviously speculative fictional fantasy, it is nevertheless loosely based upon what I believe is a theological thread revealed in the Bible that becomes clear upon closer inspection of the text.

Taking a look at the first passage, Genesis 6:4, in context we read:

> Gen. 6:1-4
> When man began to multiply on the face of the land and daughters were born to them, the sons of God saw that the daughters of man were attractive. And they took as their wives any they chose. Then the LORD said, "My Spirit shall not abide in man forever, for he is flesh: his days shall be 120 years." The Nephilim were on the earth in those days, and also afterward, when the sons of God came in to the daughters of man and they bore children to them. These were the mighty men who were of old, the men of renown.

Genesis 6 is the opening lines to the story of Noah's flood. It talks about man reproducing upon the face of the earth and "sons of God" taking women as wives. I have already documented extensively elsewhere that the phrase *sons of God* in the Bible is a proven attribution to supernatural members of God's divine council. But some still attempt to change that meaning of the phrase in this passage to mean either men in the "righteous lineage" of Seth as contrasted with the daughters of men in the "unrighteous lineage" of Cain, or to mean kingly rulers on the earth who were engaging in polygamy.

In either case, these interpretations correctly acknowledge the negative connotation of the intermarriage and the violation of a separation, but they both seek to define the sons of God as natural men on earth. What both of these "humanly" interpretations miss is that the passage does not talk about a violation of separation of status or bloodline, but upon heavenly and earthly essence. The text links the "daughters of men" to the multiplication of "man" in general, *not* to a particular bloodline or royalty.

The Sethite view seeks to base its argument on an early reference in Genesis after Cain has killed Abel, and God grants a new son, Seth, to replace Abel for Eve. "To Seth also a son was born, and he called his name Enosh. At that time people began to call upon the name of the LORD (Gen. 4:26)." They believe that these ones calling upon the name of the Lord are those in the line of Seth as opposed to people in the line of Cain.

But the text does not restrict the righteousness in any way to Seth's lineage. It speaks in general of people calling upon God. In fact, the word used of "man" in Genesis 6 is "adam" which makes the population growth of

Genesis 6:1 a generic reference to humankind fulfilling God's mandate to *the* Adam as mankind's representative to populate the earth, not to the exclusive lineage of Cain. The daughters are after all, "daughters of *adam*," in the text, not daughters of Cain.

Michael Heiser sums up the arguments against the human interpretation:

> First, Genesis 4:26 never says the only people who "called on the name of the Lord" were men from Seth's lineage, nor does it say that Seth's birth produced some sort of spiritual revival. This is an idea brought to the text from the imagination of the interpreter. Second, if these marriages are human-to-human, how is it that giants (*Nephilim*) were the result of the unions? Third, the text never calls the women "daughters of Cain." Rather, they are "daughters of men [humankind]." Fourth, nothing in Genesis 6:1-4 or anywhere else in the Bible identifies those who come from Seth's lineage with the descriptive phrase "sons of God."[1]

There is simply no explicit reference in the Bible to sons of Seth being sons of God or daughters of man being only daughters of Cain. One must bring a preconceived theory to the text to make it fit. But in so doing, one must ignore the more explicit Biblical passages about the sons of God as God's heavenly host. And in so doing, one must affirm a racial righteousness based on human blood lineage. The emphasis in the text is on the separation of heavenly and earthly flesh.[2]

The New Testament agrees with the supernatural interpretation of divine/human cohabitation because it actually alludes to this very violation of fleshly categories and resultant punishment in 2 Peter and Jude, letters that show a strong literary interdependency on one another. If you compare the two passages you see the sensual violation of human and angelic flesh that is located in Genesis 6:

---

[1] Michael S. Heiser *The Myth That is True: Rediscovering the Cosmic Narrative of the Bible*, unpublished manuscript, 2011, p 70. Available at www.michaelsheiser.com.
[2] For a refutation of the sons of God as human rulers, judges or potentates, see Appendix A, "The Divine Council and the Sons of God."

2Pet. 2:4-10
For if God did not spare <u>angels when they sinned</u>, but cast them into hell (*tartarus*) and <u>committed them to chains of gloomy</u> darkness to be kept until the judgment; if he did not spare the ancient world, but preserved Noah, a herald of righteousness, with seven others, when he brought a flood upon the world of the ungodly; if by turning the cities of <u>Sodom and Gomorrah</u> to ashes he condemned them to extinction, <u>making them an example of what is going to happen to the ungodly</u>;... then the Lord knows how to rescue the godly from trials, and to keep the unrighteous under punishment until the day of judgment, and especially those who <u>indulge in the lust of defiling passion</u> and despise authority.

Jude 6-7
And angels who did not keep their own domain, but abandoned their proper abode, he has kept in eternal chains under gloomy darkness until the judgment of the great day— just as Sodom and Gomorrah and the surrounding cities, which likewise indulged in gross immorality and pursued strange flesh, serve as an example by undergoing a punishment of eternal fire.

Both these passages speak of the same angels who sinned before the flood of Noah, and who were committed to chains of gloomy darkness. 1 Peter 3:19-20 calls these imprisoned angels "disobedient." According to our study, the angelic sons of God are spoken of as sinning in Genesis 6, so these must be the same angels referred to by the authors of the New Testament. But just what is their sin?

Both Peter and Jude link the sin of those fallen angels with the sin of Sodom and Gomorrah, which is described as indulging in "gross immorality" by pursuing "strange flesh." The Greek words for "gross immorality" (*ek porneuo*) indicates a heightened form of sexual immorality, and the Greek words for "strange flesh" (*heteros sarx*) indicate the pursuit of something different from one's natural flesh. This "strange flesh" cannot be a reference to homosexuality for several reasons. First, homosexuality is not the pursuit of *hetero* or different gender, it is the pursuit of *homo* or same gender. Secondly, homosexual behavior involves the *same* human male flesh (*sarx*), not different flesh as it would with angels. Thirdly, when the New Testament refers to the unnaturalness of homosexual acts it uses the Greek phrase, *para physin*, which means "contrary to nature" (Romans 1:26). The Bible certainly does condemn homosexuality as sin, but the sin of Sodom that that Jude and Peter focus on is not so much homosexuality, as interspecies sexuality between angels and humans.[3]

Angels on earth can have a physical presence. The angels who visited Sodom were clearly spoken of as enfleshed in such a way that they were physically present to have their feet washed and even eat food with Abraham and with Lot (Gen. 18:1-8; 19:3). Bible students know that the men in Sodom were seeking to engage in sexual penetration of these same angels who visited Lot in his home. So here, men seeking sex with angels is not merely a homosexual act, it is a violation of the heavenly and earthly flesh distinction that the Scriptures seem to reinforce. So Peter and Jude link the angels sinning before the flood to the violation of a sexual separation of angels and humankind. The New Testament commentary on Genesis 6:1 affirms the supernatural view of the sons of God as having sex with humans.

It has been long known by scholars that the letter of *Jude* not only quotes a verse from the non-canonical book of *1 Enoch* (v. 14 with 1 Enoch 1:9),[4] but that Jude 6-7 and 2 Peter 2:4-10 both paraphrase content from *1 Enoch*, thus supporting the notion that the inspired authors intended an Enochian interpretation of "angels" called the Watchers (sons of God) having sexual intercourse with humans. *1 Enoch* extrapolates the Nephilim pre-flood story from the Bible as speaking of angels violating their supernatural separation and having sex with humans who bear them giants.[5]

---

[3] This observation is qualified by the fact that in Genesis 19, the Sodomites do not apparently know that the two men are angels. In Judges 19, the same exact scenario as Sodom is played out with Benjaminites in Gibeah seeking homosexual copulation with a visiting Levite (angels are not involved). Jude seems to draw out the angelic/human copulation angle in his interpretation. In full Biblical context, it may be most consistent to say that the sin of Sodom includes both homosexuality *and* angelic/human violation.

[4] Richard J. Bauckham, Vol. 50, *Word Biblical Commentary: 2 Peter, Jude*. Word Biblical Commentary. Dallas: Word, Incorporated, 2002. Here is the Jude passage: "[T]hat Enoch, the seventh from Adam, prophesied, saying, "Behold, the Lord comes with ten thousands of his holy ones, to execute judgment on all and to convict all the ungodly of all their deeds of ungodliness that they have committed in such an ungodly way, and of all the harsh things that ungodly sinners have spoken against him." Here is 1 Enoch 1:9, the text from the actual book that Jude quotes: "And behold! He cometh with ten thousands of His holy ones to execute judgement upon all, and to destroy all the ungodly: And to convict all flesh of all the works of their ungodliness which they have ungodly committed, and of all the hard things which ungodly sinners have spoken against Him.

[5] See 1 Enoch 6-19 and 86-88, especially 7:1-2; 15-16; 106:17. Richard Bauckham observes, "This was how the account of the "sons of God" in Gen 6:1–4 was universally understood (so far as our evidence goes) until the mid-second century A.D. (*1 Enoch* 6–19, 21, 86–88, 106:13–15, 17; *Jub.* 4:15, 22; 5:1; CD 2:17–19; 1QapGen 2:1; *Tg. Ps.*-

Any question regarding the authenticity of this interpretation in Jude and Peter is quickly answered by another commonality that the New Testament authors share with the Enochian interpretation. Their combination of the angelic sexual sin with the sexual sin of Sodom is a poetic doublet that does not occur in the Old Testament, but does appear in multiple Second Temple Jewish manuscripts circulating in the New Testament time period. Jude and Peter are alluding to a common understanding of their culture that the angelic sin (and its hybrid fruit of giants) was an unnatural sexual violation of the divine and human separation. Here are some of those texts:

> Sirach 16:7-8
> He forgave not the giants of old,
> [the fruit of the angelic sin]
> Who revolted in their might.
> He spared not the place where Lot sojourned,
> Who were arrogant in their pride.[6]

> Testament of Naphtali 3:4-5
> [D]iscern the Lord who made all things, so that you do not become like Sodom, which departed from the order of nature. Likewise the Watchers departed from nature's order; the Lord pronounced a curse on them at the Flood.[7]

> 3 Maccabees 2:4-5
> Thou didst destroy those who aforetime did iniquity, among whom were giants trusting in their strength and boldness, bringing upon them a boundless flood of water. Thou didst burn up with fire and brimstone the men of Sodom, workers of arrogance, who had become known of all for their crimes,

---

J. Gen. 6:1–4; *T. Reub.* 5:6–7; *T. Napht.* 3:5; *2 Apoc. Bar.* 56:10–14)." Bauckham, Richard J. Vol. 50, *Word Biblical Commentary : 2 Peter, Jude.* Word Biblical Commentary. Dallas: Word, Incorporated, 2002, p 51. Other Second Temple Jewish writings support this ancient interpretation of pre-diluvian Nephilim/human offspring as giants: 3 Baruch 4:10; Wisdom 14:6; 3 Maccabees 2:4; Sirach 16:7.

[6] *Apocrypha of the Old Testament, Volume 1,* ed. Robert Henry Charles, Sir 16:7–8. Bellingham, WA: Logos Research Systems, Inc., 2004, 372.

[7] Charlesworth, James H. *The Old Testament Pseudepigrapha: Volume 1.* New York; London: Yale University Press, 1983, 812

and didst make them <u>an example to those who should come after</u>.⁸

[notice "making an example for those after" that is also referenced in Jude 7]

Jubilees 20:4-5
[L]et them not <u>take to themselves wives from the daughters</u> of Canaan; for the seed of Canaan will be rooted out of the land. And he told them of the judgment of <u>the giants</u>, and the <u>judgment of the Sodomites</u>, how they had been judged on account of their <u>wickedness</u>, and had died on account of their <u>fornication, and uncleanness, and mutual corruption through fornication</u>.⁹

This is critical for understanding the Nephilim as unholy giant progeny because the Nephilim are the result of this sexual union between angel and human.

Some respond that angelic beings cannot have sex with humans because of Jesus' statement in Matthew 22. Jesus is confronted by Sadducees who are trying to force Jesus to deny the future Resurrection of the dead. They construct a hypothetical of a woman with multiple husbands due to their multiple deaths, and then ask him whose wife she is at the Resurrection,, hoping to stump Jesus on the horns of a dilemma. Jesus replies, "You are mistaken, not understanding the Scriptures nor the power of God. "For in the resurrection they neither marry nor are given in marriage, but are like angels in heaven (Matt. 22:29-30)." Because of this, it is alleged that angels cannot have sexual intercourse with humans.

But this is not at all what Jesus is concluding. Firstly, Jesus is not talking about sexual intercourse, but the religious law of marriage connections between husband and wife. Secondly, he is not talking about what angels *cannot* do, but what they *do not* do. Angels in heaven who obey God do not marry. This has no implication on what a fallen angel is capable of physically doing when coming to earth. Thirdly, Jesus is talking about angels in heaven, their natural abode, not angels on earth who left that abode to engage in unnatural liaisons with human flesh (as we saw in 2 Peter 2 and Jude). The

---

⁸ *Apocrypha of the Old Testament, Volume 1.* ed. Robert Henry Charles, 3 Mac 2:5. Bellingham, WA: Logos Research Systems, Inc., 2004, 164.
⁹ *Pseudepigrapha of the Old Testament Volume 1.* ed. Robert Henry Charles. Bellingham, WA: Logos Research Systems, Inc., 2004, 42.

angels in heaven that Jesus is talking about are not the angelic sons of God who left heaven, came to earth, and violated God's separation of those domains by having intercourse with human women.

Returning to Genesis 6:1-4, let's take a look at the second part of the passage:

> Gen. 6:3-4
>
> Then the LORD said, "My Spirit shall not abide in man forever, for he is flesh: his days shall be 120 years." The Nephilim were on the earth in those days, and also afterward, when the sons of God came in to the daughters of man and they bore children to them. These were the mighty men who were of old, the men of renown.

Some believe that the Nephilim were not the result of the sexual union between the sons of God and the daughters of men, but rather Nephilim were simply mighty warriors who happened to be around during those times before and after the incident of the sons of God. But this view would make nonsense of the text by inserting something (Nephilim) that has no connection to what is being talked about, namely the sexual unions and the flood. The pericope of verses 1-4 are a lead up to the proclamation of the flood in verses 5-8. The contextual reading of this concise unit of text begins talking about the sexual union of the sons of God with the daughters of men, then makes a reference to God's announcement to destroy the world in 120 years, which then references the Nephilim in context with that judgment, and then bookends the pericope with a reference back to the supernatural sexual union again, thus linking everything between those "bookends" as a sidebar explanation of what it was all about, which leads to the flood in verse 5-8. The Nephilim were around before and after *the flood*, not just the intermarriage incident, and they were the offspring result of that union.[10] Numbers 13:33 confirms this interpretation by saying that the Anakim at the time of Joshua were descendants of the Nephilim, so the Nephilim were clearly around before *and after* the flood.

---

[10] C. Westermann concludes, "There is every reason to think that the Nephilim in 4a refers to mythical semi-divine beings, the fruit of the marriages of the gods with humans, who are connected with the overstepping of the bound presumed in the divine judgment of v. 3. "They came to (them)": " 'to come to' refers in this connection only to the male who visits a woman's quarters, 30:16; 38:16" (E.A. Speiser, AncB). This sentence states expressly that children were the fruit of the union of the sons of the gods with the daughters of men, and clearly, they must be something special; they could not be just plain ordinary mortals." Claus Westermann, *A Continental Commentary: Genesis 1-11*, (Minneapolis, MN: Fortress Press, 1994), p 378.

But the question remains, what does the Hebrew word *Nephilim* mean? Some scholars looking at the root word claim that it means "fallen ones" because that is what the Hebrew means, "to fall". But there is a problem, and that is that the Septuagint (LXX) which is sometimes quoted by the New Testament authors as authoritative, translates this word as "giants."[11] Did those ancient Hellenized Jews not know the true meaning of the word? Or did they know something we do not?

Biblical scholar Michael S. Heiser has revealed a Biblical reference that virtually seals the proof that *Nephilim* are giants, not "fallen ones." In his article "The Meaning of the Word *Nephilim*: Fact vs. Fantasy"[12] he explains that Hebrew is a consonantal language, which means it only spells words with consonants and leaves the reader to fill in the vowels. The ancient language of Aramaic is also consonantal and has an influence on the Hebrew text at various places. There are many Aramaic words in the Bible, and some chapters, such as Daniel 2-7, are written in Aramaic. In later copies, vowel markers were added to the consonants in order to aid in pronunciation. He then explains that the Hebrew word NPHL which is translated into English as *Nephilim* has different meanings depending on the morphology or form of the word. Evidently the morphological form of the word in Genesis and Numbers is not that of the Hebrew meaning "fallen ones," but that of the Aramaic meaning "giants." And the Bible clinches this argument in Numbers 13:33:

> Num. 13:33
> And there we saw the Nephilim (the sons of Anak, who come from the Nephilim), and we seemed to ourselves like grasshoppers, and so we seemed to them."

Heiser shows that the first spelling of Nephilim in the verse is the Hebrew spelling, but the second spelling of Nephilim is a variation that is clearly the Aramaic spelling of "giants." And should there really be any question when the text then describes these Anakim who are descendants of the Nephilim as being gigantic in stature such that they felt like small grasshoppers?

---

[11] Genesis 6:4; Randall Tan, David A. deSilva, and Logos Bible Software. *The Lexham Greek-English Interlinear Septuagint*. Logos Bible Software, 2009.
[12] Michael S. Heiser, "The Meaning of the Word *Nephilim*: Fact vs. Fantasy" http://www.acidtestpress.com/

Now, let's take a look at the Anakim and the other giants that the Bible speaks about. The Anakim or "sons of Anak" are unquestionably defined as giants throughout the Bible because of their tall height (Num. 13:33; Deut. 1:28; 2:10, 21; 9:2). One of the most famous of all those Anakim giants was Goliath.[13] He stood at 9 feet 9 inches tall.[14] His coat of mail alone weighed about 125 pounds, the weight of his spearhead was 15 pounds (1 Sam. 17:4-7). There is no doubt Goliath was unnaturally huge in stature. And his brother Lahmi was of the same genetic material (1 Chron. 20:5). Philistia had a big problem with these Anakim giants, as 1 Chronicles 20:4-8 attests to no less than four of them who had to be killed by King David's men in an apparent campaign against the giants.

But if we go back in time from David to Joshua and the conquest of the Promised Land, we see that the giant Anakim that David was fighting were merely the leftovers from Joshua's own campaign to wipe them out:

> Josh. 11:21-22
> Then Joshua came at that time and cut off the Anakim from the hill country, from Hebron, from Debir, from Anab and from all the hill country of Judah and from all the hill country of Israel. Joshua utterly destroyed them with their cities. There were no Anakim left in the land of the sons of Israel; only in Gaza, in Gath, and in Ashdod some remained.

As it turns out, the Anakim were not the only giants in the land. Evidently the land in and around Canaan was crawling with giants that were called by different names in different locations, such as the Emim, Rephaim, Zamzummim, Horim, Avvim and possibly Caphtorim:

> Deut. 2:10-11, 20-23
> (The <u>Emim</u> formerly lived there, a people <u>great and many, and tall as the Anakim</u>. Like the Anakim they are also counted as <u>Rephaim</u>, but the Moabites call them <u>Emim</u>... (It is also counted as a land of Rephaim. Rephaim formerly lived there—but the Ammonites call them <u>Zamzummim</u>— a people <u>great and many,</u>

---

[13] Joshua 11:21 says that the only Anakim left by the time of David were in Gaza, Ashdod and Gath, Goliath's home.
[14] David Tsumura, *The First Book of Samuel, The New International Commentary on the Old Testament* (Grand Rapids, MI: Wm. B. Eerdmans Publishing Co., 2007), 441.

The Nephilim

and tall as the Anakim; but the LORD destroyed them before the Ammonites, and they dispossessed them and settled in their place as he did for the people of Esau, who live in Seir, when he destroyed the Horites before them and they dispossessed them and settled in their place even to this day. As for the Avvim, who lived in villages as far as Gaza, the Caphtorim, who came from Caphtor, destroyed them and settled in their place.)

King Og of Bashan is described as one of the last of "the remnant of the Rephaim" whose bed was over 13 feet long and made of iron (Deut. 3:11). That is no kingly bed alone; that was a large strong iron bed to hold a giant.

The Rephaim have an interesting Biblical history that connects them literarily to the Nephilim in the Bible. First, the Nephilim are described as *gibborim*, or "mighty men," "men of renown" in Genesis 6:4. This word *gibborim* is used extensively throughout the Old Testament of warriors such as David's "mighty men" (2 Sam. 16:6) and even of the giant Goliath (1Sam. 17:51) and many others.[15] The Nephilim were mighty warriors. The Rephaim were mighty warrior kings.

In the Bible, *Rephaim* were Anakim giants, descendants of the Nephilim (Deut. 2:11; Num. 13:33), who were so significant they even had a valley named after them ("Valley of the Rephaim," Josh. 15:8). But there is more to the Rephaim than that. Og, king of Bashan, was a Rephaim giant, and all his portion of the land of Bashan was called "the land of the Rephaim" (Deut. 3:13), an ambiguous wording that could equally be translated as "the 'hell' of the Rephaim."[16] Bashan was a deeply significant spiritual location to the Canaanites and the Hebrews. And as the *Dictionary of Deities and Demons in the Bible* puts it, Biblical geographical tradition agrees with the mythological and cultic data of the Canaanites of Ugarit that "the Bashan region, or a part of it, clearly represented 'Hell', the celestial and infernal abode of their deified dead kings," the Rephaim.[17]

Mount Hermon was in Bashan, and Mount Hermon was a location in the Bible that was linked to the Rephaim (Josh. 12:1-5), but was also the

---

[15] Josh. 1:14; 6:2; 8:3; 10:2, 7; Judges 11:1, 1Sam. 2:4; 14:52; 2Sam.23:16-17, 22; 2King 5:1; 24:14; 1Chr. 7:5, 7, 11, 40, and many others. Nimrod was noted as being the first Gibborim mighty warrior on earth after the flood: Gen. 10:8; 1Chr. 5:24.
[16] K. van der Toorn, Bob Becking and Pieter Willem van der Horst, *Dictionary of Deities and Demons in the Bible DDD*, 2nd extensively rev. ed., 162 (Leiden; Boston; Grand Rapids, Mich.: Brill; Eerdmans, 1999).
[17] "Bashan," *DDD*, p 161-162. "According to *KTU* 1.108:1–3, the abode of the dead and deified king, and his place of enthronement as *[Rephaim]* was in *[Ashtarot and Edrei]*, in amazing correspondence with the Biblical tradition about the seat of king Og of Bashan, 'one of the survivors' of the Rephaim, who lived in Ashtarot and Edrei' (Josh 12:4)."

legendary location where the sons of God were considered to have come to earth and have sexual union with the daughters of men to produce the giant Nephilim.[18]

There are two places in the Bible that hint at the Rephaim being warrior kings brought down to Sheol in similar language to the Ugaritic notion of the Rephaim warrior kings in the underworld:

> Is. 14:9
> Sheol beneath is stirred up to meet you when you come;
> it rouses the shades [The Hebrew word *Rephaim*] to greet you,
> all who were leaders of the earth;
> it raises from their thrones
> all who were kings of the nations.
>
> Ezek. 32:21
> They shall fall amid those who are slain by the sword… The mighty chiefs [*Rephaim*] shall speak of them, with their helpers, out of the midst of Sheol: "They have come down, they lie still, the uncircumcised, slain by the sword."

Hebrew scholar, Michael S. Heiser concludes about this connection of Rephaim with dead warrior kings in Sheol and Bashan:

> That the Israelites and the biblical writers considered the spirits of the dead giant warrior kings to be demonic is evident from the fearful aura attached to the geographical location of Bashan. As noted above, Bashan is the region of the cities Ashtaroth and Edrei, which both the Bible and the Ugaritic texts mention as abodes of the Rephaim. What's even more fascinating is that in the Ugaritic language, this region was known not as Bashan, but *Bathan*—the Semitic people of Ugarit pronounced the Hebrew "sh" as "th" in their dialect. Why is that of interest? Because "Bathan" is a common word across all the Semitic languages, biblical

---

[18] The non-canonical book of Enoch supports this same interpretation: "Enoch 6:6 And they were in all two hundred [sons of God]; who descended in the days of Jared on the summit of Mount Hermon, and they called it Mount Hermon, because they had sworn and bound themselves by mutual imprecations upon it."

Hebrew included, for "serpent." The region of Bashan was known as "the place of the serpent." It was ground zero for the Rephaim giant clan and, spiritually speaking, the gateway to the abode of the infernal deified Rephaim spirits.[19]

List of Giants

The Bible reveals that there are many different clans that either were giants or had giants among them that were ultimately related in a line all the way back to the Nephilim of Genesis:

Nephilim (Gen. 6:1-4; Num. 13:33)
Anakim (Num. 13:28-33; Deut. 1:28; 2:10-11, 21; 9:2; Josh. 14:12)
Amorites (Amos 2:9-10)
Emim (Deut. 2:10-11)
Rephaim (Deut. 2:10-11, 20; 3:11)
Zamzummim (Deut. 2:20)
Zuzim (Gen. 14:5)
Perizzites (Gen. 15:20; Josh. 17:15)
Philistines (2 Sam. 21:18-22)
Horites/Horim (Deut. 2:21-22)
Avvim (Deut. 2:23)
Caphtorim (Deut. 2:23)

The following are implied as including giants by their connection to the descendants of Anak in Numbers 13:28-29:

Amalekites
Hittites
Jebusites—The word means "Those who trample"
Amorites (Amos 2:9-10 links the Amorites as giant in size and strength)
Hivites (Has the same consonants as a Hebrew name for snake)

---

[19] Michael S. Heiser *The Myth That is True*, p 169. Available online at www.michaelsheiser.com.

Here were the towns, cities or locations that were said to have had giants in them:

Gob (2 Sam. 21:18)
Hebron/Kiriath-arba (Num. 13:22; Josh. 14:15)
Ar (Deut. 2:9)
Seir (Deut. 2:21-22)
Debir/ Kiriath-sepher (Josh. 11:21-22)
Anab (Josh. 11:21-22)
Gaza (Josh. 11:21-22)
Gath (Josh. 11:21-22)
Ashdod (Josh. 11:21-22)
Bashan (Deut. 3:10-11)
Ashteroth-karnaim (Gen. 14:5)
Ham (Gen. 14:5)
Shaveh-kiriathaim (Gen. 14:5)
Valley of the Rephaim (Josh. 15:8)
Moab (1 Chron. 11:22)

Many significant individuals are described in the Bible implicitly or explicitly as giants being struck down in war against Israel:

Goliath (1 Sam. 17)
Lahmi, Goliath's brother (1 Chron. 20:5; 2 Sam. 21:19)
Ishbi-benob (2 Sam. 21:16)
Saph/Sippai (2 Sam. 21:17; 1 Chron. 20:4)
Arba (Josh. 14:15)
Sheshai (Josh.15:14, Num. 13:22)
Ahiman (Josh. 15:14, Num. 13:22)
Talmai (Josh. 15:14, Num. 13:22)
An unnamed warrior giant (1 Chron. 20:6)
And unnamed Egyptian giant (1 Chron. 11:23)
Og of Bashan (Deut. 3:10-11)

The ubiquitous presence of giants throughout the narrative of the Old Testament is no small matter. When God commanded the people of Israel to enter Canaan and devote certain of those peoples to complete destruction

(Deut. 20:16-17), it is no coincidence that most of these peoples we have already seen were connected in some way to the Anakim giants, and Joshua's campaign explicitly included the elimination of the Anakim/Sons of Anak giants. Could these giants that were from the lineage of the Nephilim (who were the offspring of the Sons of God) be the very Seed of the Serpent that would be at enmity with the promised messianic Seed of the Woman (Gen. 3:15)? You will have to read the sequels to *Noah Primeval* to find out.

CHAPTER 37:
LEVIATHAN

In my novel *Noah Primeval*, I have a sea dragon called "Leviathan" that is crucial to the plot of the story. While it is a monster of the waters, a symbol of chaos, it nevertheless is providentially used by Elohim and tamed for his own purposes. I found this character in the pages of the Bible itself and had always been befuddled by its presence. It kept popping up in strange places like the book of Job and the Psalms. Was this a mythical creature in holy writ? Was God's power over Leviathan as described in Job just a poetic way of saying God is in control and nothing is too powerful for him? I would soon find out that this recurring sea dragon was so much more.

Job 41 is devoted to this strange creature. Here is that chapter in its entirety:

> "Can you draw out Leviathan with a fishhook
> or press down his tongue with a cord?
> Can you put a rope in his nose
> or pierce his jaw with a hook?
> Will he make many pleas to you?
> Will he speak to you soft words?
> Will he make a covenant with you
> to take him for your servant forever?
> Will you play with him as with a bird,
> or will you put him on a leash for your girls?
> Will traders bargain over him?
> Will they divide him up among the merchants?
> Can you fill his skin with harpoons
> or his head with fishing spears?
> Lay your hands on him;

Leviathan

remember the battle—you will not do it again!
Behold, the hope of a man is false;
he is laid low even at the sight of him.
No one is so fierce that he dares to stir him up.
Who then is he who can stand before me?
Who has first given to me, that I should repay him?
Whatever is under the whole heaven is mine.
I will not keep silence concerning his limbs,
or his mighty strength, or his goodly frame.
Who can strip off his outer garment?
Who would come near him with a bridle?
Who can open the doors of his face?
Around his teeth is terror.
His back is made of rows of shields,
shut up closely as with a seal.
One is so near to another
that no air can come between them.
They are joined one to another;
they clasp each other and cannot be separated.
His sneezings flash forth light,
and his eyes are like the eyelids of the dawn.
Out of his mouth go flaming torches;
sparks of fire leap forth.
Out of his nostrils comes forth smoke,
as from a boiling pot and burning rushes.
His breath kindles coals,
and a flame comes forth from his mouth.
In his neck abides strength,
and terror dances before him.
The folds of his flesh stick together,
firmly cast on him and immovable.
His heart is hard as a stone,
hard as the lower millstone.
When he raises himself up the mighty are afraid;
At the crashing they are beside themselves.
Though the sword reaches him, it does not avail,
nor the spear, the dart, or the javelin.

> He counts iron as straw,
> and bronze as rotten wood.
> The arrow cannot make him flee;
> for him sling stones are turned to stubble.
> Clubs are counted as stubble;
> he laughs at the rattle of javelins.
> His underparts are like sharp potsherds;
> he spreads himself like a threshing sledge on the mire.
> He makes the deep boil like a pot;
> he makes the sea like a pot of ointment.
> Behind him he leaves a shining wake;
> one would think the deep to be white-haired.
> On earth there is not his like,
> a creature without fear.
> He sees everything that is high;
> he is king over all the sons of pride."

As this chapter describes, this is no known species on earth. From the smoke and fire out of its mouth to the armor plating on back and belly, this monster of the abyss was more than a mere example of showcasing God's omnipotent power over the mightiest of creatures, it was symbolic of something much more. And that much more can be found by understanding Leviathan in its ancient Near Eastern (ANE) and Biblical covenantal background.

In ANE religious mythologies, the sea and the sea dragon were symbols of chaos that had to be overcome to bring order to the universe, or more exactly, the political world order of the myth's originating culture. Some scholars call this battle *Chaoskampf*—the divine struggle to create order out of chaos.

Hermann Gunkel first suggested in *Creation and Chaos* (1895) that some ANE creation myths contained a cosmic conflict between deity and sea, as well as sea dragons or serpents that expressed the creation of order out of chaos.[1] Gunkel argued that Genesis borrowed this idea from the Babylonian tale of Marduk battling the goddess Tiamat, serpent of chaos, whom he vanquished, and out of whose body he created the heavens and earth.[2] After

---

[1] Hermann Gunkel, Heinrich Zimmern; K. William Whitney Jr., trans., *Creation And Chaos in the Primeval Era And the Eschaton: A Religio-historical Study of Genesis 1 and Revelation 12* (Grand Rapids: MI: Erdmans, 1895, 1921, 2006), xvi.

[2] "He cast down her carcass and stood upon it."

this victory, Marduk ascended to power in the Mesopotamian pantheon. This creation story gave mythical justification to the rise of Babylon as an ancient world power most likely in the First Babylonian Dynasty under Hammurabi (1792-1750 B.C.).[3] As the prologue of the Code of Hammurabi explains, "Anu, the majestic, King of the Anunnaki, and Bel, the Lord of Heaven and Earth, who established the fate of the land, had given to Marduk, the ruling son of Ea, dominion over mankind, and called Babylon by his great name; when they made it great upon the earth by founding therein an eternal kingdom, whose foundations are as firmly grounded as are those of heaven and earth."[4] The foundation of Hammurabi's "eternal kingdom" is literally linked to Marduk's foundational creation of heaven and earth.

Later, John Day argued in light of the discovery of the Ugarit tablets in 1928, that Canaan, not Babylonia is the source of the combat motif in Genesis,[5] reflected in Yahweh's own complaint that Israel had become polluted by Canaanite culture.[6] In the Baal cycle, Baal battles Yam (Sea) and conquers it, along with "the dragon," "the twisting serpent," to be enthroned as chief deity of the Canaanite pantheon.[7]

Creation accounts were often veiled polemics for the establishment of a king or kingdom's claim to sovereignty.[8] Richard Clifford quotes, "In Mesopotamia, Ugarit, and Israel the *Chaoskampf* appears not only in cosmological contexts but just as frequently—and this was fundamentally true right from the first—in political contexts. The repulsion and the destruction of the enemy, and thereby the maintenance of political order, always constitute one of the major dimensions of the battle against chaos."[9]

After he had slain Tiamat, the leader…He split her open like a mussel into two parts; Half of her he set in place and formed the sky… And a great structure, its counterpart, he established, namely Esharra [earth]."
(Enuma Elish, Tablet IV, lines 104-105, 137-138, 144 from Heidel, *Babylonian Genesis*, 41-42)

[3] Heidel, *Babylonian Genesis*, 14.

[4] W.W. Davies, The Codes of Hammurabi and Moses: With Copious Comments, Index, and Bible References (Berkeley, CA: Apocryphile Press, 1905, 2006), 17.

[5] John Day, *God's Conflict with the Dragon*. Day argues that the Canaanite Baal cycle implies a connection with creation, since it is a ritual fertility festival (cyclical creation) falling on the New Year, traditionally understood as the date of creation. But his strongest appeal is the argument in reverse that the Canaanite myth makes a connection between creation and *Chaoskampf* because the Old Testament does so.

[6] "Then the word of the LORD came to me, saying, "Son of man, make known to Jerusalem her abominations and say, 'Thus says the Lord GOD to Jerusalem, "Your origin and your birth are from the land of the Canaanite, your father was an Amorite and your mother a Hittite." (Ezek. 16:1-3)

[7] Most recently, David Tsumura has argued against any connection of such mythic struggle in the Biblical text in favor of mere poetic flair: David Toshio Tsumura, *Creation And Destruction: A Reappraisal of the Chaoskampf Theory in the Old Testament* (Winona Lake, IN: Eisenbrauns, 2006).

[8] Bruce R. Reichenbach. "Genesis 1 as a Theological-Political Narrative of Kingdom Establishment." *Bulletin for Biblical Research* 13.1 (2003).

[9] Clifford. *Creation Accounts*, footnote 13 p 8.

The Sumerians had three stories where the gods Enki, Ninurta, and Inanna all destroy sea monsters in their pursuit of establishing order. The sea monster in two of those versions, according to Sumerian expert Samuel Noah Kramer, is "conceived as a large serpent which lived in the bottom of the "great below" where the latter came in contact with the primeval waters."[10] The prophet Amos uses this same mythopoeic reference to a serpent at the bottom of the sea as God's tool of judgment: "If they hide from my sight at the bottom of the sea, there I will command the serpent, and it shall bite them" (Amos 9:3). One Sumerian text, *The Return of Ninurta to Nippur*, refers to "the seven-headed serpent" that must be defeated by the divine Ninurta to illustrate his power to overcome chaos.[11]

Perhaps the closest comparison with the Biblical Leviathan comes from Canaanite texts at Ugarit as John Day argued. In 1929, an archeological excavation at a mound in northern Syria called Ras Shamra unearthed the remains of a significant port city called Ugarit whose developed culture reaches back as far as 3000 B.C.[12] Among the important finds were literary tablets written in multiple ancient languages, which opened the door to a deeper understanding of ancient Near Eastern culture and the Bible. Ugaritic language and culture shares much in common with Hebrew that sheds light on the meaning of things such as Leviathan.

A side-by-side comparison of some Ugaritic religious texts about the Canaanite god Baal with Old Testament passages reveals a common narrative: Yahweh, the charioteer of the clouds, metaphorically battles with Sea (Hebrew: *yam*) and River (Hebrew: *nahar*), just as Baal, the charioteer of the clouds, struggled with Yam (sea) and Nahar (river), which is also linked to victory over a sea dragon/serpent.

---

[10] Samuel Noah Kramer. *Sumerian Mythology: A Study of Spiritual and Literary Achievement in the Third Millennium B.C.* Philadelphia, PA: University of Pennsylvania Press, 1944, 1961, 1972; p 77-78.
[11] *The Return of Ninurta to Nippur*, Black, J.A., Cunningham, G., Robson, E., and Zólyomi, G., The Electronic Text Corpus of Sumerian Literature, Oxford 1998-. < http://www.gatewaystobabylon.com/myths/texts/ninurta/nippurninurta.htm>
[12] "Ugarit," Avraham Negev, *The Archaeological Encyclopedia of the Holy Land*. 3rd ed. New York: Prentice Hall Press, 1996.

Leviathan

UGARTIC TEXTS	OLD TESTAMENT
'Dry him up. O Valiant Baal!	Did Yahweh rage against the rivers,
Dry him up, O Charioteer of the Clouds!	Or was Your anger against the rivers (*nahar*),
For our captive is Prince Yam [Sea],	Or was Your wrath against the sea (*yam*),
for our captive is Ruler Nahar [River]!'	That You rode on Your horses,
(KTU 1.2:4.8-9)[13]	On Your chariots of salvation?
	(Hab. 3:8)
What manner of enemy has arisen against Baal,	In that day Yahweh will punish Leviathan the fleeing serpent,
of foe against the Charioteer of the Clouds?	With His fierce and great and mighty sword,
Surely I smote the Beloved of El, Yam [Sea]?	Even Leviathan the twisted serpent;
Surely I exterminated Nahar [River], the mighty god?	And He will kill the dragon who lives in the sea.
Surely I lifted up the dragon,	(Isa 27:1)
I overpowered him?	
I smote the writhing serpent,	"You divided the sea by your might;
Encircler-with-seven-heads!	you broke the heads of the sea monsters on the
(KTU 1.3:3.38-41)[14]	waters.
	You crushed the heads of Leviathan.
	(Psa 74:13-14)

Baal fights Sea and River to establish his sovereignty. He wins by drinking up Sea and River, draining them dry, which results in Baal's supremacy over the pantheon and the Canaanite world order.[15] In the second passage, Baal's battle with Sea and River is retold in other words as a battle with a "dragon," the "writhing serpent" with seven heads.[16] Another Baal text calls this same dragon, "*Lotan*, the wriggling serpent."[17] The Hebrew equivalents of the Ugaritic words *tannin* (dragon) and *lotan* are *tannin* (dragon) and *liwyatan* (Leviathan) respectively.[18] The words are etymologically equivalent. Not only that, but so are the Ugaritic words describing the serpent as "wriggling" and "writhing" in the Ugaritic text (*brh* and *'qltn*) with the words Isaiah 27 uses of Leviathan as "fleeing" and "twisting" (*bariah* and *'aqalaton*).[19] Notice the last Scripture in the chart that refers to Leviathan as having multiple heads *just like the Canaanite Leviathan*. Bible scholar Mitchell Dahood argued that in that passage of Psalm 74:12-17

---

[13] Wyatt, *RTU2*, pp 69-70.
[14] In Wyatt, *RTU2*, pp 79. Charioteer of the Clouds also appears in these texts: KTU 1.3:4:4, 6, 26; 1.4:3:10, 18; 1.4:5:7, 60; 1.10:1:7; 1.10:3:21, 36; 1.19:1:43; 1.92:37, 39.
[15] KTU 1.2:4:27-32.
[16] Though this verse is spoken by the goddess Anat, Baal's sister, as if she accomplished these exploits, it is described as Baal's actions in other texts (KTU 1.5:1:1-35) that lead scholars to conclude that Anat's claims are a kind of sympathetic unity of action between her and Baal.
[17] KTU 1.5:1:1-4. Wyatt *RTU2*, p 115.
[18] Walter C. Kaiser, Jr. *The Ugaritic Pantheon* (dissertation). Ann Arbor, Mich: Brandeis University, 1973, p 212.
[19] Michael Fishbane, *Biblical Myth and Mythmaking*, Oxford University Press, 2003, 39.

the author implied the seven heads by using seven "you" references to God's powerful activities surrounding this mythopoeic defeat of Leviathan.[20]

The Apostle John adapted this seven-headed dragon into his Revelation as a symbol of Satan as well as a chaotic demonic empire (Rev 12:3; 13:1; 17:3). Jewish Christians in the first century carried on this motif in texts such as the *Odes of Solomon* that explain Christ as overthrowing "the dragon with seven heads... that I might destroy his seed."[21]

Thus, the Canaanite narrative of Lotan (Leviathan) the sea dragon or serpent is undeniably employed in Old Testament Scriptures and carried over into the New Testament as well.[22]

And notice as well the reference to the Red Sea event also associated with Leviathan in the Biblical text. In Psalm 74 above, God's parting of the waters is connected to the motif of the Mosaic covenant as the creation of a new world order in the same way that Baal's victory over the waters and the dragon are emblematic of his establishment of authority in the Canaanite pantheon. This covenant motif is described as a *Chaoskampf* battle with the Sea and Leviathan (sometimes called *Rahab*[23]) in this and other Biblical references.

> Psa. 74:12-17
> You broke the heads of the sea monsters in the waters.
> You crushed the heads of Leviathan;...
> You have prepared the light and the sun.
> You have established all the boundaries of the earth;
>
> Psa. 89:9-10
> You [Yahweh] rule the raging of the sea;
> when its waves rise, you still them.
> You crushed Rahab like a carcass;
> you scattered your enemies with your mighty arm.
>
> Isa. 51:9-10
> Awake, awake, put on strength, O arm of Yahweh;

---

[20] Mitchell Dahood S.J., *Psalms II 51-100 The Anchor Yale Bible* (Yale University Press, 1995) 24.
[21] Odes of Solomon 22:5. James H. Charlesworth, *The Old Testament Pseudepigrapha and the New Testament, Volume 2: Expansions of the "Old Testament" and Legends, Wisdom, and Philosophical Literature, Prayers, Psalms and Odes, Fragments of Lost Judeo-Hellenistic Works* (New Haven; London: Yale University Press, 1985).
[22] See also Isa 51:9; Ezek 32:2; Rev 12:9, 16, 17;
[23] An Akkadian equivalent of "Rabu" can be found on the Babylonian Map of the World describing a sea serpent. Wayne Horowitz, *Mesopotamian Cosmic Geography*, Winona Lake; IN: Eisenbrauns, 1998, 35; "Rahab," *DDD*, 684.

> Awake as in the days of old,
> the generations of long ago.
> Was it not You who cut Rahab in pieces,
> Who pierced the dragon?
> Was it not You who dried up the sea,
> The waters of the great deep;
> Who made the depths of the sea a pathway
> For the redeemed to cross over?

Isa. 27:1
> In that day the LORD with his hard and great and strong sword will punish Leviathan the fleeing serpent, Leviathan the twisting serpent, and he will slay the dragon that is in the sea.

The story of deity battling the river, the sea, and the sea dragon Leviathan is clearly a common covenant motif in the Old Testament and its surrounding ancient Near Eastern cultures.[24] The fact that Hebrew Scripture shares common words, concepts, and stories with Ugaritic scripture does not mean that Israel is affirming the same mythology or pantheon of deities, but rather that Israel lives within a common cultural environment, and God uses that cultural connection to subvert those words, concepts and stories with his own poetic meaning and purpose.

Chaoskampf and creation language are used as word pictures for God's covenant activity in the Bible. For God, describing the creation of the heavens and earth was a way of saying he has established his covenant with his people through exodus into the Promised Land,[25] reaffirming that covenant with the kingly line of David, and finalizing the covenant by bringing them out of exile. The reader should understand that the Scriptures listed above, exemplary of *Chaoskampf,* were deliberately abbreviated to make a further point below. I will now add the missing text in those passages in underline to reveal a deeper motif at play in the text—a motif of creation language as covenantal formation.

Psa. 74:12-17
> Yet God my King is from of old,

---

[24] Psalm 18, 29, 24, 29, 65, 74, 77, 89, 93, and 104 all reflect *Chaoskampf*. See also Exodus 15, Job 9, 26, 38, and Isa 51:14-16; 2Sam 22.
[25] John Owen, *Works*, 16 vols. (London: The Banner of Truth Trust, 1965-1968), Vol. 9 134.

working salvation in the midst of the earth.
You divided the sea by your might;
[A reference to the Exodus deliverance of the covenant at Sinai]
You broke the heads of the sea monsters in the waters.
You crushed the heads of Leviathan;...
You have prepared the light and the sun.
You have established all the boundaries of the earth;

Psa. 89:9-12; 19-29
You rule the raging of the sea;
when its waves rise, you still them.
You crushed Rahab like a carcass;
you scattered your enemies with your mighty arm.
The heavens are yours; the earth also is yours;
the world and all that is in it, you have founded them.
The north and the south, you have created them...
I have found David, my servant;
with my holy oil I have anointed him,
so that my hand shall be established with him...
and in my name shall his horn be exalted.
I will set his hand on the sea
and his right hand on the rivers...
My steadfast love I will keep for him forever,
and my covenant will stand firm for him.
I will establish his offspring forever
and his throne as the days of the heavens.

Isa 51:9-16
Was it not You who cut Rahab in pieces,
Who pierced the dragon?
Was it not You who dried up the sea,
The waters of the great deep;
Who made the depths of the sea a pathway
For the redeemed to cross over?...
[Y]ou have forgotten the LORD your Maker,
Who stretched out the heavens

And laid the foundations of the earth...
"For I am the LORD your God, who stirs up the sea and its waves roar (the LORD of hosts is His name). "I have put My words in your mouth and have covered you with the shadow of My hand, to establish the heavens, to found the earth, and to say to Zion, 'You are My people.'"
[a reaffirmation of the Sinai covenant through Moses]

Isa. 27:1; 6-13
In that day the LORD with his hard and great and strong sword will punish Leviathan the fleeing serpent, Leviathan the twisting serpent, and he will slay the dragon that is in the sea...
In days to come Jacob shall take root,
Israel shall blossom and put forth shoots
and fill the whole world with fruit...
And in that day a great trumpet will be blown, and those who were lost in the land of Assyria and those who were driven out to the land of Egypt will come and worship the LORD on the holy mountain at Jerusalem. *[the future consummation of the Mosaic and Davidic covenant in the New Covenant of Messiah]*

In these texts, and others,[26] God does not merely appeal to his power of creation as justification for the authority of his covenant. More importantly, He uses the creation of the heavens and earth, involving subjugation of rivers, seas, and dragon (Leviathan), as poetic descriptions of God's covenant with his people, rooted in the Exodus story, and reiterated in the Davidic covenant. The creation of the covenant is the creation of the heavens and the earth which includes a subjugation of chaos by the new order. The covenant is a cosmos—not a material one centered in astronomical location and abstract impersonal forces as modern worldview demands, but a theological one, centered in the sacred space of land, temple, and cult as the ancient Near Eastern worldview demands.[27]

It has been noted by scholars that the motif of *Chaoskampf* is absent from Genesis 1 where God creates the heavens and the earth, painting a very different picture of the Hebrew creation story than its ANE neighbors.

---

[26] See also Psa. 77:16-20; 136:1-22.
[27] N.T. Wright, *The New Testament and the People of God* (Minneapolis, MN: Fortress Press, 1992), 306-307.

However, its very absence in that text is most likely a part of the covenantal polemic in the text. For a close look at the original Hebrew shows us that the word for dragon that we have been talking about (*tannin*) is in fact used of the "great sea creatures" (*tanninim*) that God created on Day five:

> Gen. 1:21-22
> So God created the great sea creatures (*tanninim*) and every living creature that moves, with which the waters swarm… And God saw that it was good. And God blessed them, saying, "Be fruitful and multiply and fill the waters in the seas, and let birds multiply on the earth."

The ancient Near Eastern audience would read this text and know full well what was being implied against their cultural familiarity with the sea dragon. Apparently, the ANE notion of struggle against the dragon is subverted in this text by depicting God creating the dragon by the mere words of his mouth, rather than wrestling with a preexistent monster for control over the sea. And then God blesses that dragon as one of the many "good" creations that he commands to reproduce. This picture amounts to the reduction of the dragon to a mere domesticated pet in the language of Genesis 1.

In this text, the conspicuous absence of the struggle of *Chaoskampf* is evidence of its subversion to the greater purposes of the Hebrew creation story. Sometimes Leviathan is used as a covenantal expression for the establishment of God's world order out of chaos, and sometimes, it is used as a symbol of God's authority over pagan religious expressions. In any case, its Biblical meaning is connected to its ancient Near Eastern symbolic context, not to a modern interpretation of a merely physical sea monster.

CHAPTER 38:
MESOPOTAMIAN COSMIC GEOGRAPHY IN THE BIBLE

In my novel, *Noah Primeval*, I depict the universe as it was thought to be through the eyes of ancient Mesopotamians, as a three-tiered universe with a flat disc earth, surrounded by waters, which includes the watery Abyss and beneath that, the underworld of Sheol. Above the earth is a solid dome of the heavens, beyond which is the waters of the "heaven of heavens" where God's throne sits on the waters. A generic illustration of this cosmography is the old public domain image depicted below. I decided to use this cosmic geography as creative literary license to capture the way the ancients saw and experienced the world. This essay explains the Scriptural expression of this worldview as held by the Biblical writers.

Cosmography is a technical term that means a theory that describes and maps the main features of the heavens and the earth. A Cosmography or "cosmic geography" can be a complex picture of the universe that includes elements like astronomy, geology, and geography; and those elements can include theological implications as well. Throughout history, all civilizations and peoples have operated under the assumption of a cosmography or picture of the universe. We are most familiar with the historical change that science went through from a Ptolemaic cosmography of the earth at the center of the universe (geocentrism) to a Copernican cosmography of the sun at the center of a solar system (heliocentrism).

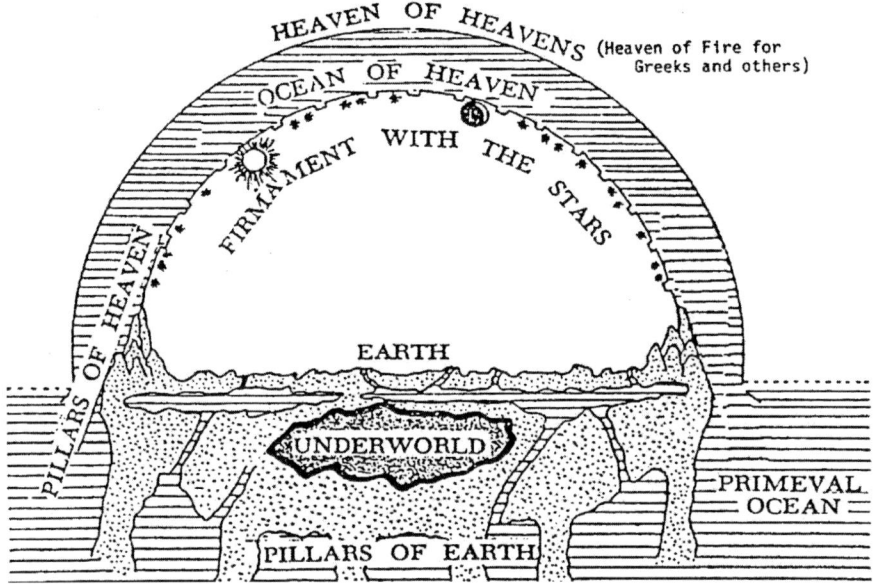

This antique drawing represents the Mesopotamian picture of the universe used in this story.

Some ancient mythologies maintained that the earth was a flat disc on the back of a giant turtle; animistic cultures believe that spirits inhabit natural objects and cause them to behave in certain ways; modern westerners believe in a space-time continuum where everything is relative to its frame of reference in relation to the speed of light. Ancients tended to believe that the gods caused the weather; moderns tend to believe that impersonal physical processes cause weather. All these different beliefs are elements of a cosmography or picture of what the universe is really like and how it operates. Even though "pre-scientific" cultures like the Hebrews did not have the same notions of science that we moderns have, they still observed the world around them and made interpretations as to the structure and operations of the heavens and earth.

A common ancient understanding of the cosmos is expressed in the visions of 1 Enoch, used in the novel *Noah Primeval*. In this Second Temple Jewish writing, codified around the third to fourth century B.C., and probably originally written much earlier, Enoch is taken on a journey through heaven and hell and describes the cosmic workings as they understood them in that day. Here is just a short glimpse into the elaborate construction of this ANE author:

> 1 Enoch 18:1-5
> And I saw the storerooms of all the winds and saw how with them he has embroidered all creation as well as the foundations of the earth. I saw the cornerstone of the earth; I saw the four winds which bear the earth as well as the firmament of heaven. I saw how the winds ride the heights of heaven and stand between heaven and earth: These are the very pillars of heaven. I saw the winds which turn the heaven and cause the star to set—the sun as well as all the stars. I saw the souls carried by the clouds. I saw the path of the angels in the ultimate end of the earth, and the firmament of the heaven above.[187]

The Bible also contains a picture of the universe that its stories inhabit. It uses cosmic geographical language in common with other ancient Near Eastern (ANE) cultures that shared its situated time and location. Believers in today's world use the language of Relativity when we write, even in our non-scientific discourse; because Einstein has affected the way we see the universe. Believers before the 17th century used Ptolemaic language because they too were children of their time. It should be no surprise to anyone that believers in ancient Israel would use the language of ANE cosmography because it was the mental construct within which they lived and thought.[188]

The Three-Tiered Universe

Othmar Keel, leading expert on ANE art has argued that there was no singular technical physical description of the cosmos in the ancient Near East, but rather patterns of thinking, similarity of images, and repetition of motifs.[189] A common simplification of these images and motifs is expressed in the three-tiered universe of the heavens, the earth, and the underworld.

Wayne Horowitz has chronicled Mesopotamian texts that illustrate this multi-leveled universe among the successive civilizations of Sumer, Akkad, Babylonia, and Assyria. The heavens above were subdivided into "the heaven of

---

[187] James H. Charlesworth, *The Old Testament Pseudepigrapha: Volume 1*, 1 En 18 (New York; London: Yale University Press, 1983).
[188] The book that opened my mind to the Mesopotamian cosmography in the Bible was *Evolutionary Creation: A Christian Approach to Evolution* by Denis O. Lamoureux, Eugene; OR, Wipf & Stock, 2008. I owe much of the material in this essay to Mr. Lamourcux's meticulous research on the ancient science in the Bible. But one need not accept his evolutionary presuppositions to agree with his Biblical scholarship.
[189] Othmar Keel, *The Symbolism of the Biblical World*, Winona Lake; IN: Eisenbrauns, 1972, 1997, 16-59.

Anu (or chief god)" at the very top, the "middle heavens" below him and the sky. In the middle was the earth's surface, and below that was the third level that was further divided into the waters of the abyss and the underworld.[190]

Let's take a look at the Scriptures that appear to reinforce this three-tiered universe so different from our modern understanding of physical expanding galaxies of warped space-time, where the notion of heaven and hell are without physical location. Though the focus of this essay will be on Old Testament context, I want to start with the New Testament to make the point that their cosmography did not necessarily change with the change of covenants.

> Phil. 2:10
> That at the name of Jesus every knee should bow, of those who are <u>in heaven</u>, and <u>on earth</u>, and <u>under the earth</u>.

> Rev. 5:3, 13
> And no one <u>in heaven, or on earth, or under the earth</u>, was able to open the scroll, or to look into it… And every creature <u>in heaven and on the earth and under the earth</u> and in the sea…

> Ex. 20:4
> "You shall not make for yourself a carved image, or any likeness of anything that is in <u>heaven above,</u> or that is <u>in the earth beneath,</u> or that is in the <u>water under the earth</u>.

> Matt. 11:23
> Jesus said, "Capernaum, will you be <u>exalted to heaven</u>? You will be <u>brought down to Hades</u>. [the underworld].

Both apostles Paul and John were writing about the totality of creation being subject to the authority of Jesus on his throne. So this word picture of "heaven, earth, and under the earth" was used as the description of the total known universe—which they conceived of spatially as heaven above, the earth below, and the underworld below the earth. And not only did the inspired human authors write of the universe in this three-tiered fashion but so did God Himself, the author and finisher of our faith, when giving the commandments on Sinai.

---

[190] Wayne Horowitz, *Mesopotamian Cosmic Geography*, Winona Lake; IN: Eisenbrauns, 1998, xii-xiii.

One may naturally wonder if this notion of "heaven above" may merely be a symbolic or figurative expression for the exalted spiritual nature of heaven. Since we cannot see where heaven is, God would use physical analogies to express spiritual truths. This explanation would be easier to stomach if the three-tiered notion were not so rooted in a cosmic geography that clearly was their understanding of the universe (as proven below). A figurative expression would also jeopardize the doctrine of the ascension of Jesus into heaven which also affirms the spatial location of heaven above and the earth below, in very literal terms.

> Acts 1:9-11
> He was lifted up, and a cloud took him out of their sight. And while they were gazing <u>into heaven</u> as he went, behold, two men stood by them in white robes, and said, "Men of Galilee, why do you stand looking <u>into heaven</u>? This Jesus, who was <u>taken up from you into heaven</u>, will come in the same way as you saw him go <u>into heaven</u>."

> John 3:13
> No one has <u>ascended into heaven</u> except he who <u>descended from heaven</u>, the Son of Man.

> John 6:62
> Then what if you were to see the Son of Man ascending to where he was before?

> John 20:17
> Jesus said to her, "Do not cling to me, for I have not yet <u>ascended to the Father</u>; but go to my brothers and say to them, 'I am <u>ascending to my Father</u> and your Father, to my God and your God.'"

> Eph. 4:8-10
> Therefore it says, "When <u>he ascended on high</u> he led a host of captives, and he gave gifts to men." (In saying, "<u>He ascended</u>," what does it mean but that <u>he had also descended into the lower regions, the earth</u>? He who <u>descended is the</u>

Mesopotamian Cosmology

<u>one who also ascended far above all the heavens</u>, that he might fill all things.)

The location of heaven being above us may be figurative to our modern cosmology, but it was not figurative to the Biblical writers. To suggest that they understood it figuratively would be to impose our own modern bias on the Bible.

Now let's take a closer look at each of these tiers or domains of the cosmos through the eyes of Scripture in their ANE context.

Flat Earth Surrounded by Waters

I want to start with the earth because the Scriptures start with the earth. That is, the Bible is geocentric in its picture of a flat earth founded on immovable pillars at the center of the universe. Over a hundred years ago, a Babylonian map of the world was discovered that dated back to approximately the ninth century B.C. As seen below, this map was unique from other Mesopotamian maps because it was not merely local but international in its scale, and contained features that appeared to indicate cosmological interpretation.[191] That map and a translated interpretation are reproduced below.[192]

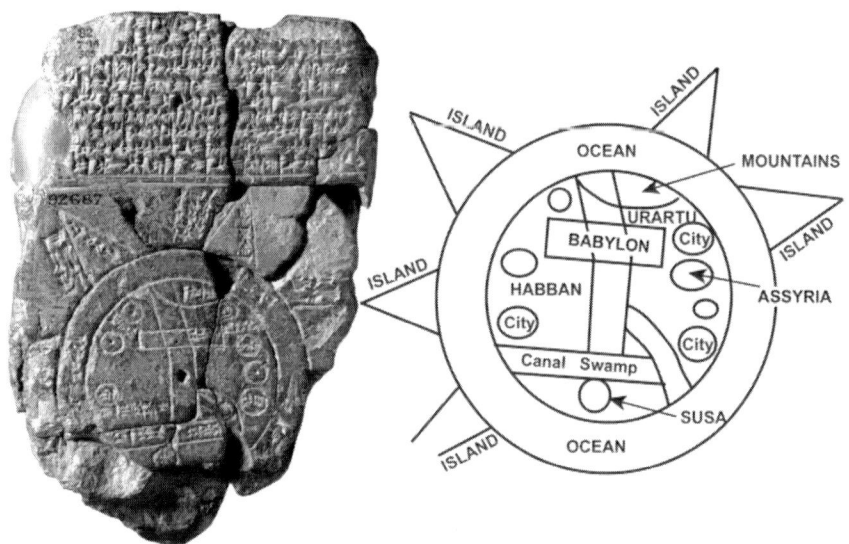

---

[191] Horowitz, *Mesopotamian Cosmic Geography*, 25-27.
[192] Photo is public domain (Courtesy of the British Museum). Illustration is my own based on Horowitz, *Mesopotamian Cosmic Geography*, 21.

The geography of the Babylonian map portrayed a flat disc of earth with Babylon in the center and extending out to the known regions of its empire, whose perimeters were surrounded by cosmic waters and islands out in those waters. Of the earliest Sumerian and Akkadian texts with geographical information, only the Babylonian map of the world and another text, *The Sargon Geography,* describe the earth's surface, and they both picture a central circular continent surrounded by cosmic waters, often referred to as "the circle of the earth."[193] Other texts like the Akkadian *Epic of Gilgamesh,* and Egyptian, and Sumerian works share in common with the Babylonian map the notion of mountains at the edge of the earth beyond which is the cosmic sea and the unknown,[194] and from which come "the circle of the four winds" that blow upon the four corners of the earth (a reference to compass points).[195]

The Biblical picture of the earth is remarkably similar to this Mesopotamian cosmic geography. When Daniel had his dream *from God in Babylon*, of a tree "in the middle of the earth" whose height reached so high that "it was visible to the end of the whole earth," (Dan. 4:10) it reflected this very Babylonian map of the culture that educated Daniel. One cannot see the end of the whole earth on a globe, but one can do so on a circular continent embodying the known world of Babylon as the center of the earth.

"The ends of the earth" is a common phrase, occurring over fifty times throughout the Scriptures that means more than just "remote lands," but rather includes the notion of the very physical end of the whole earth all around before the cosmic waters that hem it in. Here are just a few of the verses that indicate this circular land mass bounded by seas as the entire earth:

> Isa. 41:9
> You whom I took from the ends of the earth, and called from its farthest corners

---

[193] Horowitz, *Mesopotamian Cosmic Geography*, 320, 334. This interpretation continued to maintain influence even into the Greek period of the 6th century B.C. (41).

[194] A Sumerian hymn to the god Enlil, Lord of the Wind, represents these ends of the earth within the context of the god's rule over all the earth: "Lord, as far as the edge of heaven, lord as far as the edge of earth, from the mountain of sunrise to the mountain of sunset. In the mountain/land, no (other) lord resides, you exercise lordship. Enlil, in the lands no (other) lady resides, your wife, exercises ladyship." Horowitz, *Mesopotamian Cosmic Geography*, 331. "Circle of the earth" in Egyptian understanding meant the disc of the earth unto the horizon "(These) lands were united, and they laid their hands upon the land as far as the Circle of the Earth." "Inscription on the second pylon at Medinet Habu," J.H. Breasted, *Ancient Records of Egypt*, Part Four, University of Chicago, 1906, p 64.

[195] Horowitz, *Mesopotamian Cosmic Geography*, 195-97, 334.

Psa. 65:5
O God of our salvation, the hope of all the ends of the earth and of the farthest seas

Zech. 9:10
His rule shall be from sea to sea, and from the River to the ends of the earth.

Mark 13:27
And then he will send out the angels and gather his elect from the four winds, from the ends of the earth to the ends of heaven.

Acts 13:47
'I have made you a light for the Gentiles, that you may bring salvation to the ends of the earth.'

Job 28:24
For he looks to the ends of the earth and sees everything under the heavens.

Remember that Mesopotamian phrase, "circle of the earth" that meant a flat disc terra firma? Well, it's in the Bible, too. "It is he who sits above the circle of the earth, and its inhabitants are like grasshoppers" (Isa. 40:22). Some have tried to say that the Hebrew word for "circle" could mean *sphere*, but it does not. The Hebrew word used here (*ḥûg*) could however refer to a vaulted dome that covers the visible circular horizon, which would be more accurate to say, "above the vault of the earth."[196] If Isaiah had wanted to say the earth was a sphere he would have used another word that he used in a previous chapter (22:18) for a ball (*kaddur*), but he did not.[197]

Two further Scriptures use this "circle of the earth" in reference to God's original creation of the land out of the waters and extend it outward to include the circumferential ocean with its own mysterious boundary:

---

[196] "*ḥûg*" Harris, R. Laird, Robert Laird Harris, Gleason Leonard Archer, and Bruce K. Waltke. *Theological Wordbook of the Old Testament*. electronic ed. Chicago: Moody Press, 1999, p 266-67.
[197] Even the Septuagint (LXX) does not translate the Hebrew word into the Greek word for sphere. "Isaiah 40:22," Randall Tan, David A. deSilva, and Logos Bible Software. *The Lexham Greek-English Interlinear Septuagint*. Logos Bible Software, 2009.

> Prov. 8:27, 29
> When he established the heavens, I was there; when he drew <u>a circle on the face of the deep</u>… when he <u>assigned to the sea its limit</u>, so that the <u>waters might not transgress</u> his command, when he marked out the foundations of the earth.
>
> Job 26:10
> He has inscribed a circle on the face of the waters at the boundary between light and darkness [where the sun rises and sets].

Even when the Old Testament writers are deliberately using metaphors for the earth, they use metaphors for a flat earth spread out like a flat blanket.

> Job 38:13
> <u>Take hold of the skirts of the earth</u>, and the wicked be shaken out of it.
>
> Job 38:18
> Have you comprehended <u>the expanse of the earth</u>?
>
> Psa. 136:6
> To him who <u>spreads out the earth</u> above the waters.
>
> Isa. 44:24
> "I am the LORD, who <u>spread out the earth</u> by myself."

Geocentricity

In the Bible, the earth is not merely a flat disk surrounded by cosmic waters under the heavens; it was also the center of the universe. To the ANE mindset, including that of the Hebrews, the earth did not move (except for earthquakes) and the sun revolved around that immovable earth. They did not know that the earth was spinning one thousand miles an hour and flying through space at 65,000 miles an hour. Evidently, God did not consider it important enough to correct this primitive inaccurate understanding. Here are the passages that caused such trouble with Christians who took the text too literally because it did not seem to be figurative to them:

> Psa. 19:4-6
> Their voice goes out through all the earth,
> and their words to <u>the end of the world</u>.
> In them he has set a tent for the sun,
> which comes out like a bridegroom leaving his chamber, and,
> like a strong man, runs its course with joy. Its rising is from the end of the heavens,
> and its circuit to the end of them.

> Psa. 50:1
> The Mighty One, God, the LORD, speaks and summons the earth from <u>the rising of the sun to its setting</u>.

> Eccl. 1:5
> The sun rises, and the sun goes down,
> and hastens to the place where it rises.

> Josh. 10:13
> And the sun stood still, and the moon stopped,
> until the nation took vengeance on their enemies...
> <u>The sun stopped in the midst of heaven</u> and did not hurry to set for about a whole day.

> Matt. 5:45
> Jesus said, "For he makes his <u>sun rise</u> on the evil and on the good."

Two objections are often raised when considering these passages. First, that they use phenomenal language. That is, they describe simply what the viewer observes and makes no cosmological claims beyond simply description of what one sees. We even use these terms of the sun rising and setting today and we know the earth moves around the sun. Fair enough. The only problem is that the ancient writers were pre-scientific and did not know the earth went around the sun, so when they said the sun was moving from one end of the heavens to the other they believed reality was exactly as they observed it. They had absolutely no reason to believe in a "phenomenal distinction" between their observation and reality.[198]

The second objection is that some of the language is obvious metaphor. David painted the sun as a bridegroom coming out of his chamber or of being summoned by God and responding like a human. This is called anthropomorphism and is obviously poetic. But the problem here is that the metaphors still reinforce the sun doing all the moving around a stationary immobile earth.

> 1Chr. 16:30
> Tremble before him, all the earth;
> yes, the world is established; <u>it shall never be moved</u>.
>
> Psa. 93:1
> Yes, the world is established; <u>it shall never be moved</u>.
>
> Psa. 96:10
> Yes, the world is established; <u>it shall never be moved</u>."

Understandably, these texts have been thought to indicate that the Bible is explicitly saying the earth does not move. But the case is not so strong for these examples because the Hebrew word used in these passages for "the world" is not the word for *earth* (*erets*), but the word that is sometimes used for the inhabited world (*tebel*). So it is possible that these verses are talking about the "world order" as does the poetry of 2Sam. 22:16.

But the problem that then arises is that the broader chapter context of these verses describe the earth's physical aspects such as oceans, trees, and in the case of 1Chron. 16:30, even the "earth" (*erets*) in redundant context with the "world" (*tebel*), which would seem to indicate that "world" may refer to the physical earth.

Lastly, *world* can be interchangeable with *earth* as it is in 1Sam. 2:8, "For the pillars of <u>the earth</u> are the LORD'S, And He set <u>the world</u> on them."

And this adds a new element to the conversation of a stationary earth: *A foundation of pillars.*

---

[198] "The Firmament And The Water Above: Part I: The Meaning Of Raqia In Gen 1:6-8," Paul H. Seely, *The Westminster Theological Journal* 53 (1991) 227-40.

Pillars of the Earth

The notion of an immovable earth is not a mere description of observational experience by earth dwellers; it is based upon another cosmographical notion that the earth is on a foundation of pillars that hold it firmly in place.

> Psa. 104:5
> He set the <u>earth on its foundations,</u> so that it should never be moved.

> Job 38:4
> "Where were you when I laid <u>the foundation of the earth</u>? Tell Me, if you have understanding, Who <u>set its measurements</u>, since you know? Or who <u>stretched the line</u> on it? "On what were <u>its bases sunk</u>? Or who <u>laid its cornerstone,</u>

> 2Sam. 22:16
> "Then the channels of the sea were seen; <u>the foundations of the world were laid bare</u>.

> 1Sam. 2:8
> For the <u>pillars of the earth</u> are the LORD's, and on them, <u>he has set the world</u>.

> Psa. 75:3
> "When <u>the earth totters,</u> and all its inhabitants,
> it is I who keep steady its pillars.

> Zech. 12:1
> Thus declares the LORD who stretches out the heavens, <u>and founded the earth.</u>

Ancient man such as the Babylonians believed that mountains and important ziggurat temples had foundations that went below the earth into the abyss (*apsu*) or the underworld.[199] But even if one would argue that the notion of foundations and pillars of the earth are only intended to be symbolic, they are still symbolic *of a stationary earth that does not move*.

Some have pointed out the single verse that seems to mitigate this notion of a solid foundation of pillars, Job 26:6-7: "Sheol is naked before God, and Abaddon has no covering. He stretches out the north over the void and <u>hangs the earth on nothing</u>." They suggest that this is a revelation of the earth in space before ancient man even knew about the spatial location of the earth in a galaxy. But the reason I do not believe this is because of the context of the verse.

Within chapter 26 Job affirms the three-tiered universe of waters of the Abyss below him (v. 5) and under that Sheol (v. 6), with pillars holding up the heavens (v. 11). Later in the same book, God himself speaks about the earth laid on foundations (38:4), sinking its bases and cornerstone like a building (38:5-6). Ancient peoples believed the earth was on top of some other object like the back of a turtle, and that it was too heavy to float on the waters. So in context, Job 26 appears to be saying that the earth is over the waters of the abyss and Sheol, on its foundations, but there is nothing under *those pillars* but God himself holding it all up. This is not the suggestion of a planet hanging in space, but rather the negative claim of an earth that is *not* on top of an ancient object.

Sheol Below

Before we ascend to the heavens, let's take a look at the Underworld below the earth. The Underworld was a common location of extensive stories about gods and departed souls of men journeying to the depths of the earth through special gates of some kind into a geographic location that might also be accessed through cracks in the earth above.[200] Entire Mesopotamian stories engage the location of the subterranean netherworld in their narrative such as *The Descent of Inanna, The Descent of Ishtar, Nergal and Ereshkigal*, and many others.

Sheol was the Hebrew word for the underworld.[201] Though the Bible does not contain any narratives of experiences in Sheol, it was nevertheless described as the abode of the dead that was below the earth. Though Sheol was sometimes used interchangeably with "Abaddon" as the place of destruction of

---

[199] Horowitz, *Mesopotamian Cosmic Geography*, 98, 124, 308-12, 336-37.
[200] Horowitz, *Mesopotamian Cosmic Geography*, p 348-362
[201] "Sheol," *DDD*, p 768.

the body (Prov. 15:11; 27:20),[202] and "the grave" (*qibrah*) as a reference to the state of being dead and buried in the earth (Psa. 88:11; Isa. 14:9-11), it was also considered to be *physically* located beneath the earth in the same way as other ANE worldviews.

When the sons of Korah are swallowed up by the earth for their rebellion against God, Numbers chapter 16 says that "they went down alive into Sheol, and the earth closed over them, and they perished from the midst of the assembly (v. 33)." People would not "fall alive" into death or the grave and then perish if Sheol was not a location. But they would die after they fall down into a location (Sheol) and the earth closes over them in that order.

The divine being (*elohim*), known as the departed spirit of Samuel, "came up out of the earth" for the witch of Endor's necromancy with Saul (1Sam. 28:13). This was not a reference to a body coming out of a grave, but a spirit of the dead coming from the underworld beneath the earth.

When Isaiah writes about Sheol in Isaiah 14, he combines the notion of the physical location of the dead body in the earth (v. 11) with the location beneath the earth of the spirits of the dead (v. 9). It's really a both/and proposition.

Here is a list of some verses that speak of Sheol geographically as a spiritual underworld in contrast with heaven as a spiritual overworld.

> Amos 9:2
> "If they dig into Sheol, from there shall my hand take them; if they climb up to heaven, from there I will bring them down.
>
> Job 11:8
> It is higher than heaven—what can you do? Deeper than Sheol—what can you know?
>
> Psa. 16:10
> For you will not abandon my soul to Sheol, or let your holy one see corruption.
>
> Psa. 139:8
> If I ascend to heaven, you are there! If I make my bed in Sheol, you are there!

---

[202] "Abaddon," *DDD*, p 1.

> Isa. 7:11
> "Ask a sign of the LORD your God; let it be <u>deep as Sheol</u> or <u>high as heaven</u>."

These are not mere references to the body in the grave, but to locations of the spiritual soul as well. Sheol is a combined term that describes both the grave for the body and the underworld location of the departed souls of the dead.

In the New Testament, the word *Hades* is used for the underworld, which was the Greek equivalent of Sheol.[203] Jesus himself used the term Hades as the location of damned spirits in contrast with heaven as the location of redeemed spirits when he talked of Capernaum rejecting miracles, "And you, Capernaum, will you be <u>exalted to heaven</u>? You will be <u>brought down to Hades</u>" (Matt. 11:23). Hades was also the location of departed spirits in his parable of Lazarus and the rich man in Hades (Luke 16:19-31).

In Greek mythology, Tartarus was another term for a location beneath the "roots of the earth" and beneath the waters where the warring giants called "Titans" were bound in chains because of their rebellion against the gods.[204] Peter uses a derivative of that very Greek word Tartarus to describe a similar location and scenario of angels being bound during the time of Noah and the warring Titans called "Nephilim."[205]

> 2Pet. 2:4-5
> For if God did not spare <u>angels</u> when they sinned, but <u>cast them into hell [*tartaroo*] and committed them to chains</u> of gloomy darkness to be kept until the judgment; if he did not spare the ancient world, but preserved Noah.

The Watery Abyss

In Mesopotamian cosmography, the Abyss (*Apsu* in Akkadian) was a cosmic subterranean lake or body of water that was between the earth and the

---

[203] "Hades," *DDD*, p 382.
[204] "They then conducted them [the Titans] under the highways of the earth as far below the ground as the ground is below the sky, and tied them with cruel chains. So far down below the ground is gloomy Tartarus...Tartarus is surrounded by a bronze moat...above which the roots of earth and barren sea are planted. In that gloomy underground region the Titans were imprisoned by the decree of Zeus." Norman Brown, Trans. *Theogony: Hesiod*. New York: Bobbs-Merrill Co., 1953, p 73-4.
[205] 1.25 ταρταρόω [*tartaroo*] Louw, Johannes P., and Eugene Albert Nida. *Greek-English Lexicon of the New Testament : Based on Semantic Domains*. electronic ed. of the 2nd edition. New York: United Bible societies, 1996. Bauckham, Richard J. Vol. 50, *Word Biblical Commentary : 2 Peter, Jude*. Word Biblical Commentary, Dallas: Word, Incorporated, 2002, p 248-249.

Mesopotamian Cosmology

underworld (Sheol), and was the source of the waters above such as oceans, rivers, and springs or fountains.[206] In *The Epic of Gilgamesh*, Utnapishtim, the Babylonian Noah, tells his fellow citizens that he is building his boat and will abandon the earth of Enlil to join Ea in the waters of the Abyss that would soon fill the land.[207] Even bitumen pools used to make pitch were thought to rise up from the "underground waters," or the Abyss.[208]

Similarly, in the Bible the earth also rests on the seas or "the deep" (*tehom*) that produces the springs and waters from its subterranean waters below the earth.

> Psa. 24:1-2
> The world, and those who dwell therein, for he has <u>founded it upon the seas</u>, and established it upon the rivers.

> Psa. 136:6
> To him who spread out the earth <u>above the waters</u>.

> Gen. 49: 25
> The Almighty who will bless you with blessings of heaven above, Blessings of <u>the deep that crouches beneath.</u>

> Ex. 20:4
> You shall not make for yourself a carved image, or any likeness of anything that is in heaven above, or that is in the earth beneath, or that is <u>in the water under the earth</u>.

Leviathan is even said to dwell in the Abyss in Job 41:24 (LXX)[209]. When God brings the flood, part of the waters are from "the fountains of the great deep" bursting open (Gen. 7:11; 8:2).

---

[206] Horowitz, *Mesopotamian Cosmic Geography*, p 334-348.
[207] *The Epic of Gilgamesh* XI:40-44. *The Ancient Near East an Anthology of Texts and Pictures.* Edited by James Bennett Pritchard. Princeton: Princeton University Press, 1958, p 93.
[208] Horowitz, *Mesopotamian Cosmic Geography*, p 337.
[209] "[Leviathan] regards the netherworld [Tartauros] of the deep [Abyss] like a prisoner. He regards the deep [Abyss] as a walk." Job 41:34, Tan, Randall, David A. deSilva, and Logos Bible Software. *The Lexham Greek-English Interlinear Septuagint*. Logos Bible Software, 2009.

The Firmament

If we move upward in the registers of cosmography, we find another ancient paradigm of the heavens covering the earth like a solid dome or vault with the sun, moon, and stars embedded in the firmament yet still somehow able to go around the earth. Reformed scholar Paul Seely has done key research on this notion.[210]

> Gen. 1:6-8
> And God said, "Let there be an expanse [firmament] in the midst of the waters, and let it separate the waters from the waters." And God made the expanse [firmament] and separated the waters that were under the expanse [firmament] from the waters that were above the expanse [firmament]. And it was so. And God called the expanse [firmament] Heaven.

I used to think, what is that all about? Waters below separated from waters above by the sky? Some try to explain those waters above as a water canopy above the earth that came down at Noah's flood. But that doesn't make sense Biblically because birds are said to "fly over the face of the firmament" (Gen. 1:20) with the same Hebrew grammar as God's Spirit hovering "over the face of the waters" (Gen. 1:2). But the firmament cannot be the "water canopy" because the firmament is not the waters, *but the object that is separating and holding back the waters*. If the firmament is an "expanse" or the sky itself, then the birds would be flying *within* the firmament, not *over the face of* the firmament as the text states. So the firmament cannot be a water canopy and it cannot be the sky itself.

The T.K.O. of the canopy theory is the fact that according to the Bible those "waters above" and the firmament that holds them back were still considered in place during the time of King David long after the flood:

> Psa. 104:2-3
> Stretching out the heavens like a tent. He lays the beams of his chambers on the waters;

---

[210] "The Firmament And The Water Above: Part I: The Meaning Of Raqia In Gen 1:6-8," Paul H. Seely, *The Westminster Theological Journal* 53 (1991) 227-40. http://faculty.gordon.edu/hu/bi/ted_hildebrandt/OTeSources/01-Genesis/Text/Articles-Books/Seely-Firmament-WTJ.pdf

Psa. 148:4
Praise him, you highest heavens, and you waters above the heavens!

Seely shows how the modern scientific bias has guided the translators to render the word for "firmament" (*raqia*) as "expanse." *Raqia* in the Bible consistently means a solid material such as a metal that is hammered out by a craftsman (Ex. 39:3; Isa. 40:19). And when *raqia* is used elsewhere in the Bible for the heavens, it clearly refers to a solid material, sometimes even metal!

Job 37:18
Can you, like him, <u>spread out</u> [*raqia*] the skies, <u>hard as a cast metal mirror</u>?

Ex. 24:10
And they saw the God of Israel. There was under his feet as it were a <u>pavement [*raqia*] of sapphire stone, like the very heaven</u> for clearness.

Ezek. 1:22-23
Over the heads of the living creatures there was the likeness of an <u>expanse [*raqia*], shining like awe-inspiring crystal, spread out above</u> their heads. And <u>under the expanse [*raqia*]</u> their wings were stretched out straight.

Prov. 8:27-28
When he established the heavens… when he made firm the skies above.

Job 22:14
He walks on the vault of heaven.

Amos 9:6
[God] builds his upper chambers in the heavens and founds his vault upon the earth.

Not only did the ancient translators of the Septuagint (LXX) translate *raqia* into the Latin equivalent for a hard firm solid surface (*firmamentum*), but also the Jews of the Second Temple period consistently understood the word *raqia* to mean a solid surface that covered the earth like a dome.

> 3Bar. 3:6-8
> And the Lord appeared to them and confused their speech, when they had built the tower… And they took a gimlet, and sought to pierce the heaven, saying, Let us see (whether) the heaven is made of clay, or of brass, or of iron.

> 2Apoc. Bar. 21:4
> 'O you that have made the earth, hear me, that have fixed the firmament by the word, and have made firm the height of the heaven.

> Josephus, *Antiquities* 1:30 (1.1.1.30)
> On the second day, he placed the heaven over the whole world… He also placed a crystalline [firmament] round it.

The Talmud describes rabbis debating over which remains fixed and which revolves, the constellations or the solid sky (Pesachim 94b),[211] as well as how to calculate the thickness of the firmament scientifically (Pesab. 49a) and Biblically (Genesis Rabbah 4.5.2).[212] While the Talmud is not the definitive interpretation of the Bible, it certainly illustrates how ancient Jews of that time period understood the term, which can be helpful in learning the Hebrew cultural context.

When the Scriptures talk poetically of this vault of heaven it uses the same terminology of stretching out the solid surface of the heavens over the earth *as it does of stretching out an ANE desert tent over the flat ground* (Isa. 54:2; Jer. 10:20)—not like an expanding Einsteinian time-space atmosphere.

> Psa. 19:4
> He has set a tent for the sun.

---

[211] Quoted in *The Science in Torah: the Scientific Knowledge of the Talmudic Sages* By Leo Levi, page 90-91.
[212] Seely, "The Firmament," p 236.

Psa. 104:2
Stretching out the heavens like a tent.

Isa. 45:12
It was my hands that stretched out the heavens,

Isa. 51:13
The LORD... who stretched out the heavens and laid the foundations of the earth.

Jer. 10:12
It is he who <u>established the world</u> by his wisdom, and by his understanding <u>stretched out the heavens</u>.

Jer. 51:15
"It is he who <u>established the world</u> by his wisdom, and by his understanding <u>stretched out the heavens</u>.

Keeping this tent-like vault over the earth in mind, when God prophesies about the physical destruction he will bring upon a nation, he uses the symbolism of rolling up that firmament like the tent he originally stretched out (or a scroll), along with the shaking of the pillars of the earth and the pillars of heaven which results in the stars falling from the heavens because they were embedded within it.

Isa. 34:4
All the host of heaven shall rot away, and <u>the skies roll up like a scroll</u>. All their host <u>shall fall, as leaves fall</u> from the vine.

Rev. 6:13-14
[An earthquake occurs] and the <u>stars of the sky fell to the earth</u> as the fig tree sheds its winter fruit when shaken by a gale. The <u>sky vanished like a scroll that is being rolled up</u>, and every mountain and island was removed from its place.

Matt. 24:29
"The stars will fall from heaven, and the powers of the heavens will be shaken."

Job 26:11
"The <u>pillars of heaven tremble</u>, and are astounded at His rebuke.

2Sam. 22:8
Then the earth reeled and rocked; the foundations of the heavens trembled and quaked.

Is. 13:13
Therefore I shall make <u>the heavens tremble</u>, and <u>the earth will be shaken</u> out of its place at the wrath of the LORD of hosts.

Joel 2:10
The earth quakes before them, <u>the heavens tremble</u>.

Waters Above the Heavens

Now on to the highest point of the Mesopotamian cosmography, the "highest heavens," or "heaven of heavens," where God has established his temple and throne (Deut. 26:15; Psa. 11:4; 33:13; 103:19). But God's throne also happens to be in the midst of a sea of waters that reside there. These are the waters that are above the firmament, that the firmament holds back from falling to earth (Gen. 1:6-8).

Psa. 148:4
Praise him, you highest heavens, and you waters above the heavens!

Psa. 104:2-3
Stretching out the heavens like a tent. He lays the beams of his chambers on the waters.

Mesopotamian Cosmology

Psa. 29:3, 10
The voice of the <u>LORD is over the waters</u>... the LORD, <u>over many waters</u>... The LORD sits <u>enthroned over the flood</u> [not a reference to the flood of Noah, but to these waters above the heavens][213] the LORD sits enthroned as king forever.

Jer. 10:13
When he utters his voice, there is a tumult of <u>waters in the heavens</u>,

Ezek. 28:2
"I sit in the seat of the gods, in the heart of the seas."

The solid firmament that holds back the heavenly waters has "windows of the heavens" ("floodgates" in the NASB) that let the water through to rain upon the earth.

Gen. 7:11
All the fountains of the great deep burst forth, and the <u>windows of the heavens</u> were opened.

Gen. 8:2
The fountains of the deep and the <u>windows of the heavens</u> were closed, and the rain from the heavens was restrained.

Isa. 24:18
For the <u>windows of heaven</u> are opened, and the foundations of the earth tremble.

So, What's Wrong With the Bible?

The sheer volume of passages throughout both Testaments illustrating the parallels with Mesopotamian cosmography seem to prove a deeply rooted ancient pre-scientific worldview that permeates the Scriptures, and that worldview consists of a three-tiered universe with God on a heavenly throne

---

[213] Robert G. Bratcher, and William David Reyburn. *A Translator's Handbook on the Book of Psalms*. Helps for translators. New York: United Bible Societies, 1991, p 280. Psalm 29 takes place in heaven amidst God's heavenly host around his throne.

above a heavenly sea, underneath which is a solid vaulted dome with the sun, moon, and stars connected to it, covering the flat disc earth, founded immovably firm on pillars, surrounded by a circular sea, on top of a watery abyss, beneath which is the underworld of Sheol.

Some well-intentioned Evangelicals seek to maintain their particular definition of Biblical inerrancy by denying that the Bible contains this ancient Near Eastern cosmography. They try to explain it away as phenomenal language or poetic license. Phenomenal language is the act of describing what one sees subjectively from one's perspective without further claiming objective reality. So when the writer says the sun stood still, or that the sun rises and sets within the solid dome of heaven, he is only describing his observation, not cosmic reality. The claim of observation from a personal frame of reference is certainly true as far as it goes. Of course the observer describes what they are observing. But the distinction between appearance and reality is an imposition of our alien modern understanding onto theirs. As Seely explains,

> It is precisely because ancient peoples were scientifically naive that they did not distinguish between the appearance of the sky and their scientific concept of the sky. They had no reason to doubt what their eyes told them was true, namely, that the stars above them were fixed in a solid dome and that the sky literally touched the earth at the horizon. So, they equated appearance with reality and concluded that the sky must be a solid physical part of the universe just as much as the earth itself.[214]

If the ancients did not know the earth was a sphere in space, they could not know that their observations of appearances were anything other than reality. It would be easy enough to relegate one or two examples of Scripture to the notion of phenomenal language, but when dozens of those phenomenal descriptions reflect the same complex integrated picture of the universe that Israel's neighbors shared, and when that picture included many elements that were *not* phenomenally observable, such as the Abyss, Sheol, or the pillars of earth and heaven, it strains credulity to suggest these were merely phenomenal descriptions intentionally unrelated to reality. If it walks a like a

---
[214] Seely, "The Firmament," p 228.

Mesopotamian Cosmology

Mesopotamian duck and talks like a Mesopotamian duck, then chances are they thought it was a Mesopotamian duck, not just the "appearance" of one having no reality.

It would be a mistake to claim that there is a single monolithic Mesopotamian cosmography.[215] There are varieties of stories with overlapping imagery, and some contradictory notions. But there are certainly enough commonalities to affirm a generic yet mysterious picture of the universe. And that picture in Scripture undeniably includes poetic language. The Hebrew culture was imaginative. They integrated poetry into everything, including their observational descriptions of nature. Thus a hymn of creation such as Psalm 19 tells of the heavens declaring God's glory as if using speech, and then describes the operations of the sun in terms of a bridegroom in his chamber or a man running a race. Metaphor is inescapable and ubiquitous.

And herein lies a potential solution for the dilemma of the scientific inaccuracy of the Mesopotamian cosmic geography in Scripture: *The Israelite culture, being pre-scientific, thought more in terms of function and purpose than material structure.* Even if their picture of the heavens and earth as a three-tiered geocentric cosmology, was scientifically "false" from our modern perspective, it nevertheless still accurately describes the teleological purpose and meaning of creation that they were intending to communicate.

Othmar Keel, one of the leading scholars on Ancient Near Eastern art has argued that even though modern depictions of the ancient worldview like the illustration of the three-tiered universe above are helpful, they are fundamentally flawed because they depict a "profane, lifeless, virtually closed mechanical system," which reflects our own modern bias. To the ancient Near East "rather, the world was an entity open at every side. The powers which determine the world are of more interest to the ancient Near East than the structure of the cosmic system. A wide variety of diverse, uncoordinated notions regarding the cosmic structure were advanced from various points of departure."[216]

John Walton has written recently of this ANE concern with powers over structure in direct relation to the creation story of Genesis. He argues that in the ancient world existence was understood more in terms of function within a god-created *purposeful order* than in terms of material status within a natural physical

---

[215] Horowitz, *Mesopotamian Cosmic Geography*.
[216] Othmar Keel, *The Symbolism of the Biblical World*, Winona Lake; IN: Eisenbrauns, 1972, 1997, 56-57.

structure.[217] This is not to say that the physical world was denied or ignored, but rather that the priority and interests were different from our own. We should therefore be careful in judging their purpose-driven cosmography too strictly in light of our own material-driven cosmography. And in this sense, modern material descriptions of reality are just as "false" as the ancient pictures because they do not include the immaterial aspect of reality: Meaning and purpose.

Biblical writers did not *teach* their cosmography as scientific doctrine revealed by God about the way the physical universe was materially structured, they *assumed* the popular cosmography to teach their doctrine about God's purposes and intent. To critique the cosmic model carrying the message is to miss the meaning altogether, which is the message. God's throne may not be physically above us in waters held back by a solid firmament, but he truly does rule "over" us and is king and sustainer of creation in whatever model man uses to depict that creation. The phrase "every created thing which is in heaven and on the earth and under the earth" (Rev. 5:13) is equivalent in meaning to the modern concept of every particle and wave in every dimension of the Big Bang space-time continuum, as well as every person dead or alive in heaven or hell.

The geocentric picture in Scripture is a depiction through man's ancient perspective of God's purpose and humankind's significance. For a modern heliocentrist to attack that picture as falsifying the theology would be cultural imperialism. Reducing significance to physical location is simply a prejudice of material priority over spiritual purpose. One of the humorous ironies of this debate is that if the history of science is any judge, a thousand years from now, scientists will no doubt consider our current paradigm with which we judge the ancients to be itself fatally flawed. This is not to reduce reality to relativism, but rather to illustrate that all claims of empirical knowledge contain an inescapable element of human fallibility and finitude. A proper response should be a bit more humility and a bit less hubris regarding the use of our own scientific models as standards in judging theological meaning or purpose.

If you liked this book, then please help me out by writing an honest review of it <u>here on Amazon</u>. It's usually pretty easy. That is one of the best ways to say thank you to me as an author. It really does help my exposure and status as an author. Thanks! — *Brian Godawa*

---

[217] John H. Walton, *The Lost World of Genesis One: Ancient Cosmology and the Origins Debate* (Downers Grove, IL, InterVarsity Press, 2009), 23-30.

·····

More Books by Brian Godawa

See https://godawa.com/ for more information on other books by Brian Godawa. Check out his other series below:

Chronicles of the Nephilim

Chronicles of the Nephilim is a saga that charts the rise and fall of the Nephilim giants of Genesis 6 and their place in the evil plans of the fallen angelic Sons of God called, "The Watchers." The prelude to Chronicles of the Apocalypse. Learn more here. (paid link)

Chronicles of the Apocalypse

Chronicles of the Apocalypse is an origin story of the most controversial book of the Bible: Revelation. An historical conspiracy thriller trilogy in first century Rome set against the backdrop of explosive spiritual warfare of Satan and his demonic Watchers. Learn more here.

Chronicles of the Watchers

Chronicles of the Watchers is a series that charts the influence of spiritual principalities and powers over the course of human history. The kingdoms of man in service to the gods of the nations at war. Completely based on ancient biblical, historical and mythological research. Learn more here.

·····

Biblical & Historical Research

For additional free Biblical and historical scholarly research related to this novel and series, go to Godawa.com > Chronicles of the Nephilim > Scholarly Research.

CHAPTER 39: GREAT OFFERS BY BRIAN GODAWA

Get More Biblical Imagination

Sign up Online For The Godawa Chronicles

https://godawa.com

Special Updates on the novels of Brian Godawa
Special Discounts, Free Articles,
Cool Artwork and Videos!

CHAPTER 40: ABOUT THE AUTHOR

Brian Godawa is the screenwriter for the award-winning feature film, *To End All Wars,* starring Kiefer Sutherland. It was awarded the Commander in Chief Medal of Service, Honor and Pride by the Veterans of Foreign Wars, won the first Heartland Film Festival by storm, and showcased the Cannes Film Festival Cinema for Peace.

He also co-wrote *Alleged*, starring Brian Dennehy as Clarence Darrow and Fred Thompson as William Jennings Bryan. He previously adapted to film the best-selling supernatural thriller novel *The Visitation* by author Frank Peretti for Ralph Winter (*X-Men, Wolverine*), and wrote and directed *Wall of Separation,* a PBS documentary, and *Lines That Divide*, a documentary on stem cell research.

Mr. Godawa's scripts have won multiple awards in respected screenplay competitions, and his articles on movies and philosophy have been published around the world. He has traveled around the United States teaching on movies, worldviews, and culture to colleges, churches and community groups.

His popular book, *Hollywood Worldviews: Watching Films with Wisdom and Discernment* (InterVarsity Press) is used as a textbook in schools around the country. His novel series, the saga *Chronicles of the Nephilim* is in the Top 10 of Biblical Fiction on Amazon and is an imaginative retelling of Biblical stories of the Nephilim giants, the secret plan of the fallen Watchers, and the War of the Seed of the Serpent with the Seed of Eve. The sequel series, *Chronicles of the Apocalypse* tells the story of the Apostle John's book of Revelation, and *Chronicles of the Watchers* recounts true history through the Watcher paradigm.

Find out more about his other books, lecture tapes and dvds for sale at his website **https://godawa.com/**.

Mesopotamian Cosmology

Mesopotamian Cosmology

Brian Godawa

Made in United States
Cleveland, OH
11 January 2025